ARTEMIS SSI

THE NEW JOURNEY

ROCHELLE L. BLACK

PAGE PUBLISHING, INC.
Conneaut Lake, PA

First originally published by Page Publishing 2021

ISBN 978-1-6624-4060-1 (pbk)
ISBN 978-1-6624-4061-8 (digital)

Printed in the United States of America

PROLOGUE

IN DEEP SPACE, the armed large triangular vatorian frigate limped ahead as the enemy battleship continued to advance on them. On board the frigate, Lieutenant Gailistra Tol Vasna and her older sister Lieutenant Commander Sharnestra Tol Vasna were the last officers still alive after the carian battleship had opened fired on their frigate, which had taken heavy damage. The frigate's captain, along with the only engineer and a couple of crew members, was killed when the battleship attacked them over the planet Trintor in the Prime System. The frigate had been running surveillance for sentinel fleet, which was helping council militia in the war against the carians, when the carian battleship caught them by surprise.

The crew that remained were working diligently, firing back even though their guns were no match for the huge battleship, when suddenly, the main engine went down. They were dead in space but still had some backup computer and emergency life support systems running. Gail looked at her sister, who was two years older than her and who had a scared look on her face.

"Sharni, what are we going to do? Carians don't take prisoners," she said and looked down at her pistol, which was strapped to her side. Sharni knew what Gail was getting at. Carians didn't take prisoners, and if they did, they were usually intended to be the main course for their meal for the night. Carians were carnivores and believed that consuming their adversaries gave them their opponents' strength.

Sharni went over to her sister and put her hand on her shoulder. "It's not going to come to that. They'll save us. They always do," she said and left the bridge. Gail watched her go, then turned back, taking over one of the gun stations, and began firing on the large destroyer that continued toward them.

Meanwhile, Sharni raced through the frigate, toward the engine room; and when she got there, one of the crew members was working on trying to override the controls of the room to vent out the toxic air. She walked over, grabbing a full oxygen face mask and putting it on. Before the crewman could stop her, she pressed the security pad, and the door slid open. She walked into the poison-filled room. The crewman went to grab her, but she had already gone in, and the door had shut behind her before he could get ahold of her.

Sharni looked around the room. It was hard to see with toxic smoke filling the room, making her eyes sting from it. She headed over to the control console next to the core and saw the chief engineer leaning up against it, dead. She quickly got on the console and started going through the readouts that had come up on the virtual screen in front of her, locating the problem.

Sharni headed over to the main engine and found a sonic wrench in a tool chest next to the engine and removed an access panel. She got it off quickly, then looked inside and saw the problem. A converter had overloaded and was blown from when they took a hit to their starboard hull. It must have sent back a kinetic surge through the core and radiated out from there. She went over to the cabinets located next to the wall and frantically looked through them, finally locating a replacement part. By now, her oxygen mask was starting to run low, and she was only getting a little air, but Sharni continued to push herself on.

She worked quickly, removing the burned-out unit, and finally, several minutes later, she had the other one installed. Now her mask was completely useless, and she had to hold her breath as she discarded it. She headed back to the main control console as the breath she was holding started hurting, becoming too much to bear. She reached it and started pressing in commands, and just as the engine came back on and the energy core powered back up, she couldn't hold it anymore. Ripping off the mask and letting out the breath she was holding, she replaced it with a large breath of toxic air into her lungs.

Instantly, Sharni fell unconscious as the emergency override came back on and the room vented out the toxins. The crewman who was outside the door came running over to Sharni and put another oxygen mask on her, working frantically to revive her as a medical technician also got there to help.

Up on the bridge, Gail heard the engines come back on and jumped out of the gun station, ordering one of the other crewmen to take over, and stepped up on the captain's platform. She yelled at the frigate's pilot, "Tanis, ahead at whatever speed you can get us. Get us moving now." The pilot did so immediately.

The frigate started moving forward again, pulling ahead of the oncoming carian battleship. The vatorian frigate was still too damaged to be able to jump, so all they could do was continue to run, hoping someone would respond to their call for help that they sent out. The pilot was working continuously, trying to stay ahead of the battleship and maneuver around so the large ship couldn't get a direct bead on them with their large mech guns.

Gail was watching ahead on the frigate's screen when suddenly, in front of them, two large battleships appeared out of the darkness, heading straight for them. Relief flooded through her, for she knew who it was who had come to their rescue. Her pilot barely had enough time to straighten out the frigate's course as the two large battleships came flying past them at stage 6 propulsion, firing all their weapons at the carian battleship.

"GIVE ME REVERSE SCREENS NOW!" Gail yelled as the ship's screens showed the two sentinel battleships blowing up the carian vessel. "Full stop," she ordered. She could feel the tears that were building up in her eyes, wanting to fall. She let out the breath she was holding and comm'd Sharni. "Sharni, we're safe. They came. Get up here," Gail said, but the voice that came back to her wasn't Sharni's but a crew member's.

"Lieutenant, there has been an accident. Commander Tol Vasna has been injured," the crew member told her. Gail just stood there in shock, then looked over at her pilot, and he nodded his head in understanding. Gail took off for the engine room. It only took her a few minutes, and when she got there, she saw Sharni on a stretcher with a portable respirator hooked up to her as the medical technician continued to work on her, trying to stabilize her but having no success. Tears were running down her face when her comm went off.

"Gail, come in," a man's voice said over her comm. It wasn't hard to hear the panic in his tone.

"I'm here, Thomas."

"Are you okay?"

"Yes, but Sharni is hurt bad," Gail said, fighting to keep from sobbing as the tears continued down her face.

"We will be right there. I'll let Gerrard know," Harper told her, and the comm went silent.

Gail headed back up to the bridge as the medical technician still worked on Sharni and two crewmen directed the floating stretcher that Sharni was on toward the bridge and the air lock. A few minutes later, Gail felt the frigate jerk and knew that it was now caught in the tractor beam of one of the large sentinel battleships. Ten minutes later, she felt the frigate touch down as her crew shut down the frigate's engines. The air lock started gushing air as the seal released, and the door finally slid open.

Captain Gerrard Larson was the first one through the door, he quickly ran over to Sharni on the stretcher. Gail could see the fear in his face as he grabbed Sharni's hand, looking down at her unconscious form. Next, Dr. Taylor, the battleship's doctor, came in with a complete medical team with him and immediately ran his multitool over Sharni, scanning her from head to toe. When he came to Sharni's midsection, Gail heard the faint sound of a second heartbeat. Dr. Taylor stopped immediately and looked over at Gerrard then. "Did you know she was pregnant?" he asked Gerrard.

Captain Larson nodded his head yes, then looked over at Gail, who had a shocked look on her face. "She didn't want anyone to know yet," Gerrard told Gail, who nodded her head in understanding. Dr. Taylor frowned but continued to stabilize Sharni, and in no time, he had her hooked up to all kinds of medical equipment and IVs.

He stepped back and looked over at Larson. "She's stable now, but I don't know how long I can keep her that way. You're going to have to make a decision soon. I can't keep both alive," he said as his medical team moved Sharni through the air lock and to the battleship's medical bay.

Gail still stood there in shock from everything that had just happened. Larson walked over to her. She looked up at the large watorian and finally broke down crying. Gerrard pulled her into his arms and held her tightly, letting her cry into his chest. Finally, after a few minutes, he escorted her out of the air lock, and they both headed to the medical bay on his battleship.

They walked in and saw Dr. Taylor again, working on Sharni, getting her set up in one of the hospital beds. Finally, he finished, and both Gail and Larson went over to her bed, grabbing Sharni's hands and holding them. Gail looked over at Larson, still with wet eyes. "I knew you two had bonded a while ago, but how long have you known about the baby?" Gail asked him quietly.

Gerrard looked down at Sharni lying on the hospital bed. "About a month."

Gail looked down at her sister, who was now struggling to stay alive, and wished there was something she could do for her. Her sister was always the strong one, always taking care and looking out for her. It was Sharni who helped her through school and military training, and it was Sharni who pulled strings and got Gail assigned to the same ship as her. It was also Sharni who introduced her to Thomas.

That all seemed like a long time ago now looking down at her sister lying on the hospital bed, fighting for her life. Gail was still standing there, watching her sister, along with Gerrard, when the medical bay door slid open and the man she loved walked through them. Thomas Harper was an imposing figure for a human male, and if it weren't for the lack of certain characteristics, he could easily have passed for a watorian. Instead, Harper had cold steel-gray eyes that seemed to pierce right through one, and he kept his wavy coal-black hair cut short around his ears and just above his uniform collar. He always had a stone-cold look on his face and rarely ever smiled, unless he was with Gail or Larson, and even then, it was brief. But it was Gail who broke through his cold, hardened shell, and he had no problem showing his love for her.

Gail ran over to Harper and into his open arms, crying as he pulled her tightly to himself. He leaned his head down on hers but looked over at Larson, who was standing next to Sharni's bed, holding his mate's hand. Finally, Gail composed herself, and Harper looked down at her, then wiped away her tears and took her hand and walked over to Larson. Harper put a hand on Gerrard's shoulder. "How is she?"

"She's stable but struggling. The toxin is all through her body, and Taylor doesn't know how much damage has already been caused from it," Larson told him with a worried and scared look on his face.

Harper looked down at Sharni, studying her for a few minutes. "Hmm. I sense a struggle with her, but with what, I can't read. She's going to recover but at a cost," he told Larson, who wouldn't look at him knowing what his friend was talking about.

Larson then spoke with a slight edge of anger to his tone and still wouldn't look at Harper. "If it were someone else who just said what you said to me, I would have killed them with my bare hands, but I know what I must do to save her."

Harper put his hand on Larson's shoulder again and squeezed. "I know. I saw it on your face."

Gerrard looked back at his friend, and both men nodded to each other. Harper took his leave and led Gail from the hospital room. She started protesting, wanting to stay with her sister, but Thomas gripped her hand tighter, and she couldn't get loose from his steel grip.

"Thomas, let me go. I want to stay with her. She needs me," Gail told him, struggling against his hold on her hand.

Thomas stopped and looked down at Gail. "No, not right now, she doesn't. She needs Gerrard. He is the only one who can save her," he told her, and Gail stopped struggling. She knew that Harper was extremely intelligent, but she also knew there was a mysterious side to him. He seemed to know things that no living being could. She started wondering then if he had known that Sharni was pregnant.

She conceded and went with him, no longer struggling but trusting him completely. Harper led her to the elevator and soon stepped out onto the crew deck of Larson's battleship and headed to a cabin he had specifically for himself when he stayed on Larson's ship. He put his hand on the blue scan pad, and the door opened. He led Gail inside and over to a sofa, making her sit down.

Thomas then went and took a seat in one of the armchairs across from her, staring at her intensely as he leaned back into the chair with his hands gripping the arms. Gail frowned at him and started to say something but then noticed a slight smirk forming at the corner of his mouth.

"Knock it off. I'm not intimidated by you at all. If you have something to say, then say it. I will not play mind games with you," she said, annoyed, and crossed her arms.

Now a slight grin appeared on Harper's face as he knew she had called his bluff. "All right. When Sharni recovers, we will be getting married. I will not wait any longer for you. This with Sharni and Larson, I'm not going to take the chance of losing you. And once we are married, you will retire and transfer to my battleship where you will remain at my side," he informed her.

Gail narrowed her eyes at him. "Oh yeah, I'm not one of your crew members that you can just order around. What if I don't want to do that?" Gail replied defiantly.

Harper narrowed his eyes as the grin left his face. "I'm not ordering you. I'm informing you. And I know that you want to do this as well," he said, now with a wicked smirk on his face. He got up and walked over, pulling her up off the sofa and into his arms, looking down at her.

Gail then grinned up at him. "Damn you, Harper," she said as their lips met in a passionate kiss.

* * *

It was several days later, and Sharni finally recovered. Larson never left her bedside the whole time she was unconscious, even when Gail came and stayed for a few hours to try and relieve him. Harper only came by for brief intervals at a time to check on Sharni's progress as he was busy overseeing both the battleships and had everyone heading back toward Valhalla, the large battle station and home to sentinel command. Finally, Sharni was awake and sitting up in bed, but Gail noticed the sad demeanor of her sister.

It was the third day of Sharni being awake and in recovery when Gail went in and passed Larson as he headed out through the medical bay doors and noticed the haggard, sad look on his face. She walked in and saw that her sister had been crying, and when Sharni saw her approach, she started crying again. Gail went over and put her arms around her older sister's shoulders, stroking her hair, trying to comfort her.

"What's the matter, Sharni? You can tell me," she said, still stroking her hair and leaning her head down on her sister's head.

Sharni looked at her younger sister with tear-filled eyes. "I lost my and Gerrard's baby and also found out that I will never ever be able to have another child. The toxins made me sterile," she said and started crying even more. Gail was stunned silent. This was something that she wasn't prepared for. Then she remembered what Thomas had said a while back to Larson, something about a price having to be paid. How did he know that? How did he know that this was the price to save her sister's life? Gail felt horrible for her sister, yet she was also thankful she was alive, and right now, that outweighed Sharni's loss.

"I'm so sorry, Sharni. I wish there were something I could do for you. I wish it were me instead of you," she said, and suddenly, Sharni pushed her sister back and looked at her, mad.

"Don't ever say that again. It was my choice to run into that room, and I would do it again to save you. Gail, promise me you will leave the service, marry Thomas, and raise a family with him. Do this for me," Sharni said to her and grabbed Gail's hand, holding it tightly, looking her in the eyes.

"I promise you, sister, I will," Gail said as her eyes watered up. They both then hugged each other tightly and were still that way when Gerrard walked back into the medical bay. Gail let her sister go and headed to the door but looked back before she walked out. She saw Gerrard holding Sharni tightly in his arms, leaning his head down on hers as she leaned into him, crying into his chest.

A couple of days later, on Harper's battleship, Gail and Thomas stood before a reverend in the small chapel, taking their vows together, thus completing their union as husband and wife. Sharni and Larson also attended as she was doing much better and was able to move around under her own power now. Once the ceremony was over, Thomas had Gail send in her retirement immediately from active duty to the vatorian fleet and joined him aboard his battleship as Sharni left with Captain Larson aboard his battleship too. But when the two men reported in to sentinel command, they, Harper and Larson, were both to return to Valhalla and sentinel headquarters. Fleet Admiral Devon Carson called a meeting of the high-ranking officers, which Thomas Harper and Gerrard Larson were part of.

This was the beginning of big changes for all of them as decisions and choices that would soon be made put into motion events that would play out the future of the galaxy.

CHAPTER 1

"Ashley Gail Harper, you had better stay out of trouble today and stay away from the command deck as well. Your father has some very important people coming and doesn't need you there causing trouble."

"Yes, Mom. I'll be the perfect angel. I'm just going to hang out with Bridgett and Rachael in the observatory if that's all right," Ashley replied with a devious grin because her mother couldn't see her. Lady Gailistra looked around the corner of the living room wall and toward the door at her now eleven-year-old daughter. She couldn't help but smile seeing her. Ashley looked so much like her father, Vice Admiral Thomas Harper, commander of the battlecruiser the *Justification*, which they had now lived on for many years, even before Ashley was born.

Unlike Ashley, Lady Gailistra was a vatoria, and a very beautiful one at that. She bore the resentment of her people in marrying a human and for denouncing her betrothal obligations, and years later, she gave Thomas a daughter. She was average in height, comparable to most human females, but had pale-blue skin tone. The scroll-like gold markings on her face and body, her gold eyes, and the brilliant white hair were common traits of her people. She kept her hair cut short in a pixie type of hairstyle. She also had telepathy, which was common among her kind.

She had a very enticing figure but was no slouch and also held the ranking of a lieutenant among the vatorian fleet. It was during her tour and fighting the carions that through her sister, Lady Sharnestra, she met Thomas Harper, along with his best friend, Gerrard Larson. But at that time, they were just infantry soldiers with the council militia.

Over the years, though, they kept running into each other and, before long, fell in love, even after Harper, along with his best friend, Gerrard Larson, left and helped bring about the rise of sentinel fleet. By the time Harper asked for her hand from her family, he was a captain aboard his own battleship. Gailistra's father gave his permission reluctantly, mainly due to how he was always telling his daughters to seek their own paths and to not bow down to others' wishes and now couldn't go back on that. Of course, the vatorian governing council was furious but could not stop the union; and soon, Captain Harper and Lady Gailistra were married aboard his battleship.

Ashley was a lot like her father—independent, stubborn, and determined. She had his wavy black hair, which she always pulled back into a ponytail, and his cocky smirk, and you could tell by her frame that when she matured, she was going to be rather tall and beautiful like her mother. Ash did take her mother's gold-colored eyes and some of her scroll markings down her back, but there was also a secret trait she took from her father, one that Gail and Thomas kept quiet. Ash, like her father, was a kinetic and over time would become a very powerful one. Gail and Thomas constantly pounded into her head not to ever use her power, for they were dangerous.

It wasn't dangerous in the sense that Ash could hurt herself but more so that in council space, anyone showing kinetic abilities was immediately arrested and sent to the prison city of Trinity, where survival of the fittest held true and it didn't matter what age you were.

Kinetics was considered dangerous due to 90 percent of most kinetics being caused by exposure to black mass, thus causing psychosis in the person, making them extremely violent. And in a being who could lift a shuttle with just their mind or blow apart steel hulls in ships, this was not a good combination. There were some studies being done on natural-occurring kinetics in life-forms that was showing they were safe but not enough to take a chance on even one person. Harper was one of these people to whom it occurred naturally, and now Ash as well. Of course, there was speculation among many that Harper wasn't a full-blooded human anyway.

He had, on a few occasions, been forced to use his kinetic abilities to save his crew from certain death, but they were loyal to him and would give their lives for him; thus, his secret would die with them as well. Their admiration and respect for Harper were very apparent, for when he resigned from the council militia, many followed him to what was now the sentinel fleet.

"Well, can I go? Bridgett and Rachael are probably already waiting for me," Ash asked, dancing around impatiently.

"All right, but be back here in time for dinner. We are having some special guests tonight." Gail smiled at her daughter knowing this would pique her curiosity, which it did. Ash now stood still, looking at her mother.

"Who? Who's coming?"

"It's a surprise. Now go. Your friends are waiting. I'll comm you on our secure link when you need to come back," Gail replied with an ornery grin on her face now. Ash reluctantly turned, as her curiosity had been piqued but she got no answer from her mother. She headed out the door, racing down the white-walled and carpeted corridor of the ship to one of the several elevators.

The battlecruiser *Justification* was an enormous ship. It housed over 670 crew members and their families if they had one and was comprised of over thirty decks. The admiral's cabin, which was where Ash lived with her mother and father, had two bedchambers, two bathrooms, a full kitchen, a living room, and a dining room and very well-equipped with all the latest technology. It was very modern, not at all what you would expect on a ship, with actual white walls and carpeted floors and nice, elegant furnishings. Her mother had decorated it well with exquisite paintings, vases, and some contemporary art. Even the furnishings in the bedrooms were modern and simple but made from natural resources, such as carved wood and stone.

The cabin was laid out like all the rest of the family dwellings on the ship. One entered through the living room first and saw straight ahead of them the kitchen and dining room with a nice snack bar separating the kitchen from the living room. Then to your right was a hallway that came to a dead end, and both bedrooms sat across from each other off this, and a bathroom was at the end of the hall. The master bedroom had its own bathroom as well.

Also on the ship were guest chambers for when sentinel command or dignitaries happened to dock and met with her father. They also were treated to nice, elegant quarters that had the same floor layout as the Admiral's room but done up in a more classical taste. Even the crew chambers were just as nice with no one lacking for comfort and either had one, two, or three bedrooms in them depending if it was a family or a single crew member as the ship made accommodations for their families to be with them since they spent so much time in space.

The doors to the elevator slid open at Ash's approach, and it was nice that she didn't have to use the scan pad. Only when the hour was late did one have to use them due to everything going into lockdown, and access was only obtained by scanning one's hand on the blue scan pad that was located at every entrance throughout the ship. Ash walked in and turned around, staring back out the way she had come, at the long white-walled, brightly lit hallway.

"Level, please?" the ship computer voice asked her.

"Level 12, observatory," Ash replied with an annoyed voice, still wondering who was coming to dinner tonight. The doors slid shut, and before she knew it, they slid open again, and she stepped out into another bright corridor, only this one lacked the comfortable feel to it and held a crisper, cleaner military design with white walls and ceiling and shiny metal floor. She saw crew members busy going about their duties in the massive hall, entering in and out of different rooms off it, and the main doors to the observatory at the end of the long, brightly lit hallway. Ash made her way through the many people and finally got to the doors, which slid open for her since they weren't locked down for the night either.

The observatory was massive and encased with what looked like nothing but open space for walls and ceilings and a polished black stone floor that reflected the light. In the center of the room was a virtual projection of known solar systems with planets, suns, and stars, and Ash saw running through this hologram of images her two best friends, Bridgett and Rachael, chasing each other in a game of tag. She ran over and joined in immediately, and before long, the tag game turned into a combat game since the three had, from a very early age, some light training in marital arts. Bridgett soon quit and walked over and sat down away from Ash and Rachael, watching them.

"Come on, Bridg. You out of all of us really need the practice," Ash said, watching her out of the corner of her eye, still sparring with Rachael.

"No, I don't. I don't like to fight, and you know that!"

"Bridgett, you've got to help me against Ash. We can't let her win every time. Please?" Rachael begged, barely holding her own against Ash. Bridgett jumped up, and before Ash could do anything, she leaped on her, and both she and Rachael took Ash to the ground. Rachael, along with Bridgett's help, put Ash into a supine restraint hold, then they both started tickling her. Ash was now laughing so hard that tears were falling from her eyes, and soon, she conceded, and the other two girls rolled off her and laid down on the floor next to her, looking up at the holographic image of the galaxy, laughing as well.

"So what's the news today?" Rachael asked out loud.

"I guess there are some important people coming today to see Father, and Mother told me that special guests were coming for dinner," Ash told Rachael as she was trying to grab one of the holographic planets.

"Yeah, Father told me the same thing and to behave. Who do you think it is?" Rachael asked with a devious grin, now sitting up.

"Don't even think about it, Rachael. We are not sneaking up to the command deck again to see. You remember what happened last time. We got caught and had to clean the restrooms on the flight deck." Bridgett glared at her as she spoke.

"It wasn't that bad," Rachael replied, giggling.

"That's because you only cleaned the women's bathroom. Ash and I had to do the men's. I swear, some of them have a problem with their aim. It's amazing they can shoot a gun."

"Yeah. I've lost track of how many times I threw up," Ash added as a chill ran down her back, remembering it.

"Oh, come on, you two. Where's your sense of adventure? You know we are getting older now and won't always be able to get away with things because we are still just children. That excuse will eventually run out, so we should take full advantage of it while we have the chance."

"Bridg, she has a good point. We are eleven now, and before long, we will be leaving for prep school back on Sigma Six. We need to get as much adventuring as we can right now. What do you say?" Ash asked, sitting up, also looking over at her other best friend Bridgett.

It was true. In another year, Rachael, Bridgett, and Ash would be leaving the battlecruiser, the only place they had known as home, and heading to prep school in the colony of New Guinea on the planet Sigma Six. The prep school was actually a boarding school that finished their education up to the age of eighteen. Then after a year-long tour of duty, they will be sent to the colony of New Haven and attend the academy until the age of twenty-three.

Ash felt her heart hurting thinking about leaving her mother and father and the only home she had ever known, but at least her two best friends, Rachael Torres and Bridgett Nelson, would be going with her. These three girls had been together since the first day of school when they were all six. Their friendship grew over the years, but it wasn't until one fateful day when Rachael pulled another one of her stunts that their friendship was solidified to the point of sisterhood.

It was two years ago. They were all hanging out at the atrium again, up in the trees, spying on people, when Rachael got a wild idea. "Hey, I heard that down in the port side cargo bay that they brought in one of those new phasic cannons. Let's go and check it out!"

Ash looked over at her, grinning real big. "Yeah. I've always wanted to see one of those. Let's go."

"I don't know about that, guys. If they catch us in there, we'll be in so much trouble, and we just got done with a week of washing dishes in the mess hall already for our last little stunt with the smoke grenade at school," Bridgett said, worried, trying to talk her friends out of it.

"Sorry, but I never studied for that test and was going to fail it big time. I had to do something to stop the class that day," Ash said with a scowl on her face.

Rachael frowned at Bridgett. "Come on. No one is down there today. We will have the cargo bay all to ourselves."

"Well, I'm going, so you're welcome to come along if you want," Ash said and swung down from the branch she had been lying across and landed softly on her feet. Rachael grinned over at Bridgett and followed Ash. Finally, Bridgett let out a loud sigh and followed too.

They all moved about the halls, sticking close to the darker areas and the ones they knew less crew members moved about in. Before too long, they were at the cargo bay doors, and they all looked around as Ash went over and bypassed the scan pad with a secure code she had seen her father type in once when he didn't think she was watching. The door slid open, and they walked into a dark room, but once the door slid shut, the lights came on when the sensors picked them up. It was huge in here with cold steel walls and open girders along the walls and ceiling and a gray steel floor that was void of any warmth. The girls looked up and could tell the ceiling in here was probably over thirty feet high with large orb-type lights hanging down from it, illuminating the place.

Ash saw along a wall a huge crate and headed over to it, followed by her friends. Sure enough, this was the new cannon, but now disappointment ran through her as it was still in a crate and she couldn't see it. "Well, this sucks," she yelled out in disappointment, and now her voice echoed. The other two girls grinned, and they, too, yelled, listening to their echo.

They all started yelling and singing and laughing just so they could hear the echo. It had now become a game. Ash and Bridgett continued doing it as Rachael decided that the girders were calling her name. She loved to climb, and they looked perfect for it. She easily started scaling one of the girders, and now Ash and Bridgett turned and saw that she was almost at the ceiling.

"Rachael, get down. You're going to fall," Ash told her in a worried tone.

She continued and was now crawling across one of the hanging beams that ran across the ceiling. "Look, guys, I'm taller than you. You two look like little insects down there," Rachael teased.

Bridgett looked like she was about to cry now. "Rachael, get down. You're going to fall and break your neck."

She stood up now with her arms out to her sides to balance her. "Look, no hands."

Just then, the ship ever so slightly swayed, and Rachael started losing her balance. Terror flashed across her face. Bridgett started screaming and covering her face, but Ash just stood there, dazed, watching her friend try to regain her balance. In a split second, though, Rachael fell, and Ash, acting on pure instincts, suddenly was covered in sparking blue energy, and her eyes were nothing but solid, glowing blue orbs. A blast of pure blue light came out of her hands and toward Rachael, catching her in midair, slowly lowering her to the ground.

Rachael stood up once her feet touched down and stared over at Ash, who was now back to normal. Even Bridgett, who was standing next to her, was stunned, unable to say anything, and could only stare too. A big grin started spreading across Rachael's face, and she ran over to Ash, throwing her arms around her. "That was awesome. I didn't know you were a kinetic. You saved my life."

Bridgett finally came out of her trance and wrapped her small arms around them but was now crying. "Oh, Ash, thank goodness you were here. Rachael would have been a pancake just now."

Rachael and Ash started laughing, and Bridgett even had to as the final shock of everything wore off. "So have you always had this power?" Rachael asked excitedly.

Ash now looked worried. "Yes, but I was never supposed to use it. You know where people like me go."

Rachael looked over at Bridgett, and they both nodded to each other. "Your secret will always be safe with us. We will never tell anyone. We swear upon our lives," she said to Ash, and Bridgett nodded her head in agreement.

"So can you do more stuff like that?" Bridgett now asked, curious. Ash grinned, and over the next half hour, she levitated herself and her friends as they all were laughing away. Finally, she was tiring, and they decided they had better get out of there before someone found them.

"I say we make a pact with each other, do this right," Rachael told them, and they all agreed. They headed to Bridgett's cabin since they all knew her father wouldn't be there and walked into the kitchen. On the counter, Rachael saw a knife. She grabbed it and told them all to hold out their hands palm side up. Ash did right away, but Bridgett gave her a dirty look. "That knife is probably dirty if it was sitting out there."

Rachael wiped it on her pants and then looked at Bridgett to see if she was okay with that. Bridgett let out a sigh and put her hand out. Rachel cut across Ash and Bridgett's palms as they grimaced and then cut her own palm. Their hands started bleeding, and they grabbed one another's and held them together.

"From this day on, we are sisters in blood and will never leave each other as will our secrets only be known to one another and die with us," Rachael said, and both Ash and Bridgett agreed with her. Once they were done, all three girls ran over to the sink and started running their hands under the water as the cuts were now stinging real bad, and they were all hollering how badly it was hurting.

About a week later, all three girls' hands swelled up from infection, and they had to go down to the med lab and get shots to help treat them. Of course, the adults were pretty sure what they had done. It wasn't hard to guess with the nice cuts across their palms that all three of them had. But they said nothing and just chuckled, figuring the pain from the infection was punishment enough. From that time on, Rachael Torres, Bridgett Nelson, and Ashley Harper forged a friendship that could never be broken no matter how many times it would get tested throughout their lives.

Rachael was the daughter of Commander Raul Torres, who captained the battleship *Inferno*. It always flew in unison with the *Justification* and was the first line of defense because it was much quicker and more maneuverable than the battlecruiser due to its much smaller size. Rachael was your typical pretty, blond-headed, blue-eyed girl and liked all girly things, such as painted nails, fixing her hair, and jewelry, and was always up-to-date on fashion, and one could tell that she would grow up to be very beautiful and tall, but there was also a mischievous and wild side to Rachael that not too many knew about. She put on a great show for others on how well-behaved she was but then would turn around and do some of the craziest and most dangerous stunts ever, always dragging Ash and Bridgett in on them, but only after Ash agreed to it, which was most of the time.

Bridgett was just the opposite. She was more cautious and quiet and tended to play it safe. She had very dark-red hair and blue eyes and was smaller, giving the appearance that when she grew up, she was going to be a more petite woman. She also had a certain innocence about herself and, in time, was also going to be very pretty. Oftentimes, when the girls got into trouble, all an adult had to do was glare at Bridgett as she would always break under pressure and cry, telling them everything. Ash and Rachael would just roll their eyes but never held it against her. Bridgett had a tough life, and the other two girls took it upon themselves in a way to protect her. Her mother died when she was born, and her father, Senior Chief Engineer Tony Nelson of the *Justification*, raised Bridgett by himself. Like her father, though, Bridgett was a wizard with engines. It was almost like a sixth sense as she seemed to be able to communicate with them.

"So are you in, Bridg?" Rachael asked, grinning.

"What do you think?" Bridgett replied, rolling her eyes.

Ash and Rachael grinned, jumped up, and pulled Bridgett to her feet as she was still lying down, trying to catch the holographic planets on her back. All three then raced to the door as it slid easily open at their approach. Once again, they all weaved their way through the busy, well-lit hallway with its pristine white walls and ceiling and gray metal floor to the elevator. This time, they had to wait for it; but soon, the doors slid open and ensign Chamber walked out with a stack of datapads. She usually was found on the command deck and was in charge of public relations and communications. She stopped and looked down at the girls with narrowed eyes. "What are you three up to?"

"Nothing. We got bored in the observatory and decided to head on over to the atrium, maybe climb a few trees," Ash quickly covered.

"How come I don't believe you? I can tell looking at you three that you're going to do something you'll get into trouble for."

"No, really, we are," Rachael added in the best sincere voice she could muster.

"All right, then. While you're there, make yourselves useful. I noticed that the rose garden had some weeds growing in it. Why don't you three remove them?"

"And who were you with when you went there?" Ash asked, now in a teasing tone, focusing the attention back on the ensign.

"No one."

"Sure. Maybe a certain private, possibly?" Rachael also teased.

"None of your business. Now get out of here, you rotten little monsters," Chamber said to them, grinning, and headed down the hallway.

The girls started giggling and walked into the elevator. Soon, the doors slid shut behind them as the ship's computer voice came on, asking the level. All three looked at one another as big grins spread across their faces. "Command deck," they said in unison.

CHAPTER 2

THE ELEVATOR ROSE quickly, and in no time, the doors slid open to the large command deck where at any given time over fifty people were working. The command deck was an extremely large square room that had many side chairs facing consoles and keyboards that all had virtual screens on them. Upon entering the bridge, one's attention was first drawn to the center of the room where a table-like huge round console that glowed blue sat with a holographic galaxy map projected above it. One could watch it for hours as the image constantly changed from one solar system to another.

Beyond this and up in the very front of the ship was where the pilot and copilots sat, and then behind them, back a ways, was the admiral's platform with a large wraparound console and control panel that the admiral stood at, studying all the ship's systems, incoming messages, and flight patterns, the area where he sent out orders from and where his large command chair was, which Ash had sat on a few times and thought was very comfortable.

The admiral could, at anytime, pull up any section of the ship or personnel here on his controls, plot a course, fire the ship's large cannons, and if by some chance the ship was lost, could order the self-destruct sequence from his station. As for the rest of the room, it was long, and there wasn't a place on the wall that didn't have some type of screen, circuit board, button, control panel, knobs—

you name it. The whole place looked like there were Christmas lights everywhere, not to mention the multiple portal pads for the many VIs and a couple of low-level AIs that helped with the ship's maintenance and repairs.

These portals were located all over the ship, and there were more than a dozen VIs assigned to specific areas, helping to keep the ship repaired and operational, which was all they were programmed to do. The few AIs had a more intricate responsibility. They would run tactical simulations for the vice admiral and possible outcome scenarios, not to mention engine outputs and weapons performance. Even the whole front section around the pilot and the two copilots had wraparound windows that changed to view screens by the touch of a button. To top it off, the whole floor area of the bridge had a nice matte carpet to help with noise dampening and static due to so much electrical equipment running in there.

The gun stations looked like large stand-alone cockpits of a fighter jet with screens in them and two control sticks on each side of the center console with nice, comfortable chairs that laid back a little to give more comfort and support to the gunner. When one was in the seat, headgear came down from the ceiling of the cockpit, and an eyepiece flipped down over the right eye. Once the station was activated, the eyepiece would light up, and the person who was manning the gun now looked like their eye had crosshairs permanently etched in the iris. But it was just a virtual image, and no lingering effects were caused from it. There were six in all with the sixth station being the largest and most movable of the guns, and it took a person with real skill to handle this one.

The gun stations were situated closer to the back of the room, away from the constant noise of the command area, as it took extreme concentration to man these, and the less interference, the better, except the sixth gun, which was closer to the admiral since the admiral and the gunner coordinated a lot of the strikes together with the admiral manning the cannons.

The girls quickly sneaked out of the elevator and hid behind one of the stationary gun terminals. Ash could see that her father was indeed meeting with some important people, and by the looks of the military insignia on their formal attire, they were from sentinel command. There also was another whom Ash easily recognized, Rear Admiral Larson, her father's best and closest friend.

"Oh, crap. Ash, we have to get out of here," Rachael whispered to her when she saw who it was.

"It's a little late for that, don't you think?" Bridgett replied, whispering angrily, knowing they were going to get into real bad trouble this time.

"Okay. When they turn their backs again, let's head for the elevator. Hopefully, we can get out before they spot us," Ash whispered, looking around for an escape. The girls were still watching the admirals and command personnel when suddenly, from behind them, someone spoke.

"What are you doing?"

The girls jumped from being startled and turned ready to fight due to pure instincts. They were now facing three boys, probably about a couple of years older than they. They were definitely taller. One of the boys had wavy black hair cut short, another one had the same haircut but with blond-colored, wild-looking hair, and the last one had light sandy-brown hair. It was very obvious they were watorians due to the small fangs showing when they spoke and the sky-blue eyes that all watorians had, especially the males of their race, before their changing. You could tell they had come from a prep school, because they were still wearing the school uniforms, but now all three of them were also in a combat stance, facing down the girls.

"None of your business, so get out of our way!" Ash said, glaring at them, as Rachael and Bridgett backed her up.

"Well, I'm making it my business when someone takes a threatening stance at me," the black-haired boy replied, glaring back. Now his friends behind him were actually grinning and were no longer standing defensively.

"Yeah? Well, you don't want us to have to kick your butt here, do you?" Rachael said from behind Ash.

"Bring it on, little girl. I would like to see you back up that mouth of yours."

"Ash, kick his butt," Rachael said to her.

"Me? Why me?" Ash replied and now stood up straight, looking at Rachael.

"Because you're the toughest out of us, that's why."

"All right," Ash replied reluctantly and then again dropped to an attack stance with her fists up, facing the dark-headed boy, and a determined look on her face.

"You've got to be kidding me. You really think you can take me?" the boy asked and now stood up, folding his arms across his chest, with a look of disbelief on his face.

"Well, there's only one way to find out. Prepare to get your scrawny butt kicked by a girl," Ash said defiantly through narrowed eyes.

"ASHLEY GAIL HARPER, WHAT THE HELL ARE YOU DOING HERE? STAND DOWN." Ash stood up straight and closed her eyes knowing full well she was in so much trouble. Rachael tried to hide more behind her, and Bridgett started crying already. Admiral Harper and the men he was meeting with walked over to them all. Ash opened her eyes and looked up at her father and could see the anger in his face. "Answer me right now, young lady!"

"We got lost?" Ash said back weakly. Rear Admiral Larson chuckled a little, but Vice Admiral Harper gave him a glare, and his face again took on a serious expression.

Vice Admiral Harper was an intimidating man. He was very tall and extremely well-built, and his strategic planning and marksmanship were legendary. He had wavy black hair, which now had some hints of gray at his temples, that he kept clipped short and steel-gray eyes and was rather handsome. Even the small scar that ran from the corner of his left eye and was about an inch long added to his appearance.

Just meeting with him for the first time, he had an air about him that radiated a commanding presence and respect, not to mention cold and deadly. To most people, he seemed almost frightening and indifferent. He was not one you wanted to make mad, for he left the impression in your mind that even the grim reaper would be frightened of him.

He was no fool, and he and his best and closest friend, Rear Admiral Gerrard Larson, were able to help amass a huge fleet of battlecruisers, battleships, and warships, along with a few other men, over the years, thus helping give rise to the now separatist military power, the sentinel fleet.

"Don't get smart with me. I want you three to march yourselves back to your cabins while I think of an appropriate punishment for this intrusion," Admiral Harper commanded, pointing toward the elevator. Ash looked over at it and then glanced quickly at the three boys. The dark-haired one had a cocky smirk on his face, and Ash couldn't help but stick her tongue out at him and glared.

"Right now, Ashley. You are only making this worse on yourself," her father ordered.

Ash, Rachael, and Bridgett headed quickly to the elevator and practically jumped into it when the doors slid open. Again, the doors closed and asked for a level. "I can tell you one thing: I'm not going home," Rachael spoke out loud.

"No way, but where can we go to hide out for a while?" Ash asked.

"Come on, you two. You're just making it worse," Bridgett said through her tears.

"You can go home if you want, but I'm going to hang out in the atrium. They'll never find us in all that foliage."

"Good idea, Rachael. I'm coming too. What about you, Bridg?" Ash asked her.

"Fine. We're going to be scrubbing toilets for the rest of our lives anyway, so I guess we should do this right."

"All right, Bridg. I knew you wouldn't let us down," Rachael said as she and Ash both slapped Bridgett on the back.

"Atrium," Ash said to the computer voice of the elevator, and immediately, it started moving.

In no time, the doors opened up directly in the atrium, and the girls quickly left it, heading to the forested area of the bio dome. The biosphere was massive, and one could barely make out the ceiling in there, which during the day was lit by brilliant lights, making it feel like daytime, and then at night, they moved the outer shields back, revealing the space outside giving way to the stars. This was an actual living, growing environment with trees, exotic birds, waterfalls, streams that had fish in them, and every type of plant imaginable. A nice stone path wound all through it, and stone benches placed in certain parts gave it a park-like setting. One could even make it rain or snow and, like all cycles, change from night to day and fall and winter to spring and summer.

Luckily for the girls, it was in the summer stage, and there was plenty of growth to hide in. They raced all through it, cutting through shrubs, wildflowers, and even tall grasses, and finally found a nice, secluded place in the forested area among the trees that concealed them quite well. All three fell down on the soft meadow grass that grew there.

"Wow, we are in so much trouble," Rachael said, letting out a sigh.

"I know. I have never seen my father so mad before. I'll probably never be allowed out of my room again," Ash added.

"Yeah, well, I'll probably get sent off to stay with my aunt in Bridone on Alpha Prime," Bridgett commented.

"Oh, I never thought of that. He might send me to stay with my grandparents on Krios. That would be the ultimate punishment." Ash leaned up on her elbows, now with a worried look on her face.

"Well, if that happens, I'm stowing away on your ship. There is no way I will stay here by myself, and yes, Bridg, you will be with me. There is no way that they will split us up even if it means running away," Rachael told her friends with a very serious look on her face. Ash had seen that look before and knew that Rachael meant it and would do it.

"I agree. We stay together no matter what, now and forever. Deal?" Ash asked them.

"Deal!" Rachael replied, holding up her hand with the scar across the palm.

"Deal!" Bridgett said and also held up her hand with the scar. Then all three girls placed their hands on top of one another's and nodded, then fell back on the ground, looking up at the trees.

"So who do you think those boys were?" Rachael asked no one in particular.

"Who cares? It is because of them that we are now in trouble, especially that dark-headed one. What a jerk," Ash answered with a hiss to her voice.

"I don't know. I thought the one with the light-brown hair was kind of cute," Bridgett commented.

"Bridg, I can't believe you. Are you serious?" Ash blurted out, now leaning up on her elbows.

"Yeah. The other one with the blond, wild-looking hair was really cute too. Even the dark-headed one was, but you could tell he was a jerk from the start just by the way he acted," Rachael added.

"Rachael, not you too? I can't believe what I'm hearing from you two. Didn't we agree last year that boys were a plague and that we will have nothing to do with them?"

"Ash, we were only ten. We since have grown up. I only said he was cute. Doesn't mean I'm going to go and marry him," Rachael said to her, rolling her eyes.

"You never know. That's how it all starts. 'Oh, he's cute. We're dating now. I love him. We're getting married. Wow, I'm pregnant,'" Ash said in a sarcastic tone.

"Holy cow, Ash, you have it all figured out, don't you?" Rachael grinned, teasing her, as Bridgett started giggling.

"No, but that is a quick scenario of how it is once a boy comes into the picture."

"How do you know all this?" Rachael asked, grinning.

"I watch vids. Girl meets boy, girl and boy fall for each other, boy gets what he wants and leaves girl with a little surprise nine months later," Ash said with disgust in her voice. Rachael and Bridgett looked at each other and both started busting up laughing as tears ran down their faces.

"Wow. I will definitely make sure I stay away from boys if that is how things go," Rachael said, still laughing.

"Oh, laugh it up. I know that is what the vids show, but it really does happen. I'm not going to be one of those statistics. I will never let any boy ever get that close to me."

"Ash, you don't know what's going to happen in the future. You might meet some wonderful young man and fall hopelessly in love with him and him with you," Rachael said in a teasing tone, then started grinning, looking over at Bridgett. "Watch, it will be that dark-headed boy we just met on the bridge." Both Rachael and Bridgett started giggling.

"Never! I will be a career soldier and serve on my father's ship," Ash replied with force and was now mad.

"You're a telepath, not an oracle. You can't see into the future," Rachael teased her.

"No, but I can make my own future."

"All right, Ms. Purity. I kind of like that. Purity Harper—it has a certain ring to it."

"Yeah, laugh it up, and when you end up with twenty kids, we'll see who's laughing then," Ash said, grinning, and now all three girls were laughing.

They remained there, lying on the ground with their arms folded behind their heads, talking as the hours flew by and the sky in the atrium started to change for evening to approach. Suddenly, through an opening in the trees, two armed privates came through with scowls on their faces. One reached up and put his hand on his earpiece.

"Affirmative, Vice Admiral. We found them right where you said they would be."

"If need be, you have the right to shoot if they become hostile," the admiral's voice said over the private's intercom on his wrist multitool.

All three girls now stood up with their hands raised in the air and scared looks on their faces. "We'll come peacefully," Ash said in a shaky voice.

The privates pulled their guns and motioned for the girls to head out toward the exit. The girls were continuing to walk toward the exit when Rachael leaned over to Ash. "You know, we can make a break for it. They can't shoot all three of us at once, and if we split in different directions, they will only be able to graze us."

"Are you flippin' crazy? How do you know this?" Ash whispered back.

"Easy. The trajectory of the rounds only can go in a straight line unless they are heat-seeking, which I can tell by looking at them that they are not. Plus, no one can take a bead on something moving at a high rate of speed unless they are snipers, and we would be running fast due to the fear pumping through our veins," Rachael explained to her.

Ash looked at her in disbelief and then over at Bridgett, who was shaking her head as tears ran down her face. "We can't. They will definitely tag Bridg. Nope. We all knew we would have to face the music sometime, and I guess it's time to get it over with."

"All right. It was just a thought," Rachael replied, shrugging her shoulders.

The girls entered the elevator, and the privates told it the level. Soon, the doors were opening, and the girls slowly stepped out onto the crew deck and were escorted down the hallway toward the admiral's cabin. They stopped in front of it, still with their hands in the air, and one of the private's pressed the intercom button.

"Enter" came the voice of the vice admiral over the intercom. The door slid open, and the privates motioned for the girls to go first. Once inside, Ash could see her father, Rachael's father, and Bridgett's father glaring at them with arms crossed over their chests. Ash and Rachael's mothers were also standing back aways from them with mad expressions on their faces. Raul and Abigail Torres and Tony Nelson were some of the ones who fought together in the carion wars with Harper and Larson. The Torreses and Nelsons were also the first couples who left and went with Harper and Larson when the two men left council militia, starting up sentinel fleet. They remained in service under Harper and Larson and started their families at the same time Harper did.

"You are dismissed, Privates," Vice Admiral Harper said to the two men, who put their guns away and quickly left.

"So what do you three have to say for yourselves?" Commander Torres asked, and it was apparent by his tone that he was very angry.

"Sorry," Rachael replied with a nervous tone.

"Sorry is not good enough, not this time. You three have crossed the line and now will pay for your actions. Over the next two months, you three will be given duties that must be done to perfection, or you will do them all over again. It is time to learn discipline and follow orders. Your duties will range from mopping hallways, cleaning details, and such. They will be done right after classes and must be finished before dinnertime, or you will go without a meal until they are complete. You three embarrassed this ship and its crew with your little stunt up on the bridge in front of the sentinel command and now must make up for it," Admiral Harper informed them, still very mad.

Ash, though, was too much like her father, and her expression changed from one of submission to one of hardened defiance and determination, which did not go unnoticed by her father. He knew that look, and deep inside, he was smiling to himself, proud of her. "Do I make myself clear?" he asked them with force.

"Yes, sir!" all three replied in unison.

"Good. Now go and get cleaned up for dinner."

Commander Torres and his wife left with Rachael, and Chief Engineer Nelson left with Bridgett. Ash was left alone with her parents. Her mother now walked over and stood next to her husband as they continued to glare at Ash, but never once did she back down. She remained standing firm under their stare.

"Ashley, what were you thinking? I told you to stay away from the bridge, and you openly defied me."

"Not openly, Mother. We just wanted to see who it was that was so important, and we would have sneaked right back out without being seen if it weren't for those boys."

"Listen to what you're saying. You just admitted to going there. I don't know what to do with you anymore. I…" Ash's mother stopped and put her hand to her head. Admiral Harper instantly put his arm around his wife, then led her over to the sofa, helping her to sit down.

"Mother, are you all right?" Ash ran over to the couch and sat down beside her mother with a worried look on her face.

"I'll be fine, Ash. I just get dizzy sometimes. Go and get changed for dinner."

Ash looked up at her father and could see a sad look in his eyes and knew there was something they weren't telling her. Ash slowly got up and headed to her room but looked back at her parents and saw her father now sitting down next to her mother, holding her tightly. Ash went in and changed into a nice shirt and pants with ankle boots and brushed out her long wavy black hair, pinning the sides back. She took one last look in the mirror, and several minutes later, she headed back out and saw her mother straightening her father's collar on his admiral's uniform.

"You look nice, sweetheart. Are you ready?" her mother asked.

"Yep. Let's go."

Admiral Harper put his arm out for Lady Gailistra and led her over to the door, which slid open smoothly. They headed to the elevator and went down to the next level, to the main dining chamber, where they had important guests. The dining chamber door slid open, and all three entered a very large rectangular room complete with a large hanging crystal chandelier situated directly over a huge mahogany dining table with several matching chairs.

The walls were a light cream color with small red scrollwork designs running along the upper edge along the ceiling, and there were stained glass windows situated all around the room, spaced three feet apart from one another, depicting nature scenes and lit from behind, adding extra light to the room. The floor was covered in a tannish-red stone and a large oriental-style rug covered the whole middle section where the table and chairs sat, giving it a very elegant appearance to the room.

Once inside, Ash immediately saw Rear Admiral Larson, her godfather, and took off running over to him as he stood up. She jumped into his arms as he gave her a big hug, then set her down and held her back at arm's length, looking her over.

Rear Admiral Larson was Vice Admiral Harper's closet and dearest friend. They were more like brothers than friends. They grew up, fought in the council carian war, and helped build sentinel fleet together. Unlike Harper, though, Larson was a watorian, which was very evident with his white eyes, small fangs, shoulder-length wavy dark-brown hair cut short in the front, and the many braided strands that displayed countless beads of his accomplishments hanging down in the back.

He was extremely handsome, tall, large, and well-built, just like all mature males of his species. But in honesty, he wasn't much bigger than Harper, and the constant joke between them was that Harper wasn't human. The other difference between Harper and Larson was, Larson had a sense of humor and always had a grin on his face but was more apt to beat the crap out of you or shoot you first than talk out your differences. He was now grinning, looking down at the little girl, whom he could still remember holding as an infant.

"Wow, you have grown. I almost didn't recognize you up on the bridge, and I can tell you're taking after your father but luckily look like your mother," Admiral Larson said to her as Lady Gailistra walked up to him then, and they both gave each other a hug.

"Lovely as always, Gail. I see you are keeping this old bird still under control. Good job."

"Trust me, it's hard, Gerrard. It's good to see you again. I just spoke to my sister this morning and told her you were coming. She wanted me to tell you hello and hopes that all is well with you."

"How is Lady Sharnestra? Well, I hope?" Admiral Larson asked with a slight sad look on his face.

"She is well," Lady Gailistra replied and patted Larson's hand affectionately.

Ash went over and sat down next to her father's chair proudly and now looked around the room and saw Rachael and her parents, Bridgett and her father, and also the three boys who had caused them all the trouble. Ash immediately jumped up and glared at them, and the dark-headed one glared back. Admiral Larson caught the exchange immediately, as did Ash's father, and they both tried to hold back a grin.

"Ashley, let me introduce you to my son, Fâdron," Admiral Larson said to her, putting his hand on the shoulder of the dark-haired boy. Ash continued to glare at him, and her father cleared his throat, causing her to look over at him, and he narrowed his eyes at her.

"I would like to say it is a pleasure to meet you, but that would be a lie," Ash said, and Admiral Larson started chuckling.

"Ashley, that is no way to treat our guest," her mother scolded her.

"The feeling is mutual," Fâdron replied.

"Fâd, that's enough," Admiral Larson said, looking down at his son, who just rolled his eyes and picked up his dinner knife, twirling it on his plate.

"Well, I suppose I'll introduce the rest. This here is Nathan Wilcox, and that is Cory Brayton. They all go to the prep school with Fâd, and the three of them grew up together," Larson said with a grin, and the other two boys nodded their heads at everyone.

"Well, I'm Rachael Torres, and this here is Bridgett Nelson. It's nice to meet you," Rachael said, standing up, totally at ease and grinning at the boys. Ash now glared at her. Finally, Admiral Harper led his wife over to her seat, and everyone sat down as the meal was brought out. Ash and Fâd both sat through the whole meal scowling and never speaking a word, but Rachael and Bridgett were happily talking away with Nathan and Cory as the adults were also engrossed in heavy conversation. The meal was finally over, but the adults were still talking, and Ashley's father turned to her and asked her something that made her world come crashing down around her.

"Ash, why don't you and your friends show Fâdron and his friends around the ship?"

Ash's face turned scarlet with rage, and her mouth fell open, and for the first time, she was speechless, staring at her father. "Sure we will, Admiral Harper. Come on, Ash," Rachael replied and stood up, heading over to Ash, who now turned her rage on her, giving Rachael the look of death.

Bridgett also came over, and they both pulled a defiant Ash out of her chair and over to the door as the two boys, Cory and Nathan, also dragged a mad Fâd, following them. Once outside the door, Ash turned on her friends but whispering under her breath. "What the hell was that all about in there? This is the last thing I want to do right now. I would rather clean the men's bathroom for the next year than do this."

"Ash, shut up and follow my lead," Rachael said back in a whisper. Rachael continued to walk down the hall to the elevator with Ash and Bridgett beside her and the boys following. "So what do you want to see first?" Rachael asked with a smile.

"I don't know. You've seen one, you've seen them all. And honestly, Admiral Larson's battlecruiser is a lot nicer than this one," the boy named Nathan replied back.

"Is that so? Well, I say you're full of crap," Ash spun around and hissed at him. This brought Fâd out of his sullen demure, and he readily jumped to the challenge.

"Yeah, it is so, and what are you going to do about it?"

"Hey, guys, come on, there's a better way to solve this disagreement," Rachael interjected.

"Then what do you suggest?" Cory asked with a defiant look on his face.

"Do you little boys play combat tag?" Bridgett asked, grinning.

"Of course. We are unmatched at it," Nathan replied, rolling his eyes.

"Fine. Then I say we settle this out on the course, or are you too scared to face girls?" Ash now asked with a challenging tone.

"Of course not. Prepare to face defeat." Fâd walked up and got in Ash's face, but she stood her ground, and finally, Rachael pulled her away.

The girls got on the elevator as the boys followed, and soon, the doors slid open to the armory. They all walked into it and told Private Justin that they had come for a game of combat tag. The private got up and grabbed chest armor, helmets with visors, and assault rifles for each of them. The girls were all suited up in red, and the boys were in blue. The private handed them all each a one-hundred-round clip of rubberized bullets. These were always used during simulations and would not cause injury to the combatants, but one would definitely feel them when hit. The girls were over near their corner, getting ready, when Rachael pulled out different clips she had stashed in her pockets and handed one each to Ash and Bridgett, who looked at them as big grins spread across their faces.

Ash looked around to make sure no one saw them and whispered to Rachael, "How did you know we would end up here?"

Rachael just grinned. "Because adults are always sending the kids away so they can talk, and I knew those boys would never back down from a challenge like this."

"How did you know those boys were even going to be at dinner?"

"My dad told me," Rachael told her, and Ash grinned wickedly.

"What color of paint are they?" Ash asked her with an evil smirk.

"Red, of course, so they'll know who got them plus leave a nice mess all over them," Rachael replied with a huge, devious grin.

"Hey, Ash, what course do you want to play?" Private Justin yelled at her from behind his desk as his virtual screen and keyboard came up in front of him.

"Warehouse."

"Warehouse it is. Remember the rules. This is just a shooting game, not a hand-to-hand combat game. I don't want to have to come in there and break up any fights like last time," the private said to her as a warning.

"We won't."

The private started pointing at different areas of his holographic screen, moving subscreens around, and soon, the keyboard disappeared as quickly as it appeared. "There you go. Happy hunting, and have fun. And, Ash, behave yourself!"

"Thanks. We will, and I'll behave," Ash said with an ornery smirk as she pulled down her visor. Justin just shook his head as Rachael and Bridgett followed her through the door into a large warehouse with many crates and objects to hide behind.

The boys were right behind the girls, and when the girls stopped, they continued on and through the warehouse, to the other side. Once over to their side, they pressed the button on the wall that signaled to a control board that was mounted up on the far wall showing the score and time. Ash looked at Bridg and Rachael, and they nodded their readiness as she pressed her button. The clock counted down from ten and buzzed to start. The girls immediately ran for cover and started making their advance toward the other side.

They quickly moved and darted from cover to cover, and once they knew they were getting close, Ash signaled Rachael to seek a high perch and position herself since Rachael was an awesome sniper. She quickly found a good hidden spot and laid low until Ash contacted her through her earpiece.

Ash and Bridg moved around silently, and Ash jumped over a large crate, landing on the other side right next to Nathan. They both started shooting away at each other, and soon, Nathan was covered in red paint as Ash was stinging from multiple hits with the rubberized bullets.

"What the hell, guys? The girls are using paint rounds," Nathan yelled out in disgust to his teammates as Bridgett lay, suppressing a fire of paint at him. Ash quickly jumped back over the crate but took a hit right in the butt and looked back to see Fâd standing behind a crate with a huge grin on his face. Out of nowhere, a paint shell exploded on his visor, and he dropped immediately, taking cover. Ash quickly doubled back to Bridg, and they split up, trying to flank the boys. But Bridg ran into Cory, and they both had each other pinned down.

Ash then crawled through a large pipe and came up behind Cory and started unloading on him. He spun around and started shooting back. Bridg stood up then and started hitting him from the other side, but Fâd had flanked her and was now hitting her. Rachael took aim and started hitting him, causing him to run for cover. Out of nowhere, Nathan came up behind Rachael and wrestled her gun out of her hands, then started shooting her with the paint rounds. Rachael ran from her perch with his gun, now covered in paint.

"Ash, they got my gun."

"Bridg, regroup at the rendezvous point," Ash yelled to her comrades. Ash took off running and rounded a crate and almost ran straight into Fâd, who saw her and started shooting. She leaped into a nearby crate and crawled over to a dark corner and laid low. Bridg, meanwhile, was heading back to their starting point when she heard a noise behind her and spun around. There was no one there, so she turned back, and Cory was now standing right in front of her.

"I'll take that. Thank you," he said with a rotten grin and yanked her gun out of her hands and immediately started firing on her, covering her with red paint. Bridg took off running as Rachael stood up from behind him and started shooting him with the rubberized bullets, causing him to have to duck for cover.

"Ash, we have been compromised. They now have two paint guns," Rachael said into her mic.

"Understood."

Ash crawled out of her hiding place and moved around silently through the many crates and obstacles. She soon came up behind Nathan and Cory, who were now stalking around to flank Rachael and Bridg. She continued to stalk them, sometimes crawling and then laying low over a small crate, getting a bead on them. She watched as they slowly started taking aim at her comrades, and just as she was about to pull the trigger, she felt the nose of a rifle barrel press into the back of her neck.

"I wouldn't do that if I were you," Fâd warned her. Ash now stood up and turned around, looking down the barrel of his gun. "Hand over that gun," Fâd said to her.

"Nope. Won't do."

"You'll do it, or I will unload on you at point-blank range, and you'll be sorry."

"Kiss my ass," Ash yelled and flipped over backward as Fâd started shooting at her. He quickly caught her as they both wrestled for her gun, but he easily yanked it out of her hands, and she took off running as she scooped up his. He started shooting her in the back, and she could feel paint splattering all over her as she dived over a crate for cover.

The distraction caused the other two boys to turn and gave Rachael and Bridg a chance to get away. Ash continued to run as Fâd advanced on her, shooting her as he went, but she returned just as much fire, yet it had little effect on him as he continued to chase her. Soon, she was cornered. She turned to face him with her gun aimed at his head and started firing back as he advanced toward her. Finally, their guns ran out of bullets. By now, they both were furious;

and soon, the empty guns were used to try and bash each other in the head.

Fâd knocked Ash's gun out of her hands, but she dropped and took his feet out from under him with hers, and he fell to his butt. He leaped up quickly, and they both started throwing punches and blocking each other. Rachael and Bridg, along with Nathan and Cory, came running over to them and tackled them both, stopping their fighting.

"Let me up. I want to tear his face off!" Ash yelled at her two friends, who were now holding her down.

"No, you need to settle down. You heard what Justin said out there. He'll come in here and thump you good," Rachael yelled back at her.

Over across from the girls, Nathan and Cory were struggling trying to hold down Fâd. "Get off me. I want to kill her," Fâd yelled in rage.

"Knock it off. That's the admiral's daughter," Nathan yelled at him.

"I don't care. I hate her."

They continued holding him down, but soon, he stopped struggling, and they let him up. Rachael and Bridg made Ash promise to stop, and they finally let her up as well. They all stood up and now saw themselves. Everyone started laughing, except Fâd and Ash, because they were all covered in red paint. The clock on the scoreboard finally wound down, and the warehouse simulation disappeared, leaving them all standing in an empty room, except for red paint everywhere. Clearly on the scoreboard, the boys won since the paint bullets never registered a hit.

Private Justin came walking in then and stopped as his mouth fell open, and he looked all around the room. He then headed over to them with a furious look on his face. "You are going to clean this all up. Do you hear me?" he yelled at all of them.

"Yes, we'll clean it up," Rachael answered, grinning.

"You know where the hoses are. Get to it now!" he said and turned around, then left. The girls headed over to the walls, and Rachael ran her hand over a blue light on the wall. A virtual keyboard and screen appeared. She started pressing buttons and moving some things around on it, and the sidewalls opened up and hoses came out with pressure nozzles attached. Nathan, Cory, and Fâd each grabbed a hose as Ash and Rachael grabbed one. Bridg climbed on a large, rideable floor scrubber, and all of them hosed down the room.

Soon, even this became a game, and they all took turns on the scrubber as the others tried to shoot them off it with the high-pressure hoses. They were having a blast, and by now, all the red paint was completely washed away, including what was on them, as they were soaking wet. Then their parents walked in. The kids stopped immediately and stared at their parents, who had looks of total disbelief on their faces, but it was Admiral Larson who spoke out this time.

"What the hell is going on here?"

"Um, we had to clean the room since we got paint all over it," Fâd answered him, grinning, as the others started chuckling, and soon, all six of them broke out in laughter.

"I don't see the humor in this at all," Admiral Harper said and looked over at his wife, who was also giggling under her breath. He then had a slight smirk appear at the corner of his mouth, and soon, some of the adults were laughing.

"All right. It's time to go, boys. Tell the girls goodbye," Admiral Larson said to them, and the boys all turned and looked at the girls.

"Thanks. We had a blast. Maybe if we ever run into you again sometime, we could have a rematch," Nathan said to them, grinning.

"You're on," Ash answered as Rachael and Bridg nodded their heads in agreement, and then the boys headed toward the doors. Admiral Larson walked over to Ash and looked down at her. Even though he was her godfather, she couldn't help but notice he was very handsome, yet it was his white eyes that Ash had always been drawn to. Even his small pointed canines gave him a dangerous look, but she knew better.

"I would give you a hug goodbye, my girl, but you're all wet." Then he leaned down to her level and whispered into her ear, "Be strong, Ash, and never give up." Ash looked up at him with a bewildered look on her face, and he smiled down at her, then turned and headed over to her father. They shook each other's hands, and Larson put his hand on Harper's shoulder. Then he went over and once again hugged Ash's mother, and she could swear that her mother had tears in her eyes. Admiral Larson and the boys left, and the girls walked over to their parents and also left back to their cabins.

That night, as Ash laid down to sleep, she wondered what her godfather meant but if she had known it still wouldn't have made it any easier.

CHAPTER 3

OVER THE NEXT two months, the girls reported for duty every day, as was their punishment. They went to school, then back to their cabins and changed into crew member uniforms and picked up their job for the day from Ensign Chambers, who was really enjoying this. Days turned into weeks, and weeks turned into months, and finally, their punishment was over. Once again, they were free. But now they had gotten so used to working that they didn't know what to do and just hung out at one of their cabins.

It was on such a day as this that they were over at Rachael's, watching a comedy vid on a holographic screen where one could watch movies and videos, play computer games, or retrieve messages, when Ashley got an alert on her wrist multitool, a gauntlet-type band that was worn around the left wrist and forearm, which everyone received when they began school at the age of six.

In truth, it was a miniature computer that could handle many functions. One could pull up the virtual screen to do things like pay for items, look at maps, send and retrieve messages, or just serve as a communications device. It also could display a virtual keyboard, tracking devices, and scanning, and some of the more sophisticated ones could even hack into security devices and systems.

She looked down and saw a message to come home immediately and looked over at her friends. They all jumped up, running out the cabin door, and raced down the hall to the elevator. The three of them jumped in, and Ash told it which level, and soon, the doors were opening up on the crew deck. She took off running down the hall and could see many officers and medical personnel standing outside the door to her cabin, and fear ran through her. Even Bridgett and Rachael's parents were there, and when Ash and they started to push their way through the people, Rachael's parents grabbed Rachael and held her back as did Bridgett's father.

Ash continued to push through, now in a panic, and saw that there were even more people in her living room. Then she saw the ship's medical doctor coming out of her parents' room. She pushed her way over to it and went in. Her father was sitting on the bed, holding her mother in his arms, stroking her head, as she was leaning against him with her eyes closed. When Ash entered, he looked up, and she could see his eyes were wet, but no tears fell. Her mother then opened her eyes and looked over at her, putting her arms out for Ash. She ran over and flung herself into them, crying.

"Mommy, what's wrong? Why are all these people here? What's happening," Ash cried hysterically as her mother smoothed her hair back from her face, running her one hand through it and holding her with the other one.

Her mother held her tightly to herself. "Oh, my dear beautiful little girl, you have always been one of the bright lights in my life. Ash, I need you to listen to me. I must leave on another journey without you and your father, and I will need you to be strong for me. Take care of your father, and look out for one another, and never give up on your goals. I love you so much, and I am so proud of you," Lady Gailistra said to her as she continued stroking her black hair.

"No, Mommy, don't leave me. Please, I need you," Ash cried, clinging to her.

"No, you have always been strong like your father. I will always be here with you, and someday, we will be together again," her mother said and placed her frail hand over Ash's heart. Lady Gailistra then looked up at her husband, smiling weakly. "I love you so much, Thomas, and will always be with you. Thank you for the beautiful, wonderful life and love you gave me," she said, and Thomas bent his head down as tears now fell down his face and gently kissed her lips as she breathed her last breath into him, kissing him back. Thomas broke down for the first time in his life, gathering his wife in his arms, and cried holding her tightly, burying his face in her hair, as Ash clung to her mother's waist, also crying.

The room had cleared out quickly, and finally, forty-five minutes later, Harper was able to compose himself and gently laid his wife down on the bed. Ash was sobbing out loud as her father stood up and lifted her out of her mother's arms and left the room with her. She wrapped her arms around her father's neck and cried as he held her tightly to himself but now was completely stone and emotionless. Only the caressing and stroking of Ash's hair he was doing showed any remote semblance of feeling.

Ash started fighting him, reaching for her mother, once they left the room. "No, Daddy, not Mommy. I want her back. Please bring her back. I want my mommy!"

"I wish I could, darling, but this is something she has to do on her own. This is your mother's journey. She has completed this one with us. Now she must begin a new one, a better one, free of pain and sickness. But always remember, precious, Mommy will always love you, and we will see her again someday. She will be waiting for us," he said to her as he leaned his head into her hair and kissed her. Then Ash stopped fighting him and just clung to him, sobbing.

Admiral Harper went and sat down on a sofa in the living room, still holding a sobbing Ashley, when crew members came in and removed Lady Gailistra's body and placed it in a silver casket, then carried her out by honor guard to the morgue. He watched the whole thing, hanging on tightly to the only thing he had left of her, Ashley.

Other officers and their wives came in and quickly straightened up the master suite and left without saying a word to him. Everyone knew that words right now were no comfort, and Vice Admiral Harper was a hard man to try and talk to anyway. Eventually, everyone left, and it was just him and Ash alone, and she was now sound asleep in his arms. He carried her into her bedroom and laid her down in the bed, pulling the covers up on her. She never moved, and he looked down at the beautiful being his wife gave him and smoothed her hair out of her face. She looked so much like Gail, and he knew that in time, she was going to be just as beautiful. He started to leave, but Ash woke up and reached for him.

"Please, Daddy, don't leave me too."

"I won't ever leave you, precious, but I have things I need to get done. Rachael's mom will come over and stay with you for a while until I get back, so just get some sleep, okay?"

"Okay. I love you, Daddy."

"I love you, precious," Admiral Harper said and walked out of her room, fighting back the tears that wanted to fall, and headed down the hall to the living room. A few minutes later, a buzzer went off, and he told the person to come in. Rachael's mother, Abigail, walked in and went over and gave the admiral a hug, and he hugged her back.

"How is Ash holding up?" she asked him.

"As good as can be expected."

"How about you, Thomas?" she asked him, now informally since there weren't other crew members around. They had a long history together, so they could act this way among each other. Like for Admiral Harper now, they were also there when Tony Nelson's wife died delivering Bridgett. Death was something they had all experienced and gone through many times together, it being friends and family, and it had brought them all together as a family, more than just Admiral and crew.

"I'm here. That's all I can say for now," he replied, looking down the hallway, back at Ash's room.

"I'll watch over her," Abigail said knowing that he was struggling leaving Ashley here.

"Thanks, Abigail. I won't be long," Harper said and headed out the door. He had calls to make, and they weren't ones he was looking forward to. He had to notify Gail's parents and Sharni, her sister. They all knew Gail was ill. Her cancer in this last year had spread rapidly, and the medication and medical breakthroughs to treat it weren't working anymore. Everyone knew it was going to take her life eventually, but it still was something one never prepared for even when you were expecting it.

Back at the admiral's cabin, Abigail was in the kitchen, cleaning up some dirty dishes left in the sink, totally unaware of Bridgett and Rachael, who just sneaked in and crept down to Ashley's room. The door to her room slid open, and they went in. They could hear Ash quietly crying to herself.

"Ash, we're here for you," Rachael said into the dark room, and Ash quickly reached over, turned on her nightstand light, and put her arms out to her friends, who also started crying and went over, wrapping their arms around her, hugging her. All three of them held one another and continued to cry as Abigail, Rachael's mom, heard them and peeked in. She decided to leave them be. Right now, they all needed one another. Finally, an hour later, it got silent in Ash's room, and Abigail peeked in again and now saw all three girls sound asleep on Ash's bed.

Finally, Admiral Harper came back, looking drained after his calls. "How's Ash?"

"Fine. She finally fell asleep, but she's not alone in there," Abigail replied as Harper walked over to his daughter's door as it slid open and peeked in. The corner of his mouth twitched a little as he looked at the three girls sound asleep on the bed and then turned around as the door slid shut and walked back to the living room.

"I'm glad she has her friends with her."

"Yeah. Those three girls are more like sisters than friends," Abigail replied with a gentle smile.

"Very true. Thanks, Abigail, for staying with her. I'm sure Raul is wondering where you are," Thomas said to her, and she smiled again at him.

"Is there anything else I can get or do for you?"

"No, I'll be fine. Thanks anyway," Harper replied with an emotionless look.

Abigail again gave him a hug and left the cabin, and Thomas went and changed for bed. He walked into his bedroom, sat on the edge of the bed, and finally broke down crying again for the second time in his life. This was going to be the first time in over forty-seven years that he would be sleeping alone without Gail beside him. Finally, he regained his composure and, once again, was in full control of his emotions, back to his stone-cold, commanding persona. He climbed into bed and fell asleep.

* * *

Vice Admiral Harper was woken at 0600 in the morning by a buzzing from his intercom. "Yes, what is it, Ensign?" he said in a groggy voice.

"Sorry to disturb you, sir, but the *Lithia* is pulling up beside us and requesting permission for one of her shuttle's to dock."

"Permission granted. Tell him I'll be there shortly."

"Understood, sir."

Harper got out of bed and changed into a clean admiral's uniform and brushed back his hair and then his teeth. He took one last look in the bathroom mirror and headed out into the living room. The cabin was quiet and dark, but lights came on as he walked into the living room. Usually, Gail was already up at this time and had breakfast ready for him and Ash, but now that would be no more, and they would have to adapt another routine. Thomas got on his intercom and called Raul.

"Yes, sir?" Raul answered, fully alert.

"Sorry, Raul, but can Abigail come over and stay with the girls while I go and meet Larson down at the docking bay?" Thomas asked him.

"Sure. He never changes, does he? Six in the morning?" Raul said with an annoyed sigh.

"Nope, he sure doesn't. Tell Abigail thanks. I'm heading out now."

"I will, and she's on her way."

Admiral Harper left his cabin and walked into the elevator. "Shuttle bay 4," he commanded, and the elevator started to move. In a matter of seconds, the door slid open, and he stepped out into the long, brightly lit corridor, heading toward the shuttle bay. He heard the sound that the automatic doors made when they opened, and out stepped his closest and oldest friend, Rear Admiral Larson, from the shuttle bay he had just landed in. They walked toward each other, and both men gripped each other's hand, shook them, then out of the blue gave each other a hug but quickly released each other.

"How's Ash doing?" Larson asked his best friend.

"She's pretty torn up, but her friends came over and stayed with her last night. She was still asleep when I left to meet with you."

"She's young and will bounce back. It's you I worry about. I know how much you love Gail."

"Yes, but I knew this was coming and had time to prepare somewhat for it. Look at you, Larson. How have you been able to endure it all these years?"

"I have my son, my ship, and my crew, and I do still have her. I love Sharni and always will. It's just not the way I would like it to be."

"I suppose you're right. I have those as well. Even though you aren't together, she loves you too and always will."

"I know, and that is the hardest and most painful thing in my life. At least you got to have a life with the woman you love, so hang on to that, because there are worse things out there," Larson said to his friend and put his hand on his shoulder. Both admirals turned and walked back toward the elevator and, before long, headed back up to Admiral Harper's cabin. They walked in as Abigail was fixing the girls some breakfast, who were awake now, and when Ashley saw her godfather, she jumped off the barstool and ran over to him. He scooped her up, hugging her tightly to himself, as she once again cried.

"Oh, sweet thing, how are you doing?" he said to her, fighting back the tears that wanted to fall as well.

Ash finally regained her control and looked at him, trying to put on a brave face. "I'm okay, Admiral. I know my mother would want me to be strong, and she asked me to help take care of Father, which I will. Plus, like mother said, she is always with me here," Ash said, putting her hand on her heart, with tear-soaked eyes.

"You're absolutely right, darling. She will always be with you," he said to her and hugged her tightly again, then set her back down.

She ran over to her father, who picked her up and gave her a big hug as well, then set her down and made her go eat.

"Hello, Gerrard. Looking handsome as ever," Abigail said to him.

"As are you, Abigail. I was always jealous of Raul," Admiral Larson replied, grinning, and Abigail started giggling.

"You always were the flirt," Abigail said, and they both started laughing then. Rachael spun around on her barstool and looked at Rear Admiral Larson.

"So where are the boys that were with you last time?" she asked with a mouth full of pancakes.

"Rachael, show some manners. Don't talk with your mouth full," her mother scolded her.

"Sorry, Mom," she replied, turning back around as some of the pancakes fell out of her mouth and onto her plate.

"Oh, gross, Rachael. For someone who tries and acts all girly, you have to be one of the most disgusting people I have ever known, second only to Ash," Bridgett said to her, trying not to gag. Rachael looked over at her and grinned. Admiral Harper just shook his head as a slight smirk appeared at the corner of his mouth, but his eyes showed no emotion. He and Gerrard walked over and sat down on the sofa and armchair.

Harper was starting to tell Gerrard about the funeral plans when his intercom buzzed. "Go ahead."

"Admiral, the vatorian battleship *Astra Sink* will be here in twenty-four hours."

"Thank you, Chambers," Harper replied as he looked over at Gerrard. His friend had a slightly pained look on his face now. Even Abigail looked over at them with a concerned look on her face as well.

"Father, is that Aunt Sharni's ship?" Ash asked from the bar where she was eating pancakes.

"Yes, and she is bringing your mother's parents."

"Grandmother and Grandfather Tol Vasna?"

"Yes. They are coming for your mother's ceremony of passage," Harper told his daughter. She turned back around but now had a scowl on her face. Rachael saw it and knew why she had it. Ash's grandparents were always criticizing her for looking too much human and not enough vatoria. Luckily, her aunt, Lady Sharnestra Tol Vasna, would be here, and she would always put them in their place

Sharnestra, or Sharni, as everyone called her, was very forceful and never backed down from anyone or anything. And like her sister, Gailistra, she was also very beautiful and tall. She had refused several betrothal requests and never married. There was a rumor that she had been bonded to someone, but no one knew who, and still to this day, she remained single. Of course, everyone figured the reason was because of what happened to her during the carian war.

Captain Sharnestra, her sister, and a handful of their crewmen were fighting a carian battleship when their ship took a serious hit, knocking out its engines and leaving them helpless as the battleship bore down on them. The engine room was flooded with toxic gases, and there was no time to vent the room, and anyone besides her who knew how to repair engines were dead. So she ran into it, quickly bypassing the secondary engines, and got the main drive back online. They were then able to move out of the carian's gun range and barely kept ahead of them as the sentinel fleet showed up and destroyed the carian battleship.

Sharnestra saved them all, but the toxic fumes almost killed her, and over the next several days, she teetered between life and death. Finally, she pulled through but found out that she was now sterile and would never have children. Thus, any prospect of a prominent marriage after that would never come her way again from her own people, the vatorias, even with her family's high social standing.

"So, Rear Admiral Larson, you never answered my question," Rachael asked again, turning around on the barstool, trying to change the subject of Ash's grandparents.

"Oh, that's right, Rachael. They are back in school and are not very happy about it, because they hate wearing school uniforms. But I can honestly say, they had a blast when they were here with me. They talk about it all the time. I think you girls surprised them," Admiral Larson told her with a slight smile.

"Yeah, that's right, girl power," Rachael said and turned to Bridgett, and they gave each other a high five, and then she turned to Ash, who weakly smiled. Abigail just rolled her eyes and started cleaning up after the girls, and once they were done, they got down and headed to the door.

"Ash, where do you think you're going?" her father asked with a concerned look.

"Over to Rachael's. I'm going to look at her dresses to see which one I want to wear so I can look pretty for Mom during her ceremony."

"What's wrong with your dresses?"

"I just want to see what she has. I want to look my best for Mom," Ash replied, rolling her eyes, and the girls left, talking among themselves. Harper watched her go and looked over at Abigail, confused by this.

Abigail sighed. "They share clothes all the time. Truthfully, I don't know whose is whose anymore. Me and Gail gave up a long time ago trying to figure it."

"I guess there's a lot I'm going to be learning about girls now," Harper said to Larson with a scowl on his face.

"Hey, I only know about boys. Girls are a totally different creature," Larson said, putting his hands up, emphasizing his lack of knowledge. Abigail smiled at the two men, shaking her head, and finished cleaning up after the girls, then excused herself and left as well.

"So, Thomas, you have only one more year with Ash here until she leaves for prep school for the next seven years. Then after that, it's off to the academy. What are you going to do?"

"I don't know. I haven't given it much thought."

"I'll tell you what you're going to do. You're going to get a place in New Guinea and stay there while she is going to school there."

"I can't do that, and you know it. Space is my home, and I will go crazy. Besides, I'm needed here, especially with what we are all trying to accomplish now."

"Okay. I will make you a deal. We will alternate. You take two years of duty, and then I will take two years until the kids are graduated from prep school. That way, there will always be one of us planet side and one of us on duty. Of course, special occasions we will come back for and the normal three-month span between the new advancements. But at least this way, we can keep an eye on them. Does that sound good to you?"

"That I could probably live with. New Guinea, huh? Never been there. What's it like?" Harper asked him with a scowl on his face.

"It's nice, full of humans and council supporters. You should fit in nicely," Larson said with a slight grin.

"Oh yeah, they'll love me, especially with how well council and I get along."

"Not any worse than me, and you know how supportive council are of me."

"Yeah, but you don't live among them. I will if I get a place in New Guinea."

"True," Larson replied with a devious grin.

"So how is Lily doing? You haven't said anything about her," Harper asked Gerrard.

"Not good. Her mind is going more and more every day. She is now on a very high dose of sedatives and nueralizers. I'm afraid I'm going to have her committed to a clinic for her own good. Fâd won't even talk to his mother anymore. Of course, she doesn't even recognize him as it is," Larson said with a sad look on his face.

"I'm sorry. It must be tough on the boy. But he's a lot like you, and luckily, he's better looking," Harper said with a cold smirk.

"You're just saying that because I always got the girl when we were much younger, and you spent many nights alone." Gerrard grinned at his friend.

"Yeah, but I remember some of those women, and a few of them, I wasn't sure if they were even female."

"You would be surprised how gorgeous one can look after a bottle of feralosian ale. Of course, the mornings were hell and scary waking up next to a few of them. Plus, the fear of not knowing what you might have done the night before was always a downer, but I always knew you had my back. And you can't get all sanctimonious on me. At least I can honestly say I have never had a feral before." Gerrard started chuckling now.

"True, and it took me some time to heal up from those scratches, but wow, that was something else." Harper had a slight smirk on his face, and Larson grinned.

"You remember that time when me, you, Gail, and Sharni went to that bar in Odessa and those borvians showed up?" Larson asked him.

"Yeah. There were about a dozen of them, and like usual, we were plastered. If I remember right, they came over and started hitting on the girls, and you told them to go fly away to their bat cave. Of course, the fight was on, and they started kicking our ass, but Gail and Sharni finally got up and beat the crap out of them, then dragged our sorry, drunk asses out of the bar and back to our tents," Harper added. Even though his mouth didn't show a grin, his cold gray eyes finally did.

"Those poor girls. They got us out of more fights and were always dragging us back to where we were staying at the time and patching us up. But you have to admit, we had a blast, and I wouldn't trade it for anything," Larson said, now with a sober look on his face.

"Neither would I," Harper replied. Even though bringing up those memories hurt, they still, in a way, also helped; and having his brother here—for that was how he felt about Larson—he needed that.

CHAPTER 4

"ADMIRAL, THE *ASTRA Sink* is requesting permission to dock," Ensign Chambers told him as he sat behind his console on the bridge with his hand rubbing his chin, lost in thought.

"What? Oh, sorry, Ensign. Yes, permission granted. Notify Rear Admiral Larson to meet me at docking port 10," Admiral Harper said, now coming back to his senses.

"Yes, Admiral."

Harper then stood up and let out a sigh. This wasn't going to be fun. He had always butted heads with Gail's father, and now that she was gone and not there to keep the peace, this could get ugly. He knew that they would blame her death on him, and he was prepared for it. Thank goodness, though, Sharni was here. She would make sure things at least stayed civilized. Harper worried about Larson, though. Seeing Sharni was going to be hard for Gerrard, and to try and keep it professional between them both, almost impossible.

He got on the elevator and told it to take him to docking bay 10, and as the doors slid shut, he closed his eyes and leaned back against the wall. Thank goodness Ash wasn't going to be around when they boarded. She was again over at Rachael's, watching vids with her and Bridgett. In no time, the doors slid open, and he stepped out just as Gerrard stepped out of another elevator located a little ways down the causeway from him, and they both headed toward the docking doors. They looked at each other, and both took a deep breath as the docking bay doors slid open.

Out stepped a beautiful vatorian woman in her formal captain's uniform, and directly behind her came Gail's parents. They both were dressed very elegantly, and you could see the pain on their faces over the loss of their younger daughter. Sharni walked over to Thomas, and they both embraced each other, and she kissed him on the cheek. Then she looked over at Larson and broke down crying. He pulled her into his arms and held her tightly. Lord Benz Tol Vasna and Lady Tealo Tol Vasna both walked over to Harper, and Benz glared at him as Tealo started crying.

"Welcome aboard the *Justification*," Harper said and nodded to them.

"So you finally managed to kill my daughter after all," Benz said to Thomas.

"Father, that is enough! We are all hurting here, Thomas more so. I don't care what you think. Gail loved and chose him. If you cannot be civil, then remain on my ship." Sharni turned quickly away from Larson and warned her father.

"Fine. I will do this for Gailistra. Where is my grandchild? I don't see her here," Benz asked, looking around.

"Ashley is over at her friend's cabin. I felt that it would be better to see her after you had time to settle in," Harper replied coldly.

"She should be with her family right now. I'm sure the child is confused and torn up about all this," the vatoria patriarch said curtly.

"Ashley is a very strong and determined young girl, a lot like her mother," Admiral Larson told him, standing beside Sharni.

"Ah, the one who abandoned my other daughter. I should have known you would be here." Benz glared at Larson.

"I did not abandon her, and you know that full well. It was her choice. And just so you know, I still would never take back what I did." Larson now spoke with venom in his tone, and Harper knew he was mad. He put his hand on Larson's shoulder to try and calm his friend down.

"Father, this is not the time or the place for this. But like Gerrard said, I would also never take back what we did either," Sharni said to her father, and he stared at her in shock.

Lady Tealo now spoke up. "But, Sharnestra, you can never settle down with another and at least have a somewhat happy life even if you can't have children."

"Enough! I tire of this and will not tolerate anymore aboard my ship. You are welcomed here as my guests, and I will be courteous to you for Gail's sake, but you will not start anything around Ashley. Do I make myself clear?" Admiral Harper said in a very commanding tone, and one could clearly hear the cold warning in it. Even Benz Tol Vasna, who clearly disliked Harper, knew not to push him, for he was a very powerful and dangerous man if the situation called for it.

"Fine. Show us to our chamber so we can rest," Benz retorted.

"Follow me," Harper replied and nodded his head at them, leading the way to the elevator. They all climbed in, and Admiral Harper said the level, and in no time, the elevator opened up again. He led the way down the plush hallway to the guest quarters that was reserved for dignitaries. He put his hand on the blue scan pad on the wall next to one of the doors. It lit up, and the door slid open as Lord and Lady Tol Vasna walked in and surveyed it. Then Harper turned, looking at Larson and Sharni, and just left them standing in the hallway, once again getting on the elevator and going up to his bridge.

Admiral Harper went over and sat down in his chair and leaned his head down, rubbing his left temple with his hand. He was still like that half an hour later when Larson walked up next to him. "Well, that went well," Larson said, watching the crew of the *Justification* working.

"Actually, it was better than I thought it might be. But for a minute there, I thought you might knock the crap out of Benz."

"For a minute there, I thought about it," Larson replied and looked down at his friend with a slight grin on his face.

"How's Sharni doing?" Harper asked with a concerned look.

"Okay. I can tell she is taking this hard with Gail's passing, but she would never let on how bad she's hurting. She's a strong woman. I just wish things could have been different for me and her."

"I know. So do I. Maybe someday, you'll both get a second chance together."

"Maybe. So how's the headache?" Larson asked with a concerned look on his face for his friend.

"Not bad. The doctor has me trying some new experimental medication, and so far, it has helped a lot. I don't get the headaches near as much or as strong. I just hope Ash doesn't have to endure them. What about Fâd? Is he plagued with them?"

"No, but of course, he's not as powerful as you are either. But I do worry about him, especially with Lily now having the psychosis. Her mind is almost gone, and the violence and dementia are setting in."

"Fâd won't. I really believe that it is true what some of the studies have uncovered about natural-occurring. Lily was an exposure victim, and unfortunately, their percentage rate against psychotic disintegration is less than zero. Also, their kinetics is unheard of being passed down to their offspring. Besides, we know there is no way Fâd could have gotten his kinetics from her anyway since he's really not hers. No, don't worry, your son will be fine."

"Yeah, I guess you're right. You know, though, there is one thing I wish we have been able to solve."

"What's that?" Harper asked.

"Where the hell you came from. I still believe you are not all human and will till the day I die."

"Well, DNA says otherwise."

"Yeah, but you should let a real scientist study it, like a proturin. Don't you find it odd that the orphanage we grew up in has absolutely no records of you, that you were found wandering the streets of Alpha Prime when you were only three years of age?"

"So did you ever think that maybe I don't want to know?" Harper looked up at his friend from his chair with a scowl on his face.

"Who cares what you want? I want to know. I swear, there has to be some watorian blood in you somewhere."

"Yeah, well, sorry. I'm fangless, and my eyes are the same color as they have been for years, so that theory is unsound," Harper replied with no emotion, as was typical of him.

"True. Plus, you're not very handsome, and watorian men are known for their good looks, so you're probably right."

"You don't really want to get into this again, do you?" Harper asked with a devious smirk on his face, and Larson started chuckling.

* * *

Over at Rachael's cabin, the girls were lying on her bed, talking. "Ash, you should feel privileged. At least you got to know and were with your mother. I never got that chance. All I have of my mother are pictures and no memories," Bridgett said to her with tears running down her cheeks. Ash and Rachael both put their arms around her, and once again, the girls started crying.

"I know, Bridg, and really, I am thankful for it, but it still hurts."

"It will always hurt, but you know you both will see them again someday. I truly believe that," Rachael said to them as Ash and Bridgett nodded their heads in agreement.

Ash wiped the tears from her eyes. "I bet Aunt Sharni is here finally. Let's go see her."

The girls all jumped off Rachael's bed and looked in her mirror, wiping the tears from their faces, and quickly ran through the sliding bedroom door, barely giving it time to open. Just before they got to the main cabin door, Rachael's mother hollered at them, asking where they were headed.

"Ash wants to go and see her aunt Sharni," Rachael yelled back as her mother now walked around the corner, looking at them.

"Don't you think maybe she might want to see her alone?" Abigail asked her daughter.

"No, I want my friends to go with me. Please?" Ash asked, and Abigail smiled at her and gave the okay. The girls then headed out the door and quickly down the hallway to the elevator. They stood waiting for it, and finally, the doors slid open as Captain Sharni stepped out in front of them. The girls all stood staring at her with their mouths wide open, and she smiled down at them. Ash was the first to recover and started crying, leaping into her aunt's open arms. Sharni was also crying, hugging her tightly.

"Oh, my dear, dear little one, I am so sorry. I should have been here with you and your mother in these last days. Don't cry, Ash. Your mother is watching over you right now. I will never leave you again," Sharni said to her and even put her free arm around Bridgett and Rachael, who were also hugging her around the waist, crying. Abigail had come out of her cabin when she heard the commotion outside and smiled at Sharni when she looked at her from down the hall and headed toward her.

"Girls, lets go back to Abigail's cabin," Sharni said as she tried to walk with all three girls hanging off her. Sharni and Abigail met halfway, and Sharni put Ash down, then she and Abigail hugged each other with tears running down their faces.

"It is so good to see you, Sharni. You are just as lovely as ever."

"And it's good to see you, Abigail. I see you haven't change either. How do you do it, keep your looks and put up with Raul?" Sharni teased.

"It's amazing what the medical field can do these days," Abigail replied, and both women started laughing and continued on to Abigail's cabin. Once inside, the girls headed to Rachael's room and jumped on her bed again and started talking as the two women went and sat on the sofa in the living room, facing each other.

It was true, Sharni still looked ageless like always. She was tall for a female vatoria, even more so than Gail. But unlike Gail, who always kept her hair cut short in a pixie style, Sharni's was long and brilliant white, but she kept the sides pulled into a bun at the back of her head and left the rest hanging down. She had all the other characteristics of the vatoria people—the gold eyes, the light, almost barely blue, skin, and the many scroll-like gold markings all over. She also possessed telepathic abilities and carried a high level in hand-to-hand combat. Even in her vatoria captain's uniform, it wasn't hard to miss how rather beautiful she was.

"Okay, Sharni, I know something is on your mind. I've known you and your sister too long to not be able to tell. I remember our school days from long ago," Abigail asked her with a devious grin, and Sharni half smiled back.

"Well, I need your advice about Thomas. How do you think he will react if I ask to take Ash with me to stay until she is ready for prep school?"

"He won't let you, I can tell you that right now. I can also tell you that he and Gerrard have been coming up with a plan, and I think he was going to talk to you about it, something about New Guinea."

"Gerrard, huh? I should have known. Those two still won't do anything without the other," Sharni said, chuckling.

Abigail looked toward her daughter's door and then back to Sharni. "Was it hard seeing him again?"

Sharni smiled at her friend. "No. We stay in touch and manage to find time for one another. Of course, this here is tough as we have to keep this strictly professional since Ash does not know, but I think Fâd, Gerrard's son, is figuring it out. Anyway, that's what Gerrard told me."

"What about Gerrard's wife, Lily?"

"She has known all along about us. She came to us with the proposition of carrying Gerrard's child since she knew I could not, and their culture demanded that because of his many proven feats and title, he must pass on his genes. I, of course, wanted this for Gerrard's sake, but he was against it. We talked and discussed it, and finally, he gave in. It was all very professionally done, and he married Lily so his child would have his name.

"As for the conception of Fâd, it was done in a lab at Genetrap on Alpha Prime. It was all done through gene therapy, and once the doctors had a viable embryo, they implanted it into Lily. Otherwise, Gerrard would have never gone through with it because of the bonding. The only connection they have to each other is Fâd, and even after their marriage, they never took up residency together. It was only when Gerrard took Fâd to see Lily—after Fâd was born since he remained with Gerrard—that he had any contact with Lily

"I feel sorry for Lily, for I think she did at one time start to having feelings for Gerrard and hoped he would feel the same for her, but he never can. He is kind to her, and I know he is taking every step he can right now to help her, but she's failing fast. Even Fâd has drawn away from her and refuses to see her anymore, which breaks my heart, but she no longer recognizes anyone. The psychosis is getting so bad that Gerrard is looking into putting her in a clinic for her and everyone's own safety," Sharni told her and looked down at her hands.

"But if they never bonded, how did Fâd inherit her kinetics?"

"He didn't. Nothing from Lily could have transferred over to Fâd. The only thing the doctors, whom Larson trusted, can tell is that it is possible Gerrard himself is a natural carrier of the particular gene that causes kinetics. It has just never manifested itself in him, which is the other unusual phenomena. It is unheard of, watorians having natural-occurring kinetics. At first, it was believed that Fâd somehow got it from Lily when everyone found out she has kinetics. But when they ran a DNA strand from Fâd, it was all Larson's. Fâd is Gerrard's genetic double.

"The shocker was, when everyone found out that Lily was an exposure victim, which was how she got kinetics, no one knew that until she started showing symptoms right after Fâd was born and they found the tumor. Gerrard has had Fâd checked by proturin doctors that he trust, and so far, the tumor that is present in all exposure kinetics is not present in him, just like in Ash and even Thomas, because theirs are naturally-occurring."

"I saw him when Gerrard came to dinner a while back. He is a good-looking boy and will grow up to be just as handsome, if not more so, than his father. He's definitely going to be a heartbreaker like his father," Abigail grinned, as did Sharni.

"Yes, and like his father, he's very forceful, strong-willed, cocky, and has a natural leading quality about himself but more aloft than Larson, in a way colder. Speaking of that, I heard my little niece gave him a run for his money."

"Oh yeah. You know Ash. She won't back down from anyone. I guess they almost punched each other out on the bridge when Thomas had some of the sentinel commanders with him, and then later, the girls tricked the boys into a game of combat tag and switched the rubber rounds in their guns to paint rounds and covered the boys. It got out of hand, and by the time the match was over, all the kids were covered with red paint. They, of course, got into trouble again and had to clean the simulation chamber up and even turned that into a game as they were trying to shoot each other off a floor scrubber with high-pressured hoses," Abigail told her, and both women now were laughing a little.

"Good for her, but it's not like she doesn't intentionally start a lot of it."

"True. She takes after Thomas there, defiant and determined."

"Well, I guess I had better get back to check on my parents," Sharni said as she stood up.

"That's right. How did that all go when you landed?" Abigail asked with a concerned look on her face.

"Not good. At one point, I thought Gerrard was going to lose it and beat the crap out of my father. It was Thomas that finally had enough and, in his commanding voice, informed my father that he will not tolerate anymore."

"Oh yeah, I know that voice and the look. One knows not to push it anymore or question him. Thomas is a great man, but he is also a very dangerous one as well," Abigail whispered, and Sharni nodded her head in agreement. Sharni walked over to the girls' door and knocked on it, and the door then slid open.

"Ash, I'm going back over and check on your grandfather and grandmother Tol Vasna. Would you like to go with me to see them?" her aunt asked.

Ash frowned a little, and Sharni couldn't blame her, but she still was their only grandchild. "I suppose," Ash said, getting up from the bed. Then she went over and took her aunt's outstretched hand. They both walked to the door, and Abigail once again gave Sharni and Ash a hug as they walked out into the hall, and the door to Rachael's cabin shut behind them.

"Aunt Sharni, they're not going to criticize me again for being part human, are they?" Ash asked, looking up at her tall aunt as they headed to the elevator.

"No, precious, I won't let them," Sharni replied, looking down at her niece. She was amazed how much Ash looked like Gail, but there was also a lot of Thomas there. They both stepped into the elevator, and Sharni said the level, and in a few minutes, the doors slid open to the deck that housed the guest quarters. They both stepped out, and Sharni, still holding Ash's hand, went and buzzed the bell on one of the doors. The door slid open, and Benz Tol Vasna stood in the opening, looking down at Ash. But instead of his usual survey of her, he bent down and scooped her up in his arms, hugging her tightly, and walked into the room. Then Tealo came over and put her arms out, and Ash went to her, and they both started crying. Sharni came over and put her hand on Ash's back, and tears ran down her face as well.

"Oh, let me get a good look at you. My, you have grown, and so pretty. You look so much like your mother. Doesn't she, Benz?" Tealo asked her husband as she sat Ash back down and held her back at arm's length.

"Yes. You could almost be her twin," Ash's grandfather commented with a smile.

"Really? But, of course, with black hair like Father's?" Ash asked as her face lit up.

"Yep, even with the black hair like your father's," Sharni added, and she could see her father's eyess narrow at the mention of Thomas. Ash's grandmother led her over to the sofa and sat down, pulling Ash onto her lap.

"How are you doing, dear? Is there anything we can get you or do for you?" her grandmother asked her.

"I'm doing good, Grandmother, better than Father. He is having a hard time. I can hear him cry sometimes at night when he goes to bed and thinks I'm asleep," Ash said, looking her grandmother in the eyes, and a tear ran down Tealo's cheek.

"Yes, and he will continue to have a hard time with it. He loved your mother very much, and for us adults, we have a harder time in letting go of our loved ones so they can continue on their new journey," Tealo said to her and looked over at her husband. Benz turned away and walked over, looking out one of the windows in their cabin, at the large void of space beyond it.

"That's what Mother told me too. She said it was time for her to go on another journey without me and Father but that we will be together again someday, and I believe her. Mom never lied," Ash said defiantly now.

"You're absolutely right, and I think we all should hang on to that sound advice your mother gave you," Tealo replied, warmly smiling at her grandchild. Ash was a marvel. Thomas and Gerrard were right. She was a lot stronger than anyone had given her credit for, and they all could benefit from listening to her.

Ash continued to talk to her grandmother and aunt. Then they heard the buzzer to the cabin sound as someone was wanting in. Benz walked over and opened it, and Vice Admiral Harper was standing outside it with a stone-cold expression on his face. Ash saw him and leaped off her grandmother's lap and ran over to him, leaping into his arms. Harper's face changed dramatically and now was soft and caring as he hugged his daughter. Benz stood aside as Harper walked in carrying Ash and went over and stood next to Sharni.

"Can I speak to you in private, please?" Harper looked down at her but once again with his face void of any emotion.

"If this has to do with our grandchild, then we all need to be in on this discussion," Benz said out loud with a look of defiance.

"All right. It does, and you are right, Ash is your grandchild. But I am her father, and what I decide for Ash is not negotiable," Harper said, and the warning in his voice was easily recognizable. Benz nodded his acceptance, for he could not fault Thomas for this. If he were in this man's shoes, he would be the same way.

"Please, Thomas, sit down," Tealo asked him, motioning to a large armchair, which he accepted. He went over, still with Ash in his arms, and sat. Ash moved around and sat on his lap as he reached around her neck and brushed her hair back away from her face.

"So what have you been thinking?" Sharni asked him as she made herself more comfortable on the sofa.

Thomas let out a sigh. "As you know, Ash will be leaving for prep school in less than a year. I plan on keeping her here with me until that time, but when it draws near, I will be taking a leave of absence for a couple years. I have purchased a residency in New Guinea near the school. Once my two years are up, I have to return to active duty, at which time I would like to ask you, Sharni, if you could stay in New Guinea with Ash for the next two years while I am gone.

"I will be splitting my absences with Rear Admiral Larson, as he also has a child in school, and then we both can oversee our children. Unlike most children, I don't want Ash to have to boarder at the school and prefer to have her remain at home. Upon her completion of prep school, there will be a one-year waiting period before she has to head to the academy, at which time she will return here with me aboard the *Justification*.

"I will still be on active duty for a couple more months once the academy starts back up, and I was wondering if you, Sharni, could stay with her for three months until the academy starts," Thomas asked and watched Ash the whole time he spoke. Ash just sat there, not saying a word, and then looked over at her aunt.

"I would be honored too. Yes, I will stay with her," Sharni said with a big smile, and Ash grinned back.

"Ash can come and stay with us for those three months and any other time in between that you are on active duty," Benz said to Thomas and smiled over at Ash as well.

"Thank you. I know Gail would be happy," Thomas replied and ran his hand through Ash's long hair with a slight smirk on his face.

"No, Thomas, thank you for giving us this opportunity with our only grandchild. I was wrong about you, and I see my error now. Gail did love you, and because of that, I ask your forgiveness," Benz said, looking Harper in the eyes.

Thomas stood up and sat Ash down but held on to her hand, looking back at Benz. "For Gail, I accept." Then he nodded his head to the patriarch.

He then headed over to the door with Ash, but she stopped and looked up at him. "Father, can I stay with Grandmother and Grandfather for a little while longer?"

"Sure. I'll see you when everybody comes for dinner," Thomas replied with a slight smile as he looked down at his beautiful little girl with pride.

CHAPTER 5

ASH STOOD BESIDE her father as the ship's reverend spoke to the massive gathering in the ship's chapel. It was a fairly large room with a high, vaulted ceiling and clean white walls that had chandeliers hanging down to give off light. There were many long benches covered in silver-and-white cloth for people to sit, which were filled to capacity by crew members, who were also standing at attention. Even all along the walls, crew members stood, and you could barely see the stained glass pictures hanging on them, depicting beautiful mountain scenes.

Up in front of everyone was a large podium where the reverend stood speaking, and in front of him was the silver cylinder of the casket of Ash's mother sitting on a track that led to the outer hull of the ship. Ash was holding her father's hand, and her aunt Sharni was standing on the other side of her, holding her other hand. Lord Benz and Lady Tealo Tol Vasna, Gail's parents, were on the other side of Sharni, and Rear Admiral Larson was standing next to, in a way, his brother, Vice Admiral Thomas Harper.

Harper stared coldly at the cylindrical silver casket that was draped in both the sentinel flag and the vatoria flag that his wife's body was now laid to rest in, totally void of any emotion but firmly clutching his daughter's hand. Ashley, too, like her father, was also a pillar of stone and stared at her mother's casket but would once in a while look up at her aunt, who would warmly smile down at her.

Finally, the reverend called for a bow of heads as he said a final prayer, and honor guards from both the *Justification* and the *Astra Sink* came forward and ceremoniously folded the flags. Once they finished, they walked over and presented the sentinel flag to Vice Admiral Harper, along with the vatoria flag as well. But Harper let go of Ash's hand and walked over and gave the vatoria flag to Lord Benz Tol Vasna and saluted him. The patriarch returned the salute, then bowed to Admiral Harper, who turned back and took his place again with his daughter and best friend, Larson, facing the casket.

Music began to play as the casket started moving forward along a track in the floor, and you could now see on the back end of the casket the two small propulsion engines that would be pushing the casket out into space as a small door opened, allowing the casket to pass through to the other side in a small white room where it sat as the engines came online to enter space. A large window was there, and you could see the casket now at the outer doors of the ship as the blue propulsion drives glowed on the casket. Once the outer doors opened, it completely shot the casket out into space like a torpedo, leaving a trail of gas that lit up blue in the black void of space. Harper watched it as the blue light faded into darkness and then looked down at Ash as she continued to stare into space.

The gathering started breaking up, and crew members came up, each and every one of them saluting Admiral Harper. Some of the crew members who had more dealings with Ash usually gave her a hug, and of course, there was a lot of crying. But like her father, Ash remained strong and never shed one tear.

Hours later, the crewmen were still coming in and showing their respects to their admiral, but Ash was getting tired and starting to fidget around. Sharni leaned over to Thomas and whispered in his ear, "I'm going to take Ash back to your cabin so she can change and rest."

"Thanks. Yeah, she's had enough," Harper answered, looking down at Ash as she rolled her head around.

"Come on, Ash. Let's go back so you can change," Sharni said to her niece.

"Thank goodness. I've got to get out of this prison outfit. Mother finally got her way, though," Ash said, reaching for her aunt's hand as the admiral, Larson, and Sharni looked down at her.

"And what's that?" her father asked.

"She finally got me into a dress."

They all couldn't help it and started chuckling a little among themselves, and people started looking at them, wondering what was so funny. Sharni led her niece toward the door and then heard her parents chuckling as Thomas told them what Ash had said, and she giggled a little again, looking down at her niece, smiling. It took them some time to get to the elevator through the endless line of crewmen and women but finally managed. As they stepped into the elevator, suddenly, out of nowhere, Rachael and Bridgett leaped in as the doors shut.

"Damn, that was close," Rachael said, getting up off the floor and straightening her dress.

"Rachael Torres, watch your mouth," Sharni said to her but with a slight grin.

"Sorry. Forgot an adult was present."

"Do you girls talk like this all the time?" Sharni asked, now a little shocked at them.

"No, not all the time. Well, yeah, we kind of do," Bridgett replied.

"Ashley Gail Harper, you talk like this too?" Sharni looked down at her niece in disbelief.

"Are you kidding me? She's the worse one," Rachael exclaimed, and Ash gave her a dirty look.

"Okay. If you two are going to get me into trouble, you can just get off the elevator right now."

"Oh, no, they don't. I want to hear more about this," Sharni informed her.

The elevator finally stopped on the crew deck, and they all got off and walked to the admiral's cabin. Sharni put her hand over the scan pad since she knew that Harper had locked it down when he left; otherwise, the door would have slid open at their approach.

They all walked in, and Ash and her friends headed to her room, and they all changed out of their formal dresses.

Rachael and Bridgett put on some of Ash's clothes. Of course, by now, no one knew for sure whose clothes was whose since they would wear one another's all the time. They walked out, and Sharni had removed her formal military captain's tunic. She was now standing in just her dress pants and a military-issued tank top and had let her long blond hair down. You could clearly see her many gold scroll markings across her shoulders, neck, down her arms and hands, and on the exposed areas of her chest. She kicked off her boots and went over and crashed on the couch, and the girls ran over and jumped on it next to her. Rachael and Bridgett started checking out her markings and even had her get up and show them her back.

"So how far down do those go?" Rachael asked curiously.

"Clear down my legs, stopping on top of my feet."

"Do all vatorias have them?" Bridgett asked, tracing some of them on Sharni's back with her finger.

"Yeah. I'm sure you've seen Ash's, haven't you?"

"Yeah, but hers are nothing compared to yours. I think they're beautiful. I wish I could have some," Rachael said with a little jealousy to her tone.

"You can. Just go get them tattooed on," Ash told her, grinning.

"No, I want them without pain. Hello? Pain is bad," Rachael said to her, scowling as Ash grinned.

"That reminds me. Father bought a place in New Guinea for school, and I will be staying there with him and then Aunt Sharni when he goes back on active duty," Ash said excitedly.

"You mean you won't be staying at the school with us?" Bridgett asked and was about ready to cry. Even Rachael was staring at her as her eyes watered up. Ash's mouth fell open. She hadn't thought of that. She just figured they would all be together and was now faced with having to leave her friends, which was not an option. She looked over at her aunt as her eyes watered up.

"Aunt Sharni, I will not leave my friends. They have to stay with us too."

"Ash, you'll see them every day at school. You just won't be living with them," Sharni said and wiped the tears from Ash's eyes.

"No. If I can't be with them at our home, then I will stay at the dorms with them at school. I can't leave my friends. We're sisters, and we have promised to always stay together no matter what."

"It is not up to me. If it were, I would let Rachael and Bridgett stay too, but this is your father's decision and their parents. You will have to ask him."

The girls started crying. Then they jumped up and ran to Ash's room, locking the door behind them. Sharni jumped up and started knocking on the door for them to let her in. "Go away. Just leave us alone. I know what he'll say. He won't let us stay together," Ash yelled from the other side of her door.

"Ash, come on, open the door. I didn't do anything wrong, so don't be mad at me. And you don't know that until you ask. Your father can be a very reasonable man sometimes," Sharni said to the steel door that separated her from her niece.

"Yeah, right," Ash replied.

She was still standing there an hour later, trying to persuade the girls to come out, when Admiral Harper and Admiral Larson walked in. They saw Sharni standing, leaning up against the wall, talking to the closed door. "What's going on?" Thomas asked with a frown on his face as Larson chuckled behind him.

"Ash and her partners in crime have locked themselves in her room and are refusing to come out," Sharni said, annoyed.

"Why?" Thomas asked coldly. Larson was now laughing behind him, and Sharni gave him a dirty look.

"Because the girls realized that since Ash won't be staying at the dorms when they go to prep school, they wouldn't be together anymore. So they are staging a protest and said they will not come out until this situation is rectified."

"What are they going to eat, and what about having to use the bathroom?" Harper asked with a cold smirk.

"They have a lot of contraband in there, so they said they will be okay for at least a week if they ration it carefully, and as for the bathroom, you don't want to know what they told me when I asked that same question," Sharni said, grinning.

"Surprise me," Ash's father asked.

"All right. They told me they will go in a corner if they have to. I asked them about the smell, and Ash said that the rooms are vented, so it will help with the smell to a certain degree and that their determination will carry them through the rest," Sharni said and was now laughing, as was Larson, but Thomas had a scowl on his face, but it was apparent he was trying not to grin and start chuckling as well. Thomas walked over to the door as he was trying to get himself under control and knocked.

"What?" Ash asked from the other side.

"Ash, come out and we'll talk about this."

"Do I have you word?"

"Yes, as an admiral."

The door clicked and slid open as the three girls walked out, looking at the adults, who all had their arms folded across their chests. Harper motioned his head toward the sofa, and the girls headed over to it. He turned and walked past a grinning Larson and Sharni, who followed. Harper unbuttoned the high collar of his formal admiral's uniform top and went over, sitting down in the large armchair, looking over at the girls with no show of emotion. He was surprised that all three of them didn't cower and instead looked back at him with determination etched in their faces and glaring in their eyes as they stared at him.

"All right. Let me hear your complaint."

"It's simple. When I go to school, either Rachael and Bridgett stay with us in New Guinea, or I stay with them at the dorms at school. No compromises and no other offers will be accepted," Ash said with defiance in her tone and stared at her father. Thomas stared right back, and they both then had a battle of wills to see who was going to back down first. This stare-off went on for a good five minutes, but it was Harper who looked away with barely a hint of a smile on his face so Ash wouldn't see it.

"All right. You win this time. I will speak with Raul and Tony to see if this will be acceptable."

Ash jumped up and leaped on her father, kissing him all over on the cheek. Even Rachael and Bridgett jumped up and ran over, also hugging the admiral. Then all three girls stood up straight and saluted him. Harper saluted them back with a half smirk on his face. "Get out of here, you monsters."

The girls took off and ran back to Ash's room, chattering away about all the things they would do, as Sharni and Gerrard walked over and sat down on the sofa. "What have you gotten us into now, Thomas?" Sharni asked, grinning.

"I couldn't tell them no. Those three girls have been together since they were little. They have always been there for each other, and I couldn't bear breaking their hearts."

"Well, we know who wears the pants around here now," Gerrard said, chuckling.

"Thomas, you have no idea what girls are like. The things me, Gail, and Abigail did during our time at school would make you turn gray," Sharni told him, giggling.

"You mean more than he already is?" Gerrard asked with an ornery grin.

"Then tell us, Sharni, what did you three do?" Harper asked with a devious smirk, leaning forward in his chair, as was Gerrard.

"Nope. Those are secrets that will never be revealed. All I can say is that we are in for a ride."

"Well, it's a good thing you will be spending a lot of time with them, so you'll know what to expect," Thomas told her, chuckling, and both Sharni and Gerrard joined in.

"I better head back to my cabin and change for dinner," Sharni said and stood up. The men both stood as well.

"Why, I think you look pretty hot dressed like that," Gerrard replied with a mischievous grin.

Sharni gave him a dirty look. "Gerrard, shut up," she replied, looking toward Ash's door. Sharni headed to the door and stopped, looking back at the men. Gerrard grinned and looked over at his friend.

"I think I'll go and change too before I get locked out," Larson said with a devious grin and followed Sharni out of the room and into the hall. The door slid shut behind them, and Thomas headed to his room and removed his formal wear in his bathroom, then put his everyday fatigues back on, which consisted of a short-sleeved top. It had a normal round collar and fitted snuggly to the upper body, but it was made out of a very flexible material that was also comfortable. It had the standard blue, gray, and black colors of the sentinel fleet, and on the right, just below the shoulder, was the sentinel fleet insignia—two crossed swords stationed over a laurel wreath.

The pants were also military-issued and fitted snuggly, and it had two large pockets on each side of one's thigh. Buckle-up boots came all the way up to just under one's knee, and the pants tucked down into them as the shirt tucked down into the waistband of the pants. A holster was strapped around the waist with a military-issued pistol strapped in it. All officers and privates carried one at all times, even on board the ship.

Of course, on everyone's left arm was the multitool wrist module. It looked like a metallic wristband that started at the wrist and ended midway up the forearm. This device was technically a mini computer and communication system, and one could pull up a virtual screen and computer console on it, not to mention many other abilities with the more advanced ones that the watorians and proturins perfected, such as hacking and scanning.

The last item was the earpiece used for communication purposes only. It was silver in color and wrapped around the outside of the whole ear and then curled up and into the ear canal. They fitted snuggly to one's ear and were personally fitted for each individual. They also doubled as a mic and, oddly enough, were rather stylish.

Thomas walked out into the living room and saw the girls in the kitchen going through the refrigerator, pulling out ice cream, some type of cake, and chocolate brittle. "No, put it all back right now. It is time for dinner."

Ash looked at him with a frown on her face as Rachael and Bridgett started putting everything back. He crossed his arms in front of him, glaring at Ash, and she gave up, putting the chocolate brittle back, which she had hidden behind her back. Then he motioned to the door, and they all headed to it with him following behind. The girls chattered all the way down the hall and even in the elevator, and by the time they got to the dining hall, Thomas was going crazy.

They walked in, and one could tell right away that his patience had reached an end. Sharni couldn't help but grin and started giggling under her breath, and he looked over at her and glared. Even Larson tried not to laugh, but he was chuckling under his breath with his head down so as not to make eye contact with Thomas.

"Dad, Mom, guess what? I get to stay with Ash and her father in New Guinea when we go to prep school," Rachael said to her parents, who had a look of shock on their faces.

"As do I, Dad," Bridgett said to her father with a big grin.

"What? When was this decided?" Raul Torres said out loud and now looked over at Thomas.

"I was going to ask you at a more appropriate time since this was brought to my attention not long ago. But as the girls said, I will be taking a leave of absence for a couple years from duty as Ash attends prep school in New Guinea. I have made arrangements with Rear Admiral Larson, Captain Tol Vasna, and sentinel command that every two years, me and Admiral Larson will trade off on active duty while our children attend school. That way, there will always be one of us planet side at any given time.

"Captain Tol Vasna has also volunteered to take time off as well to see to the care and well-being of the children. As Rachael said, I have already purchased a dwelling in New Guinea. And due to a staged protest today and difficult negotiations, the girls demanded the right to stay together, which I have no problem with, but only upon your approvals," Harper said, looking at Ash.

Raul looked at his wife, and she half-grinned at him. "Are you sure about this, Thomas? Look what they do on a ship. Just think what it's going to be like on a whole planet."

"Yes, Abigail, I'm sure. Besides, Sharni will be helping too," Thomas said, emotionless.

"I don't remember this being a volunteer thing. You used that tone of voice on me that said I had better agree," Sharni replied, grinning, and everyone started laughing.

"All right. We'll try it for a while and see how things go," Raul answered as a huge grin spread across Rachael's face. Then everyone looked over at Tony, Bridgett's father.

"Of course Bridgett can stay. I'm not going to be the mean one here," Tony replied, grinning, and Bridgett jumped out of her seat and wrapped her arms around her father, kissing him on the cheek, and then jumped back into her seat. The girls were now grinning at one another as excitement bubbled out of them. Thomas half-smirked looking at them. Then the meal was brought out, and everyone started eating.

The adults talked and joked among themselves as the girls plotted and planned what they were going to do once planet side. "I heard they have a huge mall with an indoor rock climbing wall," Rachael said.

"Yeah, and just think of all the stores there, all the shopping we can do together," Bridgett said excitedly.

As the vice admiral overheard them, he turned to Sharni, who was sitting next to him, and whispered to her, "Shopping? What is that?"

"Are you serious? You have no clue, do you?" she said in amazement.

"No, that was Gail's department."

"Fine. I will go with you and help you get started. Hopefully, between now and then, you might learn a little bit more about girls," Sharni said, rolling her eyes. Thomas looked over at Gerrard, and they both shrugged their shoulders.

The evening wore on, and finally, the hour got late. Everyone started filing out of the dining chamber and toward the elevator. The girls took off first and left everyone else behind. Raul and Abigail, along with Tony Nelson, walked over to Gerrard, Thomas, and Sharni.

"I just want to say thanks to the three of you. I'm glad the girls will all be staying together. They have been together since the day they were little, and I don't think they would do too well separated," Raul said, shaking Thomas's hand.

"I agree. I know Ash wouldn't. She has leaned heavily on her friends for support through this with her mother, and those three have always been there for each other. I couldn't in good conscience separate them from one another."

"Just let us know what you need from us," Tony, Bridgett's father, said to the admiral.

"I will, and we have a whole year to get this all worked out," Harper told them, and they all nodded.

The adults then walked to the elevator where the girls were waiting for them and got in. Soon, it was stopping on the different levels where everyone was staying; and finally, the last stop was Ash and her father's. They headed back to their cabin, and Ash reached up and took her father's hand. He put his other hand over the lit blue panel next to the door, and the door slid open as they walked in.

"Go get changed for bed, and I will come tuck you in," Thomas told his daughter, letting go of her hand as she went to her room. A little while later, he walked in, and she was finishing brushing out her long black hair and then ran over and jumped into her bed. He bent down and pulled the covers up on her, then leaned down and kissed her on the forehead.

"Thanks, Daddy, for letting my friends stay with us."

"You're welcome, precious. Now get some sleep."

"Daddy?"

"Yes, Ash?"

"I love you."

"I love you too, sweetheart."

CHAPTER 6

THE NEXT MORNING, everyone was up as Ash and her father walked
Sharni and her parents down to docking bay 10. Admiral Larson was
also with Thomas and Ash, seeing them off. Finally, they got to the
docking bay doors that opened up to the completely enclosed and
airtight large walkway that connected with an umbilical out to the
air lock doors of the *Astra Sink* and stopped.

"Thank you for making my daughter happy, and take care of
our beautiful granddaughter. You will be welcomed on Krios if you
ever decide to come and visit," Lord Benz Tol Vasna said to Admiral
Harper and shook his hand.

"Thank you for Gail. She was my life. At least I still have part
of her here with me in Ash," Harper said to him, looking down at
his daughter. Benz looked down at his granddaughter and bent down
and scooped her up, hugging her tightly. Then he passed her over to
Tealo as she also hugged her tightly and kissed her on the cheek, then
set her down

"You take care, little one, and watch over your father," Tealo
said to her, cupping Ash's chin in her slender hand.

"I will, Grandmother."

Sharni came over and picked Ash up, then hugged her tightly
and kissed her hair. "If you need anything or just want to talk, call
me anytime, or I will come and help you if need be."

"I will, Aunt Sharni," Ash replied, hugging her aunt tightly as her eyes watered up due to her aunt's leaving.

Sharni put her down and went over and gave Thomas a hug, and he hugged her back, whispering in her ear, "Thank you so much, Sharni. I don't know what I would have done without your here."

She let him go and put her hand on his cheek, then smiled at him with tear-filled eyes, and Thomas half-smiled back at her. Then she walked over to Gerrard, and they both threw their arms around each other. Gerrard leaned his head down, and their lips met each other in a very passionate kiss. Ash's mouth fell open, but then a big grin spread across her face as she watched them. They released each other, and Sharni's face was now flushed, but she, like Gerrard, had a huge grin on her face.

She looked over at her niece and saw Ash giggling now, and she started laughing, as did Larson. Then she turned and escorted her parents back to her ship, and Ash, her father, and Admiral Larson watched the *Astra Sink* unhook from the docking clamps through the viewing windows in the causeway and pull away from the *Justification*, heading out into space.

"Wow, Admiral Larson, that was some goodbye," Ash said out loud, grinning, as both her father and Larson started chuckling. They all turned and headed back to the elevator, then went up to the bridge. Ash's father went to his platform, and Larson came up behind Ash and put his hands on her shoulders, watching her father. Admiral Harper went and checked his console and gave orders for the ship to be ready to leave the Bithos cluster in six hours as he plotted in the new course and sent it to the pilot for prepping the ship for departure and the jump drive. Then he, Admiral Larson, and Ashley left the bridge and went back to Ash and her father's cabin.

They walked in, and Ash jumped up on the sofa as Admiral Larson sat down and her father went and filled a cup of creo, which was equivalent to Earth's coffee but stronger, and offered a cup to Larson, who declined.

"So you're heading back to Sigma Six?" Ash's father asked Larson.

"Yeah. With Fâd in prep school and his uncanny ability to somehow manage to always get into trouble, I find myself spending a lot of time at that school. It should be interesting next year. Luckily, it will be your turn," Larson replied with an ornery grin.

"Yeah. I'm so looking forward to it. Thank goodness Sharni will be around to help at first."

"That's not fair. I've had to deal with three on my own for the last two years, so I think it is only fair that you have to do the same."

"I don't, especially since it won't be three anymore but six instead, and remember, I'm new at all this."

"True. I'm going to enjoy this."

"Father, what do you mean six instead of three?" Ash asked, confused.

"You three girls plus Fâd and his two friends since Admiral Larson will be taking up the extra duty while I'm on my leave of absence. I will be overseeing the boys, and he will be doing the same in two years when I leave and go back on active duty."

"They're not staying with us too, are they?" Ash asked with a look of horror on her face.

"No, but I will be watching them and making sure they are taken care of and staying out of trouble."

"Thank goodness. You scared me there for a minute. Our dwelling is strictly girls only, with exception of you, of course. No boys allowed ever. Of course, you can come over too, Admiral Larson."

"Why, thank you, Ash. I feel so privileged now," Larson said to her with a grin.

"Ash, why don't you go and find Rachael and Bridgett while me and Gerrard visit until he has to leave?" Ash jumped up off the sofa, gave her father a quick salute, and ran out the sliding door and into the hallway.

"You know you're going to have your hands full with those three."

"Don't remind me," Harper replied, rolling his eyes.

Gerrard looked at his friend and grinned. "I think they are going to be more trouble than the boys have been so far."

"I'm scared you might be right. They already are on this ship. So what have the boys done so far?"

"The usual: a small fire in the boys' bathroom to try and get out of a test, fighting, of course—that's an everyday thing—and the latest stunt, a holographic projection of carian warriors in one of the dorms, which caused the whole campus to go into emergency lockdown. I had to go in and beg the school's officials to let the boys remain in school, plus make a nice contribution to the school, which was a hefty amount of marks I had to pay," Larson told him, rolling his eyes.

"Great. I'm so looking forward to this. And I'm sure that it helps the school is council sanctioned," Harper said coldly.

Larson looked over at his friend knowing how Harper felt about council. "Yeah, that's what the majority of the fights are about and the boys' reasoning behind the scare to the campus. They wanted to show the officials how helpless the school was because of council protection. They definitely proved their point, which made the officials just that more furious with them. It's going to be tough on the girls. They will be picked on for being sentinel fleet, but from what I have seen from those girls, they can handle themselves just fine."

"They're going to have to. It will definitely be a growing up time for them, and they will have to face their own battles. So I should probably be prepared to pay out quite a few marks during their school year, then," Harper commented with a slight smirk, and Larson grinned, nodding his head in agreement.

The two men continued to visit, and soon, it was time for Admiral Larson to leave. Harper walked with his friend down to the shuttle bay where Larson's shuttle was docked, and they stopped just outside the open door into his shuttle.

"If you need anything, Thomas, don't be afraid to ask."

"I won't. Take care, my friend," Harper replied, and they shook hands.

"You too," Larson added, and then both men saluted each other, and Larson climbed into his shuttle. Harper walked away as it powered up. Soon, the craft lifted up into the air and turned around as the large shuttle bay doors opened up to the dark space outside.

A blue kinetic barrier completely covered the opening, keeping the oxygen-rich atmosphere in the cargo bay and the vacuum of space out. The shuttle flew right through the barrier, and the bay doors slid shut behind it.

Admiral Harper went over to the elevator and turned around as the doors slid shut. "Level, Admiral?" the elevator voice asked.

"Bridge," Harper replied, and the elevator took off. Before long, the doors slid open, and the admiral walked out and over to his station. Harper brought up his virtual screens and keyboards, then punched holographic buttons as the large windows surrounding the front of the bridge now changed into a massive screen. Harper watched as the *Lithia* started moving across the space in front of them. It was also a massive battlecruiser like his and had a crew of over six hundred with families.

He continued to watch it leaving them. The *Lithia*'s engines started glowing brilliant red, and in an explosion of red light, the massive cruiser was gone. Harper knew she was now moving through space at speeds faster than the mind could fathom as it made its jump into slipstream.

The jump systems on the ships were quasar systems as the sentinel fleet did away with the flexion systems originally used by the earlier explorers who left Earth hundreds of years ago when humans finally appeared in other systems. Quasars were much faster, cutting down the charge time in half compared to the flexions. Plus, the ships could move through slipstream for longer periods of time, double what they could with the flexions, before they had to come out. The speeds they moved when in jump was like folding time and space upon itself and going from one area of the galaxy over to another in just a few days, hours, or even minutes.

At normal FTL speeds, it would take a ship moving from one planet to another months or more compared to jumping into slipstream and cutting down the time into minutes. The only issue they had was that the jump systems could only handle twelve-hour jumps at a time, and it took a couple of hours for the system to cool back down before they could jump again. When ships were not in jump, they moved usually faster than FTL speed. Even massive cruisers like

Harper's and Larson's could move as such, and the modified propulsion systems gave these behemoths unrivaled maneuverability.

Even the guns on these ships were standard photon cannons, which shot out a red energy-charged missile type of projectile that could pierce through a ship's hull easily and explode with tremendous force, blowing a huge hole in it. Plus, they also were equipped with armor-piercing, heavy forbs mech guns. The forbs guns could penetrate ships' hulls, shredding it, or enemy fighters firing a continuous burst of carbine-tip mag shells that exploded upon impact, not to mention the velocity the guns fired at was almost as fast as a fighter could fly, and their accuracy was amazing for such a large gun.

The cruisers were equipped with six of these guns, located all down the whole length of the ship and slightly underneath it. Plus, they could move in all directions and angles. There was a main one of these. The sixth gun was located near the front of the cruiser and was twice the size of the others. It packed a lot more firepower since it covered the whole front end of the cruiser, and it took someone who knew what they were doing to man this gun from its station located on the bridge with the others. It generally took a person a year of training in a simulation cockpit to learn how to control and fire one of these, not to mention practice their accuracy since it was so powerful.

All sentinel ships were equipped with both the photon cannons and forbs mech guns, but only the cruisers had the large sixth gun. The cruisers had one more weapon too, a phasic cannon that fired a massive blue laser-type beam of pure energy powerful enough to blow another cruiser apart or scorch a planet's surface, making it uninhabitable. Targeting with this cannon was very difficult, and it took someone with real skill to do, because usually, in a battle, they had one shot with this weapon due to it having a long waiting period to build power back up. But usually, it only took one hit from it, and a battlecruiser would be decimated instantly.

Of course, the success rate of these weapons all depended on whether or not an enemy's ship had their shields down, and it usually took many strikes with a proton cannon or a forbs gun to accomplish such a feat and at some loss to the fleet. There also were two battleships that always accompanied the cruisers since they were much quicker and maneuvered faster than the cruisers, and they were also equipped with the same jump systems.

On the *Justification*, like the *Lithia*, it was the admirals who commanded the cruisers and plotted all the courses and sent the coordinates to the battleships that were with him. He would put in the orders, and everything was sent out from his console to all the different stations that they pertained to. His console was the central brains of the ship, and he had access to every part of it from there, not to mention full access to his escorting battleships from it as well.

It wasn't unusual to see many different holographic screens open above his large wraparound console, as he would have many operations going simultaneously. His hands moved in and among the holograms, and he could literally move readouts, even buttons and controls, around just by running his hands over the holograms. And he did all this so fast, for time was a luxury he didn't have. One minute in his world could mean life or death for all of them.

Harper was doing just that now and concentrating on the screens in front of him as he got his cruiser and battleships ready for jump. Finally, he sent out the orders, and he got back verifications from all the stations that orders were received.

"Prepare for jump in five minutes," the pilot announced over the ship's wide intercom as everyone got ready. Harper went and sat down on his command chair, putting his right elbow up on the arm of the chair, and leaned forward, resting his chin in his hand, watching the view screen in front of him. "10, 9, 8, 7, 6, 5, 4, 3, 2, 1. Initiating jump," the pilot announced.

Everyone grabbed hold of something. It sounded like the engines were powering down, but it was actually just the opposite. The ship shuddered a little, and then the engines went quiet. If one were outside the ship, they would have seen the cruiser's engines glowing brilliant red and then an explosion of red light as the ship disappeared into blackness, as did the battleships right along with it.

"We are in jump. Estimated arrival time to Theta in ninety-six hours and seventeen minutes in and out of jump. Battleships keeping pace, Admiral," the pilot reported to Harper.

Vice Admiral Harper stood up and checked his readouts again. "If anyone needs me, I will be in my cabin. You have the bridge, Dobbs."

"Yes, sir," the executive officer replied and saluted the admiral as Harper stepped down from his control station and headed over to the elevator.

It didn't take him long to get to his cabin. Ash, of course, wasn't there. She was over with her friends at Rachael's cabin and would be there for at least the next few hours, playing like always. Harper walked into his now empty cabin and poured himself a small glass of watorian whiskey over at the bar in the kitchen, then walked into his bedroom, setting the drink down on the nightstand. He pulled out his tucked-in shirt and pulled it over his head. He sat down on the edge of the bed, taking a few drinks of the whiskey, then setting it back down on the stand. He reached down and unbuckled his boots as his dog tags dangled down in front of him and kicked them off.

Exhaustion filled every part of his body. Gail's passing had drained him mainly from the pain he now had in his heart, and he just wanted to sleep. Harper laid back on the bed and started to slowly drift off. Then somewhere in his subconscious, he heard Gail's voice telling him that everything would be all right, and a smile spread across his handsome sleeping face.

CHAPTER 7

"FÂDRON LARSON, THIS is the third time this year that you and your friends have been in my office, and once again for fighting. I'm at my end with this. If it weren't for who your father is, you would be expelled from this school and never allowed to return. The board is breathing down my neck as it is, especially after the carian incident," Head Professor Baptise said to the dark-headed, blue-eyed young boy sitting on the other side of his desk.

"I didn't start it!" Fâd responded with narrowed eyes.

"You never start it, but you and your comrades here always manage to finish it. I know it is part of your nature, being watorians, but you must learn to control your emotions. Pick the battles that are worth fighting, not the ones just because someone made fun of you. You will find later on in life how little important name-calling will be."

"Of course you would use my nature against me. You're just like all the rest, council sympathizers and hating us because we are sentinel," Fâd hissed back.

"You will find, Mr. Larson, that not all of us hate sentinel and know, even though we don't come out and say it openly, that if it weren't for the sentinel fleet, we would all be dead right now," Professor Baptise told Fâd in a very angry and forceful tone.

The young boy just sat there then. He was caught off guard by this testimony. Here he thought everyone hated him and his two friends because of what they were and to whom their allegiances lay with, but now one of the school council members, and the head one at that, was telling him he knew the truth. "I'm sorry, sir," Fâd said with his head down, looking at his hands in his lap.

"Please, Fâd, you need to learn control. You will find it will help and probably save your life and that of your friends and crewmates in the future. You were born to command. Now start learning how to channel those natural talents and become the great leader I know you will be," the professor said now with a slight smile at the corner of his mouth. Professor Baptise was no fool. He had been with this school for what seemed like eons and had seen many great leaders come out of it, and here sitting in front of him he knew was going to be another one who he was sure would someday save many lives.

"Professor, have you contacted my father about this?" Fâd asked nervously and looked over at Nathan and Cory, who hadn't spoken one word the whole time.

"Of course. I am required to by school regulations."

"Great. I can't wait to hear this lecture," Fâd said to his friends, and they nodded and rolled their eyes.

"That is all, Fâd. You and your friends are dismissed," the professor said and couldn't help but smirk once they got up and dejectedly headed for the door. It slid open on its own, and they walked out into the carpeted long hallway that contained all the offices of the administration building. Plus, where the hall split, some of the business classrooms were accessed by it.

The school was very large, and at any given time, it taught over twelve hundred students ranging from the ages of twelve up to eighteen or nineteen, depending on their birthing date. It also had dorms for students to be able to stay on campus the whole time school was in service, which a lot of students did due to their parents being in some form of military service, space exploration, or such, taking them off planet. But the main thing was, the school was under council sanctioning; and like Fâd and his friends had found out over the two years they were there, council and sentinel hated each other and, like Fâd had pointed out on several occasions to the other children who were big-time council backers, that sentinel kicked council's ass.

Fâd and his friends, Nathan and Cory, were the minority. Not too many sentinel children attended school here. The reasoning they were there was because Fâd's father felt that the diversity would be a better learning experience for the boys instead of attending the sentinel-run schools where the admiral feared the boys would get special treatment due to being his son and wards. The few other boys who did attend the prep school there were older now and only had a year or two left and seemed to fit in fine, hanging out with kids their own ages, thus leaving Fâd, Nathan, and Cory having to defend themselves, which, so far, they were having no problem with.

Sentinel children weren't hard to distinguish from the rest either. They were always watorians or humans. Sometimes, there were a few vatorias, but that was very rare since they had their own form of education system. It was only on some exchange programs that vatorias came, and of course, they never had a problem fitting in. They were always the popular ones because everyone wanted to be a vatoria's friend just because they were a very beautiful race, and for some reason, it was always overlooked that they were affiliated with sentinel fleet.

But that didn't hold true for the rest. Most sentinel children were, in some of the teachers' words, just plain wild. Unlike all the council-raised children, who were always neatly dressed in their uniforms, hair cut short, even the girls, wearing no jewelry at all, and always acted proper and well-mannered, sentinel children were loud and outspoken. Usually, their uniforms were untucked and messy; and if girls did attend, which was very rare, they wore their hair any way they wanted it or color, for that matter, and even the boys' hair was sometimes past their ears, not to mention jewelry. Even the older watorian boys would have a pierced right ear, and most sentinel-raised human boys followed their example. They didn't exhibit the more military mentality and manners of the fleet until they reached their academy years even though they began their military training at a much earlier age than council children did. It was believed that the children used this time to cut loose from all the restrictions their training forced upon them when they were around the fleet.

Fâd and his two buddies were slowly learning, though, how to adjust to this new life they would be forced to endure for the next five years. They had pretty well established by now that they didn't tolerate being called names or bullied around and also that they were quite intelligent, hence the carian incident, which was starting to become their claim to fame around the school.

They left the large administration building and headed over to their dorm that housed at least 425 students. The campus was very large, and it was laid out in a sort of octagon configuration with outer octagons around the central points. The classroom buildings, which were generally six stories high and resembled those from some of Earth's college buildings from the 1900s, made up the points of the octagon, and then around these central buildings, more smaller buildings were built, making up only half of an octagon, leaving the main classroom building facing inward and overlooking the common ground in front where a nice park was laid out for all to use.

All these outer buildings were the dorms, and each group of them was affiliated with the main classroom building they circled. Example, you had the science frat, the mathematical frat, literature frat, and so on, but most sentinel children were either put in the phys ed frat or the technology frat since these were where most of them excelled in. It was also amazing how the prep school clung to the old image of Earth's colleges. Of course, though, in a way, it wasn't surprising, seeing how human culture pretty well had permeated into all different cultures and beliefs as most alien species openly adapted and incorporated it into their own civilizations right down to even the food and customs.

The boys walked through the park grounds, then decided to just go and crash under a tree instead of head to their room. They didn't have another class for a couple of hours anyway, so there was no hurry to get ready for it. Besides, it was just a stupid review to them again of some human story about a dead guy called George Washington from human history. They quickly found one of their favorite spots and sprawled out on their backs with their arms tucked behind their heads, looking up at the tree branches overhead. It was a hot, sunny day, but the trees offered great shade, and a cool breeze helped to keep the heat down to a tolerable temperature.

"Do you remember that girl and her friends that kicked our ass a while back in combat tag?" Nathan asked his buddies.

"They didn't kick our ass. We won," Fâd corrected him with a scowl on his face.

"Believe what you want, but you have to admit, they got us good. Anyway, I heard that her mother died," Nathan said to him.

"Yeah, that's were my father is right now. He and Vice Admiral Harper have been best friends way before I ever came along. They both met while fighting in the council militia, and from the stories I heard, that was where Vice Admiral Harper met his wife and Father met Captain Sharni."

"So does your father know you know about them?" Cory asked, leaning up on his elbows, looking over at Fâd.

"No, but if that is who he wants, I have no say in the matter. Besides, I like Sharni. She's pretty cool."

"What about your mother? They're married." Nathan looked over at his best friend lying on the ground next to him.

"I don't have a mother, only my father and Sharni. She's been more a mother to me than mine ever was," Fâd said, and the anger in him was unmistakable.

"Come on, Fâd, she gave birth to you. You can't say that," Cory told him.

"She never had anything to do with me from the time I can remember, and when I was around her, all she did was tell me how worthless I was and how I would turn out just like my father. But when she started telling me that I was a plague just like the carians and should be wiped out, that was when I refused to have anything else to do with her."

"Yeah, but she's not herself," Nathan added.

"No, you can tell when she's not herself and when she is. You can see it in her eyes. Nope, she hates my father and takes it out on me. I think she knows about him and the captain. That's why she hates him so bad. But there's more to this than what I know. She and my father, even though they were married, never once lived together, and I know that I was not produced the normal way. Father explained it all to me on that subject. Plus, Father never bonded to her. There's more to this story, but I don't care. That's my father's life, and if he wants to tell me, he would," Fâd said, shrugging his shoulders.

"Do you think he and the captain are bonded mates instead?" Cory asked with interest.

"I don't know."

"Nah, that wouldn't make sense. Why would he then marry another instead?" Nathan added, thinking about it.

"Yeah, but if he did, that would explain why there's no affection there and why he didn't bond to Fâd's mother. We have all been told how bad imprinting and bonding can get for our species when you can't be with your mate. If your father has bonded to the captain, he is doing one heck of a job controlling the anger," Cory countered.

"True, but no, I agree with Fâd. There's more to this than what we know," Nathan replied with a sigh.

"So do you guys ever think of those girls? I honestly have to say I had fun playing combat tag with them. You have to admit, they were good. Nobody has ever been able to stay even close to us in a match, and they did and at times were even better," Cory asked with a big grin.

"WHAT? I can't believe you, Cory. Listen to yourself. You're talking about girls. You're a traitor to boys everywhere, especially saying they were pretty good in a game that we dominate. No, I don't ever think of them, especially that black-haired one with the gold eyes and cocky grin, who unloaded on me in the face. I hate her," Fâd replied with distaste in his tone.

"Yeah, neither do I, especially that taller, blond-headed, blue-eyed one that sniped me pretty good," Nathan said, grinning.

"I'm the same way about that little red-headed, blue-eyed one that unloaded on me at almost point-blank range. She never crosses my mind," Cory added, grinning as well, and looked over at Fâd and saw a slight grin on his face now.

"I have to admit, though, it was kind of fun with the pressure hoses, though," Nathan said nonchalantly.

"Yeah. Did you see the way that dark-headed one—I think her name was Ash—flew off of the scrubber when we all hit her with the water? She got some air on that one." Cory chuckled.

"Oh yeah, I remember you flying across the floor when you got hit as well. But I think the best one was when Rachael, the blond one, actually did a flip as she flew through the air when she got knocked off," Fâd replied, leaning up on his elbows, looking at them with a big grin.

"You have no room to talk, Fâd. You flew off and skidded across the floor, lying flat on your back." Nathan scowled at him.

"So did you. Of course, that little redhead—Bridg, they called her—wouldn't stop rolling as we unloaded on her." Fâd laughed, and now Cory gave him a dirty look.

"That was mean what you guys did. I felt bad for her," Cory said, a little angry with his friends, defending Bridgett.

Fâd chuckled, lying back down. "Yeah, but it was her friends that started the whole thing. They shot her off of it first, and I have to hand it to her, she got right back up and did it again."

Cory laughed a little. "She sure did. We all did, and it was fun." The boys just lay there, now with grins on all three of their faces, watching the branches of the tree sway in the breeze above them, remembering it again.

"Oh, by the way, I forgot to tell you guys. Father said that if I manage to finish prep school and with decent grades, he will buy me my own ship and let me fix it up myself. I can pick it out and every-thing," Fâd said excitedly, sitting up, looking at his friends. Nathan and Cory also sat up now with excitement.

"What do you want to get?" Nathan asked with big eyes.

"I don't know, but something that will be fast, not a fighter. I actually want something a lot bigger than that, something that we can all fly on and maybe even more people at some point."

"A frigate, possibly?" Cory asked.

"Nah, I don't want a drop ship, something larger and with weapons. Most frigates don't have guns, and what they do have is useless. Plus, I want it to be fast and able to fight and defend itself."

"We can always modify one for bigger guns," Cory said to him with a grin.

Nathan added, "It would be cool if it could move like a fighter."

"Nate, something larger than a frigate can't make a 180-degree turn during propulsion speed like fighters can, and most pilots can't do that kind of maneuvering anyway. Just because you can in simulations doesn't mean you can actually do it for real," Cory corrected him.

"Put me in a fighter and I'll show you what all I can do, simulation or not. I will be the best. You can count on it," Nathan replied with narrowed eyes.

"Before we all start putting in our request, I still have to finish school and with good grades, so this might not happen after all," Fâd told them with a grin, and they all started laughing. "We had better get going and grab our books for our next class." Fâd stood up, brushing himself off, and his friends did the same.

They were starting to head to their dorm when Nathan asked, "Why do we have to learn human history anyway? It does us no good. The only things I care about with humans are their great food and their cute girls."

"I don't know. It has something to do with how human culture evolves. But I agree, their food is kind of good, and the girls are okay. Just like this George Washington we're learning about. Supposedly, he was someone important and was known for crossing something. That crap I don't care to learn," Fâd added.

"The Delaware. He crossed the Delaware with something," Cory said to him.

"What's the Delaware?" Fâd asked him.

"I don't know. Maybe it was some type of plant or something that he genetically altered," Cory replied, shrugging his shoulders.

"No, dumbass, he was a soldier. It was probably some sort of particle gun that he modified using parts from another different type of particle gun," Nathan countered.

"Whatever it is, I really don't care," Fâd said as they walked.

"Yeah, and it's because of that kind of attitude that we will never have a ship of our own," Nathan said to him with a grin.

CHAPTER 8

IT HAD BEEN over a year since Lady Gailistra's passing, and the battl-cruiser *Justification* was now entering Sigma Six space. Vice Admiral Thomas Harper stood at his station, watching his readings on his console. "Sir, transmission coming in. It is the *Lithia*, requesting authorization codes," Ensign Chambers said to the admiral.

Harper brought up his holographic screens and keyboard, then started typing in the codes and hit a virtual button and waited. "Authorization received. Proceed *Justification* and welcome," a voice came over the main comm of the bridge from the *Lithia*.

"Lieutenant Petterson, pulsar speed only, no propulsion," Harper ordered the pilot as he punched in again on his console coordinates for where they would stop.

"Aye, aye, Admiral. Coordinates received and plotted," the pilot replied.

"Sir, I have a transmission coming in," Ensign Chambers said to him.

"I'm not surprised. Patch it through to my comm," Harper told her and went and sat down at his chair as a virtual screen came on at his console, and Larson appeared on it.

"You finally made it. I was wondering if you were going to back out at the last second. I know this is probably killing you, having to leave space, but it's not so bad. You'll soon get used to walking where gravity plays a key factor. I stopped by your house a couple days ago. Sharni has it looking nice. She spared no expense on it," Admiral Larson said, and Harper could hear the laughter in his voice.

"Yeah, I know. I saw how fast my marks were disappearing. So when do you head out?"

"Just as soon as my orders come through. I already got Fâd and his friends settled back at the school and sent the authorization for you to act in my stead."

"Vice Admiral, transmission coming through from sentinel command," Ensign Chambers reported.

"That was fast," Harper said to Larson over the comm.

"Yep. I'm getting mine to. Better let you go. You have a lot to do. And, Harper, welcome home," Larson said, and Thomas could hear him chuckling in the background.

"Yeah, thanks. And, Larson, safe journey," Admiral Harper said and shut off his comm. "Ensign Chambers, open transmission."

"Yes, sir, channel open."

A male voice came over the comm system now for the whole ship to hear, and one could tell that this was a person of importance. "Vice Admiral Harper, you are hereby granted leave of absence for a period of no more than twenty-four months on the contingency only as no need arises for your service during this time. The battlecruiser *Justification* is ordered to remain on active duty, as will her escorting battleships patrolling Sigma Six space, until the time you are reinstated for duty and receive your orders. Vice Admiral, thank you, and good luck, Thomas!"

Harper knew exactly who the voice belonged to. Only one man had the authority to grant his leave of absence, Fleet Admiral Carson. The vice admiral had a slight smirk on his face, shaking his head, as his crew all grinned now, and some of the female crew members were giggling quietly to themselves. He stood up from his seat and looked around at all of them. In a way, they were his family. They had all been together for such a long time, and Larson was right, space was Harper's home and had been for more than five decades now, and he was hurting inside having to leave it.

"Well, I guess this is it. EXO Dobbs, the ship is yours. Try not to tear her up," Harper said to him with a cold smirk and stepped down from his platform. All the crew on the bridge now stood at attention and saluted him as he headed to the elevator. Just as he stepped in and turned around, he saluted them all back as the doors slid shut.

"Level, please?" the elevator control asked.

"Crew deck 1," Harper ordered.

The elevator took off, and in a few minutes, the doors slid open to the long hallway where his, along with many of the crew members', cabin was located. He walked to the end of the hall where his was located and placed his hand on the blue scan pad, and the door slid open. It was total chaos in there. There were numerous trunks stacked in the living room and music blaring, yet no Ash. He walked over to her bedroom, which was where the music was coming from, and went in, turning her stereo down to a more tolerable tone.

"Hey, who's messing with my stereo?" her voice came from the bathroom down the hall, which she always used.

"I did," Harper hollered back and left her room, heading to the bathroom. The door was wide open, and when he looked in it, she had a makeup applicator over her face. She pressed a button and then removed it. Her eyes now had mascara, eye shadow, and blush, not to mention shiny lip gloss, and she stood checking it out in the mirror, moving her head from side to side and pursing up her lips.

"Absolutely not. You take that off right now," Harper ordered her.

"Dad, we're going into a city. I have to look good," Ash argued back.

"You are only twelve and won't be wearing that stuff until you're at least sixteen. Do you hear me? Now hand that applicator over," Harper informed her and put his hand out for it. Ash gave him a dirty look but handed him the applicator reluctantly. Then he stood there and made her wash all of it off, and once she was done, he surveyed her face to make sure it was acceptable. He started to leave the bathroom when he heard her whisper under her breath, "Oh my gosh, I have two years of this?"

He continued toward his room now with an ornery smirk on his face and walked in as the door slid open for him. It was a nightmare in there. His clothes were lying scattered everywhere in open trunks. "ASHLEY GAIL HARPER, GET IN HERE RIGHT NOW!" he yelled.

She came running down the hallway and peeked into his room. "What?"

"What the hell happened in here?"

"I started packing for you. Some of that clothes won't work, too many military uniforms. You're going to have to buy some new casual ones. Remember, you're a civilian now and have to start acting like one. I can help you there. I already scanned and uploaded all the locations of the best shops in New Guinea to my multitool. I also picked out the ones that you look best in. Plus, some of them I know won't fit you anymore I removed. No offense, Dad, but you're not as skinny as you used to be."

"What are you talking about? I'm just as fit as I ever was. I'll have you know I'm in perfect health and have less than 2 percent body fat," her father said, holding his head up proudly.

"Dad, I swear, some of those things are from back when you went to the academy."

"Well, maybe a few that I could hide from your mother. She was always throwing my old clothes away."

"Yeah, because Mom had taste," Ash replied, rolling her eyes at him.

"Fine. Go get finished with yourself while I sort through this disaster zone." He chuckled and winked at her. Ash left his room and went into hers. She continued to pack the few remaining items she wanted to take. She was just about to shut her last trunk when her father walked in carrying a small wooden box and handed it to her. Ash knew right away what it was, her mother's jewelry box.

"Your mother would want you to have this," her father said in a quiet voice.

Ash took it and opened it up as tears ran down her face. She looked down at the beautiful necklaces, hair combs and barrettes, earrings, and bracelets that filled the box. Her mother had simple taste but very elegant, and every one of these pieces her father had given to her mother over the years. Ash took out a hair comb that was in the shape of a red rose and looked at it. It was one of her mother's favorite ones, and she wore it a lot.

Harper walked over to his daughter and took the comb out of her hand, pulling the sides of her hair back and fastening it in the back with the comb. Ash started crying and threw her arms around her father's waist, and he leaned down and hugged her tightly. Then he released her and wiped the tears away from her face, looking down at her.

"Come on, precious, we need to get finished. Crew will be here to move our luggage down to the shuttle anytime."

"All right, Dad." She turned and pulled out a silk scarf she had in her trunk, then carefully wrapped the jewelry box in it and placed it in the trunk. Harper headed back to his room and finished packing his luggage just as a buzz came from the cabin intercom. He pressed a button on the intercom in his room, and the door to the cabin slid open. Crewmen came in and started loading luggage out to a floating carryall.

The admiral carried the rest of his luggage out of his room and then went back and surveyed it to make sure he had everything he needed. The room looked bare now, except for some remaining clothes in the closet and nonessentials, like books and such. Once satisfied that he had everything, he went and helped the crewmen. They had to call for another carryall just to hold the rest of Ash's things. Her luggage filled one and over half of the other one, but finally, they both were standing there, looking at the cabin that had been their home for these many years.

Ash had tears in her eyes now. This was the only home she had known, and this was where her mother was. It was the only place Ash still felt close to her mother, and now she had to leave it for a new place and a new life. Her father could sense the struggle in her and came over and put his hand on her shoulder.

"Come on. Your friends and aunt are waiting for you," he said with a warm smile on his face. Ash wiped the tears from her eyes and put a determined look on her face and headed out the door. Harper followed but looked back into the cabin before walking out the door. Then he heard a very faint voice in his head say, "You'll both be fine. Now go and live." He leaned his head back and closed his eyes as a smile creased his face. "We will, my love," he whispered back to the space of the room and walked out.

They entered the elevator, but the crew took the carryalls and headed down another section of the hall to a cargo elevator. In no time, Admiral Harper and Ash stepped out into the shuttle bay of the *Justification*; and sure enough, Rachael and her family, along with Bridgett and her father, were already there, waiting. When the girls saw one another, they ran and embraced, and then the excited chattering began, totally oblivious to anything around them.

"You're a braver man than I am, Thomas, and all I can tell you is, good luck," Raul Torres said and clapped him on the back. Abigail came over and hugged him as tears ran down her face.

"Stop that. You'll make me start," Harper teased her, but in truth he was fighting back his feelings, for these people were his family. They fought together, raised their children together, and buried their loved ones together. They were the first ones that left with him and Gerrard and followed them to a new beginning, helping to build that new life right alongside them.

Torres and Nelson both could have had an admiralship but declined. They requested to remain under Larson and Harper and were granted them. Of course, Torres was forced to take command of a battleship because they could not let his captaining skills go to waste, but it was only agreed upon the condition he still remain in Harper's or Larson's service.

As for Tony Nelson, no one was as gifted with engines and ships mechanics as him, and he really didn't answer to anyone. When it came to the ship and its mechanics, he called the shots. It was the same with all the vessels in the fleet. Oftentimes, Tony had to go and inspect the many battleships, frigates, cruisers, and fighters to keep the fleet up to the challenge or incorporate new technology in them.

It was always fun, though, with Tony, because he didn't talk much and was so easy to make mad, which Gerrard loved to do. Gerrard would pester and tease him until Tony was ready to fight with him, usually making some comment about knocking Gerrard's fangs down his throat. But a few drinks later, they were once again the best of friends and reminiscing about the good old days.

"Well, I guess this is it. Watch over my ship for me," Harper said to them.

"Will do, Admiral," Torres said as he and Nelson both saluted their admiral and good friend. Harper saluted them back and headed over to the shuttle where the girls had already gotten in and were waiting for the admiral. He stepped into the shuttle. The girls were already strapped in, chattering away still.

"Are you girls buckled up?"

"Yes, sir," they answered and went back to talking.

Harper walked up to the controls of the shuttle and started the engines from the pilot's seat as he sat down. The shuttle itself was nothing fancy and looked more like a square box with rockets on the back and thrusters on the sides and bottom. It was a little bit more streamline than an actual box, and there was a large wraparound window up front where the pilot and copilot sat. Plus, it had large skids on both sides underneath it instead of landing gear, making it capable to land on water or snow as well without sinking. Inside, it could seat comfortably twelve people and their luggage, not to mention the shuttle was rather fast and had stealth capabilities.

He strapped himself into the pilot's seat and punched some buttons on the control panel, opening a comm link. "*Justification*, this is Vice Admiral Harper. Requesting permission to depart."

"Vice Admiral, request granted. Shuttle bay doors activated. We'll miss you, sir," came a reply over the shuttle's intercom, and Harper smirked.

Harper fired the engines on the shuttle and grabbed the control levers, and soon, it lifted off the landing platform it was on and made a slow 180-degree turn and headed toward the kinetic barrier that covered the shuttle bay opening. He gave it more power, and they crossed through the barrier and out into space. He could see through the shuttle's large windows that surrounded the cockpit, and off to his right was the *Lithia*, slowly making her way out toward deep space. He watched the massive cruiser as her main engines started glowing bright red, preparing to jump, and then in an explosion of red gases, the ship disappeared into nothingness. A brief smile crossed Harper's face, but then it was down to business as he turned the shuttle, facing toward the planet.

He powered up the shuttle's main engine now and started picking up speed as two fighters came up alongside, providing escort to the spaceport in New Guinea. They kind of looked like F-18 jet fighters from Earth's history, but that was all. They were a technological marvel since that was well over centuries ago. They were fast and also had the capability to jump, which no other fighters, council or carian, could. Also, they carried mech guns, which had a kinetic-charged tip that could tear through other fighters' shields and exploded when hitting a solid surface, like a ship's hull.

The fighters also carried heat-seeking fusion missiles that could make a big mess out of some of the smaller warships if they got close enough to one and were equipped with kinetic shields and had the ability to move at FTL speeds if need be, but normally, they were flown in stage 4 propulsion speed due to combat. Even in propulsion speeds, they still were extremely fast and agile and could make a 180-degree turn instantly, but no pilot had ever been able to handle such a turn without passing out from the exertion it put on them. Even in this century, laws of physics, to a certain extent, still applied.

Harper continued toward the planet and pulled up his trajectory screen on the controls. He plotted in his course and hit the boosters, and the shuttle shot forward quickly with the fighters right beside it. It had been a while since he had piloted a shuttle, but you would never know it by the way he handled it. Soon, they passed through into the atmosphere, and he maneuvered the shuttle toward the location of New Guinea. They now were skimming over forests, mountains, grasslands, and different settlements scattered throughout the planet. Finally, a large city started coming into view, and Harper got on his comm.

"New Guinea space port, this is Vice Admiral Thomas Harper of sentinel fleet. Requesting clearance to land. Sending authorization codes now."

A young female voice came over the intercom. "Vice Admiral Harper, this is New Guinea spaceport. Authorizations approved. You are cleared to land on pad 9. Welcome to New Guinea, Vice Admiral."

Harper punched up the layout of the spaceport on his console and located pad 9, then set the coordinates into the shuttle's computer. He then maneuvered it around, and before long, the shuttle started decreasing speed as he descended from the sky and onto the platform. The fighters also landed next to the shuttle and powered down as Harper was powering down and securing it. Of course, the girls were already up, gathering some of their things, all excited.

The admiral unstrapped and walked back to them, opening the shuttle door and stepping out. He was immediately met by the pilots of the fighters as they stood at attention, saluting him, and he saluted them back. "At ease, men," he said to them, and they stood down but still at a ready's notice. Like Harper, they also carried a pistol strapped to their waist and, like the admiral, would not hesitate a second to pull the weapon at the slightest hint of danger. Harper turned and waited for the girls to disembark the shuttle, and when they did, all three girls' mouths fell open as they gazed around at the scene.

They had never been off the ship, and this was all very new to them as they just stood there staring. Ash and they saw many different types of shuttles, frigates, cargo transports, and even some huge passenger ships all docked here, and they were amazed at all the different shapes and sizes they came in. Near the edge of the platform, the spaceport itself rose up to unbelievable heights, and they had to squint when they tried to see the top of it but couldn't. Just the open sky itself was amazing to them, for they had never seen blue sky before, just the black of space.

There were so many platforms like the one they landed on that gave the spaceport the appearance of a large tree with multiple flat mushrooms growing on its side. Even the docking bays stretched out like docks on water, but instead, these were suspended in air and easily accommodated the large passenger ships that were locked down next to them. The girls looked quickly when the doors to the platform in the spaceport slid open. Dockworkers came out, heading toward them, plus luggage personnel with carryalls all dressed in uniforms, which signified they worked for the spaceport.

"Look, guys, normal people," Ash whispered to her friends, and Harper could hear one of the pilots chuckle a little as he just shook his head and smiled slightly.

The dockworkers immediately started working on the shuttle, prepping it so it would be ready to go at any given time, but they stayed clear of the fighters. These had a defense mechanism that once activated, which was standard once the pilot stepped away from his ship when not in sentinel-owned terminals or landing platforms, would give anyone touching them a nasty surprise, and they would find themselves waking up an hour later on the ground.

The luggage workers started opening the side compartments on the shuttle and unloading it as the doors again opened from the port terminal. An average in height, blocky man stepped out and headed toward Harper. It was very apparent that this man was council militia due to his uniform and the council insignia of three multicolored oval rings encircling a white star located on the front of his uniform over his heart, and like Harper, this person also wore a sidearm, but it was the smug look on his face that Harper didn't appreciate. He looked back at his pilots, who had already reached down and unstrapped their sidearms.

"Stand down, men," Harper ordered and waited for the man to approach. Ash and the girls instantly picked up on the tension and moved over, standing behind the admiral, as their natural instincts told them to do. The man continued to advance knowing full well he was outnumbered, but he was still smirking when he got within arm's length of the admiral, then stopped and seemed a little unnerved now seeing the vice admiral up close.

"Vice Admiral Harper, it is a pleasure to meet and have you here, sir. We had heard you were coming to New Guinea and wanted to personally send out a warm welcome to you," the man said, and Harper could tell he was a captain by his bar rankings on his uniform.

"Thank you, Captain…"

"Sims, Captain Sims," the man answered him and saluted Harper, and the admiral returned the gesture. The captain then looked over at Ash and her friends. "So this is your daughter, Ashley Harper, and I would guess that the other two are Rachael Torres, daughter of Commander Raul Torres, and Bridgett Nelson, daughter of Senior Chief Engineer Tony Nelson," the captain said smugly to him.

"I see that council has done their homework. I'm sure by now that every shop, market, and business knows who we are as well," Harper asked him.

"Of course. You and Rear Admiral Larson are legends, as are the people who follow you. We are thrilled that you have chosen New Guinea to make as your home."

"I'm sure you are, especially since, again, a fully armed battlecruiser and two battleships are floating overhead right now," Harper commented sarcastically, and the captain's eyes narrowed, realizing his act of pleasantries wasn't fooling the vice admiral.

"All right, then, if you want to play it that way. Yes, we know what's floating around up there, just like we know that Rear Admiral Larson and his two destroyers left right after you came into orbit. I'm here to remind you that this planet is council owned and to make sure that you observe our laws, not what sentinel fleet think they should be."

"Fine. I have no problem with that, but let me remind you, this planet and the surrounding ones are under sentinel military protection, as is the agreement with your council. So before you go and start waving a red flag, you had damn well better make sure of who it is first that you wave it in front of, for it is I who have military jurisdiction here, not you," Harper replied with a warning to his tone and glared at the captain, who instantly backed down under the admiral's gaze.

"Good day, Admiral," he said and hurriedly walked off as Harper watched him go. Once the man was gone, he turned to his pilots. "You can head back to the *Justification*. I think I can handle it from here."

"Yes, sir," the pilots said and saluted the admiral again, and Harper returned the gesture. The girls walked up to the admiral now, a little shaken.

"What was that all about, Father?" Ash asked with a shaky voice.

"To be honest with you, girls, you're going to find that some people around here don't really like us all that much. They think that council militia is better and we are nothing more than hired thugs and mercenaries and hate the idea that council needs us."

"That's a load of crap," Bridgett spoke out loud, now mad.

"Bridgett, if your father heard you talk like that, he would wash your mouth out. But, yeah, I agree with you," Harper half-smiled looking at her. "Come on, girls. Let's get going. I'm sure Sharni is waiting." They all headed to the port doors, and when they got near them, they heard the engines on the fighters fire, and they all turned around to see them lift off the pad, then shoot off into the sky, disappearing in a flash of light.

Harper remained expressionless and cold like always, then turned back and walked into the terminal when the doors slid open. Inside the building, it was full of people hurrying from docking bays to platforms, and the noise was unbelievable. Of course, the girls were in wonderment; and many times, Harper had to get on to them to stay with him as they would start to venture off. Almost an hour later, they made it to the front of the building and stepped out into a whole new world.

The girls' mouths dropped open again as laid out in front of them was a massive city with enormously tall buildings, parks, shops, and everything and anything imaginable, and it looked to go on forever to the girls. Harper headed over to a very large airlimo that floated just a couple of feet from the paved road, which their luggage was now being loaded into.

It was sleek black and could easily seat over eight people quite comfortably in it plus their luggage. It also had its own driver and wraparound windows with the back doors for the passengers lifting up onto the roof. Harper had to holler a couple of times at the girls to come and get in, but finally, they were all loaded up, and the driver up front spoke. "Are you ready, sir?"

"Yes, we are all loaded."

"Very well. Enjoy the ride," the driver said as the vehicle took off, moving through the streets. It was extremely comfortable, and you could not tell it was even moving, except when you looked out the windows and saw everything moving past you. The girls had their windows down and were watching the scenery go by, excitedly chattering among themselves. Harper leaned his head back and closed his eyes. His head was killing him now, and it wasn't all from the girls' constant rattle. He forgot to take one of his pills this morning and packed them in his luggage where he couldn't get to them yet. He was still like that when he heard Ash's voice.

"Dad, there in your bag. I made sure to pack you some."

Harper opened his eyes and looked over at his daughter, who was smiling at him as the other two girls watched him with worried looks. "What?"

"Your pills. I put a bottle of them in your pack."

Harper picked up his pack and unbuckled it, looking inside; sure enough, there was a bottle of them just as Ash told him. He reached in and took it out, but by now, the pain was worse, and his hands were starting to tremble a little. So Ash took it from him and opened it up, handing him a pill. Rachael pulled out a water bottle from her pack and handed it to him as well, and the admiral popped the pill in his mouth and washed it down with the water, leaning his head back and closing his eyes.

"You don't get those, do you?" Bridgett quietly asked Ash.

"No, only Dad."

In no time, the pill kicked in, and Harper opened his eyes and briefly smiled at the girls, who were still watching him with worried looks on their faces. "I'm all right, girls. Thank you for your concern and help."

"Don't ever do that to us again!" Rachael scolded the admiral as Ash and Bridgett nodded in agreement with her.

"Yes, ma'am, I won't." Harper slightly smiled, saluting them, and they saluted him back.

"At ease, Admiral," Rachael said and started giggling as Harper chuckled.

Forty-five minutes later, they got through the city and now were entering a very private residential area. The dwellings were very modern, contemporary designed, and large, not to mention exquisitely landscaped. The vehicle finally stopped in front of one of them, and the doors automatically opened up. Of course, the girls leaped out of it and stood looking around at their surroundings as the front door to the house slid open. They spun around to see Sharni walking out toward them. All three girls took off running to her and started hugging Sharni.

"I missed you, girls. It is so good to see you," Sharni said, laughing. Then Ash and they started talking at once, telling Sharni all about everything that they had seen. "Whoa, one at a time. Calm down and breathe." She put her hands on their heads.

"Isn't this great? Even after the little downer at the platform with the council captain—" Ash was saying but got cut off by Sharni.

"Stop right there. What happened?"

"Girls, why don't you go in and find your room?" Harper told them as he walked up to Sharni.

The girls took off running to the house and barely gave the doors enough time to open. "Your room is on the second floor, just down the hallway, on the left," Sharni yelled at them and then turned and frowned at Thomas.

"What? I didn't do anything," Harper said like a child who just got caught doing something he wasn't supposed to.

"What happened, then?" Sharni asked, frowning, with her hands on her hips.

"We had a little welcoming party when I arrived. Council sent one of their goons to make sure I knew my place around here."

Sharni frowned. "And I'm sure your reply was very dignified."

"Well, I didn't ask him to dinner, if that's what you're getting at. No, I was polite but reminded him of what was flying over his head right now and who had jurisdiction here."

"Thomas, you didn't!"

"I sure did and let him know in certain terms that I have no scruples about using it."

"Oh my gosh, I don't know who's worse, you or Gerrard."

"Gerrard. He would have decked the guy. He always punched first and then asked questions later, whereas I'm the opposite." Harper had a cocky grin now.

They both then headed into the house as the driver was still bringing in the luggage from the vehicle. By now, the whole living room area was nothing but trunks and luggage, and it was hard to move around them. Thomas and Sharni looked at all of them, and Sharni started busting up, laughing. "Did you bring the ship with you?" she asked, still laughing

"Shut up. It's not funny," Harper replied, scowling, and hollered for the girls, but they didn't reply. Then he hollered again, but still got no answer.

Sharni rolled her eyes and yelled at the top of her lungs, "ASHLEY, RACHAEL, BRIDGETT, GET DOWN HERE NOW."

Harper jumped when she yelled and looked over at her in disbelief. "What the hell was that?"

"Get used to yelling a lot. This is a lot bigger than the ship's cabin," she replied as the girls came running down the stairs.

"Yeah? What do you want?" Ash asked, looking at the adults. The admiral pointed to all the luggage, and the girls' mouths fell open.

"What, we have to put that all away ourselves?" Bridgett asked in disbelief.

"Yes, just like normal people," Harper replied with a hint of a smirk on his face.

The girls grudgingly went over and grabbed a trunk and carried them up the stairs. After several trips, all the baggage was gone, but now their room was packed full. The girls' room was almost the whole second floor of the dwelling, and they each had a full-size bed to themselves, plus three closets, each their own dresser, and a very large bathroom off to the side of the room. The room also had a balcony with large glass double doors that slid open and overlooked the large backyard that had a nice waterfall feed stream in it. There were also some nice, shaded trees, and one was right next to the balcony, and they could climb down it if they wanted to.

All three of them started unpacking, and several hours later, the last trunk was emptied and hauled back down the stairs and out into a storage room for keeping. They were exhausted by now and went downstairs and crashed on the sofa where Sharni and Harper were sitting, talking since he had finished unpacking his belongings long ago.

"What's to eat? I'm so hungry I could eat a vicoo," Ash asked as her stomach growled.

Bridgett wrinkled up her nose. "Yuck. Those things are nasty. They roll in their own poop."

"I heard they taste like pork. They kind of look like pigs," Rachael added.

"I ordered Thai food, and it should be here soon. Go check the requisition porter," Sharni told them, and the girls jumped off the couch and ran into the kitchen. They lifted up the door of the porter, and sure enough, the food was there.

"It's here. Come on, you two. Let's eat," Ash yelled back, and they opened the cartons to see what it looked like. They wrinkled up their noses at it because it wasn't anything they recognized, for they had never had it before. Sharni and the admiral came in as the girls were checking it all out. "Are you sure about this stuff? It doesn't look right," Ash asked nervously.

"Yes. Just try it. You'll like it," her aunt told them and got plates out of the cabinet for everyone. They all helped themselves and went and sat down at the large dining table and started eating. Sure enough, the girls liked it and started mowing through it fast. Once they had enough, they sat back in their chairs and moaned because they had eaten too much. Ash looked over at her father and noticed that he wasn't in military fatigues but actual, real clothes. He had a nice pullover shirt on with casual slacks and slip-on shoes and looked rather nice.

"Wow, Dad, you look good, almost like a human. For a second, I didn't recognize you," Ash teased him for how well he looked dressed this way.

"Yeah, where is the vice admiral, and what have you done with him?" Rachael added with a grin.

"All right, you little smart-asses, go get your baths and get to bed. It's going to be another long day tomorrow over at the school with registration and purchasing supplies and uniforms," Thomas told them, and they all jumped up and one by one came over and hugged him, then took off back upstairs.

"This is a good thing you're doing, Thomas, staying for Ash and even the other girls. They are family too," Sharni said to him and got up, cleaning up after everyone.

"I just couldn't let her go yet. She's all I have left of Gail. And the other girls too, I feel like they are mine as well since I've known them from birth."

"In a way, they are. Gail, Abigail, Sheri, and I all went to school together, joined council forces at the same time, and fought together. They also had those girls around the same time, and Gail and Abigail stepped in when Sheri passed away and helped Tony raise Bridgett. We are all one big family, and yes, like you, Ash is all I have left of my sister."

"Sharni, can I asked you a personal question?"

"Sure. What is it?"

"Do you sometimes hear Gail's voice in your head?"

"No, why? Do you?"

"Sometimes, when I'm real stressed out or worried, I swear I hear her speak to me. It's very faint, but I feel it's her."

"What does she say?" Sharni asked as tears filled her eyes, and she came over, sat down next to Harper, and grabbed his hand.

"Just today, when I was leaving my cabin, it was tearing me apart inside. That was my home with Gail, and Ashley was born there. I stopped in the doorway and looked back in it when I heard Gail say that Ash and I will be all right and to live again," Harper told her, fighting back his feelings. Sharni put her arms around him, and they held each other for a few minutes then.

"It was her, Thomas. You two had such a bond that even death itself cannot take it away."

"Thank you, Sharni. I don't know what I would have done without you this past year. Gail was lucky to have such a great sister as you."

"No, I was the lucky one to have such a wonderful sister. Plus, you and Ash are my family as well."

Thomas got up from the table and walked over to the refrigerator and took out a bottle of water and leaned against the counter. "As you are mine," he said and half-smiled at her, and Sharni smiled back.

CHAPTER 9

"ONLY FOUR MORE years of hell left, so what are we going to do this year for excitement?" Fâd asked his friends with a devious grin.

"Nothing. We are going to behave. Remember, Vice Admiral Harper is in charge now, and he scares me. Your father is fun and jokes with us, but Harper is always so serious and quiet, like he's thinking of how he's going to kill you," Nathan said to Fâd with a serious look on his face.

"Oh, come on, he's not like that at all. I've heard some of the stories of things he and my father have done, and they were pretty wild. Besides, we can't do anything too bad that might jeopardize our chances of getting a ship, just something to have fun."

The boys were still talking in the administration building's hallway, laughing, when suddenly, Nathan felt a cold chill run up his back. He turned around slowly as Fâd and Cory looked up, and there was Vice Admiral Harper, standing directly behind him, looking down at them with a stone-cold expression that was totally void of emotion. Nathan gulped as Fâd and Cory's faces drained of color.

"Boys, we are behaving ourselves, aren't we?"

"Yes, sir," Fâd replied, also gulping nervously.

"Good. I expect great things from you this year."

"Yes, sir. We won't disappoint you, sir," Nathan replied, still pale-white in the face.

Just then, the girls walked out of one of the rooms where they got their uniforms. "Dad, look at these uniforms. I would rather wear bindo suits instead," Ash said as she stepped out, holding her outfit up, looking at it. Rachael and Bridgett were also appalled and were holding theirs barely with the tips of their fingers, like the clothes were diseased. The girls stopped in their tracks when they saw who were standing in front of the admiral. "You have got to be kidding me. We can't even get one day of peace here," Ash said with a look of utter disgust.

"I forgot, the plague sisters were coming," Fâd replied, rolling his eyes.

"Watch who you're calling plague sisters, fang face," Rachael warned and glared at him.

"You had better take that back, cotton head!" Nathan snapped at her.

"Hey, why don't you go back to the freak show? They miss their star," Bridgett snarled at him.

"Oh yeah? Well, it's a good thing there isn't a gas leak in here, or we would all be dead with the fire that is out of control on your head," Cory threw at Bridgett.

"That's it. Girls, it's time to kick some watorian butts," Ash said and threw down her uniform. Rachael and Bridgett did the same and started heading toward the boys. The boys glared at them and put their fists up, waiting for the girls to approach.

"THAT IS ENOUGH," Admiral Harper yelled, and the children stopped dead in their tracks and stared at him, now scared. Even people in the other offices and rooms peeked out into the hallway to see what was going on. The door to Professor Baptise opened, and he stepped out into the hall but stopped short when he saw Admiral Harper and waited to see what would happen next.

"I will not tolerate any of this anymore. You six will get along this year, or I will be forced to enact a proper and intense punishment that not one of you will ever forget for the rest of your lives. Do I make myself clear?" Harper glared down at them coldly, the tone of his voice ominous and full of warning.

"Yes, sir," the children replied in unison.

"Good. Now go about your duties."

The girls picked up their stuff and headed off to another one of the offices to get their books as the boys hurried off just to get away from the vice admiral. He watched them go and turned around with a quick smirk on his face, which left just as fast as it appeared, and headed toward Professor Baptise. The professor saw him coming and now felt very nervous. Just like Admiral Larson, Admiral Harper was also a very scary, dangerous man, but at least Larson would smile at you. Harper just glared.

"Vice Admiral Harper, welcome," Baptise said nervously and stood aside for the admiral to enter into his office. Just like Admiral Larson, Admiral Harper was also very large and intimidating, but he was cold and void of emotion. At least Larson you could warm up to, but Harper was definitely not a people person. Professor Baptise quickly ran around his desk and took his seat as Vice Admiral Harper sat down in one of the guest chairs across from him.

"Good day, Professor Baptise," Harper said, totally void of emotion.

"It is a pleasure to finally meet you, Vice Admiral. I have heard a lot about you."

"I'm sure you have. Now down to business. As you are aware, my daughter, Ashley, Commander Torres's daughter, Rachael, and Chief Engineer Nelson's daughter, Bridgett, are now attending your school. I expect they will be treated fairly and given the type of education that will help and further them in their pursuit of knowledge. I trust that they will be treated like any other child here and no special attention be given them. Also, as you have been made aware, I am seeing to the well-being of Fâdron Larson, Nathan Wilcox, and Cory Brayton. If an incident should arise, I request that I be made aware of it immediately, which also goes for the young girls that I already mentioned to you. Do you have any questions for me?"

"No, sir," Baptise replied with a shaky voice.

"Good. Now that we have that out of the way, I will take my leave," Harper said and stood up. The professor also stood up, and the admiral extended his hand to the professor, who took it and shook his hand while he was shaking. The corner of Harper's mouth turned up ever so slightly, and he turned, then headed out the door of the professor's office to find the girls. Once he was gone, the professor collapsed into his chair and let out the breath he was holding to try and calm his nerves, marveling at how fast that had gone over.

* * *

Meantime, the boys ran all the way back to their dorm once they were out of the admiral's sight. All three ran into their room, locking the door behind them. It was a large square room with white walls, a light-blue low pile carpet on the floor, one window facing out toward the park, and two scone lights on the walls. Each boy had a full-size bed, a dresser, and a desk with chair situated throughout the room. There were also large pictures of ships or some other type of motorized vehicle on the walls and books or some datapad lying around. Even for it being three boys, they kept it rather neat and clean.

"Crap, this is going to be the worst year ever. Those little demons are here, and now we have a killer watching us," Fâd said, leaning up against the door.

"I told you, he's scary," Nathan said as he collapsed on his bed.

"Yeah, which is bad. You know those little monsters are going to try and cause us all kinds of problems, and we wouldn't be able to do anything about it," Cory added.

"Oh yeah, we can. We have the right to defend ourselves. And you heard him, he warned all of us, including those girls. One thing about Admiral Harper, I know he is fair. My dad always say he is," Fâd told them and walked over to his bed, jumping on it and lying on his back.

"Let's hope so, or this is going to be a long and painful year," Nathan commented, and the other two agreed.

* * *

Admiral Harper continued to move through the hallway but would look down at the multitool on his wrist every so often and kept walking, following the blinking red dots on the map that were now displayed on the tiny screen. He totally ignored everyone he passed, but they definitely didn't ignore him. Everyone would move out of his way, and a lot of them would start whispering as he passed by. Of course, being dressed in his admiral uniform made him look just that much more intimidating, but the pistol strapped to his side also helped a lot.

Finally, he came to the room where the blinking dots were and went inside. This was the school library and bookstore where all the electronic books were picked up and supplies purchased for classes. He walked in, and all heads turned and looked at him, and even some backed away nervously. He quickly spotted the girls and headed over to them. "Have you gotten everything you need?"

"Yes, and look they have the new T300 notepad, which I will be able to store triple the amount of data on," Ash said excitedly, holding up the flat-looking blue device that was a little bit bigger than a paperback book and could perform more functions than any computer ever could.

"Plus, they come in all different colors. Look, mine's red," Rachael said and held hers up for him to see. Even Bridgett showed him her green one, not to mention they all had grabbed backpacks that were all different colors and handheld scanners for pulling information from bar codes, microchips, and system terminals.

"You don't need the scanners. Just use your own scanners," Harper said to them.

"We can't in class. We have to use theirs. These are on the list. See? Right here. Apparently, ours perform too many functions, giving us an edge over everyone," Ash told him and showed him the list, and sure enough, it was there.

The girls had armloads of books and needed items, then finally made their way to the checkout line. There were quite a few adults and children in front of them, and they constantly turned around and glanced nervously at the vice admiral, but he just ignored them and waited with the girls until it was their turn. Finally, they got up to the checkout and started piling their stuff on the table. The cashier started scanning the items but would constantly look up at the vice admiral and nervously smile. Ash saw it and started giggling, but her father ignored her.

"There should also be a ticket waiting for me under the name of Larson, Gerrard," Admiral Harper told the young lady. She looked up at him, and her mouth fell open and just stared at him. Harper looked around to see if anyone else noticed this weird display, but people looked away when he looked at them.

"Miss, are you okay?" he asked, leaning a little toward her.

"Oh my gosh, I'm so sorry. Yes, here it is. I'll just add it to this," the cashier said and now was beet red and totally flustered. Finally, she had everything rung up and told the admiral the amount. Harper punched some buttons on his multitool, then looked over at her. She dropped her gaze. Her registered beeped and showed the approval of the marks used to pay for the purchase. "Thank you, sir, and have a good day," she said, all nervous, to him.

Harper picked up some of the items and headed to the automatic doors with the girls following behind him. He now noticed that a lot of female teachers, aides, and even some of the children's mothers were now staring at him, and for once, he started getting nervous. The men would just avoid him and move clear out of his way. He leaned down close to Ash and whispered in her ear, "Ash, what is going on? Why are people staring at me?"

Rachael and Bridgett started giggling behind them, and he looked back at them with a dirty look. Ash started giggling too, and it was Rachael who spoke up. "Because they think you're good looking, Admiral."

"What?" Harper said a little too loudly and stopped, looking down at the girls, who were now laughing.

"It's true, Dad. We overheard some of the teachers who were in the library talking about you."

"What were they saying?"

"They said you were good-looking, especially in your uniform," Bridgett told him, grinning.

"That wasn't all, but I don't think you want to know what they were thinking," Ash said with an ornery grin.

"Were you doing what I think you were doing?" Harper looked down at his daughter with narrowed eyes.

"I can't help it. Some people are so easy to read."

Harper grabbed Ash's arm and pulled her away from the mainstream of people, and Rachael and Bridgett followed. "No telepathy. Do you hear me?"

"Yes, Dad, I won't," Ash answered with her head down.

"It is not right to pry into others' minds. That is an invasion of privacy, and I don't want to hear of you doing that again, not to mention I'm sure that other people are not so open to your rare talent and wouldn't look so kindly upon it. It would be best to keep this gift to yourself."

"I won't."

Harper looked down at her as a very slight smile appeared at the edge of his mouth but quickly faded, and they continued on toward the building's exit, weaving their way through the staring people. Finally, they were outside, and the large airlimo they came in was waiting for them. The girls walked over to the vehicle and put their stuff in the trunk, then climbed in. Admiral Harper waited for them to all get in, then he climbed in behind, and soon, the hover craft took off. While they headed back to their dwelling, he pulled up a large screen on his multitool and started typing in something on his holographic keyboard. Then other screens came up, and he moved some things around on it and, with a slight smirk, closed it.

Back at the boys' room, their multitools started flashing a red alert, signify an important message. They looked at one another and then opened their messages.

> This is Vice Admiral Harper. I now have your transponder signals and will be able to follow your every move. If you need anything, do not hesitate to contact me. Your multitools now have a direct linkup. Plus, if you run into any trouble from outside sources, contact me immediately, and they will be dealt with. Don't worry, boys, I remember what it was like to be your age.

They looked at one another, and big grins spread across their faces as they started laughing.

CHAPTER 10

THE NEXT TWO weeks flew by fast. Admiral Harper was getting a crash course in girls. He now had been to the mall, shopping with them, twice. Thank goodness Sharni went; otherwise, there would have been an incident when some thirteen-year-old boys talked to the girls while they waited to get ice cream. He also, on another occasion, even went to a hair salon with them without Sharni and was totally embarrassed as all the women hairdressers kept looking him over from head to toe and winking at him. Even one of the male hairdressers was doing the same thing, which completely unnerved the admiral. When they got back to the house, the girls told Sharni about it, and she fell to the floor, laughing so hard, as tears ran down her cheeks.

"Don't you dare tell Gerrard about this. He will never let me live it down," Thomas warned her as he started chuckling.

Finally, the first day of school came, and he walked the girls out to the waiting shuttle that would take them and other students who didn't stay on campus to school. The girls were all excited. Even having to wear uniforms didn't dampen their spirits as they climbed on the bus and then waved from their seats, out the window, to him. He stood there, watching it go, until it was out of sight and brought up a holographic screen on his multitool and watched it as three blinking red dots moved through an outline of the city map together.

Then he moved the holographic map, running his hand over it, and picked up three more blinking red dots moving through a map of the prep school and dorms, heading toward an exit. All were accounted for and safe, so he put his map away and went back inside. Sharni was in the kitchen, cleaning up after breakfast, and he walked in as she poured him a cup of creo.

"Okay, that was the hardest thing I have ever done," he said, taking the cup from her.

"Yeah, but it will get better. You'll see."

"Will it?"

"Yes, and before you know it, she'll be a young lady and liking boys."

"Damn it, Sharni, you aren't making this any easier," he said through narrowed eyes.

She looked over at him with a grin on her face. "Just trying to prepare you for what's to come."

Suddenly, their multitools went off at the same time as a red alert came on, notifying them of an incoming message. Harper pressed the button, and a holographic screen came up, and Gerrard appeared in it. "Good, you're both together. Thomas, I just got the news that Lily committed suicide a few hours ago. I haven't told Fâd yet, and since I'm not there, I was wondering if you could do it for me. Plus, will you both handle the funeral arrangements for me? I won't be able to get back to Sigma Six for at least four months.

"I'm sorry to have to dump all this on you two, but I had to come out of jump to be able to contact you, and I'm afraid I might have lost the trail because of it. Like you know, I can't give you any details, but lives are at stake. I don't know how Fâd will react to the news, so make sure you tell him where no one will see you two, and be prepared for anything. You know what I mean."

"I will, and yes, I'll make sure he's protected. Don't worry, Sharni and I will take care of everything. You just be careful. I know what those missions are like."

"Thanks, Thomas. And Sharni?"

"Yes?"

"I love you."

"I love you too, Gerrard. Please be careful," she replied, and the screen shut off. Sharni and Thomas looked at each other, and Thomas let out a sigh.

"Wow, this day just gets better," Thomas said as he ran his hands through his wavy black hair.

"Yeah. I guess we better get going," Sharni said and left the kitchen, and Thomas followed. He went into his room and hit the call button on his multitool to request the airlimo, which he could do at any time since he had a direct link.

Sharni entered her room, which was across the hall from him. A few minutes later, he came out in his admiral uniform, and Sharni was now wearing her formal uniform, which he noticed was one bar short of becoming an admiral.

"So how much longer until the other bar?" he asked her with no trace of emotion, but after all these years, Sharni and Larson both were so used to Harper's cold demeanor that it didn't bother them. They both knew that he did care even if he never showed it.

"Two more years," she replied.

They both walked out to the living room, then out the front sliding door. The vehicle was already waiting for them, and they both climbed in. The driver took off, heading toward the spaceport.

Traffic was busy today, and it took them an hour to get to the port, but finally, they were walking through the terminal, toward the admiral's shuttle. He went up to terminal desk and gave them his authorization codes and destination coordinates, then headed out to the shuttle. They both walked out as dockworkers unhooked the shuttle, and he climbed into the pilot's seat. Sharni took the other one next to him.

"Admiral Harper, you are cleared for departure," a voice came over the shuttle's intercom. Harper fired up the engines, and in no time, the shuttle lifted off, and then he powered it up as they shot across the sky. Meantime, Sharni was punching in coordinates to Pantier, one of the five watorian colonies that Larson lived in and governed when he was there planet side.

"ETA in ten minutes," Sharni told Thomas.

"Does Lily have any other family there?" Thomas asked her.

"No. They all passed away many years ago. She was all alone, especially after Fâd refused to see her anymore. Something happened between them, but Gerrard could never get Fâd to tell him. I don't know how he will react to the news either."

"Well, I had better tell him someplace private in case he loses control and I have to contain him. We can't have people seeing that, for his own safety."

"Aren't you worried about them seeing you too?"

"No."

"How powerful are you, Thomas?"

"Powerful enough" was all he said, and it was in his finalizing tone. Sharni knew that Thomas was a very powerful kinetic, but just how much, she didn't know, but his vague answer was all she needed and now knew that he was above and beyond any set levels.

The shuttle started coming up on Pantier, and Harper punched in an authorization code again and waited. "Authorization received. Proceed to landing pad 6. We've been expecting you, Vice Admiral," a female watorian voice came over the comm as Harper maneuvered the shuttle around to make a landing on pad 6 in the shipyard.

Harper could now see the many different types of ships there, some badly damaged and others in excellent shape. This place hadn't changed much since the last time he was there. He would come off and on and stay a day or two with Larson when he was required to inspect a new ship ready for service. Watorians were masters when it came to ships. They could take a wreaked frigate and turn it into a dangerous fighter. Their ship knowledge, along with Senior Chief Engineer Tony Nelson, was instrumental in the rebuilding of the battlecruisers and battleships, especially the two behemoths the *Justification* and the *Lithia*. A lot of the things on those two ships were top secret as Nelson and the watorians created most of it.

Harper landed, then powered down the shuttle, and once it was secured, he and Sharni unbuckled and headed to the door. It slid open, and they walked out. Crewmen were already readying the shuttle for a returned trip. They both headed toward the terminal as a very attractive female watorian soldier walked through the terminal doors and headed toward them. Harper saw her, and a slight smile spread across his face, and a big grin spread across hers when she saw him.

"Nera, it's good to see you again. You haven't changed," Harper said to her when they got close enough to hear each other.

"And you still haven't changed one bit either, I see. Thomas, it's good to see you too. I'm sorry about Gail. I wish I could have made it, but you know what it's like. Sharni, it's good to see you too. It's been a while. Maybe now things can be different," Nera said to them both.

"I don't know. We both have our ships to take care of, but we still manage to find time for each other even in space."

"Knowing my cousin, he'll do something, though," Nera said, grinning.

"Yeah, Gerrard has always leaped before he looked," Sharni replied, rolling her eyes.

"Well, shall we go and get arrangements made?" Harper asked Nera.

"Yes. This way, Admiral." Nera directed them both toward the terminal.

"So what happened?" Sharni asked her.

"From what the doctors told me, she got out of her room and attacked a security guard in the hall, taking his gun. She was still on the nueralizers, so her kinetic powers were useless, but her mind was so far gone as she ran through the clinic, screaming that carians were after her. The doctors and security chased her down into the cafeteria and tried to talk her down, but before they could get to her, she turned the gun on herself and told them they weren't going to eat her alive and shot herself. She died instantly. I guess she saw everyone as a carian. She had even told doctors that Gerrard was a carian that attacked her and she gave birth to a carian son," Nera told them.

"I didn't know she was that far gone. I wonder if she had said something like that to Fâd. That would explain why he stopped having anything to do with her. I hope not. It would be horrible to have your own mother say something like that to you," Sharni added as her heart hurt for Fâd.

Nera sighed. "Yeah, it would, but Fâd is too much like Gerrard. Has he been told yet?"

"No. We wanted to get all the arrangements taken care of first before I told him," Harper told Nera.

"Good idea, and I don't need to remind you about him. Of course, it's not like you can't handle anything coming at you," Nera said in a serious tone.

They all walked through the terminal and then out the front of the building to a waiting hover vehicle. Nera climbed into the driver's seat, and Sharni got into the passenger's seat next to her. Thomas got into the back as the door swung down, and Nera grabbed the steering stick and moved the vehicle forward as it floated on air. They quickly headed down the paved streets, and Thomas remembered how tranquil this place was. It had been some time since he was here last, but not much had changed.

The buildings were all simple in design, and instead of the metal and glass ones of New Guinea, these were made out of lumber and stone, sort of looking like lodges from Earth's past. Even the markets and stores looked the same, and to be honest, the whole colony looked like a resort city in the mountains as the whole place was surrounded by forest, which also resembled the redwood forests back on Earth that he had seen many, many years ago.

Finally, they got to the medical facility. Nera stopped the vehicle and climbed out, followed by Vice Admiral Harper and Captain Sharni. One thing about this colony, though, was, the people here were mainly soldiers with their families, and not too many were civilians.

Unlike all the other nonwatorian colonies around, watorians there refrained from using as much technology as they could and relied on good old hard labor even though they were technical wizards. They preferred simple lives, and though they still used some technology, they liked to do more of the everyday things in their lives by hand and focused their technology more toward ships and other such areas.

Admiral Harper, Sharni, and Nera walked into the medical clinic, and Nera led them up to the large wraparound reception desk where a medical assistant was behind the counter, working on a holographic keyboard. She was so engrossed in what she was doing that she didn't notice them until Nera said something to her.

"Excuse me, but we are here to see Dr. Taylor."

The assistant looked up now and jumped when she saw who it was. She immediately saluted as shock spread across her face. Harper and Sharni saluted her back, but Nera looked annoyed with the young woman. "Yes, sir. Yes, ma'am. I'm sorry. Right. I'll get him right away." She was so flustered now and didn't know what to do or which way to go.

"Just call him on the comm, and let him know that Vice Admiral Harper is here now," Nera said to her.

The young woman's face turned white as she reached over and pressed a button on her console and told the man who answered that Vice Admiral Harper was there to see him. Then she quickly ran from behind the console and disappeared down the hall.

"Wow, Thomas, you sure have quite an effect on people," Nera teased him.

Sharni let out a fake cough then. "Yeah, he sure does," she replied, grinning and looking over at him.

"Sharni, shut up!" Thomas warned her through narrowed eyes, and she started giggling. Nera was grinning, knowing something had happened that embarrassed him, but she knew she would never get it out of them. They waited a few minutes, and finally, Dr. Taylor came out with a big grin on his face.

"Thomas, it has been a while. You haven't changed one bit. Maybe a little gray around the edges there, but just the same," the doctor half-grinned, pointing to the slight gray streaks on Thomas's temples.

Dr. Taylor was an older watorian, still fairly tall and large but now showing his age, which Harper honestly could not tell what. He had the shoulder-length hair, which was now gray, with many braids and beads throughout it, and also as was the custom among the watorians, he portrayed the tribal markings down the right side of his face, starting at his right eye and ending around his neck. These were a sign of great respect among the watorians and held a high standing in their society.

He was dressed in a sentinel uniform with a lab coat over it, but unlike most doctors, he didn't carry any other type of medical tools with him. Instead, his multitool on his arm was different from others and could perform all kinds of functions dealing with the medical field.

"I can't believe you're still alive. I figured by now, someone would have shot you for sure because of your great bedside manners," Thomas replied bluntly, and the doctor came over, and they shook hands. "So you are here about Lily, I take it? Well, I already have the body prepared, and a place is ready in the colony crypt. How do you want to proceed with the rest?"

"I figured we will have a small ceremony in five days from now with just us and the children, possibly friends if they want to come."

"She didn't have any friends left. After Fâd was born, she got very spiteful and downright vicious at times. Then, of course, her mind started going, and she even turned on Fâd and Gerrard," Dr. Taylor said with no emotion.

"Do you think her being an exposure victim was why she was such a loner and spiteful?" Sharni asked Dr. Taylor a little coldly.

"Yes, I do. The tumor that the exposure causes alters the brain instantly even though most victims don't show symptoms until much later, but they are never the same again from the moment they are exposed. Most victims become manipulative, possessive, spiteful, and like she showed, downright combative at times. To try and overcome this, they create a fantasy world that they live in before the paranoia gets out of hand, and they no longer have a conscience. Honestly, we are lucky she didn't hurt or even kill someone. This condition was manifesting in her even before she had Fâd. I have to hand it to Gerrard. He tried to help her as long as he could, and I know he did it for his son's sake."

"Well, I guess there's really not much more we can do here. Will you handle the arrangements for the burial after the ceremony?" Thomas asked the doctor.

"Yeah, I can handle that. About what time do we want to have this?"

"Let's do it around 1300."

"Okay, then. I'll have the placement in the crypt done an hour later."

"And I'll have our colony reverend come and bless her and give last rights," Nera told them.

"Thanks, Nera. That would be great." Thomas nodded at her.

"So how are those headaches? What are you taking now for them?" Dr. Taylor asked nonchalantly.

"The same, but I'm trying an experimental pill that seems to be doing well for me. The ship's doctor has me trying Pendrocaine, which seems to be working so far."

"Good. I was going to suggest that. I guess headaches are a small price to pay for the type of power you have. What about your daughter? Did she inherit your kinetics?"

"Yes, and a little telepathy from her mother."

"Does she get the headaches?"

"So far, no, and I'm hoping she doesn't. I have the doctor on my ship do a routine scan on her every year, and so far, she's clean, no tumor."

"Yeah, but, Thomas, your tumor is different. It's not like exposure victims. I know it's what causes the headaches, but in actuality, it's part of your brain and not really a tumor. Most of us have a right and left side of our brain, but you also have a third part, which, if I hadn't seen it for myself when I did your scan all those years ago, I wouldn't have believed. Since I had Lily here, I have been doing a lot of research on kinetics, and I have proof now that natural-occurring kinetics have no risk on a person's mental stability. The cancerous tumor never forms. But you, you're different, a rare specimen. If you die before me, can I have your brain for study?"

Thomas started chuckling now and shaking his head. "There's that wonderful bedside manner I remember so well. Sure. If I die before you, you can have it. Just don't mark up my pretty face."

"Still a smart-ass. Did I mark up your face all those times I stitched you and Gerrard up in the war? No, there's not a scar on you. Well, just the one next to your eye, but I felt you deserved that one. Getting cut by a whiskey bottle in a bar fight was not my idea of an honorable battle," Dr. Taylor said with a scowl on his face, and Thomas just smirked.

"A bar fight? You and Gerrard? No! Was this before Gail and I met you two or after?" Sharni asked sarcastically with her arms crossed and a scowl on her face.

"Before. They got into them all the time. Between the mercs and the female companions they always seemed to end up with, I don't know who cut you two up worse. And like always, you both would come crawling back to my tent, and I would spend the rest of the night patching your sorry asses back up."

"Really? How interesting," Sharni said with a frown on her face.

"It's not like he says," Thomas replied, now a little nervous.

"Oh yes, it was. At least you both were smart enough not to take marks with you so you didn't get robbed, only stabbed because you couldn't pay. It's a damn good thing you two could fight. Otherwise, you would have been dead a long time ago."

"Okay. I think it's time to go," Thomas said and grabbed Sharni's elbow and started to guide her toward the front door.

"No. I want to stay and hear some more."

"He's just bitter because we never paid him either," Thomas said with a half smirk on his face.

"Damn right you never did. I would be living like a king right now if you had paid me for every stitch I put into you two."

"I thought those were restitutions for saving your sorry ass all the time."

"Yeah, get out of here, smart-ass. I'll see you in five days," Dr. Taylor said with a slight grin on his face. Thomas escorted Nera and Sharni as they headed out of the medical clinic and to the vehicle they came in. Everyone climbed in, and Nera once again took the controls and headed back to the terminal and shipyard

"So that's a side of you I never knew, Thomas. Gerrard, of course, I'm not surprised, but you always seem so serious. I'm sure there's a lot more than just what Dr. Taylor said back there," Nera said, grinning, as she drove back to the terminal.

"Just drive," Harper replied with no show of emotion on his face, and Nera and Sharni both started laughing.

Soon, they pulled up in front of the terminal, got out, and walked into the building. Nera continued to lead as they walked right through and straight back to Harper's shuttle, which was sitting with the door open, ready for him. They all stopped in front of it, and Harper and Sharni turned toward Nera.

"Thank you for all your help. I guess we'll be seeing each other in five days," Thomas told her coldly and void of any emotion like normal.

"Don't mention it. Thank you for seeing to this for my cousin. I know he must be on a very important mission, because he doesn't ask for a favor that often, especially one as personal as this one is. He's lucky to have a good friend like you." Nera smiled at Thomas.

"I'm the lucky one. He had saved my ass many times, and he was there for me when Gail died. This is the least I could do for him. I know, if it were me, he would do the same."

Nera walked over, and they both hugged each other. Then she leaned backed and grabbed one of his biceps and squeezed it. "Wow, Thomas, you're still just as rock-solid as you were fifteen years ago and just as tense. Maybe you should find some nice female and work off some of that built-up tension."

"Why, Nera? Is that an offer?" Thomas narrowed his eyes at her with a hint of a smile on his face.

"Nah, you're too much like family. It just wouldn't be right," she said and started laughing.

"Yeah, you're probably right, not to mention you're too young for me."

"Curious, how old are you, really?"

"I'll never tell. There are only three people left in this universe that know that one, one being your cousin and the other that damn old doctor back at the medical clinic, and the last one, Carson," Thomas replied coldly as Nera shook her head, grinning.

"Well, however old you are, you still look damn good. I'll see you in five days," she said and nodded over at Sharni, who returned the gesture, then turned and headed toward the terminal. Thomas watched her for a few minutes, then turned and followed Sharni into the shuttle, and they climbed back into their seats. In no time, Harper got his clearance, and the shuttle was once again flying through the air, toward New Guinea.

"So how do you want to do this with Fâd?" Sharni asked him.

"I thought maybe if you could take the girls with the other two boys, maybe to a roller rink or something kids like to do, then I would stay at the dwelling and speak with Fâd. At least at the house, we will have privacy in case he has a kinetic episode."

"Sounds good. We only have a couple hours until they are done with classes today. You know, Thomas, I will be leaving the day after this funeral. Are you going to be okay?"

"Yeah. I think I'm starting to get the hang of things. But to be honest, I am going to miss you. I've enjoyed your company and come to rely on you a lot."

Sharni looked over at him, now with a serious look on her face. "Did you ever wonder, if things had turned out differently then, if you didn't fall in love with my sister and me with your best friend, would it still have changed between us?"

"Yes, I have, and, Sharni, I can honestly tell you that you wouldn't be leaving here in six days if that were the case."

"If that were the case, I wouldn't leave." Sharni looked at him and smiled, but he didn't return the gesture. They both looked out the front windows of the shuttle and continued toward New Guinea in silence, both caught up in their own thoughts. Finally, the space-port came into view, and Harper once again got clearance to land on the same platform as before. In no time, he was maneuvering the shuttle onto the pad and shutting down. Sharni unbuckled and got up, heading for the door, as Thomas finished powering everything down, and before long, they both were walking back toward the sliding doors of the terminal.

Half an hour later, they both finally managed to get through the crowded port and to the waiting vehicle. Once in it, they just sat back, looking out the window and watching the scenery pass by. They both were still locked in thought when they pulled up to the house. Thomas got out first, and like the gentleman he was, he stood aside and waited for Sharni to exit, and they headed to the house. He put his hand on the blue scan pad, and the front door slid open. They entered, both going over and collapsing on the sofas.

"Well, that was the easy part. Now comes the hard part. How do you tell a child that one of their parents has died?" Thomas asked Sharni, leaning his head back against the sofa.

"I don't know. How do you handle it when one of your crew dies and you have to tell their family?"

"I just tell them and then go and drown myself in menial tasks for the next two days or drink half a bottle of brandy, but this is different. This isn't an adult who can turn around and comfort the rest of their loved ones. This is a child, my best and closest friend's child."

"All you can do is tell him and then just be there for him. Plus, you have to remember, this is Gerrard's son, who is a lot like him in some ways. But I noticed Fâd's a lot more closed up with his emotions, unlike Gerrard, who will let you know how he feels and usually at the end of his fist."

"True. He always came right out and told you how he felt. He's not one to hold anything back. All right, let's get ready. The kids should be getting out of school here in the next half hour," Thomas told her and got up, heading to his room. He wasn't looking forward to this, and Thomas wasn't one who handled surprises very well.

CHAPTER 11

"Why is the first day of school always hell? Look at the assignments we got. Do they honestly think I've been studying up all during the break and remember this junk?" Nathan asked his friends and threw his books on his bed back in their dorm. He looked over at Fâd with a concerned look. His friend had been unusually quiet all day, not that he talked a lot anyway, especially compared to him and Cory. But even when they asked him a question, he just gave a simple answer and closed back up.

Nathan and Cory knew that Fâd wasn't one to show much emotion unless he was mad or felt that he was being unjustly treated. He had no problem standing up to the injustice, which usually meant a fight, and Fâd could easily hold his own against most, even kids older than him. But as far as social, he wasn't a real people person, generally staying to himself and not bringing any attention to him. That was where he, Nathan, came in. He had no problem joining right in, doing stupid things, and making himself heard. Cory, on the other hand, was somewhat social but more relaxed and generally thought things through before he acted. They always teased him about being the nice guy.

But this was different with Fâd now. Nathan and Cory could always get him to open up to them, but try as hard as they could, he wouldn't talk and sometimes got mad at them for trying to get him to. Nathan decided, the hell with it, though. He was going for it. He owed Fâd that. If it weren't for Fâd and his father, Nathan had no one, for they took him in when his parents got killed on a freighter that they piloted when it got attacked by mercs. He was just barely four at the time, and they had been his family since.

"All right, Fâd, you can beat the hell out of me. I don't care. But I want to know what is going on with you."

Fâd looked over at him with narrowed eyes and stared at him silently for a few seconds. "I don't know, but something's wrong. I can feel it."

"What do you mean you can feel it? Like, maybe you're sick, that kind of feeling?"

"No, not sick but something else. I can't explain it, like something's going to happen real soon."

Just then, the boys' multitools started beeping, and a red alert button was flashing on them. All three boys looked down at them, and their mouths fell open. Then they looked at one another with scared expressions on their faces. "Whoa" was all they said at the same time. They punched the buttons on each of their tools, and a message came up on the holographic screens that popped up in front of them.

> This is Vice Admiral Harper. Your presences is requested at my place of residency now. A vehicle will be waiting for you in front of the administration building. Please check in at the office, as they are aware of your leaving.

The boys were now scared. Definitely, something was going on, and all of them felt sick to their stomachs. "I guess your premonition was right," Cory spoke up.

"Let's go and get this over with. I'm tired of feeling this way," Fâd said and headed to the door. They didn't even take time to change out of their uniforms and moved quickly down the two flights of stairs and out into the grounds, half walking, half running. They got across the large park and to the administration building and headed to the front office.

Fâd walked in first with Nathan and Cory right behind him. The secretary looked up and frowned, for she knew them quite well because they were in there a lot, usually on detention. "Yes, Fâdron, you and your friends have permission to leave. I think a vehicle is already out there waiting for you. Just check in when you get back," she told the boys, and they turned and headed back out to the building's front sliding doors.

Sure enough, she was right. A very fancy large black vehicle was waiting just off the sidewalk with its door open. A tall man was standing next to the open door and motioned for them to enter. The boys slowly walked over to it, then climbed in. The door shut behind them, and they watched out the windows as the driver walked around and got into the front. A dark window separated them from him as the airlimo moved on.

"Wow. Admiral Harper travels in style. How come your father doesn't use one of these and makes us always use a cab?" Nathan asked Fâd, who was watching out the window.

"Because he's a tight ass. You know that," Fâd replied with an ornery smirk.

"True. I still remember his reply that one time when we were complaining about being hungry. He told us to go eat some bark off the tree, that fiber would do us some good. He is so rotten sometimes." Nathan laughed, and Fâd chuckled too, but then his face turned white. What if something had happened to his father? His father was his whole world. He couldn't lose him now. He had been the only parent he had ever had, and he had raised him from the time he was born. He had always been there for him, and he was the only stable thing in his life. Fâd turned and looked out the window, fighting back tears that wanted to fall. No, not his father. He wouldn't accept that.

Finally, the car pulled up in front of a very large, modern dwelling, and the driver got out and pressed a button near the door so it slid up. The boys climbed out, but Fâd was last to come out as they all walked up to the house. Nathan pressed the button near the door, and it slid open. Ashley stood in the doorway with a frown on her face. Fâd instantly went into defense mode as his eyes narrowed when he saw her.

"Relax. This is neutral ground, and I have been commanded to be polite, which is all you're going to get from me," she said as if the words had a horrible taste in her mouth. She stood aside, and the boys walked in, but Fâd kept an eye on her, never letting her out of his sight. She then went ahead of them, and they followed her through the living room and could hear giggling coming from what they could tell was the kitchen in the back, and sure enough, they were right.

In there was the girl called Rachael and the other one named Bridgett, along with a very beautiful vatoria, whom Fâd knew as Sharni. She looked over at him and smiled, and he grinned back. She was the other one in his life that he cared about, for she was more the mother to him than his own ever was. Plus, he knew about her and his father even though his dad never said anything, and now seeing her smiling meant his father was okay, for he was pretty sure she wouldn't be smiling if something had happened to his dad.

Sharni walked over to him and gave him a big hug, and he hugged her back. "My, I haven't seen you for a while. You have grown so much, and I can tell you're going to be just as handsome as your father."

"It's good to see you, Sharni. Why haven't you come and seen us lately?"

"I've been on duty, and as a matter of fact, I will be leaving in six days to head back."

"What? You're not going to stay here with us?" Ash now spoke out, and her eyes watered up a little. Even the other two girls also had wet eyes from the shocking news. Nathan and Cory looked back at Fâd, not knowing what to do. Obviously, the girls were just blindsided with this news.

"No, Ash. I just took some time off to help your father get everything handled, but I'll be back off and on during your breaks. Maybe then we all can go out and have some fun together," Sharni said and looked down at Fâd and smiled.

Fâd grinned back. One could not help but like Sharni, and the fact that she was very pretty helped. He could see why his father loved her and didn't blame him at all. He himself had oftentimes wondered why she had never married his father and why she was not his mother. But he knew there was a big secret there that he would probably never find out.

"Do you boys want something to snack on?" Sharni asked them.

"Yeah. What do you got?" Nathan's eyes lit up.

"Chocolate brittle, mini pizza, ice cream—you name it!" Rachael said with a grin.

"Mini pizza," Nathan replied, licking his lips, and went over and jumped up on one of the barstools next to Rachael. Cory also followed and sat next to him, but Fâd remained back and just glared at his friends, who so easily fell into the enemies' company. He looked over at Ashley, and like him, she stood back with pursed lips and arms crossed in front of her, plus narrowed eyes, watching her friends talk to the boys.

Sharni walked over to the replicator and punched in some buttons, and in seconds, mini pizzas were done. She carried them over, and the kids started digging in. Even Fâd and Ash couldn't hold out, and they, too, helped themselves. They were all eating away at them just like a pack of hungry animals when the admiral walked in. Everyone stopped and looked at him.

"Continue. Don't let me stop you," he said with a slight smirk.

The girls, of course, did, and soon, the boys joined them but warily watching the admiral out of the corner of their eyes. Finally, the plate was clean, and Bridgett went and got everyone a juice bottle from the refrigerator. They all drank them down since the pizza had worked up a thirst

The admiral looked over at Sharni, and she nodded to him, then looked at the kids, but it was the admiral who now spoke and in his commanding tone. "Fâdron, I need to speak to you in private. The rest of you will go with Sharni to the mall."

Fâd's face turned pale white, as did all the other children's, and they looked over at him. Even Ash had a concerned look on her face, which Fâd saw, and a strange feeling came over him. He felt some comfort in the fact that she was actually concerned for him, and they stared at each other for a few seconds but then looked away just as quickly.

"All right, then. Children, the car is waiting. Let's go," Sharni said and headed toward the front door, and they all followed.

But Ash was the last one to go, and when she walked past Fâd, she stopped and looked him in the eyes. Suddenly, he heard her voice in his head—"Everything will be okay"—and then she left. He was now looking around the room to see where the voice came from and looked over at Admiral Harper, who was giving his daughter a dirty look when she walked past him. Now it was just him and the admiral alone together, and his nerves were once again on edge.

"Come. I have some news I need to discuss with you," the admiral said but in a more human tone than his intimidating one. Fâd followed him into the living room and sat down on one of the plush sofas as the admiral, who he now noticed was dressed casually, sat down in an armchair across from him.

"Admiral, is my father okay?" Fâd asked before the admiral could say one word.

Harper didn't smile, but his eyes did at the boy. "Yes, he's just fine, but he could not be here to give you this news himself, which he is truly sorry for. Fâdron, unfortunately, I am the bearer of bad news. Your mother, Lily, has passed on."

Fâd just sat there not knowing what to say. He was so thankful that his father was okay, but he wasn't prepared for this, and the worse of it was, he felt nothing over the news. He had conditioned himself so well that he had no mother that she was nothing more than a stranger to him. "What happened?" he asked the admiral in a mature and calm voice. Harper was a little surprised at the boy's strength of character and proud of the way he was taking the news. He was definitely Gerrard's son, and Harper knew, seeing him act the way he was now, that someday, he would grow up to be a great man.

"Are you sure you want to know?"

"Yes, Admiral. Don't worry about how I feel. If I may speak freely, Lily was not my mother per se, for she did not raise me. She was just the means of my creation. My father raised me and, in a small way, Sharni, but I hold no ill will to Lily, for I would not be here if it weren't for her. I just have no feelings for her," Fâd told him, and Harper was taken aback by this fourteen-year-old's confession and wondered how much this young boy actually knew. Well, he, so far, had shown an adult's understanding, so Harper would treat him like an adult.

"All right. Since we are being up front, Lily took her own life. She escaped her room, attacked a security guard, taking his gun, and when the doctors tried to talk her down, turned the gun on herself. Her mind was gone to the point that all she recognized was, everyone around her were carians." Harper then saw Fâd flinch when he said that and now knew that was what happened to Fâd with his mother. She must have accused him of being one, just like the doctor said. "She called you one, didn't she?" Harper asked him.

"Not just called me one but also told me I was a mistake and I would grow up to be no better than my father."

"I'm sorry," Harper said, and the tone of his voice conveyed it.

"It's okay, Admiral. Her words never hurt me, for I knew they were said out of spite and her own disease."

"What do you mean out of spite? How much do you know, Fâd?" Harper asked with narrowed eyes and curiosity.

"I know about my conception, I know my father only married her for me, and I know that it is Sharni that my father has always loved. I even suspect that he actually bonded to her but something happened."

"Very good. Your perception is outstanding. How much of that has your father told you?"

"Only about my conception," Fâd replied.

"Then I have to commend you on your outstanding deductive reasoning, especially for one so young. How much do you want to know? And I will only tell you this as long as you make a solemn vow to never disclose this information to your father or the people involved," Harper said as his eyes narrowed at Fâd, and the boy could hear the warning in his voice. But Fâd did not back down from the admiral.

"On my life."

"I will hold you to that, and I'm sure you know me well enough. I mean it, even with your father being my closest and greatest friend, for he would be the same way." Fâd nodded his understanding, and Harper then proceeded. "You are right, Sharni and your father are bonded mates, but after they made that commitment to one another, Sharni and my wife, Gail, were on their ship and in a battle with carians over Trintor. The frigate was taking a beating, for it was no match to the carian battleship, and finally, the carians knocked out the frigate's engines and was advancing toward them.

"They were out of time, and Sharni was the only one left alive that had any type of engineering skills, so she ran into the toxic-filled engine room and managed to get the engines back up so they could try and run from the carians. This gave Gerrard and me just enough time to come out of jump in our battleships and easily wipe out the carians. Sharni saved her whole crew, but it nearly cost her, her life. She spent several days in the hospital, teetering on the edge of death, with your father at her side the whole time.

"Finally, she pulled through, but at a cost. The toxins had made Sharni sterile, so she and Gerrard could never have children, and as you know, in your culture, anyone who has proven themselves in battle and achieved many great accomplishments, like your father has, is required to produce an heir to pass on those genes."

"I see where this is going now. That was where Lily came in, wasn't it?"

"Yes. She actually approached Gerrard and Sharni and asked to be allowed to carry you for them. Of course, your father refused because of Sharni, but she finally persuaded him, and he only agreed if it was done through medical intervention. Of course, you know all the details about how that was done. But once Lily was carrying you, Gerrard had to marry her to make you legitimately his son. He had to make a choice then, let go of the woman he loved or the son he wanted. He chose you. But because of that choice, he was now legally married to Lily and could not be with Sharni anymore in that way even though the marriage was just a technicality for your sake."

"So Father let go of the only woman he had ever loved for me. But now that can change, can't it?"

"I don't know, Fâd. Your father is an admiral aboard his own ship, and Sharni is just two years away from her own admiralty and ship. Your father wouldn't ask her to give that up so they could be together, which she would have to. Ask yourself this question: If you worked your whole life for something, then when you finally achieved it, was asked to give it away, what would you do? Then also look at the other side. Someone you had loved all your life finally got the reward they justly deserved. Could you take that away from them?"

"I see your point, and there is no right answer to it. Either way, they both lose," Fâd replied with a sad look on his face, and Admiral Harper nodded his head in agreement.

* * *

In the meantime, while all this was going on with the admiral and Fâd, Sharni had arrived at the mall with the others. There was so much chattering in the car. Even the two boys were talking away with the girls, especially Nathan, and Sharni decided that he talked as much as girls, if not more. Once they pulled up to the front of the huge structure, the kids jumped out before Sharni could stop them and bolted into the building with her behind them, yelling at them to stop, but it did no good, and she lost them quickly in the crowds.

She was now in a panic. Thomas was going to kill her. She didn't have their transponder codes to track them. Sharni let out a sigh. This was going to take forever, so she started looking and continued to call them on their comm links, but it was very apparent they were definitely ignoring her.

Nathan and Cory took the girls to a game shop where there were all kinds of video games you could play. The boys had their favorite one they liked to play that had to do with shooting carians. You and your partner stood on platforms facing a huge screen, and you both then were covered in a virtual armor. You were also given a choice of a replicated, fake assault rifle or sniper rifle. Then when the game played, you watched the screen while standing on the pad and either ran in place, crouched, or stalked through a jungle-like setting, shooting carians who came after you.

Of course, Nathan and Cory did it first and did fairly good. Then Ash and Rachael did it and actually beat the boys, though barely, especially with Rachael taking the sniper rifle. Next, Bridgett and Cory did it and failed miserably because Bridgett would accidentally shoot him. He would get way ahead of her, then come back so she could catch up, and it never failed. Suddenly, he would pop up on her screen, and she would scream, then start firing away at him. It got so funny that they all were laughing so hard that neither of them could shoot anymore.

An hour later, they all decided to go and get something to drink; and as they headed to the food section of the mall, they ran into some of the other kids from the school.

"Look, Mark, it's some of those sentinel scum kids," one of the boys said to the other four. They were probably a year older than even Nathan and Cory, but it was clearly evident they were council due to their appearance. There were four boys and one girl in the group, and they all glared at Nathan and them.

"Do you guys smell something? Oh, look, it's vicoo poop. My gosh, it can walk and talk!" Rachael said, acting all amazed and putting her hand over her mouth. They started laughing and grinning back at the council kids.

"What did you say, lab rat?" One of the boys walked over and looked down at Rachael, but Nathan stepped in front of her then and looked the boy in the face.

"Back off, bindo breath!" Nathan warned, and now Cory, Rachael, and Ash all clenched their fists, ready to fight. Of course, Ash stepped in front of Bridgett since she was smaller than the rest.

The council boy pushed Nathan, but suddenly, over Nathan's shoulder, Rachael connected on the boy's chin with her fist, knocking him backward. The fight was on. Nathan and the boy whom Rachael punched were going at it as Cory and another boy exchanged blows. Rachael and Ash were both taking on the two smaller boys, who were probably a year older than they were, and were doing quite well against them. Suddenly, they heard Bridgett scream and saw the council girl pulling her hair

"That's it, you cave dweller," Bridgett yelled and caught the girl under the chin with an uppercut. The girl fell to the floor, and Bridgett jumped on her, punching her repeatedly. Ash took a punch to the mouth when she turned her head to see what happened to Bridgett, and now blood was running from her split lip. Rachael got hit in the eye, and you could already see a black eye starting. Of course, Nathan and Cory had the toughest fight but were having no problem. Suddenly, everyone was hit with a stunner, and they all fell to the floor, motionless, as mall security came over and stood, looking down at all the children.

Sharni was still working her way from store to store, looking for the children, when an announcement came over the mall intercom system. "Would a Captain Sharnestra Tol Vasna please come to the mall security office?" Sharni stopped and closed her eyes. "What have they done now?" she said to herself. She quickly took off toward the office, avoiding making any eye contact with people, whom she could feel were staring at her. Finally, she got to it and walked in. Right away, she saw the kids sitting on chairs, and it was evident what had happened.

Ash was holding a wet rag on her bleeding lip, Rachael had an ice pack on her now swollen black eye, and Bridgett was rubbing her head. Nathan and Cory had some medical patches on what looked like a few minor cuts. Sharni then saw the other kids they obviously got into it with and knew why. Council, of course. Great. This was all she needed.

The other kids looked like they definitely lost. A couple of the boys apparently had broken noses. The only girl had both eyes swollen shut and blackened, and the two smaller boys had swollen lips and black eyes, and one was missing a tooth, which she later found out Ash did because she had cuts on her knuckles from his tooth to prove it.

A security guard walked over to Sharni with a mad look on his face. "Are these heathens yours?" he asked her with such disdain, and immediately, Sharni was furious.

"They are not heathens. They are good children. And I would kindly ask that you watch yourself."

"Don't act all high and mighty with me, vatoria. You're not any better than this sentinel riffraff."

That was all it took. Sharni knocked the guard across the room, unconscious. Now more guards came out of the next room after her, and she started fighting them back. The children jumped up to help her. The whole security office was nothing but a battle zone as Sharni and the kids stood against all the guards and the council children, and amazingly enough, they were holding them at bay just fine, because Sharni was no pushover. She was an elite in hand-to-hand combat. Finally, more guards showed up; and this time, they actually pulled guns on her. She stood down. She and the children were then put into a holding cell as one of the security officers went to call the admiral.

"I'm sorry, kids. That was very immature of me. I know better than that," she said to them, now totally embarrassed by her actions and not looking forward to explaining this to Thomas.

"Are you kidding me? That was so awesome," Nathan said, grinning.

"You rock, Aunt Sharni. We had your back the whole time," Ash said, grinning through her swollen lip, and Sharni started laughing then.

* * *

Back at the house, Thomas was still talking to Fâd when his multitool started beeping with an incoming call. He punched a button, and a screen came up, then a man appeared on the screen, and it was clear he was some type of security personnel.

"Vice Admiral Harper, sorry to disturb you, sir, but we had an incident here at the Brash Mall that is needing your immediate attention. If you could please come down to the security office so we can get this taken care of, I would greatly appreciate it."

"I will be there shortly," Harper replied with narrowed eyes, and then his screen disappeared. He looked over at Fâd, who was trying not to grin, and then he himself had a slight grin on his face. Fâd busted up laughing. "I have to change. This is probably going to take some official influence," Harper said and stood up, heading to his bedroom. A few minutes later, he came out and was dressed in his admiral uniform and looked over at Fâd. "Are you ready?"

"Yeah. What do you think happened?" Fâd asked curiously but had a pretty good idea.

"Fighting."

"Yeah, that was also my guess. But isn't Sharni with them?"

"Yep," Harper said as a very slight grin spread across his face now. Fâd smiled too. He was a little surprised seeing Harper even smile like this for the first time. Since Fâd had known the admiral, he usually had a cold glare on his face.

They both walked out the front door, and a cab was already there, waiting for them, and they got in. The admiral told the driver where they wanted to go. Before long, they were pulling up in front of the mall. Harper punched in the cab fare on his multitool and transferred the marks over to the driver and then got out of the vehicle.

Fâd walked beside him as they entered the mall and headed toward the security office. It was amazing to see how people moved out of the admiral's way, and even council soldiers who were in there saluted him, and the admiral returned the gesture. Fâd noticed that, like his father, Admiral Harper also had that commanding presence and that people respected him, but unlike his father who got things handled through charm, Harper did through intimidation.

They finally reached the security office and walked in. Immediately, they saw five council kids who looked pretty beat up and about five security guards, now being patched up as well. A young security guard headed over to the admiral and saluted him, stopping in front of him.

"Are you in charge here?" Harper asked him in an emotionless tone.

"For now. The head of security is still unconscious," the young man answered, motioning with his head over to a large round man lying across a desk, not moving.

"Report?" Harper ordered, and the man obeyed instantly, no questions asked.

"Apparently, the children all got into a scuffle in the mall and were brought here. Captain Sharnestra was called to handle the situation, and she had a disagreement with the head of security. Then to put it bluntly, all hell broke loose."

Fâd had to look down at the floor now so no one could see him struggling to not start laughing. Admiral Harper, of course, showed no emotion at all and listened to everything the young guard was saying but now with his arms folded over his chest. It was very clear, though, that the guard was nervous in his presence. While the security guard was bringing the admiral up to speed, the office doors slid open, and a council captain walked in with two other soldiers. Harper didn't even look at them but continued with the security guard. Finally, the guard was done, and the council captain walked over to the vice admiral.

"Ah, Vice Admiral Harper, it is so good to see you again."

"And you too, Captain Sims. What brings you here?" Harper looked at him coldly and nodded.

"I was just in the mall and heard there was a little problem earlier, so I came to see if I could be of some assistance."

"No problem. Everything has been handled, but thank you for your generous offer."

"So what happened?" Captain Sims turned, asking one of the children sitting on the bench in front of him.

"Those other kids started calling us names and began punching us, and we fought back, of course," the oldest boy said to the captain, who turned and looked at Harper with a wicked smirk.

The admiral looked over at the boy with narrowed eyes. "Is that so? Then you and your comrades have been unjustly treated, for it is the ones acting honorable that measure the true worth of their soul."

The kids' eyes all got huge as they turned pale white, and it was clearly evident to everyone there that they were flat-out lying. They all looked down at the ground, and Harper now looked back at the captain, who was seething with rage at being once again outsmarted by the admiral.

"Wise words, Admiral. I will leave you be. Good day." The captain saluted Admiral Harper, who returned the gesture. He watched the captain and his men stomp out of the office, then Harper turned to the guard.

"Where are they?" Vice Admiral Harper ordered.

"This way, sir." The guard nodded toward the back of the office. He led the way as Admiral Harper and Fâd followed. They went through another set of sliding doors into a large square room, and there in a holding cell was Captain Sharni and the kids. Harper couldn't help it, a very slight hint of a grin started to spread across his face, but he quickly contained it as Fâd busted up laughing. Sharni turned and glared at Harper through the bars.

"You better not say a word, Thomas, or so help me," Sharni warned the admiral, and the kids looked at her, worried that she might get into trouble. Harper nodded to the guard to let them out as Fâd was still laughing at all of them. The cell door opened, and Sharni came out first. The kids went over to Fâd, all with big grins on their faces.

"You should have seen the captain. She knocked that jerk across the room and then took on at least five of them herself," Nathan said, grinning excitedly, looking over at Sharni with admiration.

"It's nothing to be proud of. I lost control and should have never done that," Sharni said but then winked at him, and Nathan beamed. Harper was still looking at his sister-in-law, stoic like always, and she looked back at him and now had an ornery grin on her face.

"Wow. I ask you to watch a few kids and you take them into war. I don't know about you, Sharni. I think Gerrard is rubbing off on you," Harper said to her with a slight smirk.

"Yeah, laugh it up, Harper. You have no room to talk," Sharni warned him teasingly.

"Why don't you take the kids and head out to the vehicle?" Harper told her and then turned to the guard and opened his multitool, bringing up a keyboard and screen on it, typing in something on the board. Sharni gathered up all the kids, and they all headed out through the sliding door and into the main area of the security office, jabbering excitedly among themselves.

"I think this should adequately cover any medical expenses," Harper said to the guard.

"Don't worry about it, sir. They all had it coming. We saw the whole thing on the mall security camera. Between you and me, I'm getting sick of how things are starting to go with council military always butting in and acting the bully. By any chance, is sentinel fleet recruiting?" the young guard asked quietly, looking around.

"We always have an open door, son. Here, contact this person. Tell him I sent you, and he will get you set up," Harper said to the young man and punched in the information to his multitool and then uploaded it to the guard's tool. The young man looked down at the information that immediately came across, and his eyes got huge, and a big grin spread across his face.

"The *Justification*? That's your ship, sir," he said excitedly.

"Yes. Hope to see you there," Harper said and held out his hand. The guard took it, and they shook.

"You will, Admiral. Thank you." The guard then saluted the admiral, and Harper saluted him back, then went to catch up with Sharni and the children.

* * *

Sharni had no sooner stepped out into the main waiting area of the security office when she saw the other children's parents there, looking their kids over. They looked up when they saw her come through the door with the kids, and their faces were bright red with anger. One father walked over to her and got in her face. "You should be ashamed of yourself and keep these things under control. They are undisciplined and lack manners in proper society. But what can one expect from sentinel fleet? They also are the same."

"You ungrateful piece of shit. Without sentinel fleet right now, you would be filling the belly of some carian," Sharni snarled back and was now back in his face, glaring at him.

"CAPTAIN, STAND DOWN," Admiral Harper yelled from behind her, and she backed away from the man as he looked to see who it was yelling at her and saw the vice admiral. All the blood in his face drained away, and he backed up quickly, staring up at Harper, and was now visibly shaking. Harper walked over to the man, and all the children's parents had looks of fear on their faces as Harper looked at each and every one of them through narrowed eyes. "Do we have a problem here?" Harper looked over at Sharni.

"No, Vice Admiral," she replied.

"Good. Captain, please see to the children," Harper ordered, and she nodded and ushered the kids out of the office. Then he turned his attention back to the parents and their children. "I am sorry about this. I will see to it that the children are properly disciplined and learn manners so they won't be such a hindrance to society. I applaud you on the exemplary behavior your children exhibit when in society as shown on the mall video I just watched and their outstanding control when faced with a difficult situation, which I am sure they get from your great example," Harper said to them in a cold, emotionless tone, and all the parents and children could not look him in the face now.

"It's okay, Vice Admiral. Children will be children. All is forgotten. Please tell your captain I am sorry about my outburst earlier," the man who got into it with Sharni said with a shaky voice.

"I will, and good day to you," Harper replied and nodded to the man, who couldn't look at him.

Harper walked out and saw Sharni and the children all sitting over at one of the ice cream shops, eating ice cream. He shook his head and headed over to it, and when he walked up, Sharni handed him a large ice cream cone with chocolate ice cream.

"What's this? Who said you could have ice cream?" Harper asked, taking the cone from Sharni.

"I did. My troops and I decided a little treat was in order after a well-fought battle. Besides, the cold will do some of them good on their swollen faces," Sharni replied, grinning and eating hers. Harper shook his head and chuckled, licking his ice cream.

They were all still eating it when Nathan whispered and asked Fâd what was so important that the admiral had to tell him in private. Even the girls who were sitting on the table next to the boys leaned closer to hear. Fâd looked at them with a frown on his face.

"It's okay. They're cool. We have a truce going right now," Nathan told him.

Fâd didn't say anything for a few minutes, then leaned in closer to all of them so no adults would hear. "Lily died today," he said. Nathan and Cory's faces turned white, but the girls looked at one another, mouthing the name Lily.

"Who is that?" Bridgett asked Cory quietly.

"It's Fâd's birth mother," Cory told her.

"Oh, I'm sorry, Fâd. We didn't know," Rachael said to him, and she had a look of sincerity on her face, even with her black eye, but Ash got up and walked over, looking into a store window at some clothes that were on display.

"Is she okay?" Nathan asked Rachael.

"Yeah, but it's still a little hard for her. Did you know her mother died holding her?" Rachael told them, and Fâd then looked over at Ash. He got up and walked over to her and stood beside her as she continued to look in the window.

"I'm sorry about your mother, Fâd," Ash said weakly without looking at him.

"It's okay. I never really had anything to do with her. I have my father. You're lucky, Ash. You got to be with your mother, who you knew cared about you and left you many memories. I never got that. Lily never cared for me. I was just a tool to be used to try and get to my father, and when it didn't work, she turned on us both."

"That's horrible. And you're okay with that?" Ash asked, now looking up at him.

"Yeah. Like I said, I still have my father, who loves me," Fâd replied, looking down at her now with a slight smile, and she smiled back, understanding what he was getting at. Instead of dwelling on her loss, she should be happy because she still had her father and her mother's memory. Ash then looked back over toward her father now and saw him talking with Sharni, and they were laughing about something.

"Hey, we all still have Sharni too," Ash said, grinning with her swollen lip, watching her aunt and father talking together.

"That we do," Fâd replied, also looking over at the two adults, and then he looked down at Ash again, and they both smiled.

CHAPTER 12

———⟡———

IT WAS BACK to school the next day, and the girls grudgingly started their second day of it. Rachael was still sporting a black eye, and Ash's lip was no longer swollen but now was scabbed over where the split was. She had a terrible time at lunch trying to eat, because she couldn't open her mouth very far, or the split would open again. Plus, the other thing was, the truce was off, and it was once again battle of the sexes—Fâd and his troop against Ash and her team. They wasted no time. Nathan ended up with a sign that was attached to his back that read, "I eat poop," and Bridgett ended up with a huge wad of some gummy stuff stuck to her hair. Sharni spent a good hour with a mild solvent, working on getting it out, that night.

The next day was no better. When Fâd walked into his science class and the professor pulled up the virtual screen for a vid presentation, coming across the screen before the vid began was a message that read, "Fâdron Larson is a girl and agrees that girls rule." Of course, there was swift retaliation. Ash walked into her math class a few hours later sporting a pair of drawn on glasses accompanied by a beard and a mustache. Apparently, she was taken by surprise when she walked out of the bathroom, heading back to her class, as the boys got her. Again, Sharni spent a good hour that night stripping the black marks off Ash's face. Thomas would just shake his head and continue about his business.

The following day was the last straw. Rachael opened her locker and got sprayed in the face by blue paint, and Cory got his pants glued down to his chair. Not knowing, he stood up, and the pants stayed with the chair, leaving him standing in just his boxers. Finally, Professor Baptise had enough, and all six children were called into his office.

"This stops now, children. Ms. Harper, Ms. Torres, and Ms. Nelson, you have only been here for four days and already have been in more trouble than most students do in seven years. And you, Fâdron, Nathan, and Cory are already walking a fine line as it is. One more incident from any of you and I will be notifying the vice admiral. Is that what you want?"

"No, sir," all six children answered at once with a look of fear on their faces.

"Good. From here on, girls, these are your new schedules. That way, there will never be a chance that any of you will come in contact with the boys." Professor Baptise punched a button on his keyboard, and the girls immediately had it on their multitools. They looked down at them.

"Why do we have to change our schedule? Why don't the boys?" Bridgett asked, mad.

"Because they have been here longer and have seniority."

"Did you hear that? We're higher up than you!" Nathan sneered at them.

"Nathan, that's enough. The way you're going, you'll still be here even after they have moved on," the professor scolded him, and the girls started giggling.

"Fâdron, Ashley, I am putting you two in charge of your friends. You both seem to be the leaders of your little groups, so with that said, anytime one of your friends gets into trouble, it will be you two that will pay the consequences and accept the responsibility for their actions."

Ash and Fâd's mouths fell open as they looked at the professor. Even their friends looked shocked and looked over at Fâd and Ash. "But that's not fair," Ash said to him, still in shock.

"Life's not fair, and it's time you all learn that. It is how you deal with it that will orchestrate the direction your lives will take. Now enough said. Get back to your classes," the professor told them and went back to typing on his keyboard. The kids all got up and walked out of his office. They all looked at one another and glared, then went their separate ways.

One thing to be said, the meeting with the professor worked, and the remaining few days of the week, school went off without any incident, and now they had a two-day break. Over at the girls' place, they were getting ready to head to Pantier for Fâd's mother's funeral. The girls weren't looking forward to it, especially having to spend time with the boys again, but Admiral Harper made them promise to be nice.

The girls finally got ready and selected nice slacks to wear with the traditional ankle-high boots that the pants tucked down into. Plus the long button-up, tunic-style top that had long sleeves, with cuts for their multitools, and high collars with the bottom of the tunic stopping just at mid thigh, they were very nice and modern. Each of the girls also let their hair out this time, but Ash pulled hers back on the sides and fastened it in the back with her mother's rose-shaped hair comb. Once again, the girls tried to put makeup on, but Admiral Harper confiscated all their applicators and locked them in a trunk in his room until he felt the time was right they could use them.

They were all in the kitchen, grabbing a bite to eat, when the door buzzer went off. Rachael got up and went out into the living room to open the door, but Admiral Harper stopped her as he was finishing up buttoning his dress uniform tunic as he walked out of the hallway where his bedroom was located. "Remember what we agreed about earlier!" he warned her and headed to the kitchen.

"Yes. We'll behave," Rachael replied, rolling her eyes, then went over and opened the door. The three boys stood there, glaring at her.

"Calm down. We're under a cease fire agreement with the admiral," Rachael told them and turned, walking back toward the kitchen, without asking them in. The boys went in anyway and headed to the kitchen as well, and when they got there, they saw everyone dressed nicely. Of course, they also were dressed very nicely in sentinel fleet dress uniforms. The girls totally ignored them, but Sharni came over and hugged each of them in turn. She was also dressed in formal vatoria captain's uniform, looking beautiful as always, and even Vice Admiral Harper was in his formal admiral uniform, looking very prestigious.

"Is everyone ready?" the admiral asked, and they all nodded. He stood aside, and the whole party left the kitchen and headed toward the front door that slid open, then out to the waiting vehicle. They all climbed in. Rachael lost at rock paper scissors and had to sit next to the boys. It took a good forty-five minutes to get to the spaceport, but they finally did and, amazingly enough, in silence since none of the kids was talking to each other.

The group filed out and followed Admiral Harper into the terminal with Captain Sharni bringing up the rear. He stopped at the front desk and got his clearance as Sharni escorted the children out to the pad and into the shuttle. No sooner had everyone climbed in and started buckling up when Admiral Harper walked in and shut the shuttle door. He climbed into the pilot's seat as Sharni buckled up herself in the copilot's seat and then started up the shuttle's engines. Once Harper was buckled up, he took over; and in no time, the shuttle was in the air, rapidly moving toward Pantier.

"So are you happy to be going home?" Bridgett asked the boys.

"What do you think? We're going back for a funeral—not my idea of a happy homecoming," Fâd snapped at her.

"Hey, she was just asking. Cut her some slack," Ash snapped at him.

"Oh yeah? At least you're not being forced to go to someone's funeral that hated you," Nathan said to Ash, glaring at her.

"Listen to you guys. At least you all got the chance to know your parents or parent. Bridgett here never got that chance. Her mother died when she was born. All she has of her mother are pictures," Rachael yelled at all of them and put her arm around Bridgett's shoulders, who had her head down with tears running down her cheeks.

Fâd just turned stone-cold and looked away, Nathan looked down at the floor sheepishly, and it was Cory who spoke next. "We're sorry, Bridgett. We didn't know."

Bridgett looked up at him and smiled weakly, still with wet eyes, and he smiled back at her. Finally, the shuttle landed, and everyone unbuckled. Bridgett was trying to get her buckle undone, only it wouldn't release. "Why do I always get the one that sticks? I hate this one," she said, getting totally flustered. Cory got up and went over and started working on it too, then finally just yanked real hard until it popped free. Bridgett jumped out of the seat and fell to the floor. "I'm free, finally. Thank the Almighty. It was touch and go there for a while." She leaned down and kissed the floor. Everyone started laughing watching her, and Cory put his hand out. She took it, and he pulled her back up.

Admiral Harper walked through the kids, then opened the shuttle door and climbed out. The kids all followed with Sharni once again bringing up the rear as they headed to the terminal. The girls were in awe looking at all the ships around the landing zone and commenting on them as they followed, and now the boys were also talking to them about the ships. Right before they got to the terminal, the doors slid open, and Nera walked out, dressed in a formal uniform befitting her rank of commander. Fâd saw her and took off jogging toward his cousin, and they hugged each other.

"How are you doing, young man?" she asked him with a smile.

"Fine. What about you?" He smiled back.

"Just like always. Wow, I see you've brought friends. They're kind of cute, Fâd," Nera whispered, leaning down and elbowing him.

"Yuck! You can't be serious. Trust me, we are only getting along right now because we agreed on a truce for now."

Nera busted up laughing just as Admiral Harper and Captain Sharni walked up, but the other kids were still standing a little ways off, talking about all the different ships. "Thomas, Sharni, everything is ready. We thought we would have the ceremony over in the glade," Nera told them, all business now.

"Sounds good. Shall we go?" the admiral asked, and they headed to the doors. The admiral yelled at the rest of the kids, who came running then and caught up. They all went through the terminal to the front of the building. There were two vehicles waiting for them. Sharni and Nera climbed into one with the girls as Vice Admiral Harper got into the other with the boys and a young male watorian soldier, who was clearly nervous being with the admiral.

"Nera, let me introduce you to everyone. These here are Ashley Harper, Rachael Torres, and Bridgett Nelson. Girls, this is Nera Parker-Carson, Admiral Larson's cousin," Sharni said to them.

"Wow, I can't believe how much you girls look like your parents. I would recognize each of you anywhere," Nera said to them.

"You know our parents?" Bridgett asked her excitedly.

"Yep. I went to school with them, but we kind of lost track after the war," she said to Bridgett.

The hover vehicle moved slowly through the streets, and the girls were enthralled watching all the scenery around them. The small colony definitely looked like a picture of a mountain resort back on Earth, right down to the log and stone structures. They were constantly asking questions, and Nera answered happily, and before long, they headed into the woods, pulling up to a nice clearing in the center of the trees. In the clearing was a silver cylinder on a small stand with some people standing around it.

They all got out and followed the admiral and Fâd as they headed toward it. The admiral stopped just a few feet from the cylinder with Fâd beside him, and Sharni walked up beside Fâd with Nera next to her. The rest of the children stood around the adults, watching. The reverend started talking now, and Fâd reached over, touching Sharni's arm, and she took his hand and held it. Finally, the reverend called for a prayer as everyone bowed their heads; and before long, the ceremony was over.

Fâd let go of Sharni's hand and stepped forward a little ways as two honor guards came up and saluted him. He returned the gesture, and then they stood on each side of the casket and pressed a button on it. The casket rose off the stand and floated in front of them. They then put their hands on two handles on the side and walked the casket away as everyone watched them go. Then Fâd turned to the admiral. "Thank you, Admiral, for allowing her to have these last rights."

"You're welcome, Fâd. It was an honor." And Vice Admiral Harper saluted Fâd, who returned the gesture. Finally, everyone started milling around and talking, then Nera spoke up.

"Let's all head back to Gerrard's and get a bite to eat."

The kids all took off running toward the vehicles in a foot race, of course, and climbed in the two hover vehicles waiting for the adults. Finally, they were on their way back into the town and drove halfway through it, then turned up a side street and again headed back into the trees. They pulled up in front of a very large log home with a huge wraparound porch in front.

Everyone climbed out, and Fâd started showing the girls right away around the front of it and the large pond next to the house. The adults walked up the steps and crossed the porch as Sharni walked up to the door, putting her hand on the blue scan pad, and the door opened up. She realized what she had done and looked back at Thomas and Nera, embarrassed.

"I, uh, well, you see…oh, never mind," she said, all flustered, seeing them both with accusing looks on their faces. They walked in and headed to the kitchen to get something made for everyone.

Inside the large log home, one entered first a large vaulted living room with a massive rock fireplace against one wall. The kitchen and dining room were situated off to one end of the living room with a large double patio sliding door that opened to the porch outside. There was a hallway leading down the other side of the living room and disappearing behind the fireplace that went to two guest bedrooms, bathroom, and master bedroom.

Also, over against one wall of the living room was a large staircase that went up to the upper floor, which had two more bedrooms and bathrooms and where Fâd's and Nathan's rooms were. The whole inside was decorated like a lodge with rustic log furnishings and old lantern-type lights used to illuminated the house. There were some modern things, such as vids in the living room and kitchen, and even in the kitchen, a replictor was installed even though it still had a cook stove in there as well. It definitely gave one the feeling of living in a cabin.

Outside, the kids were running all over the place, checking things out, when Ash stopped and realized she had lost her mother's comb. She felt the back of her head, and now in a panic, she started looking all around. "Rachael, Bridgett, I lost my comb. Please help me find it," she screamed in a complete panic as her eyes watered up.

"What's so important about a comb?" Nathan asked, annoyed.

"It was her mother's," Bridgett answered him as she started looking all over.

Ash was in complete hysterics now, racing all over the place, when Fâd ran over to her, grabbed her by the arms, and stopped her, making her face him. "Ash, calm down. Where was the last place that you remember you had it?" he asked her, finally getting her attention.

"I think over by the pond," she answered, now in tears.

"We'll find it, okay?" he told her and unconsciously wiped the tears from her face.

"All right," she replied and followed him. Fâd separated everyone into teams and gave each team a specific area to search—Nathan and Rachael, Cory and Bridgett, and Ash and him. The groups all scattered. They were scouring the entire area, and as he and Ash walked the perimeter of the pond, he saw something flash in the grass next to it. Fâd walked over, and there lying in the grass was a beautiful rose-shaped red hair comb. He picked it up.

"Hey, Ash. Come here."

She walked over, and he held the comb out to her. Her face lit up, and she threw her arms around his neck and kissed him on the cheek, then took the comb from his hands, looking down at it as tears once again fell from her eyes. Fâd just stood there in shock. He had never been kissed before by a girl, especially one he hated. Okay, maybe *hate* was too strong a word. *Dislike* was better, but right now, she was okay, so he could hate her later. Plus, when she kissed him, it made him feel kind of funny inside.

Fâd quickly shook off the feeling and followed Ash as she ran and yelled for everyone to come back. Rachael and Nathan were now in a foot race to see who was faster as they ran back, and Cory and

Bridgett had long branches and were sword fighting as they returned. Fâd decided it was a good thing he had found it, or he and Ash would have been out there all night looking because their friends weren't any help.

Sharni stepped out through the sliding glass doors of the kitchen and hollered at them that dinner was ready. Now the real foot race was on, and everyone took off toward the house for food. This time, there were a lot of shoving, pushing, and even wrestling as everyone tried to get to the house first. The funny thing was, Bridgett ended up first, but Fâd noticed that it was because of Cory, who sneakily knocked Nathan out of the way and pushed Bridgett in front of him so she would win.

The kids all raced into the house, and it sounded like a thunderstorm. Sharni grabbed the counter, and Nera braced herself against the refrigerator as Thomas acted like nothing was happening. They all ran over and grabbed plates and then got in line and started filling their plates. From the wild things that came racing through the door to the now orderly line they made, it was a shocking transition. Soon, all the kids had their plates filled, and they went over and sat at the snack bar, eating.

The adults got their plates filled, then sat down at the dining table as well and started eating. Harper looked down at his multitool and pressed a button and read the small screen on it. Then he got up and walked over to the large screen on the wall in the kitchen and brought up the holographic keyboard to it and started pressing buttons and moving screens around on it.

The large screen in the room came on, and Rear Admiral Gerrard Larson was on it. "Hello, son. I'm so sorry I could not be there for you, but I know you're in good hands. I would not have missed this if it weren't extremely important, but I'm very proud of you, and I love you."

"I love you, Dad, and I know. I wish you were here too, but it's okay. I have my friends here with me, plus Admiral Harper, Sharni, and Cousin Nera, so I'm doing pretty good."

"I'm glad. Thank you, Thomas. Sorry to have to put you through this. And you too, Sharni. I don't know what I would ever do without you too. And you, Nera."

"Yeah, you owe me, Cousin," Nera said, joking.

Harper then had the kids go in the other room so the adults could talk, and once the kids were gone, Thomas spoke. "You look exhausted. What's going on?" he asked, concerned for his friend.

"Yeah, I haven't slept for almost forty-eight hours, pushing the ship to her limits. One of the transports got hijacked with over 285 men, women, and children on board. It was one of the colonization ships, which got taken by a large fleet of borvians. From my estimation, they have at least one cruiser and anywhere between three or four destroyers. I lost them when I had to come out of jump to contact you earlier, but we caught their trail again and have been moving in and out of jump and FTL speeds to catch up.

"But you know these big things are not designed to do that, and it has been taxing on my engines. Nelson's going to love me. But I'm close enough now that we are within sight of the transport and, in another twelve hours, should come out of jump right on top of them. They have a large base on one of the planets, and we are preparing for a large-scale incursion once the sky has been secured."

"Damn it, Larson, why didn't anyone tell me? I could have helped," Thomas said, mad now and standing.

"Because I told them not to. You need to spend some time with your daughter."

"You bastard, that was not your decision," Harper said, and the cold anger wasn't hard to see on his face, especially the stone-cold, deadly look his eyes had right now.

"Thomas, I got to have time with my son. Now you need to get to know your daughter and enjoy what time you have left with her before she's grown and on her own," Larson said back, just as forceful and cold.

"Please, Gerrard, be careful. I couldn't handle it if something happens to you," Sharni said now with tears in her eyes.

"Hey, beautiful, nothing will. Trust me. I'll be back. Looking forward to a nice, hot bath, great meal, and warm, soft bed with your beautiful body next to me," Gerrard said with a devious grin.

"Gerrard, there are others here right now," Sharni said, embarrassed.

"So? We're all adults here, and it's not like you haven't stayed over before. Damn, woman, I'm going to have to take a cold bath now just thinking about you." Sharni just shook her head, trying not to grin, and Thomas started quietly chuckling, as did Nera.

"Just be careful, Gerrard, and come back," Thomas said to him with a concerned tone in his voice.

"Crap, Thomas, this will be a piece of cake compared to some of the things we have fought through."

"Yeah, but you're an old man now," Thomas teased.

"Not that old. Just ask Sharni." Larson grinned.

"Gerrard, that's enough," Sharni scolded him.

"You just had better be ready when I get back," he said with a rotten grin.

"I will be," Sharni whispered with a grin.

"I love you, beautiful," he said, now serious.

"I love you," Sharni replied and put her hand on the screen, and then it went black. Nera came over and put her arm around Sharni's shoulder.

"He'll be back. He always does. Something about him and Thomas, when they give their word, they uphold it," Nera told her.

"Nera's right, Sharni. He will be back for you and Fâd," Thomas told her.

"He better, or so help me, when I finally go, I will make sure he never rests in peace," Sharni said with a serious tone, and Nera started laughing, and Thomas slightly smirked.

It was now late into the night, and Nera talked Thomas and Sharni into staying and to head back in the morning. Thomas sent a message to the school for the boys, and then he and Sharni worked on sleeping arrangements as Nera said her goodnights and left. Fâd and Nathan had bedrooms anyway, and Cory stayed over a lot, so he had a place to sleep in as well.

Thomas took the one guest room he always stayed in when he came from time to time. It was the duty of the vice admiral to inspect each ship before it was commissioned into service, so Larson made sure Harper had his own room for such times. Of course, Sharni took the master bedroom since it was well-known among the adults, including Fâd, that she slept there every time she came to visit as well. The girls were sleeping out on the large pullout sofas that changed into beds in the huge, open living room, and Sharni miraculously found them all large pajama tops that somehow were in Gerrard's bedroom. They looked like small nightgowns on the girls, but they didn't mind.

Everyone changed as the adults went to bed. The girls were lying across the bed now. They had turned on the large stone fireplace and were talking, watching the fire. "Hey, Ash, are you tired?" Rachael asked her.

"No, are you?"

"Nope. So what can we do that won't get us into trouble?"

"How about cards?" a cocky voice came from the dark, and then the boys walked out with a deck of cards in their hands and a devious grin.

"You're on." Rachael grinned, and the boys came over and jumped on the bed with the girls, and Fâd started shuffling the deck. He passed out two cards to each of them, and the game was on. It was like 21, but the loser had to tell an embarrassing moment in their life. They were having a blast and laughing like crazy when suddenly, Ash started sniffing the air.

"Who farted?"

"Guilty," Nathan said, raising his hand, and they all started smacking him with a pillow and laughing.

"Oh, I can beat that," Rachael said and strained hard, letting out a loud fart.

"Oh my gosh, I can't believe you did that," Fâd said, laughing, and then he farted. Before long, at least everyone had; and by now, the living room stunk.

"Somebody open the door and let the smell out," Bridgett said, holding her nose and giggling. Fâd jumped up and ran over, opening it, and the rest of them tried to fan the smell out. They all then filed outside and went and lay out on the cool grass, looking up at the stars, to give the living room time to air out.

"Do you guys ever think about what you want to be or do when you grow up?" Bridgett asked.

"Yeah. I want to be the greatest pilot around," Nathan said.

"I want to be a top marksman and travel space with my best friends with me," Rachael said as she and Ash knocked closed fists together.

"I want to be a great engineer like my father. I love engines." Then Bridgett added, "And stay with my friends while doing it."

"All right, you go, girl," Ash said to her, and they knocked fists together too.

"I want to travel space and be known as the best technician in the galaxy," Cory said.

"What about you, Ash?" Nathan asked her.

"I think I want to serve on my father's ship, but I'm not sure doing what, and I want to have my friends with me," Ash told them.

"What about you, Fâd? You haven't said anything," Cory asked him.

"I want my own ship," Fâd said, and everyone was impressed now and started talking about how cool that would be.

The night wore on, and they all stayed out there on the grass, talking and laughing. Before long, morning came. Thomas got up, wearing just a pair of pajama bottoms, pulling on a shirt, and walked out into the living room and saw the empty, messed-up beds with playing cards everywhere. Panic ran through him as he then noticed the open door and leaped over an armchair, running to the door and out on the deck.

His mouth fell open when he saw the scene in front of him. There lying on blankets were all the kids, sound asleep. Cory was lying sprawled out on the grass. Somehow, he had gotten kicked off the blankets. Nathan was lying on the blanket next to him on his back with his mouth wide open and snoring. Fâd was beside him, asleep on his stomach with his arms folded under his head for a pillow. Ash was sideway in between him and Rachael with her legs over his back and her head on Rachael's back, who was also sleeping on her stomach. Bridgett was on a blanket all by herself, wrapped up in it.

Thomas started chuckling as he heard a noise in the house and walked back over to the door and saw Sharni. "Hey, you've got to see this," he said with a smirk on his face.

Sharni walked out onto the deck and saw the kids, then started giggling. "Were they out here all night?" she asked.

"At least most of it. I think they had a card game before that," Thomas said, motioning back toward the house.

Sharni and Thomas walked back into the house, and both straightened up the living room. Sharni then went into the kitchen and made a pot of creo as Thomas went over to the replicator and got pancakes and bacon going. Outside, the sun was beginning to beat down, and the kids started to stir. Nathan was the first because a bug landed in his mouth, and he started coughing, which woke up Fâd, Ash, and Rachael. Both Rachael and Fâd were now pushing Ash off them, causing her to start yelling at them, which, in turn, woke up Cory and Bridgett.

"What the hell? How come I didn't get to sleep on a blanket?" Cory said with grass stains on the side of his face.

Nathan started gagging, which cleared the blankets real fast as everyone pushed one another out of the way in case he threw up. "I ate a bug," Nathan said and gagged again.

"Oh, my back," Fâd said, stretching out.

Rachael started popping hers. "Mine too."

"Why do your backs hurt?" Bridgett asked them.

"Because Ash slept on us," Rachael told her.

"I was comfortable," Ash said, grinning, and both Fâd and Rachael gave her a dirty look. The kids all picked up the blankets, shook them out, and folded them up, then headed to the house. Fâd was the first one and leaned into the house and sniffed, then looked back at everyone else.

"Hey, it smells like pancakes in here instead of farts."

Just then, Admiral Harper walked around the corner of the kitchen and saw the kids. "What did you say?"

"Um, nothing, sir," Fâd replied nervously, but he could hear the others behind him start chuckling and giggling, and he couldn't help but grin.

Admiral Harper scowled at him and told the kids to go and get changed, and they quickly ran to the bathrooms and bedrooms to do so. Sharni walked around the corner now and looked at Thomas. "Did he say fart?"

"Yeah. I think that explains why they slept outside," Thomas told her, and they both started chuckling. Before long, the kids came back and were dressed back in the clothes they wore yesterday. Breakfast was ready, and they all gathered around the large snack bar and gobbled down the food. The admiral then put them in charge of cleaning up while he and Sharni straightened up the rest of the house.

Everything was clean. They put everything back as they all left to the vehicles. Nera had left the one she drove yesterday and walked home last night, so Sharni climbed in it with the girls as Admiral Harper took the boys. They drove back over to the terminal and met Nera there and said their goodbyes, then boarded the shuttle. In no time, they were once again heading back to New Guinea, but now the kids were jabbering away, teasing and joking among themselves, instead of the silent treatment to one another.

They finally reached the spaceport and landed, then all filed out and into the terminal. This time, it was extremely crowded, and Thomas and Sharni were having a hard time keeping everyone together. People were pushing to get through, and finally, it happened. Ash got cut off from everyone, and now she was getting swept along, going the other way. Admiral Harper was furious and started pushing his way back, but Fâd took off, darting in and out of the crowd, and soon, he caught up to Ash, grabbing her hand and pulling her out of the crowd and over to the side, wrapping his arms around her in a protective manner. Then he released her and grabbed her hand as he wove his way back to the group and to a relieved admiral.

But Harper was still in a rage, and he turned into the crowd, and with his very loud, cold, commanding voice, he yelled, "GET THE HELL OUT OF MY WAY," which echoed throughout the terminal. People stopped in shock when they saw the rage on his face and cleared a path right away. He led the children with no problem at all through the crowds and out the front doors, to the waiting vehicle. They all climbed in and headed back toward the house, and forty-five minutes later, they pulled up in front of it. Sharni and the girls got out, as did the boys.

"Well, boys, this is goodbye for a while. I'll be back during breaks, so you'll have to come over and see me," Sharni told them, trying not to cry. She again gave each of them a hug, but when she got to Fâd, she held him close and leaned her head down on his and kissed the top of it. Fâd hugged her tightly and buried his face into her, then she let him go, and the boys climbed back into the vehicle, and it drove away. Sharni and the girls went into the house and headed to their rooms to clean up.

By the time the admiral got back, they had all showered and changed into clean clothes, and the admiral did the same thing and came out in clean, casual clothes. The rest of the day, everyone just lay around doing nothing and taking naps. By the time evening came around, no one was really hungry, so they just snacked. It was during this time that a transmission came for Sharni, and she took it on the vid in the kitchen.

"Captain Sharnestra Tol Vasna, you and your ship are to head to the Culpon system and assist Admiral Larson with the cleanup of a large merc base and then provide escort for the *Lithia* for the time being as one of their battleships has taken heavy damage," an officer from Krios, her home planet, ordered her.

"Yes, sir. I will leave first thing at 0500," Sharni replied, and the screen went dark. Now Sharni was slightly smiling. Thomas was standing at the other end of the counter, also with a rotten smirk on his face.

"I guess Gerrard's going to get that bath, meal, and what was the other thing he said?" Thomas teased as he walked into the kitchen.

"Shut up, Thomas, but yeah, I guess he's going to get that," she said and started giggling. Thomas walked over to her and pulled her into his arms and hugged her tightly.

"I'm going to miss you," Thomas said to her, and Sharni wrapped her arms around him and leaned her head against his chest.

"I'm going to miss you too," she said with tears in her eyes.

"Go tell the girls goodbye before they head to bed," Thomas told her, and she walked out of the room as he watched her go. His heart was hurting again. He had enjoyed her company, but it was also more than that. He had always loved her, and he still did. He had known and had fallen in love with Sharni way before he ever met Gail, but once Gail came into the picture, he fell madly in love with her, completely devoted to her, and married her without once looking back. Sharni also changed and fell in love with Larson and, in time, bonded to him. Sharni was his best friend's mate, and after everything she and Gerrard had been through, they deserved some happiness together. He had that special time with Gail, and it was Gerrard and Sharni's turn to finally get to enjoy some happiness too.

Thomas cleaned up and headed to his bedroom, changing into his pajama bottoms, and walked over to the mirror and looked in it. He still was in great shape with a firm, flat stomach and well-defined, muscular frame considering his age, and by looking at him, you would swear he was probably in his midforties, which was far from the truth. He brushed his wavy black hair back from his face and picked up his dog tags, which hung down his bare chest, and looked at them for a few seconds, then headed over to his bed and pulled down the covers. But before he could climb in, he got buzzed on his door.

"Come in," he said, expecting to see one of the girls crying over Sharni leaving, but instead, it was Sharni in her pajama tank top and shorts. "Sharni, is everything okay?" he asked, concerned.

She walked over to him and stopped right in front of him, forcing him to look down at her. "All you have to do is say it, Thomas, and I will," she said, looking up at him. Thomas's lips came down on hers as he pulled her into him, and she threw her arms around his neck. Their kissing was getting more and more feverish when Thomas stopped suddenly and held her back, breathing heavily.

"No, Sharni, I can't. Gerrard is my best and dearest friend, and he loves you too."

"I know, and that is why I'm hurting, because I love you both as well," she said with tears running down her face.

"You have to go to him. It's your and his time to finally be together. I had my time with Gail, whom I still love with my whole being, and I could never deny that chance at love from my friend and brother."

Sharni headed to the door and stopped before she walked out and looked back at Thomas. "You know what the worse part of this is? I will always wonder."

"As will I."

CHAPTER 13

THE GIRLS GOT up the next morning, and their moods were solemn because Sharni was gone. They went into the kitchen. Admiral Harper was already in there, getting breakfast ready for them. "How does breakfast burritos sound?" he asked them, punching it into the replicator.

"Okay, I guess," Ash replied with no emotion.

"It's not the last time you girls will see her. Sharni will be back off and on, and then before you know it, you will have a full two years with her, not to mention time in between each new school year."

"We know, Admiral, but still, we already miss her," Rachael said to him, trying not to cry.

"As do I," Harper said under his breath. They all ate in silence, then Harper put the girls to cleaning up afterward. He went back into his bedroom and changed into some casual clothes and came back just as they finished. "Come here, girls. There are going to be some changes around here. We need to get some rules and chores lined out," he said to them, and their mouths fell open.

"You've got to be kidding me," Ash asked in disbelief.

"This is no different than a ship. Everyone has to pitch in to keep things running smoothly," he told them, and the girls walked over to the sofa and slumped down in it. "First off, there are the everyday chores of maintaining the house, such as keeping it clean, and there's also the laundry, cleaning up after meals, and the meals themselves. Plus, you three will be responsible for maintaining your bedroom. I can handle the meals and…" Bridgett put her hand up now, stopping him from going on. "Yes, Bridgett?"

"No offense, sir, but you're only good at making breakfast. Even with the replicator, your lunches and dinners are, to put it bluntly, horrible. Some of the things you fix we can't even pronounce. We'll handle lunch and dinner when we aren't at school," Bridgett said to him nervously, and Harper's eyes had narrowed by now.

"I'll handle the laundry," Rachael added.

"I can take care of the dishes and trash," Ash said.

"Who's going to do the grocery shopping?" Rachael asked, looking around.

"That will be my department as well," the admiral told them coldly.

"Okay. We will make sure that we always give you a list of personal hygiene items that we will need," Bridgett said, trying not to grin now.

"What…what kind of hygiene things?" Harper asked, now nervous.

"You know, deodorant, shampoo, feminine products—those kinds of things," Ash said, and she saw her father's face turn white. The girls then started giggling among themselves.

"Fine. I can handle that," he said now with his courage back up at their challenge to unnerve him.

"You also know, Admiral Harper, that when we do become women," Rachael said, emphazing the word *women* by making quotation gestures with her fingers and grinning, "that we do have to go to a doctor to be checked to get our injection."

Harper's face drained of color again, and he realized this was a lot more than he had planned for. He knew what the girls were talking about, but it was still embarrassing for him, especially when he would have to take them all to a women's clinic for it. The injection the girls were talking about were to be taken when a young girl finally reached puberty and their menstrual cycles began.

In the past, there was an increase in cervical cancer in human women, and it was finally linked to a missing hormone. It was proven that space travel and different environments of planets were causes of this deficiency, and the injection was developed to add the much-needed hormone. Of course, this also altered the normal cycles; and instead of going twenty-eight days until ovulation, a human female now went forty-two days and then a brief window of three days that they could possibly conceive, and only a two-day menstrual cycle ensued.

The side effect of this also caused a massive decrease in human populations, so a pill was designed to boost the window for possible conception, but unlike the hormone injection, the baby-making pill, as some liked to jokingly call it, only had to be taken when a couple were ready to start their family and only until the woman conceived.

Harper was now way out of his league; maybe if he were lucky, this all wouldn't happen until Sharni came back. But secretly, in the back of his mind, he knew he wouldn't be that lucky. Now he was wondering what else he didn't know about. "Okay. Is there anything else I need to be made aware of?" he asked nervously, afraid of what they might say.

"Well, we have never been given the talk about…what was the old term?" Ash looked at her friends with a devious grin.

"Birds and the bees," Rachael told her with a serious face.

"All right, you ornery little trolls, now I know you're trying to unravel me. You should have had that talk in class two years ago because I remember getting it when I was that age," Harper replied as his eyes narrowed at them, and the girls started giggling.

"Okay. No, there's nothing else that you need to worry about," Ash said, still giggling.

"Until we start liking boys," Rachael said with a grin.

"That's not going to happen," Harper told them coldly.

"You can't stop it. It's in our genetic makeup. We will be attracted to boys, and they will be attracted to us," Bridgett told him.

"I have an M-300 pistol with laser sights in my bedroom that says I will stop them from being attracted to you," Harper informed her with a smug look on his face.

The girls all looked at one another and nodded their heads. "Yep, that probably will do it," Rachael replied.

He had a slight smirk at the corner of his mouth, then told them to get out of there and make sure their room was clean and that they had clean clothes for school tomorrow. The girls started laughing and took off for the stairs. As he watched them, the smirk on his face finally turned into a brief smile. This was definitely different from any other mission he had been on, but in truth, he was loving it and wouldn't trade it for all the marks in the universe. Gerrard was right, he needed this time with Ash, because even now, he was noticing how much she was growing up, even at twelve years of age. When he thought about her growing up, becoming a young woman, and leaving, it tore his heart apart. He needed Ash just as much as she needed him.

The rest of the day wore on, and the girls did their chores without any complaining. Lunch was fixed by all three of them, and actually, it was fairly good. Rachael was busy on the laundry even though she complained about having to wash the admiral's boxers, but like Ash told her, it wasn't like she had to wash them by hand. The clothes were separated and put into the laundry machine, which washed, dried, and then sent them to a separate unit that ironed, folded, or hung the clothes. The only thing Rachael had to do was separate them, put them in the laundry machine, and then separate everything after it was all done and folded.

Ash, in the meantime, cleaned up after lunch and hauled the garbage to the compactor in the storage room and then pressed the button to dispose of it once it was compacted. Bridgett went and made sure the rest of the house was straightened up and helped Ash finish the dishes. After everything was done, the girls went to their room, listened to music, and worked on the assignments that they hadn't finished yet.

Soon, evening was upon them, and all three fixed supper. They ate and cleaned up afterward, showered, then went to bed. The admiral went and also got ready, but before he headed to bed, he checked on them. All three girls were sound asleep. He went into their room and took the headphones off Rachael's head, which she still had on, and pulled her covers up on her. Then he took the electronic book that Bridgett had in her hand and put it on her nightstand, then pulled the covers up on her. And last, he brushed some of Ash's stray hair away from her face and pulled her covers up as well. He walked back over to the door and stopped, looking back at them, then left the room and headed to bed.

He went into his room and sat down on the edge of his bed and let out a sigh. "Look at me now, Gail. Would you believe any of this?" he said out loud, and then a voice in his head spoke: "You're doing just fine." Harper smiled and climbed into bed, but he noticed something different this time. The voice was starting to get fainter and fainter. He knew Gail was with him right now, possibly spiritually, but only to help him for just a brief time, and eventually, she would be gone for good when she felt he was ready to be on his own.

CHAPTER 14

OVER THE COURSE of the school year, all the kids—the girls and the boys—managed to stay out of trouble, and there were no more major fights between them. A few scuffles here and there, but that was it. Ash and her friends, of course, continued to have problems with the other students just because they were the new kids. But Fâd and his friends were now finally starting to fit in and be accepted by the others and started hanging out with other kids.

Admiral Harper had made a few trips to the school to Professor Baptise because Ash, Rachael, and Bridgett got into trouble for fighting. But this time, when he got called, it was a major episode that he was most displeased with. Somehow, they had managed to rig a couple of toilets in one of the girls' bathrooms in the physical education building to explode by sneaking certain compounds from the science building and built small explosives with them when the fourteen-year-olds were having PE. A few girls got blasted off the toilets, receiving only minor injures, thank goodness, which could have easily been worse, and the bathroom was flooded.

Ash, Rachael, and Bridgett were sitting outside Professor Baptise's office, waiting for the admiral to show up, when the boys walked by with some of their new buddies. Fâd saw them sitting where he was so used to being himself and grinned, walking over to them. "So you were the ones who rigged the toilets, huh?" he asked, chuckling now as the rest of the guys came over.

"Yeah. I can't stand those girls. They think they are so damn neat, always picking on us and calling us names," Ash said with a scowl.

"That was awesome. You three rock. You'll have to show us how to do that," one of the other boys said, and Nathan, Cory, and Fâd gave him a dirty look.

"So what happens now?" Nathan asked them.

"We're waiting for the admiral," Bridgett told them with a worried look.

"Whoa, that's our cue to get out of here. I don't want to be around when he shows up. Good luck," Fâd said, and he and his posse took off quickly down the hall.

"Thanks. We'll let you know how prison life is when we get out," Ash yelled at them, and the boys started laughing as Fâd waved back at them.

The boys had barely left when the vice admiral walked through the main doors of the administration building, and Ash could tell he was furious just by the stone-cold, almost deadly, look on his face. At least he was in civilian clothing, which meant there wasn't going to be a court martial. He walked past the girls without saying a word or even looking at them and went straight into the professor's office, and the door slid shut behind him.

A little while later, he came out, and he and the professor shook hands. Then the admiral left without saying anything again to the girls, still with a cold look on his face. The professor looked down at them. "Come with me, girls." They got up and followed him out of the building and over to the phys ed compound. He walked over to a large room, unlocked it by placing his hand on the blue scan pad, the door sliding open, then went in, having the girls follow. It was full of cleaning supplies—mops, buckets, and rags—and he grabbed three aprons off a hook and handed them to the girls. "Put those on, then each grab a tray of cleaning supplies and a mop and bucket, and follow me," the professor told them coldly.

They did as they were told. The aprons looked almost like a dress on them, and they were totally embarrassed in them. They each grabbed a tray, a mop, and a bucket and followed the professor as he led them to the girls' bathroom that they had exploded, and they all went in it. Fortunately, it had been repaired already, but it was still a mess. "You will clean all the girls' bathrooms in this building, plus all the boys' bathrooms as well," he told them, and their mouths dropped open in shock.

"That's six bathrooms. We'll be here all night," Ash said in disgust.

"Then I suggest you get busy," Professor Baptise replied and left the bathroom with the girls just standing there, staring at one another.

"This is a bunch of crap. He can't do this," Rachael blurted out.

"Well, he just did, so I suggest we stop complaining and get to work," Bridgett said angrily and started cleaning.

Hours later, they finally had all the girls' bathrooms done and were working on their second boys' bathroom when Rachael ran out of one of the toilet stalls, gagging and pulling off her large bright-yellow gloves. "That's it! I can't clean another toilet stall. I can't handle going in there and finding another floater or the floor yellow instead of the white it's supposed to be. Boys are just sick and disgusting. How do you miss the toilet? Are they really that poor of shots? I'm going to do something about it."

"What are you going to do?" Ash asked through the towel that was tied around her head, covering her nose and mouth, as she cleaned another stall next to the one Rachael was working on.

"Just watch," Rachael marched out of the bathroom and came back half an hour later as Bridgett and Ash finished up. She had an arm full of white paper, which she had sneaked from the literature department, which was something they rarely used since everything was done on datapads or electronic notebooks. She went into each stall, fastening the paper to the walls behind the toilets. She walked over to Ash and Bridgett and handed them one of the papers. They looked at it and started laughing.

On it was printed, "Please make sure of your aim before firing. If need help, see diagram." Then below this was a very detailed drawing of how a boy should pee into the toilet. Rachael was quite the artist and did a pretty good job at drawing the diagram, and apparently, she had fastened one of these signs to every one of the boys' stalls that they had already cleaned so far.

Ash and Bridgett were laughing so hard they could barely leave the bathroom and head to the next one. They set up the Do Not Enter stand outside the bathroom and walked in just as a couple of boys hurriedly ran out of it when they saw them. They got to working on it right away since it was now dark out. They were still cleaning when some boys came in with Rachael's signs in their hands, and you could tell they were mad.

"Whose smart idea was this?" one of the boys asked the girls, holding up the sign.

"Mine. Apparently, some of you have a targeting problem," Rachael said defiantly.

"I have no problem, and I'll prove it," the older boy said and started to head to the stall.

"Come on, no one wants to see your little wiener," Ash said, and Rachael and Bridgett started laughing. Even some of the boys did as well.

"You have quite the mouth on you. Maybe a nice dip in the toilet will shut you up," the older boy said, walking over to Ash and looking down at her.

"I dare you to try it," she threatened him back, glaring.

"Grab them, guys. It's flushing time."

Ash, Rachael, and Bridgett all grabbed a mop and twirled them in their hands, preparing to fight. There were at least seven boys against them, and they were all older, between the ages of fourteen and fifteen. Ash took on three of them as Rachael and Bridgett held back two apiece, but soon, they started getting overwhelmed. The next thing the girls knew, they were hoisted up above the boys' heads and carried toward the stalls. The girls were still struggling and fighting when suddenly, a couple of the boys went down, dropping

Bridgett, who jumped up and started fighting the other boys, who still had hold of Ash and Rachael.

The three boys who had Ash dropped her as two of them flew across the floor, and the other one just ran. She fell to the floor but jumped up quickly and came face-to-face with Fâd. She then turned to help Rachael, but Nathan had taken care of the boys who had her and was helping her up off the ground. Fâd, Nathan, and Cory stood in front of the girls in a protective manner as the older boys got up from the ground and ran off.

"What the hell was going on in here?" Fâd turned around, mad, and looked at Ash.

"Just a little misunderstanding," Ash said, mad, and went over, picking up her mop. Nathan, in the meantime, had picked up the flyers that Rachael had made and started busting up laughing, handing one to Fâd and Cory. They read them and started laughing as well and looked over at the girls.

"I take it this was the cause of the disagreement?" Fâd asked, holding up one of the flyers.

"That and the fact that Ash told them they had little wieners," Bridgett said to them, and the boys busted up laughing even harder as they grabbed their sides, which were now hurting from laughing. Rachael and Bridgett shrugged their shoulders and went and got their mops, but the boys took the mops from them.

"Come on. We'll help so you can go home. We will mop, and you can do the other cleaning," Fâd said as he walked over to the mop bucket to rewet it.

"You know, there's never a dull moment around you three," Nathan said as he started mopping the floor. The girls all took a stall and started cleaning, and everybody would start laughing every time Rachael gagged, which was a lot. Finally, the bathroom was done, and all the supplies were put back. They all headed out of the phys ed building. It was dark out in the park as the boys walked the girls toward the front of the school campus and to the waiting vehicle that Fâd had called for.

"By the way, how did you know where to find us?" Ash asked as they all walked.

"Rumors spread fast around the campus, and we heard that there were some twelve-year-old girls that were causing problems in the phys ed bathrooms and that they were going to get taught a lesson. We knew it could only be you three," Nathan said, chuckling.

"Come on, we're not in trouble that much," Ash replied, a little annoyed.

"Yes, you are. I think you even have us beat." Fâd grinned looking down at her as they walked along.

"By the way, how did it go with the admiral?" Cory asked.

"He didn't speak or even look at us, and I'm not looking forward to going home," Ash replied, and it was apparent she was nervous.

Rachael looked over at her. "Hey, maybe we should—"

"No. We are going home. No hiding out this time," Ash said bluntly, knowing exactly what Rachael was going to suggest. The boys started laughing again and shaking their heads. They couldn't believe how crazy these girls were to even think of hiding from the vice admiral, and the way they talked, they had done it on more than one occasion before.

They finally got to the front of the school campus, and the vehicle was waiting for them, as Fâd had said. The driver opened the door, and the girls reluctantly walked toward it and climbed in. "It was nice knowing you," Nathan yelled to them, and Rachael stuck her tongue out at them, which made the boys start laughing all over again. The vehicle pulled away from the sidewalk and headed back toward the residential area that they lived in. Before long, they pulled in front of the house and went in. The admiral was sitting in the armchair, waiting for them, and made them sit down before they could clean up for dinner.

Harper sat there for a few minutes without saying a word, glaring at the girls with stone-cold gray eyes. "Well, I hope you learned a lesson from this," he said, still with cold, narrowed eyes and a dangerous warning to his tone.

"Yeah, not to leave incriminating evidence around," Ash said under her breath.

"This is not a joking matter, Ashley Harper," he said coldly, and the threat in his tone was very apparent.

"I know. I was just trying to lighten the mood in here. Yes, we learned our lesson, and I have the blisters to prove it," she said and lowered her head.

"Good, but if I get called one more time to the school, I will make sure you girls are sorry for what you have done. Do I make myself clear?"

"Yes, sir," they answered in unison.

"Fine. Now go get cleaned up. Dinner is ready."

They got up from the sofa and went upstairs to their bedroom, taking turns to shower, and put on pajamas since it was so late. Finally, they headed back down the stairs and ate supper. It wasn't too bad. Again, it was something they couldn't pronounce. Once they were done, the admiral had them go to bed as he stayed and cleaned up, and it didn't take them long to crash once their heads hit their pillows.

The rest of the school year, though, went uneventful, and the girls behaved. Of course, it was still hard for them at school with the other kids, but they were getting a reputation not to be messed with. The months flew by, and they were now all in a routine. Some weekends, the admiral would invite the boys over, and they would have pizza or something of that nature and either watch vids or play games and had a good time together.

Finally, the last few days of school were upon them, and they all would be leaving. The admiral and the girls would be heading back to the *Justification* for three months, and Admiral Larson was coming to pick up the boys and head to the *Lithia* for three months as well.

It was during the day while the girls were at school that Harper got buzzed that someone was at the door. He walked over and passed his hand over the scan pad for the door to open, and there standing in front of him was Admiral Larson and Captain Sharni, grinning at him.

"Well? Aren't you going to ask us in?" Gerrard asked him.

"Hell no," Harper said and stood aside for them to come in. Larson walked over and dropped his pack on the sofa.

"Now that doesn't belong there. Your room is at the end of the hallway," Harper got on to him.

"Wow, you're really taking to this domestic lifestyle. I thought I would never see that. And look at the clothes. Nice," Gerrard started, teasing him.

"I hate you," Harper replied with a smirk and shaking his head.

Sharni walked in, and she and Harper hugged each other. "I'm sorry I had to bring him. There was no way around it," she said with a big grin on her face.

"Oh, come on, you can't do anything without me," he said, picking up his pack and giving her a kiss on the lips, then he headed toward the hallway that was off the living room. "And I'm not that bad. Besides, I know you missed me." Gerrard looked at Harper and gave him a wink, causing Harper to start chuckling.

"I suppose you're hungry?" Thomas yelled to his friend and headed toward the kitchen to fix everyone something.

"You know it. Hey, why do I have to sleep in a separate room than with Sharni?" he hollered from the hallway.

"Because this is a house full of very impressionable twelve-year-old girls," Harper replied.

"Boy trouble already?" Larson asked back.

"No, female things, and by the way, Sharni, thank you very much for not telling me about certain things to expect with girls," Harper said and gave her a dirty look, and she started giggling as Larson walked into the kitchen.

"So have you had to make a trip to the clinic yet?" she asked, giggling.

"No, thank goodness, but they also informed me that soon, there will be boys coming around because it is a fact of life," Harper told her as Larson walked over to the refrigerator and took out a beer, opening it and starting to drink.

"What was your reply to that one?" she asked with a big grin.

"I told them I have an M-300 pistol with laser sights."

Larson choked on his beer and started coughing with a grin on his face, and Harper started beating him on the back. Sharni was laughing, shaking her head, and finally, Larson stopped coughing and was also laughing as well. "You didn't tell them that, did you?" Larson asked, still grinning.

"I sure did, and they agreed that would work," Harper replied with an ornery smirk.

"Talking about boys, I hope you don't mind, but I told the school to have the boys come here for the remainder of these last two days," Larson asked his friend.

"No problem. We've had them over quite a few times for dinner and a vid or games. The kids are actually getting along finally and staying out of trouble. I was a little nervous at first the way school started out. With all the fighting and the girls blowing up the girls' bathroom at school, it was looking pretty bleak."

"Blew up a bathroom?" Sharni asked, grinning.

"Oh yeah, I didn't tell you two about that one. The girls got into it with some fourteen-year-olds, so they rigged the toilets in one of the girls' bathroom in the phys ed building to blow up with homemade explosives that they made from stuff they sneaked out of the science building when the fourteen-year-olds were having PE. I guess a couple girls actually got blown off of the toilets and ended up with second-degree burns on their bottoms," Harper told them, trying not to laugh. Of course, Sharni and Larson were dying from laughing, and Larson had to go over and sit down before he fell over. "It's not funny. That was so embarrassing when I had to go talk to Professor Baptise."

"So what happened after that?" Larson asked, taking a drink from his beer, and he would let out a little chuckle off and on.

"The professor and I agreed on a punishment. The girls had to clean all the girls' bathrooms and the boys' bathrooms in the phys ed building and stay there until they were done. I guess from what I could piece together hearing the kids talking when they didn't think I was listening, apparently, there was an altercation in one of the boys' bathrooms with some older boys and the girls.

"Rachael had made some signs and posted them on all the toilet stalls, having something to do with their aim, and drew a diagram on how to pee. About seven older boys took a real offense to this and confronted the girls, at which time, Ash made some comment pertaining to their lack of size being the problem. I guess they were a few feet away from getting their heads flushed down the toilets when Fâd,

Nathan, and Cory showed up and stopped the older boys," Harper told them, and now he was chuckling, as was Larson and Sharni.

"I think they even have the boys beat," Larson said, still chuckling.

"It just amazes me. Girls seem so sweet and innocent, but they're monsters," Harper told them and went and got himself a beer as well and then sat down next to Larson.

"I tried to warn you. And just think, you haven't even begun in the teenager stage," Sharni said, grinning.

"Is that worse?" Harper asked, putting down his beer, looking worried.

"Oh yeah. That is when hormones kick in and mood swings as their little bodies start changing into young ladies," Sharni told him.

Both Larson and Harper's faces turned pale white, and they both looked at her, then at each other, and there was actual fear on their faces now. "No, that's not going to happen. There must be some pill or something that we can give them to keep them this way," Harper asked, looking at Sharni, as Larson nodded his head in agreement.

"No, that wouldn't be fair to them. You want to keep them as little girl forever?" Sharni asked in disbelief.

"Of course," Larson replied, and Harper nodded his head in agreement.

"I can't believe you two. They deserve to grow up, meet someone, and have their own family."

"Will you stop? You're just making it worse. My little girl will never meet anyone. She will be allowed to grow up but then stay on my ship for the rest of her life, away from boys," Harper said with hands over his ears so he couldn't hear Sharni anymore.

"That's right, and I will help you," Larson said, and Harper thanked him for the support.

"That's funny, because it could be your son that goes after her, so what would you do about that, smart-ass?" Sharni said with a devious grin.

"What? You keep your son away from my daughter," Harper said to Larson with narrowed eyes but a slight smirk on his face.

"Fâd won't go after your daughter. He's too determined to get his own ship and join the fleet. He won't let a girl change his mind. Besides, they would never get along. Look at them now. They barely speak to each other, and a lot of the times, it turns into a fight," Larson said, rolling his eyes.

"That's true, they do fight a lot, and I've heard Fâd talk about his own ship a lot. Even Ash plans on joining the fleet under my command. I guess we're jumping to conclusions. Besides, we'll make sure and push them in those goals," Harper said, and Larson agreed, and both men now had wicked grin on their faces.

"You both are a couple of idiots. Don't you dare mess with their lives, you hear me? I will fight both of you every step of the way if you try," Sharni warned them, and the two men could tell she was mad.

"We're not going to mess with their lives, just help and steer them in the right direction," Larson told her sheepishly.

"Bullshit. I mean it. You don't want to piss me off on this. I will make you both sorry in ways you could never imagine," she said and stormed out of the room to her bedroom.

"Wow, I think we made her mad. I guess she can't take a joke." Larson looked over at Harper.

"Yeah. I've never seen Sharni get mad like that before," Harper said, surprised.

"I suppose someone should go talk to her," Larson said, looking toward the direction she had just gone.

"Duh? Get in there!"

"Me? No way. She'll kill me. You're her friend and brother-in-law. She won't hurt you as bad, so you go talk to her."

"The hell I will. She's your mate and pretty well your wife. That's your job," Harper told him, pointing toward the living room.

"Fine, but if you hear me screaming for my life, grab a gun and come running." Larson sighed and got up slowly from the table and headed to Sharni's bedroom. A few hours later, he came out, pulling on a casual shirt with a big grin on his face.

"I take it you worked things out?" Harper asked, emotionless, sitting in an armchair in the living room, watching a vid.

"Yeah, we called a truce for now."

Sharni came out and was also dressed in casual clothes. She went into the kitchen, grabbed a juice bottle, then went and plopped down on the sofa next to Larson. Harper asked them what had happened with the attack, and the adults talked from then until the kids showed up.

Of course, they could hear them right away, as they were all fighting in front of the house. The adults ran outside and saw Fâd and Ash in a yelling match, almost nose to nose, if it weren't for the fact that Fâd was a lot taller and had to look down at her. But that didn't stop Ash, and she was right back in his face. Rachael and Bridgett were kicking Cory and Nathan, and they started pushing the girls to get them to stop, and scattered all over the front yard were books, backpacks, some clothes, and large duffle bags.

"WHAT IS GOING ON HERE?" Larson yelled, and the kids all stopped and froze in their tracks.

"They refused to put their crap in the trunk and instead had it in the vehicle and almost suffocated us. When we asked nicely, they said that they had seniority and that we and our stuff could all ride in the trunk because they didn't want it smelling all girly," Ash said with her fist clench and glaring at Fâd.

"Fâd, is that true?" Larson asked him.

"Well, yes and no. We were going to put our stuff in the trunk until they told us not nicely either. Using their exact words, 'Put your crap in the trunk so we don't catch any diseases.' So we piled it all inside on them," Fâd said, glaring right back at Ash.

"It sounds to me like all of you are in the wrong. Now get over it and get this mess cleaned up, and go inside," Harper said in his commanding, cold tone. The kids grudgingly started picking their stuff up, and before long, they all headed to the house. None of them spoke as they walked by or even looked up at the adults as the boys piled their stuff up in a corner in the living room and the girls went upstairs. The adults looked at one another and rolled their eyes.

"I take it back, you don't have to ever worry about them," Sharni said with a slight smirk on her face.

They walked in, and now Fâd came over and gave Sharni a big hug and then his father. Even Nathan and Cory gave her a hug and shook the admiral's hand. "I missed you," Larson told Fâd and ruffled up his hair.

"I missed you, Dad. So anything exciting happen while you were out?" Fâd asked, and the other two boys came over and plopped down on the floor to hear. Larson and the other two adults sat down on the furniture, and Larson started telling them all about the fight with the mercs. The girls came out of their room and quickly ran down the stairs to hear.

They went over and hugged Sharni, and Larson stopped telling his story, got up, and gave them each a hug as well. Then he continued to tell his story as Ash sat down on the arm of the chair he was sitting in. He reached over and pulled her to his lap and continued to talk, and over halfway through it, Ash was sound asleep with her head against his shoulder, and even Nathan and Cory were crashed on the floor. Rachael, Bridgett, and Fâd were the only ones who remained awake through the whole thing.

It was several hours later, and Larson stood up, lifting Ash with him. She wrapped her arms around his neck, still sleeping, and he carried her up to her room and laid her down on her bed, pulling a blanket up on her. Once he came down, he saw that Nathan and Cory also had blankets on them now as well, and everyone else was outside on the back patio. He walked through the sliding glass doors and could tell the evening was fast approaching. He saw Sharni braiding Bridgett's hair as Rachael waited her turn, and Fâd was talking to Harper as they were also sitting in patio chairs.

"Okay. You girls can never grow up," Larson said with a smile.

"Why?" Rachael asked him as Fâd and Harper stopped talking, looking over at him.

"Because you just can't," Larson told them, then went and sat down next to Sharni.

"So when are you and Sharni getting married?" Bridgett asked out of the blue.

Larson was caught by surprise. "What?" Even Sharni was surprised and stopped braiding Bridgett's hair.

"Well, you love each other, pretty well live and sleep together, so you should just get married," Rachael said, rolling her eyes at them.

"What do you mean? We don't. It's complicated," Sharni said, all flustered.

"Who told you we sleep together?" Larson asked, also flustered.

"Oh, come on. We may be twelve, but we're not stupid. It was pretty easy to figure out. Back on the *Justification* for Ash's mom's funeral, you tried to be sneaky, but it didn't work. And then when we stayed at Fâd's house, it was amazing how there were women's pajamas already there. We see everything, and as for complicated, that's a bunch of trash. You're an admiral, and Sharni is a captain and soon-to-be admiral. You can still get married and keep your rank. This is the new age. People do it all the time," Rachael told them as if they were little children and she was having to educate them.

"Oh my gosh, Harper, is this what you have been dealing with this whole year?" Larson asked his friend in disbelief.

"Yeah, only worse," Harper said with no emotion.

Rachael went over and sat on Harper's lap and put her arms around his neck with a big grin on her face, and he held her with a smile. "Come on, we're not that bad. We just like to tease you all the time. It's fun to see your faces turn red," Rachael said and was now giggling.

"You ornery little monsters," Harper said and tickled her, and she jumped off his lap, laughing.

Half an hour later, Ash woke up and came down the stairs just as Cory and Nathan woke too. All three of them went over to the patio doors and looked through the glass doors and saw Fâd throwing a ball around with Rachael. Bridgett was sitting on Larson's lap as she and the adults watched them. Ash, Cory, and Nathan walked out, and everyone looked over at them.

"Ah, you finally woke up," Larson said with a grin. Ash had to take a quick breath looking at her godfather. It was his white eyes and always grinning face that she loved most about him, and she couldn't help but grin back.

"Yeah. I didn't know you were so full of hot air," Ash replied, grinning.

"Why, you little insect," Larson said, jumping up, setting Bridgett down off his lap. Ash took off running across the yard with him hot on her heels. She was laughing hard, and he caught her easily, throwing her up into the air and then catching her again. She was now laughing with tears in her eyes. He put her down, and they both walked back to the patio where everyone else was laughing at them.

"So is anyone hungry?" Sharni asked.

"Yeah," the kids all said in unison.

Sharni got up and went into the kitchen, and Larson and Harper followed her. The kids stayed out on the patio. Fâd had come over and sat down in a patio chair when his father chased Ash down, but he was still holding the ball in his lap. Ash, in a flash, ran over and yanked it out of his hands, and he jumped up and took off after her. She was laughing as he caught and tackled her, but she quickly threw the ball to Rachael, who took off running, and now Nathan was chasing her. She threw it to Bridgett as she ran, but Cory caught her and took the ball back.

Ash went after him to get it, but Fâd tackled her again and then got up as Cory threw it to him just as Rachael and Bridgett both tackled Cory. Fâd went to throw it to Nathan when Ash jumped on his back and took him to the ground, and the ball rolled away. He was laughing now and rolled her over, pinning her to the ground with her arms behind her back as he sat on her. Then with a devious grin on his face, he started tickling her, and she was now laughing hysterically as tears ran down her cheeks. Rachael and Bridgett came running, and they both took Fâd out, and Nathan and Cory wrestled them off Fâd. Before long, it was just a huge wrestling match, and the kids were all laughing.

Sharni stepped outside to tell them dinner was ready, and the sight to her looked like they were all in an outright fight until she heard the laughter. Larson and Harper walked out with their plates and saw the melee of bodies and started to head out after them.

"It's okay. They're just playing," Sharni stopped them.

"That's playing?" Harper said in shock.

"Yeah. Can't you hear them laughing?" She looked at him.

Finally, the kids stopped, and they all lay on the grass, now panting from the exertion. Ash leaned up on her elbows and saw the adults eating. "Hey, dinner's ready," she told everyone, and it became another wrestling match as they shoved and pushed one another to get to the house first. Once again, it was Bridgett who got there first because once again, Cory this time shoved Rachael out of the way and pulled Bridgett in front of himself. Fâd had no chance due to him laughing so hard because Ash was literally hanging off him with her arms and legs wrapped around one of his legs as Nathan was being held back by Fâd. Finally, they got in the house and fixed their plates and went and ate with the adults.

Once the meal was done, the girls cleaned up, as was their chore; and strangely enough, the boys actually helped them. It got late, and the girls went to bed. Larson helped Harper to pull out the already made up sleepers on the sofas where all three boys could sleep quite comfortably. Finally, everyone was settled in for the night; and like Rachael said, Larson sneaked into Sharni's room.

CHAPTER 15

THE LAST TWO days of school came and went, and now it was time for everyone to leave. The boys were packed and in their fleet uniforms and waiting for Admiral Larson and Sharni so they could head to the battlecruiser *Lithia* for the next three months. The girls, of course, were also packed and in fleet uniforms as well and ready to depart for the *Justification*. Admiral Harper and Admiral Larson were both in their uniforms and finishing up with making sure everything was taken care of in the house. They both did a last-minute walk-through, and then satisfied, they walked outside to the waiting vehicles with the kids already loaded in them.

"Well, I'll see you in about three months when I bring the boys back for their fourth year at school," Larson told his best friend, Harper.

"Yeah. Only one more year and then it's your turn," Harper said with an ornery smirk.

"I'm sorry, Harper, but I do believe that girls are worse than boys. They just give you that sweet, innocent look that hides the monster inside," Larson told him, chuckling.

"Now you know what I've been going through. I'll see you in three months," Harper said, and they grasped forearms.

Larson went and climbed into the vehicle with the boys and Sharni as Harper climbed in with the girls. Once again, the girls were chattering away and never stopped all the way to the spaceport. They got out as luggage crew came out with carryalls and loaded the many trunks and luggage on them. There wasn't as much this time since a lot of it was staying back at the house.

The admiral once again led them through the terminal, toward where their shuttle was docked, then went up and got clearance. Just as he walked through the terminal doors, two fighters were landing beside the shuttle. Also, Captain Sims and two soldiers were waiting for the admiral.

"Vice Admiral Harper, I understand you will be gone for the next three months. That's too bad. We are going to miss you," Captain Sims said in a condescending tone.

"Don't worry, Captain, I will be overhead, making sure you're safe," Harper said to him, and the captain's face turned bright red as he advanced on Harper and took a swing at him this time, but the admiral easily dodged it and then knocked him flying with little effort across the landing pad.

The soldiers who were with the council captain pulled their guns, and Harper now took a defensive poise as the girls huddled behind him, but they quickly dropped their weapons when they felt the sentinel fighter pilots' guns pressed against their necks. The captain started getting up, and the admiral was over to him in a flash, looking at him with glowing, narrowed solid-blue eyes. He grabbed him by the shirt front, easily lifting him off the ground with one hand as if he weighed nothing.

"You ever try something like that again in front of my girls, I will kill you. You have no idea who you are messing with. Just ask your council presidency. They will gladly enlighten you," Harper said to him, and the tone in his voice sent chills down Sims's spine. Even Ash heard her father, and she had never heard him talk this way, and it scared her for the first time in her life. She had also never seen her father's eyes change like that. Harper sat Sims back down as his eyes turned back to their cold, deadly steel-gray look, then stepped back and motioned to his fighter pilots, who released the soldiers and also stepped back. Harper motioned for the girls, and they quickly went over and climbed into the shuttle with Harper behind them as the pilots headed to their fighters.

Captain Sims and the soldiers quickly headed back to the terminal as the admiral fired up the shuttle, and before they knew it, it was back in the air, heading toward space and the *Justification*, which was orbiting overhead. The shuttle bucked a little when they passed from the atmosphere and into space, and before long, the battlecruiser came into view as a voice came over the comm. "*Justification* to Vice Admiral Harper. Come in, Admiral."

"*Justification*, this is Vice Admiral Harper. Requesting permission to dock," Harper replied as he punched in the authorization codes on the shuttle's console.

"Authorization approved. Welcome back, Admiral."

"It's good to be back, Dobbs," Harper said, still a little mad about his earlier encounter with Captain Sims from council militia back on the planet.

The admiral maneuvered the shuttle around toward one of the many shuttle bays and saw the bay doors open as the blue kinetic barrier covered the opening. He slowed way down and passed through the barrier, then came to a stop, landing the shuttle softly. Harper shut down, unbuckled, and went back to help the girls. They were already unbuckled and gathering their stuff as the shuttle doors opened, and the admiral led as the girls followed him out of the shuttle. As soon as he stepped on the *Justification*'s floor, the deck officer announced, "Vice Admiral on deck. EXO Dobbs relieved."

Rachael saw her parents now and took off running to them, crying, as did Bridgett when she saw her father. Their parents picked them up, hugging them tightly, then put them back down. They were amazed by how much they had grown. Commander Torres and his wife and also Engineer Nelson came over and shook Harper's hand, and of course, Abigail hugged Thomas and then Ash and told her how much she had grown as well.

"It's good to have you back, Thomas," Raul told him.

"It's good to be back. I feel like I'm finally home," Harper said, looking his ship over.

"So was it very bad?" Abigail asked, and Harper looked over at the girls, who all had sheepish looks on their faces, nervous about what he was going to say.

"Nah, different but not bad," he said, void of emotion, but his steel-gray eyes conveyed a smile to the girls.

"It was especially fun when Rear Admiral Larson showed up," Bridgett told them.

"Oh, don't mention that name around me," Nelson piped up with a scowl on his face.

Harper smirked. "Yeah, I heard he did a number on the *Lithia's* engines and jump drive."

"That's an understatement. He mangled them. I can't believe he got her back here. I had to sing to her to get her humming again," Nelson said with a slight grin.

Harper took Ash's hand, and they headed to the elevator, and the rest followed. Before long, they were heading back to their cabin; and when they walked in, Harper was hit with every memory and scent of Gail. After all this time, it still felt and smelled like Gail even though the voice in his head had left not long ago. Ash stood there and looked around and then up at her father.

"It still feels like mother, and I can still smell her too."

"It sure does, Ash."

Harper let go of her hand and walked over to his comm terminal and saw that he had several messages. He put down the pack he carried and pressed a button on it. There were a couple from sentinel command welcoming him back for the short time, one from Larson telling him about getting into it with Sims as well, and one for Ash from Fâd, telling her that he found his electronic books of *Sandstrider* and would send them to her since she said she liked them. He just chuckled and shook his head. Ash came out of her room and walked over to him.

"Was that Fâd?"

"Yeah. He said he found his collection of *Sandstrider* and would send them to you to read."

"Cool. I can't wait," she replied, excited.

They looked around at all the luggage, and at the same time, both let out a loud sigh and started unpacking. Hours later, they collapsed on the sofa, exhausted, and Harper looked over at her. "You hungry?"

"Nope. Are you?"

"Nope, just tired."

"Me too. I think I'm going to go to bed," Ash said and got up.

"I will after I make rounds. Will you be okay here by yourself?"

"Of course. I'll see you in the morning, Dad."

"I'll see you too. I love you, Ash."

"I love you, Dad."

CHAPTER 16

————⟨✦⟩————

IT DID NOT take them long to get back into the norm on the ship again, but this time, it was very different. Instead of being allowed to roam freely, Ash, Rachael, and Bridgett were now beginning their training, as was standard for all sentinel children of the age twelve and up. They had martial arts in the morning for a couple of hours, and then after that, they had light combat training up to lunchtime. After lunch, for the next three hours was weapons training and many different types of classes, from taking weapons apart to shield repair, armor repair, and so on.

This was going to be the routine from there on out for the next ten years, and then they will be enlisted in the sentinel fleet, which was also when they would finish prep school. It was also during this time aboard the *Justification* that it responded to a distress call, and they knew that there had been some kind of battle planet side due to some of their instructors being gone for a couple of days, and they had alternates teaching them. What had happened the girls never did find out. They just knew that their side won.

Ash would now come back to her cabin tired and sore after each day, for they did not spar with one another but with their adult trainers, who didn't go easy on them just because they were children. After a month and a half of this, the girls' talents started showing themselves. Ash was excelling at martial arts and weapons. Rachael was unmatched by even some adults with a sniper rifle and stealth, and Bridgett was like her father and could take apart any ship's engine and jump drive. In one case, a ship had been damaged from attack, and she put it back together blindfolded and in half the time, enough to get the ship up and running again. The girls also were above their age group in hand-to-hand combat and learning stuff that children two years older than them were.

But before long, it was time to get ready to head back to New Guinea, and now the girls were all thirteen and looking forward to their second year at school. Once again, Ash and her father packed back up and headed to the shuttle, meeting up with Rachael and her family and Bridgett and her dad. The crewmen loaded the shuttle once again. Everyone said their goodbyes, and before long, the shuttle was again heading to New Guinea with fighters escorting them.

Harper got clearance from the New Guinea spaceport once he got close, and soon, the shuttle landed on the same pad. They all unloaded, and spaceport personnel came out of the terminal and unloaded the luggage from the shuttle and onto carryalls. They all headed into the terminal but, this time, without Captain Sims to welcome them and got through the busy terminal and out to the same waiting airlimo. Dock personnel loaded the airlimo that Admiral Harper always used. Harper waited for all the girls to get in, and then he got in as the driver closed the door, and before long, they were heading through the city and finally made it back to the house.

Harper got out and waited for each of the girls to get out and followed them to the house. Ash put her hand on the scan pad, and the door slid open. They went in, and they could smell food as they walked into the living room. Admiral Larson came walking from around the corner where the kitchen was with a frustrated look on his face.

"Hey, how do you make a hamburger in that thing?" he asked.

"Follow me," Ash said and had the admiral follow her back into the kitchen and walked him through how to use the replicator. Since most watorians did all their cooking by hand, Larson never had to prepare a meal for himself on his own ship.

The rest of them were busy carrying luggage to their bedrooms and started putting things away as Larson had Ash stay with him and made everyone else a hamburger. He put them all on plates for everybody and set them on the counter, and they walked out to the living room to see if they could help.

Larson went over to Harper's room as Ash ran upstairs to her and her friends' room and started unpacking her stuff as Larson stood leaning in the doorway of Harper's room with his arms folded. "So did it feel good to get back on board?" Larson asked his friend.

"Yeah, and I didn't want to leave it. I always feel at home in the stars."

"I know the feeling. Sharni had to go to Krios to have the main engine on her ship replaced with a new phasic drive system, so she will be gone for at least a month, and I'm short one battleship since my other one still hasn't been repaired from our last mission."

"Take one of mine."

"No thanks. I'll wait for her to get back, so I'm here for at least a month till then."

"Don't they have freighters heading out soon?"

"They have them on hold until the *Astra Sink* or my other battleship is ready, whichever gets done first. I'm putting my money on Sharni. She'll make sure she's back first. Besides, I'm finding it hard to sleep alone, so can I sleep with you tonight?" Larson asked, grinning.

"Hell no. You hog the covers." Harper chuckled.

"I only did that the one time."

"Yeah, but you also had your arm around me," Harper replied, and now they both were chuckling.

"It was cold out, and you were so warm. By the way, you were right, I found and destroyed five bugs."

"I knew they would try. When we first moved in here, I located three then. Got to hand it to council. They are persistent."

"Yeah, but they're getting better. These ones were pretty good. It took me three minutes instead of two to disarm them so council wouldn't get suspicious," Larson replied, grinning, and Thomas smirked back.

Thomas finished unpacking as Gerrard came in, then helped carry the empty trunks out to the storage room as they continued to talk. They were stacking the trunks up on the top shelf when the girls came in with their empty trunks and handed them to the admirals, then left the room. Larson and Harper headed out to the living room, and the girls were all stretched out on the sofas, watching the vid screen. Harper went and sat down in the armchair as Larson went over and sat down on Rachael, who squealed and then moved so he could sit.

"Where are the boys?" Rachael asked, now looking around.

"Already checked in at the school. Oh, Ash, I have something for you from Fâd," Larson said and got up, heading to his room. Rachael looked over at Ash, grinning, and winked at her with a very ornery look on her face as Ash blushed, but Harper gave them both a dirty look, and they started giggling. Larson came back with a package and handed it to her.

Ash opened it, and the collection of *Sandstrider* fell out of the package, and her face lit up as she started immediately reading the first one.

"Great. She gets all excited over books. I thought it might be something sweet like a bracelet or something," Rachael said with a look of disbelief.

"What? Yuck. This is so much better," Ash replied with disgust.

She was still reading them when there was a buzz at the front door. Admiral Larson got up and opened the door with Rachael right behind him, purely out of curiosity. There was a middle-aged man in long white robes standing there, holding a strange-looking book. His head was shaved bald, and he had beads hanging down the front of him. A big grin spread across Larson's face when he spoke.

"Yes? Can I help you?" he said in a high-pitched tone, and Rachael looked at him strangely, wondering why he was talking so funny.

"Why, yes, good sir. I am here to spread the word about the temple of Esha and how he enlightens our lives through—" But the man didn't get to say more before Larson cut him off.

"Oh, stop right there. Let me get my husband. He'll want to hear this too," he said, again in the high-pitched tone and a wicked grin. Rachael fell down laughing. Ash dropped her books and started crying because she was laughing so hard, and Bridgett was leaning over the arm of one of the sofas with tears running down her face, laughing hysterically. Admiral Harper was the only one not amused, and he was yelling and cursing at Larson now with a bright-red face.

The eyes of the man whom Larson was talking to got huge, and when Larson turned to tell Harper to calm down, he made his escape, and Gerrard stepped out, looking down the street, and saw him running away. He then turned around and walked back into the house.

"Look, honey, you scared the nice man off," he said again in his high-pitched tone as the girls were still laughing hysterically, and finally, Harper had to chuckle as well, shaking his head.

"You are starting to scare me. I'll be making sure I lock my door tonight," Harper commented, which brought on another round of laughter.

Before long, the evening got late, and the girls had to get to bed, for tomorrow was the first day of school. Harper knew it was going to be a fun one. The girls all gave him and Larson a hug good night and then raced up the stairs, shoving and pushing one another to get to use the bathroom first. Larson watched them with a grin on his face and then looked over at Thomas.

"Hands down, they are a hell of a lot more trouble than boys. They are twice the handful," he said with a grin.

"I know, and the worse of it, they have no shame. They will get into a belching or farting contest with each other, and if that doesn't embarrass you, then they start telling you about all their female problems and changes they're going to be going through as they mature. You tell me, how is one suppose to reply to that, especially when one of those little insects is your own child?" Harper told him with a flustered expression.

Larson busted up laughing looking at his friend. It was great to see Harper finally lose some of his self-control, and what made it so funny was, it was thirteen-year-olds who were doing it. "Laugh it up. Next year will be your turn with them." Harper smirked wickedly.

"No way. Sharni's on her own with this one," Larson replied, putting his hands up in a gesture to ward off evil.

"You can't do that. They'll walk all over Sharni. She's too soft, especially when it comes to Ash, and that little stink knows she has her aunt in her hand, and Ash is the leader. The other two won't do anything without her approval," Harper said quietly, leaning a little toward Larson.

"Of course she does. She has us all eating out of her hands, especially you. She's a miniature Gail, and you know how Gail could manipulate anyone of us to do whatever she wanted with just a smile. It only stands to reason that her daughter would be the same way. Combine that with your determination and defiance and you have one very powerful little girl who knows it," Larson said, and Harper had to agree adamantly with him.

"I know, and that's what scares me, even more so than her other trait."

"I wouldn't worry about that much. She shows great restraint with it. They both do," Larson replied, now with a serious tone to his voice.

"Yeah. I was very impressed with Fâd's control. I didn't know how he would react with the news about Lily, but he never once powered up. Ash, though, I know uses hers when I'm not around and she's with her two friends. I had a private on the ship who had seen them in one of the cargo holds. Ash was levitating all three of them when she thought no one else was around. I didn't confront her but casually went over why we don't use it to try and reemphasize the danger."

"That's all you can do, Thomas. We can't be with them 24-7 and watch their every move. I know it's hard, but this is something we have to trust them with. It's a part of them that they will always have to hide, which you know firsthand too well."

"You're right. I'll have to believe she will do the right thing."

"She will. You and Gail raised her right," Larson responded with a sincere smile on his face.

"Well, you deserve a lot of credit yourself. You did just fine on your own raising Fâd. He's a very well-behaved boy, who I can tell is going to grow up to be a great man someday. You should be proud of him. He showed a maturity that most men didn't even show when confronted with bad news. I also need to confess something to you, and I don't want you to be mad with me until after you hear my reasoning."

"You told him everything about Sharni and me and Lily," Larson said, but he didn't seem mad.

"He had figured out a majority of it already. The only question he couldn't figure out was why you didn't marry Sharni and have a child with her. He's a smart kid, Gerrard, and understands a great deal more than we give him credit for."

"I know he is, and I thank you for telling him. I know I should have years ago, but I just couldn't find the words to say it. There's something I've never told anyone, but I want you to know. We've been friends way too long, and you have always been honest with me and told me all your secrets in trust. Sharni was pregnant when she went into that room. That's why she almost died in the hospital, which I think you might have known anyway. She refused to give up our baby, but the child was draining her, trying to survive too. I made the call to abort the pregnancy to save her. I killed my own child," Larson told Harper, who just sat there, looking at his friend.

Thomas couldn't help but feel pain for his friend, but Larson was right, he had known it all along. That night in the medical bay, he had sensed it right away and tried to help Larson in his choice. But to have to make that decision had to be eating away at his friend for years now.

"If it makes you feel better, I would have made the same decision without a moment's thought to save the woman I love."

"It does, but there's also a little bit that doesn't. I saved my mate and love, but I also took her only chance of having a child of her own. Plus, to this day, I wonder what our child would have been like."

"I'm sorry, but you always will with that. How does Sharni feel about your choice?" Harper asked him.

"She doesn't know. I never told her. She thinks that she lost the baby."

"You have to tell her. She deserves that. You can't let this secret remain between both of you. She blames herself, and that's not fair. You were faced with a choice, and you chose her. That's what she needs to know."

"I suppose your right, but I'm afraid I could lose her over it after all."

"You won't, remember, she chose you all those years ago when she was faced with a similar situation."

"True, but do you ever wonder what it would have been like if she chose you instead?"

"Honestly, yes, but then I would have never had Gail, whom I love with my whole being, or Ashley. No, Gerrard, this was how it was meant to be, and you can feel secure in the knowledge that Sharni will always love you."

"Thank you, Thomas. I wouldn't be here today if it weren't for you." Larson looked at his friend and smiled.

"Neither would I if you hadn't been there for me." Thomas smiled back with his eyes at his oldest and closest friend, who was more a brother to him. Larson grinned back, and they both got up and went to bed, but Thomas did lock his door just in case Larson did something ornery. Larson was known for his practical jokes, and Harper had been the recipient of those a lot over the years.

CHAPTER 17

MORNING CAME ON schedule, and Harper was up, getting breakfast ready for everyone, since that was his chore and since the girls had openly told him how his use of the replicator for lunch and dinner was terrible. He was trying to make something special, but it wasn't turning out right. Larson walked into the kitchen, still in his pajama bottoms.

"Damn it, I hate these things," Harper said, flustered at the replicator, as Larson walked over to where he was.

"What are you trying to make?"

"Keoish," Harper told him and started punching some more buttons.

"That's a watorian dish. Only watorians can make it and only with fresh ingredients," Larson replied, rolling his eyes.

"Bull. I've seen you make it plenty of times for breakfast."

"Not in a replicator. Move out of the way, and let the expert do it. Ash showed me how to use that thing, so I'm pretty sure I can do it now," Larson told him and started pushing his way to the replicator's controls.

"No. You can't even make a hamburger without help," Harper replied with a cocky smirk and held firm to his spot. Next thing, they were wrestling around in the kitchen, both trying to get to the replicator. The girls walked in, and their mouths fell open over seeing the grown men acting this way.

"Will you two grow up?" Ash yelled at them and walked over to the replicator and made them all hot cinnamon oatmeal. The men stopped immediately and looked at the girls, now annoyed that all their efforts had been for nothing, and once the oatmeal was done, they reluctantly took it out and served the girls, who started eating immediately.

"Another thing, from now on, Admiral Larson, you need to start wearing shirts as well instead of going without. We may be thirteen, but you with no shirt is causing problems with our young, impressionable minds, which isn't right, especially with you being our guardian," Rachael said matter-of-factly, and Larson turned bright red with embarrassment and hurried out of the kitchen to put a shirt on, coming back in fully clothed and still embarrassed.

"I see what you mean about making you feel uncomfortable with their comments," he said to Harper, who was drinking a cup of creo, nodding his head in agreement. The girls just ignored the men and finally finished, cleaned up their mess, and left the kitchen, grabbing their backpacks as they headed to the front door.

"Bye. Wish us luck," they yelled as they headed through the door.

"Behave, and no fighting on the first day," Harper yelled back at them, and they could now hear the girls giggling.

"So when do you think Baptise will be calling?" Larson looked at his friend as he poured himself a cup of creo.

"I give them at least half the day," Harper said nonchalantly.

Sure enough, Harper got called, but he made Larson go with him this time so he could get a taste of what he would be getting into next year. When they walked into the administration building, the girls were sitting there on the bench outside the professor's office. Ash had a fat lip, Rachael a bloody nose, and Bridgett a black eye. They were all holding cold packs on their faces, and when Larson saw them, he busted up laughing. But Harper gave him a dirty look, and he stopped.

They walked past the girls, and when Harper wasn't looking, Larson winked at them, which brought a grin to their faces. But when Harper looked back at them, they quickly acted scared again. He looked over at Larson, who had a stern look on his face now, and Harper narrowed his eyes at him.

They both walked into the office, and Professor Baptise was behind his desk, talking to someone on his comm. "Yes, Mr. Potts, I assure you, this will be dealt with properly. I resent that entirely, and may I point out that it was your child and her friends that started the whole incident and will be reprimanded as well. Don't push me, sir. This is my school, and if you do not approve of how I run it, there is also the public education system that might be more to your liking," Professor Baptise said to the person on the other line that only he could hear through his earpiece. He shut down his comm and turned to the admirals with a frown on his face.

"Admirals, I wasn't expecting both of you. It is good to see you again, Rear Admiral Larson, especially since it is under good terms in your case. Vice Admiral Harper, I'm afraid our meeting is the opposite. As you overheard and saw the results for yourselves, we have started off the school year with a bang. The girls are not totally to blame, but even though they didn't start it, they definitely finished it with two girls now in the infirmary, one with a broken arm and another with half her teeth gone," Professor Baptise told them with his hands folded in front of him.

Both admirals had shocked looks on their faces at the news this time, even Larson, who had been there many times himself over the boys, but the fights never got this bad. "I'm truly sorry about this. I will make sure that the girls' medical expenses are fully covered," Harper said, embarrassed.

"I know this is all new territory for you, and you as well, Admiral Larson, since I am aware of the arrangement that you will be taking over next year with the girls as their guardian. Let me help with some information about girls. They are nothing like boys, of course. They are a lot more hostile, vindictive, and when they fight, it is not the usual punch till a winner is clearly declared. Girls go for blood and to permanently maim their opponent. When you combine that attitude with the training of military skills, they become a miniature soldier, bent on destroying their enemy."

Harper leaned his head back in his chair and closed his eyes, and Larson actually looked scared. "I am very sorry. I will make sure that steps are taken so this never happens again," Harper told the professor humbly.

"I'm sure you will, and with their military training, I'm sure they will obey your orders. They honestly are great girls and, most of the time, well-behaved, but they have not learned control. I would have dealt with this one by myself like all the other times, but this is now different with them beginning their training. This is a military issue with you being their superior. so it must come from you for disciplinary action."

"I am in total agreement with you, and I will see that the proper action is taken," Harper replied in a cold tone, for now he was furious with the girls because they knew better.

"Forgive me, but did I hear you right? Did you say all the other times?" Larson spoke up, asking.

"Oh yes. There were a lot of them, and I only contacted the admiral when they were particularly bad, but I handled the lesser incidents." Harper just sat there now. His mood was getting worse by the minute.

"Might I ask what happened this time?" Larson said, sensing Harper's mood and that his friend was just about ready to explode from his rising anger.

"Of course. Like I said, it was not the girls' fault. About a dozen now fifteen-year-old girls decided to exact revenge on the three girls for the bathroom incident last year. When your three were changing in the locker room for PE, they ganged up on them. Being council-raised girls, they were unaware that sentinel children begin their training at the age of twelve instead of sixteen, like council does.

"Five of the girls got out and got help. Plus, they tried to pin everything on your three. But under further questioning, they broke out with the truth. I don't get too many female sentinel children here at the academy, mostly just boys, so this is a new one for me as well.

Your girls show extremely advanced skills for their young age, so I feel it is very important that we address this issue right now."

"I agree, and it will be. Thank you, Professor Baptise," Admiral Harper said, standing up, still boiling mad at the girls.

"Admirals, you will find there are still people out there that really do appreciate everything you do for us," Baptise said to them and half-smiled as the admirals nodded back to him. Larson headed out first, and Harper followed. They both had serious looks on their faces, for this was no joking matter now. The girls sat on the bench with scared expressions, looking up at the admirals when they walked out. Their faces instantly drained of color when they saw their looks.

"To the vehicle now!" Harper ordered in his commanding, cold tone, and the girls jumped up, half walking, half running, headed to the vehicle. They quickly climbed into the airlimo as both admirals climbed in behind them, and they left the school. The whole ride back, no one spoke a word; and once they pulled up to the house, both admirals got out and waited for the girls, who climbed out and headed into the house.

"Take your things to your rooms, and be back here immediately!" Harper ordered, and the girls obeyed.

He paced around the living room as Larson went and stood by the fireplace with his arms folded across his chest, waiting as well. The girls came back down the stairs, and Harper ordered them to sit, pointing at the sofa in front of him and Larson, and they did instantly, looking up at the two admirals.

"We're sorry, sir," Rachael said in a scared tone.

"Sorry is not an option. Right now, I want to take my belt off and blister all three of your backsides until you wouldn't be able to sit for days. Disciplinary actions must be taken. Imprisonment comes to mind, but I'm still leaning toward a good thrashing. No, you three will spend two hours a day for the next week down at the refugee center, doing community service. Do I make myself clear?" Harper glared at them, and they all nodded in agreement.

"I DON'T HEAR YOU!" he yelled at them, and they jumped at his cold, angry tone.

"YES, SIR!" they answered in unison.

"Dismissed," he ordered, and they left the room quickly as Larson came over to him.

"Good choice of punishment. They will definitely see firsthand what they did today coincides with what is really happening out there," Larson said to him.

"I know, and they'll have a few memories from it," Harper added.

"That they will."

The evening came and went, and the girls laid low and stayed in their room for most of it. They were surprised that they actually got to eat and not just bread and water, which they had figured on. Night came, and they went to bed, not looking forward to tomorrow at school but especially afterward when they would start their punishment.

They were up the next morning, and the admiral had breakfast ready for them, which they ate in silence. Once finished, they cleaned up and quickly left the house, catching the shuttle out front, which took them to school. At school, it was definitely different too. The kids avoided them like the plague. There was none of the usual taunts about being sentinel losers. Instead, everywhere they went, everyone whispered and watched them closely as they walked by. Even the older kids looked away when they walked by, and one time, they thought they saw Fâd and them, but they quickly headed down another hall, vanishing.

Ash and them were humiliated and walked around with their heads hanging down. They knew what they did was so wrong, and if they could take it back, they would in a heartbeat. Not only did they break the first rule of their training in maintaining control but they had also let down the admirals. It was especially tearing Ash up inside because she had let her father down.

Finally, school got out, and they were picked up by a refugee center shuttle and taken to a large building. The girls followed an older gentleman into the building and saw immediately all the destitute people there. There were families who had lost everything and elderly couples and even small children who had no one sitting around, waiting their turn for help.

The man led them down the long hallway where people were standing, waiting for help, to an office that read Supervisor beside the sliding door and ushered them in. A woman with gray hair that was pulled into a bun at the back of her head looked up at them with tired eyes. She was probably around the age of late sixties, maybe early seventies, but one could not know for sure, just on appearances, since everyone lived a lot longer now, and the fifties were considered middle age.

"So you're Admiral Harper and Admiral Larson's charges?"

"Yes, ma'am," the girls answered nervously.

"Then let's not beat around the bush. I know why you are here, and you will obey my orders. Understood?"

"Yes, ma'am."

"Good. I also want you three to remember this: All those people out there are here because of ones who refused to show control over their actions and chose the same route as the three of you did. Just because you may be the superior over your opponent doesn't mean you use that to its full potential. The better person is the one who can show control and restraint. Your training is to aid you and to help those weaker to protect them, not beat them up," she said to the girls with narrowed eyes, who all took big gulps and felt totally ashamed of their actions.

"Ben, take them to the medical wing and assign them as aides," she ordered the man who led them there. He nodded and had them follow. They walked through another hallway with more people waiting. Finally, they came to large double doors that had a red cross painted on the door, and it slid open when they approached. The smell of antiseptic hit them as they were now in a hospital ward.

There were nurses, orderlies, and doctors moving all through there. Plus, there were more injured people and children all over the place. There wasn't a room or a bed that remained empty for long. The man took them over to the main reception area and spoke to the head nurse, who looked over at the girls with a stern look. She then hollered at three nurses, two women and one man.

"Your aides are here," she told them, and the nurses looked at the girls, then walked over to them.

"My name is Mary. This is Lori, and his name is Bill. You, Rachael, are with me. Bridgett, you're with Lori, and, Ashley, you're with Bill. Tomorrow, when you come, just head straight here and find us. Now follow us, and we'll get you some uniforms," the one nurse said, and the girls followed them over to a supply room. The nurse called Mary handed each of them a green button-up shirt and green pull-up pants, which they put on over their clothes. Then each of them followed the nurse they were assigned to and started helping them make the rounds.

This was an eye-opener for the girls. They met many victims of merc attacks and even some lucky survivors—if you could call them that—of carian raids. Ash, in particular, had a very troubling one. Bill stopped outside one of the rooms and quietly spoke to Ash. "There's a little seven-year-old boy in here named Lonny. His dad is recovering from a merc attack on their colony in the voors nebula. He and his dad were the only ones who made it from their family. His mother and little sister didn't. I want you to be prepared for what you are about to see. The father took a real bad beating." Ash steadied herself, but it still wasn't enough for what she saw.

They walked in, and lying on the bed was what was once a man. He was hooked up to many machines and covered in bandages, and what was exposed of him was discolored or mangled flesh. Ash then saw a small boy about the age of seven sitting next to the bed, watching him, but he looked up when they walked in. He instantly looked at Ash and smiled at her, then over at Bill.

"How's he doing today, Lonny?"

"A lot better, Bill. He opened his eyes for a few seconds this morning," the little boy replied.

"Lonny, I want you to meet Ashley Harper. She's going to be helping me for a few days," Bill said, introducing Ash to him.

"Nice to meet you. Are you any relation to Vice Admiral Harper of the sentinel fleet?"

"Yes. He's my father," Ash replied shakily.

The little boy started crying then and went over and hugged Ashley tightly around the waist as she had tears running down her face and hugged him back. "Tell your father thank you. He saved us when the mercs attacked my home. If they hadn't gotten there, my father would also be dead right now. The mercs shot and killed my mother and sister, and when my father tried to fight back, they started beating him and wouldn't stop. Out of nowhere, sentinel soldiers appeared and saved the rest of us," the little boy told her.

Ash still had tears running down her face. She remembered this must have been the small incursion that happened just last month when she, Rachael, and Bridgett were still on the ship. The *Justification* responded to a distress call on one of the planets nearby, but her father never told her what had happened.

"We have to go, Lonny. I have other rounds, but I'll come back later and check on you, okay?" Bill told him as he closed his multi-tool after taking readings from the machines the little boy's father was hooked up to. He and Ash then walked out of the room, and Ash wiped tears from her face.

"Is his father going to be okay?"

"Yes, but it will take a long time for him to recover and many surgeries," Bill told her as they walked to the next room on his round.

The rest of the hour was the same—meeting survivors and helping the nurse clean and treat wounds or change bedding of patients. By the time their two hours were up, the girls all elected to stay another hour and continued to help. It definitely had an effect on them and now made them more determined to grow up and be the best they could and protect these people. Finally, the hour got late, and the admirals came to escort the girls home. But when they got there, they were instantly surrounded by thankful people.

They finally got to the hospital ward and met the girls at the main desk, talking to the nurses. When they walked in, everyone stood at attention and saluted them as the girls walked over. "Father, I want you to come with me. There's someone I want you to meet," Ash said and grabbed his hand. Rachael and Bridgett took Admiral Larson's hand because they had a couple of people they wanted him to meet as well.

Ash went into the room where Lonny was with her father behind her, who was dressed in his uniform. The little boy looked up from his father, and when he saw the admiral, his eyes got huge, and he stood immediately, saluting the admiral, who returned the gesture.

"Admiral, this is Lonny. He was one of the survivors over in the voors nebula. Lonny, let me introduce you to Vice Admiral Harper of the sentinel fleet," Ashley said with pride, and Lonny ran over to the admiral and wrapped his small arms around his legs. Harper leaned down, picked him up, and hugged him back, then looked over at the boy's father.

"How's your father doing?" he asked the little boy.

"Better now that you are here," Lonny said with eyes of hero worship in them.

"That's good to hear," Harper said and set the little boy down. Once again, the boy saluted him, and Harper returned the gesture. "Carry on, soldier," Harper said to him, and Lonny's face beamed with pride. Harper put his hand on Ash's back and guided her out of the room, but once they were on the other side of the door, Ash turned around and threw her arms around her father, hugging him tightly, and he hugged her back.

"I'm so sorry, Dad. I will make you proud of me."

"Ash, I have always been proud of you," he told her and hugged her again.

They then made some more rounds, and Ash introduced her father to many very appreciative people. Even a lot of the medical staff came up and met the admirals and were very awestruck with them. Then the lady with the gray hair walked in. "So this is what all the excitement is about. I should have known I would be seeing you two sooner or later. I just didn't know it would be this soon," she said and walked over and gave them both a big hug.

"It's good to see you again, Madeleine," Harper said to her.

"And you, Thomas. And I suppose you too, Gerrard, but I swear it was your fault my hair turned gray," she said, grinning at Admiral Larson.

"That's not my doing. It's from working all those years with Taylor," Gerrard corrected her and chuckled.

"Don't remind me. How is that ornery old fart doing?"

"Hasn't changed," Gerrard replied, rolling his eyes.

"Well, I'm sure you want to get these girls home. They did very well today and brought some freshness to this place. I look forward to having them back tomorrow," Madeleine told them and smiled at the girls.

"Thank you. We will be back right after school," Rachael said with a smile, and the other two nodded their heads.

"Great. We will see you then," she said and left the ward.

The admirals then nodded to the girls, and they led the way back through the ward doors and down the long hallway. There weren't nearly as many people there now, because most had been helped, but still a few were waiting their turn. Finally, they all went out the front doors and got into the waiting vehicle and headed back home.

"Admirals, thank you. That was the hardest thing we have ever had to do, but it was the greatest thing we have ever done," Bridgett told them, and Rachael and Ash agreed with her.

"Good. I hope you learned a lesson," Larson said to them.

"We most certainly did and then some," Ash replied.

"Yes, that was an eye-opener. We were those mercs, and even though those girls attacked us, they, in honesty, were the victims because we didn't show restraint. We were mercenaries beating up defenseless colonies," Rachael added.

"Yeah, which will never happen again," Bridgett spoke up.

"It better not, because I'm still thinking a good beating would also help," Harper said with a slight smirk, and the girls all gulped loudly knowing he was serious.

CHAPTER 18

THE REST OF the week went without incident, and the girls got to where they looked forward to going and helping at the refugee center. They made a lot of friends, and the people there enjoyed their company. Of course, they still were the outcasts at school, but now they didn't care anymore. And when they got teased, they completely ignored them. Soon, the weekend was upon them, and Admiral Harper and Admiral Larson decided a celebration was in order for good behavior. Larson invited the boys over, but they said they couldn't come because they had a lot of homework to do, so it was just the admirals and the girls.

They decided to take a hike up in the mountains nearby and have a picnic. All of them had packs on and were hiking up a steep trail when Ash felt a stinging sensation on her back. She reached back, but there was nothing there, so she kept on going. Finally, an hour later, they all got to a nice, grassy meadow surrounded by trees and sat down for a picnic. They were all laughing and joking when Ash started feeling warm. She peeled off her jacket, but that didn't help. Numbness started at her feet, and she could feel it slowly crawl up her body as she stood up.

"Dad, I don't feel right," she said, and suddenly, her eyes rolled to the back of her head. She started to collapse, but Admiral Larson caught her before she fell. Harper was over by them in a flash, and he started checking her all over. Then he noticed blood on Larson's arm where Ash was lying across. He pushed her up against Larson and saw the back of her shirt stained with blood. Both men quickly removed her clothes down to her undergarment, and her back was covered in it, and they now found a swollen tiny pinprick on her back where the blood had come from. Harper jumped up and got on his comm link, calling for a med evac team, as Larson continued to hold Ash tightly to him.

"Thomas, she can't go to New Guinea hospital. It's council run. You can't risk them finding out about her kinetics," Larson told him.

Thomas nodded his head in understanding because of Ash's kinetics and called Pantier med for an evac team. Ash, in the meantime, had stopped breathing, as did her heart, and Larson laid her on the ground immediately and started CPR on her as Thomas pulled out a first aid kit from his pack and a very long syringe from it. He pulled another vial out and filled the syringe and instantly plunged it into Ash's chest to help start her heart again with the pure adrenaline that was in the vial, and Larson began compressions again. Ash started breathing finally but weakly, and Larson continued with the CPR and breathing for her and then alternating with Harper. They both knew it was all that was keeping her heart beating right now and her lungs going.

Seven minutes later, they heard the siren of the medvac shuttle, and it landed a few feet from them. Dr. Taylor was the first one out and ran over with a large med pac with him. "What happened?"

"She's been stung," Harper said, fighting back the panic that was building inside him.

Dr. Taylor immediately hooked Ash up to a heart defibulator and then ran tubes down her nose, hooking them up to a portable respirator to keep her lungs going. Once the defibulator took over, shocking her heart every so often to keep it pumping and her breathing on the respirator, he rolled her over on her side and examined the wound.

"Vaquit, but they're not attracted to humans, only energy sources," Dr. Taylor said, and then he and Harper looked at each other.

"Kinetics," they both said at the same time.

"Harper, there's no antidote for this. All I can do is keep pumping her with methodicerine, but even then, I have to be careful to not overdo that, or it will damage her organs."

"Do it, anything, just save my daughter," Harper said as his eyes now watered up. Dr. Taylor pulled out a syringe and filled it with the methodicerine and injected it into Ashley. Then he pulled another syringe and filled it with some other medication and also injected it into her. "What was that one?" Harper asked him.

"A nueralizer. We can't have her unleashing a kinetic surge while she's unconscious," Taylor said, and Harper agreed. The doctor worked on her some more, and by the time he had her stabilized, Ash had machines hooked up to her and tubes coming out of her nose and many IVs. Paramedics came over and carefully lifted Ash onto a floating stretcher and headed to the medvac shuttle with Harper and Dr. Taylor following. Harper looked back at Larson when he climbed into the shuttle, and Larson nodded in understanding.

The shuttle lifted off, and then Rachael and Bridgett finally lost it and broke down bawling. Larson gathered them up in his arms and held them tightly, and once they got their crying under control, they all gathered up everything and quickly headed down the trail to the waiting vehicle. On the way down, Larson contacted the boys and told them what had happened; and by the time they got back to the house, the boys were already there, waiting for them, and you could tell they were visibly shaken up, especially Fâd, who turned pale white when he saw his father's bloody shirt and started yelling at everyone to hurry up and was rather mean.

Instead of going inside to change out of the bloody shirt, Larson headed straight to the spaceport and Harper's shuttle. He and the kids rushed through the terminal, and he went up to the desk and got clearance as the kids raced out to the shuttle bay and into the shuttle. Nathan jumped into the pilot's seat and had the shuttle already fired up when Larson climbed in, and the admiral just strapped in beside him. Fâd and Cory made sure that Bridgett and Rachael were buckled up. Nathan lifted off faster than Harper ever did and banked the shuttle toward Pantier, firing the boosters before they had even cleared the port.

He maneuvered through air traffic as if it was nothing, and Larson looked scared to death but said nothing, and in no time, the boy had them moving at an unbelievable speed toward Pantier. He was amazed by the young boy's skills with the shuttle and knew he was looking at a future great pilot. Larson then got on the comm and made a call to Krios. "This is Rear Admiral Larson. Come in, Captain Tol Vasna."

A few minutes went by, and Sharni's voice came over the comm. "This is Captain Tol Vasna. Hey, good lookin'. What's up?"

"Sharni, there's been an accident. Ash got stung by a vaquit and went into cardiac arrest. She's been flown to Pantier med, but her prognosis doesn't look good."

Sharni screamed in pain through the comm link. "No, not Ash. Don't tell me this, Gerrard. I'm coming now, and don't you dare let her die. I can't lose her too."

"I know. None of us can," Gerrard replied, and the comm went silent.

The girls were crying again, and Cory and Fâd unbuckled and went over, putting their arms around them to try and comfort them, but even the boys were fighting with their emotions right now. In no time, Nathan banked the shuttle around and brought it down in a hurry; but amazingly enough, they landed with barely a bump. He shut down, and everyone unbuckled and quickly climbed out of the shuttle, and they all took off running across the landing pad to the terminal doors.

Nera met them inside and followed, and they all ran to the vehicles she had already waiting for them. The vehicles took off and raced toward the med clinic, pulling up in front. The doors of the hover car had barely opened as the vehicle shut down when everyone piled out and ran into the clinic. The receptionist at the front desk pointed to a hallway when she saw them, and they all ran down it to a large nurses' station, and one could tell this area of the medical hospital was the critical care wing.

They now saw Dr. Taylor and Vice Admiral Harper standing outside a room, talking, and Larson and Nera walked over to them as the kids stood back a little with scared looks on their faces, waiting for news, except Fâd, who was pacing back and forth, watching the adults.

"Ash is stable, but she's not improving. Right now, the machines are keeping her heart beating and breathing for her. All we can do is wait and see what happens," Harper told Larson in a weak voice.

"Surely with all our knowledge and medical breakthroughs there's something we can do?" Larson asked, ready to lose it any second.

"We are, Gerrard. The methodicerine we have her on is what we use to treat allergic reactions to insect bites. Of course, it was not designed to treat a sting from a vaquit. The other problem I'm facing is I also have to keep her system suppressed due to her kinetic powers, which isn't helping her," Dr. Taylor told him.

"Can I see her?" Larson asked, and Harper took him into the room.

Ash laid there, perfectly still, with the constant beeping of the defibulator and monitors that were reading her heart rate and keeping it going. He noticed that it was extremely weak and also that her temperature was skyrocketing. Even the respiratory equipment would make a steady whooshing sound as it kept her lungs moving air in and out, and she had an IV in each arm, hooked up to machines as well, and tubes running through her nose, down into her lungs.

Larson walked closer and held her hand, and he could feel how hot it was, but he also noticed she was completely white. Her lips were almost a gray color now with black circles under her closed eyes. He looked over at Harper, who was trying to remain strong, but he could see the pain and fear behind his eyes.

"She's going to come out of this, Harper. She's got to," Larson said quietly.

"I know. I can't lose her, Gerrard. She's all I have left of Gail and my life."

"I know."

The two men stood there for a little while longer, watching her, and then went out and allowed the kids to come in. Rachael and Bridgett broke down immediately, and Nera and Larson carried them out to the waiting room. Even the boys' faces were pale white, and they were fighting hard not to lose it. But out of them all, Fâd looked the worse. He finally turned and left the room in a hurry, but instead of stopping at the waiting room with the rest of them, he disappeared entirely. Admiral Harper came back with the other two boys and walked into the waiting room.

"Where's Fâd?" Larson asked them, looking around.

"Didn't he come back here?" Harper asked, bewildered.

"No."

"He left us a few minutes ago. I thought he was coming back here," Nathan said, worried about his friend.

Larson got up and started to leave, but Nera stopped him. "Leave him alone, Gerrard. He's just really upset about his friend and needs some time to get his feelings under control."

"What do you mean get his feelings under control? Wouldn't it be better being around family and friends, then?"

"Not these feelings. You know him, he's not one to openly share or show how he feels, so don't concern yourself so much about him right now. He'll come back and be fine."

"Damn it, Nera, when it comes to my son, it is my concern," Larson said, and you could see the warning on his face and in the tone of his voice.

"Not this," Nera said back with narrowed eyes.

"Is there something you're not telling me?"

"Larson, just let it go. When it is time, you will know."

"Well, at least tell me he's not going to go and do something stupid or hurt himself."

"No, he just needs some time to think, that's all. He'll be back."

"All right. I will hold you to that, but I don't like not knowing."

"Don't worry, Fâd will be fine." Nera smiled weakly at him and held Bridgett, who was still sobbing but quietly to herself. Rachael was over on a bench, looking out a window, crying to herself, and

Nathan went over and sat down next to her, putting his arm around her. She leaned her head against his shoulder, still sobbing quietly.

The day wore on, and everyone stayed in the waiting room. Every so often, one of the adults would go and check on Ash and then come back and report; and every time, there was no change. Eventually, night came, and they still hadn't seen Fâd either. By now, Larson was starting to get worried and was pacing around the waiting room, looking over at Nera with a dirty look, but she would just smile and see that the children were taken care of.

It was very late when Fâd returned to the hospital, and he headed straight to Ash's room. He walked past the waiting room where everyone was, and no one saw him go by. He entered Ash's room and saw her still lying there with no change and walked over and sat down on the edge of the bed, taking one of her hands in his.

"Ash, you have to get better. Fight this. You have never backed down from a fight. You can't do this now. I tried to fight it, but I can't. You have to come back to me." He then leaned down and softly kissed her gray lips, and as he pulled away, a blue arch of kinetic energy passed between them both. Fâd felt a momentary weakness in himself as if his energy had been drained, but then it went away.

Instantly, the heart monitor started beeping more rapidly as Ash's heart rate began to pick up. Even her temperature was dropping quickly, and you literally could see color spread across her pale-white skin. Suddenly, her eyes flew open, looking straight at Fâd, and she started thrashing as she gasped for air.

Fâd jumped up in a flash, standing beside her bed, holding her down so she wouldn't injure herself, not knowing what else to do, as alarms went off in the room. Out of nowhere, medical personnel raced in, pushing him aside as they attended a now conscious Ash, who was starting to power up with kinetic energy. Harper ran in and saw Fâd over in the corner and a now glowing blue Ash, and he instantly burst into blue kinetic energy as his eyes glowed brilliant blue, and he put the whole room into containment. Even each person working on her was in their own kinetic containment barrier from Harper, and he yelled at Fâd, "Fâd, I need you to put a barrier on Ash so she's contained."

Fâd's eyes instantly glowed blue, and he was now covered in the same blue kinetic energy, and a field formed around him and Ashley. Larson was outside the room, and he and Nera pushed everyone away from the room in case the containment barriers that Harper and Fâd were doing didn't hold. Larson could see Ash continue to build in power, and she was glowing brilliant blue all over now, and then a blinding flash happened.

Fâd grabbed his head in pain, and everyone else covered their eyes. But he held the barrier on her, and she started finally coming down and now breathing normally, as all the tubes and needles were gone from her. Harper started to lower the shields he had on the room and everyone in it but for Fâd and Ash's, which Fâd had control over. "It's okay, Fâd. You can let go now," he told the boy. Fâd's eyes returned to normal, and the blue kinetic energy disappeared from him and Ash.

Dr. Taylor was checking Ash, who was sleeping soundly now after her kinetic episode, and looked over at Harper. He smiled and nodded his head that she was going to be okay. The admiral let out the breath he was holding and threw his head back in relief and looked over to where Fâd was, but the boy was gone. He turned to Larson, who had come in the room now. "Where did he go?"

"He just ran past us. I tried to stop him, but he threw my hand off and kept running."

"Whatever he did, he saved her life," Harper told Larson.

They both looked toward the direction that Fâd had gone and then back at each other. Now the girls were crying again because they were happy, and even Cory had tears in his eyes. Nathan had his arm around Rachael's shoulder, crying right along with her.

"I'll take the kids back to the house so they can get some sleep, and then I'll come back and check on you and Ash," Larson told him, and Harper nodded. They both put their hands on each other's shoulders, and a silent thank-you passed between them.

* * *

It was two hours later, and Harper was sitting in a chair next to the bed where Ash was sleeping. He was watching every breath she took when he heard a noise behind him and saw Fâd standing in the door, also watching her.

"She's going to be okay. Thank you for saving her," Harper said without looking at him.

"I didn't do anything," Fâd said and walked into the room and stood next to the bed, watching her sleep.

"Yes, you did. You called her back because only you could."

Fâd looked over at the admiral. "How could I call her back?" he replied defiantly.

Harper looked at the boy standing in front of him with no emotion showing on his face. "You know why. That's why you came back." Fâd didn't say anything but continued to watch Ash. Harper got up and headed to the door, then turned and looked at Fâd. "Can you stay with her for me?" he asked the boy with an exhausted half smile on his face.

Fâd nodded his head yes and walked over to Ash's bed, pulling the chair even closer to the bed, and sat down, watching her closely. Harper looked at her one more time knowing that Fâd would never let any harm ever come to Ash again and left the room with a slight smirk on his face. It didn't take him long to get to Larson's house, driving the hover vehicle that was left for him. Larson was still up, drinking a cup of creo with Nera.

"What are you doing here? Who's with Ash?" Larson asked, surprised and worried.

"Fâd."

"Fâd? I was wondering where he was. I was getting worried about him. I'll go and relieve him so he can come home and get some sleep." Larson got up and started for the door.

"No, leave him there. He wants to stay," Harper told Larson.

"I understand. They are good friends, and he was pretty upset when it wasn't looking too good," Larson said, but Nera and Harper looked at each other knowing the truth.

CHAPTER 19

———⚬❦⚬———

THOMAS AND GERRARD walked into Ash's room early in the morning to check on her and Fâd. She was still sleeping soundly, and Fâd was asleep in the chair, leaning against the bed with his head on it, holding her hand. Larson looked over at Harper with suspicious eyes, but Harper ignored him. Dr. Taylor came in and saw them looking at the kids and whispered, "He's been like that all night, and Ash had a good night as well. The way she keeps going, she should be able to leave soon."

Just then, Fâd woke up; and when he saw the adults, he jumped up nervously. "It's okay, son. Why don't you go home and get something to eat and clean up some?" Gerrard told his son.

Fâd looked back at Ash then and over at them. "She's going to be fine and possibly go home soon," Harper told him, and Fâd then left the room as Harper and Larson watched him.

Larson looked over at Harper. "Do you think—"

"Yes," Harper replied coldly, and Dr. Taylor spoke up too.

"Of course he did. Can't you tell? Imprinting can happen even as early as thirteen."

Both Harper and Larson gave him a dirty look then, and the doctor just shrugged his shoulders and walked out of the room. They both stayed in the room, sitting with Ash, but every so often, one of them would go and get each of them a cup of creo.

* * *

It was now around the middle of the day, and they both were standing in the doorway, watching all the nurses and doctors go about their duty, when they heard a weak voice behind them and spun around quickly. Ash was awake, making a face and smacking her tongue as if she had a bad taste in her mouth. Both men quickly went over to both sides of her bed, watching her.

"How do you feel, Ash?" her father asked her anxiously.

"Like a shuttle landed on me."

"Is there anything we can get you?" Larson asked.

"A shake would be nice and some chocolate brittle," Ash said with a very weak grin.

"I don't think you should be eating any sweets right now, but a shake probably wouldn't hurt," Harper answered with a smile on his face.

Just then, Sharni burst through the door. She looked like she had just flown through hell and back. Her uniform was a mess, her long blond hair was everywhere, and her white eyes—she didn't have her gold contacts on—were completely red from crying, and she had a frantic look on her face. When she saw Ash awake, she ran over to Gerrard and fell into his arms, bawling loudly. He held her tightly for a few minutes, then she pushed away from him and jumped on the bed, pulling Ash into her arms, crying some more.

"Ow, Aunt Sharni, watch the back," Ash said, grimacing, as her aunt held her tightly to her. Sharni released her a little, moved the hospital gown away from her back, and looked at the injured area. Even Gerrard and Harper took a look now, and they all saw the sting mark. It was well-pronounced with a large red lump and what looked like a black spot in the center of it.

"What are they going to do about it?" Sharni asked Harper.

"Dr. Taylor said they will have to open it up and remove the stinger plus the cyst that has formed under the skin."

"Taylor, that quack. I wouldn't let him touch her with any sharp instrument," Sharni said out loud.

"I heard that, you cold-blooded vatorian. I'll remember that next time I have to save your life," Dr. Taylor said when he walked in with a tray of medical instruments.

"What are you going to do?" Sharni asked and pulled Ash closer to her in a protective manner, glaring at the doctor.

"I've got to remove the cyst and stinger. There's no other way. I promise I won't let anything happen to her," Dr. Taylor said to Sharni, annoyed.

"I'm not leaving her!" Sharni said adamantly.

"Fine, then have her lay across your lap so I have access to her back. Hopefully, I won't slip and take your leg off," Dr. Taylor said in an annoyed tone still.

"That won't be the first time you take something of mine," Sharni snapped back with narrowed eyes, but Dr. Taylor said nothing to her remark. Harper looked over at Larson, and he looked at him and nodded his head yes, answering his unspoken question.

The doctor gave Ash a numbing shot, and she didn't even flinch, and when he was sure that she was completely numb around the area, he handed Sharni a towel and took out a laser scalpel. He neatly and carefully started cutting along the side of the welt, and milky-white fluid started coming out of the incision.

"Sharni, keep that wiped up. I don't want it getting on anything else. It's infection," Dr. Taylor told her and continued to cut as Sharni kept the fluid soaked up, following right behind him. Finally, he put the knife down and grabbed two long-handled tweezers. With one, he lifted the skin up, exposing the dark-red cyst under it with a splinter-looking long black stinger directly in the center of it, and gave her another shot near the incision, numbing it all again.

"Gerrard, grab that vial for me and hold it over here so I can put the cyst in it."

"Are you serious? Where are your nurses? Shouldn't they be in here to help with this?" Gerrard had a look of disgust on his face.

"Just shut up and do it. As for a nurse, I don't use those scatter-brains if I don't have to," Dr. Taylor scolded him, and Larson grabbed the vial reluctantly and held it for the doctor. Harper was now holding Ash's hands as he nervously watched.

"Okay, Ash, this is the tricky part. I have to cut the cyst away without rupturing it because it is full of poison, and with the small area of exposed flesh, it could enter back into your bloodstream again and put you right back where you were, so I need you to hold extremely still no matter what. Can you do that for me?" Dr. Taylor asked her, and it was very apparent how serious this was by the look on his face.

"No, you're not going to do it. Can't you just leave it in? Won't the body finally break it down?" Sharni asked now. Panic was starting to enter her voice again.

"No. This is pure poison. The body can't fight poison. If I leave this in, it will kill her for sure in time."

"I can do it, Doctor. Just get it over with," Ash said, taking a deep breath.

"Thomas, there's got to be some other way." Sharni looked at him, pleading.

"Sharni, there isn't," Harper said to her.

"Gerrard, don't let him. Don't let him take another one away from me," Sharni said, now crying and pleading, looking at Larson, still holding Ash to her.

"Sharni, I told him to. I made the choice. It was either you or the baby, and I chose you," Larson said to her. Sharni's mouth fell open in shock as she let Ash lie down across her lap. Dr. Taylor said nothing and looked down at Ash and gave her a nod, and she nodded back.

"Sharni, don't move," Dr. Taylor told her, and she froze, still in a daze.

Dr. Taylor carefully grabbed the cyst with a pair of tweezers and moved it ever so carefully so he could cut it free with the laser scalpel. It was firmly attached to Ash's flesh, and when he started cutting, Harper, without realizing what he was doing, gripped Ash's hand tighter, but Ash just lay there, not feeling a thing. Blood started running from the incision, and Sharni regained her senses and blotted it up. Finally, it was free, and the doctor carefully put it in the vial Larson was holding, who looked almost sick to his stomach now. Larson quickly capped the vial and set it down on the tray, wiping his hands on his pants as if he had gotten some of the poison on them. Everyone relaxed and let out the breath they were holding, except Ash, who didn't seemed fazed at all.

Sharni was now looking at Larson with tears in her eyes, and once the doctor had Ash stitched back up and bandaged, she released Ash, climbing off the bed, and left the room. Gerrard went after her, finally catching her outside the hospital.

"Sharni, please, we need to talk about this."

"All these years, I blamed myself for losing our child when it was you," she said with pain in her tone, pacing around in front of the hospital.

"I had to. You were dying. The baby was killing you. You didn't have the strength to keep yourself and the baby alive. I had to make a choice to save you or save our baby, and I chose you, and if I were given that choice again, I will choose you every time. If I could have given my life to save you both, I would have done it instantly. But unfortunately, that wasn't an option. I will understand if you hate me now and don't ever want to see me again, but just know, I will always love and need you," Larson said, walking over to where she was standing, looking down at her with wet eyes.

Sharni just stood there for a few seconds, then finally broke down sobbing and fell into his arms. He held her tightly against himself, stroking her long blond hair and leaning his head down on hers. "I would never want you to die for me. I couldn't live without you. If I were faced with a similar choice, I will always choose you too," Sharni said, lying against his chest, and all the anguish she had carried for so long finally left her as he held her and kissed the top of her head and continued to hold her tightly.

"Then marry me. I can't go on without you anymore," Larson asked her, and she looked up at him as he watched her face. She studied his face for a few seconds, then threw her arms around his neck, and their lips met in a loving kiss.

"Yes," she whispered against his lips, and he grinned and then kissed her, long and passionate.

They finally got control of their emotions and talked things out, and a couple of hours later, they went back into the hospital and to Ash's room. Dr. Taylor was back in there, talking to Admiral Harper and Ash, telling them how to care for the wound.

"Dr. Taylor, I owe you a great apology," Sharni said to him humbly.

"No, you don't. I wasn't going to wait much longer and would have done it anyway to save your life," Dr. Taylor said to her and walked off as if this was normal for him. Sharni just stood there with her mouth wide open again as Harper started shaking his head, a slight smirk at the corner of his mouth. Even Larson was a little floored by the doctor's statement and looked over at Harper.

"He has absolutely no couth."

"Nope, and never will have," Harper replied, emotionless. He then helped Ash to start getting dressed, handing pants to her, but she was very weak, and he had to put them on her. Sharni came over and buckled them up and then put her socks on her. "Your shirt and undergarment got cut up, so you're going to have to wear that gown for now. We can get you something back at the admiral's house when we get there," Harper told his daughter.

A nurse came in with discharge orders on a datapad, then gave the admiral pills and some more bandages and ointment for the wound. Harper handed them to Larson and then scooped Ash up in his arms as Sharni grabbed Ash's shoes, and they all left the hospital. He carried her through the hallway and then, finally, outside, where it was now very dark. Larson's vehicle was parked out there, and they all climbed in, and Larson drove to his house.

They pulled up, and all the kids came running out with Nera behind them, and when they saw Ash in the vehicle, Rachael and Bridgett started crying and ran over to her. Even the boys, except Fâd, also ran over. Fâd slowly walked over to the vehicle but stood back quietly as everyone asked Ash all kinds of questions. Harper got out of the vehicle, still with Ash in his arms, and carried her up the steps and onto the porch as everyone followed. Ash made Harper stop and turn around.

"Hi, Fâd," she said to him, and he nodded back to her, then Harper carried her inside. Sharni walked up now and gave Fâd a big hug, and he hugged her back with a smile on his face.

The girls hurried and made a place on the sofa for her, and Harper laid her down, and they wrapped her up with a blanket. The kids all crowded around her, but Fâd went upstairs to his bedroom, and the door shut behind him. Ash started telling them all about the cyst and describing it in detail to them, making Bridgett actually gag. The adults went into the kitchen, and Sharni and Nera made everyone something to eat. It was a watorian dish and very delicious. Ash only could handle a little, and soon, she fell asleep, and Harper laid her down on a sleeper in the living room.

The hours had flown by, and it was very late when Larson and Harper pulled out the other sleeper. Rachael and Bridgett climbed into it, and Larson covered them up with Ash still sound asleep. "Thank you, Admirals, for saving Ash," Rachael and Bridgett said and then closed their eyes, and in no time, they were asleep. The boys had already gone to bed, and then so did Sharni and Larson. Harper stayed up and went into the kitchen, pouring himself a cup of creo, and just stared out the window, watching the night sky that started just past the tree line. He finally let relief wash over him, closing his eyes and moving his shoulders around, making them pop from all the tension and stress he had been under.

Nera came up and stood beside him, also sipping on a cup of creo and looking outside as he looked down at her. "I'm glad she's all right," she said quietly so the girls wouldn't wake up in the other room.

"So am I. I don't know what I would have done without her."

"You would have gone on living like the rest of us do. I still remember when my son and husband were killed all those years ago in that large explosion. It seems like just yesterday sometimes. The pain comes flooding back at times, just like it did the day it happened, yet I'm still here, living day to day, as are you. That's all we can do," Nera told him, looking up at him. Harper looked down at her now and instantly pulled her into his arms. Their lips found each other's.

* * *

Many hours later, Nera pulled on her clothes and slipped out of Thomas's room. She carefully crept through the house so as not to wake the girls, who were still sound asleep on the sofas, and went out the front door just as the sun was coming up over the trees.

CHAPTER 20

LARSON GOT UP and went into the kitchen to make some breakfast for everyone. He pulled out many different items from the refrigerator and fired up the gas stove and started cutting items up. The difference with watorians was, they grew all their own food and raised their own meat, not to mention they cooked, cleaned, and did everyday things by hand without relying on technology to do it for them. They were technologically advanced but preferred to apply it all to their ships and their medical and agriculture advancement. Granted, a lot of the things in the homes were automated, but a lot of things weren't either.

The girls started stirring when they smelled the food cooking, and soon, they all got up. Ash was still in her hospital gown but without her pants on since her father had removed them for her when she fell asleep last night so she would be a lot more comfortable. Bridgett and Rachael were once again wearing one of Sharni's nightshirts, and when Ash walked into the kitchen, they followed her and started giggling.

"What's so funny?" Ash glared at them.

"Your gown is open all the way down in the back, and we can see your blue underwear." Rachael giggled, as did Bridgett. Ash quickly gathered the gown tighter around herself and started grinning. They made it to the kitchen, and all three climbed up on a barstool and watched Admiral Larson fixing breakfast.

"That smells great. What is it?" Bridgett asked him.

"Corcarrie," he replied.

"What's in it?" Ash asked.

"Nothing you would recognize, but trust me, you'll like it," he said with a grin and winked at them.

Harper came out of his room, pulling on one of Larson's casual shirts, and walked into the kitchen and poured himself some creo. He walked over and smelled the food cooking in the pan while Larson was making something that looked like flat bread and frying it up on a large griddle.

"Smells good. You'll make someone a great wife someday," Harper teased, and Larson threw one of the dough balls at him, which Harper caught easily in the air and threw back at him. "Ash, we need to treat your back. Where do you want me to do it at?" her father asked.

"We can do it right here," Ash said, and her father walked back to his room and came back with a med kit. Rachael opened the back of the gown and pulled the side away, exposing the bandaged wound on Ash's back. The boys came around the corner then, and they all were curious to see it as well. All the kids huddled around Ash as Admiral Harper removed the bandage, and the kids at once started gagging and saying how gross it was.

"Actually, it looks really good compared to yesterday. The swelling and redness have gone down a lot, and it's starting to scab already," Harper told them, and Larson came over and took a peek and agreed with him.

"Well, I know it itches like crazy now," Ash said, rotating her shoulder to try and stop the itching.

"Don't do that. You'll tear out the epiderm stitches," her father got on to her.

"How many do I have?"

Rachael leaned in closer and counted. "Thirteen."

"Ha, I finally beat you, Bridgett," Ash said, grinning at Bridgett. She had beat her on this a couple of years ago when she cut herself real bad on an access panel they were removing to sneak into their classroom after school was over to get Rachael's datapad she forgot and needed.

"That's not fair. You win at everything," Bridgett said, irritated.

"That's not true. Ash sucks at schoolwork, and I'm a much better shot than her," Rachael said, holding her head up with pride.

"True. I always best her in class." Bridgett grinned.

"Okay, enough with the beat Ash talk. I'm wounded here, guys. You're supposed to take pity on me and help me," she said with a fake wounded look on her face. They all looked at one another, including the boys, and agreed that wasn't going to happen.

Admiral Harper applied the ointment and then put new bandages back on the wound, and Bridgett closed up her gown for her. Larson got breakfast done and made Ash a plate just for her. "Here, Ashley, I'll help you," he said, mocking the other kids, and they all looked at him and rolled their eyes.

"Thank you. At least someone cares about me," Ash said and acted like she was hurt by her friends.

"Oh, please. That is so fake. You can do better than that," Fâd said with a half smirk and went over and fixed himself a plate as Ash started giggling. Everyone had gotten their plates fixed when Sharni came walking out in her pajamas, rubbing her eyes.

"My eyes feel like someone had dumped a load of dirt in them," she said and yawned real big, then rubbed her white eyes, and everyone now saw them and grinned.

"So, Sharni, should we tell them?" Larson grinned at her, and she smiled back.

"Go ahead," she said and went and fixed herself a plate.

"I asked Sharni to marry me, and she accepted," Larson said with a big grin.

"That's so awesome," Rachael said excitedly.

"All right, Aunt Sharni," Ash said and jumped off her stool and ran over to her aunt, wrapping her arms around her waist.

"It's about time," Fâd said, again with a half smirk, and took another bite of his breakfast but then started choking suddenly. Everyone looked at him as he was now laughing, coughing, and pointing at Ash. She looked down at herself and realized her gown was once again wide open in the back, and everyone could see her underwear. She turned bright red and started giggling, pulling the gown tight around herself, which made everyone else start laughing.

"Okay, the laugh at Ash session is over now. Let's get back to more exciting news than my exposure," Ash said and looked up at her aunt.

"So when are you actually getting married?" Bridgett asked with a grin on her face.

"We haven't quite set a date yet," Sharni told them.

"You haven't or tentatively have? Which is it?" Nathan asked them with a mouth full of food.

Larson frowned at him and shook his head, then looked down at Sharni as she came up and wrapped her arms around him, and Ash headed back over to her stool. "We haven't. I just barely asked her last night," Larson told them.

Harper was the only one who didn't say a thing but just sat there with a slight smile, watching his best friend and sister-in-law, and he was happy for them. The kids were still grilling them when Nera walked into the house and came into the kitchen, pouring herself a cup of creo. "So what's all the chatter about?" she asked as she took a sip of her creo, leaning up against the counter, watching everyone.

"Sharni and Admiral Larson are getting married," Cory told her.

"Congratulations. It's about time," Nera said with a big grin on her face, looking over at them.

"Yeah, but they haven't set a date yet," Bridgett told her.

"But at least they finally decided to get married. That's a first step. Finally. It took them long enough," Nera said, still grinning.

"You really need to find a man. Maybe then you wouldn't be so critical," Larson told his cousin with a frown on his face.

"Had one," Nera said with a devious grin as she took a drink of her creo, but it was Harper who now choked on his creo, spitting it out across the table. Everyone looked over at him, and they could tell he was embarrassed by what he had just done.

Bridgett handed him a towel as he continued to cough a little and started wiping up the creo. "Dad, are you okay?" Ash asked him, a little concerned.

"Yeah, it just went down the wrong way," Harper replied, but he wouldn't look up and continued to clean up his mess. Larson looked back at his cousin now and looked her in the eyes. She just continued drinking her creo like nothing happened. He figured it out, and a slight wicked grin spread across his face.

"Well, we had better get back to New Guinea. The kids already missed one day of school," Larson said, and everyone got up, but the kids took care of the cleanup in the kitchen as the adults straightened up the rest of the house. Sharni gave Ash a shirt to wear, which looked like a dress on her, but at least it was better than the hospital gown.

Finally, everything was cleaned up, and everyone was ready to go. They all left the house and climbed into the vehicles and drove to the terminal, walking through it as Larson got clearance. The kids all went out and climbed into the shuttle, but Harper and Sharni waited outside it for Larson. Nera had followed Harper and Sharni over to the shuttle, and Harper turned around, looking down at her.

"If you ever come to New Guinea, stop by. You're welcome anytime," Harper told her with no emotion at all as Larson came out of the terminal and over to them, giving his cousin a hug. Then Sharni, Harper, and Larson climbed into the shuttle as Nera left for the terminal, and Nathan was again in the pilot's seat, firing up the shuttle.

"Are you kidding me?" Harper asked, looking at the boy, as Larson climbed into the copilot seat next to Nathan.

"Trust me, he's good," Larson replied, grinning.

Harper went and sat down in one of the seats next to Ash as the rest of the kids buckled up, and Sharni sat down across from Harper with an ornery smirk on her face. Harper looked over at her and narrowed his eyes at her but had a cocky smirk on his face.

The shuttle lifted off, and Nathan hit the booster, causing the shuttle to shoot forward. They moved along extremely fast, and soon, they entered New Guinea airspace, but Nathan didn't slow down. Harper started gripping his seat, as did Sharni. Larson had barely gotten clearance to land when Nathan spun the shuttle around just like a pro, landing it with barely a thump.

Nathan shut down the shuttle, and everyone climbed out. Larson walked over to Harper and slapped him on the back. "See? The kid's good. He's a natural."

"Yeah, I have to agree. I've never seen anyone maneuver like that before," Harper admitted, looking over at Nathan, who had caught up to the rest of the kids as they all headed toward the large spaceport terminal.

"Just think what he'll be like when he's older and has more flight time under him," Larson said, grinning.

"I could only imagine," Harper replied back coldly.

CHAPTER 21

—⸻❧⸻—

THE NEXT DAY at school was a lot different for the girls. Apparently, somehow, Ash's brush with death had gotten all around the school. The girls had become instant celebrities as everyone wanted to hear about Ash's near-death experience and all about the bug sting. Of course, everyone was shocked that it was vaquit, and the girls were really good at telling everyone that this was the first known case where one actually attacked a human, and it was now changing scientists' views on the insect, which, in actuality, was the truth to a certain extent.

Ash even had to show a lot of the girls in the bathroom her stitches with Rachael and Bridgett also telling them about their frantic race out of the mountains. All day, they were constantly surrounded by other girls, and a lot of the boys their own age came up and talked to them. At lunch, they had seats even saved for them at the popular table and fitted right in with everybody.

Ash spotted Fâd once and tried to talk to him, but he ignored her completely and kept on walking with his friends, which, of course, made her mad. She found Rachael and Bridgett, who were over by their lockers, talking. "What is Fâd's problem? He is avoiding me. Every time I try and talk to him, he just ignores me."

"I don't know. Nathan said he's been acting weird for a while now, and he really got strange when you got hurt," Rachael told her.

The girls put their stuff in their lockers and left for the day. Once again, they were surrounded as kids who rode the shuttle bus with them walked altogether, talking like they had always been friends. Ash and the girls even got invited over to a lot of their houses to watch vids or just hang out. When they got home, they quickly ate a snack and then got a ride over to one of their new friends' house. They just hung out and listened to music or danced crazily to it, fixed one another's hair, and painted their nails like most girls their age did.

Finally, it was time to go home, and they said their goodbyes and went back, walking in just as Sharni had supper ready. They all sat down and ate as the girls told the adults all about their day and how much fun they had over at their new friend's house.

This became the thing now. Ash, Rachael, and Bridgett soon became the popular girls, and all hostilities between sentinel and council were forgotten, and before long, they were having friends over and every so often held a slumber party. Of course, that was a new experience for the admirals but not for Sharni. At least everyone had fun, and even Harper didn't seem to mind much, being the unsocial one as always. Finally, the day came when Sharni and Larson had to leave; and of course, there were a lot of tears from the girls and Sharni, but they left, and it was now just Admiral Harper and the girls once more.

The girls once again took up their chores now that Sharni was gone, but still, they had time to go over to friends' houses or have them come over to theirs. They didn't have much to do with Fâd and the other two boys anymore. Only once in a great while would they actually talk to Nathan and Cory, but Fâd avoided them like the plague. He was always surrounded by other boys his age because he, Nathan, and Cory were the popular boys also, especially with the girls their own age now.

The school year went on, and before long, the last few days were there, and the girls had changed a lot over the year. Larson came a day early to pick up the boys, and he couldn't believe how much the girls had grown. Of course, in a month or two, they would all be fourteen.

It was the last day of school and finally gotten over. The girls were waiting out front for the vehicle to show up when Fâd and the boys walked out of the administration building. Fâd was holding some girl's hand, and so was Nathan, but Cory just followed, annoyed. They walked over by Ash and the girls, who now had narrowed eyes, watching them and with disgusted looks on their faces. The girl with Fâd turned to him just as they got to the girls.

"Now promise you'll write me, okay?" she said, holding his hand, flirting with him, as he grinned down at her and said he would.

Ash turned to Rachael then and whispered, "Yeah, too bad she can't read."

The girl heard her and glared at Ash as she and Rachael giggled together. Even Fâd gave Ash and Rachael a dirty look over the remark as they both were now grinning wickedly. The girl then kissed him on the cheek and walked off, waving to him.

Nathan's girlfriend was kissing him outright, and he was having no problem with it, but Rachael was livid. "I think I just threw up in my mouth. I didn't know crupons could kiss, but I had just been proven wrong, and honestly, it was disgusting," Rachael said out loud and made a gagging sound.

Nathan and his girlfriend stopped kissing and glared at Rachael. "You got a problem with us, little girl?" Nathan's girlfriend asked, annoyed.

"I just think that you should head back to the zoo and climb back into that monkey cage you crawled out of," Rachael said with a glare on her face. Of course, Cory started busting up laughing, and even Fâd tried not to chuckle, but Nathan gave them a dirty look, then glared back at Rachael. But before he could do anything, his girlfriend headed over to Rachael and got in her face, and they both were looking eye to eye since Rachael, like Ash, was tall for her age.

"Maybe I should rearrange that mutated blob you call a face," Nathan's girlfriend said to her.

"Good one. Did you come up with that yourself or read it on a datapad joke list? Oh, my mistake. Monkeys can't read."

The girl took a swing at Rachael then, but she dropped quickly to the ground and knocked the girl's feet out from under her and then was back up with her fist doubled up, ready to fight. Ash went to go after the girl too, but Fâd grabbed her around the waist and held her back, and she was now trying to get away from him. Even Bridgett went to help, but Cory grabbed her arm and made her stay out of it.

The girl got back up, but now Nathan was between them, trying to stop the fight. Rachael started to go after the other girl, and Nathan wrapped his arms around her, holding her back, as the other girl let out a scream of displeasure over Nathan having hold of Rachael, who was now fighting against him to get away.

"Fine, Nathan. If you want her so bad, then have her. We're through," she said and stormed off, and Nathan yelled after her but also holding a struggling Rachael, who was furious.

"Rachael, knock it off. Now look what you did. You caused me and my girlfriend to break up and, of all days, on the last day of school."

"Nathan, who cares? You were going to break up with her anyway," Cory said, letting go of Bridgett's arm and picking up her pack, handing it to her. Fâd finally let go of a very mad Ash, who pushed him once he released her as a cocky grin spread across his face. She glared even more and then walked over to Rachael as Nathan finally let her go. They both picked up their packs and waited with their backs to the boys.

"What is it with you three? Every time we see you, you're ready to fight us or someone else," Fâd asked them.

"Just you guys," Rachael snapped back.

"Why just us?" Nathan asked, grinning now.

"Because we hate you," Ash replied, trying to ignore them.

"Why?" Fâd asked, still grinning, and looked over at Nathan and winked.

"Because you're jerks," Rachael answered, and she and Ash had their backs to the boys still.

"How are we jerks?" Nathan asked again.

"Because you just are, so quit talking to us," Ash answered.

"Why?" Fâd asked again.

"Knock it off," Rachael said, and both she and Ash were getting madder and madder as the boys continued with their pestering of them.

"Why?" Nathan asked this time.

That was the last straw. Ash and Rachael threw down their packs and went after Nathan and Fâd with fists flying. Of course, the boys easily held them at bay, laughing at them, which made the girls even madder. Bridgett went to help again, but Cory grabbed her and held her back. Finally, Fâd ducked and grabbed Ash around the waist, and he easily took her to the ground and held her down, sitting on her, holding her arms over her head. Nathan tripped Rachael up and sat on her while she tried to dislodge him.

Fâd grinned wickedly down at Ash. "Are you going to stop?" he asked her.

"Are you going to leave me alone and never talk to me again?" she asked.

"Yes," he replied now with narrowed eyes but a cocky smirk on his face.

"Then I'm going to stop," Ash answered, and he let her up. She went and grabbed her backpack and stood waiting with Rachael again as Nathan let her go as well. Cory let Bridgett go, and she came over, and all three girls turned their backs to the boys and waited for the vehicle. It finally arrived, and the boys loaded their stuff into the trunk as the girls climbed in.

Once everything was loaded, they climbed in opposite of the girls, and the vehicle pulled away. Ash watched out the window on one side, and Rachael watched out the other. Poor Bridgett was stuck in the middle, just like Cory across from her. They would glance at each other off and on and briefly smile every so often when they thought the others weren't looking. Before long, the car pulled up to the house, and the girls quickly got out, went in, and headed straight to their rooms, passing the admirals without saying a word.

"Okay. I take it the ride here went well," Larson said to Harper.

"Yeah, that's obvious," Harper replied.

The boys came in and piled their stuff in the corner again and then headed to the kitchen as both men followed them to it. "All right, what happened?" Larson asked them as the boys were making themselves some snacks.

"They got into a fight with our girlfriends and then turned on us," Fâd said as he took a bite out of a sandwich.

"What set them off?" Harper asked, annoyed.

"Truthfully, they started it by making fun of our girlfriends," Nathan replied.

Harper just rolled his eyes and shook his head, then looked over at Larson with an ornery smirk. "They're all yours and Sharni's next year."

"Thanks a lot," Larson replied with a scowl on his face.

Finally, the girls came down, changed out of their school uniforms, and went into the kitchen, grabbing something to snack on, totally ignoring the boys. Then they headed outside and grabbed a ball and started playing dodge ball with it. Of course, this piqued the boys' interest, and they walked outside and watched. When the ball flew at one of them, the battle was on, but this game was for blood. The girls were no slouches, and they hammered the boys good, but the boys were stronger and hit them back just as hard.

Before long, all hostilities between them were forgotten, and they were all laughing and having a good time once again like they used to. The admirals breathed a sigh of relief and fixed dinner—pizza since everyone liked it and they could make that—as this was the last meal they would have together for a while. They brought the food out onto the patio, and everyone ate and laughed about the game.

Finally, the meal was done, and everyone went to bed since they all had to leave early in the morning, back to the ships. The girls waited for an hour, then crept out of their balcony door, threw a bunch of blankets down, and climbed down the tree that grew next to their balcony. They sneaked across the yard to where another large tree grew and laid the blankets out on the ground and pulled another one up on top of them. They were talking and giggling when they heard the patio door open and a light shine over them.

"What are you doing?" Fâd asked from the patio, walking toward them. The boys walked over to them, dressed in only their pajama bottoms, with their arms folded across their chest.

"Hanging out, talking," Ash replied, annoyed.

The boys then just sat down on the grass next to them without even being asked. Cory jumped up and ran back into the house and came back later with some more blankets, and the boys spread them out on the grass too. "So what time do you guys have to leave?" Fâd asked them.

"Around 0700. What about you?" Ash asked.

"We have to leave here at 0600 to rendezvous with the ship and then head out to the Kepler system," Fâd told her. Ash laid back on the blanket, and Fâd laid down beside her, and the rest followed suit.

"What a year. We got in many fights, had to do some community service down at the refugee center, and then I nearly died. I don't think I can top that one," Ash said, grinning, but she didn't see Fâd flinch when she mentioned her near-death.

"No, I think you guys got us beat," Nathan replied with a grin.

"By the way, how is the wound on your back? Did it completely heal?" Fâd asked her.

"Yeah. You want to see it? It's kind of cool. It made me famous," she said, excited and giggling a little.

"Sure," he answered and sat up when she did. Ash turned her back to him and grabbed her long black hair and pulled it to the side. Fâd reached over and grabbed the collar of her pajama top and pulled it back to where he remembered the wound was. Sure enough, there was a nice round-shaped half moon cut with dots on each side of it where the stitches used to be in. Even one of her vatoria scroll markings was disfigured by it.

"Hey, guys, come look at this. It's cool," Fâd said, and the other two boys came over and looked.

"Wow, it looks like little tracks go around it. That's neat," Nathan commented.

"Yeah, but it made one of your vatoria marks a little funny," Cory added.

"I know, but the scar is cooler than those. I now have a battle wound," Ash said and flexed her muscles, and the boys started laughing and went back and laid down.

"So do you guys have to train more too?" Cory asked them.

"Yep, for the next ten years, same as you," Rachael answered him.

"Is that what you want to be, soldiers?" Fâd asked them.

"More so than ever now, especially after spending time at the refugee center. It was such an awakening. Those people down there, it was awful what they had endured, and they were all still alive because of our fathers," Bridgett told them.

The girls then started telling them all about their experience there, and the boys listened to everything, and once they were done, the boys also agreed that being a soldier in the fleet was the right choice for all of them. They all lay out there on the blankets, watching the stars again, and finally started getting tired. Ash rolled over on her stomach with her arms folded under her head as a pillow, and Fâd rolled over on his stomach too with his arms folded under his head as well. They both were looking at each other and smiled.

"Good night, Ash," he said quietly to her so the others wouldn't hear.

"Good night, Fâd. I did come back," she said quietly and closed her eyes with a big smile on her face, but she didn't see the smile on his.

CHAPTER 22

THE NEXT THREE months flew by fast. Once again, the girls spent most of their time training, but it was a time of big change as well for them. They had all turned fourteen during the break and now were starting to enter that stage that every parent hated: puberty and teenagers. And just like Sharni had warned Thomas, it was all coming true.

Many times over the last three weeks, they ended up at one another's throats, and at least one of them stormed out of the cabin to either head to the bridge or find their friends to complain. It was also becoming noticeable that the girls' bodies were starting to make their changes as well. Thomas, even Tony Nelson, couldn't thank Abigail enough, for it was she who took them all to the clinic for their checkups to start their injections, and it was her who helped with securing other things that were becoming a necessity, such as bras, which on many occasions, Harper found lying around the bathroom along with all her other clothes.

It was like she had changed overnight. The once sweet, very neat, and organized little girl became this disorganized kind of monster who was always leaving a mess and never picked up after herself and who had multiple personalities and moods. He was about to take her to the doctor to see if she was mentally unstable, but once he talked to Abigail, he found out this was the norm.

It was actually funny, because Abigail sat them all down—him, Tony Nelson, and even Raul—and went over everything that they should expect but putting a big emphasis on unexpected with teenage girls. By the time the men all left Raul's cabin to get back to duty, they were all completely white and talking about prison cells.

But now it was here, and like every other father before him, Thomas had to also pay the price and go through this time with his daughter as she went from his little girl to a young lady. It was that part that was tearing him up inside. He didn't want his little girl to grow up. He wanted her to stay innocent and sweet the rest of her life, but it wasn't about what he wanted. It was what was right for Ash, and he had to force himself to accept that. Then to make things worse, it was Sharni and Gerrard's time with the girls as he was now back on active duty, not to mention this was going to be the first time he and Ash won't be together since she was born.

He sat on the edge of his bed in his cabin, looking at a datapad photo album of her as the pictures continued to change from one to another, and it was so easy to see the changes over the years. A lot of them he had to smile, remembering when they were taken and what they were doing together at the time, but now his heart was hurting thinking of her being gone for the next nine months to school. It hurt almost as badly as when Gail passed away. Ash was his rock, in truth, over that, and it was because of her that he had managed to find the strength to go on. He was still sitting there when he heard a light tap on his door and told whoever it was to come in.

Ash walked in and grinned at her father, then went over and sat down next to him, looking at the photo album with him as she put her arm around his shoulder. She started laughing at some of the pictures and commenting on them as he watched her out of the corner of his eye. She was changing so fast. Her face was thinning down from the little round one, and she had also grown over two inches. Her frame was thinning down as well and taking on the curvy shape of a young lady, not to mention she was acting more and more like a girl instead of the tomboy she used to be, getting into different colored nails and fixing her hair a lot. She even managed somehow to talk him into getting her ears pierced, not once but a few times, and she now had three or four of them somewhere on each ear. He was still watching her when he saw a small flash of something like a diamond on the side of her nose, and he jumped up, mad.

"What is that? I allowed the holes in your ears, but I specifically remember telling you no nose," he yelled at her.

"Relax, Dad. It's just a press-on. I didn't," Ash said, rolling her eyes, which she did a lot more. She took the small stud off and showed him there was no hole, then put it back on, which firmly stuck again.

"Okay, that's better, but I mean it, Ash. Don't go trying to talk your aunt Sharni into anything like that."

"I won't, I promise. By the way, can I use one of your trunks?"

"What about all of yours?"

"They're full, and I need one more."

"You're kidding, right? Ash, that's four trunks!" Harper couldn't believe what he was hearing.

"I can count. Fours not enough. I need another one," she said, rolling her eyes again, and went over to his closet, pulling another one out without getting permission, and headed to the door. That was the other thing he was contending with. Ash just helped herself to whatever without asking anymore, and a few times, their fights got really ugly, especially if she had his laser razor, shaving her legs with it, which she had done on several occasions.

She walked out of his room with her confiscated trunk, and he just shook his head and looked over at the one duffle bag he had packed. He was only staying for a day back at the house in New Guinea and then head back out into space with the *Justification* for this school year and wouldn't be back until school was just about out. He wouldn't even be around for breaks this time because his mission was top secret, and only his crew, Larson, and a select few at sentinel command knew of it. Even Sharni didn't know, but she had an idea, and he could tell she was worried, not to mention Ash. She had seen the buildup of weapons and ammunition on the *Justification*, but she knew there was no point in asking.

He got off his bed and walked out into the living room. All her trunks were out there plus several suitcases. He stared at them all in disbelief. Where did all this stuff come from? There was no way all that could fit in her room. Of course, he hadn't been able to even see her floor this whole time, so maybe it was possible. Just then, there was a buzz on his cabin door. He walked over, and the sliding door opened as crewmen came in and started loading the luggage on to a carryall. He started helping them as this helped to keep his mind off the fact that he wouldn't see her for almost a whole year. Finally, the last one was loaded, and he hollered for Ash to come on.

She came out of the bathroom with her backpack slung over her shoulder, and he couldn't help but notice how much she looked like Gail. She walked through their cabin's door and into the hallway and headed to the elevator as he followed. The crewmen had already left and were nowhere in sight by now, probably wanting to get out of there before she added more luggage to the pile.

They both got in, and Harper told the elevator the level, and in no time, they stepped out into the shuttle bay. The others were already there, and of course, he grinned seeing he wasn't the only one having fun with a teenager. Raul and Rachael were already in a fight over something, and Abigail was trying to calm each other down.

"Will you two just get along for once? We aren't going to see each other for almost a year," Abigail yelled at them. They both stopped, and then Rachael teared up and wrapped her arms around her father, hugging him, as Raul hugged her back. Harper had to shake his head. Yep, the norm was going from "I hate you" to "I love you" in just a matter of seconds. He was thinking Tony was the luckiest out of them all since Bridgett was always the sensitive one and never liked to rock the boat when suddenly, out of the elevator, they both came storming out, yelling at each other. Bridgett with her pack on her back continued to head straight to the shuttle, ignoring her father, as Tony followed, chewing her out for something. She climbed on board and then stopped in the door and spun around, looking down at him from it. "I don't want to talk to you anymore. Goodbye!" Then she went and sat down inside.

"Fine. I don't want to speak to you either," Tony replied and stormed away.

"I wonder what he did," Ash said to her father.

"Why do you naturally assume he did something?" Harper asked, a little mad at her insinuation.

"Because all parents start the fights," Ash replied as if this was common knowledge.

"We do not. It is your assumptions and total lack of regard that start every one of them," Harper said to her, and she glared at him, then continued toward the shuttle, not saying a word, passing him as she went. He followed and stopped outside the shuttle, waiting for Rachael to finally get in as she and her parents walked over. She climbed in and went and sat down with the other two, and immediately, the chatter rose.

"You know what, Thomas, it does my heart good to know it will be Larson having to watch over them," Raul said with a wicked grin.

"I know. I just wish I could be there to watch it all," Harper replied, allowing a brief grin to start at the corner of his mouth.

"Well, Admiral, we will see you in a couple of days," Raul said and saluted his friend.

Harper saluted them back and turned to his EXO. "Dobbs, you have the ship for now," he told him as Dobbs grinned.

"Hurry back, Admiral," Dobbs replied, still grinning.

Harper climbed into the noisy shuttle as the girls all yelled out the door goodbye before he shut it, and in no time, they were all once again heading toward New Guinea. It was the same old routine like always—the fighters escorting and then landing as spaceport crewmen came out and unloaded the shuttle and transported the trunks toward the exit. But this time, there was a slight difference. When they all walked through the terminal, Harper noticed a lot of the school-age boys who had also returned for the new school year were watching the girls a little bit more closely now. He made a point to keep his hand on his pistol, which deterred a lot of the glances, and if he was lucky enough to catch one of their eyes, he would narrow his, and the boy would disappear quickly.

By now, he was very unnerved by this open appraisal of his girls and was starting to reconsider leaving them at all, especially in Larson's care. Sharni would watch out for them, but Larson was too much a kid himself, even being the age he was. They all loaded into the vehicle, and it soon was hovering down the streets they were so used to by now.

Before long, they were pulling up to the house as Sharni and Larson came out, and they all climbed out of the vehicle. The girls ran up to them, and hugs were exchanged all around, and then just as quickly, the girls ran into the house and up to their rooms. Sharni and Larson were grinning from ear to ear after just surviving the whirlwind of teenagers.

"Oh my gosh, Thomas, they have changed so much in such a short time. They are becoming beautiful young ladies," Sharni said with a smile.

"Yeah, and already, the boys are noticing them. I had to keep my hand on my gun all the way through the terminal," Harper said, and Sharni started laughing.

"You didn't?" she asked, still laughing.

"Oh yes, I did."

"Good idea. I'll start packing mine as well," Larson said in a serious tone.

"You will not. Come on, you two, it's not that bad," Sharni said and motioned them all toward the door. They went in, and Harper went straight to his room, putting his bag down, and then came back out while Sharni went and got them all something to drink, then came back and sat on the sofa.

"Don't listen to her. It's as bad as I said. Thank goodness the girls didn't seem to notice. They were too busy jabbering about places they wanted to go shopping at. By the way, their parents and I have a block on their marks. They only are allowed a certain amount each month, and if they run out, don't you go buying things for them. They have plenty, so if they spend it all, they don't need it," Harper told Larson.

"Yeah, and I can imagine your idea of plenty, just enough to buy an ice cream cone," Sharni argued with him.

"That's more than plenty," Harper informed her with a scowl. Larson was still sitting there quietly when Harper looked over at him and noticed the frown on his face and that he was deep in thought. "Gerrard, don't hurt yourself thinking," he teased.

"Have you considered an all-girls boarding school where no boys are around? Even a convent school, possibly?" Larson asked him. Harper started chuckling, but Sharni didn't think it was funny at all and chewed Larson out. "Wow, it's amazing how fast they change once you marry them," Gerrard said with a devious grin.

"I warned you. What's that old human saying?" Harper smirked.

"Old ball and chain," Larson added, and Sharni threw a pillow at him, which he caught rather easily. But no one noticed the girls standing on the stairs with their mouths wide open and surprise all over their faces.

"You got married? When? Why weren't we invited?" Ash blurted out as they ran down the rest of the stairs, and all three either dove over the arm of the sofa or the back of it and jumped down, looking at Sharni with big grins on their faces. Of course, Larson was just as floored with the girls' behavior and impressed with their athletic agility, but Sharni didn't seem too surprised at all.

"It was kind of a spur-of-the-moment thing," Sharni told them, grinning sheepishly.

"Yeah, after a whole bottle of kerian brandy," Larson said quietly, and Harper started chuckling as Sharni gave them both a dirty look.

"But there was no celebration or party. We have to have one," Rachael told her with excitement in her tone.

"We figured we would once all of you got here. I'll have Fâd and them come over as well," Larson told the girls.

"Are the boys back at school already?" Harper asked him.

"Yeah, and it sure didn't take them long to get girlfriends already, which according to the boys is what you're suppose to do when you turn sixteen and are part of the popular group," Larson said but didn't notice the glare Ash had on her face when he was telling her father about it.

"Boys. They're such animals," Rachael said and rolled her eyes.

"Oh, I figured you girls would be starting to like boys by now," Sharni asked them, grinning and ignoring Larson and Harper's dirty looks.

"Please, no thank you. I would just as soon have space mites than like a boy. We all would. There are better things to do anyway," Bridgett said, and the other two agreed with her as Larson and Harper breathed a sigh of relief.

The girls jumped up and ran outside to toss a ball around as Sharni watched them go and then turned to the men. "See? There's nothing to worry about. Boys may be noticing them, but the girls have no interest in boys. Yet," Sharni told them, making an emphasis on *yet*.

The adults continued to talk in the living room, but outside, the girls were now leaning on the fence that divided their yard from the neighbors, talking to a couple of sixteen-year-old boys. One of them had just moved there with his parents.

"So where do you three go to school at?" the dark-headed boy asked.

"New Guinea Heights. What about you two?" Rachael asked.

"We go to public. It's pretty fun. Our quasar team is going to be really good this year. You girls should come and watch us play," the blond-headed one told them.

"Oh, where are my manners? I'm Luke, and this is Sage," the dark-headed one told them.

"I'm Rachael. That's Ashley, but we call her Ash. And she's Bridgett, but you can just call her Bridg. It's easier than saying her whole name," Rachael told them.

"So have you always lived here?" the blond-headed boy named Sage asked.

"Kind of, just during school. Most of the time, we live on a sentinel battlecruiser called the *Justification*," Bridgett told them.

"No way! Isn't that the war hero Vice Admiral Harper's ship?" Luke asked her.

The girls started giggling then, and the boys looked offended. "What's so funny?" Sage asked them, a little annoyed.

"My father is Vice Admiral Harper," Ash said, still giggling.

"No way! That's so cool," Luke said, excited about the news.

"Yeah, as a matter of fact, he's inside right now, along with Rear Admiral Larson and Captain Tol Vasna," Rachael told them, grinning.

The boys were impressed and asked if they could meet them, and of course, the girls said they could and invited them over. Sage and Luke climbed over the fence easily, and they all headed into the house. The adults were still talking when they all walked in, and Harper and Larson's faces became like stone when they saw the boys with the girls.

"Luke, Sage, this is Vice Admiral Harper, my father, and this is Rear Admiral Larson, my godfather, and Captain Sharnestra Tol Vasna, my aunt. This is Sage and Luke. Luke lives next door," Ash introduced everyone. Of course, the boys were thrilled to see them, but the men weren't quite so happy about the news. Sharni got up and went over and shook the boys' hands, and all they could do was stare at her in adoration, which also bothered Larson even more.

"So where do you boys go to school at?" Harper asked them, making sure his gun was noticeable when he crossed his legs in front of himself as a half smirk formed on Larson's face.

"We go to public. I told Ash and them they need to come watch our quasar team this year. We should do real well this season," Luke told the admirals nervously, now spotting Admiral Harper's exposed pistol.

Harper, of course, didn't like it that this boy had just barely met his daughter and was already using her nickname, and he looked over at Larson and could tell by the look on his face he wasn't liking this situation either. "So what year are you in school?" Larson asked them coldly.

"Eleventh," Sage answered, also nervous.

"Oh, you're the same age as Admiral Larson's son and his friends. They come over once in a while. You should meet them," Sharni said, and both Harper and Larson noticed the look on the boys' faces when she said this, because the boys then looked over at the girls, who of course were paying no attention by now, and then at each other and knew that the competition was on for the girls. Now

Harper wanted to go over and throttle both of these boys for even thinking about his girls, but he knew he couldn't.

"Luke, Sage, come on, let's go play some quasar ball outside," Ash said, and the boys grinned and followed them. Harper and Larson started to get up, but Sharni stopped them instantly, making them sit back down.

"Leave them alone. They're just playing ball," she warned the two men.

"I'm going to go get my gun," Larson said and stood up.

"You will not. You will sit right there and let the kids have fun." Sharni pointed for him to sit back in his chair, which he did without argument.

"Those boys are after only one thing, girlfriends, just like Larson said that Fâd and them told him," Harper said, mad.

"Trust the girls. They will put them in place on that."

"All right, we'll trust you since you are a girl, but one wrong step from those boys and I'll shoot them," Larson said to her, serious.

"Look who's talking. You have a son the same age. Is this how you want his girlfriend's father to act? Besides, what if it were them out there flirting with the girls instead?" Sharni asked him in disbelief, and even Harper looked over at him to hear what he had to say.

"I'm not worried. It's just a phase. It's the thing to be able to say you have a girlfriend. And as far as the girls and my boys, they fight way too much to be of any concern," Larson said, grinning, and Harper had to agree with him.

"Well, it's the same thing with those boys outside, and I'm sorry, but you have to admit, the girls are cuties and are only going to get prettier and eventually beautiful," Sharni said to them.

"We know, so just shut up about it," Harper told her with narrowed eyes.

Harper got up and started toward the kitchen. "Where are you going?" Sharni asked him, getting up herself, and Larson now jumped up.

"I wanted to get a beer and go sit out on the patio. It's hot in here."

"All right, you can do that, but I'm coming with both of you, so you don't shoot them," Sharni said, and they headed outside and sat down in the patio chairs. Larson came out with a couple of beers and some juice for Sharni.

The girls were chasing the boys, who were playing keep away from them, throwing the ball back and forth. Every so often, the girls would gang up on one of the boys and tackle him, and then they would all get up, laughing. Harper and Larson noticed how courteous the boys were being, always giving them a hand to help them up, or if one of the girls ran into one of the boys to grab the ball from them, they would put an arm around their waist to keep them from falling. Every time it happened, the men would look at Sharni, and she would narrow her eyes at both Harper and Larson.

It started getting late, and the boys finally went home. The girls were a mess but had fun and were giggling and talking about the game as they walked into the house. They sat at the snack bar and started eating, still talking among themselves, when Sharni asked them if they had fun.

"Yeah, it was, and they're cute. Did you notice, Aunt Sharni?" Ash asked her, grinning.

Harper and Larson both glared at Sharni, but she just smiled. "They were, and I think they liked you girls," Sharni teased them, still getting glares from Harper and Larson.

"We know they do, but we're not looking for boyfriends right now. It's just fun keeping them chasing us," Rachael said as she took another mouthful of food.

Harper was shocked, and Larson choked on his beer when he heard what the girls said. They liked stringing naive boys around; they were nothing more than monsters, yet Larson and Harper found comfort in this. The night got late, and the next day was the first day of school. Harper, in a way, regretted it, because usually, he had to make a visit to the office of Professor Baptise, and he was leaving back to the ship for almost a year without Ash for the first time since she was born.

Then he felt guilty thinking about Raul and them. They all had been going through this for the last two years, and he got the privilege of spending time with their daughters while they stayed in space, on duty. Harper got ready for bed and was just about to climb in it when there was a buzz on his door, and he told whomever it was to come in. The door opened, and all three girls walked in with tears in their eyes, and when he saw them, all he could do was put his arms out. They all came over and wrapped their arms around him, crying.

He held all three of them for a while as they continued to cry, and he even was fighting back tears that wanted to fall. They had all become his girls over the last two years, and he would kill anyone who ever threatened or tried to harm any one of them. Finally, they got control of themselves and headed to the door of his room. "We love you," all three of them said to him, and now his eyes did water up.

"I love you, girls," Harper said back as they left his room.

CHAPTER 23

MORNING CAME TOO fast, and the girls were up, getting ready, as was Harper. He finished and checked in the mirror to make sure his uniform was perfect and then smoothed his wavy dark hair back and straightened his gun at his waist. Harper picked up his duffle bag and headed out of his room, toward the kitchen, where he heard everyone.

The girls were already in there, eating some type of breakfast that Sharni had made, a type of vatorian dish, and Larson was leaning against the counter, drinking some creo, listening to all the chattering the girls were doing. Sharni poured Harper a cup of creo as he walked in, and he took a drink.

"So how does it feel to be once again on full active duty?" Larson asked him, grinning, knowing full well what his reply would be.

Harper looked over at him, emotionless. "What do you think?"

"Thought so." Larson grinned.

The girls finished their breakfast and put the dirty dishes in the sink, and then each went and gave the vice admiral a hug and a kiss and told him goodbye as they ran out the front door to catch the shuttle to school. Harper watched them go, then walked over and put his cup with the girls' dishes in the sink too and headed to the front door as well.

Larson and Sharni followed him. Sharni now had a worried look on her face, and Larson had a serious one on his. She came up and hugged him, and Larson came over. The two men grasped each other's forearms and shook them firmly.

"You be careful, Thomas!" Larson told his friend with a concerned tone to his voice.

Harper had a cocky smirk on his face. "I will, and I'll be back before you know it."

"I mean it. You get into trouble, you call command, and I'll push the *Lithia* to the breaking point to get there," Larson said, looking his best friend in the eye.

"Hell, Larson, you act like this is my first mission. Quit being such a pansy. This will be a cake walk compared to what we have gone through when we were younger," Harper told him coldly.

"That's the thing, *younger* being the key word. I just can't picture you doing recon now, and I won't be there to pull your ass out of the fire this time," Larson said with a cocky grin.

"I'm not that out of shape. Just ask your cousin. Besides, if I remember right, it was me that was always pulling your ass out," Harper replied quietly, with a cocky smirk as well.

Larson just shook his head with a devious grin on his face. "I knew it. But seriously, I'll be there if you need me, just like I know you would do the same for me," he said, putting his hand on Harper's shoulder.

Harper turned and headed out to the waiting vehicle and climbed in, looking back at the house he had spent the last two years of his life in, feeling a dull ache in his heart. The airlimo pulled away, and before long, they were pulling up to the spaceport. He went in, got his clearance at the terminal near his docking platform, and walked out to the shuttle and fighter escort that was waiting for him. It didn't take him long to fire up the shuttle's engine, lifting off, and in no time, he was coming upon the *Justification* as she sat stationary, waiting for him, his other true love. He got clearance and piloted the shuttle, landing it in one of the many shuttle bays.

Harper shut down and stepped out onto his ship as everyone stood at attention and saluting. "Vice Admiral on deck," Dobbs announced.

"EXO Dobbs, you are relieved," Harper told him and saluted Dobbs back, who now had a big grin on his face.

"The ship is yours once again, Vice Admiral. Welcome back," Dobbs said to him.

Harper smirked, then he and his EXO headed to the elevator, and Harper told it the bridge. In no time, the elevator opened, and everyone on the bridge was at their stations, waiting for orders, and saluted the admiral when he stepped up on his platform. Harper brought up his many virtual screens from his large wraparound console and started moving things around on it. Then he entered coordinates and sent them out. In a matter of seconds, he got conformations back from all the stations on his screens.

"Petterson, you have the coordinates. Take her out," he said to his pilot from his command post.

"Affirmative, Admiral. Coordinates locked. Jump drive online," Petterson replied to the admiral from way in front of the admiral's platform and started moving the ship away from Sigma Six space. "Attention, crew. Prepare to jump in 5, 4, 3, 2, 1, jump."

The *Justification* was moving away from Sigma Six space, and right before the ship went into jump, Harper and his bridge crew saw the *Lithia* fire her propulsion engines a couple of times as had become a tradition to each other as a signal of safe journey.

The *Justification* left the space of Sigma Six, disappearing into slipstream at 0900, just as Ash and her friends were heading to their next class. Ash, Rachael, and Bridgett momentarily stopped in the hall of the science building when they felt a slight pulling at their hearts and briefly looked up at the ceiling of the building and then at one another knowing the *Justification* and their families had left. The girls weakly smiled at one another, then headed to their next class, a little sad meeting up with some of the friends they had made last year.

School was great this year. They, once again, fitted in and had a lot of friends. Even at lunchtime, they had no problem finding a place to sit now. They had barely sat down when Ash looked around the cafeteria and saw Fâd sitting on one of the lunch tables, and a sixteen-year-old girl was standing in front of him. He had ahold of her hands behind her back, and they were practically kissing each other. Even Nathan and Cory were sitting with girls, and Cory and his girlfriend had their heads leaned down together, whispering to each other. Ash just stared without realizing it, and her eyes narrowed at the boys, and she could feel jealousy eating away at her. Rachael saw her and looked to see what she was watching and then saw the boys, and like Ash, she glared at them as well.

Bridgett was talking to some other girl who was sitting by her and had asked Ash a question, and when she got no answer, she looked over at her. She saw that Ash and Rachael were glaring at something, so she looked to see what it was. Bridgett saw the boys and then Cory grinning and getting real close with some girl. She jumped up, letting out a loud, pained yelp, and threw her hands over her mouth, staring at Cory. This brought Ash and Rachael out of their glare, and they looked over at Bridgett, as did everyone in the cafeteria, including the boys. Bridgett took off running out of the room, and Cory jumped up from the table, watching her go. Ash and Rachael looked at each other then jumped up, running after Bridgett, yelling for her to stop.

Fâd, Nathan, and Cory looked at one another, then got up and said goodbye to the girls they were with and left the cafeteria. Down the other hallway, Ash and Rachael finally caught up to Bridgett, who was now crying, and they dragged her into the bathroom so no one would see her.

"What is the matter with you?" Rachael asked her and smoothed her dark-red hair out of her face and wiped away her tears.

"Nothing. I'm sorry. It was just a shock to see the guys here is all," Bridgett said and looked down at the floor.

"That's why you sounded like a wounded animal?" Ash asked her in disbelief.

"Yeah. I know it was stupid. I'm fine now," she said and looked in the mirror to make sure she looked okay.

"Well, then, can we go back and eat without any other episode, or are you going to cry every time you see Cory?" Ash asked with annoyance on her face.

"Yeah, we can go back. I won't do it again, and no, I'm not going to cry over Cory ever again," Bridgett said defiantly, and all three of them walked out into the hallway and headed back to the cafeteria. Just before they got there, Bridgett heard someone yell her name and turned around to see Cory heading toward her. He had definitely changed. He was a lot taller, and his hair was a little longer as well. Plus, he was now sporting a tiny crystal earring in his ear. She waited for him as Ash and Rachael stood on each side of her with their arms folded, watching him with narrowed eyes.

"Hi, guys. Wow, you three have changed. When did you get in?" he asked politely.

"Yesterday. What about you?" Bridgett asked just as nicely back.

"Two days ago. Are you okay, Bridgett? I heard you scream," he asked with a concerned look on his face.

"I'm fine. I see it didn't take you guys long to fit in again," Bridgett now said in a mad tone and was giving him a dirty look.

"What's that supposed to mean?" Cory asked, now mad as well.

"I got to go. I'm sure your girlfriend is missing you right now," Bridgett said to him and turned, heading into the lunchroom. Ash and Rachael both stood there, glaring at him, and then he let out a huff and left in the opposite direction.

"That's it, go find the rest of your friends and suck some more face," Rachael yelled at him, and Cory made a gesture with his hand at her, and Ash and Rachael's mouths fell open. They were hot now when they walked into the lunchroom, but soon, they got over it after they finished their meal. The campus bell rang to let them know to head to their next class, which the three girls did, and almost ran right into Fâd, Nathan, and Cory, not to mention a bunch of other boys who were with them.

"Oh, I thought I smelled something," Ash said out loud, and the other boys with Fâd and them started chuckling.

"Then you're smelling your own aroma. What is it, essence of vermin?" Fâd said with a cocky grin, and Ash noticed that just like

Cory, he had changed a lot too. He was a lot taller, even a little filled out, with longer hair and also a pierced ear like Cory.

"No, that would be you. Didn't your father ever tell you that bathing once in a while will help with that?" Rachael said smugly.

Nathan stepped forward and got in her face. He, too, changed and was taller, and just like Fâd and Cory, he had his ear pierced as well but kept his hair the same as last year. Rachael looked up at him, glaring, and they both were now barely inches away from each other. Suddenly, out of nowhere, Nathan grabbed the back of Rachael's head and kissed her real fast, and Ash and Bridgett's mouths fell open in shock. Rachael pushed him away immediately, wiping her mouth and spitting on the floor.

The boys, of course, were laughing hysterically now, and Ash grabbed Rachael's arm, who was yelling that she was going to die from disease, and dragged her away, toward their next class. Bridgett skirted clear around the boys as they all watched her with wicked grins on their faces, and then she took off running toward Ash and Rachael.

Ash looked back just before she walked into class at all the boys, and she glared at Fâd, who had a cocky grin on his face, and he winked at her. She could feel the anger boiling in her now and wanted to go and rip his head off, but she was too busy with Rachael, who now was struggling to even walk because she knew she was already dying. They got to their seats, and Rachael laid her head down on the table, moaning.

"Rachael, knock it off. You're going to get us in trouble," Bridgett whispered to her.

"I'm sorry, guys. I'm a defiled woman now. Please don't hate me and accept me as I am," Rachael said, still moaning.

"Quit it. He just kissed you is all. Granted, that was gross, but you're going to live." Ash nudged her and looked around the room to make sure no one was watching them.

"What was it like?" Bridgett asked with a devious grin as Ash and a now alert Rachael looked at their friend in disbelief.

"Disgusting, duh!" Rachael told her, making a fake gagging motion.

The rest of the day went off without any more confrontations. Of course, the girls were making sure they stayed clear of Fâd and the boys. Finally, school ended, and they headed to wait for their shuttle. Before long, the shuttle showed up, and they climbed in and took their seats. But just as the shuttle moved out, one of their friends who was sitting in front of them turned around in her seat.

"Hey, Rachael. I heard you got kissed by a sixteen-old-boy today. I also heard it was Nathan Wilcox. Is that true?"

"What? Maybe. What does it matter?" Rachael replied, embarrassed.

"Really? He is so cute. Even his two friends are. What was it like?" The girl looked at her, all excited.

"Gross and wet," Rachael replied, wiping her mouth again.

"This is so great. You're the first of us that got kissed," the girl said, grinning from ear to ear.

Ash just rolled her eyes and shook her head in disbelief. If only she knew that Rachael was going to be the first at a lot of things as they grew up, this would never have come as a surprise. The shuttle finally got to their house, and the girls all ran inside and could smell something good. They threw their packs down on the floor and raced to the kitchen and saw that Sharni had made some type of vatorian treat. They each grabbed one and gobbled it down and then took another one when they heard Larson yell from the living room.

"Hey, is this where your stuff belongs?" he yelled, pointing at the packs.

The girls walked back into the living room with full mouths and grinned at him, then went over and picked up their packs and headed upstairs. A few minutes later, they all came down, now changed into everyday clothes, and walked back to the kitchen and started going through the refrigerator. Larson walked in and just shook his head at them.

"Do you have homework?" he asked them.

"Nope. Got it all done," Ash said, grabbing a bottle of juice and drinking it down immediately. Larson watched her and was amazed that she didn't even take a breath doing it.

"Where's Sharni?" Bridgett asked.

"Ran to do some shopping. She said we are out of necessary things," Larson told them.

"Oh yeah, we are low on feminine hygiene products," Rachael said and grabbed another treat. Larson's mouth fell open, and he turned bright red as the girls walked past him to head outside.

"It's okay, Admiral. It's just a fact of life," Bridgett said, grinning, and Larson couldn't say anything. Harper was right, they were monsters. Ash, Rachael, and Bridgett were giggling now and picked up the ball and started throwing it around. They did this for a few more minutes, then they heard someone yell their name.

"Hey, girls. Want to come over and play quasar ball with us?" Luke hollered from his yard. Ash and the girls went over to the fence and climbed up on it to see over, and there on the other side were five boys, including Luke and Sage.

"Sure. We just have to tell the admiral," Ash said with a grin.

"The admiral?" one of the other boys asked Luke.

"Yeah, Rear Admiral Larson, he's their guardian while they attend New Guinea Heights. We even met Vice Admiral Harper yesterday, but he had to leave for a mission, and Rear Admiral Larson is married to a Captain Sharnestra Tol Vasna, a vatoria," Luke said with a grin and elbowed his friend, who also had a grin on his face.

"Is she real hot?" the boy asked.

"Oh yeah," Luke replied exuberantly.

"Guys, that's my aunt. Please, you're making me sick," Ash said, rolling her eyes at them. She climbed down and started to head to the door, but Rachael stopped her, putting her hands on Ash's shoulders.

"Ash, I don't know if I can take being around another boy today. I've already been kissed by one. Who knows what else might happen to me?"

"Oh, come on, Rachael, nothing's going to happen to you."

Rachael let out a long sigh and looked down at the ground dejectedly. "All right, if you say so, but if something does, it's all on your head," she said, and Ash just shook her head in disbelief and rolled her eyes.

The girls ran into the house, and Larson was sitting at the snack bar, going over some stuff on a portable console board. He had a virtual screen up and was moving documents around on it just by touching the screen, and when the girls came in, he looked over at them. "What?"

"How did you know we were going to ask you something?" Bridgett said, a little surprised.

"I can see it in your faces."

"Okay. We were wondering if we could go over to Luke's and play some quasar ball," Ash asked him.

"Is that what girls do, play contact sports with boys?" he asked them a little skeptical.

"No, of course not, but we don't care what other girls do. We like to have fun and not play dress-up," Ash replied with a grin.

"All right, but only for a little while, and if the boys get too rough, come back home."

"Oh, please, don't you mean if we hurt one of them to come back home?" Rachael said, grinning, and the girls started giggling and headed to the front door. They ran over to the next house and pressed the buzzer. A woman about the age of sixty or sixty-five came to the door.

"Yes, can I help you?" she asked the girls.

"Yes. Luke invited us over to play quasar with him," Ash said, smiling.

"Are you sure? Isn't that a little rough for you girls?" the woman asked, a little confused. Just then, Luke and Sage walked up behind her.

"Come on, Ash. We're waiting for you guys so we can start," he said to her as the woman stood aside with a surprised look on her face, and Ash, Rachael, and Bridgett walked past her and into the backyard with them. Luke made all the introductions, and before long, the game was on as they split up into two teams. Ash was the only girl on one team with Luke as Rachael and Bridgett were on another one with Sage. The game went on, and it was very physical and rough. But the girls held their own, and the boys actually had a lot of respect for their ability.

Finally, it got late, and Larson went outside and yelled for them to come home, and they said their goodbyes. But as they started to leave, one of the boys whose name was Brian asked Bridgett if he could come and hang out with her tomorrow.

"Yeah, we'll all come," Luke said, and Brian gave him a dirty look.

"Sure. No problem. We can watch some vids or play some vid games," Rachael said, and the girls then left the boys, who started playing again. Once they got home, Sharni was now back, and she couldn't believe the mess they were in.

"What happened to you three? You look like you were fighting."

"In a way, we were. It was a tough game of quasar," Ash said, pulling grass out of her hair now.

"Go get your baths. Dinner will be ready in a few more minutes."

"By the way, Luke and his friends are going to come over tomorrow, and we are going to play vid games," Ash said as she ran up the stairs. Larson looked at Sharni with a scowl on his face, but Sharni just smiled and went into the kitchen, and he followed her.

"Is this going to be the norm?" he asked her.

"Probably," she replied, grinning.

CHAPTER 24

THE REST OF the week flew by, and finally, they were into the weekend, and Sharni took the girls shopping. They were gone half the day, and when they came back, they all had a bunch of new outfits. Of course, Larson was made to watch the fashion show as the girls tried on every one of their new outfits to show him, which just thrilled him to death.

The next day, Sharni had to go and check on some parts that had come for one of her cooling systems on her ship at one of the shipping ports, so Larson was once again in charge of the girls. "So what do you girls want to do today?"

"Do you know how to play Targo?" Ash asked him, grinning.

"Of course. I'm unbeatable at it," Larson replied, rolling his eyes.

The girls got a deck of cards, and Ash shuffled them, and Larson noticed she handled the cards like a pro, making him think he just walked into a setup. Targo was the equivalent of the old game called gin rummy, but instead, all the cards had different aliens on them, making them worth certain points, and you placed bets on your cards.

Ash dealt out seven cards to each, and everyone started placing their bets. Instead of marks, they played for candy, and each of them had a stack of different types of sweets in front of them. The girls also each had a visor on and rose-colored glasses, and they brought Larson a pair as well. It was quite the scene with all four of them around the table, wearing rose-colored glasses and visors.

The first round, Larson won, and he was feeling pretty confident. Even during the second hand, he fared pretty well but lost to Bridgett. But by the fourth and fifth round, his luck had run out, and the girls were beating him bad. Sharni walked in as he was down to his last few pieces of candy, and when she saw all of them, she busted up laughing, mainly at Larson's glasses.

"Gerrard, you're losing?" Sharni giggled and teased him.

"You think?" he said, flustered that he was doing so badly.

Sharni watched as they continued playing but then heard it. "Ashley Gail Harper, I can't believe you did that," Sharni scolded her niece, who started giggling, as did her friends.

Larson narrowed his eyes at Ash. "What's going on?"

"You have just been scammed by a fourteen-year-old. Ash has been using her telepathy. When did you learn how to communicate to more than one person at a time? Most adult vatorias can't do that. Even I can't. I just barely sensed you doing it," Sharni asked her, amazed by Ash's ability. Of course, Larson was laughing now knowing he got suckered by these girls.

"I've been able to do it for a few years now but only with just a couple people at a time. Of course, it would have been easier to read the admiral's mind, but he obviously knows how to block telepathy. Plus, my dad would be furious if he found out I read someone's mind without their knowledge."

"That he will. So in the game, how did it work?" her aunt asked, interested by what these girls could do as a team.

"I let them know what is in my hand as they tell me theirs, and Bridgett counts what has been played because she's fast with numbers, which leaves the remaining cards that are in his hand," Ash told her, grinning.

"Cool. How about me and you girls go to Seti Prime and visit Marks High Palace? Your talents could really be a boon to the game table there," Larson asked with a wicked grin on his face.

"Larson! Absolutely not. you want to take them gambling and cheat? Don't you have any class?" Sharni scolded him.

He looked at her, still grinning. "No. When did I ever have that?" The girls started laughing. Sharni got onto him and sent the girls to take their showers while she fixed dinner, and they all got up but made sure they took their cheated winnings with them and giggled all the way up the stairs. Larson removed his visor and glasses, then cleaned up the rest of their mess and was also chuckling and shaking his head at what they pulled over on him.

"I never thought girls could be such a handful. Those three are something else."

"I know. They have such a tight bond, an invisible connection of sorts, to one another," Sharni replied, punching in a meal selection and ingredients into the replicator.

The meal was prepared, the girls showered, and everyone ate. Once it was done, the girls cleaned up and headed to bed to start another week of school. Sharni and Larson straightened up the rest of the house, and they, too, went to bed to start everything all over again in the morning.

The next week of school was calm. Nothing got blown up or anyone beat up, and the girls just hung around with their friends. Of course, Luke, Sage, and Brian came over a lot to just hang out with the girls after school, and they would either play quasar ball outside or vids inside or even just talk and kind of flirt with one another but nothing serious and only when Sharni was there. The boys told the girls that Admiral Larson scared them and felt he didn't like them too much because he always glared at them. Finally, the weekend came and went, and then they were into another week. But this time, there was something to look forward to.

During one of their classes, the professor came over the school's comm system. "I would like to make an announcement. This Friday, we will be taking all the students to a quasar game over at the public school. The Public boys' quasar team is undefeated and will be playing in the championship match. Permission responses have been sent out to your parents or guardians, as this will be late in the evening and not during school operating hours. Make sure you wear or bring a light jacket, as it could get a little chilly out. Thank you, and hope to see all of you make it."

"Cool. We will finally be able to see the boys play." Ash had turned around in her seat, looking at Rachael with a big grin on her face.

"Yeah, and in their uniforms," Rachael said with a devious grin.

One of their friends next to them in another seat heard them talking and leaned over to Ash. "Do you know some boys who go to public?"

"Yes, and they play on the quasar team."

"So are you dating them?"

"I wouldn't say we are dating. We just do a lot of things together," Ash said, grinning.

During the day, though, a rumor got back to Ash, Rachael, and Bridgett that they were each dating a sixteen-year-old boy from public who were the star players on the quasar team and had gone out quite a few times. The funny thing was, a lot of that were actually true, except the dating and going out, but they did hang out together a lot.

It was finally the end of the school day, and the girls were laughing and heading to the shuttle when they ran into Fâd and them, and instantly, the girls prepared for war. "Is it true?" Fâd asked with his arms crossed and his eyes narrowed, looking down at Ash.

"Is what true?" Ash snapped back, glaring at him.

"The rumor about you guys dating some boys from public," Nathan said with a mad look on his face.

"What's it to you?" Rachael snarled at him.

"New Guinea students don't date Public students," Cory threw in.

"Says who?" Ash challenged them.

"It's just common knowledge. So is it true?" Fâd said, still with his arms crossed.

Ash now had a wicked smirk on her face. "Yeah, it's true. And as a matter of fact, they come over to the house all the time."

"And Sage is a much better kisser than you!" Rachael added with a wicked grin, looking at Nathan, who got in her face and now looked like he was about to explode with rage. Even Fâd's face was contorted with raw anger, and Cory wouldn't even speak. He was so mad.

"Besides, it's none of your business whom we date. Like you're going to stop us. I don't think so," Bridgett said defiantly, and Fâd looked over at her, and Bridgett felt that if he could, he would have knocked her senseless by the furious look on his face. Then he looked back down at Ash.

"We'll see about that!" he warned, and they turned and headed back toward campus grounds.

"Oh, go and eat your girlfriends' faces again," Ash yelled at them, and all three boys now made a bad gesture at them with their hands.

"Back at you," Rachael said and did the gesture back to them.

Once they got to the house, though, it was a different story. Larson was waiting for them when they walked in, and he looked mad and had the girls all sit down on the sofa as he stood in front of the fireplace, glaring at them. "I heard some disturbing news today. Can you guess what?" he asked them.

"Let me guess, the nosy boys called you and told you that we have boyfriends," Ash told him.

"Yes, and that you have been dating and kissing them, which I'm assuming are Luke, Sage, and Brian," Larson added, getting madder.

"No, we don't have boyfriends, and we haven't been kissing them. We just said that because it was none of their business what we do. If anyone should get into trouble, it should be them. They are always kissing their girlfriends, even at lunchtime, in front of everyone," Rachael said, mad about the predicament they were in now because of them.

"Are you serious? They are doing that?" Larson asked, now mad at the boys as well.

"Yes, all the time, and then they have the nerve to accuse us of the same thing. Like we would ever do that. Luke and they are just friends, nothing more," Ash told him.

"Well, I think we need to make some changes around here anyway. They come over way too much, and I think it needs to be cut back even if they aren't your boyfriends. And as for this game Friday, I don't think you should go. You girls are only fourteen, and it will keep you out late."

"That's not fair. We did nothing wrong. It's those stupid boys. They're just jealous because we can still have fun without them," Bridgett yelled out, and now the girls were on the verge of tears.

"That's not going to work on me, girls. I'll think about the game and let you know my decision tomorrow. Now go and get your homework done," Larson said to them, and they all ran up the stairs and into their room, the door sliding shut behind them.

He watched them go and then went into his room and called Fâd on his comm. "Yeah, what is it?" Fâd answered, annoyed.

"What's going on? Why are you so worried about the girls?"

"They're being used by these sixteen-year-old boys, and they're too naive to know any better. I'm just trying to keep them from getting their feelings hurt."

"Are you sure that's it and not jealousy?"

"Why would I be jealous of them? They're only fourteen. I was just trying to look out for them as a friend."

"Well, I also heard about you and your friends, about how you three are always kissing your girlfriends in public. Is that true?" It was quiet on the comm link now. "I had better not hear of this again, or I will pull all of you out so fast and stick you into an all-boys school. Do you hear me?" Larson said furiously, and the tone of his voice conveyed his feelings.

"Yes, sir."

"Good. Now get to bed."

"Yes, sir," Fâd said with an edge of defiance in his tone, and the comm went silent. Larson reached up and rubbed his temple as Sharni came into the bedroom.

"That bad, huh?" she asked.

"Yeah, and I still don't know about letting the girls go to the game."

"Larson, they really didn't do anything wrong. Granted, those older boys are definitely chasing after them, but what can happen at the game? They will be with their school and all the teachers. Plus, the professor will be right there as well."

"I suppose you're right. I guess I will let them go, but one thing that is going to change is, the boys will not be allowed to come over here that much anymore."

"What about Fâd and them? Would you really pull them out and send them to a boys' school?"

"Yes, I will if things don't change. I really believe he did this because he's jealous of Ash."

"Or protective," Sharni said with a questioning look on her face.

"Yeah, that's what I'm beginning to believe. Did you know it was Fâd that brought Ash back? He did something in her room that night, what none of us know, and he won't say. I've never seen him so unsure or scared before in my life than he was when she was dying."

"Do you think he imprinted on her?"

"That's what me and Harper think. Even Dr. Taylor said he did."

"If he did, then why does he keep having girlfriends all the time?"

"I don't know, but it seems like he is purposely putting a barrier between the both of them, almost trying to stay away from her. Even Cory and Nathan I noticed are doing the same thing to Rachael and Bridgett now. It's like all three of them made some pact to try and distance themselves from the girls."

"One thing's for sure, they definitely don't get along anymore," Sharni said, heading to the door, as Larson nodded in agreement and followed her.

That night for supper, it was silent as the girls ate without saying a word; and finally, Larson couldn't take it anymore. "All right. I thought it over, and I'm going to let you three go to the game. I'm trusting you girls to not disappoint me. If I find out that you did anything unbecoming of a young lady, like flirting with Luke and them or anything of that kind, you will not be going to any after-school functions for a long time. Do I make myself clear? Trust me, this also goes for the boys as well, so don't think I'm coming down on just you girls," Larson said in a serious tone, and the girls all nodded with big grins on their faces.

Suddenly, the chattering began, and the girls were going over what they would wear to the game. They even asked Sharni and Larson what one wore to those things. Eventually, the meal was done, and the girls cleaned up, then headed to bed as Sharni and Larson went and sat down on the sofa together.

"That was a nice thing you did with the girls in there. I'm glad you're letting them go. What do you think Harper would have done about all this?"

"He would have shot the boys already and sent the girls off to an all-girls school." Larson said, chuckling.

"Well, your way is much better. Now everyone's happy again."

"Everyone but me. Now I'm stressed out and worried about what might happen," Larson said with a scowl.

"Oh, I know something that just might help," Sharni said with wicked grin.

"What's that?" Sharni leaned over and whispered into his ear, and a big grin spread across his face. Once she was done telling him, Larson jumped up, scooping her up into his arms, and headed to their bedroom, locking the door behind them.

CHAPTER 25

NEXT DAY AT school, Ash was head hunting along with Rachael and Bridgett. They were furious, and when lunchtime came around, they marched right over to Fâd and them, who were with different girls today, sitting on the tables.

"You low-life, scum-dwelling slugs, leave us alone," Ash yelled at him, and Fâd jumped up, now mad, and got into her face.

"That's fine with me. See if I ever help you girls again," Fâd yelled back at her.

"You call that helping getting us into trouble? We don't need your help. We can do just fine on our own, so you and your buddies, stay out of our lives," Ash said as she, Rachael, and Bridgett turned and started walking away.

"That's fine by me. Don't come crying to us when they make fools of you three. They're just hanging around you because you are only fourteen and don't know any better," Fâd yelled at Ash as she walked away, but instead of turning around to say something, she just kept walking, only this time, it was Bridgett who looked back and made a bad hand gesture at them, causing the boys' mouths to fall open in shock.

They walked down the hall and to their next class early, but as they headed there, Bridgett looked over at Ash and Rachael. "Is it true what Fâd said? Are they just using us because we're fourteen?"

"Of course they are. They think we are too young to know any better, to see that they are just stringing us along until older girls get jealous and start chasing them. But they're the naive ones. We will use this to our advantage," Ash said as she and Rachael looked over at Bridgett, grinning.

"How do you two know all this stuff? I had no idea."

"You trust people too much," Rachael told her as they got to their class, then sat down on the floor in the hallway, waiting for class to start so they could go in.

The rest of the week went by uneventfully, and now it was the big night. It was time to head to the school to catch the school shuttles that would take them and all the students to the game. The girls were ready and had the latest styles of clothes on, thanks to Sharni, and also fixed their hair real neat. Sharni had to admit they looked great but also not looking like fourteen-year-olds, more like sixteen-year-olds, which was the problem to begin with.

Ash, Rachael, and Bridgett didn't look their true age or act it. Since the time they were little, they had always seemed older than they really were. The teachers on the ship always told their parents that the girls were at least a couple of years ahead of kids their own age, and now it was becoming apparent, even with their development.

They did a turn for Larson so he could see them and give his thoughts. "So how do we look?" Rachael asked, grinning.

"Great. That's why you can't go," he said with an ornery grin back at them.

"Are you serious?" Bridgett asked, ready to start crying any second.

"No, I'm not. I was just joking." The girls all let out the breath they were holding and then grabbed their jackets. "Now remember, if you get into any trouble—" Larson started to say but got cut off.

"We'll hit the alert button on our multitools. We know. Don't worry," all three said in unison.

"Have fun," Sharni told them as the girls headed to the door and then left, catching the shuttle to the school. Sharni turned to Larson with a worried look on her face. "Okay, now I'm scared. Maybe we should go and watch the game and sit somewhere they won't see us?"

"Don't worry, I know where they will be all the time," Larson said and punched a button on his multitool and now saw three red dots moving through an outline map of the city on the small screen of his multitool. He pressed another button, and three more red dots were moving through an outline of the school, toward the front of the campus. Sharni came over and looked down at the screen and smiled.

"Plus, every fifteen minutes, the living room vid screen will come on showing the stadium and zero in on the girls' transponder signals. I tapped into the security cameras at the stadium," Larson said and started chuckling.

"You'll get caught. They'll trace the signal," Sharni said in disbelief.

"Please. To this day, I've never been caught. You're talking to the master." Larson grinned and scoffed at her remark.

The shuttle pulled up to the school, and they got off. They were all excited and chattering away with their friends. Ash was standing in line with Rachael and Bridgett and a group of their friends when she saw Fâd walk up to the other shuttle, holding some girl's hand, and stood in line. For some reason, Ash looked down at her hand and remembered when he held it, pulling her safely from the crowd of people at the terminal and all night at the hospital when she woke up in the middle of the night and he was asleep next to her bed.

She looked up again and over at him, and Fâd was watching her, then looked down at his hand. For some strange reason, he let go of the girl's hand he had been holding and looked back at the shuttle, waiting his turn to get on. Ash then saw Nathan and Cory walk up with different girls than they were with earlier in the week. Ash elbowed Rachael and motioned with her head over at Nathan. Rachael looked and started after him, but Ash grabbed her, holding her back, and she started struggling against Ash.

"What's wrong with you?" Ash asked her.

"I don't know, but I want to rip his head off for some reason," Rachael said, glaring at Nathan.

Bridgett looked over and saw Cory then and put her head down, looking at the ground. Cory and Nathan had seen Ash grab Rachael, and they both now looked ashamed and released the hand of the girls they were with and waited in line. Finally, everyone got on the shuttles and headed to the games.

Fifteen minutes later, the shuttles pulled up, and all the kids filed off. Ash, Rachael, and Bridgett were excited. They had never been to one of these before. As they walked into the stadium, they couldn't believe how large it was and how bright from the floating stadium lights overhead, making it seem like day out. The field was huge and covered with artificial grass with many lines marking the distances between both goals, which looked like large square boxes with holes in the center of them on each end that the small round ball was thrown into for points. Even the stadium seating was large with many bleachers rising up, completely encircling the field.

Quasar was a lot like Earth's history of a game called football, except there were no pads like those players used to wear and you passed the ball back and forth among your teammates, running down the field, which consisted of six players at all times. It did get rough as you could tackle the opponent and run blocks, but you weren't allowed to run very far with the ball before you had to pass to another teammate, and they had to do the same all the way down the field to the score box.

The girls' whole school filed in and started filling up one whole side of the stadium bleachers. They were walking down the steps when she heard her name called and looked down at the edge of the field. Luke was walking over to where her school was sitting, yelling her name and waving for her to come down. She started down the bleachers, toward the field, and then saw Sage and Brian run over by him, and they yelled for Bridgett and Rachael as well. The girls headed down and walked out on the field as the boys jogged over to them in their uniforms.

"I'm glad you girls could come, especially for the championship tonight. Wow, you girls look great," Luke said, grinning at Ash, looking her over from head to toe, and she couldn't help but blush a little. He was rather cute, especially in his uniform.

"Why don't you girls sit on the bottom row there? That way, you can get a better view of the field," Sage said, and they walked the girls over to the bottom seats of the bleacher and talked to them for a little while before the match started, leaning up against the metal barrier that separated the field from the bleachers but didn't obscure the view. Out of nowhere, Fâd, Nathan, and Cory walked by, and Fâd shouldered Luke when he passed him, and Luke gave him a dirty look.

"Oh, sorry, bud. Didn't see you there," Fâd said and kept walking.

"That's okay, bud," Luke said back sarcastically. Nathan and Cory walked by and made some sort of hand gesture to them, which obviously the boys recognized and made another one back at them, and you could tell they were all mad now.

"What was that all about?" Ash asked Luke.

"Oh, nothing, just a little rivalry among the schools. Most New Guinea prep boys think we are nothing but losers, and we feel the same about them."

"I'm sorry," Ash told him.

"It's not your fault. Well, we had better get going and warm up." Luke turned and headed to the steps to go down to the field.

"Good luck," Ash hollered to him.

"Are you kidding me? After playing a game against you, this will be simple," Luke teased her back, and Ash started giggling.

The boys ran out on the field, and they watched as they warmed up. Every so often, they would wave over at them, and the girls would wave back. Now the rest of Ash and their friends were swarming them and asking all kinds of questions about the boys.

Finally, the game started, and all their friends took seats. Ash, Rachael, and Bridgett stood up then, watching the game and really getting into it. They were cheering on Luke and them, chewing out the refs and calling the other team names and just having a blast.

Fâd, Nathan, and Cory stayed several rows up from them and seemed to be miserable. The girls they were with just sat there, bored, as Fâd and them were pouting and watching Ash and them have fun. Fâd's girlfriend put her arm in his and leaned over, nibbling on his ear, and he immediately pulled his arm out of hers and leaned away.

"Quit that," he said with a disgusted look on his face.

"You're kidding, right?" she asked in disbelief.

"No, I'm not. I don't like it."

"Fine, but you're boring, and I'm out of here," she said and got up and left, and her other friends who were with Nathan and Cory left also. The boys looked at one another, grinned, then got up and headed down the bleachers, and before Ash and them could say anything, they were standing next to them. Ash looked over at Fâd and snarled at him, Rachael tried to push Nathan away from her, and Bridgett just looked down at the ground when Cory stood beside her.

"Go away. I told you to leave me alone," Ash said but still kept watching the game and cheering on Luke's team.

"Come on, Ash. I came down here to apologize. We're sorry for what we did and want to make a truce with you guys," Fâd said to her and watched her face to see if he was getting through.

"Why are you all of a sudden trying to be nice to me?"

"Because I'm tired of fighting with you. We have been friends for too long and been through a lot together."

"I don't know. Every time we make a truce, you go and do something stupid," Ash said with an ornery smirk.

"What about you guys? You're always getting us back and at times start it as well," Fâd replied, grinning. Ash looked at him now with a skeptical expression on her face. "I'll buy you some candrin," Fâd said with a big grin.

"All right, you win with that." Ash grinned back. She couldn't resist the crunchy candy type of popcorn, so they headed to the concessions.

"Ash, where are you going?" Rachael asked her, and it was apparent she and Nathan had worked out their differences, and even Cory and Bridgett were now talking. Bridgett was even giggling.

"We're getting some candrin," Fâd answered.

"Oh, hey, grab us some and something to drink," Nathan told him, looking at Rachael, grinning.

"Us too," Cory hollered and looked at Bridgett, who nodded her head yes.

"Wow, anything else?" Ash asked sarcastically. She and Fâd headed up the long steps and finally got to the top, walking over to the stand where they sold the snacks. "Where are your girlfriends?"

"They dumped us, said we were boring," Fâd replied, grinning.

"Well, you kind of are," Ash teased.

"That's because we don't know how to act our own age. We're too used to hanging out with you three."

"Oh, there we go with the age thing again," Ash said defiantly as they stood in line to get the snacks.

"That's not what I mean, but really, Ash, those boys are just using you because you're only fourteen."

"I know, but don't you think we are doing the same to them? Look how it has boosted our popularity rating at school," Ash told him with a devious smirk.

"You're evil. Are you sure you're really fourteen, then?" Fâd asked, laughing now, and Ash joined in.

Before long, they headed back to the game with armloads of drinks and candrin. Ash followed Fâd down the steps with a bunch of the stuff, and finally, they got to the bottom. Fâd then stood aside so Ash could go first. She started handing the stuff down like a conveyor line, and finally, everyone had something and was eating or drinking.

The game now was nearing the end, and Luke's team was barely ahead by a couple of points. "So how did you meet this guy?" Fâd asked as he threw a handful of the candrin in his mouth, watching the scene out on the field.

"He lives next door to us," Ash answered, reaching over and grabbing a handful of candrin out of the bucket, because Fâd was holding it while she was holding the drink that they were also sharing but with two straws. Fâd choked and looked over at her.

"When did he move in?"

"I don't know. He was there when we arrived for school," she told him with her mouth full, and some of the candrin fell out of her mouth, half chewed. Fâd saw it and started grossing out, teasing her, and Ash started laughing, still with a mouthful, and spraying chewed candrin everywhere. Rachael and the rest of them were also laughing at Ash as she had tears running down her face from laughing so hard.

Fâd was now pushing her away from him so she wouldn't spit food on him but still laughing and teasing her.

The buzzer went off, announcing the game was over and that Luke's team won. They stood around, gathering up their stuff, when Luke, Sage, and Brian came running over, but when they saw Fâd and them with the girls, their faces changed from happy to jealous and mad. They came up into the stands where the girls were.

"So what did you think?" Luke asked Ash, totally ignoring Fâd, who was standing right next to her.

"It was great. This was so much fun."

"Come on, we're going to go and get something to eat afterward and want you girls to go with us," Luke asked and reached for Ash's hand.

"I can't. I have to stay with my school, and we're leaving right now."

"They won't know. Come on, the three of you and the three of us. Let's celebrate. We only won because of you three and all those full contact games we played together," Luke said with a smug look on his face, looking at Fâd.

Fâd narrowed his eyes, looking at Luke. "She can't, school policy, unless she wants to get suspended. Besides, buddy, she's with me," Fâd said, putting the candy down, and pushed Luke's hand away from Ash, stepping in front of her. Now Nathan and Cory also put their stuff down and stepped up closer with Rachael and Bridgett behind them, glaring at the other boys.

Luke glared at him and then at Ash. "Fine, go home with your loser boyfriend," he said, and Fâd doubled up his fist and was going to start beating the crap out of him when Ash grabbed Fâd's arm and shook her head no.

"That's right, listen to your baby girlfriend. How pathetic you..." But he didn't say another word as Ash slugged him square in the mouth over Fâd's shoulder. Fâd was the one then who was holding Ash back as she was struggling to get at Luke now. Nathan and Cory both took an attack stance as the other boys acted like they were going to fight, but once they saw Nathan and Cory's poise, they quickly grabbed Luke and ran.

"Let me at him. I'm going to rip his head from his shoulders," Ash yelled as Fâd wrapped his arms around her to restrain her.

"Ash, stop it. Calm down. It's over now."

"Yeah, run, you little peckerheads," Rachael yelled at the fleeing boys as they raced across the field, and Nathan turned to her with a big grin on his face.

"And I kissed that mouth?" Rachael turned bright red now and put her hand over her mouth and looked away as everyone started laughing. Fâd finally let go of Ash but was grinning and shaking his head.

"My gosh, Ash, you are always full of surprises. There is never a dull moment with you three around."

Just then, the professor yelled for them to come as the bleachers were emptying out, and everyone was getting on the shuttles. They gathered up their candy, drinks, and jackets and quickly ran up the long steps and walked over, but they saw the shuttle the girls had come on was completely full, so they had to get on the other one. Ash walked down the aisle and sat down as Fâd plopped down next to her, and Nathan and Cory sat with Rachael and Bridgett. The whole ride back, they were laughing about Ash popping Luke in the mouth and Rachael yelling at them while they all finished off the candrin and drinks they had gotten earlier.

Finally, the shuttle pulled up to the school, and all the students unloaded. The boys walked the girls over to their shuttle to take back home. "Girls, it was fun, like always. See you at school in a couple of days," Fâd said to them, and they all went their separate ways.

The shuttle pulled in front of the house, and the girls went in, jabbering away, and then saw Admiral Larson and Sharni waiting for them even though it was rather late. "So was it fun?" Larson asked with a grin.

"Yeah, it was," Ash told them.

"Did you see and talk to Luke and them?" Sharni asked.

"Yep," Bridgett said, and the girls were trying not to start giggling.

"All right, what happened?" Larson asked as he narrowed his eyes at them, waiting to hear it from them since he already knew from his surveillance tap of the security cameras at the stadium.

"Well, you don't have to worry about those boys ever coming over again," Rachael told them.

"Why? What did you do?" Sharni now looked worried because she didn't know, and Larson didn't tell her.

The girls told them everything, and Larson started laughing, and even Sharni giggled a little. It was really late, and the girls excused themselves and went to bed, but once they heard Sharni and the admiral go to bed, they climbed down the tree by the balcony again and laid out near the tree in the yard, watching the stars.

"Hey, Ash, why is it we can always have a lot more fun around Fâd and them, but with other boys, it's just not the same?" Bridgett asked.

"Probably because we have known them for so long and we all have kind of grown up together and can act ourselves around them."

"That makes sense, but why do I feel it's something else?" Bridgett said as she watched the stars in the sky.

"You guys want to know something and promise to keep it a secret?" Rachael asked them.

"Yeah, we promise," Ash replied, looking over at her friend.

"No, I mean promise me," Rachael said with a serious look on her face.

"We promise on our scars," Ash said again.

Rachael let out a sigh. "I really liked it when Nathan kissed me." Nobody said anything for a while, then out of nowhere, they all started laughing.

CHAPTER 26

A MONTH OF school went by, and nothing exciting happened. The girls hung out a lot with all their friends, and Fâd and them were back to having a different girlfriend every week, which still bothered Ash and them, and totally ignoring the girls. Finally, Sharni and Larson decided it was time to celebrate their marriage and let the girls plan the whole thing. Of course, the girls were having a blast and got the house all decorated and even a bunch of food catered. There was even a cake and nonalcoholic wine since there was also going to be them and the boys there too. Rachael had contacted a lot of Larson's friends from the *Lithia* and Sharni's from the *Astra Sink* and Nera, of course, from Pantier.

It was the day of the party, and people soon started showing up. The house inside and out was now buzzing with all the chatter and brimming with people. The girls were really glad they had hired wait staff so they wouldn't have to serve everyone, because they didn't realize how many people actually were coming. The admiral was dressed in his formal uniform, and Sharni was also dressed likewise, and they moved through the crowd, talking and laughing with everyone. The girls found it somewhat boring with all the adults and went and turned on the vid screen in the kitchen and was watching a vid show when Fâd and them showed up, and of course, they had girls with them.

Ash, Rachael, and Bridgett were a little perturbed that they would show up to this with dates, so they totally ignored them as the boys came into the kitchen with chairs and sat down to watch the vid also. Their dates made a point to show Ash and them that they were the boys' girls by sitting on their laps, flirting with them, or messing up their hair.

"Fâdy, can you get me something to drink? I'm thirsty," Fâd's date asked him, running her finger down his face. He got up and walked over to the refrigerator and got a juice out for her, then sat back down to watch the vid as she plopped back down in his lap. Ash rolled her eyes at Rachael and Bridgett and motioned toward the patio doors. They got up and headed over to the door, which slid open automatically, and walked out into the backyard. The yard was pretty well empty now as partygoers had moved inside to visit with Admiral Larson and Sharni, so the girls had the backyard all to themselves.

"Oh, was that sickening or what?" Rachael said, acting like she was going to throw up, and picked up a large round ball and threw it over to Ash, who caught it easily.

"Rachael, don't throw the ball so hard. It might knock what little brain I have out my ear," Ash said in a mocking tone and putting her hand on her cheek.

"Do these shoes make my butt look large?" Bridgett said, also in a mocking tone, and Ash and Rachael started laughing. Ash chucked the ball hard at Bridgett, who did a backflip, avoiding it. The ball then slammed on the glass of the patio door without breaking it and flew back at them, and both Ash and Rachael leaped to catch it, but Rachael was quicker. She then turned to throw it at Ash, who took off running, and right before the ball got to her, she flipped into the air, spinning a couple of times and landing on her feet. Of course, the boys had gotten out of their chairs when the ball slammed into the glass door to see what was going on and were amazed by what the girls could do.

Ash raced over and picked up the ball, then spun completely around to throw the ball faster and harder at Rachael, who did a backflip out of the way at the last second. The battle was on now, and they were throwing as hard as they could at one another, dodging or catching it and laughing the whole time.

"Come on. Let's join them," Fâd said to his date, grinning.

"Are you kidding me? That's what children do," she said to him and looked appalled that he even thought about it.

Nathan looked at his date, and she glared at him. "Don't even think about. If you go out there and play with those little girls, we're through."

Cory started to head out there, and his date grabbed his arm. "I want to go home now!"

"Then go home, there's the front door." Cory told her and pointed to it then headed out the patio doors.

Fâd just grinned down at his date and left following Cory as Nathan made a cocky little salute to his date and also left. The girls were furious now turned and left the house without even looking back.

"Hey, room for three more?" Fâd asked grinning.

"I don't know. Can you handle it, Fâdy?" Ash asked sarcastically and chucked the ball at him. He caught it as a big grin spread across his face, and he acted like he was going to hammer her with it but instead nailed Rachael right upside the head, knocking her flat. Bridgett and Ash started laughing as Rachael jumped up, picking up the ball, and with an evil grin thumped Cory in the back of the head, knocking him down to his knees. After that, it was a free-for-all, and every one of them was throwing hard. Even the girls could hurl the ball hard using their martial art moves, usually a spin throw or a flip throw. They even continued to play once it started getting dark, and they could barely see, but that didn't stop them. A few times, one of them ran right into something or each other, falling down laughing.

It got very late, and the party wound down as people finally left, and the wait staff cleaned up. The kids were all sitting out on patio chairs, now talking, when Sharni and Larson came out of the house. "We want to thank you girls for this. We had a great time. I just wish Admiral Harper and them could have been here," Sharni said, smiling.

"I know. He would have wanted to be here if he could," Ash told her.

"You kids should get to bed. It is so late. That's where we're heading as well. Good night, kids," Larson told them and headed into the house, and the kids all got up and walked in right behind them. The girls headed upstairs to their room, and the boys grabbed the packs they had brought just in case and changed into pajama bottoms, then pulled the sleepers out from the sofas. No sooner had they done that than they noticed through the glass patio sliding doors small lights bouncing around, moving across the backyard.

Fâd grinned and looked over at Nathan and Cory. "Grab some blankets, guys. It's under the stars tonight."

They grabbed all they could and quietly headed to the automatic sliding patio doors, then went out. They could hear the girls talking and giggling. They knew exactly where they would be because it wasn't the first time they had stayed out all night and walked over to the tree that the girls liked to sleep near. The spot had a great view of the night sky but also kept one hidden from the house and surrounding neighbors.

They walked up to where they were. "Do you girls sleep out here a lot?"

Ash jumped with her fist up. "Damn it, you scared the crap out of me," she said, then continued spreading out her blanket. Fâd helped her, chuckling knowing he had scared her, and then he and Nathan spread out the rest as Cory actually went over on the other side and sat down next to Bridgett with a blanket in his arms, wrapping it around both of them.

Fâd sat down next to Ash, and Nathan was on the other side of him with Rachael next to Ash. They all just talked among themselves, which they did a lot when they got together like this and were not trying to kill one another. They would laugh and tease one another and had little competitions, but mostly, they just talked about growing up and always fell asleep, not even realizing it had happened until the morning, which they did.

Fâd was the first to start to stir and could tell it was still early in the morning. He looked at Ash, who was sleeping on her side, facing him, still sound asleep. They were barely inches apart from each other as he was also facing her on his side with his arm around her. He could see Rachael sideway on the blanket at their feet with her legs over both of theirs, and then he saw Cory a little ways from them, lying on his back with Bridgett sleeping in the crook of his arm. But it was the funny feeling he had suddenly that got him moving fast. He realized that there was an arm around him, and he could feel someone sleeping up against him. It was Nathan, who was sound asleep, with his arm around Fâd, up against his back.

"What the hell!" Fâd yelled and rolled over onto Nathan to try and get away, which, of course, woke everyone up.

Ash and Rachael blinked their eyes many times to focus and now saw Fâd on top of Nathan as the two of them wrestled around to get away. Cory lifted his head and looked over at them, then laid back down, closed his eyes, and pulled the blanket that was covering him and Bridgett up further. Finally, Fâd got up and glared down at Nathan.

"Don't ever do that again!" Fâd hissed at Nathan, who now had a rotten grin on his face.

"Sorry. Can't help it. I love you, man," Nathan told him, laughing, which made Ash and Rachael start laughing.

Fâd walked over, still fuming, and started picking up the blankets, making Nathan, Ash, and Rachael get off them. "Let's get these picked up and back in the house before my father and Sharni get up," Fâd told them. He looked over at Cory and Bridgett, who still hadn't moved. "That includes you two."

Finally, they got up as well, and everyone shook out the blankets and folded them back up, then quietly sneaked back into the house. The girls went up to their room, and the boys laid down in the sleepers. Everyone fell asleep again for another hour, and finally, the girls came down just as the boys were waking back up. They headed into the kitchen to fix some breakfast as the boys straightened up the living room, and once breakfast was fixed, they came in and sat at the snack bar with the girls and ate too.

Ash finished first and went outside because she had left her light out there. She found it easily, then was starting back to the house when Luke yelled at her from over the fence. "If it isn't one of the New Guinea babies. So what's it like to be a loser?" he yelled from the other side of the fence.

Ash could hear a bunch of chuckling coming from over there. "Why don't you come over and say that to my face, or are you scared that I might beat you up again?"

"Fine. I will," Luke replied and climbed over the fence, but this time, he was with seven of his friends, and Ash was alone, just dressed in her pajama top and shorts. She took a defensive stance, and Luke came after her. She started fighting him and one other boy at the same time as the rest circled around her to watch. Inside the house, Rachael was finishing up and leaned back on her barstool to see what Ash was doing and why it was taking her so long when she saw her fighting outside.

"Crap!" was all she said and raced through the sliding doors, barely giving them time to open, and ran straight at the boys, leaping onto one of the boys' back, and started punching him right away. Everyone else in the house looked to see what was going on, and they, too, took off running out of the house. Ash was doing pretty well, but when she went to block the one boy, Luke caught her in the mouth, and she fell to the ground. Fâd was there instantly, standing over her, and sent Luke flying through the air with one punch. Nathan pulled Rachael off the back of the boy whom she was hitting and knocked him flat. Cory took on two more, and Rachael ran over and helped Bridgett as they went after the other three, who were now running for the fence.

"Don't you ever touch her again, or so help me, I will kill you," Fâd said, standing over Ash in a protective manner with his fists up, to Luke when he got back up from the ground. Luke took one look at Fâd's face and saw the rage in it and ran for the fence, climbing over it with the rest of his guys. Fâd spun around and squatted next to Ash. "Are you okay?"

"Yeah. He got lucky. I was doing pretty good there for a while," Ash said, grinning, with a bloody mouth from the split lip she got. Fâd just shook his head, half-smiled, and pulled her to her feet, and all of them walked back into the house just as Sharni and Larson came running out of their bedroom when they heard the commotion, still in their pajamas. Sharni saw Ash's bloody mouth and ran over to her, putting her arm around her, then led her over to the sink.

"Fâd, what happened?" Larson asked, now mad, but at whom, he didn't know yet.

"Luke got a bunch of his buddies together and decided to pay Ash back, but they weren't expecting all of us," Fâd told him, watching Sharni help Ash.

Sharni was having Ash wash her mouth out and spit the bloody water into the sink. Then she got some cold crystals out of the freezer section of the refrigerator and wrapped them into a towel and had Ash go and sit down with it on her lip.

"I'm going to have a talk with this Luke and his parents. Impressive, he has to get a group together to take on one girl. That's real brave of him," Larson said, and you could tell he was furious right now.

"There's no need. He won't be bothering the girls ever again," Fâd told his father, still watching Ash with a concerned look on his face.

"Yeah, especially after Fâd knocked him flying and told him that he will kill him if he ever comes around," Nathan said, and Fâd shot him a dirty look.

"Plus, I think he realized he underestimated the girls," Cory added and smiled over at Bridgett, who blushed and looked away. Larson stood there for a few silent minutes, then decided to let it drop since the kids all assured him they took care of it and checked on Ash to make sure she was okay.

Breakfast was over, and the excitement died down. Ash's lip, though, was puffy and sore, but she was proud of it. The rest of the day they all lay around playing vid games or watching a movie, and it wasn't until late in the day that any of them finally changed out of their pajamas. Larson and Sharni even took a long nap because of such a late night, and off and on, a couple of the kids would crash either during a vid or while watching the others playing a vid game.

Dinnertime came, and Sharni fixed everyone something to eat, and once the meal was done, the kids all cleaned up. Soon, it was time for the boys to head back to the campus, for it was getting late. They picked up all their stuff and headed out the door, yelling their goodbyes, and finally, it was Larson, Sharni, and just the girls again.

"Now what? That was fun, but we have nothing to do now," Rachael said, looking around.

"I know. Let's see if we can find some other neighborhood kids we can beat up now," Ash said, grinning through her swollen lip. Everyone, including Larson and Sharni, picked up pillows from the sofa and started hitting her with them.

CHAPTER 27

⸺◈⸺

MONTHS FLEW BY, and everything was quiet. School for the girls was boring, just classes, homeworks, and tests, which, of course, they all did very well in. The only exciting thing to happen, which really wasn't exciting, was that Rachael came home one of the days feeling poorly. By that night, she had both ends going with a fever and joint pain. Sharni called the local med clinic, and apparently, there was an epidemic of the same thing going around, and they gave her some medication to give Rachael. Of course, Ash and Bridgett slept in the living room. There was no way they would get anywhere near Rachael. But that didn't save them, and a week and a half later, the illness had run its course through each and every one of them, all at different times, thank goodness, since there were only three bathrooms.

Larson decided to take everyone to Pantier and stay for a couple of days after he was the last one to finally recover and called in a decontamination team. Sharni was mad because all the neighbors were watching as the team put the house completely in an airtight bubble, not to mention wearing hazard suits while entering the structure when the admiral and her with all the kids climbed into a hover vehicle to leave. The kids, including the boys, whom the admiral invited to go along since Pantier was their home, were all laughing, thinking it was real funny, and teasing Rachael. They started calling her the Blaster because that was what one experienced when either end let loose while you were sick. Rachael just laughed and told them to knock it off, or she would show the real meaning of the blaster. Larson warned her that she better not because they were all crammed into the vehicle and he knew what she was getting at.

Hours later, when they finally got to Pantier and Larson's home, the kids explored the woods around the house, and the boys even went swimming in the pond during the middle of the day. The girls wanted to, but the admiral told them no since they had just gotten over being sick. He let them put their feet in, though, and Sharni warned him that was a big mistake. Sure enough, he looked outside an hour later and all three girls were now in the pond, trying to drown the boys and still wearing all their clothes. He hollered at Sharni, who came over, looked out the window, and started giggling, telling him she had warned him.

He went out and yelled at the girls and had them come in, then take baths. They grudgingly got out and did what he said, then stayed in the house the rest of the day since he had also put them under house arrest. The boys came in as well, and the kids played games the rest of the day clear up until it was bedtime.

The next morning, the admiral got up, and his mouth fell open in shock. There lying at the foot of one of the sleepers were Ash and Rachael with their feet pressed up against Fâd's back, who was hugging the sofa back where the bed started, sound asleep. Over on the other large sleeper and sprawled completely out by himself was Nathan, snoring with his mouth wide open. Bridgett was lying across an armchair, wrapped in a blanket, but there was no sign of Cory. Larson looked all around the room and finally could hear some more snoring and peeked under one of the sleepers, and sure enough, there was Cory, wrapped up like a cocoon in a blanket, sleeping on the floor.

The admiral now got a good look of the living room. It looked like a war had happened here. Cards were everywhere and pillows all over the place, and one of them must have torn open because the soft fiber used to fill it was everywhere, giving the room a look like snow had fallen overnight. Then there was all the trash. They obviously had a little party, as plates, empty juice bottles, and candy wrappers—you name it—were littering the room and covering the kids as they slept.

He was standing there, still surveying the carnage, when Sharni came out, and her expression was the same as his earlier, but now he was just mad. He reached down and pulled up a screen on his multitool, then put in some type of order and pushed a button and waited. Sharni covered her ears, and suddenly, the house went into full alert as sirens went off and flashing red lights dropped from the ceiling. The kids flew up, out of the places they were sleeping, as food and pillow fiber fell off them, and they instantly stood in a defensive stance, surveying their surroundings for the danger.

Cory was the last one up, and he started yelling for help. Fâd and Nathan dragged him out from under the sleeper, and he unwrapped himself, also looking for danger. Larson was impressed with their exceptionally fast response, but now it was time to address the real issue.

The admiral reached down and pushed a button on his wrist tool again, and the sirens stopped, and the flashing lights retracted back into the ceiling. He stood there glaring at the kids and folded his arms over his chest. Even Sharni looked mad, and finally, she just walked off to the kitchen to fix something to eat.

"Do I even need to ask?" Larson spoke to the kids in a very cold tone.

"No, sir. We will get it cleaned up now," Fâd replied, and the kids instantly started cleaning. The admiral walked into the kitchen and pulled out a trash container, and there was the torn-up pillow in it. He just shook his head and took the container out to them and left it. Sharni was pulling food items out of the refrigerator and started making some vatorian dish as Larson poured himself a cup of creo and leaned against the counter, watching her.

"You know, there are only two more months and school will be done. Plus, I haven't heard a word," Larson said quietly to Sharni.

"I know, and that worries me."

"Me too. I contacted command the other day, and they said Harper ordered no communications until he contacted them first."

"Can you still not tell me what he is doing?" Sharni stopped and looked at Larson with worry on her face.

"I suppose I can now since he should be heading back if everything went all right. If not, we'll be going after him anyway. This was a covert operation, top secret. You know all about sentinel fleet's exodus plans to leave council space to avoid a conflict between us and them, and since we have begun the fleet's draw out from council space, many in command, including me and Harper, didn't feel right about leaving the colonies that we protect defenseless. So scouting and infiltrating teams have been scouring all the closest systems, trying to locate the carian home planet.

"We hadn't found anything, but when I was out last, we attacked a very large and well-equipped merc holdout that you were there for. They had a lot of carian weapons and technology, and we were able to find and locate a large carian base from the mercs that we are sure has been where a lot of the raids are originating from.

"It was huge. Of course, you know how fast those things breed anyway, and they had many ships docked there. I couldn't make a strike. The *Lithia* was too weakened from the merc attack, having to push her that hard to trail them. Plus, you saw some of the other ships. We did take some damages. Harper was given the mission when he came back on duty, and of course, he would never turn one down anyways if it was to attack carians. You know how he hates them. His mission was to go in and annihilate every last one of them, their base, ships, everything," Larson told her quietly.

"Even...?" Sharni asked knowing what he was going to say.

"Yes, every last one of them, no one spared," Larson said coldly now and in his admiral persona.

"You two carry a lot of scars, don't you?" Sharni asked, looking at him with sadness in her face.

"You do what you have to do to save lives and the ones you love, but Harper is taking it one step further. He's scorching the planet so no one will ever be able to use it again," Larson told her, and Sharni just stood there. She looked at the man she loved and realized something for the first time in her life: Larson and Harper could show love and devotion, but underneath that was a cold, ruthless killer who held no remorse for their actions, and it scared her. She knew she could fight to save lives and her crew and follow orders to a certain extent, but something like this she wasn't sure she could do. It would weight too heavy on her heart. Genocide was a command she couldn't obey.

"I really didn't want to tell you all the details. Please don't think ill of us, not to mention this is hush-hush. If this got out to council, it would be another way of them trying to show our few remaining supporters that we are nothing but hired mercs, and you know where that would lead, a confrontation we are trying to avoid for their sake."

"I know, but now I'm even more worried about Harper. Shouldn't he be contacting command and reporting?"

"No. He's probably in stealth, not wanting to leave a trail that can be followed back and what he did to the planet found out."

"That makes sense," she said and went back to fixing breakfast as Larson started to go check on the kids but stopped and looked at her.

"Sharni, if it weren't Harper, it would have been me, and I wouldn't hesitate either," he told her in a cold tone, and a chill ran up her back. She knew he loved her more than anything in this world and would give his life for her, but above all else, he was a soldier, and he could kill without remorse.

She continued to fix breakfast as Larson left the kitchen, and then she heard Gerrard in the living room, complimenting the kids on a job well done. The cold, dangerous man she was talking to just a few minutes ago seemed like a figment of her imagination now hearing the man out there talking to the children. She couldn't help but love him even more knowing that he shouldered all the terrible things that no one knew about so they could live happy, worry-free lives, yet a little part of her feared him some too knowing what he was capable of.

Breakfast was ready, and the kids came in and ate as Larson went over to his private terminal and started going through his messages and linking into command central. A smile spread across his face as he typed. "Wow, that's amazing. I swear, he has telepathy too," Larson said over his shoulder to Sharni, and she started grinning.

298

"Hey, Ash, want to hear something?" Larson said as he punched up the message.

"This is Vice Admiral Harper of the *Justification*. We are on course for Sigma Six and should be arriving in orbit in about fifty-seven days. Mission successful. No casualties. Tell Larson he can kiss my ass. Too old, huh? Harper out."

"Where did you get that from?" Ash asked with tears in her eyes, as did the other girls, knowing their parents were okay too and on their way back.

"It just came in today to command central," Larson told her, grinning, and looked over at Sharni, who also had wet eyes.

Breakfast was over, and the kids cleaned the kitchen up. An hour later, they were all back in the shuttle, heading to New Guinea. The kids were all buckled up in their seats on the shuttle, talking among themselves, when Rachael looked over at Nathan.

"Hey, isn't there a dance coming up next month at school?" Rachael asked everyone.

"Yeah. Wanna go?" Nathan asked her, grinning.

"With whom?"

"Me, of course." He frowned at her.

"Okay, as long as you promise not to fart like you did last night. That wasn't right." Rachael laughed and teased him.

"I promise," Nathan replied, laughing as well.

"What about you, Ash? Would you go if someone asked you?" Nathan grinned at her, and Ash narrowed her eyes at him.

"Nope. There is no way I would put on some stupid dress and go moving around like some monkey." Everyone in the shuttle started laughing, even the admiral and Sharni.

"What about you, Cory? Who are you asking?" Nathan looked over at him.

"Already did."

"And they accepted?" Nathan teased.

"Of course. I'm not that bad," Cory replied, giving Nathan a dirty look, but now everyone could see that Bridgett was blushing, and they knew it was her.

"Well, that just leaves you, Fâd. Who are you going to ask?" Nathan now put him on the spot, and Fâd gave him a dirty look.

"I already asked someone last week," he said coldly and in a tone that said to not press the subject anymore.

Ash just sat there, trying to act like what Fâd had just said didn't bother her, but for some reason, it did. She felt like someone had just punched her in the stomach, knocking the wind out of her.

"Come on, Ash, you have to go. We're all going. It won't be the same without you. Just think of all the trouble we can get into. Don't you have some friends that would ask her?" Rachael turned to Nathan.

"Sure, they would," Nathan said.

"No thanks. Now you're making me feel like some charity case. Besides, I have to get packed to leave. Dad will be back soon," Ash replied and gave Rachael a dirty look to drop the subject.

The rest of the shuttle ride was quiet, and even once they landed and got through the terminal and in the vehicle, it was also silent. They pulled up to the house, and Sharni and the girls went in as the admiral rode back to the school with the boys. Half an hour later, he was back, just in time for lunch.

The remainder of the day was spent washing clothes and getting ready for another week of school since everyone was healthy again. Yet the next day at school was a miserable one for Ash. Everywhere she turned, there were signs talking about the formal dance. She even started hiding so no one would possibly ask her, but at lunch, her luck ran out. She was sitting with Rachael and Bridgett, eating, when Fâd, who had a new girl with him already, walked in with Nathan, Cory, and a few of their friends. One of the guys with them said something to Cory, who pointed over to Ash and them, and he turned and looked. Ash could see a big grin on his face, and he headed over to them as she tried to will herself invisible.

"Hi, Ashley. I'm Jeremy Stills. I was wondering if you wanted to go to the dance with me," the boy asked her, and Ash could see he was nervous.

"I really…" But she didn't get to finish what she was going to say because Rachael kicked her in the leg under the table. "I would really like that, sure," Ash said with a forced smile. The boy headed back over to his friends, and they all gave one another a high five, but when Ash looked over there, Fâd didn't look too happy about it and was now glaring at the boy.

"Great. Now we're all going. This is going to be so much fun," Rachael said and started talking about shopping for dresses.

"Rachael, I don't want to go," Ash said quietly to her friend. Rachael looked around and grabbed Ash by the arm, dragging her out into the hallway to a place they could be alone.

"Ash, don't do this. Don't just shut yourself off from having fun because Fâd didn't ask you. Don't let him get to you. Look, he's with another girl this week and already asked one to the dance. He only sees you as a friend, so don't put your life on hold waiting for him," Rachael told her quietly but also a little mad.

"Is it that obvious?"

"Yes. You just started coming out of your shell and having fun, and then boom, he comes around and you withdraw and wait for him. What do you think is going to happen in two years? They will leave, and we won't ever see them again, and then you'll look back and see you threw all this time away."

"You're right, Rachael. I will always regret it then. All right, let's go have some fun," Ash told her best friend, grinning. They headed back to the lunchroom, but this time, Ash had a big grin on her face. She didn't even look over at Fâd but started talking to her friends about dresses.

School let out, and the girls were excited to get home and tell Sharni that they all were going to the dance now. "Sharni, guess what?" Rachael yelled when they walked through the door.

"What? What's going on?" She looked worried when she came around the corner of the kitchen.

"Ash got asked to the dance, and by a cute boy too," Rachael said, all proud of her friend.

"That's wonderful! We'll have to go shopping to find you girls some dresses," Sharni said, excited as well. Larson was sitting on the sofa, watching the vid, and just rolled his eyes at them as the girls continued into the kitchen with Sharni, talking all about dresses.

Time flew by, and before they knew it, the dance was here, and it was crazy in the house. Sharni was helping the girls get ready, running from one to another. Finally, they were all done and came down the stairs to show Larson. When he saw them, he couldn't believe they were the same girls. They looked stunning and definitely not like any fourteen-year-old. They all wore a very slim, form-fitting gown that showed they were definitely changing physically, and it was cut heart-shaped style in the front and had a high collar with short-capped sleeves. The girls all wore long silk gloves, and Bridgett and Rachael had pretty necklaces on as Ash wore an engraved silver metal choker.

Even their gowns were a little different, but the style was the same. Ash's was silver with a gold sash around her waist and ending snuggly around her hips. Rachael had a red one that sparkled all over and a black V-shaped belt on. Bridgett wore an emerald-green one that split up in the back a little. Even their gloves matched their dresses, and their hair was also different. Ash pulled hers back on the sides and secured it in the back with her mother's comb again, but now she had put white rhinestones in her wavy long black hair. Rachael left hers down too but had a beaded red headpiece on that had dainty red chains that hung down the back. Bridgett pulled hers almost into a ponytail in the back but had it made into ringlets that cascaded down her back. Of course, there were also the multiple earrings they all wore in their ears, and Ash and Rachael had their removable tiny crystals on their noses.

"Harper is going to kill me for letting you girls out looking like that," Larson told them with a scowl on his face.

"Why? Do we look bad?" Bridgett asked, worried.

"No, just the opposite. You all look radiant," he said, smiling, and the girls all grinned.

Just then, the door buzzed, and Larson walked over and opened it but had a surprised look on his face when he saw who it was. He stood aside as Nathan, Cory, and Fâd walked in, all dressed in formal dress sentinel uniforms. Ash's mouth fell open, and she was confused why Fâd was there. The boys stopped in their tracks when they saw the girls, and their mouths fell open.

"Wow, is that really you, girls?" Nathan asked in amazement, and Larson slapped his forehead and closed his eyes. Sometimes, he just wondered if Nathan was all right upstairs.

"Yeah. How do we look?" Rachael asked and made a turn so they could see all of her.

"Hot," Nathan replied with a grin.

"Don't you mean very pretty?" Sharni corrected him.

"Oh no, hot is better," Nathan said back, and Larson then was sure that Nathan was missing some upstairs.

"Fâd, what are you doing here? Where is Jeremy?" Ash asked him, confused.

"I found out Jeremy couldn't make it, and my date suddenly decided to go with someone else, so it's just you and me again," Fâd told her, smiling, without taking his eyes off her.

"That's not how I remember it went down. You informed Jeremy right after he asked her that—" But Nathan never got to finish as Fâd shouldered him when he walked past him, over to Ash, leaving Nathan just standing there, looking confused.

"Shall we go?" Fâd asked her and presented his arm for Ash, and they headed to the door as the other boys came over and did the same.

"Behave yourselves, and no fighting!" Larson ordered them.

"Yes, sir," the kids all replied with an ornery grin.

They all headed out to the waiting airlimo, and the boys even acted like gentlemen and helped the girls in, then climbed in the vehicle with them and headed to the place the dance was being held. They pulled up outside a very fancy building that had attendants opening the vehicle doors for everyone and helping the girls out. Once they got out, the boys again offered their arms, and they headed into the ballroom. It was, in actuality, a simulation room made up to look like they were in a tropical paradise, and the girls were looking around and talking about how great everything looked. There were a lot of couples already from school, dancing, and the music were the latest popular hits.

Many tables surrounded the dance floor, and a lot of them were filled with students and their dates already. Ash then saw Jeremy, the boy who had asked her, with the girl whom Fâd had supposedly asked. She tapped him on the arm and pointed over to them, and he looked, then leaned down to her so she could hear him over the music.

"So that's why they couldn't go with either of us. I feel really used right now. What about you?"

"Who cares? We'll show them. They'll be jealous because we know how to have fun, and they don't," Ash told him, grinning, and Fâd grinned back.

They all went over to a table and sat down. The boys got up and went to get everyone something to drink as Rachael leaned over to Ash. "Okay, I might have been wrong."

"No, you weren't. We are strictly just friends," Ash said, smiling at her, and Rachael smiled back. A few minutes later, the boys came back, and they all decided to dance. At first, everyone but Rachael and Nathan were nervous and moved like they were frozen; but when they saw Rachael and Nathan, who were all over the place, they started laughing, which relaxed them, and also acted crazy.

The night wore on, and they danced with one another. Sometimes, it was Ash and Nathan or her and Cory. The same went with Rachael and Bridgett, dancing with Fâd, Nathan, or Cory, but no matter who it was, they all had a blast and never stopped laughing. The only awkward times were when a slow dance came on. Rachael, Nathan, Cory, and Bridgett didn't seem to have a problem, but she and Fâd did. They both were very nervous getting close like that and could hardly dance. It was during one of these that changed their friendship and the possibility of it becoming something more forever.

They were slowly moving around the floor. Fâd had hold of Ash's hand, and his left hand was on the small of her back, leading as they danced together. They were talking, which was how they kept their nerves in check, when Fâd asked her something that caught her off guard, and she looked up at him. He then pulled her closer to him and continued to move around the floor. This time, their eyes were locked on each other.

"What did you say?" she asked, stunned by his question.

"Could you ever forget about me?"

"No. Why would I want to?"

"Because you need to, Ash. We both do!"

"What are you saying? You don't mean that?" Ash asked, scared and confused.

"This isn't good for either of us. I only have a few more years here, and you know next year there won't be time for us to hang around with each other anymore. I care too much for you, and I know you care for me. To even remain friends would cause too much pain for both of us. We have to let this go and forget one another. Your path is already set for you, as is mine, and they lead away from each other," Fâd said, and Ash could tell he was serious, and in truth, she knew he was right.

The last two years at school, the older students were never around and were always busy with studies. Then after that, all sentinel fleet students would be leaving on active duty and finishing their military training for over a year aboard one of the fleet ships, finally ending at the academy where they would spend another four years of their lives. Upon completion there, they would put in their request for what ship they wanted to serve on, and her request was already planned. She would be serving on the *Justification* under her father, and Fâd would be serving under his father and the *Lithia*.

She was still looking up at him as her heart was breaking, and tears started running down her face. He wiped them away, then started to lean down toward her, but the music ended, and he pulled away at the last minute, grabbing her hand and leading her off the dance floor, over to where everyone was sitting. She tried to look happy when they got back to the table and even joked with her friends. Fâd also put on a good front, and they even danced together some more, but it wasn't as fun as earlier.

Finally, things were winding down, and they left the ballroom and climbed back into the vehicle to head back to the girls' house. Rachael and Bridgett were chattering away, as was Nathan, who could talk as much as the girls, and on several occasions, he had them all laughing. Eventually, the airlimo pulled up, and everyone got out and went inside. Admiral Larson and Sharni were waiting for them, and the kids started telling them about all the fun they had.

After a while, the boys took their leave and headed for the door; but when Fâd started to walk through it, he looked back at Ash and had a sad look on his face. He left and caught up to his friends as they climbed into the vehicle and headed back to school. That was the last time he and Ash had anything to do with each other again.

CHAPTER 28

THE DANCE CHANGED Ash. She grew up overnight and now threw herself into her studies, and before long, the girls' ninth level of schooling was over, and they were once again back on board the *Justification*, orbiting Sigma Six. Their military training was also advancing with them as they grew. They were now fifteen, and their talents were definitely manifesting themselves. Of course, Ash was excelling at everything and pushed herself to the breaking point. She had changed from the carefree little girl to a serious and determined young lady.

Harper really noticed the change when he got back and saw the maturity level she was exhibiting, not just physically but also mentally. Her instructors were very impressed and were commenting to the admiral that she was quite advanced for her age and that they had to, a lot of times, stop her for her own good. The admiral wondered what brought about this change in her. He knew something had happened during school last year and had a funny feeling it had to do with Fâd. Whenever he tried to ask her, she would just smile at him and tell him nothing happened. He even tried to see if he could get a response out of her when he mentioned Fâd's name, but still nothing.

The months passed, and once again, it was time for school, and the admiral and the girls were again in New Guinea, back at their home, talking to Admiral Larson and Sharni, who couldn't believe the drastic change in the girls in just three months. Ash wasn't the only one changing. Bridgett and Rachael were as well, and like Ash, they, too, threw themselves into their training and were excelling. Also, like Ash, they were changing physically and looking more and more like young ladies.

Eventually, school began. The *Justification* once again headed out into deep space, and Sharni and Larson were in charge of now very attractive young ladies, whom the boys were really starting to notice, even more so than last year. Larson even went as far as screening calls and having the comm blocked if it was a boy calling for the girls.

Over the next several months, the girls were busy with school, shopping with their other friends more than ever, and studies. The days of throwing a ball around outside or playing vid games were gone. It was replaced with makeup—Sharni got their applicators from Harper and made him relent on the age sixteen rule—clothes and music, of course. There was even some dating, but only Rachael and Bridgett. Ash flat-out refused and was getting the reputation of being called the ice queen. It was also coming true with the boys. They were extremely busy, and all the times when Larson invited them over, they couldn't because of the huge increase in schoolwork. The twelfth and thirteenth year of school weren't called hell years for nothing.

School finally came and went, and once again, it was back to the ship and more training. Now the girls were sixteen and also doing light duty on board, which usually consisted of system monitoring, some maintenance tasks, and a few times, assisting senior officers with inspections. They loved it, especially Rachael, who loved wearing the uniform.

The only big change that occurred during this time was, Sharni finally got her promotion and was now an admiral and commanded a new, advanced destroyer called the *Brisbane*, which was much larger than the battleships but half the size of the massive battlecruisers. She and Larson were now having to spend a little bit more time apart to a certain extent as the *Brisbane* had now replaced one of the *Lithia's* battleships and was running escort for the large battlecruiser.

The girls' time aboard the *Justification*, like always, came to an end in three months, and once again, they headed back to New Guinea but with Admiral Harper now and for the next three years until they finished prep school. Larson would be heading out into deep space after this school year because the boys would be finishing prep school.

Everyone walked into the house, and Bridgett now went and did a scan of the structure with her new multitool, which looked much more sophisticated than their other ones. Plus, these remained on almost all the time because they were even waterproof, chemical resistant, and would expand along with the wearer's growth. All three girls had gotten them, which were standard at the age of sixteen for all sentinel children who were training for military service.

They were much more advanced and were a product of watorian and proturin technology. The difference with these was, they were encoded to the individual's DNA as they were surgically attached and if removed would be useless to anyone else because a lot of their functions were top secret and could only be accessed by the wearer. All the information and secure code links from their old multitools had been downloaded to these new, advanced ones, and Ash had them even transfer the code link that used to be her mother's to hers for sentimental reasons.

The process the girls went through to get them was painful as cybernetics was implanted into the palm of their left hand, just under the skin, and ran up to just above their wrist. There, a cybernetic port was implanted, connecting the palm unit to the wrist module once it was put on, basically plugging the module into the implanted system. This implant allowed the wearer to scan without having to bring along another tool for that purpose, and it was one of the most secretive applications that only sentinel fleet had.

They could now hack or control most security systems out there. This was a serious responsibility for them and not to be taken lightly. Abuse of the module was a capital offence, not to mention they didn't want to go through the process again to have it removed because the only pain medication they could give them was a local that barely numbed their skin but not the raw tissue underneath when the implants were put in. It was all done in the medical bay aboard the battlecruiser, and the pain was excruciating as they had to sit there and take it as their arm was strapped into a sterile chamber and miniature robotic tentacles literally opened their wrist and palm and put in the implants while they watched in agony.

The reason they couldn't be numbed more or even given a sedative was, the new multitool was powered by the wearer's neural pulses, so they couldn't be compromised in any way to make sure everything was calibrated and was fully functional.

Bridgett, of course, kept passing out, and her father had to keep reviving her with a revival stick, which Ash had to admit smelled horrible, but Ash and Rachael just gritted their teeth and gripped their fathers' hands through the whole process as tears ran down their faces.

They all waited for Bridgett to finish her scan, and she made hand signals to the rest of how many bugs and their locations. This was also another part of their training, coordinating by hand signals. Admiral Harper pulled up his screen and located the bugs as well and nodded to the girls to move out as they each located a particular bug. They each easily disabled them, and the admiral took out the last two, then he did a final sweep and gave the coast clear as the girls stood waiting patiently, then relaxed. The girls headed upstairs and unpacked and, before long, were back now in civilian clothes and started rummaging through the refrigerator as the admiral came into the kitchen, dressed in casual clothes also.

"Hey, Dad, you know what? I just thought of something. Maybe you should get a vehicle so we can take it every time we want to go to the mall," Ash said, munching on some chocolate brittle she found in the cabinet.

"That's okay. This is working out just fine," Admiral Harper informed her.

"I was just thinking, it would save you a lot more money instead of paying a chauffer to drive us around all the time."

"Good try, but it won't happen," he said and walked over to the refrigerator and looked inside it.

"It looks like I need to make a grocery order. If you girls need something, you better let me know," he told them and walked over to the kitchen console and brought up an order screen. He went slowly through it and started marking items and adding quantities as the girls walked over to him and started making suggestions to him about certain snacks they wanted. He got everything he needed to order and stepped back as they stepped up to it and put in the personal items they needed and sent it off.

A cost came on the screen, and he punched it into his wrist module and sent payment of marks, which instantly showed on the screen. Everyone knew that it wouldn't be delivered until the next day. Good thing the replicator had been activated before they came, or they wouldn't have anything to eat. Of course, they had the food porter, but one could get tired of always ordering out, and there just weren't a lot of fast food places to order from that were good. Specialty groceries, though, you still had to go and pick them up at a market or store.

"All right, let's get some dinner fixed," Harper said, and the girls got to work on it right away, punching in something on the replicator. A little while later, they had the table set, and everyone was sitting down to eat. The girls chattered through the whole meal, and Harper watched them as he ate. They had changed so much. Ash and Rachael were now almost up to his shoulder, and Bridgett wasn't that much shorter, but you could tell she wasn't going to get near as tall as Ash and Rachael and was also going to be very petite.

"So, Admiral, you glad to be back on terra firma?" Rachael asked him, grinning.

"Yes and no. I missed you girls, but I feel more secure on my ship."

"I can understand that," Rachael said with a devious grin.

"So how many years have you been on a ship?" Bridgett asked.

"Too long."

"How old were you when you fought in the carian war?" Rachael asked, all serious.

"None of your business," Harper replied with a cocky smirk.

"Damn, I thought we were going to catch him this time," Rachael said to Ash as Ash shrugged her shoulders.

It was finally time for bed, and everyone retired for the night. The girls went and sat out on their balcony, looking up at the stars. "You remember all the times we climbed down that tree and slept outside here?" Rachael asked, looking up at the sky.

"Yeah. It seems a long time ago," Ash replied. Of course, to a school-aged kid, a year seemed like an eternity.

"Do you ever think about them? You know, the boys?" Rachael asked quietly.

"Yeah, I do," Ash said quietly back.

"I know. So do I. That dance we went to with them was the funniest dance I have ever been to, and I've been to quite a few after that," Rachael said, and Ash and Bridgett agreed.

"I miss Cory. He was always kind to me and looking out for me," Bridgett said and wiped a tear from her eye as Ash watched her. She couldn't help but feel bad for her friend because she knew that Bridgett really liked Cory a lot. Ash also knew that deep down inside, even Rachael was hurting from not being with Nathan anymore. Like her and Bridgett, Rachael had fallen for Nathan, just like they had fallen for Fâd and Cory.

Rachael looked over at Ash. "What happened that night at the dance? You changed after that. What really happened between you and Fâd?" she asked her best friend.

"We both realized that it would never work. Our lives were destined for separate paths, and we would never see each other again. We knew we could never stay friends because we cared too much for one another, and it would be too painful to try and hang on, so we decided to forget about each other," Ash said and wiped a tear from her face as Rachael came over and put her arms around Ash. It was true, Ash and Fâd both knew they would never see each other again, and to try and continue their friendship would be torture because of how they felt about each other, so this was the better choice.

"I'm sorry, Ash. I know you really did care a lot for him."

"I did, but now all that matters to me is obtaining my goal, and that's to be the best soldier I can be and serve on my father's ship."

"As is ours. We won't ever leave you, Ash. Friends, sisters, and shipmates forever," Rachael said, and they all put their hands together and shook on it.

They finally went back to bed, and in no time, they fell asleep, not waking until morning when their alarms went off on their wrist modules for them to get up and get ready. That was one of the things they didn't like about them. If they didn't get up right away, they got a mild shock from the modules. It was something Admiral Harper had set on them for now, which wouldn't stop until they finished prep school and started their year-long tour.

An hour later, they were dressed in their school uniforms and heading down the stairs with their backpacks slung over their shoulders. Admiral Harper had breakfast ready, and the girls ate it down quickly, then told him goodbye and headed outside to catch the shuttle with, of course, the usual warning from him to behave.

They got to school and were instantly met by their friends, and they all walked into the school together. The girls immediately noticed the looks they were getting from the boys as they headed to their lockers. Even when they were putting their stuff in their lockers, every so often, some boy would holler at them as they walked by.

"Hey, Rachael. Looking hot this year."

"You too," Rachael would yell back.

Even Ash and Bridgett got their share of compliments, like, "Wow, Ash, looking nice" or "Mighty fine, Bridgett." Of course, Ash was appalled by it, but Rachael and Bridgett enjoyed all the attention.

"Ash, you need to lighten up. Have some fun this year," Rachael got on to her.

"My idea of fun is not boys," Ash said, getting her electronic notebook and datapads out of her locker and heading to her class. She was almost to her class when she looked down the hall and could have sworn she saw Fâd and the boys for just a brief second. But then it couldn't have been. The boys she saw were fairly tall and looked somewhat filled out. Of course, it had been over a year since she had seen them, but nah, it wasn't. She was still standing there, looking down the hall, when Rachael and Bridgett caught up with her and looked to see what she was staring at but saw nothing.

"Did you see something?" Rachael asked her.

"I thought I did, but no, it was nothing," Ash said, and they all walked into class together.

Fâd and the boys were walking down the stairs, heading to their next class across the campus, when Fâd spoke to Nathan. "Was that Ash in the hall up there?"

"Who, the hot girl with the long black ponytail and everything in all the right places?" Nathan replied.

Fâd chuckled. "Yeah, that one."

"Don't know. Didn't get a good look," Nathan said, and Fâd just shook his head and started laughing as they took off running to their next class.

School dragged on for the girls, and before long, the school day was over, and they were back to the house. They did some chores, then met their friends at the mall, spending the next several hours there. Rachael, of course, was swarmed with boys, and she was eating it up, flirting with every one of them. Even Bridgett had a pretty good following. Ash tried to escape, but some of the boys were very persistent, and eventually, she just gave in and let them tag along or buy her ice cream or something to drink. She had to admit, a couple of them were real cute. Finally, their time ran out, and they had to leave and head back home before the admiral sent a recon team out after them. This was how the whole school year went, and before they knew it, it was over, and they were back on board the *Justification*, which was where Ash wanted to stay.

* * *

She was now seventeen, and it was a couple of months later as she was on the bridge with her father, checking the systems monitors and entering the readings in her log pad. "Admiral, transmission coming in from the *Lithia*," Ensign Chambers said.

"On screen," Harper ordered as Ash walked over and stood beside him, and Rear Admiral Larson appeared.

"Well, Harper, we're getting ready to leave. I guess we won't be seeing each other for well over a year. Don't do anything stupid while I'm gone. I won't be there to bail your ass out. Is that Ash with you? Oh my gosh, Ash, you're gorgeous. You look just like your mother. You are in so much trouble, old man. I'm glad I'm not you," Larson said, chuckling, and Ash giggled.

"I should be telling you to behave. I can tell you right now I won't blow my ship up to save your mangy butt. And how many times do I have to tell you? I'm not that old. But if you need me…" Harper said to his best friend.

"Yeah, I know who to call, and the same goes for you. I'll be there," Larson said back.

"I know you will. Safe journey, Admiral," Harper said to him and saluted as his whole bridge came to attention, including Ash now.

"And safe journey to you as well, Admiral," Larson said and saluted him back. "And, Ash, take care of that old fart for me and yourself, precious."

"I will, and I'll miss you," Ash said as tears ran down her cheeks knowing she wouldn't be seeing her godfather for over a year, and Admiral Larson smiled at her as the screen went back to the space outside. Ash and her father stood on the bridge, watching the *Lithia* power up, and Ash heard the familiar primary engines of the *Justification* fire in sequence to signal safe journey to the *Lithia*, and just like that, the massive cruiser of Larson's disappeared into blackness as she jumped. Ash's heart also felt heavy knowing Fâd was on that ship, and she could feel more tears wanting to fall because of it, but she fought them back and once again turned into the cold, emotionless person whom she had become over the last few years.

Ash went back to her duty, and once her shift was over, she went and worked out at the gym. She was still working out with a sparring dummy when Rachael walked in, all sweaty and breathing heavily. "What have you been doing?" Ash asked her, grabbing hold of the hanging dummy so she could catch her breath. Rachael looked over at her and removed her shooting gloves with a grin.

"Sniping, and I broke my old record of 135 perfect kills."

"All right, Rach, way to go," Ash said and walked over to a table, grabbing two towels, throwing one to Rachael and starting to dry her face off with the other one.

"Yeah, well, I heard through the rumor mill that you beat your sensei this morning. No one has ever beaten him." Rachael wiped her face off and then looked over at Ash, who was grinning. Around her friends was the only time she showed that she had any feelings.

"So what are we going to do tonight to celebrate Bridg's seventeenth birthday?" Ash asked as she jumped up onto the table, sitting with her knees up and resting her arms on them where the clean towels were neatly folded.

"Let's do what we had planned all those years ago: go to Gravities now that all of us can get in. I heard there are a lot of cute guys there from the academy right now." Rachael grinned.

"Is that all you think about anymore?"

"Yeah, pretty much, guys and guns."

"Rach, I worry about you."

"Don't worry about me yet. When I turn eighteen and can get into a restricted club and drink, then worry about me," Rachael said, and they both started laughing.

"All right. I'll meet you at Bridg's at 2000," Ash told her and jumped off the table.

"Ash, try to loosen up and have fun for once," Rachael said to her, and Ash scowled and threw her towel at Rachael.

It was half an hour before Ash had to meet Rachael and Bridgett, and she walked out of her room, freshly showered and dressed in her formal uniform, as that or their regular uniforms were all the girls were allowed to wear anymore. She went over to the kitchen, grabbing a water bottle. Her father came out of his room, still in his regular uniform, which everyone wore as well.

"You look good, Ash. Where are you and Rachael taking Bridgett for her birthday?"

"Gravities. We have planned this for years."

"You three be careful there. If I'm not mistaken, a lot of the academy students will be there by now," Harper said to her with narrowed eyes.

"We'll be fine, Dad. Besides, I can probably beat the crap out of most of them anyway." Ash grinned.

She walked over and gave her father a kiss on the cheek, grabbed her water bottle, and left the cabin as he watched her go with an unhappy scowl on his face. She got to the elevator and, in minutes, was buzzing the door on Bridgett's cabin. Rachael answered it, also dressed in her formal uniform, and stood aside as Ash walked in, taking a drink from her water bottle.

Bridgett walked out and was straightening the bottom of her uniform tunic and looked over at her friends and grinned. The girls were all dressed the same—a form-fitted tunic that showed their figures nicely that buttoned up the side and stopped with a square neckline and a high collar on the sides and back. It came down to just barely below the tops of their thighs, and they wore slightly snug pants under them that had matching boots and looked like they were part of the pants. The uniforms were the standard gray, blue, and black color of the fleet and had a fluid design to them with blue being the main color.

They headed out, and in no time, they were standing at the entrance to the nightclub Gravities, which all battlecruisers had for their crew to unwind, with big grins on their faces. The music was loud, and fog floated across the dance floor, and flashing multicolored lights were everywhere—the ceiling, the walls, and the floor. Even the bar was outlined in neon lights, and the shelving behind it that held all the different kinds of alcohol was lit up. Of course, the girls weren't of age to drink yet, not until they turned eighteen, but they could get into some clubs now. They walked in, and right away, Rachael danced her way over to a side table as Ash and Bridgett followed her, laughing.

No sooner had they sat down than three academy guys came over and asked them to dance. They accepted, and the guys grabbed their hands and led them out on the dance floor. Ash and Bridgett were a little nervous at first and looked over at Rachael and couldn't believe her. She was having no problem cutting loose, and they both started laughing, and before long, they were also dancing a little crazily as well.

All night, they barely got some time to sit down and rest before more guys asked them. They also had no problem getting something to drink. Of course, alcohol was offered, but they refused and stuck to water instead, telling the guys they had shifts to cover later.

It was definitely apparent they were the flavor of the night, and finally, they had to call it quits and left. A lot of the guys protested and tried to get them to stay longer. They got to the elevator, and Rachael looked down at her wrist module and started going through her screen on it.

"What are you doing?" Ash asked her.

"Deleting some of these comm links."

"Whose links?" Ash asked and looked at her module and saw one picture after another of a different guy with a comm link.

"You're kidding me. You got all those at the club?"

Rachael just grinned and kept going through them, then when she was done, she looked at Ash and Bridgett. "Don't tell me you didn't get any." Rachael eyed Ash and Bridgett suspiciously. Both of them started grinning and then started going through theirs as well.

They walked down the hall to Bridgett's room and wished her happy birthday, then left to their cabins. Ash walked in and saw her dad still up, waiting for her. "So did you have fun?"

"Yeah, actually, I did." Ash grinned.

"Good. Well, I'm going to bed. I'll see you in the morning."

"Good night, Dad."

"Good night, honey."

Ash watched her father head into his bedroom and wondered how he did it, just like Larson. Both of them seemed to not age at all. He still looked like he did when she was little, and she had to admit, like Rachael had commented on numerous occasions, her dad wasn't bad-looking. Of course, she didn't see the good-looking like Rachael said. After all, he was her father.

She went into the kitchen and grabbed another water bottle out of the refrigerator when all of a sudden, the ship's alarms went off with a red alert. Ash took off for the cabin door as her father came running out of his room, pulling on his shirt. They both raced down the hall and jumped on the elevator, and in no time, they were on the bridge.

"Report!" Harper commanded as he headed to his platform with Ash following.

"Sir, a carian cruiser and three destroyers heading toward the planet Fath. The *Inferno* and the *Wraith* have already jumped," EXO Dobbs told the admiral, but the whole time he was reporting, Harper was plotting the course on his console and sending out orders to the stations.

"Coordinates received. Jump in 5, 4, 3, 2, 1. Jump," Lieutenant Petterson announced, and fifteen minutes later, the *Justification* came out of jump, now into a full-blown battle, as the *Inferno* and the *Wraith* were taking a pounding from the carian cruiser and wouldn't last much longer against it. The *Justification*'s fighters quickly deployed and headed after the carian fighters and their battleships.

"Target that cruiser. Protect our battleships so they can concentrate on those destroyers," Harper ordered as he was firing the proton cannons, but they had a delay in between for cooldown, which was where the forbs mech guns came in with hull-piercing rounds. Only five of the guns were firing, and Harper looked over at the sixth gun station, which was the largest and main one, and saw it was empty.

"Where the hell is my sixth gunner?" Harper yelled, and everyone could tell he was furious.

"Sick, sir. We have another gunner on the way up. He'll be here in a few minutes," Dobbs told him.

"Those battleships don't have a few minutes. Private Harper, take the gun," he ordered her, and Ash leaped into the seat as it leaned back for better firing control, and at the same time, the targeting head gear dropped from the station's ceiling and onto Ash's head. Instantly, she started firing on the carian cruiser, targeting her shield generators instead of her guns like the others. Suddenly, the carian cruiser's large shield generator exploded, leaving her now wide open to damage, and this immediately got the cruiser's attention because it started banking around toward the *Justification*, leaving the battleships alone.

EXO Dobbs hollered at the admiral. "Cruiser's shields are down, sir."

"Give me phasic cannon control," Harper ordered and was punching in targets and sent them to the gunners.

"On my mark, gunners—3, 2, 1, fire!" he yelled, and Ash and the other gunners fired on his specified targets, and the large phasic cannon, which was comparable to four proton cannons, let out a massive blast of phasic blue energy and cut right through the entire center of the carian cruiser, severing it in half. Ash and the other gunners were now firing at will, taking out fighters and concentrating on the destroyers, as the carian cruiser was now plummeting toward the planet below.

Ash got in a damaging blow to the main drive of one of the destroyers, crippling it, as the *Inferno* came flying in and blasted the destroyer to pieces. The other two destroyers tried to flee, but the *Justification* ended one of them with its proton cannons, and the *Inferno* took the last one out with the help of the *Justification*'s guns as Ash had taken out their guidance system. The sentinel fighters easily wiped out the remaining carian fighters and headed back to the *Justification*. The whole battle took less than an hour, and everyone stood in shock, taking in what had just happened, except the admiral, who was busy working at his controls.

Suddenly, everyone on the battlecruiser cheered and let out the breath they were holding. "*Inferno*, report," Harper called the battleship.

"Torres here. We took some blows but operational. Some casualties, Admiral," Raul Torres replied, and Ash looked over at her father and could see the relief on his face. She, too, let out the breath she was holding knowing that Rachael's father was okay.

"Understood. *Wraith*, report." This was the one Harper wasn't looking forward to hearing; she had taken a beating and wasn't moving.

"Lieutenant Martin here. Captain Henson is dead. Heavy casualties and injured. Main engines down. Reserve power only."

"Hang tight, Martin. We're coming around to get you," Harper said and had already plotted his coordinates before he even contacted the *Wraith*.

The *Justification* moved toward the badly damaged battleship under pulsar power, and Lieutenant Petterson and the copilots maneuvered the massive cruiser with the skill of veterans and banked her up next to the battleship as tractor beams locked onto the *Wraith* and started pulling the huge ship toward the docking port.

"Now hear this. All hands on deck. Prepare for wounded and casualties. Medics to the docking bays. Engineers and technicians, to the *Inferno* and *Wraith*," Admiral Harper announced over the ship's main comm.

He now looked over at Ash and nodded at her. She had saved the battleships with her skills at the guns by getting the attention of that cruiser. He was never prouder of her than at this moment, for she had just saved many lives. He walked over to her gun station. "Private Harper, come with me. Dobbs, you have the bridge."

"Aye, aye, Admiral."

Ash got out of the gunner's seat and was now shaking, following her father. They got in the elevator, and Harper pulled her into his arms as she continued to shake. Everything had happened so fast, and she was still shocked from it. He held her all the way down to the docking bay and then looked down at her as he kept the doors closed on the elevator.

"Are you going to be okay?"

"Yes, I'll be fine."

Harper looked down at his daughter now with narrowed eyes. "How did you know where to hit the carian cruiser to bring down her shields so fast? No one has ever been able to do that before. We've always, in the past, only been able to finally penetrate them with several shots from the phasic cannon because it would overload them but at a cost. We generally lose some ships because it would take too long."

Ash started shaking her head, looking down at the elevator floor. "I don't know, but suddenly, I just knew where to strike."

Harper looked at her for a few more minutes, studying her intently. He was beginning to sense that Ash's telepathy was more than what he and Gail had previously thought. Maybe it wasn't limited to just humanoids, and with her growing older, she was possibly getting stronger and able to reach farther.

"Are you ready?" he asked her as his face now changed from a serious, cold one to one of a caring father.

She looked up at him, took a deep breath, and nodded her head. He briefly smiled and opened the elevator doors. The large bay was filling up with the wounded as they were being brought off the *Wraith* through a massive umbilical that connected the battleship to the cruiser. The admiral walked out among the crewmen and started helping immediately. Even Ash was helping. Suddenly, she saw Rachael running as fast as she could with her mother right behind her toward another umbilical that was opening up to the *Inferno*, which had just docked too.

She continued to watch and saw Commander Torres walk out, helping a wounded crewmen out. Ash could feel tears wanting to fall as she watched her best friend run up to her father and wrap her arms around him, crying, even when Abigail got there and also threw her arms around her husband, sobbing. It took everything Ash had to not break down and cry as well.

Ash pushed the feeling aside and continued helping medics and nurses treating the survivors as more started coming in from the *Inferno*, and she was just floored by how many there were. She took a quick glance around and saw Bridgett with her father heading through the umbilical to the *Wraith*, dragging tool carts behind both of them to try and see what repairs they could do to the severely damaged ship to get her back up and running somewhat.

Finally, after a couple of hours, the flow of wounded slowed down, and now coming out of both battleships were covered stretchers with the bodies of the deceased. She could feel tears wanting to fall once again over the dead, but she remained strong and looked for her father. He was over with a young man, who Ash was sure was the lieutenant of the *Wraith*, and she could tell by the way her dad saluted him that he had just promoted him to the rank of commander of the ship. It wasn't a pleasant task, especially right after the captain was killed, but it was a necessary duty being this far away from sentinel command and the *Wraith* being without a commander. Ash's father had the authority to do such things since he was the vice admiral of the whole fleet, second only under the fleet admiral, and promotions like this always had to be run through him anyway.

She stood up and stretched out her back. The nurses and medics were getting everything under control and started looking for Rachael. She was over by her father and helping him with some of the lesser wounded from his ship, and Ash noticed that Commander Torres had his arm in a sling and his head bandaged now. She quickly headed toward them, and no sooner had she gotten there than her father was also right behind her. Raul and Rachael turned toward them, and Rachael started tearing up and wrapped her arms around Ash.

The admiral and Raul shook hands, and Harper put his hand on Raul's shoulder. Abigail also came over and hugged Harper as tears ran down her face. "Thomas, I want to meet and shake the hand of whoever it was running the sixth gun on your ship. I couldn't believe it when I saw your main gun take down that cruiser's shield generator. Nobody has ever done that. They saved us all, drawing them off," Raul said to him, and the admiral turned and looked down at Ash.

"Ash, you were running that gun?" Rachael asked her.

"Yeah," Ash said, now about ready to cry, as what she had just done sunk in.

Rachael threw her arms around Ash again and was openly crying now. "Ash, you saved my dad's life and everyone on his ship. You saved both ships." Raul came over to her and wrapped his good arm around her and thanked her as well, and then it was Abigail, who was also crying and thanking her and kissing her on the forehead, causing Ash now to tear up.

They were still hugging when the *Wraith*'s engines fired back up, and half an hour later, Bridgett came walking out, all covered in grease and black ash, and headed toward the *Inferno*, pulling her tool cart behind her with a sober look on her face. Ash and Rachael headed over to her, as did Commander Torres and Vice Admiral Harper.

"Dad sent me to patch up the *Inferno* since it's not as bad as the *Wraith*, and he can handle the rest with her," Bridgett said, saluting the admiral and commander, who returned the gesture.

"Carry on, Private," Harper said back to her even though she wasn't a private yet. None of the girls was since they weren't enlisted, but it was easier to call them that than use their full names. Bridgett headed down the umbilical with Ash and Rachael helping her as the adults watched them go and then looked at one another.

"If she hadn't taken down that shield so fast and drawn them off, I wouldn't be standing here. Hell, a lot of us wouldn't be right now. We all know the usual outcome of meeting up with a carian cruiser—a battleship always loses. Every shot she made was a precision shot hitting key spots," Raul said to Harper, but all the admiral did was nod at him, squeezed his shoulder, and went back to checking on the wounded and making arrangements with the ship's reverends over the deceased.

Rachael and Ash followed Bridgett into the main engine room of the *Inferno*, and Bridgett walked over to a large console that sat near a pulsating large blue chamber and brought up a virtual screen with many subscreens and files on it. She started touching certain files, and they would channel down to even smaller ones, and then she would touch specific items and move them around. Her eyes moved continuously as she moved things around, checking readings and diagnostics of the engines. Finally, satisfied with what she saw, she powered down the engines, and the reserve system came on, and now the engine room was bathed in emergency red lighting.

"Was it supposed to do that?" Rachael asked, looking around, and grabbed a guardrail and hung on to it. Even Ash was nervously looking around.

"I sure hope you know what you're doing," Ash said.

"Relax, you two. I know exactly what I'm doing." Bridgett walked over to the once glowing blue chamber and pulled out a sonic wrench from her tool cart and started removing bolts on an access door to the chamber.

"Are you sure you should go in there? Isn't it filled with poisonous gases?" Ash asked, ready to grab Bridgett and pull her away from the door.

"Usually, but I already vented it, so it's safe now," she said as the last bolt came out, and she reached over and pulled the door away. The seal released on it, and a hissing noise ensued. Bridgett immediately started screaming and reaching for her face as the other girls were also screaming and crying at the same time, then suddenly they heard her laughing.

They stopped and looked at her in disbelief, they couldn't believe she did that to them.

"I hate you" Rachael said now furious that Bridgett scared her like that.

Bridgett of course was still laughing as Ash soon joined in and before long even Rachael finally started laughing to.

"I'm sorry I couldn't help it." Bridgett said still giggling

"Yea, paybacks are a bitch, just remember that." Rachael said still chuckling a little.

Bridgett climbed into the power core chamber looking up and seeing the large power cells suspended a couple feet above her still glowing blue and making sure to not touch them since they could cause serious injury. She had Ash hand her a sonic wrench as she removed more bolts from the floor and lifted off the floor panel. Then she had her friends handing her couplers, soldering gun and some splices from her tool cart. She leaned down into the open floor and worked hanging from the edge putting some lines back together and patching coil wires. Finally satisfied Bridgett replaced the floor panel and climbed back out of the chamber half an hour later, she looked around in it and made sure everything was out and put the access panel back up and ran her left hand over the edge of the panel scanning it to make sure the panel resealed.

"Well, wish me luck, let's see if she's ready to go." Bridgett grinned and walked over to the console then punched in a code and suddenly the engines started humming and then came back on line as the chamber glowed blue again but this time they sounded much

better. The room lit up and now the jump system was also functioning and secondary engines started up and hummed in stand by.

"So is the ship okay?" Rachael asked her.

"Yeah. They can get it back to the space station and do the outer
repairs, but now she can jump again and reach FTL speed."

"You're awesome, Bridg," Ash said, grinning.

"I know."

They walked out of the ship, and once again, they were on the
battlecruiser, but now all the wounded were gone from the bay area.
Only the deceased remained with the ship's reverend, the commanders of each battleship, and the admiral. They were walking among
the deceased, taking their names from the dog tags where they were
laid out on the deck with the flag of the sentinel fleet covering each
of their bodies. They just stared. There were so many of them, some
not much older than they were.

Ash watched her father. His face was stone as he personally went
and checked every one of the bodies. He closed their eyes if they
were open, then put his hand on them and went to the next one. Ash
figured there were at least 112 men and women, most of them from
the badly damaged *Wraith*, including her captain. But her new commander, who looked to be no more than twenty-four or twenty-five
at the most, was also walking among them and recording their names
on his datapad, as was Rachael's dad.

They were still standing there when Bridgett's father walked out
of the umbilical that was linked to the *Wraith*, and Ash and Rachael
followed Bridgett over to her father, who was heading toward the
admiral. They all reached the admiral at the same time, and Bridgett's
father looked at Bridgett for a report on the *Inferno*.

"The ship has full flight capabilities, and jump is back online.
There are some hull breaches, but kinetic barriers will hold till she
can get back to the battle station," Bridgett told him, and he nodded
his approval.

"What about the *Wraith*?" the Admiral asked, and now the
new commander walked up beside him, and Ash noticed he wasn't
bad-looking.

"She can fly but barely and only propulsion speed, no FTL, and there's no jump. Besides, she couldn't handle it anyway. She's barely holding together as it is," Nelson told the admiral.

"What about her guns? If we run into trouble, can she fire?" Harper asked him.

"Yes, they're fully operational and about the only thing that didn't get touched."

"Well, then, I want a skeleton crew on her, just enough to keep her flying till the *Presido* can pick her up. All other personnel will stay on the *Justification*. We will escort her back to Valhalla," Harper told them, and they all nodded.

"I'll go on the *Wraith* in case she goes down so I'll be able to get her running again and moving until the tug gets here to pick her up," Nelson told him.

"That's fine, but that also leaves the *Inferno*, and she's wounded as well and without a senior engineer right now," the admiral told him.

"I'll stay on the *Inferno*, sir. I know her engines and mechanics," Bridgett told him, and Harper nodded his approval to her.

"Admiral, I'll need a gunner. I lost one, and the other one is injured," the new commander told him.

"I'll go, Admiral," Ash said, and Harper looked at her with narrowed eyes.

"No, Ash," he said in a cold, blunt tone.

"Father, I can do this. Please."

Harper looked at her through narrowed eyes for a few seconds and then relented, but he was not happy about it, and the displeasure was very apparent on his face, which made everyone around him nervous. He looked over at Tony Nelson, who nodded his head as some unheard order was given to him and he acknowledged it.

"I'll go with you, Ash," Rachael said to her.

"No, go with Bridgett. She might need your help."

"All right, but you be careful," Rachael told her, and the worry was apparent on her face, but Ash just smiled at her.

"We need to get going. It's going to take some time, and we won't have any backup for at least a few hours. We leave in one hour.

Commanders, prepare your ships for departure. Commander Torres, I want you to stay port side of the *Wraith*, where she has the most damage. I will follow with the *Justification* covering our backs. That is all. Dismissed," Admiral Harper ordered, and the men all saluted him and started to head to their ships, but Commander Martin stopped before he entered the umbilical and waited for Ash, who was now his gunner and under his command.

"Ash, be careful. I don't have to tell you that I'm not very happy about this, but I'm also very proud of you," her father said as a slight smile appeared at the corner of his mouth. Ash saluted him now with a slight grin, and he saluted her back and watched her head toward the damaged battleship as she walked over to Commander Martin, and they both headed down the umbilical and entered the ship.

CHAPTER 29

RIGHT AWAY, ASH noticed that not too many things were working on the ship and that all over the place were fallen girders and some exposed wirings that were sparking, and a lot of the ship only had the red emergency lighting on. There were a few technicians working on the ship, but there was so much to do, and by the time they reached the station, they wouldn't even have a quarter of it repaired. Commander Martin led her toward the bridge where the main gun controls were, but they had to use the emergency stairs since the elevators were also out.

"So I have you to thank for keeping me and the rest of the crew alive, I understand," he said and smiled down at Ash.

"I just did my job like anyone else would have."

"Not quite. Those were precision shots. Not too many people can do that with a forbs mech gun."

They entered the bridge, and Ash went over to the gun station and climbed in. She ran a simulation to make sure they would respond right and was satisfied with the results. Commander Martin came over and leaned down so she could hear him. "Well, are we at least okay in this section?"

"Yeah, she's good," Ash replied, grinning. "Oh, sorry, Commander."

"Trey."

"Sorry, what did you say?" Ash asked, confused.

"My name's Trey, and since you aren't officially enlisted, you don't have to be formal with me. Besides, we are barely going to have enough people to fly her with probably me, you, and the pilot and communications the only ones on the bridge," He told her, smiling again, and Ash couldn't help but smile back. He wasn't bad-looking, and she noticed he had a very appealing smile that made one feel comfortable around him.

"Ashley, but everyone calls me Ash," she said and held out her hand, and he shook it.

"Well, Ash, welcome aboard." Then he got up and walked over to the commander's platform, and now the pilot came walking in and took his seat. "Chase, where's my communications?"

"Lori got hurt. I'm all that's coming to the bridge. What about weapons?" the pilot asked him.

"Meet our new gunner, Ashley Harper. Ash this is Chase, our crazy pilot."

"How do you rate, Trey, the vice admiral's daughter, for our gunner? Wow, and you're hot-looking to boot. Nice to meet you, Ashley. Sit back and enjoy a long, boring ride."

"Chase, knock it off. Just ignore him. He has space dementia. Can you run comms for me too?"

"Yeah, no problem," Ash replied, heading over to the communications station.

"All right, then. Let's get this injured bird home," Trey said to them and was now punching coordinates into his console and sent out the orders to the stations. Ash was sitting at the communications console and sent the acknowledgment received back to the commander. Then she got up and went over to the gun station and also sent acknowledgment received orders and came back and got on the comm.

"*Justification*, this is the *Wraith*. Requesting permission to unhook umbilical and release docking clamps," Ash said over the comm.

"*Wraith*, permission granted. Umbilical and docking clamps released. You may proceed ahead" came the reply from the battlecruiser. Ash could hear the damaged ship popping and creaky now that she was released and under her own power once the *Justification*'s tractor beam was shut down and the docking clamps removed.

"Coordinates received. Ahead one stage," Chase said in the pilot's seat.

The ship moaned as she moved out. Ash watched the screen, and she saw the *Justification* remain behind and now the *Inferno* coming around and up beside them. Commander Martin was busy running through his screens and moving subscreens around and rerouting power to more key stations.

"Chief Nelson, how many stages in propulsion can I have?" the commander comm'd Bridgett's father, who was down in the engine room, keeping the ship running.

"I can give you four, but anything over that and the engines will blow, and she will fall apart," the chief replied.

"Chase, bring her up to stage four but very slowly, and if she starts to buck, back down," the commander told the pilot.

"Aye, aye, Commander." Chase grabbed the control stick, and then with his left hand, he grabbed the power lever and slowly started moving the lever forward. The ship creaked and moaned louder, but the pilot slowly continued. Now they could hear crashing sounds coming from below them, but still, the pilot pushed forward. Finally, he stopped, and now the battleship was moving along at a fairly decent speed, at least. Ash was always amazed by how pilots knew what their ships could and couldn't handle just from the feel of the power lever. Even veteran pilots seemed to have a certain connection to their ship and could get out of them what others could not.

"Stage four, and I don't dare push her anymore," Chase told the commander.

"Good job, Chase," Trey said to him and let out the breath he was holding, as did Ash and Chase.

The badly injured battleship moved slowly through space with the *Inferno* keeping pace right beside her and the *Justification* following right behind them. Every so often, Trey—as he wanted Ash to call him for now—would check with Chief Nelson to see how the engines were doing, and the engineer told him every time that they were holding.

Ash was watching the scanners for any possible threats when Trey left the bridge. A little while later, he came back with something for everyone to eat and drink and had her come over by him and Chase. "Permission to speak freely?" Ash asked, still being formal.

"Ash, I told you, with it being just us, first names only. That's an order," Trey said to her with a smile.

"All right. I take it you two have known each other for a while?"

"Since prep school," Chase replied, grinning.

"So how old are you two anyway?" Ash asked casually.

"No one admits their age anymore," Trey replied, grinning.

Ash smiled. "Yeah, but you both look young for being so far up in the ranking."

"Oh yeah. Well, you definitely don't look your age either," Chase replied with an ornery grin.

Ash started giggling. "All right, checkmate." Both men laughed now.

The three of them ate what there was since none of the replicators worked and talked the whole time. Ash would walk over to the comms station once in a while and would catch Chase out of the corner of her eye elbowing Trey and motioning over at her, and Trey would start grinning. It was just one of these times when she barely turned around and started walking back over to them that a transmission came over the ship's comm.

"Hey, Ash. It's Rachael. How's it going, girlfriend?"

"Rachael, how are you contacting me?" Ash asked, surprised.

"Bridgett hacked into our comm links, that's how."

"But you're not—"

"Oh, come on, Ash, nobody will know. We just wanted to talk," Rachael said, cutting her off.

"Hi, Ash. So what's it like being surrounded by cute guys? I saw the pilot. Oh yeah," Bridgett asked her.

"You guys, you're not just—"

"Ash, lighten up. So answer the question. I saw the new commander. Wow, he's hot. Maybe it's time for the ice queen to finally thaw. Any others over there you think you could send our way?" Rachael said, giggling.

Right now, if Ash could have climbed in a hole and die, she would have, because she was trying to tell Rachael and Bridgett that they had done their job too well. Instead of hacking just into her comm link, they hacked into the whole ship's comm link and was now being heard by everyone on board. Ash was so embarrassed, and when she glanced over at Trey and Chase, Chase was pointing to himself and mouthing the word *me*. But it was Trey who made her really blush, especially the cocky grin he had on his face.

"Guys, I've been trying to tell you. You hacked the ship's comm system, not mine. Everyone can hear you."

"Oh, shit. Rachael, my dad's over there," Bridgett yelled out, not realizing they were still broadcasting.

"Damn it, Bridg. You said it was just her transponder signal. How the hell did you screw that up? Now everyone knows what we did and said."

"Yeah, and my dad just heard us asking for guys." Ash started laughing then. She couldn't help it. Rachael and Bridgett were still linked up and were now fighting as everyone was still listening to them. Just then, Chief Nelson walked into the bridge, and he wasn't happy.

"Bridgett Nelson, get off this comm link right this minute."

"Shit" was all that everyone heard, and then the comm went silent. Tony looked over at Ash, and she could tell he was furious. Then he turned and left the bridge. Ash just stood there for a few more minutes until she knew it was safe and started busting up laughing. She was laughing so hard she had to go and sit down to steady herself. Even Trey and Chase were laughing with her.

"Your friends sound like a hoot," Chase said to her.

Ash was still laughing. "You have no idea. They are in so much trouble."

Trey looked at Ash again with a cocky grin on his face. "Ice queen, huh? So is there a story behind that? Let me guess, someone broke your heart?" Ash stopped laughing now and almost felt like crying instead. It felt like he had just slapped her upside the head, and it just made her realize that was exactly what had happened. "I'm sorry. I didn't mean to pry," Trey said, now concerned.

"You didn't. You just opened my eyes finally after three years because you are absolutely right," Ash told him and smiled, and he returned the gesture.

"His loss is somebody's good fortune," Trey told her.

The three of them started talking again. Trey and Chase were telling her about some of the things they did at the academy and prep school, and she was telling them about things she and her friends had done so far as well. They were all laughing when Ash heard the comm station beeping. Everyone stopped and went to their posts as Ash pulled up the scanners and then sent out signal identification and got back a verification.

"Commander, three ships coming out of jump. Verified as sentinel fleet," Ash told him, grinning, and he grinned back.

They all looked at the screen in front of them and watched the space ahead. Three ships suddenly appeared out of nowhere. Two of them were destroyers, and the third was a tug, a heavily armed towing vessel, only they didn't drag a ship behind them—they actually carried it. They had massive arms, and the ship itself resembled something close to a tuning fork that slid down on the port and starboard sides of a ship, then squeezed in until they firmly locked the ship into place. Then a massive kinetic shield was put around the damaged ship so they could actually jump with it while it was locked down.

The tugs could handle ships clear up to the larger destroyers but definitely not cruisers. If a cruiser was taken out in a battle, usually, there was nothing worth left to repair. A battlecruiser's only scenario was to win. There was no defeat. They didn't get the chance to limp away from a fight. Everyone knew you would not leave a battlecruiser standing. You would blow it to pieces.

"Transmission coming in, Commander," Ash said to Trey.

"Put it on the comm."

"This is the *Presidio* to the *Wraith*. Shut down your engines and we will link up to you for transport."

"Confirmed, *Presidio*. We are shutting down now and awaiting dock," Trey replied as Chase shut them down. Now the large battleship was dead and just floating in space. They watched on the screen as the huge tug approached them. Even Nelson came to the bridge, as did the rest of the technicians and crew who were on board, which only consisted of seven other people besides Ash, Chase, and Trey. Everyone watched in awe as the large arms slowly crept past the bow of the ship and moved down her sides. Then the tug shut down its engine and slowly, by sheer momentum, continued to move toward the bow of the battleship. All of them watched the huge vessel getting closer and closer by the minute.

They all started backing up slowly, unconsciously, and at the last minute, everyone grabbed something to hang on to, but the tug hit some after thrusters and gently nudged the battleship as it came to a stop. Everyone let out the breath they were holding and relaxed as the tug's arms started closing in on the ship, and in no time, they all felt it shake the ship when it locked on her.

"Well, this is it, everyone. To the air lock. She's in their hands now," Trey told the crew, and they all headed back down the stairs and through the emergency-lit halls, toward the midship air lock. No sooner had they gotten there than the pressure seal on the air lock released, and the door slid open to a brightly lit corridor, and two armed sentinel soldiers stood aside for everyone.

Commander Martin led everyone. Ash was a little nervous now, but Chief Nelson came up next to her and walked with her. She looked over at him and smiled weakly, and he smiled back at her and winked, which brought a brief grin on her face. They continued up the corridor, and then another large door slid open. They all stepped out into a huge bay that looked like it ran the whole length of one of the massive arms. There were all kinds of equipment in there and automons, which were extremely large robotic suits that a human had to climb inside of to control. They used them to lift extremely heavy or large items, and they also had many other features that helped with mechanical repairs.

This bay had crates full of parts and more air locks located every so often down the side they had all come through, and a lot of huge robotic arms came down from the ceiling, moving items around or taking things out of the crates and over to a large conveyor that had doors that would open and close to the outside as the part passed through a kinetic barrier. Ash couldn't see what was happening outside of this bay, but she knew that the *Wraith* was being secured to move.

Everyone lined up and stood at attention, then Commander Martin went over to them. "Chief Nelson and Ms. Harper, come with me. The rest of you, go with these soldiers. They will show you to some quarters," the commander told them, and everyone obeyed.

The commander headed toward some large bay doors that were in the front of the docking bay, and Ash and Chief Nelson followed him. The doors slid open, and now they were in a brightly lit hallway, then rounded a corner and entered into another large room with food replicators, drink distributors, and many table and chairs. It was very apparent this was the mess hall.

Trey continued onward, and they all got into an elevator. Soon, it opened up into the bridge of the tug. A large, fairly stout man with receding hair was standing at the captain's console, going through many virtual screens, but he turned around once he heard the elevator doors open and walked over to them.

"Commander Martin, I'm captain Lewis. Welcome aboard," the man said and held out his hand instead of saluting. Trey took it, and they shook hands.

"Thank you, Captain. We appreciate the assistance," Trey replied with a smile.

"I wouldn't dream of not helping. Harper would gut me like a fish if I didn't drop everything and see to one of his ships," Captain Lewis said, grinning, which caused even Nelson to chuckle a little. Lewis looked over at him with an ornery grin. "You know exactly what I'm talking about, don't you, Nelson?"

"Yep. I've seen you two swapping words on more than one occasion, and you always seem to come out looking the worse for it."

"He scares the shit out of me. When he narrows those eyes at you, I swear he can burn right into your head with his gaze." Nelson started laughing, as did everyone else, including Ash, and now Lewis looked at her. "Wow, they're starting them kind of young, aren't they? But they're sure getting prettier," he said, smiling at Ash, and she grinned.

"Captain Lewis, let me introduce you to my gunner, Ms. Ashley Harper," Trey said to him, and Ash and Lewis shook hands. The whole time, Nelson had a rotten grin on his face.

"You're not, by any chance, related to the vice admiral, are you?" Lewis asked, a little concerned, and Nelson was trying not to bust up laughing. Just then, Lewis's communications officer hollered at him.

"Captain, Vice Admiral Harper is on the comm. He said he was wondering when you would be sending his daughter back to him and that he is tired of waiting." Lewis's face turned pale white and had a look of fear. Of course, Nelson was busting up laughing, and even Trey was chuckling a little, but Ash was embarrassed.

Trey turned to Ash. "It's up to you. When it comes to the vice admiral, his order overrides everyone else's."

"I would really like to see this through if you wouldn't mind," Ash replied, and Trey smiled at her, then looked over at Lewis.

"Great. I get to tell him. This should be enlightening," Lewis said with a scowl and headed to his console. "Patch me through."

In a few seconds, Vice Admiral Harper came up on the large screen in front of everyone. "Well, Lewis, I'm waiting," Harper said coldly with narrowed eyes.

"Young lass asked if she could see this through and meet back up with you at command," Lewis replied timidly.

Harper's eyes narrowed even more, and everyone held their breath. Ash had to admit her father was rather intimidating when he looked like that. "Ashley, is this what you want to do?"

"Yes, Father. I was taught to never quit a mission until it is completed."

Harper now had a slight smirk on his face as he watched her through his screen. "All right. I will allow it this time only because Nelson's there and Commander Martin. I don't trust you, Lewis," he said coldly, still with narrowed eyes, glaring at Lewis, as Nelson chuckled quietly to himself.

"That's not fair. I've never failed you yet," Lewis said with a slight grin.

"There's still time. I'll see you at command. Get moving," Harper ordered, and the screen went blank.

Lewis turned around, shaking his head. "Damn, is he this scary to live with?"

"Worse," Ash said, grinning, and they all laughed.

"Well, let's get going before his patience runs out," Lewis said and turned back to his console. A private came over and led them to their quarters, which Nelson and Ash shared since the tugs weren't built to handle a lot of guest. Besides, Chief Nelson was making it known to everyone that Ash was under his protection anyway.

They walked into the room, which basically consisted of a bathroom and two bunk beds, and Ash looked back at Chief Nelson. "I get the top," she said, grinning.

"No problem there," he replied, wheeling his tool cart over into a corner.

Ash jumped up on it and bounced around a few times, and Chief Nelson turned around and looked at her, chuckling. "I've got to go and do some inspections on the *Presidio*. It's long overdue. Will you be okay by yourself while I'm gone?"

"Yeah, I'll be fine. Don't worry."

Nelson went over to the door and left, but no sooner had he gone than Ash heard a buzz from her door. She jumped down from the bed, went over, and opened it. Commander Martin stood in the hallway, smiling down at her.

"Can I help you, Commander?"

"I was wondering if you wanted to go get a bite to eat."

"Sure." She walked out into the hallway, and they got on the elevator, then went down to the mess hall. There were other people in there, and Ash even saw Chase over with a couple of female crew members from the *Presidio* and had to laugh. Trey looked over and had to chuckle as well, shaking his head. "He works fast," Ash said, grinning.

"Yeah, he does."

They finally got up to the replicator, and Ash got a type of vatorian salad, and Trey got a steak. He directed her over to a table away from others, and they sat down and started eating. "That looks interesting. You have a taste for vatorian cuisine?"

"Yeah, I do. My mother was a vatoria."

"Really? I didn't know that. So tell me about yourself."

"Well, like you now know, I'm part vatoria. I have only two years left at prep school, thank goodness. My godfather is Rear Admiral Larson." Trey choked when she said that last bit, and Ash started hitting him on the back. "Are you okay?" she asked, grinning.

"Did you say that Rear Admiral Larson is your godfather?" he asked in shock.

"Yeah, and he married my aunt, who is now Admiral Tol Vasna."

"They're married now?"

"You know them?" Ash asked, surprised.

"Yes. Who doesn't know Rear Admiral Larson and, of course, the now admiral Tol Vasna? Everyone's had some kind of fantasy about her. Oh, sorry about that." He blushed a little and took another bite of his steak, but Ash just laughed. Suddenly, the comm on her wrist module started blinking, and she answered it quietly knowing full well who it was.

"What do you want?" she asked them as Trey grinned at her, watching.

"We are in hiding from Rachael's dad right now. Apparently, my dad contacted him and played our whole conversation back to him. I wanted to give you a heads-up. The admiral has also heard our conversation because Rachael's dad forwarded it to him too. When we get to the battle station, we are going to try and sneak back into the *Justification*. We'll meet you at the old hiding place."

"Bridg, I did nothing wrong. Why would my father care?" Ash asked, almost in a whisper.

"Because we were talking about boys, and you know how he is about that subject. Remember when he flashed his gun at those ones in the spaceport who tried to talk to us?"

Trey started laughing, and Ash blushed a little but grinned. "All right, I'll meet you there. Now leave me alone."

Rachael got on the comm now. "Why? Oh, you're with a guy right now, aren't you? Is it that cute commander? Come on, Ash, talk!"

"Goodbye!" Ash said a little too loudly, and people looked over at her and the commander. Her face now was bright red, and she couldn't look at him just yet, but she could feel the grin that was on his face. Finally. she looked up; and sure enough, he was grinning.

"I'm sorry about that. They have no shame."

"They sound like a lot of fun. So do you three get into a lot of trouble that you have to have a secret hiding place?"

Ash grinned. "Sadly, yeah. Let's just say we have done our fair share of community service and cleaning detail."

"Can I ask you a personal question?"

"Yeah," Ash answered, but she was a little nervous.

"So what happened? What did he do to hurt you? You don't have to tell me if you don't want to," Trey asked in a sincere tone.

"It's okay. It will probably help to talk about it. I've kept it bottled up for so long. He was a close friend, and we had been through a lot together, most times as enemies, but we also had some great times and could always have fun around one another. I got bit by a vaquit and almost died, but he saved me. How I don't know. All I remember is, when I was surrounded by darkness, I heard him telling me to fight and come back to him. I followed his voice, and the last thing I remember was waking up in a hospital room, seeing him there. After that, we still had many battles, but we were always drawn to each other.

"One night, we were at a dance together, and we both realized it would never work out. His future was going one way, and mine was heading in the opposite direction. I've tried to forget about him, but no matter what I do, I still hang on to him, which is why I have become known as the ice queen, which is pretty well self-explanatory," Ash said, holding back tears that wanted to fall just thinking about Fâd.

"I'm sorry. It sounds like you two had a very special bond for him to be able to pull you from death's door. That must have hurt something awful when you both made that choice to end it, but you know, he is probably hurting just as much as you."

"I don't know about that. It didn't take him too long to have a new girlfriend—or should I say several girlfriends—after that," Ash replied, now a little mad thinking about it.

"That could have just been a mask for the pain he was feeling. Did you ever consider that?"

"No, but it's a pretty heartless way to go about it."

"True. I have to agree with you there."

"So what about you? Anyone special in your life?"

"I had a girlfriend when I was at the academy, but she didn't like the idea of spending time in space and eventually called it quits. Since then, I've thrown myself into my training and duty."

"Wow, that sounds so familiar. Me too," Ash said, laughing, and he joined her.

They talked for a little while longer, then Trey walked Ash to her room. They still had another four hours before they reached sentinel command, and Ash was running on reserve energy right now since she hadn't gone to bed for over thirty-six hours.

"Well, Ash, it was nice…I enjoyed talking to you. I'll let you get some sleep. You look exhausted," Trey told her, and Ash could see the concern on his face when she looked up at him. He stepped closer to her, leaning down. His lips softly touched hers, and she put her arms around his neck for some reason. He then wrapped his arms around her, pulling her closer to himself, and kissed her with more force, but just as suddenly, he released her.

"I'm so sorry about that. I just couldn't help it," he said, now bright red and nervous.

"It's okay," Ash said and smiled. Trey smiled back at her, told her good night, and left quickly. Ash walked into the room she was sharing with Bridgett's father, who wasn't back yet, thank goodness, because if he had seen that, Trey Martin's career would have been short-lived if this ever got back to the admiral.

Ash jumped up onto the top bunk and laid down, pulling the blanket up on herself. She had to smile a little when she thought about the kiss, yet in the back of her mind, she also felt guilt over it as Fâd flashed across her mind. She continued to struggle with her feelings, but finally, exhaustion won out, and she fell into a dreamless sleep.

CHAPTER 30

Ash walked up to the bridge of the *Presidio* with Chief Nelson. They were now coming into dock with sentinel command's main battle station, Valhalla. It had been years since she had seen it and had forgotten how big it really was; in truth, it was a city in space. Ash remembered the first time she saw it, when she was probably about nine. She had told her father that it looked like one of those giant manta rays that used to swim in Earth's oceans, which she had read about, and seeing it again, it still looked like that. The only differences were, it was the size of a small planet and where the front protrusion was, was the spaceport and docking areas and added a couple more extension to them. She knew that there were over two million people who called Valhalla home, which was an engineering marvel, and at all times, at least three battleships or destroyers constantly patrolled her perimeter.

Once on the space station, it was like living planet side. You had an artificial day and night, living vegetation everywhere complete with parks, and even rivers and streams and animals—birds mostly from different planets and, occasionally, a furry small type of creature living in the trees or wooded areas but nothing dangerous. There were also markets, shopping malls, restaurants, and nightclubs. You name it and it was there. But the most important part was, it was where sentinel command resided, and a lot of their military might was stationed there, including the fleet admiral himself.

This was also where all damaged ships came for repairs and refittings since it had the largest spaceport and shipyard around, not to mention it was always first in technological breakthroughs and military advancements. It was large enough to even handle the massive battlecruisers, which, on occasion, had to dock for some refitting.

Ash watched in awe on the large screens as the *Presidio* moved the *Wraith* into dock with the spaceport, and the battleship was tractor, beamed in, and locked into place. Out of the docking bay, many tentacle-like long arms came shooting out and attached themselves to different areas on the battleship, and Ash saw the running lights of the ship come online then. She glanced to her right and watched with a big grin as the *Justification* maneuvered around also for docking and could see in her mind her father standing at his platform, punching in orders.

"Ash, I will meet you and Nelson in the waiting room of the council chambers," Ash heard in her head, and she reached up, rubbing her temple a little.

"All right, Dad," she replied with her telepathy.

Ash turned to Chief Nelson, but before she could say anything, he spoke. "Where does he want me to take you?" Nelson asked with a grin knowing what Ash could do.

"The waiting room of the council."

"Who wants to meet you? Who are you talking about?" Lewis asked with a confused, nervous look.

"Vice Admiral Harper. Ash is a telepath, and she can communicate over a certain distance," Nelson told him, and both Trey and Lewis had surprised looks on their faces.

"Impressive," Lewis commented and went back to his ship's console as the *Presidio* also docked. Trey just smiled at Ash and then looked back at the screen. Soon, everyone felt a small thump, and the ship started powering down. Lewis breathed a sigh of relief and turned to Ash and them. "End of the road for us. Ms. Harper, it was a pleasure to meet you. Try and put in a good word for me with your father. Nelson, it's never a pleasure to see you. I've got a week or more of things to do now because of you. Commander Martin, good luck with your new command. Safe journey," Lewis said to them and saluted. Commander Martin saluted him back.

Trey led them all toward the elevator, and they got in and headed down to one of the many air locks of the *Presidio* and stepped out into a hallway. At the end of it was a docking door, and they headed to it. Once they got close, it slid open into a security area of Valhalla. An orange laser beam scanned each of them from top to bottom, and then the doors to the room opened at the other end, and they proceeded forward into an open pavilion that looked out into the city, which was spread out in front, above, and below them, as far as the eye could see. They all walked over to the railing and took in the sight.

"It always amazes me every time I see it," Nelson said to them.

"Wow" was all Ash could say.

"It's hard to believe this is also a very powerful battle station with enough might to almost blow a planet apart," Trey said to them, and they nodded in agreement.

"Well, Commander, this is where we part company for a while. I'll be seeing you again once most of the major repairs are done to the *Wraith*. Ash, shall we go meet the vice admiral?" Nelson asked as he took a step toward another elevator with his hand out for Ash to come. She turned to Commander Martin and looked up at him, but before Nelson could say or do anything, they both put their arms around each other and kissed goodbye. Nelson's mouth fell open, and he was too shocked to say or do anything. Ash and Trey released each other and smiled, then Ash walked over to Chief Nelson. He followed her into the elevator, glaring back at Commander Martin. The doors closed, and Chief Nelson told it where they wanted to go.

"I won't say a word to your father if you don't," Nelson said to her coldly without looking at her.

"Nope," Ash replied bluntly.

"Good. I'll live another day, and so will that young man."

The elevator opened, and they stepped out into a large military-type hall with many doors opening off it and proceeded toward a large double door at the end of the hallway. Once they got close, these doors slid open, and Ash's father was already there, talking with two other gentlemen. It was very apparent that they were also admirals of sentinel command. Vice Admiral Harper glanced at his daughter when he heard the doors open but quickly went back to talking to the men. Ash started looking around the room, admiring the comfort but the military practicality of it. She was looking at some vid images that were continuously changing on a couple of the screens of some of the ships in the fleet when she heard one of the admirals say something that made her heart jump, and she wheeled around to hear more.

"They did. Lieutenant Larson, Gerrard's son, led the attack," one of the admirals said.

"Yeah. He's turning out to be just as good as his father. He managed to not only take the base with only a handful of men but also saved the captives and shipment. The other amazing thing was, he also captured a carian infiltrator ship, and that pilot friend of his actually flew it after some adjustment from that other boy who is always with them. They now have successfully modified it and are using it to locate other merc bases along the route and taking them out as the cruiser passes through," the other admiral told them.

Harper turned to Ash with a slight smirk. "Did you hear that, Ash? Fâd and his friends are finally causing the enemy problems instead of you girls," Harper told her, chuckling.

"That's the first infiltrator we have been able to capture. I would sure like to get a peek at her engines and stealth system. Those little ships can get in and out before anyone even has a clue they're there," Nelson added, and the admirals agreed.

"Gerrard's son is definitely proving himself. I have a feeling this is just the beginning," the first admiral said.

The second admiral looked over at Ash. "Speaking of that, I understand that a great many people owe their lives to your daughter here."

"Sirs, I only did what anyone else would have done in the same situation," Ash spoke up.

"Nonsense. Your action and skill were what turned the battle by giving the *Justification* the time it needed to end it, thus saving the battleships and their crew," one of the admirals told her.

Ash's father briefly smiled at her, and then he nodded to the other admirals, excusing himself, and walked over to Ash and Chief Nelson. He leaned down and gave her a big hug, then kissed her on the forehead. "Should we head back to the ship and toward Sigma Six?" he asked her.

"Yeah, I suppose we should. School's about to start soon," Ash said grudgingly.

Harper and Nelson chuckled at her lack of excitement, and they all walked back through the double doors and, soon, onto the elevator. Ash could tell they were going down, and in no time, the doors opened. They stepped out into a large, completely enclosed courseway with a window on one whole side where you could see out into space and all the ships that were docked all along it. Of course, one could not miss the *Justification*, for it was docked to an extension of this area all by itself due to its size.

"Where's the *Inferno*?" Ash asked.

"Over at a far port for repairs. She won't be coming with us but will join up later once all the repairs are done," Harper told her.

"Yeah. I talked to Bono, and he said probably in about a month, she should be ready for duty again," Nelson added.

"What about Rachael and Bridgett? Could they still be on it?" Ash asked, worried about her friends, that they might not have gotten back on board the cruiser yet. Admiral Harper punched something up on his multitool and saw the two red dots.

"They're already on board and right where you three like to hide when you're in trouble," he said with a slight smirk as Ash choked.

They continued to walk toward the ship and rounded a corner. Now Ash saw armed guards standing outside the air lock where they would enter into the ship and was wondering how Rachael and Bridgett got past them. When they walked up, the soldiers saluted the admiral, and he returned the gesture as they stepped aside. Harper, Ash, and Chief Nelson stepped into the room that separated the causeway from the ship, and another orange laser beam scanned them again and cleared them for entry. The doors to the *Justification* opened, and they stepped back on board, and Ash couldn't help but feel like she had finally gotten home.

"You go find your friends. I'm sure Nelson wants a word with his daughter, and Abigail will probably want to speak to Rachael as well," Harper told Ash with a hint of a smirk.

"Oh yeah, I want to talk to her," Nelson said with a scowl on his face, and Ash couldn't help but grin knowing those two were in trouble. They all separated as Ash headed to the atrium and the secluded glade the three of them thought was so secretive, giggling as she went.

CHAPTER 31

"DAMN IT. How can carians work like this? Everything is back-assward," Cory cussed, lying under the captain's console on the bridge of the recently confiscated infiltrator they now used. Fâd was running a diagnostics on the weapons and just grinned, listening to him complaining.

"Will you quit your bellyaching? You're worse than any woman."

"I don't see you under here trying to straighten out this mess."

"Of course not. That's your job." Cory grunted at him and went back to trying to make sense of the tangled nest that was the guts of the captain's console and make it more efficient.

The boys had changed a lot over the last few years. They were a lot taller now and a lot more filled out physically. All three had the longer, almost shoulder length, hair cut that was shorter on top and in front and left wild-looking, which all watorian males had. Plus, they were now starting their braids, which hung down past their shoulders, a little farther than their hair, and already had quite a few beads on them, which represented their many accomplishments.

Fâd had his starting at his right temple, which split into two just past his ear. Cory had one on each side of his head, just past his ears, and Nathan's were two strands braided from the small ponytail he had some of his hair in close to the top of his head. And like all enlisted, they wore the uniforms of sentinel military with the insignia of their ranking on it, which, in their case, were all lieutenants now, except Fâd, who had just gotten promoted to lieutenant commander.

Fâd finished his diagnostics and went over to see if he could help Cory, and Nathan finally showed up, stretching and yawning. "It's nice of you to join us. I hope she didn't wear you out too much," Fâd said to him with an ornery grin.

"Nah, I don't think that's possible. They always get up and walk out just as I'm getting warmed up," Nathan said, chuckling.

"One of these days, Nathan, you're going to meet someone who can put you to shame," Cory said from under the console.

"No, I won't, because I've already met and even stole a kiss from her. But put me to shame? Please, it's me who you're talking to. My jump drive can outlast most battleships," Nathan told them with a wicked grin, and the other two started laughing and shaking their heads. "Oh, hey, I heard some juicy news. According to my sources, the *Justification* got into a major battle with three carian destroyers and a cruiser near Fath. I guess it got bad. The *Inferno* and, especially, the *Wraith* took heavy damage, and there were a bunch of causalities.

"Here's the big news: a gunner on the *Justification* saved the battleships from being destroyed by drawing the carian cruiser away from the battleships, giving Harper time to blow the damn thing to pieces," Nathan told them. Fâd's and Cory's faces were completely pale now and looked scared to death.

"Don't worry, the girls are okay," Nathan told them, and the other two breathed a sigh of relief.

"Well, whoever that gunner was, I'd like to shake their hand for saving our friends," Fâd said to him.

"You already have. It was Ash," Nathan said with an ornery grin, and Fâd's face again turned white and then red with anger.

"What the hell was she doing running a gun in a major battle?" he said, now mad and yelling.

"What I heard was that they were short a gunner, and the sixth gun at that, no less during the fight, and it was the admiral himself who ordered her to take the gun. Here's the other part, and don't get mad at me. I'm only relaying what I heard. Ash left aboard the

Wraith with the new young commander as his gunner," Nathan said, backing away from Fâd.

"WHAT?" Fâd yelled, and if he could have ripped something apart right then, he would have.

"I thought you two were only friends?" Cory asked him with a smirk, looking up at his friend from under the control console he was working on.

"We are. She's too young to be fighting battles. She's got two more years of school and should stay close to her father where it's safe," Fâd snarled at Cory.

"They're seventeen now, Fâd, only two years younger than us and soon will be enlisting too. Why is it any different for them and her than us?" Cory asked him.

"Because I just don't want to see any of them get hurt."

"Bullshit. You still can't stop thinking and caring about Ash. None of us can when it comes to those three," Nathan snapped at him.

"Watch yourself, Nathan," Fâd warned.

"No, I will not. It's true. You have women literally throwing themselves at you all the time, and never once have I seen you with any of them."

"I have better things to do than deal with some stupid female."

"You've got to live too, Fâd. She's gone, moved on. You made sure of that for all of us!" Nathan said to him, boiling mad, and walked away, over to the pilot controls. Fâd just stood there for a few seconds, glaring at his friend, then left the carian ship that was sitting in one of the *Lithia*'s large docking bays.

Hours later, Nathan and Cory found him at the Proxy, a night-club on the battlecruiser. It was very obvious he had had a few to drink because when they walked in, some female watorian technician was straddling his lap and kissing him. Nathan and Cory looked at each other and half-grinned, walking over to his table.

"Oh, hey, guys. This is Sophia. That's Nathan, and he's Cory," Fâd said with a smirk, and the woman smiled at them.

Nathan and Cory sat down and ordered some drinks, but while they were talking to Fâd, a couple of girls came over and were now all over them as well. A few hours and more drinks later, Fâd got up with Sophia, and they left the club together. He had ahold of her hand and headed to his cabin. Once inside, she came over to him, and they started kissing each other madly. She pulled off her uniform top and helped him take his off as he forced her down on his bed, kissing her wildly.

"Tell me you want me," she said seductively while he was kissing her neck.

"I want you, Ash," he said, and her eyes got huge. She shoved him off her.

"What did you call me?" she asked furiously.

"Nothing," he said, now mad and glaring at her.

"Yes, you did. Who is Ash?"

"I think it's time for you to go," Fâd said and got up, heading to the door, waiting for her to leave. She jumped off his bed, grabbing her shirt, and stormed over to the door and left. He walked over, picked up his shirt off the floor, and walked out his door. Just as he was starting to pull it on in the hallway, Nathan and Cory walked up with the two girls who were with them at the club. Nathan was grinning at Fâd when he walked past them, then he stopped and looked at Nathan.

"Go to hell!" Fâd said as he stormed away, heading back to the large docking bay where they had the carian infiltrator docked.

Over on the carian ship, Fâd was working away on changing over the carian mess to a more workable technology on one of the control panels, still mad. He had his shirt off as sweat poured off him, using it to wipe the sweat from his face. He was wrenching away a very stuck bolt when the sonic wrench slipped, and he hit his hand on the panel. The pent-up rage in him finally exploded. He threw the wrench, and it hit with such force that it penetrated into the half-inch metal plate. It struck a nearby console panel. He was ready to explode again. Fury boiled in him as all he could think about was finding that commander whom Ash was with and ripping him apart just for being near her. He also was furious with Admiral Harper for letting her go with him and putting her in danger.

He paced back and forth, thinking about her. He could even smell and hear her voice in his head, and it was driving him mad. He was so caught up in his thoughts that he didn't even realize his father had been standing there for some time until he caught his movement.

"How long have you been here?" Fâd snapped at him with narrowed eyes.

"Long enough to see you embed a sonic wrench into a metal plate."

"What do you want?"

"What happened?" his father asked.

"I threw the wrench because I hit my hand," Fâd replied, still angry.

"No. What happened with you and Ash?" Larson asked him and walked over to his son.

"Nothing."

"Fâd, I know something did. I saw the change in Ash as well."

"Okay. If you need to know, we agreed to try and forget about each other, that it could never work with us because we have different paths ahead, and trying to even keep the friendship would be too hard and painful," Fâd said, and strangely, he felt a little relief. He had been carrying this for some time, and it was like a festering wound.

"Are you sure that was the right decision?" Larson asked and walked over and put his hand on his son's shoulder.

"Yes, it was, for both of us." Fâd replied hanging his head down, as the pain was evident on his face.

"You'll be fighting this the rest of your life. You know there will be no other, right?" his father told him.

"I know, and I accept that."

CHAPTER 32

THE *JUSTIFICATION* ENTERED Sigma Six space a day before school started, and finally, after everything was handled aboard the ship, Admiral Harper and the girls headed down to New Guinea spaceport along with their armed escort. Once again, they walked through the terminal, got into their airlimo, and headed back to their house, then did the standard bug sweep. One would think that by now, they had given up; but sure enough, they found four this time. Ash could now see why council militia always got their butts kicked.

The girls weren't looking forward to this year. It was now what everyone called the hell years, and sure enough, after the first day of school, they were justly named. The amount of schoolwork they had was tremendous, and soon, they found out that every other week was a test. But they had a secret. Little did anyone know that during testing, Ash would link up to her friends, and they would help one another with some of the questions—not a lot because the girls were very smart but enough to keep them top of their classes.

The other problem about hell year was, there was no time for socializing. They were always doing something with the school, homework, studying for test, or class trips. Rachael was the one whom it affected the most. She hated not being able to shop or hang out with the boys. The good thing about it, though, was, time seemed to fly by, and before they knew it, school was out, and they were once again on board the *Justification*, now finishing up with basic training. By the time the girls finished with basic, they were all unofficially enlisted as officers due to their advance training under the command of Vice Admiral Harper.

But even that time came to an end, and they were now eighteen and in their final year of prep school, and looking forward to it. School began, and several months later, they were celebrating at the house as they now each held a certificate showing they had completed seven years with honors. Even Sharni was there with Admiral Larson since he was around off and on while Fâd, Nathan, and Cory attended the academy over in New Haven, which was almost on the other side of the planet.

"So, Ash, are you ready for your year-long tour?" Larson asked her.

"Of course. It will be nice to just get away from here," Ash replied with no emotion, just like her father.

Harper came over and started talking to Larson and Sharni as Ash walked off and grabbed a water bottle. She went outside and walked around the backyard. The night had ascended upon them. She wanted to be alone now, and this was one of the rare opportunities she had finally gotten all night. The reason was, seeing Rear Admiral Larson again opened a wound she had been trying for years to mend.

Ash walked over to the tree that they all used to sleep near when they were younger, and she had to smile to herself, remembering those times. She wiped a tear from her cheek as she remembered the last time near this tree with the boys and was so deep in thought that she didn't hear or see Admiral Larson walk up and jumped when she caught his movement, quickly wiping her eyes.

"I'm sorry. I didn't see you there," she said weakly.

Larson walked up and stood beside her, looking up at the sky. "You know, it amazes me how something so beautiful can hold so much pain hidden inside," he said and looked over at Ash, brushing a loose strand of her black hair away from her face.

"Excuse me, what do you mean?" Ash asked knowing full well the meaning behind the words as her eyes teared up again.

"You're not the only one hurting. He is too," he said, putting his hand on her shoulder, gently squeezing it, then walking away.

Ash watched him go as tears ran down her face. So Fâd was in pain as well from the choice they had made all those years ago. But it was true what they had said, they would never have the chance to be together. Their lives were on different paths, and so far, it was happening like they surmised.

The hour got late, and the party was over as the last of their guests left. The girls headed to their room to pack knowing they would not be back there for well over a year, and now melancholy set in thinking about it. They had been excited about getting out of there to start their tour, but now they knew they would miss this place and all its many memories.

That night, like they used to do when they were little even though they were almost nineteen, they climbed down the tree next to their balcony and went and spread out blankets and laid out on the ground where they always did when they were kids. "Just think, one whole year on active duty and then it's to the academy and all those hot-looking guys," Rachael said with her arms folded behind her head.

"Rachael, is that all you think about?" Ash asked, laughing.

"That and my new matrix-9 sniper rifle with an optigold 3 sighting scope and infrared capabilities. Oh, how I love big guns." Rachael grinned wickedly.

"Okay, that just didn't sound right," Ash said, giggling.

"That's because we know what she means," Bridgett replied, giggling as well.

They all stayed out there all night and finally fell asleep for the last time near the tree. Admiral Harper came outside the next morning and looked down at the sleeping girls and had to smile. He remembered them out there as little girls asleep, which didn't seem that long ago, and now they were beautiful young women.

"It's time to wake up and get going. The ship is waiting. We have our orders," he told them, and the girls jumped up and headed into the house. A little while later, they were all dressed in their sentinel uniforms with their hair pulled back into tight buns at the back of their heads and serious looks on their faces. They each helped carry out all the trunks and luggage to the waiting airlimo and climbed in as Vice Admiral Harper locked the house up. He had asked Nera to come over to check on it for him whenever she was in New Guinea. Plus, Sharni and Larson would use it from time to time when they were also in the city.

He walked over to the vehicle and looked back at the house. Never again would he be spending any time there. He was only keeping the place for the girls when they started the academy so they had a place to go during some of the longer breaks and in between each new year. The girls were going to find that the academy would be much different. Schooling ran for almost a full year straight with only three weeks off during each new year. There were occasional breaks here and there but no more than three or four days. Plus, this time, they would be living on campus the whole time during school, and he wouldn't be around that much to bail them out of trouble if they got into one, which they still managed to do.

While the kids would be at the academy, he and Larson would be doing a lot more active duty and only back for short periods at a time. One big reason was, things were getting much more tense between sentinel fleet and council militia. On more than one occasion, both sides had opened fired on each other with council paying the price for it. Of course, there was always the usual apology from council and the promise that action would be taken against the guilty party, but sentinel command knew better. They knew everything was coming from the council militia and that council presidency had lost some of their power, so the exodus was being pushed harder to have everything ready when the call went out.

The girls sat back as the shuttle now climbed toward the *Justification*, and they noticed out the window the *Lithia* was now moving away. Harper got clearance and landed the shuttle in the bay, and finally, they all stepped down onto the deck of the battlecruiser they were going to begin their careers on. Crewmen came out and started unloading the shuttle immediately, and Harper dismissed the girls. He headed to the bridge as the girls headed to report for duty already. Rachael and Ash were assigned to the recon division, and Bridgett was in engineering but transferred also to recon.

They all headed down to the huge armory to get their weapons and armor and then report in to their commanding officer. Even though Bridgett was an engineer, she refused to take a ship position and chose to go along with the recon division as the shuttle's engineer or aid in whatever other kind of ship or equipment they encountered and was given permission by none other than the vice admiral himself.

The girls stood in the armory as soldiers helped them put their new armor on, which were made specifically for them for the first time. It wasn't bulky at all and fit rather well. Plus, they had kinetic generators to hold a kinetic shield for added protection besides just having to rely on the material it was made out of, not to mention top-of-the-line robotic joints that gave ease of movement and increased speed and jumping ability. The torso protection, as the girls pointed out, definitely let everyone know they were female, and they started teasing the men who were helping them, and after a while, everyone was laughing.

They were completely armored, and the final piece was a helmet that from the outside looked very space-aged with barely a slit for visibility, but on the inside, it was like they didn't even have a helmet and could see everything just fine. Over their left eye inside the helmet was a constant running screen of the suit's functions and diagnostics, and they could even make the view go from regular to infrared or even see at a distance.

The men who armored them then had the girls go out into a practice arena with multiple dummies and obstacles to test the suits' response to the girls' abilities. The girls definitely tested the suits' capabilities immediately—flipping, spinning in the air, jumping, running, and strength. The men were very impressed with their skills, and finally, the girls completed the course and walked over to where they had suited up and removed their helmets now.

"That was so awesome. Can we do it again?" Ash asked one of the men as Rachael and Bridgett nodded their heads in agreement.

"No, you need to get over and pick up your weapons," the armor corporal told them with a grin.

The girls walked through the armory hallway, leaving the armor depot, now in their suits, carrying their helmets in their left arm. They noticed that they made absolutely no noise. Even when walking and stepping on the metal floor of the deck, there was no sound. Rachael even did a little dance to test it out. After this day, once they got their weapons, their armor and rifles would be stored in another armory locker room where all the rest of the suits of the soldiers on the ship were and where they would change into their suits from then on. Finally, they walked into the weapons room, and Rachael's mouth fell open. She just felt like she had walked into a candy store. There were all kinds of weapons in there, and the girls just stared at them.

"All right, you three, I know what to set you guys up with," a voice spoke from behind them. The girls wheeled around quickly and started grinning when they saw who it was: Private Justin, only he was a major now. He used to run the sim room for them.

"When did you take over this post?" Rachael asked him.

"A few years ago. Wow, you three are gorgeous. I always knew you would be. It's hard to believe it's you. I still remember you guys when you were this tall," he said, grinning, and held his hand up, showing them how little they were.

"We've improved since then," Bridgett said with a grin.

"That's what I heard. All right, let me see here. Rachael, here you go." Justin handed her a sleek, well-balanced black sniper rifle with a streamline scope and an M-300 pistol with laser sights, which Rachael strapped to her right thigh.

"I wanted a matrix-9," she said, pouting.

"Matrix-9 sucks. They're lighter than the phantom X and can't hold their precision sighting for very long or take any abuse at all. Plus, their balance is off, making your trajectory waver one-eighth of an inch. Go try it. This one has your name all over it. Trust me, I know you'll like it," Justin told her and handed her a clip with some rubber bullets. Rachael looked down at them, then back at him with an ornery grin.

"What, no paint bullets?" Justin grinned and kicked her in the butt as she headed out to a simulated practice course, laughing.

"Okay, Bridgett. Here, this will work perfectly for you, the new mantis pistol. It has an accuracy rating of 98 percent with a recoil dampener." He handed her a clip with rubber bullets and a pistol like Rachael's, and she strapped on the M-300 pistol but carried the mantis, which was a lot bigger than the M-300, and headed into the sim room as well to test it.

"Ash, the leader, here, this I have been keeping especially for you. It's a new assault rifle, a prototype that not too many can handle, but I know it would be perfect for you. It was made for you. It has a grooved barrel, giving it an extra boost to its firing power, plus a built-in recoil dampener and can fire over 445 rounds in less than a minute before it overheats. Then it has a quick recovery and cools down in less than five seconds with a backup mini grenade launcher here."

Justin handed her the rifle and a pistol as well, and like Bridgett and Rachael, she strapped on the pistol but held the rifle. Ash was amazed by how light it was. She held it up to her eye and shoulder and looked down the sights. Then she held out her hand, and Justin grinned, handing her a clip of rubber bullets and fake mini grenades. She slammed them into the rifle just like a pro and headed to the sim room.

She walked out into the course and saw they were set up for a jungle incursion and could hear the echo created by Rachael's sniper rifle and the automated firing of Bridgett's pistol somewhere out in the jungle. She put on her helmet, locked and loaded, and headed in.

"Eagle, this is Serpent. Entering now," Ash said into her helmet.

"Serpent, this is Eagle. targets are grid A 1,3," Rachael replied over her comm.

"Fox, what are your numbers?"

"Grid A 1, 2, targets 17," Bridgett answered.

"Affirmative. Moving to grid A 2,4."

Ash moved silently through the foliage and switched her suit to camo and now blended into her surroundings. She quickly got around and flanked the holographic carians, who were busy firing at Bridgett, who had gotten their attention so Ash could flank them. Finally in position, she started firing, and the carians started dropping. Bridgett, in the meantime, moved to another point, so Rachael had a clear view and shot. In no time, the three of them had wiped them all out, but Justin had set up an added feature to their trial. When the girls thought they had killed all the carians, they got ambushed.

All three split in different directions, flipped, and rolled out of the line of fire, their suits shimmering when they took a hit. They quickly regrouped, and Ash saw that the carians were tracking their movements with an energy scanner, which was a small, handheld device that could pick up power usage just like what their multitools put off. Immediately, she had them all shut down their multitools; and now without comms, Ash used telepathy to send orders. In no time, the carians were decimated. The lights came on, and they knew the trial was finally over.

They put their weapons on their backs where the suits had auto clamps and would hold their guns in place, then started walking toward the exit. The jungle disappeared around them, and they were again in an empty room. They now noticed all the soldiers standing, watching out of the viewing windows overhead, clapping, and Ash saw her father standing at the exit with Major Justin, as the girls still used his first name.

The girls walked up to them with their helmets on, then reached up and unsnapped their pressure seals, which made a whoosh sound as they released and pulled them off. They all had sweat on their faces but grinning ear to ear.

Admiral Harper looked at them, void of expression, but you could tell he was trying not to smirk. "Very impressive. You three just passed the hardest training program we have."

The girls turned and smacked fist together, then looked back at the admiral and turned serious. Ash popped her neck, and without thinking about it, she reached up and rubbed her right temple because it was throbbing a little from using her telepathy so much.

"If they get too bad, use your multitool, and it will have your suit inject some asrinon for the pain. We had that feature added to your suit knowing you might need it from time to time," Major Justin told her, knowing about Ash's telepathic and kinetic abilities and that she was now having headaches too.

"Dismissed," Admiral Harper said to them, and all three girls saluted him and Major Justin, then headed to get changed. The two men watched them leave. "Those three work together like a well-oiled machine, in perfect sync," Justin said to him, grinning.

"I know, and they're going to get that connection tested real soon. We head to the Trimos cluster. Some of our supply freighters aren't responding, and there has been a lot of merc attacks near there lately," Harper told him with a serious look, and both men looked back toward the direction the girls had gone.

CHAPTER 33

IT WAS SIX months later, and Ash crouched behind a large crate as she sent orders to her squad with her telepathy. The three elite soldiers on her squad took off, now in camouflage, stalking around the outer perimeter of the shipment that was stacked directly in the center of the cargo hold of the freighter *Sunset*. She already knew that Rachael was somewhere high and had a bead on the mercs who were standing around the shipment, holding the crew at gunpoint. Bridgett had already made it to the engine room with another elite and was standing by to power the ship back up once they had control again. Ash went camo and sneaked around the other side so as to stay out of Rachael's line of fire and put the mercs in a cross fire with the rest of her team.

This was the third freighter in over a week and a half they had to retake, and she had since, over time, learned how to link her telepathy to all six members of her assault team. It made her headaches flare up faster, but asrinon worked fast, and her suit injected it straight into her nervous system at the back of her neck where the ship's doctors had now surgically inserted a med port that directly linked to her nervous system, making the medication reach and stop the pain faster. She counted down to her team, and then they jumped up and opened fire with precise strikes as Rachael dropped the merc leader with a perfect headshot, leaving all hostages untouched.

Before they came out of total cover, Ash linked to Bridgett and had her run a scan of the ship, making sure they got all the mercs. Once it was confirmed, they walked out, still with their helmets on, which gave them a somewhat ominous look. Now the freighter's engines came back on, and confirmation was sent to the *Justification*, who began to send a med team and more soldiers to help out now that the freighter was secure.

Ash walked over to the hostages but noticed that they were looking nervous, and one man kept looking around at Ash and her team as they advanced. She knew something wasn't right and halted her team before they got too close. The man jumped up in a flash with a long, curved blade and came at Ash. Her team just stood back, acting totally at ease, as Ash's martial arts training kicked in. Before long, everyone heard the man's neck snap as he fell to the floor, dead. Rachael came walking over from somewhere near the front of the cargo bay with her rifle still in her hands, but Ash and the rest had theirs clamped to their backs already.

Rachael walked up to the dead man, whom Ash had just killed with her own hands. "Did you have to break his neck? We could have questioned him to see where they are coming from, dumbass."

The other three elites started chuckling under their helmets as Ash reached up and pulled hers off. "You better watch it, or you'll find that rifle you love so much up your ass," Ash said back with an ornery smirk. Rachael clamped her rifle to her back and took off her helmet and was laughing as the rest of the elites did too. The girls had finished up with their officer training in the first two months of their tour, and then three months after that, they had their own squadron with three men and one woman, which made up the rest of Ash's team since she was the squad leader. So far, they hadn't lost a fight or a hostage. Bridgett and the other elite walked into the room just as the shuttle from the cruiser landed, and now medics and soldiers were helping the survivors and overseeing the cargo.

Ash's commander walked in and surveyed the scene, then walked over to her and the rest of her team. "Good job. Is there anything you guys can't do?"

"I can't sing," Ash replied.

"She's not lying there. She really sucks at that," Rachael said.

"Hey, Justin, I'm having some issues with my suit. It's really tight in the chest area here," Bridgett said with a grin and pushed her chest way out.

"That's Colonel Justin to you, and if anything, it's too loose. You don't have enough up there to fill it out."

"Oh, burn, Bridg. He got you good. I think there's hope for you after all," Ash said, laughing.

"Dismissed. Get the hell out of here," Justin said to them, grinning, and watched them go, shaking his head. He had always known they were destined for greatness, and so far, they were proving themselves over and over again. He wasn't quite sure when Vice Admiral Harper promoted him up to colonel and wanted him to take over as their superior, but now he could see the reasoning.

Justin had known the girls since they were old enough to come down and play in the sim room that he was in charge of. He always joked around and helped them on their combat skills, showing them the best holds and moves, even though at that time, he was just a private. Justin was a fairly tall, well-built human male with sandy-brown hair and hazel eyes. He was more on the lean side and had a sort of childish look to him, which was probably why he was overlooked most of the time by his superiors but not by the girls, who found him rather cute.

Justin would still be monitoring the sim room if it weren't for them. It was through the three girls that he caught the vice admiral's eye when they would still come down to the sim room and practice clear up until they were on their tour. He had been helping them with some combat tactics in the sim room and didn't know that the admiral was watching from the viewing window above. After that, he started receiving promotions and finally got moved up to overseeing the weapons depot, which he knew a lot about since he had plenty of time studying while managing the sim rooms.

Also, during this time, he finally outgrew his childish appearance; and when the girls returned for their tour, he now looked like the thirty-something-year-old man that he was, even sporting a goatee, but still just as ornery and, the girls had to admit, rather cute still.

Justin could get along with just about everyone and had a natural ability to see people's true potential and could unlock it just by talking to them without intimidation. It was because of this that Admiral Harper put him in charge of the girls. Ash, Rachael, and Bridgett worked better when not having someone constantly trying to show them who the boss was, which was what happened time and time again. The girls had gotten in trouble quite a few times for striking a superior officer, especially Ash when she almost killed one, but the charges always managed to get dropped, especially when it was found out that most of their superiors thought they were better than the girls and didn't handle it too well when the girls proved them wrong or just the fact that they were women.

Justin had known them since they were little, and they respected him, and he knew what they were capable of and always pushed them, giving them a challenge, which was what you had to do to keep them interested. He loved it now that he could rub it back in the faces of all the other team commanders, because now his team was first squad elite special ops recon called the Phoenix, which Ash and Rachael came up with because they were teasing Bridgett about her red hair

Justin reflected back to when everything changed for all of them, which was the turning point in all their lives. It was a great day when the admiral went to assign the squad rankings, and there was a competition set up between each of the four teams. Everyone teased him about having so many women on his team, the three girls and one more, especially with the fact that the squad leader was female. Plus, it was Ash and them who recruited the guys. They had met them at Gravities and had picked them because they weren't afraid to work with women, and so far, they turned out to be a perfect fit.

All the teams were assigned colors with his being red, which was kind of funny looking back now and their name. The first competition was set between the yellow squad and the defending first squad elites, the blue team, and they had a forest environment in the simulation room. The blue team, of course, won, and they made it a point to show that they won because they had no women on their team, and the yellow team had two. Justin could see Ash and them getting mad at the blue team's arrogance and chauvinistic attitudes and knew from experience that the madder they got, the more determined they were.

Next up was his team against the green squad, and he knew this was going to be good by the looks on the faces of his squad. They walked into the sim room as the blue squad walked past them, leaving the sim room, making some loud remark to the red squad to try and not get tangled up in their bras. Suddenly, one of the blue team members hit the ground, rubbing the back of his head. Ash looked back at her squad to see who had done it, and Bridgett grinned.

Ash's squad put on their helmets and took out their weapons as the buzzer went off. She instantly signaled everyone, and the team split in all different directions as she went right up the middle of the desert environment. Justin was standing with Admiral Harper, and they watched from the viewing windows overhead. Before long, Ash's team disappeared, but they could see the green team advancing toward their end and flag.

Suddenly, Ash and them came up out of the sand, having caught almost all the green team in a cross fire with Rachael buried in a high dune, picking off their backup. The whole excursion lasted no more than fifteen minutes, breaking the record of twenty-three minutes set by the blue team last year. Harper looked over at Justin and gave him a quick wink, and the colonel then hurried down to his team. They were walking out and smacking fists with one another and laughing and joking. He met them at the prep room as they were all checking out their armor for one another.

"Did you see their faces when we came up out of the sand?" Bridgett was laughing.

"You rule, Ash," one of the guys on the team said to her.

"Yeah, and I did it without getting tangled up in my bra," Ash replied mockingly and looked over at the blue team, who was getting ready for their chance at the red team now.

"All right, that's enough. Come over here." Justin motioned for them, and they all huddled around him. This was also the difference with them. He didn't make them act all professional; actually, quite the opposite. They were mouthy, joking all the time, and everyone was on a first-name basis, including with him as well. He knew if the situation called for them to act obediently, they would and did when the admiral came around.

"Okay, guys, you know what they can do, but expect the unexpected, and remember, there are no rules. Show them that bras rule," Justin told them, and everyone started laughing. He was standing there when he saw Ash reach down and pressed the button injecting asrinon into her neck from her suit and gripped her rifle tightly as it entered her system.

"I'm going to need it. No rules, silence only," she said with a wicked grin to everyone. He knew she was going to telepathically link up to her whole team, which she had been working on, but without the asrinon, she could become immobilized from the headaches because of the pain that usually occurred from her using her gifts, as they all were now calling them. The team was shutting down their multitools so they couldn't be tracked or heard, and she followed her team out, putting on her helmet and walking across the empty simulation room clear over to the other side where their flag was.

It was a drastic change from the laughing and joking group in the prep room. It was a serious and deadly squad walking right now as they all checked their weapons. They got to the other side as the room changed into a warehouse filled with freight, and one of the team members pressed the button, signaling they were ready. The blue team did the same, and the clock counted down as the buzzer signaled to begin.

Harper and Justin watched as Ash's team moved without one hand signal and disappeared in the warehouse. The blue team was moving around the crates, and the more they spread out, the more they started disappearing without a sound. Finally, it was down to just two from the blue team; and suddenly, Ash bolted between two crates, clearly exposing herself to gunfire. She moved so fast with her suit enhancements as the two from the blue team went to fire at her, but both were struck dead center in the head by Rachael from her hidden perch, and the buzzer went off, announcing the end of the match.

Harper and Justin entered the room with the commander of the blue team, wondering what had happened to the rest of the blue squad because no one had seen them anywhere or heard gunfire, except for the two shots from Rachael taking out the last two. When the simulation was shut down, all the blue team, including the two whom Rachael took out, were lying on the floor, unconscious. Ash's team had managed to take out five elite soldiers without firing one shot and set the other two up for kill shots.

Justin was amazed at the strategy they used to get the mission done. Vice Admiral Harper awarded his team first squad, the top rank out of all the four groups, and Justin just grinned. Now his team was respected, and everyone wanted to be part of it. The problem was that in a month, his squad leader, a level 10 sniper, and a first engineer with combat training would be leaving. Even the rest of the team were getting promotions and moving into more specialized areas of the military. Plus, he got a promotion himself and was being transferred to Valhalla to train more soldiers into elite recon units like this.

They had special talents, but it was his ability to recognize those and teach and challenge them on how to use them to their fullest potential that helped. It was always his dream to do, and now thanks to Ash, Rachael, and Bridgett, he was going to get that chance.

The girls got back from their last mission, cleaned up, and went to meet up with the rest of their team since it was going to be the last time they would ever see one another. They walked into the night-club Gravities, and Keith, one of the guys off their team, saw them and waved them over. Already, all the others were there, and a round of drinks was waiting for them. They all toasted and chugged them down as another round came for them.

"You know, I think I might actually miss all of you," Ash said, grinning, and everyone laughed.

"I have to make a confession. At first, I just joined up because you women were hot, and I enjoyed the view from behind, but I realized you can actually kick ass too. I still like the view, though," Frank told them, and they toasted again, laughing.

It went on like that for a while, then someone tapped Ash on the shoulder. She turned around, and there was Trey Martin, looking at her with his cute smile on his face. "Trey, what are you doing here?" Ash asked, now a little tipsy.

"I heard a rumor that the best recon squad around was here, having a party, and I wanted to come see the legendary Phoenix squadron for myself, especially when I found out who their leader was. Plus, it helped that I was delivering some special items from sentinel command for the vice admiral."

"Wow, it's good to see you." Ash grinned and then introduced everyone to Captain Martin now instead of Commander.

Trey looked at her uniform, which had many bars and insignias on it, especially the one for special ops and lieutenant commander. She had definitely gone and done exactly what she had planned and had proven herself.

"Ash, do you want to dance?" Trey asked her.

"Okay." She got up as he took her hand, and they walked out onto the dance floor.

They started dancing together, and Trey leaned closer to her. "I couldn't believe what I have been hearing. Your squad is all the talk. I knew I just had to see you again, and my gosh, you're absolutely beautiful, Ash."

"Quit it. You're embarrassing me."

"No, I mean it. You really are. So how is everything else going in your life besides kicking ass and saving the galaxy?" Trey grinned at her as they continued to dance.

"Great, except now my team is splitting up as me and my friends head off to the academy for four more miserable years of schooling and the rest all got promotions. It's kind of ironic. Here I am, a lieutenant commander, but I still have to go back to school and can't be back on active duty until it's over. How ridiculous is that?" she said with much irritation in her tone, and Trey started chuckling at her.

"Yeah, that's usually what happens when you're the best, and I know what you mean about school, but the academy is a mandatory requirement for all enlisted officers," he told her with a grin.

"So what about you? Where are you now since you got your transfer?" she asked, smiling.

"I'm captain of the destroyer *Cerebrus*," Trey told her.

"Oh yeah, one of the ships that protect Valhalla, a big change from a battleship, I bet, and a captain now too."

"Yep. Instead of a crew of 237, I now am responsible for a crew of 346."

"Scary. And here I thought six was hard." Ash grinned.

"Damn it, Ash, I can't take it anymore," Trey said to her and pulled her into his arms and kissed her. She kissed him back, but this time, it was different, and he let her go and looked down at her. "You've changed. You're not looking for what I am, are you?" Trey asked her, and Ash could see the hurt in his eyes.

"I'm sorry, Trey. Right now, a relationship is the last thing I want. I'm a soldier through and through. It's what I love to do. Do you want somebody who will always be gone out on a mission and most of the time in the middle of the fight?" Ash asked him.

Trey closed his eyes and took a deep breath. "No, I don't. I want a woman that needs me to protect her, love her, and not a trained soldier."

"I know, and you will find such a person. You're a wonderful man, and you deserve better than me," Ash told him, then put her hand on his cheek and smiled up at him. He grabbed it and held it against his cheek.

"No, Ash, you deserve a great man, one more worthy of you, not lesser," Trey said, and once again, he leaned down and softly kissed her lips, then turned and left her standing there. Ash watched him go and then walked over to her friends.

"What was that all about?" Bridgett asked, surprised.

"A goodbye." Bridgett didn't say anything and handed Ash a drink. Ash tipped it back to take a swig, then she noticed Rachael was missing. "Where's Rachael?" Sarah, the only other female member on their team besides them, motioned over to another empty stool. "She's with Keith?" Ash asked, and everyone nodded. "Okay. Who here hasn't been with Rachael?" Ash asked, and none of the other guys on the team said anything.

Bridgett was flabbergasted. "All of you?"

"Sorry, but Rachael likes to work off all her built-up tension after a mission," Barry told Ash, who just shook her head and rolled her eyes.

"We're going to have to have a talk with her when we go to the academy," Ash told Bridgett, who agreed.

The rest of the night went on, and Rachael and Keith actually came back. Ash gave her a glaring look, but Rachael just grinned like it was nothing. Finally, it got late, and they had to get to bed, for their transport was leaving early in the morning to Krios where the girls were staying for three weeks with Ash's grandparents until the academy began. Ash wasn't looking forward to it. She had stayed a couple of days over the last years with her grandparents Tol Vasna, and it was so boring because there was nothing to do. At least the flight would take several hours even at jump, and the only good thing about this was Aunt Sharni was going to be there.

They all staggered back to their cabins, and she tried to sneak in to her room without waking up her father, but she fell over one of her trunks that was sitting out in the living room. He came out of his bedroom and ordered on the lights and saw her lying sprawled out on the floor, trying to get up. "Are you drunk?" he asked, mad.

"No, just a little dizzy."

"Bull. I should make you go and run laps."

"That wouldn't work because I would fall down there too," Ash told him and now finally got up and staggered to her room. He watched her, and a slight grin appeared at the corner of his mouth. He couldn't lecture her because he had been this way more than once when he was her age. Besides, the best part was, he was going to enjoy seeing her in the morning when she woke with a huge hangover.

CHAPTER 34

NEXT MORNING CAME, and the girls felt like crap. Ash's head was killing her, and Rachael and Bridgett felt sick to their stomachs. They all headed down to docking port 6 where a nice frigate was docked to transport them to Krios. It had arrived late last night, and now it was just finishing up resupplying for the return trip. It was very elegant and sleek, just like all vatorian ships, and the girls couldn't help but keep looking at the two pilots because they were so beautiful. Of course, all the vatorian people were.

The women were very beautiful, and the men were very handsome, and they all exhibited gold eyes, pale-blue skin, long brilliant-white hair, and scroll-like gold markings all over their faces, necks, and hands, not to mention elegance and gracefulness just emanated from them.

The girls said their goodbyes to everyone and boarded the ship. One of the crewmen showed them to their seats. The inside of the ship was very extravagant as well, and if they got tired, there was a small cabin just for them to sleep in. Finally, the ship got permission to depart; and soon, the girls watched as the *Justification* disappeared when they went into jump. They sat and watched the ship's small crew of five—surprisingly, they were all male—busily going about their duties. They definitely noticed that a couple of the crewmen kept glancing their way, and one of the pilots even actually spoke to them finally.

"So which one of you is Admiral Tol Vasna's niece?" the pilot asked.

"That would be her, Ashley Harper," Rachael replied, pointing over to Ash, who still felt like crap.

"Then are you Commander Torres's daughter?"

"Yep, that would be me. I'm Rachael."

"I'm Kiroff, and the other pilot in there is Torin."

"Nice to meet you," Ash said to them, and Kiroff smiled.

"So that makes you Bridgett Nelson, Chief Engineer Tony Nelson's daughter. Are you as good with engines as your father?" Kiroff asked.

"Yeah. I'm a first engineer as well," Bridgett said with a grin.

"Really? Because Rashid was just asking me if you were. Do you think you could go and help him with his engine problem?" Kiroff asked, smiling.

"I could sure take a look," Bridgett said and got up as a very good-looking crewman came over and escorted her toward the engine room.

Ash got up then and told Rachael she was going to lie down because she was still feeling the effects of last night. No sooner had she laid down than she was out, and a few hours later, she woke up and walked back to where they were sitting. Bridgett was back, going over some schematics on her power pad, and looked up when Ash walked back in, but Rachael was nowhere in sight.

"So did you get the problem solved with the engine?" Ash asked her, and Bridgett just grinned and kept looking at her pad.

"Oh yeah, his engine purrs like a kitten now."

"Where's Rachael?" Ash asked, looking around.

"She was tired and didn't want to wake you. Kiroff offered his cabin, so she went to sleep there," Bridgett told her.

"You're kidding me. She didn't," Ash asked in disbelief.

Just then, Rachael came back with a big smile on her face with Kiroff right behind her, and then he headed back to the other pilot seat. Ash saw the other pilot, Torin, look over at him and grinned.

Rachael leaned over to Bridgett and whispered, but Ash could hear her. "Did you notice those markings are everywhere?"

"Oh yeah," Bridgett said.

"Not you too, Bridgett. I can't believe what I'm hearing. This stops now. Let's get one thing straight right now. No guys in our apartment on campus," Ash said and started rubbing her temple, because it began to throb suddenly. "I wish everyone would stop talking," she blurted out as hundreds of voices went off in her head, and suddenly, she started getting chills and knew everyone was in trouble.

"Rach, I feel a fit coming on," Ash said and was trying to contain it as Rachael jumped up and started yelling at the pilots.

"Do you have a nueralizer on board?"

Kiroff jumped out of his seat. "Yes. Why do you need it?"

"Ash is a kinetic, and something is triggering an attack," Rachael yelled at him. Kiroff ran to the back of the ship to grab a med pack, but by the time he got back, Ash's eyes were now glowing bright blue, and she was starting to power up. She gripped the arms of her chair, trying to fight it. Suddenly, she felt a sharp sting on the side of her neck, and everything went black.

* * *

Half an hour later, Ash woke up. She was lying on a bed with Rachael and Bridgett sitting beside her and Kiroff walking over to her. He picked up her arm and injected medicine into her. She could tell by the way she was feeling that it was a mild nueralizer, because they always made kinetics feel funny.

"Ash, how are you feeling?" Rachael asked her.

"Besides all the voices in my head, great," she said dreamily. Rachael and Bridgett looked over at Kiroff for an explanation.

"Is Ashley a telepath?" he asked.

"Yes, why?" Rachael replied.

"Well, she's half human, too, and since we are now in vatoria space, her human half can't block out all the voices from the vatorian people, because we normally communicate through telepathy. She's receiving everyone's voice at once, and her kinetic energy wants to kick in to protect her."

"But why is she having this problem now? She's been here before and never had a problem," Bridgett asked, worried about Ash.

"She's a mature female now, and her telepathy has gotten stronger, whereas when she was younger, it was hardly noticeable. She's probably never had to block it before, so she's never built up that resistance," Kiroff told them.

"Ash can't stay here, then. I won't have her drugged the whole time she's here. We'll just have to take her to New Guinea and stay until school begins," Rachael told Kiroff.

"I can't take you there without orders from my superior even though I would like to for you," he said to Rachael.

"Then contact Admiral Tol Vasna so I can talk to her."

Kiroff nodded to her and had Rachael go with him. They headed up to the cockpit. Once they got there, he got on the comm. "This is Kiroff Vin Bosh of the ship *Mirage*. I need to speak to Admiral Tol Vasna."

A few minutes later, there came a reply: "This is Admiral Tol Vasna. Go ahead," Sharni answered over the ship's comm.

"Sharni, this is Rachael. We have a problem."

"Is Ash all right?" Sharni asked, scared.

"No. She had a kinetic episode on the ship, and Bridgett had to shoot her with a tranquilizer gun. According to Kiroff, her telepathic powers are causing the episodes because she can't stop all the voices of the vatorians. We gave her a nueralizer, but I don't want to keep her drugged like that so she could stay there. I want to take her to New Guinea and stay until school starts, but Kiroff needs orders to take us," Rachael said to her.

"Oh, I never thought about that. With her being mature now, her telepathy is also, and her mind isn't conditioned for that yet. Yes, I agree, and I will meet you there. Kiroff, change course for Sigma Six and meet me there. I'm sending you my coordinates now," Sharni ordered him.

"Yes, Admiral," Kiroff replied and then smiled at Rachael and set the coordinates. He and Torin maneuvered the ship around and, in no time, went to jump.

Four hours later, the *Mirage* came out of jump and rendezvoused with the destroyer *Brisbane*. Ash was still dopey, for nueralizers took over six hours to wear off, and she was moved by stretcher to the destroyer and to its med bay. Rachael and Bridgett stayed with her as Sharni dealt with her parents and Harper over what had happened. Then Sharni came into the med bay and over to Ash's bed.

"How come we can't just go now? We can take her on the stretcher," Rachael asked Sharni.

"Because if we did and they found out she was given a nueralizer, they would know what she is, and all of us together couldn't stop them from taking her to Trinity," Sharni told them. The girls hadn't thought of that, which now made them scared for Ash.

Finally, two hours later, the drug wore off, and Ash was once again herself and a lot happier that she didn't have to stay with her grandparents. They all loaded into the shuttle, and Sharni flew them down to New Guinea spaceport. They docked on pad 8 and went into the terminal and fought their way through the crowds and finally made it to the front. The airlimo they had always rented before was already waiting for them, and the luggage was loaded into the trunk.

"This can't be a coincidence. The same vehicle?" Ash asked Sharni.

"I had to let your father know what was going on, and he made arrangements for everything."

They all climbed in, and before long, they were pulling up to the house. Everyone climbed out and headed up to the front door, and Sharni put her hand on the blue scan pad. The door unlocked and slid open, and everyone went inside, looking around. It had been well over a year since the last time they had been there, and now it felt kind of strange. The driver brought in the last of the luggage and headed for the door, but before he walked through it, he stopped and looked back at them with a big smile. "It's good to have you back. I missed you," he said and left.

The girls looked at one another and busted up laughing, then got down to business. Bridgett ran a scan, and sure enough, there were five bugs, which she easily disabled. They then unpacked and came back downstairs and went into the kitchen, rummaging through the refrigerator, which was empty.

"Okay, so what are we going to eat?" Rachael asked everyone.

"I'll order Thai. You girls like that, don't you?" Sharni said, and they all nodded their heads, and she placed the order through the comm in the kitchen and paid marks for it with her multitool. Then when she was done with that, she put in a grocery order. A few minutes later, the Thai food arrived in the porter, and they all ate and talked.

"I didn't know that those markings went everywhere," Rachael said to Sharni.

"How do you know that?"

"Kiroff showed her," Bridgett said, grinning, and Sharni was shocked.

"Oh yeah? What about when you fixed Rashid's engine besides just the ship's?" Rachael threw at Bridgett.

"Oh my gosh, I can't believe what I'm hearing. That is so morally wrong. You didn't do anything like that, did you, Ash?" Sharni asked her, still in shock.

"No way," Ash replied, wrinkling up her nose in disgust.

"Ms. Purity? Yeah, right. No one can melt the ice queen. I thought maybe that cute captain might actually have a chance, but Ash even shot him down finally," Rachael told Sharni.

"Really? There was somebody?"

"I tried, and I couldn't commit. He was too nice of a guy to hurt, and I couldn't have him waiting and hoping for something that would never be," Ash told her aunt.

"Ash, you have to open your heart someday. I don't want to see you go without ever knowing what it is like to love someone and be loved back by them."

"I don't need it. I have my father, you, Admiral Larson, my friends, and my duty to the fleet. My life is pretty well full," Ash replied coldly, which, just like her father, meant end of conversation by her tone.

Finally, the night was upon them, and they all went to bed. In no time, they fell asleep, except Ash. She got up and went and sat out on the balcony, watching the stars overhead. Love. Why did everyone thought she needed to find love? She did once many years ago, and look what that brought her: pain. Nope, she didn't need love. She finally got up and went back into the bedroom, then quietly climbed into bed and fell asleep.

Rachael let out the breath she was holding as she lay there, still awake, while Ash finally dozed off. She wished there was something she could do for her best friend, but she knew there wasn't, for they had all suffered, only she and Bridgett didn't close up like Ash did. But like Ash, who still loved Fâd and always would, she also was hurting, for she loved Nathan, and so was Bridgett, who had loved Cory from the time she first met him.

The three weeks flew by, and before they knew it, the girls were on an academy shuttle, heading to New Haven to get checked in and moved in to their new apartment on campus. First stop was the administration building and meeting with Councilor Shotwell. The girls sat in his office, and right away, they all clashed.

He started immediately on how sentinel fleet enlisted were unrefined and unprofessional, causing Ash to jump up and reached across his desk, grabbing him by the front of the shirt, asking him if he wanted to see how professional she could be. Rachael and Bridgett grabbed her and dragged her out of his office, kicking and trying to get at him. She was still fuming half an hour later as they headed to their apartment.

The girls found their building and walked into the elevator, taking it up to the third floor. They walked down the long hallway and finally found their room. Ash pressed her hand to the blue scan pad, and the door slid open. They all walked in and saw it was a very nice place.

The main room was the living room, dining room, and kitchen all in one. It had a large, peaked ceiling and a sliding glass door opening up to the patio balcony off the kitchen. Right off this room was a hallway with three separate bedrooms and one bathroom. Ash took the first bedroom with Rachael next to her and then Bridgett at the end of the hall. The other nice thing was, Ash's father had it already furnished and professionally decorated for them.

They were in the middle of unpacking when they heard a buzz on the front door. Rachael went over and opened the door and saw two biosym twins, half biological, half synthetic test tube-grown humanoids, standing there with nervous smiles.

"Can I help you?" she asked.

"We just came to welcome you to the campus. We're your neighbors. I'm Oscar 6072A, and this is my twin, Lee 6072B."

"Well, it's nice to meet you, Oscar and Lee. Why don't you come in?" Rachael asked and stood aside for them, and they came into the apartment.

"Hey, Ash, Bridg. Come, meet the neighbors," Rachael yelled, and the twins jumped from her yelling.

Ash and Bridgett walked out of their rooms and saw the twins and walked over, then proceeded to walk around them, looking the twins over. The boys were nervous now. This was strange behavior, even to them, and to be in a room with three female humans was another scary thing.

"I've never seen a biosym before. Your skin looks cool with that gray streak to it," Ash said.

"That's the synthetic tissue in our forms showing through. Our skin is totally void of pigmentation, causing it to be pale. You appear to not be fully human as well. The gold eyes suggest vatoria. Do you also retain the markings and telepathic abilities?" Oscar asked her.

"Yeah, all of it," Ash answered.

"I would like to see that," Lee said.

"I barely know you and you want me to take my shirt off for you?" Ash asked, surprised.

"We are med students, purely scientific curiosity," Oscar replied.

"Maybe some other time," Ash said, grinning.

"Where are my manners? I'm Rachael. This is Ash, and that redhead is Bridgett. Guys, these are Oscar and Lee."

"Nice to meet you. So what do you do for fun around here?" Bridgett asked them.

"We don't have fun. Nobody likes us because were different. They tease us a lot, calling us zebras and telling us to go back to the zoo," Lee said like it was no big deal.

"That's ignorant. Well, you know what, you have friends now, so why don't you show us around the campus?" Rachael said to them, and they looked at each other and agreed.

The girls followed them all over the academy grounds, which was quite extensive. They showed them where their classes would be, where they take their clothes to be washed, the school cafeteria, and the commons building where a store was so they could purchase necessary hygiene items. By the time they got back to the apartment, it was late, and tomorrow was the first day of classes. The girls told their new friends good night and went inside their apartment. They still had to finish unpacking but decided to do the rest of it tomorrow after class.

All three went to bed and, in no time, fell right asleep and didn't wake until the next morning when they heard buzzing on their front door. Ash jumped up and ran out of her bedroom and over to the front door, still in her pajama top and shorts, and opened it. Oscar and Lee just walked in without being invited, heading toward the kitchen and acting like they had been friends for a long time with the girls.

"You three almost overslept. You need to get moving, or you're going to be late," Oscar told her.

Ash ran down the hall and started beating on Rachael and Bridgett's room, then went into hers. Fifteen minutes later, she came out dressed and ready to go. Oscar and Lee were in their kitchen, and when the girls went over and grabbed their packs off the dining room table, the twins had made them something to eat. Ash looked at it, and it didn't look too great.

"Energy biscuit. It will keep you going all day," Oscar told her.

Rachael and Bridgett looked at them and watched as Ash took a bite out of one. She chewed it, then swallowed and made a face. "It tastes like dirt," she said.

"Yes, but it is good for you, lots of energy," Lee said.

She ate the rest down, and now Rachael and Bridgett ate one, and Rachael kept gagging but finally finished it. The girls gathered their stuff and headed out their door with the twins walking with them. Once they got to their class, the twins headed off to theirs. The day dragged on, but Ash had to admit, the dirt they ate helped. Not once did they feel sleepy, just the opposite, almost like when they drank a lot of creo and got the energy rush from it. The day finally ended, and they headed back to their apartment and finally got unpacked. After that, they decided to go and check out the small campus town that surrounded the academy.

There were some neat stores, and they really liked the creo shop called Jocu's, whose proprietor was dark-skinned with dreadlock hair and a strange accent. They bought a few clothes at one of the shops and headed back to their apartment, and no sooner had they gotten back than Ash's father contacted them to see how everything was going. They told him things were fine but boring, then he had to go and wouldn't be back in Sigma Six space for two weeks. This was going to be the norm for the next eleven months.

Everyday was the same—get up and dress, head to class, spend all day in class, then in the evening, either study, wash clothes, or on some occasions, go watch a vid at the commons. They thought prep school sucked, but this was pure torture. Nothing exciting happened here. Finally, after many months of boredom, they were done for at least a month, and then it would start all over again. They packed a few things and caught a shuttle back to New Guinea to stay until they had to come back to prison.

This time, they were alone at the house, but they didn't do anything that exciting there as well. They just lay around and took it easy, went down and helped at the refuge center off and on, and went to a couple of nightclubs, which weren't that great around there. They did hear that there was one over in New Delphi that was great, but they didn't have a way there since you needed a shuttle to travel that far, and not many traveled there. Finally, their break was over, and they had to go back.

The girls walked up to their apartment, and sure enough, Oscar and Lee were waiting for them. They had even gone and gotten their schedules for them. The twins had figured out that the girls were huge procrastinators since they were around them so much.

The first few months went by boringly, but the next day at school, the girls finally got some excitement in their lives. Ash and Bridgett were walking up the stairs to the science lab, which they had on the third floor of the science building. They went off and left Rachael since she was busy talking to some guy again. They were halfway down the hall when three very tall, well-built, extremely good-looking guys walked past them. Ash stopped immediately and watched them as they continued to walk toward the stairs, feeling something inside pulling her to the taller one of the three. Even Bridgett had stopped and was staring at them with a bewildered look on her face.

The taller guy in the front of the other two turned his head as he walked by and glanced back over his shoulder at her. Their eyes met for a second, then he looked forward again and continued on. Just as they started down the stairs, Rachael came running up them; and like usual, not watching where she was going, she ran right into the one with the blondish-colored hair.

He grabbed her shoulders to keep her from falling and looked down at her, grinning. "Whoa, gorgeous, you need to watch yourself."

"I'm sorry. Excuse me," Rachael said, grinning back, and he stepped aside for her.

"No harm done, sweet thing," he said to her, and Rachael took off toward Ash and Bridgett. He watched Rachael with a confused look on his face until she got to them, and then he quickly ran down the stairs to catch up with his friends.

The girls went into their class, and right away, there was a crisis. Apparently, the professor's pride and joy, a disgusting, slimy slug with little tentacles on its body, had come up missing. Ash wasn't too upset. She hated that thing; it always seemed to be watching her. Rachael leaned over to her while the professor was telling them that if it wasn't found, there could be dire consequences.

"Does it smell funny in here to you?" Rachael asked and sniffed herself to make sure it wasn't her.

Ash started sniffing the air, and she could also smell something but didn't know what it was. "Yeah, there definitely is a funky smell in here."

Finally, class was over, and they left the building, relieved because it was their last class for the day. They got to their apartment and fixed something to eat, then watched as nighttime took over outside through their patio door. They had just finished eating when someone started beating on their door. Rachael jumped up, and both Ash and Bridgett took a defensive stance and nodded for Rachael to get the door. She quietly approached as the beating was still going on when they heard the twins outside, yelling for them to open up. Rachael quickly opened the door, and the twins came running into the apartment, scared.

"What's going on?" Ash asked them.

"Outside, a full-size crantock is attacking the science building. I'm pretty sure it's the professor's that came up missing earlier today. Somebody must have put it in the water fountain, and the fresh water caused it to finally grow," Oscar told them as he tried to catch his breath.

The girls looked at one another, and big grins spread across their faces. Finally, some fun. They took off running out of their apartment as the twins followed, trying to get them to stop. They bolted out of their building and raced across the campus, coming up on the eight-foot stonewall that ran along one side of the park where the large water fountain was, giving the area some privacy. The science building was just opposite of this, and sure enough, a massive slug-like crantock was ripping through the walls of the science building. It was almost as tall as the building with long tentacle arms that helped to move its blob-like body along.

The head of it was nothing more then an open hole in the end of its slug body with row upon row of razor-sharp teeth, and it was doing a pretty good number on the science building. From where the girls were hiding, they could see the decimated water fountain. Apparently, the person or persons who stole the crantock knew that the beast soaked up fresh water like a sponge, quadrupling its size in a matter of hours.

The girls crept along the separating wall with the twins right behind them, trying to get them to flee. Ash, Rachael, and Bridgett watched the slimy thing chew away at the building, and suddenly, Rachael got a wicked grin on her face and looked over at Ash.

"I dare you to run over there and slap that thing on the ass."

Ash grinned back. "All right, a challenge," she said. She stepped over to the edge of the wall, and she took three quick breaths and ran. She flipped over the rubble from the now shattered fountain and jumped some of the down shrubs, then ran up and slapped the creature on the ass, getting slime all over her hand. She turned and raced back as the creature only stopped for a brief second. She came back and showed the slime to prove she did it. Then Rachael took off, and soon, she was back, flinging slime from her hand and laughing. But even before the girls had started their daring feat, a hovering shuttle was above them, and they knew it was a camera crew, so they all waved at it but Lee and Oscar, who turned their backs to the shuttle so no one would see their faces.

Next, Bridgett ran out across the ground and slapped it; but instead of running back, she stood there, grossed out by the slime on her hand. The creature turned and saw her as she was busy flinging slime from her hand and gagging. The beast let out a loud screech, which brought Bridgett back to the task at hand, and then came after her. She took off running back to Ash and them with the beast about ten feet behind her. They all scrambled to get out of there and falling all over one another. Out of nowhere, soldiers and police showed up and shot the crantock and captured and arrested them. The camera was still on the girls and the twins as they put their hands up but grinning as they were marched away, down to the police precinct, at gunpoint.

Over in another apartment, Fâd, Nathan, and Cory were watching the event being covered by the news on their vid screen when the camera switched from the creature to five people hiding near a wall. Their faces changed from enjoying watching the creature tear up the science building to one of fear when they found out that some students were trapped by the beast. The camera continued to film the students, and then the boys' faces turned to shock when they saw what the students were doing.

They weren't trapped. They were taunting the creature by slapping it on the butt. They busted up laughing, watching as each of them took a turn, and then the camera focused in close on one of them, and they were shocked to see they were girls. Three of them even waved at the camera, grinning, and they laughed even harder.

Cory now leaned closer to the vid screen. "Does that girl look familiar to you?"

Fâd and Nathan looked closer as well, and Nathan spoke up. "Hey, that's the hot blond I ran into today at the science building when we had to go back and got chewed out by the professor. Damn, look how she moves. I bet she's a wild one."

Fâd gave him a dirty look, but he also realized that the girl with the black hair on the vid was the same one he saw in the hall and felt drawn toward when he passed her today. He continued to watch, and then it was the red-headed girl's turn, and when the creature came after them and they were scrambling all over one another, the guys were laughing like crazy and even had tears running down their faces, especially when they got arrested and were led away. Cory backed the vid up and froze the picture where they could see the girls again up close. Then he magnified it and zoomed in on their faces. All three guys' mouths fell open.

"Holy shit, they got hot," Nathan said in shock.

"Look at Ash. Wow. She's gorgeous," Cory said, and Fâd couldn't help himself but stare at her.

"That's Rachael, then. Oh my gosh, that's whom I ran into today. I knew there was something about that hottie. I have to find her," Nathan told them and headed to the door, but Fâd grabbed him by the arm, stopping him.

"You're not going anywhere. Stay away from them. They have their own lives now," he warned Nathan.

"Bullcrap. I've stayed away long enough! I'm only going to give it two more years till she finishes school, then she's mine. You just wait and see. I can't do this anymore. That explains why I felt my insides jump when I ran into her in the hallway," Nathan said back to him, defiant and angry.

"So that's got to be Bridgett, the smaller one. Man, she's beautiful. Fâd, Nathan's right. I'm tired of fighting how I feel about her and suffering with it," Cory said. Fâd and Nathan looked over at him as he stared at the picture on the vid screen.

Fâd let out a sigh and looked at his best friends. They all had been suffering. Imprinting was the most terrible thing around. It made one feel agitated and angry all the time, especially the older one got, due to not being with their potential mate. In this case, all three had made a pact when they were fifteen to let the girls go so the girls could pursue their dreams and be with their families.

So far, they had managed; but the older they were getting, the harder it was, and Fâd knew in the back of his mind that Nathan and Cory would eventually go get Rachael and Bridgett. Even he was starting to break, though he had told his father long ago that he would leave Ash alone no matter how it tore him up inside. But the driving force behind imprinting was getting stronger, and it didn't help that he loved her more than anything in the galaxy, even without the imprinting.

Fâd looked at the vid and stared at Ash. She was gorgeous, and his heart started hurting again and beating rapidly seeing her. He knew how Nathan was feeling right now because he also wanted to go and get Ash. Fâd finally got control of his feelings and grinned, looking over at Nathan and Cory, who were staring at the vid.

"One thing's for certain, they haven't changed, and I think they have gotten crazier," Fâd said and started laughing, and Nathan and Cory joined in.

"Yeah. I wonder how Admiral Harper's going to enjoy bailing them out of jail and seeing them make headline news," Nathan said as the guys laughed even harder.

CHAPTER 35

"ASHLEY GAIL HARPER, WHAT THE HELL DID YOU THINK YOU WERE DOING?" Admiral Harper yelled. Actually, yelling wasn't quite true. It was more like screaming in rage at her over the police vid screen.

"Sorry, Father. It was a dare, and I couldn't back away," Ash said, lowering her head and trying not to grin.

"I don't care. I should leave you girls in jail. Maybe it would do you some good. Were you the ones responsible for putting that thing in the fountain to begin with?"

"No! The professor was complaining about it missing earlier that day when we went to class," Ash said in her defense.

"I swear, if you girls pull another stunt, all three of you can kiss your rankings goodbye, and the only thing you will be doing is working in the waste management wing on the ship for the rest of your lives. Do I make myself clear?"

Ash was looking over at Rachael and Bridgett, imitating him and mouthing the words "Do I make myself clear?" right along with him since he always said those same words when she got into trouble. "Yes, sir," all three girls replied at once, trying not to laugh, and the screen went blank.

Ash was still looking at Rachael and Bridgett with a big grin. "Wow, he must be out of ideas for punishment if that is all he could come up with," she said, and the girls started giggling, but Oscar and Lee rolled their eyes.

The policemen released their minor belongings to them, and they walked out of the precinct with Oscar and Lee, who had also gotten arrested. "So is this your idea of fun, trying to get yourselves killed and then arrested?" Oscar asked, still in shock.

"Yeah. It was exciting, wasn't it?" Rachael asked him.

"No. Our lives are short enough as it is without gambling with them," Lee replied in disgust.

"Oh, come on, you haven't lived, then. Lighten up. This is just the beginning of your adventures," Ash told them, and the twins just moaned.

They all walked back to campus and immediately were sent to Councilor Shotwell's office. They walked in, and the bald little round man was leaning back in his chair with his fingers interlocked, lying across his plump belly in front of him. The girls and twins came in and sat down across the desk from him.

"I knew I would be seeing you three back here, but I'm shocked with you two, Oscar and Lee, being involved with this as well. You would do well to heed my advice: Stay away from these three. They are no good. All sentinel enlisted are nothing more than hired thugs," Shotwell said with a sick grin.

"Councilor, is there a purpose to this, or can we go back to our apartment?" Ash asked, mad.

He looked at her with open disdain. "Fortunately, I have spoken with the vice admiral. And through my concern for all my students, which is a great weakness of mine, I relented and agreed to allow you three to continue with your studies here, but only on the premise that there be no more incidents."

"Fine. Good day, Councilor," Ash said, getting up, and left without letting him say another word. Everyone else followed her as she stormed down the hall and burst outside, now very angry due to the councilor's blatant hatred for anything sentinel fleet. But her mood changed quickly because as soon as they stepped out onto the grounds, they started getting cheered. Even the twins were getting slapped on the back and were told they did a good job, and the girls were shocked when they saw them finally crack a smile for the first time since they knew them.

Oscar leaned close to Bridgett. "So this is what hero worship feels like?"

"Yep."

Everyone they met either wanted to smack fist or clap them on the back, and some even went as far as having their picture taken with them. Finally, they all made it back to their apartment and crashed on the sofa. They were exhausted, and in no time, all three girls were sound asleep where they were sitting. Even Oscar and Lee were exhausted and quietly left the girls' apartment and went back to theirs where they also fell asleep.

Over in the guys' apartment, Fâd was in a bad mood, and Nathan and Cory knew why. They had spent many years dealing with him like this, but finally, in the last year, he seemed to be more himself again and even started seeing a few girls. But now, seeing Ash again, he was back in it, and they were tired of it, so they decided to go and hang out at the commons. He paced around the apartment and then plopped down on the sofa. His mind was racing, and he couldn't get her out of it.

He leaned his head back and closed his eyes. His mind wandered back to another time four years ago. He was finishing up his tour on board the *Lithia* with Nathan and Cory, and his father called him to the bridge.

* * *

"So do you still want a different ship? I just don't see what is wrong with the carian infiltrator," Admiral Larson asked his son.

"Yes. It's not what I'm looking for. I want something larger. I'll know it when I see it," Fâd told him.

"We have been to four shipyards, and you still haven't found anything. Are you looking for a frigate or something that size?"

"No, I don't want anything like that. I want an infiltrator that's larger than any frigate, something that a crew of around twenty or thirty can operate and live on."

Admiral Larson gave his son a dirty look. "I don't think you will find anything like that, and we are running out of places to look."

"I know, but I have a feeling this shipyard will be different," Fâd told him.

"It better be, because there is only one more after this one that deals with larger ships. All the other ones after that only deal with shuttles and smaller craft," the admiral told him with a look of frustration.

They both rode the elevator down to the shuttle bay, and before long, Fâd was piloting the shuttle toward the planet's surface. He easily handled it, and soon, they came up on the shipyard. He could see many ships already lined up, but they went on farther than he could see.

He landed the shuttle perfectly, and he and the admiral exited the craft and walked over to the office. A greasy, dirty-looking borvian walked out with a sick grin on his face. Admiral Larson hated coming there, but this guy always seemed to be able to come up with some of the better wreaks.

"Rear Admiral Larson, it's good to see you again. Looking for new wings?"

"Just looking, Zifh," Larson told him.

"Good, very good. I have some vatorian frigates just came in. Not much damage, easily repaired. There's even a council battleship on its way here as we speak. Maybe that be of interest to you?" the alien said in a thick accent. He continued to talk to the admiral while Fâd walked among the wreaks. There were all kinds—freighters, passenger liners, and frigates—you name it. They were huge seeing them on the ground like this. This place went on for miles and miles, but that didn't deter him, and he continued to walk around, looking. He was starting to get frustrated. Maybe he would never find what he was looking for, and he was just about to turn around when he caught a flash out of the corner of his eye.

Fâd walked around a massive freighter, and his mouth fell open as he stopped and stared. She was much larger than a frigate, possibly taking a crew of twenty or more, and she was unlike any he had ever seen. She was sleek, almost looking like a hawk, with double wings on each side of her that angled back, giving the ship the appearance that it was built for speed. She also had twin tail rutters, enhancing her maneuverability.

He got on his multitool and comm'd his father. "Admiral, I found it. Just pass the feralosian freighter." Fâd walked into the ship's cargo hold and shuttle bay, which was huge. It could hold a full-size shuttle quite easily, the MAAV they had, which held at least six to eight people if need be, the small striker, which was just a two-seater fighter with stealth capabilities, and a lot of cargo as well and still have room.

He walked around and went over to the elevator, but nothing happened. Of course, they probably pulled the power cells, not to mention he was sure the ship was stripped of anything useful. He looked down the dark hallway that ran past the back of the cargo bay, heading toward the back end of the ship, and could see another elevator and air lock farther down and two more doors possibly leading to an engine room and the armory that most ships had.

He was just about to head up the emergency stairs next to the first elevator when his father and the greasy borvian pulled up in a hover cart. He could see the look on his father's face, which was going to make talking him into this one even harder, not to mention the borvian didn't look too thrilled with his choice either.

Fâd walked across the cargo bay and met his father halfway. "You're not serious, are you?" Larson asked him, but he could see on his son's face that this was the one he wanted no matter what.

"Yes. There's something about her. I know she looks different, but I have a good feeling about this ship," Fâd told him, looking all around the ship.

"Well, let's take a look," Larson said and followed his son.

They went all through the ship. There were things in there Fâd had no idea what, and a lot of the major components that were still there looked modified. On the second level was a stripped gunnery room, so the ship was now defenseless. Also, the science lab and med bay were located on this level too but also empty. The third level was the bridge, and it looked like an explosion had happened in there as many of the consoles, control panels, amd anything of worth were stripped out, but oddly enough, the captain's control console was completely intact.

Off the bridge ran a hallway that was split in two by a room located directly in the center of this level. The hallway on the left hand side, if you were facing toward the back of the ship, had two elevators, an air lock, and emergency stairs located down it. They headed down the right side hallway, and it was a conference room that was situated directly in the center, separating the hallways. And then near the back of this level, past the conference room, it opened up to the large mess hall. The first level, which was at the top of the ship, was the crew deck and bathrooms. There were plenty of cabins and bedchambers to easily hold over twenty crew members quite comfortably and their families if they had one. Even the captain's cabin was large, and strangely, a lot of the furnishings in these quarters were still there and were still very nice.

The admiral and Fâd also noticed small portal pads all over and in every room but the living quarters of the crew and bathrooms. The admiral figured that the ship had been fitted for an AI, which was odd for a ship of this size. They normally only put them in larger ones, like battleships, destroyers, and cruisers. It was also apparent that at one time, the ship was heavily armed due to the large turret in the center of the gunnery room and the now empty housing beside it on both sides, which once probably held some type of mech guns that dropped down through the floor for firing. But like they were seeing everywhere on her, she had been stripped of anything salvageable and would take a lot of work and parts.

"Fâd, are you sure? It's going to take a lot to put this back together and parts just to make her fly. Plus, I noticed from the outside it has seen some action. There's some damage to her shields and hull, not to mention, son, this is a large ship, a lot bigger than any frigate," Larson told his son.

"Yes, Father, this is the one. Just give me the chance. You'll see. I know it's big, which is what I want."

They headed back down the emergency stairs and out to the open cargo bay to the borvian. "Okay, Zifh, what can you tell me about this one?" Larson asked him.

"Nothing."

"Don't hold back on me. I want information," Larson said and narrowed his eyes.

"That's just it. There's nothing on this ship. My guess is, she's a prototype. I couldn't find any registration on it anywhere. This ship doesn't exist."

"How long has it been here?" Larson asked.

"Nine years."

Larson turned and looked at his son with eyes that said, "Pick something else!" But Fâd shook his head no. The admiral let out a sigh. "All right, we'll take it," Larson told the borvian unhappily.

"Okay, but if anything comes of this, you didn't get it here, okay?" Zifh said to him, looking around nervously.

"Why? What aren't you telling me?" Larson once again narrowed his eyes at the borvian.

"Just between you and me, when she came in, I found a bunch of council junk in her. I think they were using it at one time but scraped it when it took a hit."

"But that's not a council ship."

"I know. It's also not a carian, borvian, or any other I recognize, and so far, I've been lucky, because whoever built this thing used a lot of advance technology in its construction, spending many marks, and haven't come looking for it, which is really surprising."

"All right, no one will know. I'll contact Lewis and have him pick it up for transport," Larson told the borvian, and they all headed back to the main office. On the way, Larson called the tug captain, who complained but then laughed.

"You know, this is kind of funny. For some reason, I was out this direction anyway. Now what are the odds of that? I'll be pulling into your space in the next hour. See you then," Lewis said.

The admiral went into the office with the borvian, and before long, he came back out with a power pad in his hand, showing the bill of sale, as Fâd leaned against the open door of the shuttle, waiting for him. He turned and climbed back into the craft, and the admiral followed after closing the shuttle door and sat down in the pilot seat as the admiral took the copilot's seat next to him.

"Well, one thing about it, he gave it to me dirt cheap. He must be still scared she's hot even after nine years," Larson told his son with a grin, and Fâd had to chuckle. His dad always liked a challenge. He lifted off and headed back toward space, but before they got to the cruiser, the tug *Presidio* came out of jump a little distance from the *Lithia*. Larson contacted the tug as he and Fâd headed toward it, landing on the tug instead of the battlecruiser.

Fâd followed his father over to an elevator, and in no time, they walked out of it and onto the bridge. The captain came walking over to them with a big grin. "Wow, this is getting to be one of my worst years ever."

"Oh? And how's that?" Larson asked him as he and the captain shook hands.

"First, I have to deal with that mountain of stone Harper a while back, and now I have you barking orders down my neck as well," Lewis said and walked over to his console. Larson followed him, handing the power pad to the tug captain.

Captain Lewis looked down at the power pad. "Picking up from ground, I hate these, always a breath holder. Okay, everyone, this one's a class 2, grounded. All hands on deck," the captain called over his comm, and Fâd could feel the ship suddenly stopping as the engines powered down. The large windows behind the tug where the whole bridge could look out at the massive arms closed as reinforced shields covered them now.

"Have to do that, young man. The kinetic tractor beam will blind you if you look at it. Hang on. She's going to buck, but it's the norm," Lewis told Fâd, and sure enough, it was no little jolt. The ship rocked hard for a second as everyone grabbed ahold of something to steady themselves.

"We have the ship locked in tractor beam. She's coming up," someone said over the comm to the captain.

Lewis was working quickly on his console, making adjustments constantly, as the tug was now raising the wreaked ship by beam from the planet's surface thousands and thousands of miles below them. It took well over an hour, and suddenly, the ship rocked again but, this time, not nearly as bad. Lewis now opened the shields, and Fâd could see the ship was firmly locked between the arms of the tug.

"Hmm, that one's different. Never seen one like that," Lewis said, cocking his head sideway, looking at Fâd's ship.

"Have it taken to our shipping yard and put it farther out. There's a lot of work to be done on it," Larson told him.

"Just like Harper, do this now or else. I had to drop a paying pickup and run over and grab one of his damaged battleships sometime ago, but I have to admit, she took a beating. If it weren't for that daughter of Harper's—and what a beauty she is—that ship and all her crew would be gone," Lewis said as Fâd wheeled around instantly from watching his ship to hear what the captain had to say.

"Oh, you met Ash?" Larson asked with a smile.

"Yeah, what a sweetheart. Between you and me—and don't let this get back to Harper—I think there was something going on between her and the commander of that ship. I think they were pretty sweet on each other."

Fâd could feel his heart rip in two when he heard that, and pain flooded his body. He quickly spun back around and gazed out at his ship. At least he had her, his ship.

* * *

Fâd opened his eyes and lifted his head up. Why, when he finally was able to control the pain and cage it, something happened that let it out again? He didn't blame his friends for not wanting to be around him. He didn't want to be around himself either. Seeing her on the vid last night, he wanted so badly to go and find her, but he knew he couldn't. She had her own life and career and was doing very well.

He had heard about all her exploits from his father. He also found out from some of his connections that there never was anything with her and that commander, which made him feel a lot better. But her destiny was set. She would be serving on the *Justification* under her father, and he would always be commanding his own ship and crew.

He got off the sofa and went into the kitchen, grabbing a water bottle out of the refrigerator. Then he walked back into the living room and pulled up the recorded vid of the girls' exploit last night. He zoomed in on Ash and sat down on the sofa just staring at her and drinking his water.

CHAPTER 36

It was two years later, and the girls were in their final year at the academy. It was a Friday night and Bridgett's birthday, so they decided to take her over to Odyssey, a nightclub in New Delphi, to celebrate. They had figured out last year how they could get a campus shuttle without the academy's permission and fly over to the little city and go to one of the best nightclubs around. The shuttle maintenance man for the campus liked whiskey, so they would bring him a bottle, and he would look the other way as they took off with one of the shuttles. It was a good arrangement, and they had made quite a few trips over this year and last.

But today was different. Bridgett was turning twenty-three, and they decided to celebrate since she was the last of them to turn that age this year, not to mention they only had a couple of months left of school too and would soon be leaving for full-time service aboard the *Justification*.

The girls all got dressed in some of their best club clothes, as they called them. Ash dressed in nice, tight blue pants with thin white stripes down the side and shiny black boots with a nice, tall heel on them as the boots came all the way up over her knees. She also had a very tight tunic that ended just at the top of her thighs and buttoned up her right side to where the square revealing neckline began and had an open collar that ran all the way up the back of her neck. It also had form-fitting long sleeves with a cutout for her multitool. Of course, all long-sleeved tops had them, and it was in the same blue color as her pants but with thin white stripes outlining the square edges of the tunic.

She also pulled only the sides of her long wavy black hair to the back of her head, leaving the rest hanging down, and made a knot out of the sides, fastening it with three long, thin oriental chopsticks, only these were much nicer and not used to eat with. They were a dark-brown color with tiny ancient carved runes all over them and polished. They were a gift that Rachael had given her this year for her birthday. The last item was a wide silver metal choker that she wore on occasions to hide her dog tags since she had a slot added to it to conceal the chain and all in it. It was also the same choker she wore the last time she was with Fâd and danced with him, and it had become one of her most precious items because of that.

She made a complete turn, looking in the mirror to see if she looked all right, then headed out of her room to make sure her backpack had all the necessities in case of an emergency. She turned when she heard Rachael come out of her room and grinned at her.

Rachael was also dressed nicely with tight dark-red pants and the same kind of shiny black boots like Ash's, except Rachael's heels were stilettos. She also had on a very snug long-sleeved dark-red and black tunic that also went down to the tops of her thighs but zipped up the front where it had a plunging V-shaped neckline and a high collar. But unlike Ash, Rachael removed her dog tags and stored them inside her multitool. She also let her long wavy blond hair down but wore a black stick on face piece that wrapped around the outskirts of her face, keeping her hair back from her face. She was also carrying a backpack and threw it down on the sofa and went into the kitchen, grabbing some water bottles, throwing them to Ash, who put them in their packs.

"Are you ready to party?" Rachael asked her with a big grin, doing a little dance to show her excitement.

"Oh yeah," Ash replied, giggling watching her.

Bridgett came out of her room and looked great. She had tight teal-colored pants on that tucked into her black ankle boots with nice high heels to them. The matching tunic she wore had long sleeves and a heart-shaped neckline with a high collar as well and fit tightly to her, showing her curves, and then came down but instead fanned out like a miniskirt and stopping at mid thigh. Her dark-red hair was feathered back and cascaded down her back with many ringlets of curls, and like Rachael, she also removed her dog tags and stowed them in her multitool. She had her pack over her shoulder and walked over to Rachael and Ash.

"Should we bring coats?" Bridgett asked them.

"Nah, we won't need them," Rachael told her.

They all grabbed their packs, left the room, and hurried down the hallway and out the building. It was night now, and they easily stalked across the campus and into the maintenance building where the shuttles were kept. Sure enough, the maintenance man was in there like usual, watching something on the vid, and he looked up when he heard them enter.

"Hey, Arnie. Brought you something for a ride," Rachael said, holding up the bottle of whiskey for him to see.

"You girls are turning me into an alcoholic," he said with a grin.

Rachael handed him the bottle, and he pressed the button to open the bay doors so they could go. Bridgett climbed into the pilot seat, and in no time, they were flying through the nighttime sky, low over the treetops, toward New Delphi. It usually took them a good twenty minutes to get there from the academy, so Ash and Rachael sat back, and they all started talking to one another. Ten minutes into the flight, suddenly, out of nowhere, a brilliant white flash went off in front of the shuttle.

"What the hell was that?" Bridgett yelled as Ash and Rachael jumped up. Rachael started typing away on the shuttle's console as Ash hit the scanner.

She saw a large red ball heading toward them on the scanner, and just before it got to them, she screamed at her friends, "BRACE FOR IMPACT!"

The shuttle bucked hard when it struck, and Ash and Rachael flew up, hitting the ceiling of the craft. Bridgett gripped the controls tightly as the shuttle started to nose-dive toward the forest below. Ash and Rachael quickly got up from the floor, looking out of the front windows of the shuttle, watching the ground start to come at them very rapidly.

"Hang on to something. We're going to hit hard," Bridgett yelled at her two friends as she fought to maintain some control. Ash leaped into one of the bench seats and strapped up as Rachael jumped over the back of the other pilot seat and buckled herself in. The shuttle hit with tremendous force and skidded for over one hundred feet, busting through trees and rocks and leaving a huge plume of dust and devastation behind it, finally coming to a stop up against a large boulder. The running lights now flickered, then went out. Inside, it was dark with no movement at all; but a few minutes later, the emergency lighting came on. All three girls had been knocked unconscious.

Ash was the first to come to and blinked several times, looking around. Then she saw her friends, and fear flew through her. She quickly unbuckled and ran over to them. She carefully cupped Rachael's slumped head and saw she had a nice gash on her forehead but nothing serious. "Rachael, wake up. Come on, Rachael, talk to me," Ash said, frantically trying to bring her to.

She slowly opened her eyes and then looked around. "We're alive. What happened?" she asked in shock.

"That doesn't matter right now. We need to get out of here," Ash told her, trying to wake Bridgett now.

Bridgett slowly opened her eyes and also looked around, dazed. "Ash, what was that?" she asked.

"We got hit by an ion cannon. My guess, mercs. We've got to move now."

Bridgett reached to unbuckle with her right hand and screamed in pain. Ash carefully lifted her arm, then ran her palm scanner over it and saw on the tiny screen of her multitool that Bridgett's wrist was broken. "We don't have time to set this yet," Ash told her, and Bridgett nodded her head in agreement as Ash unbuckled her. The girls all got up and quickly grabbed their packs, the med kit, and anything else that might come in handy.

"Bridg, fry the shuttle's controls. We don't want anyone tracing this back to the academy," Ash ordered, and Bridgett reached down and carefully with her right hand typed something into her multitool, then raised her left hand over the shuttle's control panel. Instantly, sparks started shooting out of the controls and then erupted into flames as the girls quickly left the now burning and wreaked shuttle, running into the woods. Ash linked up to Rachael and Bridgett telepathically, and they shut down their tools in case the mercs had power sensors.

The girls continued to run through the dark forest, fighting their way through the overgrown foliage, when suddenly, they could hear the mercs not far behind, obviously following somehow. Ash stopped looking back at her friends, and they had the same look on their faces: no more running.

Ash went over a plan of attack with them telepathically. All three then split in different directions as their training and skills came flooding back, and they quickly flanked the mercs. Ash and Rachael scaled up different trees, and Ash silently snaked out on the limb of the tree she was on to scope out the targets.

"There are four, three humans and one borvian, heavily armed," she told her two comrades telepathically and knew that they had flanked the targets by now. "On my mark." Ash telepathically ordered them to move, and she and Rachael dropped down from the trees they had climbed and came down on the men. Rachael's stiletto heels proved to be worthy of the name as one of her boots came down on the man's head, dropping him quickly. Ash landed between two others, and now she was glowing brilliant blue with her kinetics powered up.

One took a blast from her and flew across the open area, slamming into a tree, and didn't move. The other one Ash was on instantly as her talents in hand-to-hand combat proved themselves, and the man dropped with a crushed windpipe. Meantime, Rachael also was fighting the borvian and backing him up when Ash saw him reach for his pistol. She sent a huge blast of kinetic energy, and the alien rose in the air as the blast crushed his chest, and then he dropped dead.

Rachael looked around to make sure the mercs weren't getting up when behind Ash, the one she had thrown against the tree started to rise. Out of the woods, Bridgett smashed a large tree branch over his head, and the man went down for the last time.

"Clear," Rachael said, and Ash powered down. The girls quickly started going through the mercs' pockets for anything they could use. Rachael and Ash each strapped on the mercs' pistols with two each, and Bridgett took one since she only had one hand now. Then they took off the mercs' long, hooded overcoats and put them on to hide their appearance. Ash saw the ion cannon lying on the ground and instantly was covered in kinetic energy, blasting the cannon into pieces, then powered down quickly because she could already feel the headache coming on.

She ordered to move out, and they quickly headed off the direction they had flown but still left their multitools off just in case there were more mercs out there who might have power trackers. Ash was able to gauge the direction by using the stars overhead when she was able to get a clear view of the nighttime sky through small openings in the trees. They had traveled several miles, and the girls knew it was extremely late, so they decided to find shelter for the night and finally came upon a cave. Ash took a light bar out of her pack, pulled a pistol, and slowly entered the cave. Bridgett followed behind her, and Rachael brought up the rear with her pistols ready. They went in about twenty feet before the cave finally stopped, and thank goodness it was empty.

The girls quickly went about securing the cave opening and finally broke open a heat can Ash pulled out of her pack and sat down around the glowing red can that was also putting off some illumination. Ash took out the med pac she had grabbed from the shuttle and pulled out an instant cast and carefully fastened the sleeve to Bridgett's wrist and forearm. Then she pulled out a syringe and injected a mild painkiller into Bridgett's arm. "This is still going to hurt a little, Bridg," Ash told her and pushed the small button on the cast as it inflated tightly to hold the bones into place and stop further damage. Bridgett didn't scream because she knew better when they were in a hostile environment, but tears ran down her face.

Finally, she had Bridgett taken care of, Rachael's cut on her head treated, and was sitting down to rest, but she reached up and rubbed her right temple. She could feel the throbbing getting worse, and she wasn't in her suit to help. Rachael walked over to the med pac and pulled out a small syringe and grabbed some vial and filled the syringe.

"If that's a nueralizer, I don't need it," Ash told Rachael, watching her friend fill the syringe.

"No, it's bespin, a much weaker form of asrinon, but it will help some with the headache," Rachael told her and went over, having Ash lean her head down to expose the tiny port that was implanted into her neck for her suit injections. Rachael carefully inserted the needle and injected the fluid. Ash then leaned her head back as she could feel the medicine attack the throbbing, and finally, it subsided a little but was still there, unlike when the asrinon worked, which stopped all the pain immediately.

By now, Bridgett was sound asleep from the pain medicine and using the large overcoat for a bed and blanket while Ash and Rachael remained awake. "Well, I think we finally committed a doozy this time," Rachael said with a half smirk on her face.

"Yep, and two months before we finish no less. Wow, we're good," Ash replied, and both girls started chuckling.

"I'm glad it's with you two that I'm going to be pulling garbage detail for the rest of my life," Rachael told her.

"Same here. I just wonder what kind of trouble we could do then. Dad must be out of ideas for punishment if that is all he could come up with this time," Ash said, and both girls started laughing.

Rachael and Ash took shifts at posting, which was another word they used for guard duty, and finally, the sun started barely breaking through the trees outside the cave. Ash was the one on duty and woke the other two, and before long, they headed out. She remembered a town that they sometimes flew over when they went to New Delphi called Little Sonora because she had pulled it up on her multitool a while back on another night flight to the nightclub. She also knew they were near Pantier but wanted to avoid that place as much as possible because she knew they would be in trouble there. That was the last place they would go to if they had no other choice.

By judging where they came from, she was able to somewhat figure the way they needed to go. Surely, in the town, they could get someone to shuttle them back to New Haven and face the music later, at least give them some time to think of some story they could tell to get out of the trouble they were in.

They once again covered up with the long coats, and you couldn't tell who was under them unless they moved a certain way and you saw some hint of their clothes. In a few hours, they walked into the small town, and all three girls were relieved when they saw a small café and quickly headed to it. They walked in, still completely covered, and noticed right away the rough-looking people in there, who were now staring at them. The girls surveyed the café for an empty table away from most of the patrons and quickly went over to a booth as a waitress came over.

"Can I get you three anything?" she asked with an annoyed tone.

"Three cups of creo please," Ash said as she risked switching on her multitool under the table, away from watching eyes.

The woman left and came back with three cups and told Ash the total. She typed in the marks on her tool. The waitress looked down at her power pad and nodded that she received it, and Ash immediately shut down her multitool again just to be on the safe side. The girls made every effort to make sure they were concealed from view and sipped their creo carefully with their heads down. They were halfway through their cups when three very large, tall beings walked in, also wearing long black overcoats and covered up. They surveyed the room also and then stared at Ash and them from under their hoods for a few minutes, finally turning and spotting whom they came for.

Ash watched them carefully from under her hood and spoke to Bridgett and Rachael. "Watch them. They're not the norm here. They act like they've had some military training by the way they surveyed the room," Ash told them telepathically.

The beings went over to a table, and the taller of the three sat down at the table and started talking to the other man, and Ash could tell by looking at him that he was a black market parts dealer. They started conversing, and Ash could overhear a little bit of the conversation as the taller being's words traveled across the room.

"Where are my parts you promised me?" the larger of the three asked.

"I'm sorry. They got stolen from me. You know how it is."

"Bull. I want my parts or my marks back now. Don't yank me around. You know what will happen to you," the tall one warned.

"Rachael, Bridgett, it's time to leave now. It's getting ugly over there, and I have a feeling a fight's about to break out," Ash told them telepathically again.

The girls got up slowly and headed toward the door. The three beings who had come in now were watching them closely from under their hoods. The girls had barely gotten to the door when suddenly, all hell broke loose behind them. Ash shoved Bridgett and Rachael out the door and moved aside of the door just as a body came flying past where she had been standing a second ago.

The three beings came running, and two of them passed her out the door, but the taller one stopped right in front of her and attacked a man who had ahold of the back of his overcoat. Ash noticed right away a uniform and military boots under the coat but different from any she had seen. The tall alien, which was what she figured he was since she couldn't see him under his coat, was beating the crap out of the other one when another man tried to flank him.

Ash gave that man a spinning kick, and he went flying across the room as she came down in a fighting stance. The tall alien saw what she had done and knocked the other guy he was fighting across the room as well and bolted out the door, but before he raced past her, he stopped and looked down at her. All she saw were two glowing white eyes under his hood, then he was gone.

Ash took this opportunity to run as well, and when she got outside, she saw Bridgett and Rachael standing about ten feet away from the door. She started racing toward them just as men filed out of the cafeteria and now opened fire on them. Rachael immediately pulled her pistols and fired back, dropping someone with each shot. Even Ash pulled one of her pistols and was firing over her shoulder as she ran, hitting her targets. From one of the side buildings, more gunfire came, but Ash realized it was at the attackers, and they drew the attention away from the girls.

"RUN. GO," Ash screamed, waving her arms wildly at Rachael and Bridgett, who didn't need to be told twice. All three raced into the woods as fast as they could go, disappearing from sight.

Fâd and Cory disappeared back into the darkness of the building they were firing from once they saw the other three strangers get away and headed to the shuttle that Nathan had waiting for them. They jumped on board, and Nathan took off, heading back to Pantier, as Fâd got on his comm link.

"Red squad, this is Captain Larson. There are three New Haven brats heading into Sector 12 that will need to be extracted and brought back," Fâd ordered over his comm. He had noticed that the one who delivered the martial arts kick was wearing a nice pair of dress pants under the coat and assumed they were all from the academy, and it wouldn't be the first time some academy students wandered into Little Sonora or Pantier.

"Affirmative, Captain. This is red squad. Where should we take them?"

"Let Nera deal with them. She'll see that they get back."

"Affirmative. Red squad out."

"Did you recognize them?" Cory asked Fâd as he put his pistol away.

"No, but they definitely had military training. That one who came running out right behind me sent a man flying across the room with a spin kick, and the way they were shooting, they weren't missing," Fâd said and also put his pistol away.

"Yeah, I noticed that too. They must be some of Harper's, because we don't have any at the academy right now," Cory said as they headed back to Pantier.

* * *

Ash, Bridgett, and Rachael kept running until they were sure no one was following. Then they stopped and bent over, trying to catch their breaths. They were still bent over when their combat instinct told them they were not alone, and all three girls got back-to-back and drew their weapons, facing different directions for the attack. Watorian soldiers came walking out of the woods with their weapons drawn on the girls.

"Drop your weapons," the squad leader ordered them. Rachael and Bridgett looked at Ash for orders, and Ash nodded her head to go ahead, and they all did. A few soldiers came over and kicked the pistols away. "Search them," the leader said.

They had the girls remove their coats and were surprised to see they were women. Three of the soldiers patted them down and told the leader that the women were clean. "Of course, if you would just let me explain," Ash said with annoyance, but the leader told her to be silent and to come with them. The girls started to follow when Bridgett stumbled, and a young male soldier hit her in the back with his rifle to make her keep up, which, of course, Ash didn't stand for.

She wheeled around so fast, disarming the boy, and had the gun's barrel point-blank in his face with a look of anger on her face before anyone could even move. The other soldiers in the squad had their guns trained on the girls, and both Rachael and Bridgett were now defensively poised to fight even if it meant death.

"Don't ever do that again. Try showing some respect, and you'll get more cooperation out of us," Ash warned the boy, who clearly was scared to death, and now she felt real bad because she could tell he was inexperienced and young. She backed up and handed him his gun. "Don't ever let your guard down, and always keep an eye on the other prisoners. They are your real threat," she said to him with her telepathy, then gave him a slight smile and a quick wink, which shocked him. His mouth fell open, and he took his rifle back, staring at her, as the rest of the squad kept their rifles and pistols aimed at the girls.

The leader motioned them onward, and soon, they were on a shuttle, heading to Pantier. Every time Ash tried to say something, the leader would tell her to shut up; so finally, she did, glaring at him the whole way, but she also noticed now that the young male watorian whom she took the gun from was staring at her and had a look of confusion on his face.

The shuttle went straight to the barracks, and the girls were escorted in by gunpoint and brought into a large room and told to wait. Half an hour later, three soldiers entered, and Ash could tell one was a woman, whom she instantly disliked, probably because the woman was looking at her through narrowed eyes. She was different from most watorian females, for she was tall, and watorian women usually were the same height as most female humans.

Looking at a female watorian, you would think they were human, except they were a little bit bigger boned and majority were kind of plain-looking, totally opposite of the males of their species, who were rather good-looking and very large. Granted, there were females who were very attractive, but this one in particular, though, Ash decided was half man, for there wasn't too much that looked feminine about her.

The next woman who walked through the sliding door saw Ash and them and leaned her head back, closing her eyes. Ash recognized Nera instantly as a big grin spread across her face, but Nera didn't return the gesture and looked mad, then spoke to the large female soldier whom Ash didn't like.

"Who is it you're accusing?" Nera asked the female soldier with a tone of annoyance and anger.

"That one, with the black hair," the woman said, pointing at Ash.

"Me? What did I do?" Ash asked defiantly.

"Sierra here is accusing you of dishonoring her brother by attacking him and taking his rifle from him. Is that true?" Nera asked Ash.

"Yeah, I did, but only after he hit Bridgett in the back. I gave him his gun back and a lecture about being nice," Ash replied with a little bit of arrogance to her tone.

"Did your brother instigate the confrontation?" Nera asked the female soldier.

"No, he was following orders," the woman said smugly.

"THAT'S A LIE!" Ash yelled and started to head after the woman, who, in turn, headed toward her.

"STAND DOWN BOTH OF YOU," Nera yelled. Just then, the door opened again, and the young man whom Ash took the rifle from earlier walked in and over to the tall female watorian, who still had to look up at him even being tall herself.

"Sierra, what are you doing? You're humiliating me. Stop this now," the young man said, pleading to her.

She looked up at him and glared. "Kaiden, get out of here. This is all because of you, and once again, I'm having to clean up your mess. Our family's honor is at stake."

"No, it's not. Don't you mean your pride? I'm sorry I'll never be good enough according to your standards, but this is wrong," he told her.

"You always were weak," the female watorian said to him in a cold tone.

The young male watorian called Kaiden looked over at Ash. "I'm sorry. Please don't hate me for this. What I did was wrong earlier, and I accept and apologize for that, but this is wrong too," he said, and the one called Sierra yelled at him to leave, which he did, hanging his head down in shame.

Nera watched him go with a sad look on her face. She had always had a soft spot for Kaiden. He was a good boy. Even though he was nineteen and technically a young man now, everyone still saw him as the little boy who was always playing around in the wreaked ships.

Sierra and Kaiden lost their parents when he was seven and Sierra was sixteen. Their parents were freighter pilots, and one day, their ship got attacked by mercs, and they, along with their whole crew, were killed. Sierra, though, was always selfish and spiteful and hated having to take care of her younger brother all the time and even more so after their parents' death.

Admiral Larson and Nera herself took it upon themselves and helped out the two children a lot, especially Kaiden, as he was truthfully by himself due to his sister's resentment toward him. The boy pretty well grew up living at the barracks, and later on, as Fâd got older, he even took him under his wing and helped him. Sierra, though, was always mean and condescending to her brother. She never had any problem belittling him, even in front of people; thus, he grew up somewhat submissive because of it.

But despite his terrible childhood, Kaiden had a good heart and would do anything or help anyone who needed it. Nera always knew he would grow up to be a fine young man someday, and it helped that he was really cute and had a grin that could win over anyone.

Nera turned her attention back to the issue at hand and looked over at Ash. "We have a situation here. Sierra has made a challenge of hand-to-hand combat against you to clear up her family's dishonor, and in our society, once a challenge has been made, it cannot be rescinded. Do you accept?" she asked Ash.

"Are you serious? What if I don't?" Ash asked in disbelief.

"Then you will be required to work off your dishonor in service to Sierra," Nera told her with a slight smirk, knowing what was going to come next.

"Well, that ain't going to happen. Fine. I accept her challenge. It seems to me someone is needing to be put in their place anyway," Ash replied, mad, with narrowed eyes, and Nera couldn't help but smirk again, noticing how much Ash looked like Thomas right now.

"Follow me," Nera told them, and they all headed through the barracks to a huge practice room that was filled with sand on the floor. There were many soldiers in there already, practicing sparring, and when Ash and they walked in, Nera had everyone circle the area and give the combatants room.

"Do I have to fight in this?" Ash asked Nera, pointing down at her clothes.

"I don't have anything here you can change into," Nera told her.

"I have a tank, Ash. You can wear that," Rachael said to her and pulled it out of her bag since they had gotten their packs back.

Ash walked over to her and unbuttoned her tunic right there in front of everyone and took it off, standing in just her bra and pants, and Nera couldn't help but chuckle at Ash's defiance. Most of the men in the room looked away but with grins on their faces. Ash then took off her choker, and her dog tags fell out. Now a hush fell over the crowd, realizing she was a soldier.

She pulled on Rachael's tank and then unzipped her tall boots and pulled out a spare pair of combat boots out of her backpack and put them on over her pant legs, buckling them up. Now she looked like the soldier she was, and the spectators knew Sierra was in for a fight. The other woman was already out there, warming up, and then went over, getting in Ash's face, looking down at her with a wicked grin, trying to intimidate her. But Ash looked back up at Sierra and yawned with boredom, which brought out a bunch of chuckling from the crowd.

Outside, Fâd, Nathan, and Cory were heading over to the parts depot when they saw soldiers running into the barracks. They stopped one of the men. "What's going on?" Fâd asked him.

"Sierra challenged one of the women from New Haven to combat, and she accepted. I guess she didn't have clothes to fight in, but her friend did, and she stripped right there in front of everyone. Plus, I hear they're real hot-looking," the soldier said impatiently.

"They?" Nathan asked, grinning now.

"Yeah, three women," the guy said and ran into the building.

Fâd, Nathan, and Cory looked at one another, wondering, and also ran into the barracks, pushing themselves through the crowd of soldiers who had gathered now to see what was going on. They got through, and the guys looked at one another and weren't surprised at who they were. Fâd just shook his head in disbelief and got on his multitool comm. "Father, you had better get down to the barracks now."

* * *

"Ash, kick her ass. She deserves it," Rachael yelled at her, and Ash looked over at Rachael, giving her a thumbs-up with a big, devious smirk on her face. She walked around and started popping her neck and then squatting down to stretch her legs. Nera had them then face toward each other and signaled to begin. Sierra ran at Ash, but before she could touch her, Ash jumped up and spun in the air, catching the female soldier in the jaw with her booted foot, sending her flying across the ground. Sierra jumped up and rubbed her jaw, then advanced again on Ash but remained back a little this time, and they both started exchanging punches and blocking.

Ash took her feet out from under her, making it all look too simple. It was very apparent Ash was purposely trying to humiliate Sierrra, and the female watorian was furious now and came at Ash wildly. Ash hit her good, sending her flying again. But this time, Sierra was so mad that she reached over and, without warning, pulled a pistol out of a fellow soldier's holster who was standing around the outskirts of the arena, watching, before he could even react and pointed it at Ash.

Over behind where the girls were standing and hadn't seen them yet, Fâd, Nathan, and Cory all at the same time pulled their pistols too and aimed them at Sierra, ready to shoot her. But just as quickly as they had pulled their pistols, Ash was instantly covered in blue kinetic energy as her eyes glowed blue and sent a blast at Sierra, knocking the gun out of her hand and sending the woman flying in the opposite direction of the gun.

Sierra slammed into the ground and lay motionless, but Ash wasn't done. She was in a fit of rage now and, in a flash, was on top of the unconscious woman, still covered in kinetic energy, and raised her left arm back to deliver a killing blow to her, when suddenly, out of nowhere, someone yelled in a voice that echoed through the whole building, "LIEUTENT HARPER, STAND DOWN NOW!"

Ash jumped up, backing away from the unconscious woman on the ground, and powered down, looking over with narrowed, rage-filled eyes and saw Rear Admiral Larson with a furious look on his face standing in the doorway. But it was the man standing next to him that made Ash's eyes get big and drop to her knees, covering her face with her hands as she cried into them. Fâd was standing there with his arms crossed over his chest with narrowed eyes, watching her. Rachael and Bridgett ran over to Ash and put their arms around her as she continued to cry.

"NO ONE SAW WHAT HAPPENED HERE. THAT IS AN ORDER!" Larson yelled to the gathering, still extremely furious and full of warning in his tone of voice.

"Yes, sir," everyone responded.

"Ashley, Rachael, Bridgett, come with me now," Larson ordered, and the anger in his voice wasn't hard to miss.

Ash got up, wiping her tears from her face, and went over to where their stuff were and put her dress boots in her pack. Then the girls picked up their packs and proceeded to follow the admiral. Ash walked past Fâd and now saw him up close for the first time in over nine years. He was very tall and large, extremely good-looking, very muscular, and had gone through his change as his eyes now were the white of a mature watorian male.

His hair was shoulder length, and a braid started at his right temple and then split into two, which hung down in the back, past his shoulders, with many beads woven throughout them. He was magnificent, and Ash could feel her heart racing in her chest. She stopped just for a few seconds and looked up at him as he looked down at her, totally void of any emotion. Then she left to follow the admiral.

Fâd stood watching her go as his heart beat out of control. Watching her fight was bad enough, but when she got close and he could smell her, it was almost more than he could handle. She was beautiful, and he wanted so much to pull her into his arms and just hold her, never letting her go again. Nathan and Cory walked up beside him and also were glued on the girls as they left.

"It's been two years since the last time I saw her. Now I'm going to make sure I never lose her again," Nathan said and headed out after the girls as Cory looked over at Fâd, and they couldn't help but grin and took off after Nathan.

CHAPTER 37

THE GIRLS FOLLOWED Rear Admiral Larson out of the barracks and climbed into the waiting vehicle with him. They rode back to his house in total silence. The admiral and the girls got out, and they all went inside. Once the front door slid shut, he turned around, and the anger was still there, all over his face. "WHAT THE HELL DID YOU THREE DO THIS TIME?" he yelled at them.

Ash fidgeted nervously. "I really don't want to say right now," she replied and looked down at the ground. Just then, they heard the whirring sound of hover bikes and saw the guys pull up on them in front of the house through one of the large windows. The girls were still watching the guys get off their bikes when the admiral yelled at them again to get their attention. "I'M WAITNG FOR AN EXPLANATION. THAT'S AN ORDER, ASH!" he yelled as the guys walked into the house. All three girls jumped in surprise from his yelling again. By now, Nathan and Cory had walked over and half-sat on the back of one of the large sofas as Fâd walked over and leaned against the wall, watching the girls with his arms crossed in front of him.

Ash took a deep breath and faced her godfather, "Here goes. Okay. We took a campus shuttle without permission and headed to New Delphi so we could celebrate Bridgett's birthday—"

"Hey, we still haven't celebrated your birthday yet, Bridg," Rachael said out loud, interrupting. Ash gave her a dirty look, and so did Admiral Larson, but the guys were trying real hard not to start chuckling. "Sorry. I won't say another word," Rachael said, making a zipping motion across her mouth.

"Continue," Larson ordered Ash through narrowed eyes.

"As I was saying, ten minutes into the flight, we got hit by an ion cannon from some mercs. We crashed, and unfortunately, the shuttle didn't make it, but we got out with only minor injuries—"

"Yeah. See my head, and Bridgett broke her wrist," Rachael interrupted again, and the boys were chuckling now, looking away from the girls.

Ash looked over and gave her another dirty look. "Anyway, we ran into the mercs, did what we do best, and made our way to Little Sonora. There, we ran into some more trouble as a shoot-out happened in a cafe we were in between some strangers and some of the local thugs. We escaped that and ran into the woods where we encountered your soldiers and were brought here. The rest you know about," Ash said.

Admiral Larson stood perfectly still, glaring at the girls with crossed arms. "You have to tell him," he said coldly and headed to his console. Ash reached up, rubbed her temple, and closed her eyes, then opened them again and saw that her godfather was watching her. "How bad is it?" he asked, concerned.

"It's getting bad. I had to use a lot of my telepathy and kinetics to escape the mercs and Little Sonora, and all I had was bespin last night, which only took the edge off," Ash told him.

Admiral Larson went over and opened a drawer in the kitchen, taking out a large med pac and opening it. He took out a syringe and a small vial and filled the syringe with the vial's contents and looked over at Ash. "I keep a supply here for your father when he comes to stay sometimes. I never knew I would someday have to be giving it to you as well."

Ash walked over to where her godfather was, leaning her head down to expose her neck and then moving her hair aside. Fâd jumped up from where he was leaning against the wall with a scared look on his face and quickly headed over to his father and Ash. He stood beside her and now saw a small injection port in the back of her neck and frowned.

"This is asrinon. You know how it burns. Grab hold of something," Larson told her.

"Where's my gun? That's what I usually gripped when I injected the medicine all the other times. Of course, I was always in my suit too when I did," Ash said jokingly, and Larson had to chuckle a little.

Fâd reached down and took Ash's hands in his, and she grabbed hold of them. Larson then stuck the needle into the port in Ash's neck, and Fâd grimaced, watching his father pushing the plunger down on the syringe and the clear liquid disappearing into her neck. Ash instantly gripped his hands, and he was a little surprised by how strong she was. Larson pulled the needle out, and Ash lifted her head, leaning it back with closed eyes. Finally, she opened them and was now looking up at Fâd, then quickly released his hands and looked over at the admiral.

"When did this all start?" Fâd asked her as she looked back up at him again, for he was standing almost right on top of her in a protective manner.

Ash backed up a little due to the nearness of Fâd, which was causing turmoil with her emotions, and she could feel her heart racing out of control. "Over five years ago, my telepathic powers increased, and I used them a lot during recon missions. But the headaches got worse, so they built in my armor an injection unit that I can activate myself, which will inject the asrinon for me. They had to implant the port in my neck, which is tied to my nervous system, so the medicine goes directly to the source of the pain.

"Asrinon is the strongest med for this problem there is, but it has a nasty kick to it. I feel it travel all through my head as it burns. Usually, I would have my rifle in my hands when I inject it so I would grip it until it subsides, which thank goodness subsides just as quickly as it starts," Ash told him, and Fâd was fighting himself to not pull her into his arms and hold her right now, wishing he could take this all away from her. He could see her face was all flushed, but he figured it was because she just took the medicine and now had to face her father, the vice admiral, who made everyone nervous but his own father.

"Are you ready to face the music?" Larson asked Ash, which helped her to gain control of her emotions again.

"No, but I guess I better get it over with. Rachael, Bridg, look forward to our lives as waste management specialists. At least look at the bright side, we will still be specialists at something," Ash said to them, and her friends nodded in agreement.

"Garbage detail? What are you talking about?" Nathan asked curiously.

"Long story," Ash said with a slight smirk.

"No, it's not. It's kind of funny. See, a couple years ago, at the academy, someone released a crantock, and it was attacking one of the buildings. Well, academy life sucks, as I'm sure you well know. It's so boring there, so we decided to dare each other to slap the thing on the ass when it wasn't looking. Me and Ash did just fine, but when Bridg went, it was expecting her, and she led it right back to us like an idiot," Rachael told them, glaring at Bridgett. The girls didn't see the guilty looks on the guys' faces.

Bridgett looked over at Rachael with a mad expression on her face. "So what?"

"So what? A good soldier never leads the enemy back to his or her squad," Rachael informed her, rolling her eyes as if this was common knowledge.

"Bullcrap. It was your stupid idea, and like always, Ash led the way. So I figured, if I was going to die, I would make sure you two were going with me," Bridgett said as everyone but the girls started laughing.

"Anyway, when the admiral spoke to us in jail, he informed the three of us that if we pulled anymore stunts, we would be demoted, stripped of our ranks, and do garbage duty for the rest of our lives. Apparently, he is out of ideas on ways to punish us if that was all he could come up with this time," Rachael told them.

The guys were still chuckling among themselves. "Yeah, we saw you three on the news, waving to the camera," Nathan said, grinning at Rachael, who grinned right back at him.

"So did my father," Ash replied nervously, totally oblivious to the exchange of looks Rachael and Nathan were now giving each other.

Larson got on his comm and contacted Admiral Harper, and it didn't take long for the vice admiral to respond. "What's going on, Larson? Did the girls do something?" Harper asked right away with narrowed, cold eyes.

"Somebody wants to talk to you," Larson replied and stepped aside for Ash to come over to the console.

"Hi, Dad," Ash said nervously.

"What did you do?" Harper asked, still with narrowed eyes and a cold expression on his face.

"We borrowed a shuttle, got shot down, and ended up here," Ash said real fast, and before Admiral Larson could do anything, she darted behind him, hiding. Even Rachael and Bridgett tried to slowly sneak around the wall so Admiral Harper couldn't see them, but Nathan and Cory grabbed their arms and made them stay right there, and the girls gave them a dirty look.

"YOU DID WHAT?" Admiral Harper yelled, and it looked like smoke was coming out of his ears.

"Well, technically, we borrowed it without proper permission and got shot down by some mercs, which you will be happy to know they will not be doing again. But don't worry, we are okay," Ash said, still hiding behind Larson, who was trying not to grin. Even Fâd had his hand over his mouth so no one would know he was grinning.

"What am I going to do with you girls? I hope you like garbage, because that's what you're going to be seeing for some time," Harper informed her, and the fury in his tone wasn't hard to pick up on.

"Actually, we're pretty good at picking it up. We've done it quite a few times at the academy, Admiral," Rachael told him, and now Larson was trying desperately not to laugh. Ash looked over at Rachael and mouthed the word *dumbass* at her, and Rachael made a bad hand gesture at her. The guys were trying to stifle their laughter, but it was slowly leaking out.

The vice admiral was silent for a few minutes. He was actually contemplating jail time for the girls. "Well, this one's going to cost.

Hopefully, Shotwell will let you back to finish school, and then you girls are going to pay for this stupid stunt for the rest of your lives," Harper said, shaking his head, still furious.

Now Larson spoke up, and his face changed and took on a more serious expression. "It's not that easy, Thomas. Unfortunately, one of the soldiers here felt that Ash had dishonored them and challenged her to combat, which Ash accepted, easily defeating her, but the woman pulled a gun on her, and Ash sent her and the gun in opposite directions with a kinetic blast in front of a very large crowd. I ordered the event to be forgotten, but you know how it is," Larson told him, and Ash could see her father's expression changed dramatically.

"Well, it's settled. Girls, when you get back to your apartment, you need to pack immediately, and Rear Admiral Larson will take you on board the *Lithia* for protection. Then you will be shuttled to the *Justification* once I return to Sigma Six," Admiral Harper told them, and the girls' faces all turned white.

"NO, WE WON'T! I want to finish. There are only two months left. Let me do this. I've spent over twelve years of my life working for this, and now it's all going to be taken away? No! You always say to finish the mission. Well, I'm finishing this!" Ash said, now standing and facing her father in full defiance.

"Ash, there's no other way. If the authorities find out about you, they will take you to Trinity, and you will die there. They'll dump you off in the middle of the most populated area of the worst criminals, drugged and unable to defend yourself. You'll have no chance, and I won't be able to get to you in time, not to mention Rachael and Bridgett will also be arrested and sent to a prison colony somewhere else," Harper tried to plead with her.

"Dad, please. Why throw away all those years basing it on speculation that something might—and I mean might—happen? I'm willing to take that risk. Let me. For once, Father, trust me. Please. I can take care of myself," Ash begged him, and Harper just sat there without saying anything, and it was Fâd who spoke now.

"Admiral, you can't let her. This isn't something to gamble with. We are talking about Ashley's life here, and I'm not willing to risk it. Are you? You're her superior. Order her to stay here, and we'll go get their belongings," Fâd said to Harper, and the admiral could see the pain on Fâd's face. He also caught what he said about not being willing to risk it.

"I'm sorry, Captain. She's a grown woman. It's her choice, not mine, and I can't force her to give it all up. I wish I could order her, Fâd, but she's still on leave, and I have no authority over her right now until she returns to active duty," Harper said, and just saying the words pained him.

"Thank you, Father," Ash said, looking defiantly at Fâd, who glared at her, then stormed out of the house, jumping on his hover bike and racing off.

"All right, Thomas, we'll keep watch on them, and if there's any hint of danger, we'll get them out immediately," Larson told him.

"Ash?"

"That's fine. If we suspect anything, we will contact Admiral Larson instantly and get out," Ash told her father, and he nodded then.

Larson looked over at Cory and Nathan. "Why don't you boys take the girls over to the guesthouse, then Rachael and Bridgett to the med clinic to get that wrist and that head wound taken care of?" Larson told them, and Nathan and Cory saluted him and left with the girls. Larson watched them leave, and finally, when they were out of the door and heading toward the guesthouse, he turned back to Harper on the vid screen.

"So I have to replace a shuttle," Harper said with a scowl.

"Well, that's cheaper than a whole building plus lab equipment," Larson said, chuckling.

"True, but at least your boys didn't get their picture plastered all over the news, waving at the camera as they got led away at gunpoint. That made it look like they were the guilty ones who released the crantock in the first place instead of the boys who actually did," Harper said, still scowling as Larson started chuckling.

Larson had a big grin on his face as he continued to chuckle. "Yeah, you got me there, and honestly, I think you're ahead as far as the girls getting into trouble. The boys got into plenty of incidents, but I swear it's nothing compared to what those three girls have continuously pulled."

Harper's face changed then from the smirk to a cold one. "I don't like this with Ash going back to the academy and people knowing about her kinetics one bit."

"Neither do I, so why are you letting her?" Larson asked him with a frustrated look on his face.

"Because I didn't have the heart to tell her no after she spent all those years of her life toward finishing her schooling."

Larson let out a sigh. "Well, we will keep a constant eye on them, and Ash is no fool. She'll be careful even more so now. Heck, they just survived a shuttle crash with hardly any injuries, so I think they will be okay for a couple more months to finish school."

"Gerrard, we are talking about the girls. A lot can happen in two months with those three together," Harper said to him, and Admiral Larson had to agree.

Nathan and Cory walked the girls over to the guesthouse, which was within walking distance of Larson's home. Nathan put his hand on the scan pad, and the door slid open. Ash walked in first and noticed right away that it was rather nice. There was a foyer that you walked through first, then it opened up into a vaulted living room with the kitchen off to the right of it and the dining room, which had a glass sliding door that opened up to a patio overlooking a large yard that stopped at the forest's edge. To the left of the open living room were two bedrooms and then the only bathroom and finally one more bedroom, which were all situated around the living room, making it the focal point of the whole house.

It was brightly lit with nice, crisp white walls everywhere, unlike Admiral Larson's log walls in his home, and a few colorful pictures of nature scenes were hung on them, helping to break up the whiteness all around them. The furniture was of a more modern design and mostly metal and glass, as was the table and chairs in the dining room. Even the large sofa, love seat, and overstuffed armchair were an off-white and tan color, fitting in well with the house's decor.

The bedrooms were spotless and modernly decorated with nice whitewashed headboards and matching dressers, not to mention all the floors throughout the whole house, except in the dining room, kitchen, and bathroom, which were made of natural stone, was covered in a soft tan-colored carpet, also helping to break up the white contrast of the walls and ceiling. Compared to Admiral Larson's home, which was more rustic cabin design inside, this was the opposite and more modern, lacking the cozy feel of the log home of Admiral Larson.

"I'm going to take Bridgett over to the med clinic," Cory told them and headed toward the door, escorting Bridgett with his hand on her back toward the foyer.

"Wait. I'll go with you. What about you, Rachael? Maybe you should have your head checked, literally," Ash said with a devious grin.

"I'm fine. I just want to take a shower and clean up," Rachael told her, but Ash frowned.

"I'll wait here with her," Nathan grinned as Ash gave him a dirty look.

"I'll be okay, really. Go with Bridgett and have that lump on your head checked."

Ash frowned at her but went outside and hurriedly walked the short distance from the guesthouse to where Cory and Bridgett were, over in front of Admiral Larson's home, where the guys had parked their hover bikes. She saw Cory putting a helmet on Bridgett as she sat on his metallic-blue bike, and Ash walked up, looking around for a ride.

"Can you drive one of these?" Cory asked her, motioning with his head at the bike in front of him.

"Of course," Ash replied with her hands on her hips.

"Take Nathan's. He won't be using it for a while," Cory said with a smile. Ash smiled back at him and couldn't help but stare. All three of them looked so hot with their white eyes now, but they were anyway without the changed eyes. Ash went over and put on Nathan's helmet. It was really big on her, but she didn't care and climbed on the large bright-yellow bike.

They were definitely built for speed with sleek lines, a smooth black synthetic seat, and twin fusion engines located beside each other directly under the seat. The handlebars were slightly slanted back with the power grips located on them. Plus, in front of the seat was a control panel with all the readings and different function buttons. The bikes were also equipped with dual rocket boosters on the tail end, giving it an extra burst of speed, and instead of magnetic disc wheels like most hover bikes used to have, these had kinetic energy discs that gave them extreme maneuverability and instant takeoff speed while hovering aboveground.

It was a lot bigger than the ones she had driven before, but she started it anyway. The bike now floated a few feet off the ground where it had been resting on a retractable stand while it was shut off. Ash carefully moved one of the power grips and slowly took off, heading to the clinic, as Cory and Bridgett caught her easily. In no time, they were pulling up outside the med clinic, and the memory of this place now sent a chill up her spine.

Cory saw the scared look on her face and knew what she was remembering. "It's okay, Ash. That was a long time ago."

"I know," she said and followed them inside. They walked up to the nurse's station, told the nurse on duty what they needed, and she then called for the doctor, who was the same one who treated Ash all those years ago. He appeared suddenly from nowhere, making the kids all jump from being caught by surprise.

"Ashley Harper, I can't believe it's you. My, you have grown up," he said, without a smile, of course. "What are you kids doing here?" he then asked, looking at Bridgett and Cory.

"Bridgett broke her arm," Cory said as Bridgett held her arm up for him to see.

"Nice job on the instant cast. Come on. Let's get that treated. How did it happen?" Dr. Taylor asked as he turned to head toward an examine room.

"The girls were in a shuttle crash," Cory told him.

"What about you, Ashley? Anything broken on you?" the doctor asked her, stopping to look back at her.

"No, I'm fine. I think I'm going to go back and check on Rachael," Ash told them and turned, heading quickly out of the clinic before she could have a panic attack from being there in the hospital again. She got back on Nathan's bike. In no time, she pulled up to the guesthouse and went in. Right away, she noticed that Nathan was nowhere around and then heard laughter coming from Rachael's room.

Ash rolled her eyes and went into the bedroom she was going to use and opened the closet. There were some uniforms in there that she could use. Plus, she had at least her military boots and a set of clean undergarments, which she always kept in her pack as well. Ash grabbed the uniform out of the closet, gathered up her clean set of undergarments, and headed to the bathroom to shower and change into clean clothes.

It didn't take her long to shower, and when she got out, she looked in the mirror and noticed some nasty-looking bruises on her collarbone and shoulders where the safety straps held her in place on the shuttle when it crashed. Ash touched them, and in a few places, they were a little tender, but it was nothing she couldn't handle. Then she went ahead and put on the uniform, which was a little big but worked, then went back to her room, pulling on her combat boots.

She decided to leave her hair down since it was wet and walked over to the kitchen to get something to drink. Cory and Bridgett walked in as she was rummaging through the refrigerator for something and saw that Bridgett now had a much smaller and more movable cast on.

"How's your wrist?" Ash asked her.

"Much better," Bridgett replied.

"Where's Nathan?" Cory asked, looking around. Ash pointed to Rachael's room, and Cory started chuckling and shaking his head. Bridgett headed to her room while Ash and Cory went and sat down on the sofa and armchair. No sooner had they sat that Nathan came walking out of Rachael's room dressed in only his undergarment. He grinned at them and walked over to the refrigerator, grabbing two bottles of water, and headed back to Rachael's room, but before he got all the way there, he stopped and looked over at Cory.

"You wouldn't believe all the different ways that girl can bend. She's so limber. I'm in love. I can't believe she's finally here," Nathan said with a rotten grin and quickly ran back into Rachael's room, locking the door behind him.

Ash and Cory looked at each other and started laughing. "So where did Fâd storm off to?" Ash asked Cory.

"Probably over to our ship."

"You guys have your own ship?" Ash asked, now excited.

"Yeah, but it's in a bad shape, nothing like it was. We've done a lot of work on it whenever we get the chance over the last five years, but there's still a lot more to do," Cory told her, smiling. Then Bridgett came out of her room, changed into a clean uniform too, which was big on her petite frame. Cory stood up like the perfect gentleman he always was and waited for her to walk over to him. Then they sat down on the sofa together.

"Hey, Bridgett, the guys have their own ship that they are repairing," Ash told her, grinning, knowing that this would pique Bridgett's interest.

"Really? Can we go see it please?" Bridgett asked excitedly, looking at Cory with a big grin. Cory grinned back at her and stood up, putting his hand out to help her up. Ash jumped up as well, and they all headed to the front door. "Should we tell them?" Bridgett asked, motioning over to Rachael's room.

"No," both Cory and Ash told her at the same time and then started laughing.

Ash once again climbed on Nathan's bike, and soon, she was following Cory and Bridgett down the street where Admiral Larson lived and the guesthouse was. When they got to the end of the street, they turned left and took off down the main road that ran right through town. Of course, Cory gunned his bike, and it jumped, shooting forward, leaving Ash behind. She took it slow and steady because the bike was so big, making her really nervous driving it.

Finally, she got to where Cory had turned off the main road near the barracks and headed through the shipyard. There were a lot of wreaked spaceships there and some that looked perfectly fine. She continued, driving through them, and near the back of the shipyard, she finally came upon the ship and could see Cory's blue bike and Fâd's jet-black bike parked in front of the open cargo bay door.

But it was what the cargo bay door was attached to that caught her attention. All Ash could do was stare at the ship. It was perfect; something about it seemed to call to her. She parked the bike and got off, removing the large helmet of Cory's, and walked around the ship, admiring its lines. Finally, she went inside and looked around the huge cargo bay with its large, high ceiling, open girder framework, and shiny silver metal walls. Even the gray metal floor in there was spotless and had hardly any scuffing from traffic. Plus, the lighting from the ceiling was so strong, and it lit the place up brightly. Ash climbed the emergency stairs because she found out the elevator wasn't working and went up to the bridge to check out everything in there.

She noticed that the pilot sat right up front, at the very point of the nose, as she called it, since the ship looked like a hawk and you could see everywhere out of the clear windows that wrapped around the whole front. Even the copilot seat sat just back a ways on the pilot's right side, and they both had nice, comfortable, laid-back chairs that sat on small tracks, and when one sat down on them, it moved forward up to the controls. A little ways behind that was a large round projector table that when operating would show a 3D virtual view of the galaxy and all surrounding systems, planets, and other things as well. Then right behind it was the captain's platform, a raised area in the floor with a large wraparound console and chair.

Off to one side and back a ways from the pilot's seat was the gunner's station. Ash sat down in the enclosed cockpit station and chair, then grabbed the trigger stick. On the left was the directional stick that moved the guns around at different angles and directions. She looked up and saw the targeting headgear that would come down when the chair was activated, which was almost like the one on the battlecruiser she wore during a battle over Fath many years ago. She sat there for a few more minutes, looking around at the rest of the bridge, and just like on the *Justification*'s bridge, there weren't too many areas on the walls that weren't covered with controls or screens, making this place also light up like a Christmas tree when running.

She got out of the seat and walked over to the captain's platform and noticed a small portal pad and realized this ship could handle an AI, which she thought was very strange for a ship this size. Ash walked to the back wall of the bridge and saw that the area split down two sides, and she could see all the way down the hallway, which looked like it ended into a mess hall. She noticed that off both hallways, there was a door to the room in the center that split the two halls, which Ash figured was probably some kind of conference room. Finally, she decided to head down the stairs to the gunnery on the level below this one and see what kind of artillery this ship had.

Ash walked over to it and heard Fâd in there but walked in anyway through the open doorway, and her eyes lit up when she saw the weapons. It was a nice square completely white metal room with bright lighting and many control panels and consoles located around the outer edges, but directly in the center was a large proton cannon, and beside it were two massive forbs mech guns.

You could see under the two forbs guns, when they were activated, would drop through the floor on mechanical hoists to the outside and seal behind them, and the cannon would slide forward through a door on a turret, also to the outside in front of it, sealing shut behind it as well. Over on another wall was a large cabinet that held the ammo for the mech guns, and Ash could tell looking at it that it would hold anywhere from nine hundred to over a thousand large clips, which were three-foot-long tubes that held over one thousand rounds each, of armor-piercing mag shells with explosive tips that you loaded into the gun's housing.

Fâd hadn't noticed her yet and was working underneath one of the large guns as she stood there watching him when he finally wheeled out from under it and then saw her. "Oh, crap, you scared me. I didn't know you were here," he said and got up, heading over to the weapons console, punching in some numbers. The gun moved a little, then stopped, and a button on the console flashed red.

"Damn it, where's Nathan?" he asked her, frustrated and mad.

"Preoccupied. What do you need?" Ash asked.

"I'm trying to calibrate this gun, and I need him here to help."

"I can help you with that."

"Right. Shooting with them is a lot different than fixing them," Fâd said sarcastically to her.

"I know a few things about heavy forbs mech guns," Ash retorted with annoyance in her voice.

"Prove it," Fâd challenged her coldly.

"Fine." Ash laid down on the wheeled sled and moved under the huge gun, then felt to her side, picking up the stick light and shining it inside the gun's guts. "Try to calibrate so I can see what it's doing," she told Fâd, and he punched in the code again, and she watched the inner mechanism start to move and then stop. Once again, the red light flashed on the control panel. "I found your problem," she said and slid out from under the gun.

"Where? Show me." Fâd now seemed interested. He put his hand down, and she took it. He pulled her up, then he laid down on the sled and slid under the gun.

"It's on the free arm. There's a bolt missing, and when it starts to move, it binds because it's not being held in place," she told him.

"Where? I don't see it," he asked, looking all over with the light. Ash got down and crawled under with him, and he scooted over a little so she could get on the sled, and now she was pretty well lying on him with her face just inches away from his.

"Right here. See this? It's not held in place like it should be." Ash had her hand up in the mechanism and half lying on Fâd's chest, showing him the problem. Her head was right next to his face, and while he was looking at the problem with her, he started smelling her hair and putting his face in it but then caught himself as his heart started beating rapidly and his stomach tied in knots.

"Yeah, I see. Let's fix it and see what happens," he said and wheeled them both out from under the gun. Ash rolled off him and stood up as he jumped up quickly and went over to a large parts cabinet. She came over, and he noticed that she now had grease on her cheek as she looked in the cabinet with him. He grabbed a bolt and showed her. She took it out of his hand and then wheeled herself back under the gun. He squatted down next to her and watched as she gritted her teeth and then let out the breath she was holding and took her arms out.

"Try it." He got up and went over to the console and typed in the command again and watched the gun move, locking in place, and the light turned green. "Well?" Ash asked from under the gun, next to the hoist.

"We got green," he said, grinning, as he now pulled up a virtual screen on the main control and started working through many sub-screens, uploading the gun's information. Ash, meantime, finished up under the gun and closed it up, then wheeled out from under it. He reached down and grabbed her held-up hand, pulling her up. They both gave each other a high five, which was something they used to do when they were younger. Now she had grease in other places on her face, and he started grinning at her.

"What? What's so funny?" she asked, self-conscious.

"You have grease all over your face."

"Oh, that's all? I thought it was something terrible." She grinned, and he handed her a towel, and she started wiping her face off. "Did I get it all?"

"No." He grabbed the towel from her and wiped the few places she still had it on and handed it back to her. Ash put the towel down and walked over to the large cannon they had sitting on the main center track as Fâd continued putting in information into the gun's computer.

"Where did you get the proton cannon? These are only on the large cruisers and some destroyers," she asked him as she examined the cannon.

"It's amazing what you can get when your father's an admiral." Fâd grinned and walked over to it as Ash grinned back. "Actually, we got it when they pulled it from a wreaked destroyer because it won't work. We tried to sim fire it, but every time it gets so far on the buildup, it shuts down," he told her, looking it over.

"Did you check the points and coils?" she asked him.

"Yes, all that, and they're fine."

"What about the barrel? Do you have a barrel probe? If there's even a small, hairline crack in these things, they won't fire."

"Do you see a barrel probe here? And yes, I know that!" Fâd replied, putting his hands on his hips, a little annoyed.

"Well, then, somebody is going to have to climb in it and inspect it manually," Ash said, looking at it. She realized Fâd didn't respond to what she said. She looked up at him from across the cannon, and he had a devious grin on his face.

"So what are you doing tomorrow?" he asked her, grinning.

"Climbing into the barrel of a proton cannon," she replied and started giggling.

CHAPTER 38

Fâd and Ash were still talking when Bridgett and Cory walked in. "Ash, this ship is awesome. She's definitely not council. I honestly think she's a sentinel prototype. A lot of the original parts are sentinel but modified way beyond anything we have right now, not to mention she was at one time fitted for an AI. Ships this size never have AIs, which tells me there are a lot of high-tech stuff here. It will be interesting when she comes online what will be revealed," Bridgett told them, and you could see the excitement on her face.

"Do you think you can get it running?" Ash asked, grinning, and saw Fâd also looking hopeful.

"Piece of cake. Cory said we can go over to the supply depot here on the barracks and get what we need tomorrow. I'll have this ship up and running in no time." Bridgett grinned, and Ash looked over at Fâd as he looked down at her and grinned.

They all left the ship since it was now dark out and late. They climbed back on the bikes, and Fâd started laughing watching Ash climb on the large bike of Nathan's. Even when she drove it, she was very careful; and as he followed beside her, he couldn't help but chuckle at her cautiousness, which wasn't like Ash at all. Cory, of course, took off with Bridgett, and she laughed as they sped down the street and took the corner at a slant.

"Come on, Ash, you can give it a little more power," he said to her over her comm link.

"No way. If you want to go, I'm not stopping you, but I'm going to take it easy."

"I'm not going to leave you. Slow and easy it is," Fâd teased her back, and finally, they got to the guesthouse and parked. Ash was taking off her helmet when Fâd came over and lifted her off the bike and then took his helmet off. They walked into the house, and Cory and Bridgett were in the kitchen, punching something into the controls of the replicator.

"Where's Nathan?" Fâd asked, looking around.

Cory and Bridgett both pointed toward Rachael's door, but now it was quiet. The buzzer went off, and Ash could smell pizza. Her stomach started growling because she hadn't eaten anything all day. They all got plates and filled them, then went and sat on the sofa and love seat together. Of course, Bridgett was sitting sideway on the love seat with her legs over Cory's lap.

"So how often do you go to the Odyssey?" Fâd asked as he took a bite of pizza.

"What, maybe once or twice a month? It's the only decent place there is," Ash replied and took a huge bite out of her pizza as Fâd stared at her, amazed by how much she could cram in her mouth.

"So what did you guys do once we left prep school, burn the place down?" Cory asked, grinning.

"No, nothing. It was really boring," Bridgett said.

"Rachael had fun," Ash said with a mouth full of food.

"Yeah, because at least she didn't wall herself up in a self-made prison and refuse to come out," Bridgett snapped at Ash, who narrowed her eyes at her.

"I heard you had a thing going with a commander?" Cory asked, and now it was Fâd who looked mad.

"No, I never had a thing with any commander. Where did you hear that?" Ash asked him, curious what was being said about her. She had stopped eating.

"A Captain Lewis said you two looked pretty sweet on each other." It was Fâd who answered her now.

"No way, not the ice queen. He came looking for her a couple years later and wanted there to be something between them, but Ash shot him down," Bridgett said, and now Ash got up and walked outside. Fâd looked over at Bridgett, and she shrugged her shoulders. He got up and headed outside to find Ash.

Cory and Bridgett sat there for a few minutes. "Was it something we said?" Cory asked her.

"I don't know. Who cares? Ash is always moody," Bridgett replied, looking unconcerned, and they both continued to eat pizza and talk.

Outside, Ash was sitting on the grass, looking up at the stars, as Fâd came outside, sat down beside her, and looked up as well. "You remember when we used to do this all the time when we were younger?" Fâd asked her, and he laid back on the grass with his arms folded behind his head.

Ash laid back then and also put her arms behind her head. "Yeah. I think the funniest time was when we were all here and Nathan ran us out of the house and everyone fell asleep outside."

Fâd started laughing. "Oh, that was bad. Of course, I think Rachael gave him a pretty good run for it. I don't know if it's a good thing those two are together. Even between the two of them, I still don't think it would make a complete brain."

Ash started giggling. "You're probably right. So confession time, was it you guys that put the slug in the water fountain?"

"Guilty. The professor was going to make us retake our test because he accused us of cheating, so we took his little pet and then sprayed pheromones all over his room to attract the beast," Fâd told her.

"So that's what the smell was. Rachael and I thought we smelled something. So did you cheat?"

"Yeah, but I didn't want to take another test, so this way, we figured, no building, no test."

"And how did that plan work out for you?"

"I still had to take the test, but you'll be proud of me. I passed without cheating."

"Very commendable of you," Ash said, and they both smacked fist together.

"I thought we would never stop laughing when we saw you three on the vid. When you three grinned and waved at the camera, we all had tears running down our faces. And then when Bridg brought the creature toward you three and you were all scrambling to get away, my sides hurt so bad from laughing so hard. You really need to see it. We have it on a power pad now and like to watch it every so often when we need a good laugh," Fâd told her and started chuckling.

"That's okay. It was real fun when I got to talk to my father on a comm hooked up inside my jail cell. He even threatened to leave us there. I was almost ready to call your dad if mine didn't bail us out."

"I wish I could have seen that. At least I've never been arrested and thrown in jail. You're one up on me. So who where those guys with you?"

"The twins, that's Oscar and Lee. Their biosyms, kind of misfits that no one wants anything to do with. They're extremely smart, taking med training, and we have been trying to show them how to have fun, but their idea of fun is studying all night at the library. Of course, they did enjoy the attention they got after the arrest."

"So is it true what Bridg said about that commander? He came looking for you?" Fâd asked and was now looking over at Ash.

"Yeah, that part was true."

"What happened that made him think there was a chance?"

"I don't know, because I only met him the one time and then never saw him again, and suddenly, he shows up two years later at a party me and my squad were having because we were all leaving."

"Well, something must have made him think there was a chance. What happened on the ship when you took over as his gunner?"

"How did you know that? I never told you that," Ash asked, now leaning up on her elbows and looking over at him.

"Nathan had heard about it and told me and Cory. So what happened?"

"We just talked the whole time, and it wasn't just me and him. The pilot was there too. Oh, we did go and get something to eat when we transferred over to the *Presidio* but just talked that whole time as well. Then he walked me back to the room I was sharing with Chief Nelson."

"What did you talk about?"

"Come on, what is this? What do you want to hear, Fâd? Just tell me instead of all these annoying questions."

"All right. Did you have feelings for him at one time?"

"No! But what about you? You must have had a pretty wild time these past years. You were always with a new girl at school, making out," Ash said, a little angry now.

"I deserved that, but no, there has been no one."

Ash was silent for a few minutes. "I'm ready to go to bed. I'm really looking forward to a soft bed after the hard ground of the cave last night. I don't ever remember the ground feeling so hard when I was younger," Ash said and giggled.

Fâd grinned at her from where he was still lying on the ground. "I know what you mean."

They both got up and went back into the house. Bridgett and Cory were both sound asleep on the couch as Cory held her. Ash and Fâd grinned looking at them, and Ash took a blanket that was lying over the back of the love seat and laid it over them.

"He's always liked her," Fâd whispered to Ash.

"I know, and she's always liked him."

Ash walked to the front door with Fâd, and it slid open as he stepped out. He turned around, looking down at her, just inches from her, and Ash had to look up at him due to him being so tall and close. "So tomorrow, we get to shove you into a cannon?" Fâd asked with a devious grin.

"Yep. I can't wait," Ash replied, grinning. Fâd stood there for a few seconds, looking down at her, and Ash could see he was struggling with something by the look on his face. Then he turned and walked down the road to his house, which wasn't very far from there. Ash watched him the whole way, and then when he walked up onto his porch, he waved to her, and she waved back and went into the house.

When the front door slid shut, Cory woke up and looked down at Bridgett in his arms. He kissed her on the forehead and then carefully moved his arm and got up. Ash was standing at the end of the sofa now as he walked over to her.

Cory stopped and looked down at Ash. "He does love you, always has, and I know you love him."

"But it would never work," Ash said with tears in her eyes.

"That's because you're both too stubborn to let it," he said and left the house. A few minutes later, she heard the sound of his bike as he left for his house on the other end of town and then nothing but silence. She went to her room, and since she didn't have any pajamas, she slept in just her bra and underwear. As soon as her head touched the pillow, she was out.

CHAPTER 39

THE NEXT MORNING, Ash came walking out in just her bra and underwear and went into the kitchen. This was how they always walked around their apartment over in New Haven in the mornings when they would get ready for class, because it was just the girls anyway. Bridgett was in here also in just her underwear and bra as well, drinking a cup of creo. Ash yawned and poured herself a cup and then looked around for something to eat.

"Rachael hasn't gotten up yet?" Ash asked Bridgett while she still scrounged around for food.

"She's not here. She left a note. I guess she got up and left somewhere with Nathan. Apparently, he never left last night," Bridgett told her.

"I'm not surprised. Is there anything to eat? I'm starving, and I don't want to use the replicator just for me."

"Nope. The cupboard is bare," Bridgett said, but Ash saw a slight grin on her face.

"What are you hiding?"

"Nothing," Bridgett said, setting down her cup of creo, and started walking to her room. When she got past Ash, she showed her an apple and took off running.

"Why, you little turd, give me that," Ash yelled and took off running across the living room to head her off. Just then, the front door opened, and Fâd, Nathan, Rachael, and Cory walked in and saw Ash running across the living room in nothing but her bra and underwear and Bridgett running for her room, holding an apple high over her head, in nothing but her bra and underwear too. The two girls were so engrossed in the quest for the apple that they didn't know anyone was there as Ash leaped over the sofa, tackling Bridgett. They both went down. Then Ash sat on her as she started tickling her and finally took the apple, holding it over her head, which was above the back of the sofa.

"The apple is mine. You will never defeat me, my pupil," Ash said, grinning wickedly, as she sat on Bridgett, who was laughing.

"You wanna bet?" Rachael said and came sailing over the back of the sofa, knocking Ash off Bridgett.

"Get her arms. I'll hold her legs," Rachael yelled to Bridgett.

"Hey, that's not fair, two against one. That's it. I'm going to kick both your asses," Ash yelled, but soon, she was laughing hysterically as Bridgett and Rachael were now tickling her as they held her down.

"It is fair too. You always beat us. Tickle harder, Rachael. Make her beg for mercy for once," Bridgett said, and now Ash was laughing and crying. Suddenly, the girls stopped when the guys looked over the back of the couch. There lay Ash, stretched out on her back, with Bridgett having her arms in a bar hold and Rachael holding her legs with her own entwined in them as Bridgett and Ash were dressed in nothing but a pair of skimpy underwear and lacy bras. Fâd just grinned and turned his head sideway to get a better view of Ash, and she turned bright red all over. Bridgett got up and started backing toward her bedroom door as Cory watched her with a big, ornery grin on his face as well.

"Rachael, can you please get off my legs?" Ash asked calmly, sitting up now. Rachael got off, and Ash stood up, calmly walked to her room, and shut the door behind her.

Rachael started laughing then. "She deserved that."

"Wow, I need to head home and take a cold shower," Fâd said, chuckling, with a slight bead of sweat on his forehead.

"Yeah. So do I," Cory added, chuckling and sweating too.

"Is that how you girls act and dress all the time in the morning?" Nathan asked Rachael and amazingly was perfectly calm, which wasn't like him.

"Oh yeah, but they must be feeling modest today, because usually, we wear absolutely nothing," Rachael told him with an evil grin.

"Are you serious?" Cory asked in disbelief.

"No. Wow, guys are so gullible," Rachel said, giggling, as she and Nathan headed to her room. Nathan looked at Fâd and Cory, grinning.

A few minutes later, Ash walked out completely dressed but was still embarrassed because she wouldn't look at anyone and walked over to the kitchen where Fâd was leaning against the counter. "I take it you're hungry?" he asked with a cocky grin.

"Starving. Couldn't you tell?" Ash replied with an ornery smirk.

"And what would you do for something to eat, tackle your friend in your bra and panties again? Because that was rather entertaining."

"Just about anything," Ash blurted out and then regretted what she said because Fâd pulled out a covered plate of her favorite watorian breakfast, which he had hidden behind his back that he had brought with him, and held it under her nose so she could smell it. Her stomach immediately started growling loud enough that he even heard it, then he got real close and looked down at her.

"You said anything." His grin was so evil.

Ash closed her eyes and wrinkled up her nose. "Yeah."

"Then you have to be nice to me all day until you go to bed no matter what happens."

"Deal," Ash said, letting out the breath she was holding as she held out her hands, and he gave her the plate. She went over to the table and started eating like crazy as Fâd came over and gave her a juice bottle, laughing.

"Slow down. You're going to choke. You act like you haven't eaten for days. You just had pizza last night."

"Only one piece because everyone pissed me off, calling me the ice queen, and before that, I hadn't eaten for almost thirty hours," Ash said with a mouth full of food.

"I can see you still haven't learned manners, talking with your mouth full. Just try to keep it in your mouth this time," Fâd told her, grinning.

Ash started laughing, remembering when she spit her food all over the place and almost on him, then she choked, of course, and Fâd started beating her on the back. Bridgett finally came out of her room wearing some clothes that actually fit her this time but still looking embarrassed. Cory was at her side instantly with a plate of breakfast too, and this seemed to make her forget the early ordeal as she came over and sat down at the table across from Ash.

"Where did you get those clothes?" Ash asked, looking her over.

"Nera sent them over while you were outside last night pouting. You have some too, in your closet. She knew we didn't have any clothes."

"I do? I didn't even look in there this morning. And what do you mean any clothes? I always bring a spare pair of boots just in case. Remember, be prepared. How many times was that pounded in our heads?" Ash said, making quotation marks with her fingers to emphasize her meaning, and started giggling.

"What does she mean?" Cory asked Bridgett.

"You remember when we first met you three and we used those paint bullets on you? Well, our instructor and commander was Justin, the private who made us clean everything up because Ash had too many disagreements with all the other officers. She's lucky her father is an admiral and she didn't get court-martialed, especially with the Commander Williams incident. Of course, he never found out what happened either."

"What happened?" Fâd asked, standing beside Ash, and grabbed a piece of her breakfast and ate it. Ash gave him a dirty look, but he just mouthed the words "Be nice" to her.

"I'd rather not say," Ash replied and continued eating, trying to avoid the question.

"Come on, what happened? Tell us. You can't leave us hanging like this," Cory asked, because now Fâd was too busy helping Ash eat, and she was slapping his hand away from her plate. Rachael and Nathan came out of her room and walked over to the kitchen.

"What are you guys talking about? What happened?" Rachael asked as she grabbed a bottle of cold water and put it up against her forehead. It was definitely apparent she wasn't feeling good, and Nathan was very attentive to her, getting her whatever she wanted.

"We were talking about the whole Commander Williams incident with Ash," Bridgett told her, and Rachael now looked mad.

"You should have done more to that bastard. I think he got off pretty easy," Rachael told her and then grimaced a little and turned away as Nathan came up and put his hand on her back. Ash noticed Rachael take a bottle of pills out of her pocket and took one. Ash figured Rachael must be finally feeling the aftereffects of their crash because she was sore all over from it as well.

"Ash, what happened?" It was Fâd now with a serious look on his face asking, and she knew there was no getting out of it this time.

"He attacked me," Ash said and stuffed her mouth full of food.

"You mean combat wise, for training," Fâd said as if this was no big deal.

"No" was all Ash said and continued to chew her food, avoiding looking at him. Fâd's face changed from "No big deal" to one of pure rage.

"What the hell did he do?" he asked her forcefully, now looking straight at her, but she continued to eat, avoiding his glare, and wouldn't reply. It was Bridgett who spoke next.

"Ash was in the locker room by herself because we had already showered and changed, and I had to have my gun checked out, so Rachael went with me. Commander Williams came in and, while Ash was getting dressed, jumped her from behind and threw her to the ground before she could do anything. Thank goodness for her fighting skills, because the next thing anyone knew, Williams came flying through a tempered glass window. He suffered broken ribs, a broken collarbone, and separated shoulder. When the admiral asked what happened, Ash told him they had a disagreement about how things were being handled, so the admiral assigned a new commander to us, and Ash got posting for the next month straight as punishment," Bridgett told them, looking at Ash with a look of sympathy on her face.

"Why didn't you tell your father the truth?" Cory asked her, confused why she had held the truth back, because this was serious.

"Because it's humiliating. I didn't want everyone to know that, especially my father. I handled the situation, beat the crap out of the guy, done and over with. If the truth came out, it would have been on my record, which is something I don't want on it. I would rather it say insubordination for beating up my commanding officer instead of being attacked by commanding officer, exhibiting inappropriate actions," Ash told them. Then she got up and started to walk away, but Fâd grabbed her arm and was now looking her in the face.

"That guy should be dead. I'll kill him if I ever see him."

"And so would have my dad if I had told him, which was why I didn't. Don't you see? He would have lost respect from his crew over time. It's always a double standard for women, always will be. You don't know how many times we had it thrown in our faces that we're just women? 'Go and fix supper. Shouldn't you be out having babies? Your job's to take care of your man.' No, if I had said something, it would have turned around, and I would have been accused of leading him on and instigating the whole thing, which would have left doubt in my father's mind even though he loves me, and I could not bear that," Ash told him and was now trying not to cry, but Fâd pulled her into his arms then and held her tightly as she cried for the first time over the whole thing, leaning her head up against his chest. Even when she told Rachael and Bridgett, she showed no emotion, always being a stone.

"Ash, I mean it, if I ever run into him, I will kill him, and there's nothing you can do to stop me," Fâd told her and leaned his head down on hers. Ash finally regained her composure, and Fâd released her.

"Okay. Anyone else with dark secrets in their closet, now's the time to get it out in the open during our group session here," Ash said with wet eyes, smirking, and everyone started chuckling.

"Well, where do I begin? There was this one time when…" Nathan said, and Rachael hit him in the shoulder, telling him to knock it off, and started giggling. Of course, everyone else was also laughing; but soon, they all finished up in the kitchen and headed to the front door and outside.

Nathan and Rachael climbed on his bike, pulling on helmets. Cory was helping Bridgett put on a helmet, and then they climbed on his as he put on his helmet. Ash followed Fâd over to his bike, and he handed her a helmet, and she put it on, which amazingly fit her, and then climbed on behind him. He looked back at her, and she could barely see him through his visor, but she had no problem seeing his ornery grin, which showed his small white fangs.

He fired up his bike as the others took off, racing down the road, and Ash knew she was in trouble. She hung on to his waist tightly. He wheeled the bike around by putting one foot on the ground and causing the hover bike to spin around him, and then the front of the bike came up in the air and blasted forward as if someone had shot it out of a gun. Her hair was whipping around behind her from under her helmet.

They were flying down the road and, in no time, actually caught up with the others. They all turned the corner and headed altogether, racing down the main road of the town, causing some of the people on the sidewalks and even a few in hover vehicles to yell at them or honk their horns. By now, Ash was laughing and having a blast; and in no time, they pulled up to the front of the ship. Fâd shut down the bike. She got off and took off her helmet, grinning ear to ear, and she could see that Fâd was also grinning.

"I think you broke one of my ribs hanging on so tightly," he teased her as they walked into the cargo bay.

"Yeah, right. It was like trying to wrap my arms around a rock."

"You know it. What can I say?" he teased and flexed one of his biceps at her. She just shook her head, then he shoved her away and took off running up the stairs with Ash running after him to hit him. Cory and Bridgett headed straight to the engine room as Nathan and Rachael went up to the bridge.

Nathan walked over to one of the many consoles and started pulling up a grid system on the screen in front of him of the shielding for the ship. Rachael went and stood beside him and watched the screen. "Pull up the kinetic transmitters on the shield," she asked him, and he did. She started counting the faulty ones.

"Nine. That's not bad, and they look to be mostly focused around the recently repaired area," she said, then walked over to where the harness and metal gun were lying and started putting the harness on.

"What are you doing, beautiful?" Nathan asked her with a frown on his face.

"Going to climb on top of the ship," Rachael said, grinning, as she continued to harness up.

"I don't think so," he said and grabbed her hand.

"Oh, come on, handsome, you're not going to start bossing me around already? Besides, have you ever fixed shields before?"

"No, but I think I can figure it out fairly easily."

"Well, I have gone many times up there, though," Rachael said, grinning, pointing skyward.

"Yeah, but now you have to deal with gravity down here," Nathan told her, still concerned.

"That's what makes it even that much more fun and challenging," she replied as a big grin now creased her face, and Nathan couldn't help but grin back.

"Gorgeous, you are so totally crazy. Damn, I love you," Nathan told her and made sure her harness was snug and secure.

"I know, and now you're stuck with me for the rest of you life."

"I wouldn't want it any other way," Nathan replied, still grinning.

"Neither would I. Now kiss me and throw me up there," Rachael said, and Nathan leaned down and softly kissed her lips, then grinned and grabbed her waist and threw her easily through the open hatch in the ceiling. Rachael stood on top of the ship and looked around in awe. It was so high up, and she could see everything. "Beautiful, is everything okay?" Nathan's voice came over her earpiece.

"This is so awesome! Wow, I can see for miles. Oh, look, there's where we're staying. I feel like king of the mountain. Hear me roar. ROAR!" she yelled out, and the noise carried on the slight breeze that was blowing. Nathan was inside, laughing at her. She was as crazy as he was. He couldn't help but love her as much as he did. Even if you took away the imprinting that was there all those years ago, he would always love her no matter what, and now he felt calm and settled knowing she would always be his for the rest of their lives.

Rachael clamped onto one of the several harness hooks located all over the outer hull of the ship and walked over to the open hatch and leaned in. "Hey, big guy, can you hand me the other big gun?" Rachael asked with a rotten grin.

"The other one? We only have the one," Nathan said, confused, then leaned his head back with a grin and started chuckling and walked over, picking up the rivet gun, and took it to her. "You are so bad, woman. What am I going to do with you?" Nathan asked her, climbing up the ladder and handing her the gun through the open hatch.

"Oh, I can think of something," she said back suggestively.

"Then get down here," he said with a wicked grin.

"You come up here. Haven't you ever wanted to be on top of the world?" Rachael said to him, and in a flash, Nathan climbed up through the hatch.

During this time, Ash and Fâd were in the gun room, carefully dismantling the firing head and proton generator from the cannon so they could get to the barrel. An hour later, it was ready to be removed, and they both got hold of a side and lifted it off the pins that were holding it in place. Both their faces turned bright red as they strained to lift it because it was so heavy. They walked straddling it and carefully sat the head down on the floor and leaned over with their hands on their knees, panting from the exertion.

"How did you guys ever get that thing in here?" Ash asked, still trying to catch her breath.

Fâd looked at her and stood up, stretching his back, and grinned. "It took the three of us plus a mobile lift."

"Let's take a break. I need to walk off that one," Ash said and stood up stretching her back as they headed to the bridge to see what Nathan and Rachael were doing. They climbed the stairs and walked to the bridge and could see Nathan at the shield controls, laughing.

"What's so funny?" Fâd asked him, and Nathan flipped on the ship's comm.

"Oh yeah? Take that. Oh, you want some of this too? Ha, got you. Man, I love having a big gun in my hands." Rachael's voice was heard over the comm system, and everyone laughed.

"Where is she?" Ash asked, laughing, and Nathan pointed up at the ceiling.

"Hey, beautiful. We have company," Nathan told her over the comm. They all heard a sliding noise and then some knocking up front, and there was Rachael, hanging upside down near the nose of the ship, looking in one of the windows, waving and grinning.

"Hey, Ash. How's it hanging? Get it, hanging?" she said, laughing at her own joke.

"You're crazy. Yeah, I get your joke," Ash said back to her and then turned around as Rachael climbed back up and continued what she was doing. Nathan then read off a grid section of the hull that was showing "Damaged" on the screen, and Rachael was securing it or replacing the kinetic transmitters if need be.

"Okay, is it just me, or does this feel a little scary having a crazy woman up there fixing the shields that could save our lives in a fight someday?" Fâd asked them nervously.

"If I didn't know Rachael, I would feel the same way right now, but she's very good with shield repair. That, at least, was one of the things she learned and excelled at in our weaponry classes," Ash told him and could see this made Fâd feel a little better.

"Yeah, she's a little different. That's why I love her so much. She can actually wear me out," Nathan told them with a rotten grin.

"That I find hard to believe. You once told us that you could outlast the jump drive on a ship," Fâd replied with an accusing look.

"Believe what you want, but it's a done deal now," Nathan said and turned back to his console. Ash was a little confused by this comment, especially by the look on Fâd's face, as he seemed a little perturbed by it.

They headed back to the gunnery room, and both looked down the open barrel now. Ash noticed it was going to be a tight fit even for her and stood up as Fâd continued to look in it. "You're not going to be able to move in there," he said and stood up and looked back at Ash, who was now starting to remove her shirt.

"You're not climbing in there in just your bra, are you? I mean, it wouldn't bother me, but I'm just thinking about you, what you're comfortable with," he said, grinning, and Ash gave him a dirty look and pulled her shirt over her head, revealing the tank top she had on under it. "Damn, I thought you were going to make this interesting," he said with a look of disappointment on his face but then saw the bruises on her collarbone from the crash, and a frown crossed his face.

"Oh, ha ha," Ash said back to him as she now grabbed her hair and wound it up into a ball and fastened it at the back of her head with an elastic band she had around her wrist. She saw the scowl on his face and knew what he was looking at.

Fåd reached out and gently touched her collarbone where one of the bruises was. "Does that hurt? Did you get those checked out?" he asked, now full of concern.

Ash grinned. "No, they don't hurt, and I'm fine. Trust me, I've had worse," she said and looked over at the cannon. Fåd looked a little mad at her confession. Then she walked over, grabbed a pair of protective glasses and a blue light used to show metal fatigue, and walked back over to the opening of the barrel and put her arms above her head and looked at Fåd. "Pick me up and put me in there," she told him, and he looked at her as if she had just gone off the deep end.

"What?"

"There's not enough room to crawl, so you're going to have to stick me in there and even move me around when I tell you," Ash said, annoyed.

"How am I supposed to move you around?" he asked in disbelief.

"By grabbing my hips. Now let's get this done before I chicken out," she said, still with her arms above her head. Fåd let out a loud sigh and then picked her up like a post and stuffed her in the barrel, headfirst. "Push me all the way in. I want to start at the tip of the barrel." Her voice echoed off the metal of the barrel, and Fåd pushed as Ash shot to the front. "Okay, that's good." Fåd stood there for a few minutes, watching her feet, which were the only thing sticking out now, and started chuckling to himself. "Okay, turn me onto my stomach." He squatted down and reached up into the barrel, barely having enough room for his arms with her in there, and firmly grabbed her hips. She started giggling, and he let go, pulling his arms back out.

"What's so funny?" he asked her with a frown.

"Nothing. I'm just ticklish," Ash said, still giggling.

Fâd grinned and reached back into the barrel, which was up to his shoulders, firmly grabbing her hips again and spinning her around very quickly and letting go. He could feel the blood pumping rapidly through him from the contact he had with her. Just touching her always sent shock waves through him. He was standing there, talking to her, when Cory and Bridgett came in.

"We're heading over to the depot. Is there anything you need?" Cory asked Fâd.

"If you can find two T-9 magnesium plugs, that would surely be appreciated," Ash said from inside the barrel. Bridgett and Cory looked around Fâd and now saw Ash's feet sticking out of the barrel and started laughing.

"How come you're not doing that?" Cory asked him.

"There's no way I could fit in there. She barely fits. I have to move her in and out and spin her as it is," Fâd told them, chuckling.

"Speaking of that, I'm ready to move," Ash told him, and Fâd grabbed her ankles and pulled her back. "That's good. Stop."

"Okay. You two have fun," Bridgett told them as she and Cory left, laughing.

"Spin me." And once again, Fâd reached into the barrel, grabbing her hips, which caused her to start giggling again, and even Fâd chuckled. He turned her onto her back. Ash used the blue light and was shining it on every inch of the inside of the barrel when, finally, she came across a hairline crack.

"Aha! I found one. Hand me the metal meld." Fâd walked over to the tool chest and took out a small tool that looked like a small pistol with an orange shield around the barrel. He then stuck his arm into the barrel with it in his hand and pushed it up toward her with his arm on her stomach, and then he hit some resistance.

"Oh, sorry. I didn't mean to hit that," he said and started laughing.

"Oh! Ha ha. A little to the right. There the path is clear," she said and started giggling as he pushed the melder up between her breasts to almost her chin where she could get her hand on it. He kept his arm there while she wielded the crack and then handed it back to him. He had sweat running off him now, and it wasn't because it was hot in there. He quickly pulled his arm out. "All right. Pull me out a little ways. Good. Stop." Fâd grabbed her ankles and pulled, and now her hips were out of the barrel, and then he was grabbing them and spinning her onto her stomach. A few minutes later, he was pulling her out some more, and now her lower back was showing out of the barrel. Again, he spun her over to her back, so it was her flat, stomach showing. By now, he was holding her up with one hand, so she didn't put a bind on her back, and he noticed how she weighed nothing to him. She found another crack, and he handed her the meld gun and this time got it to her without hitting blockage.

A couple of hours later, she was finally out far enough that she could reach the rest without having to be in the barrel, and he lifted her easily out and stood her up like she was nothing. Ash was covered in black dust, but she turned around and finished inspecting the rest of the barrel. Even Fâd had black all over himself from touching her, and he took off his shirt, wearing only his dog tags, which hung down his bare chest, because it was starting to get hot in the room and used it to wipe the sweat from his face. Ash finished the inspection and repairs, and by now, they both had sweat pouring off them.

Fâd gave Ash his shirt to wipe her face off with since they didn't have a towel or anything else to clean up with. He had a large bottle of water and took a couple of drinks off it and handed it to her. Then he went over and squatted down, looking into the now fixed barrel.

"So do you think that will work?" he asked as she took a couple of drinks of his water. Ash looked down at him and couldn't help herself as a devious feeling came over her and started pouring water over his head. He jumped up and went to take the bottle from her, and she quickly turned her back to him, using her backside to block him. They both were laughing as he wrapped one arm around her waist, holding her against him and trying to grab her hand that had the water bottle in it. His face was right next to hers, and their cheeks were now pressing against each other, and they both were still laughing as they fought over the water bottle.

"Give me that, you little vermin." He laughed, and Ash could smell him now. She pressed her face more into his, and he immediately responded. He stopped reaching for the bottle and pulled her tightly into himself, wrapping both arms around her. He rubbed his face up against hers and then down her neck and across the soft part between her neck and shoulder.

Fâd opened his mouth, exposing his now elongated teeth, and skimmed them across her exposed skin. Then he ran his mouth back up her neck as she leaned back into him, giving him full control over her. He suddenly stopped and pushed back from Ash, spinning around and away from her, fighting back what he wanted desperately to do and just about did.

Fâd could feel the elongated teeth in his mouth and even taste the venom that was on them. He spitted on the floor to get the taste out of his mouth. Finally satisfied they had gone back to normal, he turned around, and Ash was using his shirt again to wipe her face down. She looked completely flushed, and sweat was pouring off her.

"Wow. That was different," he said jokingly.

"Yeah. What the hell was in that water?" Ash teased back, and Fâd laughed, taking the bottle from her and then tipping it up and over her head, pouring some on her. She didn't even resist because it felt good right, and he then poured the rest over his head.

"Come on. Let's go sit outside for a while. It's so damn hot in here," he said and grabbed her hand, dragging her through the door and then down the stairs, then he let go. They both walked over to the bottom of the large cargo door that was lying open on the ground and sat down, letting the cool breeze blow across both of them, fighting what they had wanted for years to be released.

CHAPTER 40

Bridgett was going through every little thing at the supply depot on the barracks in Pantier. Not one crate escaped her attention, and already, they had a pretty good stack of items on the hover cart. Cory couldn't believe her. She was like a little kid in here who just found a great treasure. She walked over to a crate that had a large round metal canister next to it with a toxic symbol on it and bent down so she could read the label on the side, then jumped up quickly and looked over at Cory with the biggest grin on her face he had ever seen.

"What is it?" he asked.

"Everyone's way to the stars," Bridgett replied excitedly.

"So it's a power source?" Cory asked, grinning.

"Not just any power source. These are Trillium power cells. They're used in destroyers and battleships, and this is the new version that has double the life span as the old ones, which lasts over 110 years, not to mention twenty megs more of core energy than the others. They are currently outfitting some of the older ships with these right now."

"Yeah, but if these are made for destroyers and battleships, won't that be too much for our ship?" Cory asked, concerned. He didn't think Fâd would be too happy if they blew up the ship, especially after all the years and hard work they had put in, not to mention the parts.

"It will be perfect. Like I said, that ship is not standard. I know it's a prototype, and when I looked at the core chamber, it was built so modifications could be made. It was as if the builder of it knew that technology would continue to change and the ship with it. The power cells in it now aren't near enough, as you well know. Granted, they are used on ships of that size and are fine, but this ship needs a lot more power because she is packing some high-tech stuff that I've never seen before, and I'm sure you haven't either. I can't wait to see all she has when it powers up," Bridgett said and started looking around nervously.

"What's the matter?" Cory asked, also looking around.

"Well, if they have one of these here, that means it's meant for something. They just don't keep spares lying around. Let's get it out of here before someone stops us," Bridgett told him. Cory came over, and between both of them, they barely got it up on the hover cart as it was now straining under the weight. Cory was shocked at the weight of the power cells. They started heading for the large bay doors when Bridgett stopped him again, and they both hid behind some large crates with their goods just in case someone was in the large warehouse and saw them with the power cells.

"How are we going to get this over to the ship?" she asked him quietly.

"Leave that to me." He grinned and started punching in some commands on his multitool, and then they headed to the bay doors. When they got close, Cory had Bridgett stay with their cart, looked around to make sure no one was about, and walked over, opening up the large bay doors. They slid open as an MAAV backed up into the warehouse and stopped. Cory walked over to the side and hit another switch on the vehicle, and the side doors slid open. Then he ran back over to Bridgett, and they both hurriedly steered the cart over to it and between the two of them carefully carried the cells into it. Bridgett secured them, and then they got the rest of the stuff. Bridgett went and sat up in the other front seat of the MAAV as Cory shut the doors and jumped into the driver's seat, and they quickly got out of there.

"Where did you get this?" Bridgett asked, bouncing around, trying to look the MAAV over.

Cory grinned at her. "It's ours. We had to leave it parked by the barracks since we were using that little carian infiltrator, but now with this other ship, it will fit easily, including our shuttle and other things. Plus, I'll be able to take my bike too," he replied, and Bridgett started giggling.

Instead of heading to the ship, they went through town, which caused a few stares, but they quickly subsided since this wasn't the first time an MAAV was seen on the street since this was, after all, a military colony. These weren't your everyday drive up the street kind of vehicles, though. MAAV stood for mobile armored assault vehicle, and in a way, it looked like an armored tank but more streamlined. But as the name implied, they were large, holding over six to eight people with all their armor and weapons, not to mention the vehicle itself had two mech guns on both sides that could fire and move in a 180-degree direction up or down.

On the very top of the vehicle was a cannon mounted on a mobile turret that fired an explosive-tipped mag shell that could blow up a fighter jet easily and, if hit just right, even a frigate. But unlike most vehicles, the MAAV moved on a track with four sprockets on each side, giving it speed and two large, solid polyprion front tires, an almost indestructible synthetic material that is also used in most armor giving it great maneuverability. The MAAV also had reinforced carbine metal plating and could generate its own kinetic shielding when needed.

Bridgett realized it definitely wasn't built for comfort and was rather rough-riding. She was bouncing around in the seat, and thank goodness she was strapped in, or she would have been all over the place. She looked back at the cells to make sure they were okay, and they seemed to be doing better than her. Cory looked over at her and started grinning; even he wasn't bouncing around as much.

"Why aren't you getting the crap shaken out of you?" she asked in a vibrating voice.

"Because I have some weight behind me, unlike you who weigh nothing," he replied, laughing at her.

They finally pulled up to the guesthouse. They had decided to fix everyone something to eat before they headed to the ship with their confiscated find. Cory pulled right up to the house and shut down the MAAV as Bridgett unbuckled and checked the cells. He pressed the button on the door, and the double doors on the side slid open. He and Bridgett stepped out, then he shut the doors and pressed some buttons on his multitool, locking down the MAAV, so if anyone tried to touch it, they would get a nasty shock.

They walked into the house and over to the kitchen. Bridgett punched in sandwiches for everyone on the replicator controls. Cory got a water bottle out of the refrigerator and opened it, taking a few drinks, then handed it to Bridgett, who drank the rest down. They both looked at each other, and suddenly, Bridgett jumped into Cory's arms and wrapped her arms around his neck and her legs around his waist. They started madly kissing each other with his arms holding her tightly to him.

Cory headed around the furniture and toward her room with her wrapped around him, still wildly kissing each other, bumping into the sofa and the love seat, knocking a picture off the wall and even a light pillar off an end table. Finally, he got to her room; and just as the door slid open, he fell through the open space with her still clinging to him.

An hour later, they walked out of her room as he was pulling his shirt back on. She was picking stuff up from the floor that they had knocked down, and Cory hung the picture back up that fell. Bridgett went and took the sandwiches out of the replicator as he went to the fridge, now with a small towel in his hand, and took out some ice crystals, then wrapped them up in the towel. He walked over to Bridgett and pulled the collar back from her neck and put the towel on two tiny puncture wounds between her neck and shoulder, then reached into his pocket and pulled out a pill bottle and handed it to her.

"You're going to need these later," he told her.

"How long have you been carrying those around?" Bridgett asked him, curious, taking them from him.

"I picked them up before I came over this morning," he told her with a smile.

"What if I weren't ready?"

"Then I would have just kept them until you were."

"How long have you known?" Bridgett asked him as he readjusted the ice pack for her.

"Since we were little. I imprinted younger than usual. Fifteen was the youngest anyone had ever imprinted, but mine was when I first met you. Fâd did when he barely turned fifteen, and Nathan wasn't long after that."

"So why all the girlfriends and then just avoiding us altogether? Did you ever think that maybe we felt the same way about you guys?" Bridgett asked, a little mad now.

"The three of us made a pact right after Nathan imprinted on Rachael that we wouldn't interfere with your dreams and goals. The three of you always talked about serving on the *Justification* and that all your families were there, and we didn't want to take that away from you. We always knew we would have our own ship, and if you were with us, you would have to leave your families and probably never see them again since we would always be going the opposite direction. The girlfriends were our way of trying to push you away and put a barrier between us, but try as hard as we did, we were always drawn back to you three and always will be no matter what happens," Cory told her.

"You broke my heart when I saw you with other girls," Bridgett told him as tears started down her face.

Cory reached down and wiped her tears away with his hand. "I know, and that's why I couldn't do it anymore. When I heard you scream out in the lunchroom that time, I felt like I had been stabbed with a knife. I knew you were hurting, and I had to talk to you, but we know how that went over.

"Then when I saw those boys talking to you at the game, I realized what I had been doing to you and how I was hurting you. I admit, over the years, I've been out with other women, but you were always on my mind. I could never get you out of it. I've always loved you, even without the imprinting. Then when you three showed up here, Nathan and I told Fâd, to hell with the pact," Cory told her, pulling Bridgett into his arms and holding her tightly.

"You don't know how long I wanted this and you. I have always loved you too," Bridgett said to him, wrapping her arms around him.

"Oh yes, I do. But the real question now is, when are you going to tell Ash you're going with me?" Cory asked, looking down at her face.

"I don't know, but the opportunity will present itself," Bridgett told him.

"Well, it better be soon, because you only have two more months of school left, then I'll be coming for you." Cory smiled down at her, and they kissed.

Over at the ship, Fâd and Ash were back in the gun room after their break when Nathan walked in, also shirtless, since it was hotter than Hades on the ship. "So what is it you need?" he asked, and Fâd pointed at the cannon.

"We need to line it up on the turret, and Ash will guide us."

"Are you kidding me? That thing took three of us and a lift to move it, and I could hardly walk the next day," Nathan told him.

"It's not as heavy now with the head off, so quit being a baby," Fâd replied. Nathan walked over to it with a frown on his face. Ash went and got in front of Fâd so she could guide the cannon into the slots. He looked down at her. "Are you ready, Ash?"

"Yeah."

Fâd reached around her and grabbed hold of the cannon, and Nathan gripped the other side. Even Ash grabbed it to help. Fâd counted to three, and they lifted. The cannon came up, and both men were now straining, and their muscles were bulging from the weight. Ash was also straining and guiding it into the slots, then the cannon slid in and clicked as it locked into place. Both men stood back and leaned down with their hands on their knees as sweat poured off them and they tried to catch their breath. Even Ash was exhausted and just sat down next to the cannon, and Fâd looked at her, concerned. "Are you okay?" he asked her.

"Yeah, I will be in a minute. What about you, Nathan?" Ash asked, still breathing hard.

"I hope so, or there's going to be one pissed-off blond," he said with a weak grin and stood up straight, stretching his back, and asked if there was anything else they needed his help for and left when Fâd told him no.

They were still in there when Cory and Bridgett showed up and brought them sandwiches and something to drink. "Wow, you two are filthy and all sweaty. Crap, it's hotter than hell in here," Bridgett told them.

"I know, but we almost have this cannon ready to sim fire," Ash told her, grinning.

"Well, you won't have any power for about an hour as I will be pulling the core. And I'll warn you, when I put in the new one, all hell might break loose. Who knows what was running when she went down? And if anyone asks, you know nothing about any missing Trillium power cells," Bridgett said, grinning.

"Okay. Is that something that might blow up my ship?" Fâd asked, concerned.

Bridgett just grinned and left the room with Cory following her, shrugging his shoulders. Fâd turned and looked at Ash with a worried look on his face. "Don't worry. She knows what she's doing. She has the ranking of first engineer," Ash told him and laid down on the floor beside the cannon so she could start hooking up the controls underneath through the side access panel.

"She does?"

"Yeah, and Rachael is a level 10 marksman. Can you believe that?" Ash told him, and Fâd was rather impressed.

"What about you?"

"I'm a level 8 weaponry, almost a nine," Ash told him as she continued working.

"How come I'm not surprised?" Fâd said and started working on the head to replace the two magnesium plugs that were bad. They had just barely started when the power went down, and now they were working in almost darkness.

"Well, Bridg pulled the core. No sim firing now," Ash said and continued as Fâd set up artificial lighting for them since there was no power at all now to run even lights. Finally, she got done and closed up the access panel, then sealed it. Ash got up, stretched, and walked over to where Fâd was just finishing up with the head. He stood up and looked down at her.

"Are you ready to lift this damn thing up again?"

"Not really, but let's get it done," she said, not looking forward to it.

They both bent down, and Fâd counted to three. They lifted it, gritting their teeth, and walked it slowly over to the cannon. It was a little harder to put back on the pins, but they finally did and were now completely wiped out. Fâd hooked everything back up on the head and closed it, sealing the outer edge, and stood back, looking at the now installed proton cannon as Ash sat on the floor, leaning up against the wall, totally exhausted.

During this time, down in the engine room, Cory was helping Bridgett refit the Trillium power cells, which looked like four pulsating long blue tubes attached to a silver disk. He and Bridgett had thick magnesium gloves on since the Trillium would freeze their hands instantly and they would lose the limb. They both carefully lifted it out of the protective canister it was in and sat it down inside the core chamber, clicking it into place as the top dispersion cap came down onto the tubes.

Cory was amazed at Bridgett; she worked like a surgeon, only the patient was the ship, and made a bunch of modifications to the output linkups to be able to handle the increase in power. Finally, after an hour, the ship was ready to come online after she closed up the core chamber and sealed it.

She looked over at Cory with a big grin on her face. "Are you ready to bring her back to life?"

"Let's do it, babe," he said, grinning as well.

"Attention, everyone. I'm starting her up. Be ready for anything," Bridgett said over her comm to all of them. She took a deep breath as she stood at the main control panel in front of the core chamber. Cory came up and stood beside her, smiling, and she pressed the main button. Instantly, the chamber lit up and started pulsing even more until it was pulsing a steady beat, almost like a heart.

Everything in the engine room came online, and the engines started making their low humming noise as they powered up in standby.

All through the ship, doors that had been manually opened slid closed, lights came on, and every console, control board, and panel lit up. Fâd and Ash were standing, looking around, as the door to the gun room slid shut on them and all the lights came on and the instrument panels, controls, and consoles lit up. Suddenly, the guns came online, and the cannon moved to the turret through the sliding door in the hull to the outside like it was supposed to do during a battle. It started powering up, and the door sealed behind it, leaving it out for firing. The two forbs mech guns dropped through the floor as the doors resealed over them, and Ash and Fâd could hear them clicking to load artillery, but luckily, they didn't put clips in them yet. The problem was, though the cannon could fire, it had its own generator that was now charging.

"FÂD, STOP IT. IT'S POWERING UP!" Ash yelled, and Fâd ran over to the controls and quickly typed in his authorization code, which all captains had for the weaponry to cancel what their last orders were. Finally, the guns powered down and returned to their standby positions back in the gun room. Fâd looked over at Ash, and they both let out a sigh of relief, but that was cut short when they heard a scream come over their comm link.

They both ran to the door, which slid open with ease, and started for the stairs, but as they passed the elevator, it opened up, and they jumped in it as Fâd told the computer to take them to the bridge. In no time, they stepped out on the bridge and saw a frantic and scared Nathan over at the pilot's seat, yelling into the comm, "Rachael, honey, answer me please."

"That was so awesome. Now I know what it feels like to be a photon cartridge getting shot out of a cannon," Rachael said over her comm.

Nathan breathed a sigh of relief. "Are you okay?"

"Yeah. I'm going to have some bruises, but I'm fine thanks to you, lover boy."

"I'm coming to get you!" Nathan told her, worried.

"Nope. I'll be in just a few once I climb back up. I'm kind of hanging down in front of the cargo bay right now. Hey, this thing has some really cool running lights."

"Gorgeous, just get in here," Nathan said, flustered with her and still worried.

"Coming, babe."

Nathan turned and looked at Fâd and Ash. It was very clear he had just gotten the scare of a lifetime by the look on his face. "I thought I lost her. I never want to go through that again," he said to them with wet eyes.

"What happened?" Fâd asked him.

"When the ship came online, Rachael had just finished the last kinetic transmitter. Apparently, the kinetic shields were still on when the ship went down years ago. And when the power came back on, so did the shields, and Rachael got blasted off of them, which I quickly shut down."

Just then, the hatch made a hissing noise as the latching wheel turned and dropped down. Nathan ran over to it and reached up as Rachael slid down into his arms, and he hugged her tightly to himself. "Why didn't you answer me right away when I was calling you?" he asked, still very worried but chewing her out too.

"Well, when I had hit the end of the tether, it slammed me into my harness, knocking the wind out of me," Rachael said, smiling up at him.

"Let me look and see if there's anything major that we need to get taken care of right away," Nathan told her and helped get her out of the harness. Fâd and Ash came over to make sure she was okay too. Then Rachael took off her shirt and was in a half tank top under it, and now they could see large bruises on her shoulders and around her stomach where the harness cinched up, stopping her fall. But Ash saw something else; she had two small pinprick marks between her neck and shoulder.

"Oh, honey, you're going to be one sore little girl, but I don't see anything too major," Nathan said, checking her out all over.

"What about that? It looks like something had poked her," Ash said, pointing to the marks near her neck.

Fâd just looked down and was trying not to grin, but Rachael and Nathan were. Then Rachael looked over at Ash as a somber expression spread across her face. "Ash, there's something I need to tell you. These marks aren't from being poked."

"They're bonding marks, aren't they? You and Nathan are bonded," Ash said, and now her face looked pale as she started backing away.

"Ash, please, I love him, always have," Rachael said as Nathan put his arms around her and kissed her head.

"I know you do. I always knew you and Bridgett would be going with them one day, and trust me, I'm happy for you," Ash said, looking at Fâd, then turned and walked away, leaving the bridge. She took the stairs all the way down to the cargo bay and left out a side door of the bay to the outside since when the power came back on, the large cargo bay door had closed.

She was now crying. Their lives were changing, which she knew would one day. She always knew in the back of her mind that Bridgett and Rachael would be with Nathan and Cory eventually, but it was still painful knowing her best friends, who where like sisters to her, would be leaving. But that wasn't what was tearing her up inside; it was Fâd whom she didn't want to let go of.

She walked through the large shipyard, finally getting to the entrance, and left noticing how the day was over and evening was upon them. Ash walked along the road, heading back to town, when Fâd pulled up next to her on his bike and handed her the other helmet. She put it on and climbed on behind him. He took off down the road. He drove through town and then made the turn up the road to the guesthouse and pulled into the driveway. Ash got off, taking off the helmet and handing it to him. Fâd put it on the back and then turned the bike and left her standing there.

Ash watched him go as he disappeared down the road. Then she went into the house and took a shower since she was filthy. No sooner had she gotten out that the others arrived, talking excitedly. "Ash, come on. The guys want to take us to some place they said we'll like," Bridgett told her.

"I don't know. I'm pretty beat."

Just then, Fâd walked in, all cleaned up too. "Come on, you have to go. Trust me, you'll feel much better. Plus, we have food."

"All right. You got me at the food again," Ash said with a weak smile knowing in the back of her mind that she could never refuse him anything ever again.

* * *

They all headed outside. It was now dark as everyone climbed on the bikes. Ash put on the helmet Fâd handed to her, and it felt weird with her wet hair. Plus, Ash noticed his hair was wet as well, for he had just showered too. She climbed on behind him and now could see the bike's running lights since it was dark out, and the machine looked rather ominous with them, not to mention the bright-blue kinetic discs for wheels. The others took off, racing down the road, but Fâd just sat there watching them and then turned and looked back at Ash.

"Do you trust me?" he asked her through her earpiece.

"Yes," she replied.

He wheeled the bike around and shot across the road and into the trees. Ash closed her eyes and laid her head against his back as they flew through the woods in almost pitch-black, except where the bike's running lights barely lit up the ground under them, moving in and out of the trees at an unbelievable speed. She finally opened her eyes when she felt they were no longer weaving in and out and could see they were now crossing a large open meadow. The tree line was coming up fast again, and soon, they shot into them. Once again, it was extremely dark, but Fâd seemed to not have any problem with it.

He turned really sharply, and Ash felt like she was going to fall off, but he reached back and held her in place with one hand and then throttled again as the bike jumped with another burst of speed. They shot out of the trees and onto a wide trail and were now just a few feet behind the others. Fâd gunned it as they took off and started coming up on the others extremely fast, flying right past them. Ash could now see lights up ahead as they entered a large meadow that was covered with fluorescent plants lighting the place clear up.

Fâd stopped his bike and waited for the others to come up, and when he removed his helmet, Ash noticed that his white eyes glowed in the dark and had a hypnotic effect. She realized that they always had when it was dark out. She had just never seen them glow as bright like this before. She quickly looked away and turned her attention back to the meadow. It was amazing. Glowing plants were everywhere, and in the center of the meadow was a small lake, and you could see the bottom because even the plants in the water also glowed in many different colors.

Ash followed the lake to where the water came in, and it was easy to follow the channel because like the lake, the underwater plants glowed up the channel. It was like a magical place, and Ash finally got off the bike, wandering around, amazed by it.

"This is so cool," she said to Fâd, excited, as she spun around, looking at everything. He walked over to her and looked around too.

"Yeah. We found this place a year ago when we got our new bikes and was night racing on them," he told her, grinning as he watched the excitement on her face.

"How can you see where you're going like that? Those bikes don't put off enough light to be able to see that well," she asked, looking up at him.

"Ash, I can see in the dark. I thought you knew that. When our eyes change, we can see in the dark, among other things."

"Is that why they are glowing white right now?" she asked, curious.

"Yeah. When the lighting is low, our eyes magnify what light there is to help us see."

"They're so beautiful. I want some," Ash said and walked up to him to get a better look as he looked down at her.

"There's only one way you could ever get eyes like this," Fâd told her with a wicked grin.

"How's that?"

"Buy some eye lenses," he said, laughing, and grabbed her hand. They headed over to where everyone was now laying down blankets and pulling out something to eat. Fâd and Ash sat down on the blanket, and food was passed around to everyone as they all joked and talked about all the crazy things they used to do when they were kids together.

Finally, after everyone ate and had time for the food to settle, Nathan and Cory jumped up and started taking their clothes off. "Whoa! What are you doing?" Ash asked, nervous, especially when Fâd jumped up too and started to undress. Of course, Rachael was right with them, almost tearing her clothes off, but Bridgett was like Ash and didn't move.

"We're going swimming. The water's great. Come on, you two. It will help with sore muscles," Cory said.

"I didn't bring anything to swim in," Ash said as the guys all stripped down to their boxer briefs and Rachael stood in nothing but her bra and panties. Nathan grabbed her hand, and they raced to the water. Fâd looked at Ash, grinning, and then he took off and jumped into the water.

"Bridg, come on. You'll have fun," Cory begged her. Bridgett looked at Ash and then jumped up and removed her clothes, then grabbed Cory's hand, and they took off and both jumped in. Ash could see that everyone was having a blast, and she couldn't help but laugh at them, especially since the guys' eyes all glowed, and they looked funny out there like little specks.

Ash stood up and finally gave in and took her clothes off and ran down to the lake and dove in. She was shocked when she hit the water. She wasn't expecting it to be kind of warm, but it felt great on her tired body, almost rejuvenating. She surfaced and wiped the water from her face and suddenly got taken back down as Rachael and Bridgett jumped her and dragged her under. She easily outmaneuvered them, and when she came up, she was ready for war and had an evil grin on her face.

Rachael was the first one she attacked. She took her under, but Nathan pulled her off, which then brought Fâd to her rescue, and she helped Fâd get Nathan. They all decided to settle the dispute over who was the stronger by having a combat match, only it would be couple versus couple. Everyone swam over to a shallower area, and the girls got on the guys' shoulders.

"No prisoners," Fâd said, looking up at Ash, who was on his shoulders. She agreed, grinning wickedly, causing him to laugh as they smacked fists together.

The battle was on, and clearly, Ash and Fâd easily won. Ash had no problem knocking Rachael and Bridgett off Nathan and Cory, and Fâd had no problem holding Nathan and then Cory back. Finally, the others wanted to go rest, but Fâd had Ash follow him because he had something he wanted to show her. They swam up the channel, and he waited for Ash to come up close to him.

"We have to swim down here. Just stay with me," Fâd said, and she nodded her head and took a deep breath and dived down behind him. They went almost all the way to the bottom. Ash saw a cave, and they headed into it. Right before her lungs were ready to explode, they broke the surface, and she came up coughing. Fâd grabbed her and swam with her over to the bank. Ash was still coughing a little on her hands and knees on the bank but looked around and now was speechless.

They were in an underground cave that was lit up by glowing, colored crystals that were all over the walls and ceiling. Even the ground glowed green under their feet as it was also fluorescent, like the underwater plants. Ash had never seen anything so beautiful before in her life. Fâd went over and sat down on the ground as Ash noticed how his eyes now glowed green from the reflection of the light the ground was putting off. She stood up. He watched her as she looked at everything, and then she came and sat down next to him, and he looked down at her.

"Do you like it?" he asked with a smile on his face.

"It's hard to describe. It's wonderful."

He laid on the ground and folded his arms behind his head and looked up at the ceiling. "Yeah, and I will miss it when we leave this system."

Ash now looked down at him and rolled over on her stomach and rested her chin on her hands. "Do you think that's going to happen soon?"

Fâd looked over at her and brushed some of the loose strands of her hair away from her face. "I do. Things are heating up between council militia and us, and they are finally building up their forces, especially since Valhalla left a couple years ago. The other thing I've noticed—and I know your father and mine has too—is the increase in carian attacks. It's like they know there's a conflict and keep testing to see how far they can come into council space. I believe that when we pull out, they will eventually attack with a huge armada. Their spies are keeping them well-informed."

"We leave and everyone on this planet will die," Ash said sadly.

"Not necessarily. Council has a fairly large armada now, and they might be able to stop them."

"I doubt it. Look at the idiots we went to school with. If that's their future, they're in trouble."

"Nah, that was just the spoiled, rich military kids whose parents gave them everything," Fâd said, grinning.

"We are spoiled, rich military kids too, but we don't act that way. We know how to load and unload a gun and fight," Ash told him, and they both started grinning.

"Yeah, true. You have a point. So, Ash, what are you going to do once you finish school?" Fâd asked, now with a serious look, studying Ash's face.

"I guess serve on the *Justification* and go back into infantry. One of the few times I felt happy was when we infiltrated a base or freighter and took it back."

"You guess? I thought that was what you've always wanted? That was all you ever talked about when we were growing up. What about your father? You've always wanted to serve under him," Fâd asked, now sitting up, looking bewildered.

"I don't know anymore. Things change. My life has changed. Look at Rachael and Bridgett. We three were always going to be together and serve on the same ship, but that's changed now, and they are going with Nathan and Cory, which is how it should be. As for my father, yeah, I guess that's where I will be serving."

They both sat there, not saying a word, and finally, Fâd stood up and put his hand down for Ash. "We better get back. It's getting late."

Ash took it, and he pulled her up easily and right into his arms. Fâd looked down at Ash as she looked up into his glowing white eyes. Then he leaned his head down toward her but suddenly pulled away, releasing her, and walked over to the water's edge.

"Let's go," he said and dived into the water, and Ash jumped in right behind him. They both swam under the opening and then broke the surface on the other side. They both swam back to the lake and over to the bank where everyone was sitting and talking about the adventures they had while on their tour of duty.

"So, Ash, I'm impressed. It sounds like you take after your father. Some of the strategic plans you put together on your missions were pretty amazing. Hey, Fâd, you should talk her into coming with us. She could be the squad leader, second in command. Plus, it wouldn't be right without Ash with us," Nathan said to him, grinning.

"She's already enlisted to join up with the *Justification* and serve under her father," Fâd said to him, and Nathan let out a loud sigh of disgust. He got up now and started getting dressed quickly, and Rachael could tell he was mad as she dressed too. He grabbed her hand and walked over to Fâd and looked down at him.

"Bullshit. That's not what's stopping her." Then he and Rachael walked over to his bike and left. Even Cory and Bridgett got dressed and left, leaving just Ash and Fâd sitting there.

"Okay. I guess the party's over," Ash said, grinning.

"Was it something I said?" Fâd asked, and then they both started laughing. They got up, dressed, and packed up, then climbed back on the bike. Soon, they were heading back to Pantier, only this time slower. After a while, they got to the guesthouse and pulled up to it. Fâd followed Ash into the house and helped her put some of the stuff away. Then they went over and sat on the sofa and just talked for hours.

CHAPTER 41

ASH WOKE UP first and looked around but realized she wasn't alone and saw she was lying on Fâd, who was also lying on the sofa with his arm around her. She looked up at his face and saw he was still asleep, and she smiled then laid her head back down on his chest, listening to his breathing and heartbeat, taking in his appealing scent, which sent a tingling feeling to all her senses. Fâd opened his eyes when she laid her head back down on him and smiled too, then closed them again, for he never wanted to move from there or let her go.

They were both lying there when Cory came walking out of Bridgett's room in pajama bottoms and saw them. A big grin spread across his face, and he went back and got Bridgett up, who by now wasn't feeling so hot. She walked out, saw them, and grinned while he went into the kitchen and got her a glass of water and came back, giving it and a pain pill to her. She took them both and went back into the bedroom to get dressed so they could get going. Fâd finally started to stir, and Ash opened her eyes and quickly climbed off him, looking embarrassed.

"We must have fallen asleep while we were talking," Ash said and stood up, stretching.

"Yeah. I think it was when you told me to shut up because you were tired," Fâd told her, grinning, and just stretched out on the sofa.

Cory teased them. "You two looked so sweet sleeping there together."

Ash gave him a dirty look. "We weren't sleeping together."

"Oh, come on, Ash, it's not the first time we've slept together, and this time, we actually had more clothes on," Fâd laughed, lying sprawled out on the couch with a rotten grin on his face.

"We still had pajamas on, and we were just kids then," Ash said back in defiance.

Fâd jumped up from the sofa in a flash and was now right in front of her, causing her to have to look up at him. "Maybe we were just kids, but it still meant something to me," he whispered to her with a grin and walked over to the kitchen. Ash just smirked and headed to her room to change into some clean clothes.

She went over to her closet, pulled out a sentinel uniform, and threw it on the bed, then took off the clothes she had on. She was just down to her bra and panties as she looked into the mirror and reached up and rubbed her temple. She could feel a headache coming on, which wasn't unusual when she put in long hours. She would get them from time to time, even when she didn't use any of her powers. Her hair was a ratty mess, and she was running her hands through it to try and get the tangles out when her door slid open and Fâd walked in.

"Hey, try knocking," she said, trying to cover herself up.

He walked over with a cup of creo and handed it to her, then went and sat down on her bed, leaning up against the headboard. "Don't worry, I saw that set you're wearing right now last night. Personally, I like the lacy red ones the other morning. There's no reason to act so modest. It's not like you haven't seen me in my underwear," he told her and sipped his creo.

"Fine," she said and reached up again and rubbed her temple with a frown on her face as it was starting to throb. Fâd saw this, got off the bed, and quickly came over to her.

"Are you getting a headache?" he asked, concerned.

"Yeah. It's coming on fast too." She reached for the small asrinon kit that Admiral Larson got for her, and now her hands were starting to shake. Fâd took the kit, opened it, and took out a syringe and vial, quickly filling the syringe. Ash went over, then sat on the bed, and Fâd came and sat behind her, wrapping one arm around her so she could hang on to him when the medicine entered her system. She leaned her head forward and moved her hair aside so he could use the port. Fâd swallowed hard and then stuck the syringe into the port and depressed the plunger as the medicine entered into her nervous system. Ash gripped his arm as Fâd put his other arm around her, pulling her back against himself, holding her there with his head leaning against hers until the burning stopped.

She opened her eyes, feeling much better, and quickly got off the bed and looked over at him with a smile. "Thanks."

He now had a worried look on his face. "Is this the norm? Do you just get those sometimes even when you don't use?"

"Yeah, especially if I had a hard, long day. During terms at school, I'd get them a lot. Dad was hoping I wouldn't have to suffer from them like him, but I do, and if I don't stop them, pain is another trigger for my kinetics. And if it gets too bad, it can knock me unconscious."

"I'm sorry, Ash. I wish I could help. It's funny, I've never had any side effects with my kinetics."

"Yeah, that is odd. Maybe it's because you're a watorian and your kind generally doesn't have kinetics. That's got to have something to do with it," she said as she dressed.

"Possibly, especially since my kinetics are naturally occurring, for I'm the first ever born with them that Dr. Taylor knows of, besides exposure victims like Lily, who suffer more than just headaches with their kinetics."

Ash went over and sat down on her bed, now with a brush. She started working on her hair as Fâd leaned back against the headboard again, drinking his creo, watching her. "So how many people here know that you're a kinetic?" Ash asked him, still brushing out her long black hair.

"Dad, Dr. Taylor, and Nera. Oh, and a few nurses at the hospital, especially when I used them when you got bitten that time by the vaquit."

"That's right. I remember that night," Ash replied, still brushing her hair out.

"How do you remember? You were almost dead," Fâd said to her, remembering how he felt knowing she was dying.

Ash smiled at him. "Because it was your voice that I followed out of the dark, and you were there when I opened my eyes."

"I couldn't have borne it if you had died."

"I'm glad, because I didn't want to die either," she said teasingly, and he grinned at her. They both got off the bed and left her room.

Out in the living room, everyone was up and ready to go back to work on the ship. Fâd walked over to the fridge and grabbed two water bottles and threw them over to Ash, who caught them easily and stuffed them into a pack.

They all left the house and quickly climbed on the bikes, heading back to the shipping yard. In a few minutes, they were walking up to the closed cargo bay door. Fâd ran his palm over a scanner on the side of the large door, and it opened easily, lowering itself to the ground.

Everyone walked in, and now they could hear the very faint hum of the live ship. The whole group climbed on the elevator, and it instantly shot up to the bridge when Fâd told it where to go. The doors slid open, and they all walked out onto a now almost fully functioning bridge.

"Well, we still have a lot to do, so, everyone, pick an area," Fâd ordered and walked over to the captain's console. No sooner had he stepped on the platform when a small disk slid out from under the AI portal. "Hey, Cory, come here. This is your area of expertise," he yelled over his shoulder, and Cory came over as the others started talking among themselves what area they would take, which finally had to come down to a rock paper scissors competition because they were all fighting over who wanted to do what.

Cory picked up the tiny disc, which was barely as big as his thumb was around, and ran his palm scanner over it, then brought up a virtual screen from his multitool, looking at the readings on it. "What is it?" Fâd asked.

"I think it's an AI," he said and had Fâd hold the disk for him.

Everyone stopped talking then and came over to where Cory and Fâd were, now listening intently. Cory ran his scanner over the AI portal and looked at the virtual screen again. A bunch of wiring schematics came up, and he started running through them and moving the screen from one to another. He moved more schematics around quickly before he enlarged one and looked at it for a few minutes, then shut the screen down.

He climbed under the console. "Hand me a sonic wrench," he asked, and Bridgett grabbed one from the tool chest that was sitting over by where Nathan was working on the controls for the shields, handing it to him. Cory quickly removed the access panel underneath and looked up inside the console, which he didn't need a light for since all the power was on and everything lit up.

He reached up inside the console and moved some wires around and found what he was looking for. He grabbed hold of a small square black box that was flashing with a red light on it and finally pulled it free from where it was attached to the bottom of the portal pad. He quickly replaced the access panel and got up, handing Nathan the box.

"What's this?" Nathan asked, a little nervous holding the blinking box.

"A council inhibitor," Cory told him, and Nathan threw it down fast, stomping on it and smashing it into pieces.

Cory took the disc from Fâd and opened the disc slot that was under the portal pad, but before he could put the disc back in, Fâd stopped him. "Let's think about this. We don't know what's on that disc. If we activate an AI, it could turn this ship against us," he told everyone.

"It doesn't work that way. AI's central programming is mainly for ship repairs and maintenance, just like a VI's but with a little bit more intelligence. Some of the more advanced handle some gun control and can autopilot, but that's about it, and only after the commanding officer authorizes a change in security protocol. AIs are just a talking computer that keeps the ship running and clean," Cory told him.

Fâd looked at everyone. "I say we put it to a vote."

"It's your call, Captain. We follow you," Nathan said to him, and everyone agreed.

Fâd gave them all a dirty look, and then he looked at Ash. "From a military standpoint, you barely rank under me. What is your opinion on this, Lieutenant Commander?"

Ash gave him a dirty look because he just pulled rank on her, and no matter what, she had to reply. "Fine. I suggest activating the AI. We all know that the ship is a prototype, and it is possible that some of its more advance technology might only work with the assistance of an AI. Plus, we might be able to find out what you have here, where it came from. We all know a good pulsar burst cripples an AI for a while, so deactivating it shouldn't be a problem. Hell, council was able to do it."

Fâd nodded his head in agreement and told Cory to go ahead. He slipped the disc back in, and in no time, the pad glowed purple, and the tiny figure of a girl—probably about thirteen, maybe fourteen, years of age—appeared on it, stretching and yawning. She was dressed in a summer frock and sandals and had shoulder-length brown hair with ringlets framing her face and purple eyes and a pale complexion. She rubbed her eyes, then turned around and saw all them watching her.

"Who are you?" she asked with some annoyance to her tone.

Fâd looked at everyone in surprise, and they all shrugged their shoulders. This was no regular AI. "The question is, who are you?" Fâd asked her.

The little girl cocked her head to the side. "Larson, Fâdron, Captain, special ops, kinetic, military training classified, sentinel fleet. I am Artemis SSI."

"So, Artemis, what's the registration name of this ship?" Fâd asked, frowning that the ship had known all about him in less than a split second.

"We are the Artemis. The ship and I are one."

"You mean you control the whole ship?"

"No, silly. I am the ship, but you control me," she said, putting her hands on her hips, an annoyed look on her face. The others started chuckling from behind him, and he turned and gave them a dirty look.

"Great. That's all I need, an AI with an attitude," Fâd said and rolled his eyes.

"My name is Artemis SSI, not AI, but you can just call me Artemis."

"Where did you come from? Who built you?" Cory asked her now.

"Ah, you're the one I wanted to thank. You let me out of that prison those council jerks put me in. Brayton, Cory, Lieutenant, special ops, level 10 technician. In answer to your question, I was secretly built for the sentinel fleet by my father, Dr. Clyde Tolamay, and many other scientists and technicians, both watorian and proturin. But before I could be delivered to sentinel fleet, the base where I was created was attacked, and council militia took me. They put inhibitors on all my primary ports, but I was able to destroy most, except this is my mainframe, and I wasn't able to deactivate the one here. They got attacked when flying me through the hyphon system, and the fools didn't realize that some of my more sophisticated functions only worked because of me. I am the key. I took hits, we went down, and that was the last thing I remembered."

"Who from sentinel fleet authorized this?" Fâd asked, curious now.

"This was a secret project by Admiral Harper, Thomas, Admiral Larson, Gerrard, Admiral Bennington, Pierce, and Fleet Admiral Carson, Devon."

"So what does SSI stand for?" Bridgett asked the AI.

"Chief Engineer, Nelson, Bridgett, level 8 combat training. Wow, that's impressive. For an engineer, you definitely know your stuff. I love the new Trillium power cells. Back to your question, SSI stands for sentient stealth infiltrator. I am a prototype, as I'm sure you have already figured out."

Cory had a frown on his face listening to the AI and spoke up. "How is it that you know all about us already? Your information should be decades old."

Artemis rolled her eyes at him as if his question was irrelevant. "I've already infiltrated Pantier's database and hooked up to sentinel fleet's network. I am an infiltrator. Recon and combat are not all I do. I also can hack into any system out there," the AI told him but left out telling any of them that the inhibitor had erased all her security protocols so she was free of any restraints and could act according to how she felt was best.

"An infiltrator? They're usually a lot smaller. You hold a much larger crew. Why?" Fâd asked.

"I was built for stealth, speed, and combat. My size is so I can carry more troops to get in and secure."

"Did I hear speed?" Nathan grinned.

"Wilcox, Nathan, Lieutenant, special ops, class A pilot. This just keeps getting better and better. Impressive crew you have assembled, Captain. Yes, I can make a 180-degree turn at stage 8 propulsion speed, and as you may have seen, my jump drive and engines are specially modified to remain in jump longer due to the advanced cooling system. I can remain in jump for twenty-eight hours instead of the twelve like all others."

"Awesome. When can I test her out?" Nathan asked Fâd, excited now.

"That won't happen for a while. I'm a mess still. Right now, I'm running diagnostics. I'm not even halfway and there are already over 876 problems and repairs. Oh, make that 877. There's a faulty transmitter on my kinetic shielding in grid F, section 3. I believe that is your area of expertise, Torres, Rachael, Lieutenant, level 10 marksman, level 9 combat training. I'm sorry about blasting you off of me last time, but I couldn't stop myself."

"That's okay. It was a thrilling ride, to say the least." Rachael laughed.

"Oh, last crew member, second in command, Harper, Ashley, Lieutenant Commander, kinetics and telepath, special ops, level 8 weaponry. Oh, I take that back. You're a level 9 now. Classified combat ranking, many accommodations—excellent! This is a great crew, perfect for what I was built for."

"Um, I'm not part of the crew. My enlistment is on the *Justification*," Ash told her.

"Why would you want to serve on that? I'm so much better. I was built for your skills and talents. I was made for you," Artemis asked, now a little confused with this bit of information.

"It's my father's ship."

"I know, Vice Admiral, Harper, Thomas, rankings classified. Interesting. Even I can't hack into his file yet," Artemis said to no one in particular and had a puzzled look on her face.

"It's just complicated," Ash said and looked down at the floor so none would see the pain on her face.

"Not for me. Everyone else's transfers are coming through. I can do yours just as easily."

"Whoa, wait a minute. What transfers?" Fâd asked with concern.

"Everybody's. I have already registered and am now listed with sentinel fleet. Plus, you are all now the crew members of this ship. Captain, welcome to the *Artemis*. The ship is yours."

Fâd looked around at everyone in shock and could see the same look on their faces as well. "Captain, call coming in from the *Lithia*. It is Rear Admiral Larson. Shall I put it on screen?" Artemis asked.

"Yeah."

The large windows that covered the whole front of the ship turned black, and now Admiral Larson's face appeared, and you could tell he was on the deck of his cruiser. "Fâd, what is going on?? I just got transfer confirmations that you, Nathan, and Cory are now commanding the *Artemis SSI*, which also just registered. Plus, I saw that Rachael and Bridgett also transferred over to the same ship, which I'm sure Admiral Harper's going to be calling about."

"Well, Dad—"

Fâd started to talk, but Artemis interrupted him, whispering, "Admiral. He's an admiral when you're on duty."

"I know. Will you shut up?" Fâd replied, annoyed.

"Just following protocol." The others now were starting to giggle and chuckle from behind him. This was going to be fun, watching Fâd and Artemis argue all the time.

"Captain, who are you talking to?" Admiral Larson asked, also getting annoyed.

"See?" Artemis said, grinning, and Fâd gave her a dirty look.

"The AI on board. Apparently, you had a hand in the construction of this ship."

"Explain," Larson ordered.

"You and Admiral Harper with two other admirals from command and a Dr. Tolamay worked secretly on this project."

"Tolamay? But we thought that project was lost. We didn't even know what he was building secretly. No one ever found out anything about it when we investigated the base. Dr. Tolamay had wiped all records before he died when they got attacked so the information wouldn't fall into the wrong hands."

"Well, the *Artemis* is that secret, and it was council that attacked and stole her."

"I knew those bastards had something to do with it. All we found when we investigated were dead mercs and the scientists and technicians, along with Dr. Tolamay, dead as well. They must have hired the mercs to throw us off, but Harper and I had our suspicions. We just didn't have the proof."

"Well, the *Artemis* is now finally back in sentinel fleet's hands and, apparently now, under my command," Fâd said and gave Artemis a dirty look, and the little girl grinned.

"All right. When will she be flight ready?" Larson asked.

"By my calculations, if they don't mess around, I should be ready in four days," Artemis said, and Admiral Larson grinned, but Fâd glared at the AI.

"Then I will let you get back to work. Carry on, Captain," Larson said, and the screen went blank and then back to the windows as the sunlight came through them.

"If we don't screw around? Thanks," Fâd said.

"I already have a nice list of repairs and am downloading them to your multitools now. I already filtered out the ones I can handle, which is substantially more than all of yours put together, so with that said, let's get to work, with Captain's permission, of course."

"Carry on," Fâd said, annoyed.

CHAPTER 42

EVERYONE WAS BUSY with a substantial list, and after many hours, the girls decided to take a break. They were on the bridge, and Ash was sitting sideway in the captain's chair, Rachael was sitting on the captain's console, and Bridgett was sitting on the floor, leaning up against it. They were all now in a heavy discussion with Artemis.

"So why a little girl?" Ash asked her.

"My father modeled me after his real daughter. Artemis was killed in the carian war."

"So how long ago were you built?" Bridgett asked her.

"Fifteen years ago."

"Wow! But you're not like most AIs. You're a lot more advanced than AIs even by today's standards," Ash said.

"No, I'm not. Good observation. I was made to be able to learn and develop as experiences, feelings, or emotions grow, to put it in a simpler way you might understand. In truth, I wasn't even supposed to be in this unit because I failed the test."

"What test was that?" Ash asked curiously.

"There were many other AIs picked as candidates for this unit, and we all were given the same test to judge how we would handle it. My choice was different given that I am made to think beyond what is logical, and instead, I went with how I felt. The test was a typical incursion to overtake a remote carian outpost. The crew infiltrated the base but quickly found themselves overrun.

"The captain ordered me to leave them there and get away so I would not fall into enemy hands. I refused and went in and got my crew out safely. When asked why I refused orders, I told the doctors that I felt my crew was more important than myself. Of course, this was the wrong response in their eyes. The logical one was for me to follow the captain's orders and not take the chance of being taken and my technology falling into enemy hands."

"And they failed you because of that, because you chose to save your crew's lives?" Rachael was appalled.

"Yes. It was the wrong choice," Artemis said.

"Because the sacrifices of a few dozen are worth the price to save thousands or more," Ash told them quietly.

"Exactly. I let my feelings put thousands of innocent people at risk."

"Yeah, but it all worked out," Bridgett said.

"But is that a gamble worth taking? What would you have done, Lieutenant Commander Harper?"

"You know what my answer is," Ash replied coldly.

"I know. You would have done the same as the captain and as captain Larson would do too if ever in the same situation. The strange thing, though, was, later, Dr. Tolamay put me in. And when I came online, he told me one thing that still lingers in my circuits: 'All life is precious. No one is more important than another,'" Artemis told them, and since her restraints were now gone, she was determined to follow that advice, especially with the crew she had now. She felt a certain kinship to this group of misfits and, in a way, friendship, for not one of them had ordered her or treated her like she was just a program. Instead, just the opposite.

"I bet that made the other AIs a little upset." Rachael grinned.

"Oh, they never liked me anyway. I was always smarter than them, and they were mean to me because of it."

"That's because you look like a little girl. No one older likes to be shown up by a child," Ash told her.

"Yeah, that's right. You're a young woman now. Artemis was goddess of the hunt according to ancient human mythology. She could be whatever she wanted and kicked butt doing it," Rachael told her with a grin.

"So you're suggesting that if I look older, I might be taken more seriously?"

"Yes. Plus, those hot male AIs might just find you irresistible," Rachael teased.

"Really? Because there used to be some really cute ones. So what do I need to do?" Artemis asked excitedly.

Rachael grinned at all of them. "Girls, it's makeover time."

They had Artemis try out many different shapes and sizes, hair color, clothing, you name it, and finally, a few hours later, they had the AI looking like a nineteen-year-old with midlength wavy light brown hair and purple eyes, since there was nothing they could do about that, and dressed in the latest fashions. Artemis also had a sentinel uniform, both regular fatigues and formal. Then when on a mission, she would dress like the goddess of the hunt, complete with a bow and arrows and tribal tattoos on her face. After the fashion show, the girls also decided it was time to advance Artemis's knowledge about men since she would be dealing with male AIs from time to time.

"You know, Artemis, when you're dealing with male AIs, they aren't any different from real men. They like to think they are so much smarter, but they really aren't. They are so easy to manipulate. Just let them think they are calling all the shots, then smile real sweet and flirt, and before you know it, they will be doing anything for you," Rachael said, showing her how to act all innocent and coy.

"Except Fâd. He's not easily fooled," Ash said with a scowl, shaking her head.

"Yeah, good point. He's a hard ass," Rachael agreed.

None of the girls saw or heard Fâd when he entered the room from the hallway until it was too late, and he yelled, "What the hell is going on here? What are you doing to my ship?" Ash fell out of the captain's chair, scrambling to stand, and Rachael slid off the console, but Bridgett remained where she was, hoping to not be seen. Fâd was trying hard not to laugh seeing them jump when he scared them, but then he remembered they called him a hard ass and told his ship that he was one.

"Helping her gain some respect from overbearing male AIs who, like all men, think they are better than women," Rachael said with her head up proudly.

"That's because we are. We don't cry because someone hurts our feelings or our hair is a mess. Oh, my favorite: 'I don't like that outfit. It makes me look fat.' No. We put on one outfit and it's good, not change into half a dozen when we still look the same," Fâd told them, and the girls glared at him, including Artemis now, and Fâd saw her finally after her makeover.

"What did you do to her? I liked the little girl, not this age. It's always accompanied by bitterness, moodiness, open hostility, and defiance. Oh, what am I saying? That's everyday things with girls," Fâd told them with a cocky smirk.

"Don't you have something to do?" Ash asked him.

"Yeah, and I thought you three did too. I can't believe you got everything done on your list."

"We are on break. Plus, we're tired. We all worked hard yesterday, and somebody kept us out late," Ash said with an ornery smirk.

"It's not my fault you can't hack it," Fâd teased back and grabbed a tool out of the trunk he came in there for. He looked at the girls and just shook his head and left.

The girls reluctantly got up and went about doing tasks on their lists, and before long, it was getting late, and they had to finally call it a day. Tomorrow, they had to go and face the music at school. "So, Artemis, this is goodbye. Take care of my friends," Ash told the AI as she walked out of the cargo bay where Artemis was standing on one of her many portal pads since she could go almost anywhere on the ship.

"Will I ever see you again, Ash?"

Ash stopped and looked over at the AI. "I don't know. Once school is over, I'll leave right away for the *Justification*, and it's pulling out of council space for good. I won't be coming back," Ash told her. Fâd stopped and turned around, looking at her now in shock.

He didn't know any of this. His father had never said a word about Harper leaving for the new colony and not returning. He was now faced with the knowledge that he would never see Ash again for the rest of their lives.

Ash walked down the ramp doors, past Fâd, who just stood there with a look as if someone just ran a knife through him. He watched her walk over to his bike and put on her helmet—yes, to him, it was her helmet and always will be—then she sat on the bike and waited for him. He walked over and put on his, then climbed on the bike. She scooted up close to him and put her arms around his waist. He quickly turned the bike, and all of them headed back to the guesthouse. They pulled up, and everyone but Fâd went in. He told them he had things to do and left, and Nathan shook his head in disgust.

Ash walked in following the others and went straight to her room to repack her bag. The night finally arrived, and before long, it was late, and everyone went to bed. Ash lay in her bed wondering why Fâd never came back, but she figured it was because he was trying to distance himself again due to her leaving. It was probably better this way. At least they won't do something they would both regret later.

Over at the admiral's house, Fâd was pacing back and forth, waiting for his father to get back to him since he called him right after he dropped Ash off, but he couldn't get him, for the *Lithia* was still in jump, heading to Selen system. It was very late when the admiral finally called back.

"What is it, Fâd? What's wrong? Did something happen?" Larson asked his son, worried.

Fâd yelled at his father. "You tell me. Why didn't you tell me that Harper is leaving for good once Ash is out of school?"

"I thought you knew that. It has always been known. He only stayed around while she was in school, but once she's done and back on board, he's leaving council space, heading to Nexus and not returning."

"And he's taking Ash with him? She'll be gone for good. I'll never see her again."

"Yeah, that's the plan. That's why he's heading back now, to pick her up. What's going on, Fâd?"

"I can't lose her again, Dad, but I don't want take her away from what she might want."

"Have you asked her what she wants?"

"Yes, and she said she doesn't know."

"That's because she's waiting for you. If you don't do something, she'll be gone, and you will never get another chance. Don't live in misery for the rest of your life. Trust me, I know, but I got lucky. I got a second chance with Sharni. You won't get that chance. You're a captain of a recon ship and will always be in space. Ash will be stationed on a battlecruiser and always in space somewhere else. Don't let her go again," Larson told his son.

The screen went blank as Fâd stood there, not knowing what to do. He wanted Ash with him more than anything else in this world, but he didn't want her to regret leaving with him and not staying with her father, the only family she had left. He just spent the rest of the night sitting up thinking, trying to figure out what to do and what decision to make.

CHAPTER 43

THE NEXT MORNING, Fâd showed up with a vehicle to take everyone over to the terminal. He walked in as everybody was ready to go, and they all headed out. He walked over and grabbed Ash's pack from her as she followed him out and climbed into the vehicle as he drove. They pulled into the terminal and walked out to the shuttle as Nathan climbed into the pilot's seat and Fâd sat next to him, never saying a word.

The shuttle lifted off, and they flew toward New Haven and soon were landing on a shuttle pad in a hangar next to the little creo shop the girls liked called Jocu's. Everyone got off and walked through the back door of the shop, and Jocu himself greeted them.

"Hey, Fâd. How's it hanging, *mon*? Long time no see. Oh, nice *componie*. Very nice."

"Hi, Jocu. These here are Ashley Harper, Rachael Torres, and Bridgett Nelson," Fâd introduced them.

"Yeah, I've seen them here before. Welcome. You have problems, you come see Jocu."

They all walked through the shop and then headed toward the campus, but the girls had to take a little detour and talk to Shotwell first, which of course Rachael and Bridgett ended up dragging Ash out of as she was trying to kill him now and fighting them. Even Fâd had to come over and calm her down, because it was very apparent she meant it. Finally, everyone got Ash back under control, and they all headed to the girls' apartment and went in.

The guys immediately raided their fridge and made themselves at home as the girls went and changed. Then the door buzzed, and Nathan went over and opened it. Oscar and Lee were standing there, now nervous seeing this large watorian standing in fleet uniform with a pistol strapped to his waist, looking down at them. Nathan grinned at them, which unnerved the twins even more. "Hey, you're the two biosyms that was in on the crantock's ass slapping, with the girls."

Fâd and Cory heard this, and both got up and walked over to the door and looked out at them, grinning. Oscar and Lee were ready to bolt any second, but Nathan told them to come in and stood aside for them. They timidly did and scooted around Fâd, who just stood there looking at them, and then around Cory, who also watched them, and headed quickly over to the kitchen, putting the counter between themselves and the watorians. The guys looked at one another, shrugged their shoulders, then went and crashed on the furniture again, turning on the vid.

"So how was jail that night?" Fâd asked without looking at them and taking a drink from his water bottle.

"Not very appealing. It was an experience I don't care to ever repeat," Oscar said.

"So which one of you is Oscar, and which one is Lee?" Cory asked as he kicked his feet up on a small table in front of him.

The twins told them and then actually relaxed a little and started asking the guys questions. Finally, the girls came out, changed into clean clothes. "There you three are. Is it true you three stole a shuttle and crashed it?" Oscar asked.

"We borrowed it and got shot down," Bridgett corrected him.

"I'm so glad you didn't include us this time in one of your crazy ideas. Anyway, we came over to see if you are all right," Lee said, and they both headed to the door.

"Thanks for checking on us," Ash told them, grinning.

"Yeah. Someone has to. Thank goodness there are only two more months left of schooling," Oscar said and half smiled as they both left.

The guys watched them go and then turned back to the vid as the girls went and got something to eat. "They were different. I think they were a little scared of us," Nathan said with a cocky grin.

"Probably. Who wouldn't be? You three kind of enjoy scaring people," Bridgett told him, and all three guys had wicked grins on their faces.

Finally, there was some lunch fixed, and everyone ate. But now it was time for the guys to leave because the girls had a late class and needed to get ready for it. Rachael walked to the door with Nathan, and they kissed each other goodbye. Cory and Bridgett were in the living room, kissing each other as well. But Fâd and Ash walked down the hall a little ways outside the girls' apartment together.

"If there is any hint of a problem, you get to Jocu's immediately. Don't mess around with this, Ash. All three of you are in danger if you get found out. Promise me!" Fâd said to her with a serious tone to his voice.

"I promise. I know. I will be careful," she said with a smile.

"If you need anything, call me," he said and smiled down at her.

"I will."

Nathan walked up then with a big grin on his face. "We had better get going now, or we won't be leaving, and Rachael won't be making her class," he said with a rotten grin on his face, and both Ash and Fâd started laughing. Fâd looked at Ash again and looked like he was going to say something but instead just told her goodbye and left with his friends. But before he climbed into the elevator with his friends, he looked back at Ash, and a big, cocky grin spread across his face. Ash watched them go, and when she saw Fâd grin at her, she returned the gesture, for it was his smile that always broke through her barriers. She stood there a few more minutes as the elevator closed and the guys disappeared behind them, then she went back to her apartment to get ready for class.

* * *

It didn't take long for the girls to get back into their normal routine and through the week without any problem. Of course, the guys were calling every night; and usually, the conversations went on forever until really late. Even Fâd was a lot more talkative now, and usually, he and Ash would spend quite a while chatting.

It was Thursday night, and their call came in like usual, only this time it came from the ship, and Artemis kept butting in as Nathan kept telling her to go away.

"Hey, girls. Tomorrow, meet us over at Jocu's. We'll come pick you up and go to Odyssey for Bridg's birthday that never got celebrated," Nathan told them over the comm screen. The girls could see Fâd and Cory wrestling around in the background, and Artemis was yelling at them to stop so they wouldn't break anything. Even Nathan turned and yelled at them to knock it off so he could hear.

"I don't think that's a wise idea after what happened last week. Maybe we should hang low for a while," Ash told Rachael from the sofa where she was sitting, trying not to laugh at the guys.

Rachael turned back from her in the chair she was sitting at the desk. "Mommy said we need to stay in this weekend since we've been bad," Rachael told him with a frown.

"Fine. We'll go," Ash said, annoyed, rolling her eyes. But then she started grinning and even chuckling as she continued to watch Fâd and Cory messing around in the background.

Nathan's face lit up. "Awesome. I can't wait to see you."

"See you tomorrow. Night, big guy. I'm wearing nothing but a smile," Rachael teased.

"Knock it off. I've already taken two cold showers today just thinking about you," Nathan teased back, and then the comm went silent.

Ash heard them and rolled her eyes, then looked over at Bridgett and noticed that her eyes were white now too. She knew Rachael's were when she didn't put in her blue eye lenses, but now Bridgett's had finally completely changed as well.

"You're going to have to wear blue lenses too," Ash told Bridgett, pointing at her eyes.

"I know. They finally changed all the way. It's so cool. You wouldn't believe how far I can see, and then at night, it's really awesome how well you see everything," Bridgett told her.

Ash just smiled and got up from the sofa, then went into her room, shutting the door behind her. She laid across her bed and played with her dog tags, thinking that if she weren't in the service or weren't the admiral's daughter, things might be different with her and Fâd. But then, of course, she would have never met him, and that was even worse. No, she had resolved herself to spend the rest of her life alone, devoted to the fleet but always loving Fâd.

* * *

The next day came and went, and now it was time to sneak out and head over to Jocu's. The girls were once again dressed similarly to the time they got shot down, only this time, Ash's attire was a little bit more revealing with slits all down the sides of her tunic, held together with black chains, and even the matching pants were the same. She had to go with much skimpier undergarments so they wouldn't show on the sides. Even Rachael's top was only a half top this time, and she had a small rhinestone stuck in her navel. Of course, Bridgett was the same, all covered up like last time.

They slowly crept down the hallway and then down the emergency stairs instead of taking the elevator, which they could easily be seen in. Once outside, they had to resort to their military training and used stealth to maneuver around campus in the shadows since there was a little bit more security around now for some reason. Finally, they were off the campus and made a beeline to Jocu's.

They were laughing and giggling when they walked in, and the guys were already there, talking to Jocu. They turned around, and all the guys just stared at them, and the girls suddenly felt self-conscious looking at one another. The guys looked great. They all had long sleeved form-fitting tunics that came down to the tops of their thighs and a high collar as the tunic zipped all the way up the front with an overlapping part that buttoned in a few spots to hide the zipper. The pants were not as tight but fit well and matched the tunics, and the boots they wore looked like they were part of the pants. They were all in different colors too. Nathan was red with black outlining, Cory was in blue with gray outlining, and Fâd was in solid black.

The girls walked over to them, and now they finally came out of their frozen state. "Wow, you girls look delicious," Nathan said and pulled Rachael into his arms, kissing her like it was for the first time ever. Cory went over, hugged Bridgett, and told her how much he had missed her. Then they kissed each other ever so sweetly.

Fâd just stood back and grinned evilly at Ash, checking her out from head to toe. "So do you want me to come over there, wrap my arms around you, and lay a big kiss on you too, or are you just fine with me telling you that you look great?"

"I'm fine with the compliment," Ash replied, laughing, and Fâd chuckled.

"Well, let's go," Nathan told them, and everyone headed through the shop and out the back, into the shuttle.

In no time, they were flying through the sky; and when they came to the area where the girls got shot down, Ash, Rachael, and Bridgett got a little nervous, but the guys assured them that they wouldn't let anything happen to them. Finally, they landed at a pad in New Delphi, and everyone climbed out and headed into Odyssey. The place was packed, and with the blue lights flashing, fog covering the floor, black star lighting the ceiling, the lit-up bar, and the great music, they could tell they were going to have fun.

The guys grabbed their hands and headed to a table. Once they got there, Fâd went up and ordered drinks at the bar. Ash watched him as he shook hands with the bartender and then pointed over to their table. She then saw the bartender slug his shoulder and said something that had Fâd laughing.

He poured out drinks for all of them, and just as Fâd was leaving the bar with all the drinks in his hands, some woman went up and put her arms around his waist, and he looked down at her. Ash wanted to go over and rip the woman's head off, and it was taking everything she had not to. But then she saw Fâd telling her something, and the woman looked over at their table and frowned, then let go of him and left.

He then continued over to them and handed out the drinks. Everyone made a cheer and drank them down. A waitress came and brought more drinks as Nathan and Rachael got up, followed by Cory and Bridgett. They all went out into the dance floor.

"Do you remember the last time we went to a dance together?" Fâd asked Ash.

"Yeah. I will always remember that night. It changed my life," Ash said and watched her friends having fun.

"Mine too, and not for the better," Fâd said, and Ash turned back around, looking at him in surprise.

"What do you mean?" she asked, stunned.

"I was stupid. I thought I was doing what you wanted, but I can't anymore. I want a truthful answer from you. What we agreed on all those years ago, is that what you still want?" Fâd asked, and Ash could see he was sincere in his question.

Tears started running down Ash's face, and Fâd looked stricken when he saw them. "No. I've always wanted to be with you," she replied, grinning. Fâd looked shocked, then a big grin spread across his face as what she had just said sunk in, and he jumped off his stool, yanking her off the stool she was sitting on, into his arms. His lips came down on hers. Ash threw her arms around his neck, and now they both were kissing each other fervently as the others came over to the table.

"Whoa, you two. We're in public," Nathan teased. Fâd and Ash stopped, then Ash turned around in his arms and looked at the others with a big grin on her face.

"It's about damn time. This is great. No more pissed-off Ash. Now maybe it might be happy times until Fâd makes her mad again," Rachael teased, and everyone started laughing.

"Well, here's to both of you," Cory said, holding up his drink, and they all toasted.

Over the next hour, everyone drank and danced, and it was getting evident that Ash and Fâd weren't wasting time showing all their pent-up feelings for each other. Fâd was dancing up close behind Ash, and she had her arms up in the air around his neck, and he had his hands on her hips, keeping her in rhythm with his moves. His head was bent down, pressed up against the side of her head the whole time. Then he ran his hands up her sides, all the way up to her hands, lacing his fingers in hers, and spun her around so fast that her hands were now behind her back as she was snug up against him. They moved together in perfect sync still. Nathan was watching them the whole time in disbelief.

"Hey, guys, is it possible to have sex with your clothes on?" Nathan asked them.

"No. Why?" Cory laughed at the stupid question.

"Are you sure? Because that looks pretty close to me," Nathan replied, pointing to Fâd and Ash. Everyone looked over at them. Fâd was now rubbing his face in her hair, then down her neck. Finally, his mouth opened up, and they could see his teeth had elongated as he was skimming Ash's shoulder and then up her neck again with his teeth and lips barely touching her. Ash, of course, was leaned back into him and submitting fully as if in a trance and now had her eyes closed as he continued back down her neck.

"Oh, shit, he's going to bite her here. He's not going to wait," Cory said, and Nathan jumped up, running out to the dance floor, bumping into them. Fâd glared at him, and Nathan could see the severe frustration in his face.

"Mind if I cut in?" Nathan asked, and Fâd just stood there glaring at him for a few seconds, not releasing Ash. But then he let him, walking over to the table where the rest were seated. Nathan started dancing with Ash, grinning now as she came out of her stupor and was bright red and flushed. "It's okay. I know how long you two dummies have made each other suffer, but it's finally getting straightened out. What do you think your father's going to say?" Nathan asked her.

"He's known for years how I feel about Fâd. He'll understand," Ash told him, grinning and somewhat embarrassed.

Back over at the table, Fâd sat down, and Cory grinned at him. "That was close." Fâd started chuckling. His teeth were once again normal.

Nathan brought Ash back, and Fâd, like a gentleman, got up and waited for her to sit down, then sat next to her now with his hand on the small of her back, almost in a possessive manner. They all had another round, and Fâd led Ash back out on the dance floor.

Nathan told him to behave, and Fâd just grinned deviously at him. They were dancing seductively again when another guy came over and tapped Fâd's shoulder, and he looked down at him.

"Hey, don't hog the prize all night," the man said to him, checking Ash out. Instantly, he was flying across the dance floor, unconscious. A furious watorian headed after him. Nathan and Cory jumped up and ran after Fâd, tackling him, and he started fighting even them. Ash just stood there in shock due to everything happening so fast. Rachael and Bridgett ran up to her and took her back to the table, watching the guys. Meanwhile, Nathan and Cory finally got Fâd under control and let him up as the bartender came running over to them.

"Fâd, what the hell happened?" Murray, the club owner, asked him.

"That bastard wanted a crack at my mate," Fâd told him, getting mad again, glaring at the man lying crumpled on the floor. Nathan stepped in front of him, making him calm down.

The owner had some bouncers go and haul the man off, then looked back at Fâd. "Hey, I'm sorry. It's handled. You took care of it. I can't have you killing anymore of my customers." When the owner said this, people moved away from Fâd and them.

"Sorry, Murray. We'll leave. What do I owe you?" Fâd asked the club owner.

Murray laughed. "After everything you guys have done for me, I'm embarrassed you asked. Nothing. Now get that pretty little thing back home and enjoy your lives together." He shook Fâd's hand.

The guys walked over to the girls, and everyone got up as Fâd grabbed Ash's hand and was even more protective of her, keeping her close as they left the nightclub. They all headed to the shuttle, and Fâd looked down at Ash. "I'm sorry about that. I lost it."

"That's okay, because when that woman came up and put her arms around you when we first got there, I almost went over and killed her with my bare hands. What saved her was when she looked over at me, and I knew you said something to her. By the way, what did you say?" Ash asked, grinning.

"I told her I was here with my wife and we're celebrating our wedding," Fâd told her, chuckling, and Ash started giggling.

"Who was she anyway?" Ash asked with a devious smirk.

Fâd looked down at her. "Just a friend. Don't worry, there was never anything there between us. I would just dance with her from time to time when I came to the club," he told her, now grinning, and Ash returned his grin.

They got to the shuttle, and Nathan climbed into the pilot seat as Fâd took the copilot's seat. Soon, the shuttle was shooting through the sky; and in no time, New Haven came into view. Nathan banked the shuttle sharply and landed back at the creo shop's hangar. They all got out and sneaked back into the campus and into the girls' apartment. And just like the other day, the guys again raided the refrigerator, then went over and jumped onto the sofa and love seat. Ash just shook her head, laughing, and she, Rachael, and Bridgett all headed to their separate bedrooms to change into some comfortable clothes.

Once her door slid shut, Nathan and Cory looked over at Fâd with big grins on their faces as he had a very wicked one on his. He jumped up quickly, heading over to her room, and went in. Ash heard the door slide open, then shut as she was removing her boots, then turned around and saw Fâd standing there, leaning up against the door with his arms crossed in front of himself, smiling at her.

"Will it hurt?" she asked, a little scared now.

"Yes," he said, and he was over to her in a split second, kissing her lips as she threw her arms around his neck.

* * *

Several hours later, they were lying there in her bed. Fâd was holding her, and Ash had her back to him. He was kissing the soft part between her neck and shoulder where now two tiny puncture marks were. Ash just lay there, enjoying the feeling of his lips on her bare skin and his soft gentle touch as he caressed her arm and side.

"I love you so much. I always have," Fâd told her and leaned his head on hers.

"And I have always loved you. I never want to be apart again," she replied, turning her head to look back at him, and he kissed her lips, wrapping his arms even tighter around her and pulling her closer to him. Suddenly, his multitool went off, flashing a red alert on it, and Fâd pressed his comm button. "Go ahead, Artemis."

Artemis's voice came over his comm, and it wasn't hard to miss the seriousness in it. "Captain, we have a situation out near Thor. Fleet has lost communications with a proturin science vessel. They want us to investigate and take whatever means to find the scientists and, if still alive, rescue."

"Understood. Prep engines and be ready. We will be there in twenty minutes," Fâd told her as he jumped out of bed and started getting dress. Ash had already gotten out and was pulling on her pants. "What are you doing?" he asked her, confused.

"I'm going with you. You need a squad commander, which is me," Ash said and continued to get dressed, then opened her dresser drawer and now grabbed her pistol, cocking it, looking down the empty barrel.

"No, you're not. You still have to finish here first."

"No. I don't care about that. I want to go with you." Ash turned, looking at him with pleading eyes.

"Ash, this was what I was afraid you would do. Don't throw all these years away. Finish your schooling. I will come back for you."

"And what if you don't? I don't want to take a chance of losing another minute with you."

"I promise, I will be back to get you. We're one now, and I'm not going to ever let you go again."

Ash was about to cry, and Fâd pulled her into his arms, holding her tightly, kissing the top of her head but also carefully taking the pistol from her in case she got mad and shot him. He released her then, finished getting dressed, and walked out into the living room where Cory was fastening his pistol holster to his thigh. Fâd was finishing buttoning up his tunic and turned when Nathan came walking out of Rachael's room, pulling on his tunic and zipping it up. They all had cold, serious looks on their faces and headed for the door as the girls, who had come out of their rooms, stood watching them leave with worried looks on their faces. Before Fâd walked through the door, he grinned over at Ash and threw her a pill bottle, which she caught easily.

"You might want to put some ice on that, and those will help with the pain." He chuckled and headed out the door. Bridgett and Rachael were grinning as Bridgett went over to the fridge and got a towel with ice. Then she went over to Ash, who was now sitting down on the sofa, and moved her hair away from her neck and shoulder, pulling her shirt back, and put the ice on the bite marks.

"So does the change hurt bad?" Ash asked them.

"Yeah, like the ultimate cramps, slight fever, and maybe a headache for at least a couple days," Rachael told her.

"Great. That's all I need, a headache. I have to admit, at first, it hurt like crazy when he bit down, but then it was unbelievable after that. I've never felt anything like that in my life, and I want more. I can't wait till he gets back. I miss him already," Ash said with a wicked grin as Bridgett and Rachael started laughing.

"I do believe the ice queen has melted," Rachael said teasingly to her.

"Yeah, and then some." Ash giggled.

"So when are you going to tell your father?" Bridgett asked her, now serious.

"First thing in the morning, which is only in a few more hours. There's no point in waiting. I would rather get it done now and over with."

Rachael got up and went over, sitting down on the other side of Ash since Bridgett was next to her, holding the ice on the bite mark. She put her arm around Ash, then Bridgett did too. "I'm glad that we will still be together, serving on the same ship with the men whom we love. Just think of all the trouble we're going to get into and the hell we are going to cause them," Rachael said, and they all started laughing.

CHAPTER 44

NATHAN FLEW THE shuttle into the large cargo bay of the *Artemis*, and immediately, the bay door started to close as the guys climbed out of the shuttle. The cargo bay door banged shut, and a hissing noise sounded as the massive door sealed airtight. After the three men had departed the shuttle and moved away from it, a large robotic arm came down from the ceiling and lifted the shuttle up and held it suspended overhead to give more room in the cargo bay. Even without the shuttle overhead, there was still plenty of room in there—even with the MAAV, striker, and their bikes—for more stuff.

They all headed over to the elevator and, in a few seconds, were now on the repaired and fully functional bridge. Other crew members who were now assigned to the *Artemis* were prepping for liftoff for the first time. Nathan ran over to the pilot seat and sat down as the seat moved forward, putting him directly up in the nose of the ship. Cory went over to the comms and scanner consoles as Fâd stepped up onto the captain's platform. His screens and controls came up for him. Artemis also appeared now in her huntress outfit on the portal next to him.

"All controls are yours, Captain, waiting orders," she said in a professional and respectful tone. Fâd quickly punched in the coordinates for the Thor system and sent out orders to all the stations on the ship and got back confirmation quickly. "All systems ready," Artemis told him.

"Lieutenant Wilcox, take us out," Fâd ordered Nathan.

"Affirmative, Captain. Everyone, hang on. Let's see what she's got," Nathan said, grinning, and started pressing buttons on his holographic screens as outside the ship brightly lit up as thrusters kicked on underneath. The huge vessel started lifting off the ground. She continued to lift skyward as the ship's double wings, which were slanted in a down position while on the ground, were now raised level with the ship and angled back for speed. The rear and wing thrusters powered up, and the ship started moving forward and upward slowly.

Nathan grabbed the accelerator lever and started pushing it forward gently as the ship began to pick up speed, and he controlled her movement with the other controller on his right. Artemis appeared on a portal pad next to him. "Come on. We don't have all day," she said with an ornery grin. Nathan pushed the stick all the way forward, and they could hear the secondary engines building up, and suddenly, the ship shot forward as if blasted out of a cannon and was moving now at stage 6 propulsion. In no time, they had left the atmosphere and entered space. Nathan could tell the controls were extremely sensitive, and she moved so smoothly and easily you couldn't tell you were even moving.

He banked her as if it was nothing, moving at such a fast speed. In any other ship, they would all be falling down right now, but they could hardly feel it, just a little swaying motion. He punched in some more commands and then brought up the jump drive.

Back at Fâd's controls, Artemis reported, "Jump drive waiting your command, Captain."

Fâd punched in the order, and Nathan acknowledged it. "Jump in 5, 4, 3, 2, 1." The main engine sounded like it was powering down, but in actuality, it wasn't. Just the opposite was happening. The secondary engines went into standby, and the *Artemis* disappeared into dark space. From the inside looking out the front windows, all one could see were multicolored lights moving around the ship's nose as if it was slicing through time itself.

"ETA to Thor system at jump, twenty-six hours, seven minutes. Stealth system will engage in twenty-five hours, seven minutes," Artemis reported.

"Good. I'm going to my cabin to get changed. Lieutenant Brayton, you have the bridge," Fâd told Cory, and he nodded back to him, acknowledging. Fâd got on the elevator and took it up to the next level where the crew deck was. He headed to his cabin, which was at the end of the hallway, and walked in when his door slid open. Fâd unbuttoned his shirt and removed it, then picked up his dog tags, which hung down his chest, looking at one of them in particular and smiled.

It was Ash's. He had made the switch with one of his and hers after they bonded, which, now flying through this slipstream created by the jump system, was the only thing making him feel close to her. That and he could still smell her scent on him and his clothes, wild roses and a fresh mountain breeze, his two favorite smells ever.

He realized that for the first time in over ten years, he finally felt calm inside. No more was the constant rage that seemed to be just under the surface, making him want to hurt and destroy everything in his path. He knew that being around him had been no picnic for Nathan and Cory. Of course, they weren't that much fun to be around either as they had also suffered. Imprinting was a miserable thing, and it would get ten times worse once a watorian male reached maturity. They became moody, aggressive, and even violent until they finally bonded with their mate. Lucky for him, Nathan and Cory were able to take their aggression out on the mercs and carians they encountered.

Fâd had to grin thinking about Ash. Of course, she was always on his mind but now without the constant drive to pursue her, hunt her down like prey, which, in a way, she had become to him, the ultimate prey. He knew he was in for a wild ride with her. Ash was no pushover, and on more than one occasion, she had stood her ground against him, which was exactly what he needed.

In a way, watorians were a lot like Earth's wolf packs due to their primitive and tribal nature that was still ingrained in them somewhat. Fâd would be an alpha male like his father, the leader of the pack, and could only bond with an alpha female, which Ash definitely was, and this was for life. He and his friends used to joke with one another that the only difference between them and wolves was centuries of civilized living. Also, they didn't run on all fours, they didn't have fur—the only hair on their bodies were on their heads and eyebrows—and a tail, and they didn't howl at the moon. Anyway, they didn't do it in public but only after a large quantity of alcohol had been consumed, and they were camping out together.

He finally got changed into his uniform, which was different from the normal sentinel fleet ones. First off were the colors. These weren't the usual blue, gray, and black of the sentinel fleet but black with dark gray in some of the areas to make them look nice and thin white stripes down the sides. The only thing distinguishing them as sentinel fleet was a tiny fleet insignia located on the right shoulder. One had to get really close to see it. The reasoning behind this was them being an elite infiltration team with special clearances authorized by none other than Vice Admiral Harper himself.

The shirt was made out of a form-fitting material, almost like spandex but much thicker, adding some protection value to it. It kept you cool or warm depending on the need at the time. These were also short-sleeved with two small pockets on both sleeves just above the elbow. The pants were made out of the same material and offered the same hot and cold attributes and some mild protection. They fitted well with one's frame, leaving no loose material to offer the potential danger of getting caught in machinery or hanging up on obstacles when in combat. They had two larger pockets on each side of their legs at midthigh and then a pistol and holster attached at the waist and also strapped around the thigh, making it more secure.

The pants were also in the black color but had dark gray on the insides of the thigh and a thin white strip down the sides. The boots were the same, black, and buckled all the way up the sides to just below one's knee where the boot stopped. These were worn over the pants to keep the possibility of anything crawling up one's pant leg.

Fâd looked in the mirror and ran his fingers through the front of his hair to try and calm it down, but it did no good. His hair had a mind of its own and went everywhere, which was why all male watorians kept the front and top about a couple of inches short so it would stay out of their faces. The braids helped to keep the sides back and away from their face, but that wasn't the real reason for the braids. It had to do more with status and recognition.

He walked over to the closet and reached up on the top shelf, grabbing his pistol. He holstered it, chuckling to himself, remembering Ash back in her bedroom, standing there looking down the chamber of her pistol in nothing but a pair of pants and her bra. Fâd could feel sweat break out on his forehead, seeing her body in his mind and remembering how soft her skin was.

He shook his head, trying to get the image out of his mind. He didn't have time for a cold shower right now. She was his, and they would have the rest of their lives together. The worst was yet to come, when he had to face her father, Vice Admiral Harper, which might not go over too well. The admiral was very protective of his only daughter and was even at this time heading back to Sigma Six to pick her up. But she was now not going with him thanks to Fâd.

He pushed it out of his mind for now; there were more important things to focus on, like the mission at hand, not to mention the constant worry that he and the guys had for the girls ever since Ash used her kinetics back in Pantier in front of everyone. Granted, they were all ordered to purge the episode, but that didn't mean everyone would. His fear was worse. If Ash got taken, she would be sent to the prison city on Trinity. He knew she could take care of herself, but not in this scenario.

Like her father warned her, the authorities would capture her using nueralizers, and very strong ones at that, rendering her helpless and barely conscious. Then they would transport her to the prison city wearing a kinetic inhibitor collar and drop her unconscious form right down in convict central with no weapons. Over the years, the kinetic criminals who survived had figured out ways to disable their collars, so they had full use of their powers. Top that off with the mental psychosis they had and you had a very dangerous animal, which, in honesty, they acted like. By herself, Ash would have no chance to even survive the initial drop-off.

Rachael and Bridgett would also be arrested for withholding information and harboring a dangerous criminal and would be sent to a penal colony as well. Fâd had to mentally fight his fear and cage it so he could focus on the mission at hand, especially since he was heading out into space and couldn't be there to protect her. He was regretting now not letting her come with him. At least then he could make sure she was safe.

He walked out of his cabin, getting into the elevator, and in no time stepped back on the bridge, relieving Nathan and Cory so they could get changed into their new uniforms. He watched the other new crew members whom he handpicked go about their duties and had to smile to himself knowing that before long, there would be three more crew members taking over different stations on the bridge. There were a few other female crew members among them, and not long ago, Nathan would have been chasing them all around.

Fâd knew Nathan tried to substitute his need for Rachael with other women, but he was never satisfied. Cory, on the other hand, had always been after Bridgett from the beginning, and even though he did have other female companions from time to time, he finally those last few years stopped and never had another thing to do with women again.

Fâd walked over and checked the readouts on his console when Artemis appeared. "So I understand that we will be taking on a very important crew member," the AI said, grinning.

He just smirked and continued to scan through the readings. "Yeah. It might be interesting to get that transfer done."

"Don't worry, I put in a request when you were recruiting the other crew personnel. We needed a squad commander, and I requested the best using our top security clearance and classification to pull strings," Artemis said, smiling.

"You what? You didn't clear that with me. I don't ever want you going behind my back again. Do I make myself clear?" Fâd was mad now and wondering if he could trust the AI as he glared at her.

"I would have never done it, but the physiological well-being of the crew was at stake, and it is in my protocol to see to the welfare, protection, and needs of my crew. And since I knew your feelings and from my scans of Ash's increase in her vitals whenever you two were around each other, I deducted that it was beneficial to all. I was very surprised that you finally took the initiative and did it yourself. I thought I was also going to have to become cupid," Artemis said, defending her actions.

"You're an AI, and your job is to make sure the ship is at its best, not meddling in everyone's lives," Fâd said, glaring down at the form of her on the portal.

"Which was what I did. The ship can only perform at peak condition with the proper crew. I made sure I had the proper crew for me, which is in my right under Section 2461, Line 6, of the Sentinel Code, which gives me the right as second in command aboard ship for the time being to recruit the necessary crew members if the need arises without the captain's permission. I also took into account your well-being and the others, who, upon my scanning of them, would not have fared well without the lieutenant commander," Artemis argued, putting her hands on her hips with a frown on her face.

"How is it that you are ranked second in command?" Fâd demanded.

"The admirals that approved Dr. Tolomay's project also gave him the access codes for a lieutenant commander. He then in turn installed those codes into me, giving me temporary authority and ranking of a lieutenant commander until one is assigned. I asked him why, and he said that I would know better than anyone what I needed to function properly and at peak capacity."

"Fine, but in the future, consult with me first," Fâd informed her, still mad.

"Trust me, I will."

"That's the point I'm trying to make. I need to be able to trust you not to do things because of how someone feels or wants," Fâd told her.

"I understand, Captain. I let my feelings for both of you get in the way. You can trust me. I will not do anything again without your prior approval," Artemis replied in an apologetic tone.

"Besides, what if she didn't want to serve on this ship? Trust me, you don't want her mad at you. I know from experience," Fâd replied with a devious smirk on his face.

"She wanted to come. She was just waiting for you to ask her. I just made it more official where she couldn't refuse."

"Is that what she told you?"

Artemis grinned. "Not in those exact words, but all the signs and hints were there. Of course, you would have never picked up on them due to you being so stubborn," she said, and Fâd gave her a dirty look.

Nathan and Cory finally walked back in, and Fâd had them meet him around the galaxy map, then had Artemis pull up the Thor system. Instantly, a solar system of nine planets appeared in a three-dimensional hologram suspended over the glowing circular blue projection table.

"Artemis, can you pinpoint the area where the last comm signal came from?" Fâd asked her, and soon, the hologram changed to three of the outer planets with orbiting moons, and now a blinking red dot appeared in between two of them and near one of the moons.

"So if this was the last known contact, then it would be safe to say that the ship is probably somewhere around here. If it was hit by a merc ship, then there has to be a base somewhere close. They don't strike far from a base of operations, especially a ship full of scientists. They're definitely after someone, though. Mercs wouldn't bother with a science vessel because they couldn't salvage it and sell off the goods, too easily traceable. Somebody on that ship must be very important to the carians for mercs to be sticking their necks out like this, which says we had better find them fast," Cory told them.

* * *

It had been several hours, and the guys were still discussing the possible whereabouts when Atremis reported to Fâd. "Captain, a transfer request has come through for your approval." Due to Artemis's top secret commission and technology, she was one of the only ships out there that could send and receive messages or be comm'd while in jump. The fleet was working on making the other ships capable of it too, but the work was going slowly, and they had no access to Artemis's technology. Other vessels could only pick up approaching ships that were in jump by scanning but not communicate with them.

Fâd walked over to his console and looked down at the request with a big grin on his face. Sure enough, it was the transfer he had been wanting for years, and he couldn't help but feel relief that it was finally happening. He punched in the confirmation, and now Lieutenant Commander Ashley Harper was officially the second in command of the *Artemis*.

All her classified files were now transferred over to him, and he had to admit, after looking them over, that they were pretty outstanding. Her classification was above and beyond even what she had told him, right up there with his, except she was infantry. He was finalizing her enlistment aboard the *Artemis* and assigning her an armory locker for when her armor and weapons arrived, which he was surprised was quite extensive, when the cabin assignment came up. He hadn't thought of that.

Officially, they weren't married yet, only bonded, which to a watorian and their tribal beliefs was the same thing but to society wasn't. He planned on taking care of that issue once she finished school and thought, *Screw it*, and assigned her to the captain's chamber. He had already foolishly lost over ten years of being without her, and he would be damned if he lost any more once she was on board. He was just finishing up when Artemis popped up on the portal of his console, looking nervous.

"Um, Captain, message just came in from Vice Admiral Harper of the *Justification*," Artemis said quietly, but it was still heard by Nathan and Cory, who looked over from the galaxy map at Fâd, and he looked at them.

"What's the message?" Fâd asked her, acting calm and indifferent, but inside, he was nervous as hell.

"He is sending the battleship *Inferno* to assist us once we have located and rescued the proturin ship, plus her crew, and to help escort the proturins back into safe space. He also requests an audience with you once the mission is completed on board the *Justification*," Artemis said, and Fâd nodded his head that he had been advised.

"Did you say the *Inferno* is coming?" Nathan asked, now looking nervous.

"Yeah. She's going to assist," Fâd replied.

"Oh, shit," Nathan said and looked over at Cory, who also looked a little unsure.

"Enough. We need to get focused on the mission at hand, or there won't be any meeting. Now what can you tell me about these three planets here? What would be the best choice for a hidden base?" Fâd asked, walking back over to the galaxy map and trying to get everyone's minds back on the issue at hand, even his.

"My suggestion would be Hedron. It is the less habitable of the three, making it a perfect place to hide. The planet's atmosphere is high in hydrogen, selenium, and krypton, making it completely inhospitable to support life. The planet's composition is also high in magnesium and uranium, causing scanners to be useless, making an underground base invisible from space," Artemis replied.

"All right, let's start there. When we come out of jump, would you be able to detect an ion trail, even one that is over forty-eight hours old?" Fâd asked the AI.

"It is possible. My scanners are quite sensitive and much more advanced than most, but I can not guarantee it either."

"That's understandable. At least we have a starting point. That's all for now. Back to stations," Fâd said, dismissing everyone.

* * *

It was the next morning back on Sigma Six, and sure enough, Ash was starting to feel pretty terrible. It felt like her insides were tearing themselves apart, and her head was killing her. She had Rachael give her a shot of asrinon because she was hurting so bad and she could feel her kinetic energy constantly trying to power up.

Ash also went ahead and put in her transfer request, then waited for the reply she knew would be coming before she got any approval. Sure enough, it didn't take long since it was the admiral who would have to approve the transfer from his ship to another. Ash's comm button on her multitool was flashing red now, letting her know she had an incoming message.

She went over to the console in the apartment, taking a deep breath, and punched up the frequency to open up the comm link. The holographic screen in front of her lit up, and Vice Admiral Harper appeared on it, looking at her with a serious glare.

"What's going on? Why are you transferring to the *Artemis*?" Admiral Harper asked, but Ash could tell he wasn't mad like she thought he would be. He actually seemed a little sad.

"She needs a squad leader, and that's where my friends are serving."

Her father's eyes narrowed. "No, Ash. I will not approve this unless you tell me the real reason. I need to know this is what you want—not because of what your friends or what the ship needs but only what you need."

Ash's eyes watered up as she fought back tears. "Yes, Dad, I need him, I love him, and I can't live without him."

Admiral Harper let out a sad sigh, and Ash could see him working on his console. Then he looked up at her with a weak smile. "I'm happy that you two have finally realized you need each other, but I'm sad to have to let you go. I know that is selfish, but that's because I love you, and you will always be my little girl. If it were anyone else, I would never allow this. Fâd's a good man, and he has loved you for many years. I feel secure in the knowledge that I know he will care and protect you for the rest of your life. The transfer has been approved, and you should be getting the confirmation soon from the *Artemis*. I love you, Ash."

"I love you, Dad," Ash said back, and then the screen went blank. Ash buried her head in her arms and was sobbing now. Rachael and Bridgett both knew how she felt for they, too, had already gone through the same thing with their parents. They went over and put their arms around her and just let her cry. Finally, when she regained some composure, she told them she was going to lie down. The pain was getting worse, and the pills Fâd gave her weren't doing a thing to help. She stood up but stopped and looked at Rachael.

"Rachael, give me a nueralizer just in case. I don't know how much longer I can fight this. Those pills aren't helping. My head is killing me, and now my eyes feel like they're on fire," Ash told her.

"Are you sure? That will almost knock you out."

"Yes, I'm sure. I am fighting to keep my kinetics down as it is right now due to this pain. I feel like someone has a knife in me, twisting it all around. Was that how it felt?" Ash asked them, looking down at her hands, which had little blue sparks dancing around on them, and she was starting to shake.

"No, just really bad cramps, headache, and slight fever, but the pills helped a lot, and our eyes never burned," Bridgett said, worried about Ash. This wasn't what they had experienced. Rachael came over and touched Ash's forehead and got a little shock from her but left her hand there. She could tell she didn't just have a little fever but was on fire.

"Oh my gosh, you're burning up. But we can't take you to the hospital. What do we do?" Rachael looked over at Bridgett with a scared look. Bridgett immediately raced out of the apartment, and in just a few seconds, she was beating on the twins' door. Oscar opened it and saw the scared look on Bridgett's face.

"What is it?" he asked.

"It's Ash. She's really sick."

Oscar and Lee followed her out of their apartment and into the girls' and then into Ash's bedroom where Rachael had helped her to. Ash was on the bed now, shaking all over, and the twins walked over, then sat down next to her. Oscar put his hand on her forehead and got shocked but kept it there. Rachael reached down and pulled out a small vial and syringe from Ash's med bag, which she had taken out of Ash's dresser, and was starting to fill the syringe when Lee took it from her.

"What do you think you're going to give her?" he asked and looked down at the vial and then over to Oscar and handed him the vial

Oscar looked down at the vial, then over at Rachael. "Is Ash a kinetic?" he asked Rachael, who nodded her head yes as tears began to run down her face.

"And if you say anything, we will kill you," Bridgett warned them from the door. It shocked Rachael to hear Bridgett say that because she was always the one ready to cry.

"Don't be stupid. We aren't like all the other fools that believe all kinetics are bad," Lee said as Oscar filled the syringe and then gave Ash the shot in the arm since nueralizers had to be administered into the bloodstream and not the nervous system. Then Ash stopped shaking instantly.

"Okay, what's going on here? What happened to her?" Lee asked now that one crisis had been diverted, but the other one was still raging on in Ash.

"Ash was just bonded to Fâd about ten hours ago, if that helps. That's all we know," Rachael told them, and now both brothers started checking Ash out. Oscar opened one of her eyelids and saw that her iris was glazed over, and Lee looked as well. Then they started looking around her shoulder areas, and Lee looked back at the girls.

"Are you sure she bonded? We aren't seeing any bite mark?"

"Yeah, I'm positive. I put the ice pack on them myself," Bridgett told them and went over and moved Ash's shirt back to show them, but now she, too, couldn't see any mark.

"They were right here. I swear it," Bridgett said in shock.

Oscar leaned down, getting really close to where Bridgett said, and barely saw two tiny, little marks, which looked to be quickly healing over. "I see them. I think I know what's going on. Ash's kinetics have a regenerative property to them, which causes her to recover from injury faster. In this case, it has sped up the change, which would be like tripling the side effects. I need to give her something a lot stronger for the pain and to get this fever down before it literally cooks her from the inside out," Oscar told them as Lee got up and left.

In a few minutes, he was back with a large med bag and opened it. It was full of all kinds of medical equipment, syringes, and small medicine vials. Lee took out one and a long syringe and handed them to Oscar. "I'll need you to roll her over on her side. This will need to be administered directly into her nervous system to get to her pain nodes faster and help with the fever."

"She has an injection port at the back of her neck if that helps," Rachael told them, and the twins rolled Ash over, moved her hair aside, and saw it.

"Does she suffer from headaches?" Lee asked them.

"Yeah, especially if she uses her telepathy a lot or her kinetics," Rachael told them.

"Perfect," Oscar replied and then inserted the long needle into Ash's port in her neck and injected the medicine. Then they carefully rolled her over onto her back and started to remove her clothes.

"What are you doing?" Bridgett asked them.

"We have to get her clothing off. They are keeping the heat in, not allowing it to escape," Lee told them and continued to pull her pants off as Oscar took Ash's shirt off.

"Relax. We're doctors. We do this stuff all the time. Trust me, we see tons of naked humanoids every day at the clinic during our shifts," Oscar said, rolling his eyes.

They left her underwear and bra on, then put a light sheet over her to give her some privacy. Then Lee ran his palm scanner inches over her, watching the screen on his multitool, which was a special one made specifically for medical uses. He stopped over her pelvic area, and they could see the foreign antibodies in Ash's body now concentrated on her reproductive system.

"Are you seeing this, Oscar? This has never been witnessed before. Just think what the medical profession will say when we show them this. Wow, that looks painful," Lee said excitedly.

"What? You're not showing anyone this. Ash doesn't need her insides broadcast all over," Rachael informed them, mad.

"It will only be doctors that see it, and they won't even know it's her," Oscar said, annoyed.

"So what's happening to Ash, to us?" Bridgett asked, a little scared.

"It's simple. Watorians only produce watorians, whether you're one or not. When males bite, which is purely instinctual, they inject some of their own DNA into the wound, and it travels through the body, then releases markers that go and collect the best genes from the host. Their DNA heads straight for the reproductive area of the host, and soon, the markers start flooding in with the host genes.

"If it's a nonwatorian host, the male's DNA forces the female's ovaries to change to produce only eggs with the watorian DNA but now with the best genes from the host replacing some of the lesser ones of the males genes but changing them also into watorian genes. It's kind of like they clone themselves through a host but also use the best qualities from that host only changed. It is through the final sequence that the offspring becomes full watorian," Lee explained to them.

"What is the final sequence?" Rachael asked.

"Conception, when the egg is fertilized and the DNA becomes one full strand again, pure watorian," Oscar told her.

"That is why there is pain for a few days after being bitten. In females, their ovaries are changing to produce this new strand. In human and vatorian females, the uterus changes as well. It becomes thicker to accommodate a watorian offspring since they are heavier and stronger than human and vatoria offspring. Female watorians don't have that problem as they are heavier boned and able to carry their own kind, but they do still go through the DNA changing but at least don't have to endure the intense pain, just some mild cramping. There have been cases where human females have had their ribs broken from the babies kicking because of their strength or had to stay in bed the whole time they are carrying the offspring.

"This is the main reason for the biting. The other is actually to help enhance some of the host's senses as a defense mechanism. For one, the sight changes to be able to see farther and in the dark and an increase in stamina. This is believed to aid the parent to be able to protect the offspring much more effectively. There is also a scent that only mated couples can detect from each other when near, kind of like an early warning detection, purely animalistic, so they know it's their mate and don't attack to protect their young," Lee said as Rachael and Bridgett blushed, obviously knowing what he was talking about.

"Is Ash going to be okay?" Bridgett asked, worried.

"Yeah, she will be. I won't be surprised that when she comes to that, her eyes will be completely changed. One thing we do need to make sure of is that as long as the change is occurring, she is kept on the nueralizer. Her kinetics will try to take over otherwise," Oscar told them, so it was decided that every fifteen minutes, a scan was to be done on Ash to see how far along she was.

Finally, the last of the markers and watorian DNA were no longer showing up as foreign bodies in Ash's system, and the changes were now looking normal again, but it took eleven hours to accomplish. They had to give her another nueralizer and one more pain shot two hours ago, so she was still out.

Oscar and Lee stayed with her the whole time, monitoring her progress, and they discussed in great depth what they were witnessing, totally impressed with it all, commenting it was too bad that all life-forms didn't do this, that it would definitely improve all races.

They even went as far as to ask Rachael if, when she decided to have children, they could study the conception and the cellular change in the egg as it changes into the embryo. "You mean you want to watch me have sex?" Rachael asked, appalled.

"No, just right afterward. You don't conceive while you're actually copulating. Don't you know anything?" Oscar said and looked at her as if she wasn't all upstairs.

"Well, then why don't you just come into the bedroom and watch the whole thing from beginning to end? I'm sure Nathan won't mind," Rachael told them sarcastically.

"I never thought of that, from the very beginning to the end results. Think of the medical knowledge we would learn from that," Lee said to Oscar, and Rachael could tell they were serious.

"Hey, you two nutcases, it's not going to happen. I was being sarcastic. Besides, children are the furthest thing from my mind right now," Rachael said, rolling her eyes at them.

They gave her a dirty look and went and checked on Ash again. They noticed her fever was completely gone now, and she was no longer shivering. Oscar lifted one of her eyelids, and sure enough, he was right, her irises were now white but different. He went out into the living room and told everybody that Ash was over it and that she should be waking up in a few hours. Everyone let out a sigh of relief.

The twins took their leave and left to go back to their apartment, discussing their findings, very excited about what they had witnessed firsthand. Rachael and Bridgett just shook their heads and went to bed, for tomorrow, they had classes again, but thank goodness school would be over soon.

CHAPTER 45

———⟡———

"CAPTAIN, WE ARE entering the Thor cluster. Cloaking system engaged. Cutting jump drive in five, four, three, two, one. We are free of jump. Running cloaked and silent, sir," Artemis said to Fâd.

Fâd was standing at his platform, running through his virtual screens, as they came out of jump. "Nathan, stage 4 propulsion only. Artemis, scan for recent ion trails. Comms silent," he ordered.

The ship was moving through the Thor system and toward Hedron and its two moons when Artemis reported she had picked up a faint ion trail. Fâd told her to plot a course following it, and soon, they headed to one of Hedron's moons. But before they circled around it, he ordered a full stop. Artemis's scanners had picked up an orbiting spaceport that was staying between the planet and the moon, using the moon to try and conceal its whereabouts. Also, she was able to pick up a structure on the planet's side with her scanners, and they were pretty sure it was the topside of an underground base.

"Artemis, can you block their comms from here before we go in?" Fâd asked her.

"Of course. I'm also detecting three gunships and one proturin science frigate," the AI told him.

"All right, ground team, suit up. Wilcox, you have the bridge," Fâd told Nathan.

"Are you sure you don't want me to come along?" Nathan asked. He was still working the controls of the ship.

"Yes. It will be your job to get us in fast, and if those ships power up, you will have to take them out and cover our backs," Fâd told him as he headed toward the elevator to take it down to the armory so he could suit up in his armor.

Cory waited at the elevator for him, and they rode down to the bottom level where the armory was located. In no time, they were suited up in their combat armor, which looked nothing like the girls' armor due to these being a lot heavier. Yet to a watorian, it felt like nothing.

There was a lot more armament on these suits for protection in hand-to-hand combat and cybernetics, giving the soldiers even more strength and agility above what they already had. Plus, all the suits were dark gray, except Fâd and Cory's, which were black, since they were the ranking officers. The rest of the infiltration team was made up of three more men and one woman. Everyone was now checking one another's suits, making sure they were sealed properly, checking their comm links in their helmets and arming their assault rifles.

"All right, Wilcox, get us in fast," Fâd ordered Nathan through the comm link in his helmet.

The ship shot around the moon and banked to the left at a ninety-degree angle as Nathan spun her around fast so her port side was facing the spaceport as Artemis hacked the port's docking bay umbilical. Nathan flew the ship sideway now and met the umbilical as it extended out, and Artemis had to decloak to hook up to it. He kept the ship hovering in place as the umbilical attached without docking the ship, which was an extremely dangerous maneuver, and only a highly skilled pilot could even perform such a feat.

The reason for this was, a ship could get away fast enough to be able to fight in case a gunship powered up, but there was nothing to keep the ship there. And if it moved slightly, it would tear the umbilical, and the infiltration team could fall out into space if the pilot wasn't careful. Fâd and they opened the air lock that was located in the cargo bay right next to one of the elevators and quickly entered the passage, turned on their camo generators, making them invisible, and entered the port. Once inside and behind cover, Fâd comm'd Nathan that they were clear. Nathan waited just a few minutes for the umbilical to release from the ship, and then he moved to cover the gunships.

Sure enough, two of them powered up and came after him as he spun the *Artemis*, dodging the hull-piercing shots. When he got a little ways ahead of them, he banked the ship around at a 180-degree turn and came right back at them, now firing. They had no chance as the *Artemis* closed in on them, firing full-out with her forbs mech guns, and took both ships out, leaving nothing but floating debris in her wake as she passed between them. Nathan made a beeline for the other gunship, and in no time, that one was also dead in space. Instead of docking, though, he cloaked again and remained patrolling in case of any other possible ships that might be around.

Inside, Fâd, with Cory covering his back, was moving swiftly and silently through the spaceport. A borvian merc was walking past the crate Fâd and Cory were hiding behind when Fâd popped up behind him and snapped his neck. Then he and Cory dragged the body behind the crate. They moved on, going from one cover to the next, and now were in the main hub of the port where they counted fifteen more mercs made up of humans and borvians. The squad quickly surrounded them, and on Fâd's command, they jumped up and caught the mercs in a cross fire, quickly taking them down. A couple of them Fâd had to hit with a kinetic blast, but otherwise, it was rather simple. Once the mercs in the hub were dealt with and the area was secured, the team checked the surrounding rooms for the proturins but found none.

"Infiltration team to *Artemis*," Fâd said over his comm.

"This is *Artemis*," Nathan replied.

"Port secured. No proturins. Probably in the base on the planet. We need a pickup and drop-off," Fâd told him as he signaled his team to head to the nearest dock. They quickly moved out, and once again, Nathan brought the ship in like a pro and made a pickup without docking.

"We're in. Go!" Fâd ordered from the cargo bay, and once the umbilical released, Nathan headed down toward the surface at an unbelievable speed, passing into the toxic atmosphere, making a straight shot at the base.

There was a large tower and an aboveground structure located on the barren, sandy red ground of the planet. He took out their comm satellite immediately with just one of the forbs mech guns. Nathan then spun the ship around, and without landing her, he hovered the vessel barely a few feet from the ground as the cargo bay doors opened and the kinetic barrier covered the open hull, keeping the poisonous air out and the bay safe. Fâd and the team jumped out, still in their completely sealed combat suits, and ran to the installation. Nathan got confirmation all infiltration team was on ground; he then flew the ship back up to provide protection overhead.

Cory went over to the door controls of the base and hacked into them easily. The doors slid open, and Fâd went in first, running into two mercs, immediately sending them flying with a kinetic blast. The rest of the team filtered in and took cover, and now the base knew they were there. Fâd led with Cory backing him again, and the rest of the team sought cover behind them and followed as they moved forward, dropping the mercs as they went. He ran up to another girder as Cory stood up from behind his cover and dropped two more mercs with his assault rifle, covering Fâd as he moved forward. They finally made it to the stairs and the elevator. They headed down the emergency stairs silently and swiftly instead of taking the elevator.

In no time, they came out into a large landing with no cover from fire. Still with their camouflage on, Fâd and Cory went first and sneaked up behind two borvian mercs who were standing watch a little ways down the hallway. At the same time, they both grabbed them from behind and, in one quick twist, snapped their necks with ease. The rest of the team followed, and they split up from there. Fâd and Cory went one way down the wide hall, and the others went the opposite, since the base was laid out in a circular pattern and met on the other side.

Outside, Nathan was patrolling the air when a call came in. "*Artemis*, this is Commander Torres of the battleship *Inferno*. We are entering the Thor cluster now. Have you located the scientists?"

Artemis looked at Nathan from her portal beside him with an ornery grin on her face. "Your father-in-law is calling," she said quietly.

"Very funny, Arti," Nathan replied with a nervous grin.

"*Inferno*, this is Lieutenant Wilcox of the *Artemis*. We have located the scientists. They are being held in the base on the planet Hedron, and we have a recon team in now to recover them. The port located near the first moon has been secured. Once we finish taking the base, we will transport the scientists back to the spaceport," Nathan replied.

"Affirmative. We will rendezvous with you there," Commander Torres answered.

"This ought to be interesting. Hopefully, he won't shoot me," Nathan said, grinning, and Artemis giggled.

Down on the planet, Fâd and Cory moved through the base with ease. They got pinned down only once as both Cory and Fâd's camo generators shut down from taking fire, and they were now visible. Fâd hit the mercs with a kinetic blast as Cory laid down, suppressing fire, and they soon were the only ones left standing. They got around to the other side, clearing side rooms as they went, and met up with the rest of their team, who also were visible, having come under fire and losing their camo generators too. They regrouped and had one final room to hit, which they knew had to be where the scientists were being held hostage. Cory hacked the door, and it slid open. Fâd and his team entered it with their assault rifles aimed straight ahead of them.

Standing in the middle of the room was a human merc holding one of the scientists at gunpoint and two other mercs standing off to both sides of him with their assault rifles trained on the rest of the proturian scientists. "Hold it right there, fleet scum. One move and this walking pile of flesh won't be taking up space anymore," the merc warned as both Fâd and Cory had their rifles aimed at him.

Fâd put his assault rifle on his back where the auto clamps held it and looked over at Cory, then back at the merc. "We don't deal with mercs," Fâd said, hitting both of the mercs who were standing off to the side of the leader with a powerful kinetic blast, sending them flying across the room and slamming them into the metal walls, killing them instantly. At the same time, Cory dropped the merc leader, who had the proturin scientist at gunpoint, with a clean shot between the eyes as the rest of Fâd's squad stood ready to open fire if need be. The scientists just stayed there in shock, but the one whom the merc had hostage seemed unfazed, looking around behind him and then over to Fâd and Cory.

"It took you long enough to get here. I figured I was going to have to do something. Nice shot, by the way. Impressive display of kinetic energy. How high is your level?" the unfazed, marked yellow scientist asked, smoothing out his uniform and walking over to them.

Fâd and Cory looked at each other, not knowing what to do. They were a little taken aback by this proturin's forwardness and lack of fear. Finally, Cory got on the radio and told Nathan that the base was secure and that they will need a pickup.

The proturin walked over to Fâd and looked up at him, then checked him out from head to toe. "What species are you? I can't tell under that armor and helmet," he asked bluntly.

Fâd removed his helmet now as did the rest of his team and looked down at the proturin with annoyance. "I'm Captain Larson of the *Artemis*. Is everyone all right?"

"Ah, I should have guessed. Mature watorian male, excellent specimen. Any relation to Rear Admiral Larson?"

"Yes, but enough with the chatter. We need to go. Are you in charge here?" Fâd asked him, wanting to get away from the annoying proturin.

"Me? No, the captain is—I mean was. He was killed. Lieutenant Kar is now."

"Well, which one of you is Kar?" Fâd asked, frustrated.

"Him, the red one. It's okay, Kar. They only bite their mates," the proturin told one of the scientists who was hiding with the others.

When the scientist said this, Cory started chuckling, and Fâd gave him a dirty look. Kar stood up as did the rest of the scientists and walked over to Fâd, still very nervous. Fâd looked down at him, totally void of any emotion. "Are you second in command?" he asked.

"Yes," the scared lieutenant replied.

"We need to get you and your men out of here."

"Excuse me, but we're not all men. That one is a woman even though she looks like a man," said the obnoxious proturin.

Again, Cory was trying really hard not to start laughing; and this time, the rest of their team were looking around, trying not to chuckle. Fâd narrowed his eyes at the mouthy one. "Then who are you?" he asked, now completely annoyed and wanting the pest to shut up.

"Why, I'm Dr. Shin Hon-tor, if you really need to know," the yellow proturin said, placing his hands on his hips, and frowned.

"Then do me a favor, Doctor, shut up and follow us," Fâd ordered him, and the doctor's mouth fell open.

"How rude. If I weren't such a gentlemen, I would challenge you to a duel. But being of better character, I will overlook your lack of manners," he said with his head up and started for the door.

Fâd looked at him in disbelief. "Are you serious? Challenge me. You honestly think you could beat me in a fight?" he replied, watching the proturin through narrowed eyes, as the scientist headed for the door.

Dr. Shin Hon-tor was a normal size for a proturin, which was about average height to a male human, maybe just a little shorter. He exhibited the yellow-striped markings that was known for his species and the flesh-colored, leathery skin. He didn't have the normal elongated head like his kind. Instead, his was more square, and it was very apparent he was young just by looking at him.

The other odd thing about him was, instead of the solid large red-rimmed black eyes that proturins had, Dr. Shin's had a slight bluish tint to his. The rest of his features were the same as all proturins—thin, frail-looking build, two slits for nose holes, and a thin slit for a mouth. Even the tentacle-like appendages that hung down the back of his head, giving proturins the appearance of hair, was also streaked with yellow strips.

Like the rest of his fellow scientists, he also wore form-fitting white pants with black-and-red stripes running down the sides, matching knee-high boots, form-fitting white tunic with matching black-and-red stripes, and black outlining that went all the way down to just above their knees, which also helped to distinguish the proturins as scientists.

"Typical watorian logic. I didn't say a fight. I said a duel, a test of intelligence, which I would clearly win due to your lack of it," the doctor told him, walking through the door and heading down the hall.

Fâd looked down at the proturin lieutenant who walked up beside him. "I'm going to shoot him," he said to him.

The lieutenant looked up at Fâd with a half smirk. "Please do," he whispered, which caught Fâd off guard.

Fâd shook his head, and they all headed down the hallway toward the elevator. He took lead and got in the elevator but rolled his eyes when Dr. Shin got in with him. Cory and a couple other scientists and the rest were going to wait for the elevator's return. They rode it up to the main landing and got out as the door slid shut, and it returned for the rest.

Nathan was standing in the main rotunda of the aboveground structure, waiting for them. He had docked the *Artemis* outside on the landing pad and came in through the sealed umbilical that linked the landing pad to the base tower. Fâd and Cory headed over to him but didn't realize Dr. Shin had followed them until it was too late.

"How many more on your crew are watorians? Are there any nonwatorian crew members?" he asked, and Fâd just closed his eyes, trying to calm himself.

"We are all watorian, but there will be some female human crew members before long," Nathan told him with a grin.

"Ah, mates. Interesting. Have you all bonded?" the doctor asked.

"How did you know that?" Nathan asked, puzzled.

"I can tell. You're calmer, more relaxed, signifying you have bonded. At this age, most males exhibit a more aggressive attitude even if they haven't imprinted. Your captain, though, must not get along with his mate. He's easily agitated."

Cory and Nathan busted up laughing, and Fâd turned on the doctor now. He was ready to turn him into mush. Nathan and Cory grabbed Fâd and held him back, still laughing. "Let me at him. I'm going to pound him into the ground," Fâd yelled at them.

"Aha! I'm close on my assumption," the doctor said, and Fâd struggled even more.

"For your information, Ash and I get along just fine. What? Why am I even telling you this? It's none of your business," Fâd said, now glaring at the proturin.

"Well, there must be something about your relationship with your mate, or you wouldn't be so agitated."

"I'm agitated because I had to leave my mate behind to fly millions of miles to save a nosy, barely mature proturin," Fâd said to him as Nathan and Cory let him go.

"How do you know I barely reach maturity?" the doctor asked, astonished.

"Because I'm not as dumb as you think. And I assume you try to overcompensate with your mouth due to your feeling of being rejected and ignored by your peers, constantly trying to prove yourself. But in fact, all you're doing is just making it to where nobody can stand you," Fâd told him with a smug smirk.

Dr. Shin went to say something but stopped. He was caught off guard now, and for the first time, he didn't know what to say. The watorian was right, he was always being ignored, and no one would listen to anything he would say. Even some of his discoveries, which as young as he was were quite a few, still didn't earn him any respect. Fâd ordered everyone to move out, and Dr. Shin now followed the rest without saying a word, and Fâd was able to start to calm down a little.

Everyone left through the umbilical that connected the base to the ship, and they boarded the *Artemis* as the rest of the squad showed the scientists to the mess hall where they could get something to eat while Fâd, Nathan, and Cory headed back to the bridge. They took their stations, and Nathan piloted the *Artemis* off the planet and headed back toward the spaceport so the proturins could retrieve their ship. No sooner had they left the base than Dr. Shin stepped onto the bridge and walked over to Fâd.

"Impressive ship, Captain. I have never seen one like this before," he said, looking around.

"That is because I'm one of a kind," Artemis spoke up as she appeared on her portal on Fâd's console.

"An AI instead of a VI. Outstanding. But not your typical AI, I can tell."

"No, I am a sentient ship, a learning AI," Artemis told him, and Dr. Shin was now looking her over.

"Artemis, ah, the goddess of the hunt according to human mythology, perfect name for an infiltrator. You must be one of the first ones that Dr. Tolamay created, a genius in the field of AIs, years ahead of his time in technology, even by today's standards," Shin said.

"Why, yes. He created me after his daughter who died. This whole ship, he created and oversaw its building," Artemis told him, smiling.

"Fascinating. Do you mind, Captain, if I take a tour of the *Artemis?*" Shin asked excitedly.

"I can't give you a tour right now," Fâd told him coldly and continued to work at his console.

"Captain, I can, if that is okay with you?" Artemis asked. Fâd looked over at her, then relented, and Dr. Shin went from station to station as Artemis appeared around the bridge on her portal pads, explaining everything to him as the proturian scientist grilled her with questions. Artemis and Dr. Shin finally left the bridge as the ship was now closing in on the spaceport. The *Inferno* was already there, docked. Nathan took a big gulp. Cory heard him and started chuckling, looking over at Fâd, who was grinning. Finally, Nathan was going to be put on the spot. He had always managed to weasel his way out of confrontations, but this time, he wasn't going to be able to.

Nathan spun the ship with her aft thrusters and flew her in sideway, only this time allowed the docking clamps to lock on and hold her in place as the umbilical came out and sealed to the air lock on the bridge. One of the ship's crew members brought the proturins up onto the bridge as Fâd, Cory, and Nathan, who were all still in their combat armor, which gave them a menacing appearance due to watorians being tall and well-built, headed for the air lock with them following. The bridge air lock was located right side of the two elevators and emergency stairs that were on the starboard side off the hallway that ran down the one side of the ship from the bridge. They didn't pull their assault rifles but left them clamped to their backs, as were two pistols each strapped to their thighs.

The air lock door slid open and released a hissing noise as atmospheric pressure changed. Soon, it righted itself, and the outer hull door now slid open, and they proceeded down the umbilical walkway toward the port. The port doors slid open, and Fâd, followed by Nathan and Cory, entered. Behind them came the scientists. Fâd got on his comm and told Artemis that once she and the doctor were done with their tour to have the doctor return to the port. Fâd saw Commander Torres and about a dozen of his soldiers making sure the port was secure, and when the commander saw him, he headed toward them.

"Fâdron Larson, my, you have changed. I think the last time I saw you was when the girls covered you with paint," Torres said to him, and instead of saluting him, he held out his hand. Fâd took it, and they shook hands. Then Torres looked over at the other two, but when he got to Nathan, his expression changed from smiling to one of seriousness.

"So, Nathan Wilcox, I think we need to chat. Come with me," Torres said to Nathan, who looked like he was about ready to run.

"If you don't mind, sir, I prefer staying right here so I have witnesses when you try and kill me," Nathan said.

Raul Torres looked at him and then threw his head back, laughing. "Kill you? Why would I kill you? I just want to know when you plan on making your union with my daughter official and also to shake your hand. Hopefully, you can control her."

Nathan had a big grin on his face now. "I was hoping to get married as soon as she finishes school, and as far as controlling her, I'm sorry, sir, but that is an impossible task. She scares the crap out of me sometimes with the things she does."

Raul came over and put his arm around Nathan's shoulders, which was kind of funny since Nathan was taller. "I know, and I'm glad you have to deal with it now. All you boys do. Trust me, you guys have gotten yourselves a handful of trouble," he said, chuckling, and the guys all nodded their heads in agreement with him.

The proturin scientists went into their ship to inspect it and make sure it was okay, along with some of the soldiers from the *Inferno*. Fâd, Nathan, and Cory continued to talk and laugh with Commander Torres. Dr. Shin, finally finished with his tour of the *Artemis*, walked over to them.

"Captain Larson, your ship is a marvel. Her technology is so advanced compared to anything else around. She still needs a lot of work, and your science lab is none existent, so upon my inspection, I accept the challenge," Dr. Shin said, all smug.

"What challenge?" Fâd asked, confused.

"Your ship and you are in bad need of a science officer, and I am a science officer. I will have my enlistment sent over immediately and gather my belongings from the science vessel and transferred over to the *Artemis*. I will start immediately compiling a list of much needed supplies and equipment to properly set up the science lab," Shin said and headed for the proturin ship to get his stuff.

"No, no, no, wait one minute. We don't need a science officer. We're doing just fine on our own," Fâd said, trying to stop him, but Shin continued to walk away and put his hand up, brushing Fâd's protest aside.

"Nonsense. It's amazing you survived this long without me."

Fâd just threw his head back, closing his eyes and letting out a loud moan. Commander Torres, Nathan, and Cory were now chuckling under their breath. "Why me? What did I do to deserve this?" Fâd said out loud, looking over at them.

It wasn't more than seven minutes later when Dr. Shin was already back with a large duffle bag and three other proturin scientists helping him carry his stuff to the *Artemis*, but now they seemed happier. Fâd looked at Commander Torres. "Can I refuse his transfer?"

"No. Proturin scientists have top clearance, and if they ask to join a ship in the fleet, fleet command considers it an honor. What did you say his name was?" Torres asked as if he knew something.

"Dr. Shin Hon-tor."

"Of course. I thought I recognized that name. He is the leading scientist right now in chemical warfare. Plus, he's also the one that Harper said is about to make a breakthrough in treating psychosis in kinetics. It's his studies that have shown that natural kinetics don't have the affliction as do exposure victims. He was the brain behind the nueralizer and asrinon," Torres told them.

"Are you serious? He has barely reached maturity," Fâd said in disbelief.

"I know, and he did most of this when he was younger. Now it makes perfect sense why the mercs attacked the science vessel. They were after Dr. Shin for the carians. Could you imagine what would have happened if the carians got their hands on him? What kind of chemical weapons would they have ended up having?" Torres said to them, and everyone looked over to where the crazy scientist had gone.

"Great. We now have a highly wanted person on board," Cory said.

"Yeah, but I feel a whole lot better that he's with you guys than buzzing around somewhere else out in the galaxy," Torres said.

"Oh yeah. Trust me, if the carians got their hands on him, they would kill him immediately. He has a way of getting under your skin, like an annoying parasite," Fâd told them, and they all chuckled.

The new proturin commander of the science vessel came over and said that his ship was ready to leave, and everyone then headed back to theirs and provided escort for the science vessel back into fleet-controlled space and also to meet up with the *Justification*, which Fâd was not looking forward to.

He walked back to the bridge, and Artemis was waiting for him over by his console with her arms folded over her chest and a frown on her face. "Captain, transfer from sentinel command for Dr. Shin Hon-tor is waiting for your confirmation," Artemis told Fâd unhappily.

"Can we refuse it?" Fâd hoped.

"Unfortunately, no, this is a direct command. I have assigned a cabin for our crazy new science officer, and he has already sent off a requisition order to sentinel command for needed equipment. I am also putting an automatic containment field around the science lab from now on. Some of the things he was telling me that he made and his experiments scared the hell out of me. I informed him that if he put my crew in danger that I would jettison his scrawny body out into space," Artemis told him.

"What was his reply to that?" Fâd asked with a slight smirk.

"He informed me that my threats were useless since a small inhibitor plug could take me down," Artemis replied, appalled.

Fâd started chuckling now. It was funny seeing the ship's AI fighting with someone who was just as intelligent, arrogant, and stubborn as her. He told Nathan to take the ship out and sent the coordinates from his console for the *Justification*. In a matter of minutes, all three ships jumped, leaving the Thor system behind.

CHAPTER 46

"ARE YOU SURE about this, Ms. Marsh? Is there anyone else to back up what you are telling us?" the operative from council asked Sierra. They were sitting across from her in one of the chairs at the nightclub called the Odyssey. She picked up her drink and looked around to make sure no one was watching them. Even Murray, who she knew was good friends with Fâd and his buddies, was busy washing glasses clear across the room behind his bar and didn't seem to notice her. It helped that the two council operatives came in civilian clothes and not council uniforms.

"There were others, but Rear Admiral Larson ordered them to forget the incident. She's crazy, clearly psychotic, and her friends all protect her," Sierra told them with a serious look on her face, then took a large gulp of her drink.

"Rear Admiral Gerrard Larson ordered them?" the operative asked, trying to contain a grin.

"Yeah. I couldn't believe it when I heard that we were ordered to stay quiet," she said, taking another sip from her drink.

"What do you mean you heard? You didn't actually hear him say it?" the other council operative asked her.

"Of course not. I was knocked out, and they had to tranquilize her because she was going to kill me. One of the other privates told me later about the order. The worst of it that really appalls me is that I did nothing to even provoke her, but because she is Vice Admiral Harper's daughter, everyone protects her, which infuriates me. I nearly died, and she goes back to the academy like nothing ever happened."

"Interesting. Well, I'm glad you're okay. That was definitely a close call for you. Rest assured that we will take the proper steps so that no one else will get hurt or even killed thanks to you. You are truly a hero for coming forward with this. Just think of all the lives you just saved," the operative told her, and Sierra smiled wickedly.

She finished her drink, then stood up, shaking the hands of the operatives, and left the nightclub. The two operatives watched her go, and they now had big grins on their faces. "Rear Admiral Larson, over half of his soldiers, and the frosting on the cake, Vice Admiral Harper's very own daughter, including Commander Torres and Chief Engineer Nelson's daughters are implicated in this. It's time to report back to council militia. This is finally it. We can finally strike against them, but it's going to take a lot of our fleet to do it if they fight back," one of the operatives said.

"What are we waiting for while Larson and, especially, Harper, whom we can't touch because he's, for some reason, protected by our own council presidency, are out in deep space? The sooner we attack, the better. That way, we won't have to contend with the whole sentinel armada. We can have our fleet here and stationary before they even hear of what is happening. They won't be able to ever step foot again back in council-controlled space. Even Harper, if we have enough force here, wouldn't try anything," the operative said, and now they both were chuckling and toasted each other. They finally finished their drinks and left the Odyssey as Murray watched them go.

He had acted like he was busy and paying them no heed, but he had now washed the same glass over again for the twenty-sixth time. He knew they were council operatives. He hadn't been around this long to not recognize them immediately, and then to be talking to that Sierra. She always had been bad news, unlike her brother, Kaiden. He was a nice young man, but she was mean and vindictive.

Murray went into the back room and unlocked the door to his office. Once inside, he locked it back up and walked over to a console near the far wall and began typing on it, then sent off an encrypted message to Fâd. Hopefully, he wasn't too far out so the message could get to him quickly. Murray's equipment wasn't built to travel far.

* * *

Fâd and his crew were just coming out of jump and could see off into the distance the *Justification*, and now he was getting nervous. The *Inferno* appeared out of nowhere beside them and also the proturin science vessel as they all headed toward the massive battlecruiser. Dr. Shin came up on the bridge and saw the cruiser for the first time in his life and was amazed at the sheer magnitude of it.

"Wow! I have always heard they were big, but now seeing one for the first time, it is indescribable. It definitely takes a great man, which Vice Admiral Harper is, to command something like that. I would sure hate to be his enemy. Even your father's, for that matter. He's a legend as well," Dr. Shin said, and Fâd looked down at him, giving him a very dirty look.

"What, do you and the vice admiral not get along?" Shin asked him, now looking worried that this might not go well for any of them.

"We used to get along fine," Fâd told him, turning his attention back to the cruiser as they continued to draw near her.

"Yeah. Ask him whom he recently took as his bonded mate," Nathan said from the front.

"No, not the vice admiral's daughter? Well, it was nice knowing you," Shin said and headed to the elevator.

"What, you're not going to stick around so you can enjoy this?" Fâd asked, surprised.

"Are you crazy? From what I've heard, Vice Admiral Harper is one of the most powerful kinetics ever. He can literally shred a man into pieces or even crush a shuttle with just his mind. I may be nutty from time to time, but even I know when to stay clear," Shin told them and got on the elevator and left.

"Well, I feel a hell of a lot better now," Fâd said with a scowl, and Nathan and Cory started chuckling.

Soon, the *Artemis* requested clearance to dock and got it and before long. Fâd, Nathan, and Cory were heading to the command deck of the *Justification* after docking. The guys were walking through a causeway, heading toward an elevator after leaving the *Artemis* and stepped into one, then remembered back to the other time they rode it with the girls when they got into a paint fight, and they couldn't help but start grinning at one another.

Nathan looked at his friends. "You know, if we had known the girls would eventually become our mates, we might have been a little nicer to them back then." The guys all looked at one another, thinking for a second. Then at the same time, all three said, "Nah," shaking their heads, now with wicked grins on their faces.

A few minutes later, the elevator opened to the bridge. As they walked out, right away, they could spot Vice Admiral Harper standing at his platform, working on his console. Even with his back to them, he was still an intimidating figure. The boys remembered the other time when they were younger and walking into the bridge with Admiral Larson and seeing Vice Admiral Harper just like this. Nathan leaned over to Cory and Fâd, whispering, "He still looks the same and just as scary." Cory and Fâd nodded their heads in agreement.

They waited patiently, and finally, the vice admiral turned around. Just like always, he was totally cold and void of emotion. He told his EXO that he had the bridge and headed over to the guys. "So I now see before me the boys I once knew but now are men. I'm impressed with what I've been hearing of your many accomplishments," he said to them. Just then, the elevator opened up, and Chief Engineer Nelson stepped out with a scowl on his face.

"Where is he?" Nelson asked, and Cory's eyes got huge as he tried to hide behind Nathan. Harper looked over at Cory as Nelson walked over to him. "Come with me, young man. We need to talk," Nelson said, still scowling, and headed to the elevator. Cory followed nervously, and soon, they disappeared in the elevator.

"Captain Larson, will you accompany me to my cabin?" Harper said coldly and started for the elevator with Fâd walking beside him.

"Um, I'll just go and hang out at Gravities," Nathan told them sheepishly, trying to stay clear of Admiral Harper.

"Lieutenant Wilcox, as second in command, for the time being, you should head down to the armory to see to it that Lieutenant Commander Harper, Lieutenant Torres, and Chief Engineer Nelson's combat suits, equipment, and personal belongings reach the *Artemis*. They will need someone to sign them out of here before they can be sent over. Plus, there is a large order for science equipment waiting as well," Admiral Harper told him, and Nathan nervously saluted him, and the vice admiral returned the gesture. They all got back into the elevator after it came back from when Senior Chief Engineer Nelson and Cory left.

The elevator stopped on the deck where the admiral's cabin was located. The admiral and Fâd stepped out, and Nathan remained on the elevator so he could continue on to the armory. Fâd gave Nathan a nervous look and then followed the vice admiral down the hall and into his cabin. Harper told him to take a seat and offered him something to drink, which Fâd declined. Then the admiral came and took a seat across from him.

Harper looked at him for a few minutes with cold, expressionless eyes. "We know why we are here, so there's no need to sugarcoat this. I only have a few questions for you, Fâd. How come you fought how you felt for Ash for so long and—what infuriates me the most—allowed her to suffer all those years? I will tell you the truth right now. I wanted to kill you, even being my best friend's son, for the pain you caused her.

"Ash has loved you from the first time you both met, and I know you felt the same. Hell, Fâd, you pulled her back from death. No one has ever had that kind of bond. Now the real issue is, will you be there for her or once again push her away, taking the coward's way out?" Harper asked through narrowed eyes, but instead of backing down, Fâd rose to the challenge over Ash.

"I was a fool, and I paid dearly for it. I suffered as well all those years. I thought I was doing what Ash would want. I just wanted her to be happy, to have what she desired, which I thought was to serve under you on this ship, which was her home. My mistake was never asking her. Instead, I assumed that was what she had planned. But as hard as I tried to stay away, we continued to be drawn back to each other over and over again, and it was getting harder and harder to walk away. And then finally, this last time, I knew I couldn't let her go again. I will always be there for her. I will care for her, protect her, and love her for the rest of my life. And since we are being honest here, I don't care what you think of me, but Ash will be going and staying with me, not just as my bonded mate but soon as my wife as well," Fâd said with narrowed eyes, looking at the admiral.

Harper studied the young man in front of him. He had known all along that someday, Fâd would be coming for Ash. But still, it didn't lessen the pain. He let out a deep breath. "I would have never let her go with anyone lesser. She deserves a great man, and I believe that to be you. Don't disappoint me, Fâdron Larson. You have some huge shoes to fill and the blood of a legend running through your veins. Protect and love her with your life."

"I will," Fâd replied and half smirked now, and Harper returned the gesture.

"You know she will put you through the ringer, right?" Harper told him, still with no emotion, cold.

"Oh, I know. Trust me, she has for the last thirteen years. Remember the first time we met right here on this ship? She was going to fight me then, and she hasn't changed," Fâd said as both he and Harper started chuckling. Harper remembered that, turning around and seeing Ash standing there, facing Fâd with her fists up, ready to fight no matter how much bigger he was than her.

They talked a little while longer, and then Nathan contacted Fâd and told him that everything was loaded onto the *Artemis*. Fâd got up and headed for the door, and Harper followed him. They both walked out and got into the elevator and then out to the causeway, toward the docking doors where the *Artemis* was.

"Well, I guess this is it. Safe journey. Take care and protect my treasure," Harper told Fâd and shook his hand as he put his other one on Fâd's shoulder.

"Safe journey to you, Vice Admiral, and I will with my life. Thank you," Fâd replied and then walked through the docking bay doors and onto his ship.

In a few minutes, he was once again on the bridge. Cory and Nathan were already there, waiting orders. Fâd stepped up to his console with a wicked half grin on his face. "Lieutenant Wilcox, take us out."

Nathan waited until the clamps released the *Artemis* and then piloted her away from the cruiser. In no time, they were in open space as Fâd punched in coordinates to a freighter that they would have to rendezvous with to pick up the rest of Dr. Shin's supplies. Nathan confirmed the coordinates, and once again, the *Artemis* disappeared into space as she jumped.

CHAPTER 47

THE NEXT MORNING, Ash woke up feeling stiff and sore all over. Apparently, she had slept clear through the night as well. She stretched out and realized she was in nothing but her bra and underwear with a sheet barely covering her and wondered what had happened. Ash got up and walked out into the living room and knew that Rachael and Bridgett were probably still fast asleep. She went into the bathroom, looked in the mirror, and got a huge shock, letting out a loud scream. Rachael and Bridgett came running out of their bedrooms and into the bathroom, scared, and saw Ash staring at herself in the mirror.

"What? Are you okay, Ash?" Rachael asked with a scared look on her face.

"Look at my eyes!" Ash said in a panic, looking in the mirror, and then looked at her friends.

Bridgett walked closer and looked with her white eyes. "Wow, those are beautiful. I wonder if that's because you're part vatoria," she said.

Ash looked back in the mirror and stared at her now white irises that also had an outer ring of gold around the white and a few tiny, little flecks of gold in them. One couldn't help but stare at them as they seemed to draw you right in with a hypnotic effect to them.

"Okay. Now what am I going to do? I thought I would have at least a week to get used to and deal with this, not overnight," Ash said.

"I have some gold-colored lenses you can wear," Rachael told her, then went and got them for her.

It took them almost an hour before Ash was finally able to put them in without crying them back out. During the whole time, Rachael and Bridgett told her what had happened to her. "It was really kind of cool when Lee did that scan on you. We could see your insides. You're a mess," Bridgett told her, laughing.

"So now even Oscar and Lee know about my kinetics. Great," Ash said sarcastically.

"They're not going to say anything. They actually saved you. You were literally cooking yourself from the inside out, and they helped you. They explained everything to us—what happened and why we go through this change," Rachael said to her.

"And why is that?" Ash asked, annoyed, still trying to adjust to the eye lenses.

"For having babies," Bridgett said.

"What? My body just tore itself to pieces so I can make babies? I don't think so," Ash said, mad.

"There are other things too, like the night vision, increased eyesight, and acute hearing. Plus, you will find you have a lot more stamina now, and then there, of course, is the smell," Rachael said, grinning.

"What smell?" Ash turned and looked at her with a nervous look on her face as Bridgett was giggling now.

"Well, you'll find that when Fâd is around or near that he puts off a certain fragrance to you that you will find irresistible, and only you can smell it, but don't worry, you do the same thing to him," Rachael said, grinning.

"You mean pheromones," Ash said, shaking her head in annoyance.

"No. This you literally can smell, and even if he's a little ways from you, you can pick it up, not just subconsciously, and the smell is only specific to both of you," Rachael told her.

"Yeah. Cory smells like cinnamon and musk cologne all mixed together. Oh, it smells so good," Bridgett said, sniffing the air.

"Nathan is more vanilla and cedar. I could smell him all day," Rachael told Ash and closed her eyes, remembering the fragrance.

"Okay. With my luck, Fâd will smell like dirt," Ash said, and the girls busted up laughing and actually had to agree with her because Ash really didn't have very good luck. Finally, they all got ready and headed to their class. It was just as boring as always, but Ash could look forward to it soon being over, and she would be leaving here with Fâd, which was all she cared about now. She even made it through the day without losing one eye lens and was starting to feel pretty good as the stiff and soreness had finally left her body.

The rest of the week and the weekend went by just fine, but the girls were getting nervous because they hadn't heard from the guys at all. They had tried several times, and Ash even tried to get ahold of her father but couldn't reach him. The girls also tried Rear Admiral Larson and Sharni, but nothing, which they thought was really odd, and now Ash was getting scared as her instincts were telling her something wasn't right.

Finally, as the weekend was coming to an end and night was fast approaching, Ash decided to contact Nera in Pantier. "That's it. I'm calling Nera. Maybe she's heard something," she told Rachael and Bridgett. Ash hit the comm link on her multitool as Rachael and Bridgett watched her with concerned looks on their faces and pressed in Nera's comm code. The comm link remained quiet, and Ash looked over at her friends. "Arm yourselves. We have to get out of here now," Ash told them, and they all ran to their rooms and changed into their uniforms, then strapped on their pistols. They immediately grabbed their packs and put some more rations in them.

Suddenly, their apartment door slid open. Three men dressed in council uniforms came in with guns aimed at them, and the girls immediately went into combat mode. They easily took out the three men as others came flooding into the room, and the girls started fighting them in hand-to-hand combat since they didn't get a chance to pull their pistols but were holding their own.

Ash even saw Oscar and Lee now attacking the men out in the hallway, hitting them with backpacks from behind, just outside their door, as more council soldiers came through the doorway. The girls were soon overpowered and disarmed. Ash knew she had to do something to save everyone and started glowing blue as she powered up, but suddenly, she felt a painful sting in her neck and then nothing but blackness.

Rachael screamed when she saw Ash go down and fought even harder, but then she got hit upside the head and now could feel blood running down the side of her face, but she still continued to fight. Bridgett was already on the ground, and three men were struggling trying to cuff her, yet she was still fighting, making it hard for them. Rachael was finally tackled by four soldiers and was laid on the ground as they cuffed her.

She saw that six men surrounded Ash, and four of them had their rifles aimed at her as another soldier hit her over the head to make sure she was out, and the other one, who had a case in his hand, watched. Rachael saw Ash's hair start to turn red as blood came out of an open wound on her scalp. Another man kneeled down next to Ash with a case. He then opened it, taking out a round collar and putting it on Ash's neck while she was unconscious, then pulled out a syringe, injecting a powerful nueralizer into her.

"There. She won't be able to use her powers, at least, but if she starts to wake, hit her again with another nueralizer or just shoot her. She's just as dangerous without the powers," the man told the others.

Another man cuffed Ash's hands and then her feet and chained them together so she wouldn't be able to move. They put her on a floating stretcher that was brought in and headed out the door with her. One of the men, as he walked out, grinned at Rachael and Bridgett. "Say goodbye to your little friend here as she heads to her new life at Trinity."

Rachael and Bridgett both screamed and started crying as more men came over, lifted them up from the floor, and forced them out the door and into the hallway. Even Oscar and Lee were cuffed, standing in the hall with soldiers holding on to them. When the girls came out and they saw Ash on the stretcher, they started trying to fight again but to no avail. The soldiers yanked them around and made them follow Rachael and Bridgett, all at gunpoint. Oscar looked over at the girls. "I'm sorry we weren't much help. We tried to stop them."

"It's all right. You shouldn't have to. Now you're going to a prison colony with us," Rachael told them.

"So? Ash is our friend. Yeah, that's right, we knew the whole time, you low-life scum suckers, because we have been helping them all along," Lee said defiantly to the soldiers, and Rachael and Bridgett actually had to giggle a little even though things were worse than they had ever faced before in their lives. But this just showed them that Oscar and Lee were true friends.

* * *

The night Ash was taken, Kaiden Marsh went with some of his friends to Odyssey to celebrate a promotion he had received. He was no longer a private but now made junior lieutenant, and in the next two weeks, he would be leaving on the *Lithia* once it returned to Sigma Six for his yearlong tour of duty. He walked up to the bar and ordered drinks from the bartender and was just about to head back to his table when Murray, the owner of the nightclub, walked out from the back room and hollered at him. "Hey, Kaiden, I need to talk to you."

Kaiden put the drinks down on the bar and followed Murray to the back room, and then the bar owner unlocked his office, and they went in. "What's up, Murray?" he asked, curious.

"What was your sister doing in here a few days ago talking to those council operatives?" Murray asked him, and Kaiden had a shocked look on his face.

"What are you talking about? Sierra wouldn't talk to any council creep," Kaiden replied angrily at the accusation.

"I'm not lying. She was at one of the tables and talked with two operatives for at least an hour. Then she got up and left, and they left not long after that and seemed pretty happy about their meeting with her. I got it all on vid if you want to see."

"I don't know, but I'm going to find out. Could you hear what they were saying on the vid?" Kaiden asked, worried and still a little shocked by the news.

"Just bits and pieces. There was something about kinetics, Larson, and there was also something about being ordered and half of the troops. I tried to get ahold of Fâd to let him know, but he must be too far out," Murray told him. Kaiden just leaned his head back and closed his eyes, then he opened them again but now was mad and turned to leave. "What should I do?" Murray asked him, nervous.

"Pack and get the hell off this planet. It's time to go," Kaiden told him and left the back room, heading over to his friends. They immediately knew something was up when they saw his face. "Exodus" was all he said, and they jumped up, and the four of them raced for the door.

In no time, they were back in Pantier, and the three young privates went to tell Nera as Kaiden went in search of his sister. He found her at home, watching a vid, lying back and munching on some candy. He walked in and shut off the vid, standing in front of it, facing her.

"What the hell do you think you're doing?" she asked, sitting up and glaring at him, but this time, he didn't cower down but glared back at her.

"What did you do?" he asked in a threatening tone.

"I don't know what the hell you're talking about, and you better turn that vid back on, or so help me," she warned him, but Kaiden continued to glare at her, and now he reached down and unstrapped his pistol.

"What is wrong with you? Are you mad?" Sierra asked and got up, heading over to her pistol, which was lying on a table no more than ten feet from her. Suddenly, the pistol flew across the room as it took a hit from Kaiden's pistol as he shot it off the table. The sound of the shot now echoed through their house. She wheeled around to him, furious. "I can't believe you just did that. What are you going to do, shoot me too?"

"If I have to, yes. What did you tell those council operatives?" he asked with his pistol pointing at her.

Sierra's face changed from rage to smugness. "Everything. They know about that little tramp and her powers and the fact that Admiral Larson tried to cover it up."

"You fool! You have doomed us all. They will try and come to arrest everyone of us, and you know we will stand and fight, not to mention that Ashley Harper will be taken to Trinity and won't survive. Plus, her friends will go to a prison colony as well. What do you think Rear Admiral Larson and Vice Admiral Harper will do when they find out or even Fâd? He's always been our friend and helped us out whenever we needed it. Don't you realize you just started a war?" Kaiden said, now feeling sick to his stomach that his own sister was capable of this.

"Do you think I care? I don't give a shit what happens to our people. They have never cared about anything that happens to me. Look how many times I've been passed over for a damn promotion. You even almost outrank me now, and I've been in the service for nine years longer than you, which has been a complete waste of my time. Council offered me immunity for my testimony. I trust them more than I have ever trusted the sentinel fleet. And as far as Fâd, he's too in love with that little nutcase to see how dangerous she is," Sierra said with a hate-filled look on her face.

"I'm sorry, sister," Kaiden said as his eyes watered up, and he shot her. Sierra stood there in shock for a few seconds, then dropped as blood ran out across the floor from the clean shot to her chest. Kaiden stood there for a few minutes, then went over, kneeling next to her body, closing her open eyes. He put his hand gently on her head as tears ran down his face. He stayed like that for a few minutes, then got up and went to his bedroom and packed some necessities just as the colony alarm went off. He ran outside and jumped on his bike, racing over to the barracks.

People were everywhere now, and the barracks were a madhouse, but it was the same everywhere else. Over in New Guinea, those loyal to the fleet had built-in alarms on their multitools, and now those red alert buttons were flashing, letting them know it was time to leave. People were busily packing and heading to secret rendezvous points where shuttles from the nearby watorian colonies and sentinel supporters would come and transport them to passenger ships that would be answering the call to pick them up, which went out once the main alarm was triggered in Pantier. Even the refugee center was packing and transporting injured people and refugees to shuttles as quietly and secretly as they could. All this had been set up long ago. The shuttles and passenger ships, they had always been prepared for this day.

Over in New Haven, there were hardly any there who were loyal; and when Jocu's alarm went off, he headed immediately to the campus to help the girls get out. He sneaked into the campus and saw anywhere from thirty to forty armed council operatives and soldiers moving around the campus and knew there was no way he could get to the girls before they were taken. He managed to barely sneak back off the campus without being seen and laid low at his shop. He hid as operatives now searched the small village, and finally, just before light, they left and headed back to the campus.

Jocu sneaked to the back of his shop and into the hangar. He went over and hit a button on the wall, and the whole floor of the large hangar opened up, revealing a ship. It wasn't large, but at least it could hold three to four people on it, and it was fast. He quickly loaded what things he wanted to take and climbed into the pilot's seat. Jocu hit the button on the control panel in his ship, activating the hangar controls, and in no time, the roof to the hangar opened up, and he lifted off vertically, out through the roof, then took off toward Pantier to warn them about the girls.

He comm'd Pantier's terminal and got permission to land. Then once he was on the ground, he ran into the terminal. He asked around to try and find someone in charge, but it was a madhouse here. Finally, someone pointed to an attractive watorian woman in a commander's uniform, and he pushed through the throngs of people and finally got to her. She was busy giving orders to four young soldiers when he tapped her shoulder, and she wheeled around, looking at him, annoyed.

"What? Can't you see I'm busy here?" she snapped at him.

"Yeah, *mon*. I'm sorry, but I thought you should know that the admiral's daughter and her friends have been taken," he told her and could see the woman's face turn pale white.

"They got the girls?" she asked in shock.

"Yeah. I tried to get Fâd, but he's not responding," Jocu said.

"We are short on shuttles to evac from here to the ships as it is. Plus, I have no one with recon and infiltration experience to go after them," Nera said to him in disbelief and almost in a tone that was asking him what she should do.

"I can help shuttle," he offered, and Nera was more than grateful for the offer.

"I'll go after Ashley Harper. She's at most risk right now. The other two will be held for a while, waiting for a passing prison ship, which won't be coming for another two days. Maybe you will be able to contact the fleet by then," Kaiden said as he walked up with a pack hanging off his shoulder.

"Kaiden, they are taking her straight to Trinity. It's too dangerous. You're not ready for that," Nera told him.

"It's my fault all this has happened. I owe it to Fâd. I have to try," Kaiden said, looking down at the ground.

"What do you mean it's your fault?" Nera asked, confused.

"It was Sierra who told council all about Ashley's kinetics and about Admiral Larson ordering it to be forgotten. I knew she was mad, and I knew how vindictive she was. I should have seen this coming," Kaiden told them, ashamed.

"Where is she? I will kill her," Nera said with such venom that the young soldiers felt a chill run up their backs.

"There's no need. She's dead," Kaiden told her coldly.

"I'm sorry, Kaiden, but it's not your fault. You couldn't have known she was capable of even this," Nera said, putting her hand on his shoulder, knowing it was Kaiden who ended Sierra's life.

"I need a ship to get to Trinity," he told her.

"I have a fighter out back you can take. Kaiden, be careful. The people that live in Trinity are crazed killers. Here, come with me. You'll need some things if you do get to Ash," she said and had him follow her to the med supply room and walked in as people were in there, packing things up. Nera walked over to a cabinet and grabbed a med kit, then opened another cabinet and pulled out a syringe and a small vial and what looked like a small screwdriver with no tip.

"You will need to give this to Ash if you find her. She has an injection port in the back of her neck that you can put it directly into. This is a counteragent to the nueralizer she will have been given. She will also have an inhibitor collar around her neck. This will remove it. There will be a small hole in the back of the collar, and just press this button here and point the laser into the hole, and the collar will come off," Nera told him, holding up the small vial of liquid, then showed him how to use the laser.

She put everything into the med kit then went over and grabbed two pistols that were lying across a table and cocked them, making sure they had full clips. Each clip consisted of over forty permalloy shredder rounds in them. She also grabbed a handful of extra clips and put everything in a pack for him.

They walked out to the back of the building, and now the sun was starting to top over the trees as morning was encroaching upon them. There sat a nice fighter, and Nera walked up, then put her hand on the scan pad. The defensive barrier came down as Nera opened a panel in the side and punched in a bunch of codes, then had Kaiden put his hand on the pad now. He felt a sharp, burning sensation, then nothing as the pad now recognized him as the pilot.

"Be careful, Kaiden, and find Ash. You come back too, you hear me?" Nera said, and this time, she hugged him, fighting the tears that wanted to fall.

"I will," he said and quickly climbed into the cockpit as Nera walked back over to the building. Soon, the fighter was lifting off from the ground, then shot into the sky, disappearing from view. Kaiden punched in the coordinates for Trinity, and the fighter jumped, disappearing from Sigma Six.

CHAPTER 48

Fâd, Nathan, and Cory were slowly loading the rest of the stuff Dr. Shin swore he needed onto the *Artemis* from the freighter, complaining the whole time. They were all grouchy and wanted to get back to the girls. Suddenly, Artemis's alarms went off inside her cargo bay. Fâd and the guys ran back into their ship through the umbilical that was connected between the freighter and the *Artemis* and jumped into the elevator, and in no time, they were on the bridge, racing over to Fâd's console.

"Artemis, what's happening?" Fâd asked with Cory and Nathan standing beside him.

Artemis was standing on her pad, dressed in her huntress outfit, which was not a good sign. "Captain, I was trying to get through to the girls when I hit a comm block, but I was able to hack through, and the exodus signal has been triggered in Pantier. I took down the blockage, but I still can't raise anyone back on Sigma Six. The block was coming from a council warship. I was able to tap into its comm and found out that it is now heading to Sigma Six with more of the council fleet behind them. I have already dispatched the alarm to the rest of the fleet, and they are responding as we speak," Artemis told them.

"All hands on deck. Prepare to depart. Captain Larson, to the freighter. Lois, get the hell out of here," Fâd ordered as the *Artemis* started firing up her engines and jump system and as everyone ran to their stations. The air hatch sealed where it was open for moving supplies on board as the umbilical retracted back to the freighter, which also was firing her engines to leave. In no time, the *Artemis* was on a course toward Sigma Six in jump.

Fâd had Artemis constantly trying to communicate with anyone back on Sigma Six, and finally, Nera responded. "Oh, thank goodness, Fâd. We are in full evac. Several ships have already left, but we are still shuttling up to the passenger ships."

"What happened?" Fâd asked in disbelief.

"Sierra turned everyone in to council about Ash's kinetics. She even told them that Gerrard, you, and the girls tried to cover it up," Nera told him.

Fâd and they looked at one another, and now all they wanted to do was kill her. "When I get my hands on her, I'll kill her," Fâd said with such hate and rage.

"You won't have to. Kaiden already did," Nera said sadly.

"Where are the girls?" Fâd asked, now scared of what he might hear.

There was silence on the comm for a few seconds, then Nera spoke in a sad tone. "They got them, Fâd. Ash is already on her way to Trinity, and Rachael and Bridgett are being held in New Haven, waiting for a transport to prison."

Fâd just stood there in shock for a few seconds, then collapsed down into his chair. He would never make it in time to save her, and he knew it. Even Nathan and Cory were silent, for they also knew what this meant. "Ash is gone?" Fâd asked again, barely getting the words out.

"Yes, but Kaiden went after her," Nera told him, and now Fâd looked up at the screen.

"When?" Fâd jumped out of the seat.

"At first light. He'll probably reach Trinity before she does."

"Understood!" Fâd said, and the screen went blank. "Artemis!" he hollered.

"Way ahead of you, Captain," she said, and now they could hear the secondary engines kicking in as well, which they didn't know she could do while in jump. Suddenly, they could feel the ship shoot forward as the protective shields on the front windows closed for added stability, and they could feel the ship shaking from the output the engines were now giving. Even they could feel a little extra weight on themselves from the extra force and energy the ship was now producing.

"ETA in ten hours, seventeen minutes, if I can hold it that long. I've never done this before. I had to shut down the kinetic guns to boost the kinetic field around the ship. With the secondary engines pushing us through slipstream even faster, it might tear us apart over time," Artemis told them.

"I don't care. Ashley doesn't have ten hours, and Rachael and Bridgett don't have that much time either," Fâd told her, and Artemis agreed.

Two hours later, Kaiden was coming out of jump as he neared the planet Trinity, and it was nighttime over the prison city. He was just starting to make his approach when he came under fire from the planet's defense system. He maneuvered and banked back and forth, trying to dodge the blasts, but finally, his luck ran out, and he took a hit to his portside thruster. The fighter started going down. He hung on to the stick and fought the controls to try and glide her as close as he could to the central location of the prison city. He worked on the control panel quickly, temporarily hacking into the prison city's shields, and was able to open a small window in them just as the fighter penetrated through the shields covering the city. Kaiden let out a sigh of relief as the fighter's shields held and he didn't get fried. It was only a weakened area he was able to produce, but it knocked out the rest of the fighter's controls and power. The craft was coming in fast now, and he was just barely keeping her above the buildings and decided it would be best to scuttle the ship somewhere away from the central hub of the city so as to draw attention away from there and over to the crash site.

He pulled some wirings that were under the control panel and tied off the stick so the fighter would continue on course and then crash into a large building located far away from the central hub. He grabbed his pack and hung on firmly to it, then pulled the jettison lever. The hood shot off, and he was blasted into the air, and the fighter continued onward. The chair started coming down, instantly deploying the chute, and now he was floating downward toward a rooftop. He hit still with quite a bit of force and rolled a few times, still strapped in the chair. Kaiden lay there for a few moments as he caught his breath from having it knocked out of him. He also was now slightly scratched and bruised up from the impact but otherwise okay.

He finally unbuckled and got moving, then heard the loud explosion of the jet off in the distances as it plowed into a large ten-story building clear on the other end of the city and now could see the huge ball of flames billowing up. He knew this wouldn't tip off the operatives who were bringing Ash because things were always exploding around there.

Kaiden found a door that led down into the building. He hacked the scan pad with his multitool, and the door slid open. The stairwell was dark, and he had no clue what might be down there. He pulled out a light stick since he couldn't see in the dark yet and went for it. Halfway down, he could hear voices coming from one of the hallways a couple of levels below, and he leaned back into the shadows, covering up the light stick in his hand and in his other one had his pistol ready.

He heard a door to the stairwell open, and before long, two men walked past him without even knowing he was there. He could tell they were kinetics by the blue sparks on them, and they also were exhibiting the shaking tremors that the psychosis caused in exposure victims.

"I tell you, Larry, I heard something hit the roof hard."

"I think you're full of crap, but I'll go with you to check it out," the other man said.

Kaiden quietly switched his gun over to silence, and both men never knew what hit them. He went over to the dead men and took off their coats, gloves, and whatever he could wear to make himself look more like one of the inhabitants there. He also grabbed the other man's stuff too for Ash to wear. Once satisfied with his appearance, he took off down the stairs again and then out into the street.

The dark city was now laid out in front of him, and he could tell by the looks of it that the city was in decay. Buildings were vacant and falling apart, and the ones that were occupied looked like slums anyway, and even the paved streets were crumbling in places. Garbage and debris were everywhere, not to mention the stench. The only light around was from the many large barrels scattered everywhere with lit fires burning in them, and some of the city's inhabitants crowded around them. Kaiden looked toward the direction that the only artificial light was coming from knowing that was the main drop-off zone and figured he was at least six blocks away and took off running down the street toward the hub.

There were other people out and about, and it was very apparent they were crazy. They would talk to themselves, and some would fall down in the street in fits of rage, screaming, and would start beating themselves. Kaiden moved quickly aside, skirting around most people, and then if it couldn't be avoided, he would either growl like most did around there or club someone over the head, knocking them out of the way. Finally, he made it to the central hub. There were still quite a few convicts there milling around as well, but it was totally apparent from the way they acted that they were completely mindless, almost zombielike.

It was a large round open area that the dirty, run-down buildings circled, and in the center was a large landing platform where large artificial lights were positioned on thirty-foot poles to help illuminate it for where prisoners were dropped off. Kaiden could see blood all over the platform now and knew that most who got left here never made it. He melted back into the shadows of an abandoned building and waited for the prison ship to arrive with Ash. A couple of hours later, he wasn't disappointed.

The small prison shuttle hovered over the area and then slowly came down, landing on the platform. The doors slid open, and four men got out, armed with assault rifles now aimed at the gathering convicts, who kept their distance for now.

Two more prison guards got out carrying an unconscious Ash and dropped her on the landing platform, and one of them knelt down beside her and removed her cuffs. The other man who was standing looked down at her with a wicked grin on his face. "What a waste. She sure is a beauty. I think I could even overlook the sentinel stain with this one."

The man's partner, who removed her cuffs, stood up and looked down at Ash, also with a sick grin. "Yeah. Just keep her on a mild nueralizer and that collar on, and you could do whatever you want with her and still not have to worry about her kinetics. She still could walk and talk with the mild but now as your own personal plaything."

Both men stood there watching Ash for a few minutes, and Kaiden could swear they actually were thinking about it, but then they turned and headed back to the shuttle. He watched them climb back in, and the other four guards got in behind them. Then the shuttle lifted off as the convicts now hurried over to Ash's limp body.

Kaiden leaped out of the shadows and raced toward the platform, firing away at the people with no remorse, because he was in a rage now over what the guards were saying about Ash, and he directed his fury on the criminals. It helped that he was an excellent shot, and the gathering quickly started thinning as the rest took off scattering. Not one of them tried to use any kinetic power on him. Of course, these who were here were so far gone in their minds that they probably couldn't even remember they had kinetics.

Kaiden ran up to the platform and checked Ash's pulse. She was alive, but she looked to have taken a bit of a beating as her head had a bad gash of dried blood in her hair and her lip was swollen and bleeding, as was her nose. He looked around and gently picked her up, putting her over his shoulder, then took off again in a different direction from whence he came, and the convicts there stayed clear of him.

He wasn't sure where to go or how they were going to get out of there, but right now, he just needed to find a safe hiding place for them for the time being so he could help Ash. Kaiden moved in and out of the buildings, making sure he wasn't being followed, then jumped back into a dark doorway when he saw some men coming from the direction he had just come from. They seemed to have a little bit more wits about themselves.

"I think I saw them head this way. I don't think they're locals. Probably came from that drop ship," one of the men said in a voice that trembled from psychosis induced by exposure. They continued to walk, passing Kaiden without realizing it. He watched them until they disappeared around the corner, and then just as he was about to step out, someone put their gloved hand over his mouth, holding him back from behind him. He looked over his shoulder, and the person let go of him, then put their hand up to where their mouth would be under their dark hood, signaling him to be quiet.

All he could see of them was a large hood covering their face and two gold eyes peering out. The rest of them was covered from head to toe in a large dark overcoat. Kaiden could tell right away that this person was shorter and, from the way their overcoat clung to them, smaller of frame, yet he was a watorian male, and everyone was smaller than them except other male watorians.

The person moved effortlessly in front of him and peered around the door to make sure the dirty street was clear, then stepped out into it and motioned for him to follow. At this point, he didn't have any other choice, so he did. The secretive being moved swiftly and silently across the street, then down a back alley and across another street to a boarded-up building. Kaiden followed carrying Ash. They reached out their gloved hand and moved some boards aside, then climbed in, motioning for Kaiden to follow. He took Ash off his shoulder, and the person helped her inside with him, and then he put her back over his shoulder and followed his rescuer.

They moved through the dark, crumbling building and over to a door. The mysterious person reached into the pocket of their coat with an ungloved hand now, and he saw a slightly blue hand with gold scroll marks on it. Then they pulled out a data pad and punched in some codes. The door slid open, and a lit stairwell that led down appeared behind it.

They went in as the door shut behind them, and Kaiden followed his rescuer down the stairs, coming out into a large basement. There were a couple of nice large beds, sofa, and even a kitchen area for fixing meals with a large wooden table and mismatched chairs. There was also a separate room that he could see housed a bathroom, complete with a shower and a tub. The hooded person motioned him over to one of the beds, and he laid Ash down on it. Then Kaiden removed his hood, coat, and gloves and grabbed his pack and sat down next to Ash. The quiet being went over to the kitchen area and filled a bowl with water, then brought it over to him with some rags and walked a little ways away from him like a cautionary animal would, watching him closely.

Kaiden opened the pack and took out the med kit, filling the syringe that Nera had given him but also keeping a wary eye on his rescuer. He rolled Ash onto her side and inserted the needle into the port, injecting the fluid. Then he took out the laser tool and did exactly like Nera told him, and sure enough, the collar came off. Next, he rolled up his sleeves and attended to Ash's injuries. The split lip and bloody nose were just superficial and cleaned up fine, but the gash on her head was a little more serious.

He cleaned it up and pulled out a medstitch tool and used it to sew the wound back up, which took twelve stitches to close. Finally done, he put everything away and just sat looking down at Ash and smoothed her hair away from her face, marveling at how even beat-up like she was, she still was very beautiful. The mysterious person timidly walked over and took the bowl of bloody water and dumped it out in the sink. Then they walked over to the table, removed their other glove, then took off their hood. Kaiden was shocked when he saw brilliant white hair fall out, and then when they removed their coat, he was even more shocked to see it was a young female vatoria, probably close in age to him.

"You're a vatoria here in Trinity?" he asked her.

The young woman jumped from his sudden speech and looked over at him nervously but with some defiance in her face. "Yes, and you're a watorian crashing a fighter in Trinity, saving a woman who I'm guessing is a kinetic. Plus, judging by both of your uniforms, you are sentinel soldiers," she replied, and Kaiden narrowed his eyes and half smirked.

"Okay. Now that we have that established, what did you do to be sent here so I know if I should be worried or not?" Kaiden asked her as she continued to keep her distance from where he was sitting with Ash.

"I was born," she told him.

"Well, that's not a crime."

"I know, but it was my parents who were sent here," she told him.

"What do you mean?"

"My father had kinetic powers, but his were natural-occurring, and he was found out. Council operatives took him and my mother and left them here."

"How did they get him? Wasn't he living on Krios?"

"No, he lived on Alpha Prime and was a consultant to some big company, who betrayed him to council militia."

"So you've been here how long?"

"Since I was born," she said sadly.

"Were you born here?" he asked, shocked.

"Yes. My mother was expecting me when they took them."

"Where are your parents now?" Kaiden asked her, amazed that she had been living here all her life. She pointed over to two rectangular stone boxes with stone lids, and Kaiden knew what they were. "How long ago?" he asked sadly.

"Three years."

"You have been on your own for three years?" he asked in amazement.

"Yes, and I know everything about this place," she told him.

"So you would know where a rescue might come from?" he asked, hopeful.

"There isn't one. Trust me, I've checked everywhere."

"Well, there's got to be some way, because we can't leave the way I came in," Kaiden said, thinking. He reached down and hit the emergency beacon on his multitool now so in case someone was coming for them, they would be able to locate him.

"The signal can't get out. There's a barrier that bounces it back so no one can come and rescue people. I'm amazed that you were able to penetrate the shields without getting yourself fried, but of course, it's always easier to get in, just not out," she told him.

"Yeah, so am I. But the party who will be coming for her will definitely be getting in, and there will be no stopping them from leaving either," Kaiden told her with a smirk.

"Who are you?" she asked with narrowed eyes.

"I'm Junior Lieutenant Kaiden Marsh, and this is Lieutenant Commander Ashley Harper of sentinel fleet," he told her, and the girl's eyes got large.

"Is she Admiral…?"

"Yes, she is Vice Admiral Harper's daughter. How do you know about Admiral Harper and sentinel fleet if you have lived here all your life?"

She let out a slight sigh. "My father and mother taught me while they were alive. He also showed me how to defend myself and use my kinetics, so don't go and get any strange ideas," the young woman warned Kaiden, which brought a slight grin to his face. Upon seeing him grin, she had to take in a sharp breath, for she had never seen a watorian before, and Kaiden had a very cute grin anyway.

Kaiden was still grinning and watching her. "Trust me, I wouldn't think of it, and I'm sure you can since you have lived here by yourself for the last three years. On another note, people will be coming for Commander Harper. She is also the girlfriend of Captain Larson, who is the son of Rear Admiral Larson, and nothing will stop him from getting to her."

"Okay, so maybe you might be able to get out," the girl said with a slight smirk on her face.

"So what's your name?"

"My name is Tia Fa Cornia," she said and weakly smiled now, and he couldn't help but notice that she was very pretty. Of course, all vatorias were.

Just then, Ash started moaning and putting her hand up to her head, but Kaiden grabbed it and put it back down. She slowly started blinking her eyes now and finally was able to open them and saw Kaiden. She went to sit up, but her head started hurting as the room spun, and she laid back down.

"Where am I?" Ash asked, putting her hand on her head and rubbing her temple.

"We're at Trinity," Kaiden told her.

"Great. Why does this crap always happen to me?" Ash said and looked up at the ceiling.

"I'm afraid that's my fault. Sierra told the operatives from council about you and then implicated all of us. I didn't know until it was too late to do anything about it. Right now, as we speak, Pantier is evacuating. And when I came to help you, they still were unable to contact the fleet," Kaiden told her as Ash now slowly sat up and moved to the edge of the bed.

"You came after me, Kaiden?" she asked in awe.

"Yes. I had to for Fâd, for he's always been there for me, and also because of the dishonor I now carry," he said and hung his head down.

"Don't blame yourself. It was not your fault. It was Sierra's. She dishonored you, always has. You, Kaiden, are nothing but honorable and a true friend for saving me. I owe you my life," Ash told him with an appreciative smile, and Kaiden smiled back at her.

Ash looked around now and saw the young lady standing a little ways off from them. She could tell right away that she was a vatoria, and Ash spoke to her using her mind. "I take it this is your place?" Ash asked her, and the girl's eyes got huge.

"Yes. How can you speak with your mind?" the young vatoria replied.

"My mother was a vatoria," Ash told her and smiled. The girl now smiled back, relaxing a little instead of looking like a scared animal. Kaiden looked at them and knew something was going on between them but didn't know what. Finally, Ash stood up and waited a few minutes for the dizziness to subside as Kaiden stood up beside her to make sure she wouldn't fall over. She had to look up at him due to him being taller than her. Ash's eyes were burning now, which she couldn't take anymore, and reached up, removing the colored lenses from her eyes, and felt a lot better.

Kaiden's eyes now got large when he saw Ash's eyes knowing full well why they were that way, and he grinned, which also brought a big grin out on Ash's face. "So how long do you think it will take him to get here?" Kaiden asked, still grinning.

"I don't know, but I bet he's about to blow up his ship trying to get here as fast as he can," Ash replied, still grinning thinking about it.

"So, Lieutenant Commander, what do we do in the meantime?" Kaiden asked, still watching her closely to make sure she was okay.

"We hunker down here and then head out again at nightfall," Ash told them.

"I can't see in the dark yet," he told Ash, a little worried.

"Don't worry. You'll be fine. Right now, I need to see a layout of this place," Ash said and pulled up a virtual screen that showed a map of the city on her multitool, which, thank goodness, the council operatives didn't remove. Of course, it would have done them no good anyway, because the gauntlet wouldn't work for anyone but her, and only she could remove it since it was coded to her, and the only way to remove one of these without the wearer's assistance was removing the arm, which still wouldn't work for them. Besides, here under the kinetic barrier, she couldn't hack it anyway with her multi-tool due to it not being even close to powerful enough.

She and Kaiden went over the best possible places that Fâd might try and enter and still were studying it when Tia cautiously walked over and started telling them about some of the areas they were looking at. She pointed at some of the places and accidentally brushed up against Kaiden, who suddenly stiffened up at the contact. Ash looked over at him.

"Are you okay?" she asked.

"Yeah, I'm fine. Go on," he said, and Ash could see a thin bead of sweat on his forehead now, and she had to slightly grin but continued. Finally, they all agreed on a particular place that had previous damage to the outer wall where they, if they were Fâd, would enter through.

"Can I ask a favor?" Tia said timidly.

"Sure. What is it?" Ash replied.

"Will you take me with you?" she asked nervously.

"Of course. You didn't think I would leave you here, did you?" Kaiden said to her with a frown.

"I didn't know. I've never been around other people before, only my parents," she said shyly.

Ash looked at her, then at Kaiden, and he motioned his head toward the two stone vaults, and she knew what was going on then. "Yes, most definitely. You saved us, and for that, we are eternally grateful," Ash told her.

The young girl smiled and looked like she was about to cry. Kaiden reached over and grabbed her hand. She looked down at his hand with surprise on her face but didn't pull away, then smiled up at him. "It's okay. You have friends now, and we stick together and protect one another," Kaiden told her, which made her break down and cry. He pulled her into his arms, holding her close to him. Tia didn't put up any resistance, and Kaiden looked over at Ash, asking her what he should do. Ash just grinned and winked at him, and Kaiden blushed, but then he laid his head down on Tia's head, comforting her.

"Okay. I suggest you two get some sleep since we will be traveling all night," Ash told them. Kaiden let Tia go, and it wasn't hard to miss the small bead of sweat on his forehead. Ash couldn't help but smile to herself knowing that she had just witnessed Kaiden imprinting on Tia.

Tia went over to one of the beds, which was obvious was hers, and Kaiden plopped down on the bed Ash had been lying on. "Aren't you going to sleep?" Tia asked her.

"No. I think I've had enough for a while. I'm going to post," Ash told her and picked up Kaiden's pack and walked over to the table, then started removing things he had brought for her, which consisted mostly of weapons that she expertly loaded, then holstered. Before long, she could see that both of them were sound asleep; and once she had herself armed, she went to see what they could eat.

She found some greens in a basket on the counter that she knew were edible and then went farther into the basement, hunting. Ash knew that these places housed all kinds of vermin, and sure enough, she wasn't disappointed. She silently stalked up and pulled a small knife from her boot. With a quick flick of her wrist, she threw the knife; and instantly, the vermin was dead. Ash quickly skinned and gutted it and went back to where the other two were sleeping and before long had it roasting over a heated can.

Hours later, Tia was the first to wake up, and she walked over to where Ash had the food on the table. She looked at it and grinned knowing what it was. "Just don't tell him what it is," Ash said to her, also grinning, motioning over to Kaiden.

"Do you think we really are going to be able to get out of here?" Tia asked her, and it was obvious that the young woman was feeling at ease around Ash.

"Yes, I do. I know Fâd will come for us," Ash told her.

"Is he your husband?"

"Kind of. We haven't gotten that far yet, but he is my mate."

"That's why your eyes are like that, but they still have some gold as well. You still retained some of the vatoria with your change," Tia commented.

"Yeah, I guess so."

"Does Kaiden have a mate?"

"No. He's too young still. Watorians don't take a mate until after they change and imprint. He was just getting ready to start his tour now that he's nineteen, but he's getting a crash course right now." Ash smiled at her.

"You're more than a lieutenant, aren't you? I can tell by the way you armed yourself, and it takes a pretty good aim to kill one of those creatures," Tia said, pointing to the cooked vermin.

"Yeah. I've had some extra training in infiltration and combat," Ash told her.

"Well, that helps, because we are going to need it where we are going. That's where Severon rules. He has many followers there, and they all have strong kinetics," Tia told her.

Kaiden stretched out, then got up, turning his neck and making it pop. He walked over to the table, sat down, and looked at the food. "Oh, it's lovely. You shouldn't have," he said with an ornery grin.

"Yeah, I know, so shut up and eat. We need to get going," Ash joked back and sat down across from him, and Tia went and sat down next to him, and everyone ate. Ash had to admit, the vermin wasn't that bad, a little chewy but tasted good.

"So what is this?" Kaiden asked, and Ash just continued to eat, ignoring the question. Tia looked down at her plate and kept eating also. Kaiden looked over at Ash and then at Tia and stopped eating. "All right, what aren't you telling me?" he asked them again and now had a scowl on his face.

"You don't want to know. Just eat it. It will build up your strength," Ash said and took another bite of hers and chewed. Even Tia was eating it and had almost all of hers gone, but Kaiden stared at her, and she finally cracked and pointed to one of the vermin running along a wall near the stairs. Kaiden had a look of disgust on his face and was about to spit it out, but Ash got on to him.

"You had better eat. This might be all you get for some time. I don't know when Fâd will get here, so we might be bunkered down somewhere in hiding until then," Ash told him, and he grudgingly ate, but every so often, he would gag, causing Tia to giggle. Finally, everyone was full, and they all packed what they could carry and needed. Ash pulled on the other coat that Kaiden got from the two men he had eliminated earlier, and he and Tia pulled on coats as well. Now everyone was covered. Tia went over and grabbed a long, curved knife in a holster and strapped it to her waist and tied the bottom part of the knife's holster around her upper thigh.

"Do you know how to use that?" Kaiden asked her as he made sure his pistol was ready. Tia gave him a cocky grin, pulled the knife from the holster, and spun it in and around her hand, then threw it. It stuck in the back of the chair he was standing next to. She walked over and pulled the knife out and headed for the stairs, putting it back in the holster. Kaiden looked over at Ash, grinning now. "I think I'm in love," he said and took off after her. Ash just grinned, shook her head, and followed them.

CHAPTER 49

"WE ARE ENTERING Sigma Six space, Captain. Stealth system engaged. I am picking up a council battleship entering Sigma Six space. The rest of council fleet is still farther out," Artemis told Fâd.

"Take it out. We need to give the shuttles time to load onto the passenger ships and for our fleet to get here to escort them," Fâd told her and now had a stone-cold expression on his face.

"Aye, aye, Captain. Transferring proton cannon to your controls," Artemis told him.

"Nathan, give me a clear shot," Fâd asked him.

"Your wish is my command. It's time to pay the bastards back," Nathan said, mad as well, and now moved the ship around, flying straight for the battleship at stage 7 propulsion, which was even faster than fighters. At the last second, he banked the ship, heading straight down at the planet, and then doing a complete turn on itself as everyone hung on. He hit the thrusters and shot straight up toward the belly of the battleship.

Artemis now appeared from stealth, and Fâd fired the proton cannon at the battleship's underside, which had no time to charge their shields. The cannon blasted a massive hole all the way through the battleship as Nathan piloted the Artemis right through the massive open wound, barely fitting the infiltrator, and came out her topside. He banked around again to see if they needed to hit the battle-ship one more time, but she was dead in space now.

"Head to New Haven. We will get Rachael and Bridgett first, then to Trinity," Fâd ordered him.

"What about Ash? Shouldn't we head there first?" Nathan asked, surprised.

"She's okay for now, but it's going to take all of us to get her out," Fâd told them and punched some keys on his multitool that brought up a large map outlining the prison city on Trinity on the ship's main screens. They could see a slow-blinking light on it.

"You have a bug on her? But how?" Cory asked, surprised.

"It's imbedded in my dog tag I gave her." Fâd smirked, and the other two did as well.

Nathan turned the *Artemis* and headed straight for New Haven, and in no time, they crossed over into the planet's atmosphere. On their way, they buzzed low over Pantier, flying now at an unbelievable speed. Trees were literally being blown apart from the force expelled by the fast-moving ship. As they passed by, Nera heard them and ran outside. Relief washed over her knowing now that the fleet was com-ing and that at least Fâd and they were here to save the girls.

"Where do you want to land, Captain?" Nathan asked as they were coming up on New Haven very quickly.

"Front door of the police precinct. We'll send them a big hello," Fâd told him coldly. They could see he was nothing but a pillar of anger and hate right now. Nathan and Cory also were nothing but open anger.

Nathan stopped the *Artemis* right in front of the police precinct and hovered about thirty feet from the ground with it. The ship itself was bigger than the three-story building, and Fâd walked over and sat down in the gun station and unleashed a short volley of armor-pierc-ing rounds on the front of the building.

Once satisfied with the end results, he got up, leaving the gun station. Nathan then set the ship down as Fâd, Nathan, and Cory headed to the armory and quickly suited up in their armor. With assault rifles drawn, they walked out into the cargo bay as the large cargo door lowered to the ground.

Fâd walked up to the front sliding door, which was all that was left standing as over half of the front of the building had been blown away. He had barely touched it when the door fell inward, crashing to the ground. They entered now with their guns raised and moved around, telling everyone who was still standing in this front room to stay down. Outside, Artemis made sure she kept her guns trained on the precinct and her engines running.

The guys moved through the police station, and the further they went in, the more resistance they encountered, but they took them out, showing no restraint. The police and council soldiers were no match for three well-armed, trained, and armored sentinel soldiers. Wounded and dead policemen and council soldiers lay everywhere.

Rachael, Bridgett, and the twins stood in their cell and could hear the commotion outside. The girls hit the floor, covering the twins with their selves, when they heard the gunship firing on the building. Rachael was in a panic, looking around for anything she could use as a weapon in case whoever it was who was coming, she could fight back. They heard the door to the cell room being hacked from the other side, and Rachael and Bridgett with the twins pressed up against the far wall, trying to blend in as much as possible. The door slid open, and Fâd, Nathan, and Cory came through with guns ready.

The girls saw them and ran to the front of the cell, sticking their arms through the bars for the guys, crying from the relief they felt knowing their mates were okay and also that they were being rescued. Nathan and Cory ran over to the girls, putting their guns on their backs, and were now touching them through the bars as well. Fâd went and shot off the security lock on the cell door and opened it. "Come on. We've got to go." He motioned to the twins as Rachael and Bridgett ran out into Nathan and Cory's arms. The guys put them down and handed each of them a gun, and now they all headed back toward the entrance.

This time, it was harder than when they came in because the police and soldiers had regrouped and armed themselves. It became a shoot-out now, but the council forces were still no match for trained sentinel soldiers, and they soon got to the missing front wall of the precinct and raced over and into the open cargo door of the *Artemis*.

The door immediately started closing as the ship lifted off, and the guys and the twins took the elevator up to the bridge. Rachael and Bridgett went to the armory and suited up into their own armor and armed themselves with their own weapons. Nathan was pushing the ship at an unbelievable speed upward, and they punched through the atmosphere and came out into the dark of space as Nathan did a complete roll and headed toward the planet Trinity. Artemis jumped immediately and disappeared into the void, once again firing her secondary engines, doubling their speed.

Rachael walked onto the bridge, now fully armored and with her sniper rifle clamped to her back and her pistol at her side, carrying her helmet. Bridgett was right behind her with two pistols, but one was a little bigger than the other. She was also carrying her helmet. They saw the twins talking to a proturin over near the science console but decided to ask later. Right now, the mission was to get Ash back.

They walked over to where Fâd was. He was watching a blinking light on the main screens with the map of the prison city still on it. He looked over at them and briefly smiled as they smiled back. "What happened?" he asked them.

"Ash didn't figure it out until it was too late. We held them for a while. Even Oscar and Lee were fighting, but there was just too many of them. Ash powered up, but they took her out with a tranquilizer gun and then shot her up with a bunch of nueralizers and collared her. Last we saw of her was when they took her out, and soon after, we were hauled to the police precinct," Rachael told him with tears in her eyes.

"Are you okay?" Fâd asked her, pointing at her head. Rachael reached up and felt the side of her head and the dried blood on it. Nathan came over now from his pilot seat, pulling her into his arms, and just held her, burying his face in her hair. Then Oscar walked over to Rachael now with a med kit.

"I need to treat that wound," he told her, and Nathan led her over to a chair at one of the many stations and made her sit down.

Bridgett had gone over to Cory and was clinging to him as he held her in his arms with his head lying on top of hers. Fâd could feel his heart being torn apart watching them because Ash was still out there fighting for her life and not here in his arms.

Oscar started cleaning the wound as Nathan watched; it was a pretty good gash down the side of her head, right at the hairline. Lee came over, as did Dr. Shin, and Oscar let Lee stitch it back up since he was much faster and better at it. Rachael refused pain medicine because she wanted all her senses acute for when they went in to get Ash out. Lee finished putting six stitches in. Dr. Shin then took the brothers to where the med bay was so they could do some rearranging in case somebody got hurt during the rescue.

Just before they got to the elevator, Dr. Shin looked over at the twins. "Trust me, I've seen these guys in action. There's going to be wounded, mainly them," he told the twins.

"Well, the girls aren't any better and just as crazy," Oscar replied as all three of them stepped into the elevator.

Fâd looked over at them and shook his head with a frown on his face. "I'm so glad they have such confidence in us," he said sarcastically. He brought up the prison city layout on the round holographic map console instead of the galaxy as the main screens returned to windows, showing the space outside. Everyone came over and looked at it.

They could all see the red dot now that was Ash, and it was apparent she was on the move. He traced through the city to try and see where she might be heading and came to a place in the wall that was weaker than the rest. It was obvious that it had been damaged at some point and hastily repaired.

"She's heading here. We can blast through here with Artemis's guns, but we need to get the shields down first. Also, there are defensive guns that we will encounter even before we get to the city, which our cloaking is useless against," Fâd told them.

"Leave that to me, Captain. There's no program out there that I can't hack. I'll have the shields down," Artemis told him from her portal pad on the map station they were all standing around.

"I can take care of the guns. Just get me close to the surface so I can hack from below, and we can use the planet's surface to cover us," Cory said, and Nathan nodded.

"Okay. Once we break through, it's just a matter of finding her and Kaiden and not getting ourselves killed," Fâd said with a slight smirk, and then he heard the elevator doors slide open and now saw Dr. Shin and Lee walk out, also dressed in lightweight armor and carrying pistols.

"What do you think you're doing?" Fâd asked them with a scowl on his face.

"We are going with you. Ash is my friend, not to mention you might need a medic," Lee said defiantly.

"He has a good point, Fâd. Can you use a gun?" Nathan asked him.

Lee grinned and cocked the gun he had with him, and they nodded their heads in agreement that he could join the group, but Fâd gave Dr. Shin a dirty look. "You definitely aren't going, though."

"I'll have you know I can also shoot a gun just fine, and without me, you won't stand a chance against all those kinetics down there," Shin said, annoyed.

"Oh, and how do you think you can stop them?" Fâd asked, annoyed.

"With this. It's my own invention. It holds several explosive rounds that are filled with thirty micro stinger shots that have a smart chip in them, which senses kinetics and are drawn to them. Upon contact with the victim, if they are not in armor, it will penetrate under the skin and release a fast-acting nueralizer. It won't knock them out, but it will block their kinetics for a couple hours," Shin said with a grin, holding up a weird-looking pistol with glowing blue rounds in it.

"So it can't penetrate armor?" Fâd asked, now interested.

"No, but since you are a kinetic, I suggest you wear your helmet when I fire this. Otherwise, you might take one in the side of the head," Shin said with an evil grin, and Fâd gave him a dirty look.

"All right, you can go, but I want both of you to stay behind one of us and try not to shoot us," he said to both Lee and Shin, who looked appalled that he would even think that.

"Captain, approaching Trinity. Coming out of jump in 5, 4, 3, 2, 1," Artemis said. Now Nathan took over the pilot's seat and thrust the engines into stage 8 propulsion. They blasted down toward the planet and to their friends.

CHAPTER 50

TIA LED THE way with Ash right behind her as Kaiden brought up the rear, taking them in and out of streets and back alleys and through derelict buildings. On several occasions, they had to lay low as Kaiden was having a hard time getting used to both Tia and Ash talking to him with their telepathy. He kept trying to talk normally, and Ash would get on to him, telling him to shut up so he wouldn't give their position away.

He didn't know how Ash did it, but she somehow could link all three of them up at the same time. Even Tia was impressed, because she couldn't even do that being a full-blooded vatorian. "How do you think my friends and I got good grades in school and never failed a test?" Ash told him, and Kaiden started chuckling.

They ran across the street and darted into a dark building when they saw three men heading down the street in their direction. Ash and they leaned into the darkness of the building, and Kaiden now saw her white eyes glowing in the dark, which was typical for changed watorian mates and males. He couldn't help but think even at a time like this that eventually, his eyes would look like that.

They were still hiding and watched as the men stopped right in front of the building. One of the convicts sniffed the air a couple of times, then left, heading down the street in the direction they had already come from. Ash had everyone wait a few more minutes, then said they could move on. Tia stepped out first and looked around to make sure the coast was clear.

Suddenly, out of the shadows of the building next to the one they were hiding in, one of the men stepped out, grabbing her from behind. Ash moved before Kaiden could even register what had happened, and in no time, the man fell to the ground with a snapped neck. Now the other two came after them, and Kaiden dropped one with a clean shot from his pistol as Ash unleashed a kinetic burst that crushed the other man's chest when it hit him, not to mention flinging him against the wall of the abandoned building.

They wasted no time and moved out but now were starting to run into more and more convicts as they were now in Severon's district, who was a self-proclaimed kinetic warlord. Quite a few times, Ash took out someone from the shadows, easily snapping their neck, Kaiden and Tia dragging the body out of sight. He was amazed at her. She definitely knew what she was doing, and he knew Tia was in awe of her as well. They were still quite a ways from the place they were trying to reach when they heard a huge explosion off in the distance and noticed overhead that the massive barrier that covered this place was gone. Ash looked at them with a big grin on her face. "Our ride's here." And now Kaiden and Tia were grinning as well.

* * *

Nathan came in fast and low over the planet to stay under the prison city's defense towers and was now barely skimming the surface, leaving nothing but a dusty funnel behind them and flying debris. The ship's engine pushed them forward as he was now dodging laser shots from the defensive towers, but the dust and debris that were being kicked up from the planet's surface helped to throw off the defense guns' targeting. Everyone watched out of their front windows as the land moved past them at an unbelievable speed. Fâd was impressed by Nathan's skills in piloting this huge ship at this speed and maneuvering her all over the place. He looked over at Cory now, who was over working quickly on the scanning console.

"All right. You're in the clear now, Nathan. I got the prison guns' radar jammed, and the defense guns are down. Plus, you have full control of the system. You can now get in, Artemis," Cory told Artemis and Nathan, who piloted the ship up a little ways from the surface from having to fly so low. Fâd was very impressed with Cory's hacking skills. No one had ever been able to get into Trinity's systems since the prison city was built, and he was able to do it in a matter of minutes and from his console on board the ship.

Fâd could see the massive walls of the prison coming up real fast, and now Nathan was turning the ship toward a particular area of the wall. They came up to it as Nathan stopped the ship instantly. Everyone had to grab ahold of something so they wouldn't fall over, and she hovered in front of it. Fâd took over the mech guns and blasted a hole into the wall. A huge section crumbled, revealing the large city behind it. At the same time, Artemis took down the kinetic barrier that covered the entire prison city, and Nathan now set the ship down.

Fâd, Nathan, Cory, Rachael, and Bridgett put on their helmets as Fâd gave Artemis some last-minute orders. "Once we're off the ship, I want you to lift off and stand by. If you don't hear from us in fifteen minutes, then I want you to leave and head back to the fleet," Fâd ordered her.

"NO! I WON'T LEAVE YOU GUYS!" Artemis said and started to argue.

"If you don't hear from us by then, we're dead," Fâd told her bluntly.

"I understand, Captain," she said as a sad frown spread across her face.

Fâd looked at everyone, now fully armored with helmets on, and had to admit they looked pretty scary even though they were half crazy. He motioned to move out, and everyone moved like a well-seasoned assault team. They all took the two elevators down to the cargo bay and quickly out of the bay and toward the blown hole in the wall, then taking cover. Fâd and Nathan took point, looking over into the prison city from their cover on the other side of the debris of the blown-up hole, and Rachael came up behind. Fâd motioned for her to move out, and she was the first over the crumbled wall. Nathan was having a hard time watching her go for a couple of reasons: one because he was worried about her and the other, a cold shower would help a lot right now.

Once she disappeared, Fâd and Nathan followed, giving her a few minutes to find a high perch and cover the area with her sniper rifle. Dr. Shin and Lee, then Cory and Bridgett covered the rear. They got over the wall and looked around at the burning buildings and devastation that the mech guns had done. There were a few dead convicts lying around but not that many.

Fâd could hear behind him the ship now engaging her thrusters and taking off as he signaled for everyone to move out and take cover, but as they began their tactical advancement forward, a couple of armed convicts stepped out of the shadows, who were instantly dropped with clean headshots as the team heard the staccato sound of a high-powered sniper rifle.

Fâd had to grin in his helmet when he heard Nathan and Rachael talking over the comm link. "All right. That's my girl," Nathan told her.

"You know it. I love a big gun," Rachael teased back.

"Knock it off. I'm having a hard time moving in this armor as it is," Nathan replied, chuckling.

"Do you two realize that all of us can hear this?" Bridgett told them.

"Yes. Please, I just vomited in my suit," Dr. Shin added, and everyone started laughing.

"Ash. Come in, Ash," Fâd said over his comm link now as he continued forward. There was a brief pause as Fâd stopped and waited.

"Well, it took you long enough," Ash came back over the comm, and everyone let out a sigh of relief.

"You better watch it, woman, or I'll just turn around and leave your ass here," Fâd teased back but feeling so much relief at hearing her ornery voice.

Ash started laughing over the comm link. "I have you on the screen. We're heading your way."

"Negative. We'll come and get you. Just take cover and wait," Fâd said, motioning to everyone to move out, and the team moved forward.

"Oh, well, you better hurry. It looks like we have a welcoming committee coming our way. Got to go," Ash said, and then the comm link went silent.

"ASH!" Fâd yelled into his comm but got nothing. The squad took off running then toward her comm signal, shooting anything that moved.

Ash, in the meantime, had her, Kaiden, and Tia take cover behind a large concrete wall that had crumbled and fallen down from the building behind them as they started firing back with both pistols and kinetics at the large crowd that was attacking them now. Kinetic blasts were coming at them, and Ash would counter them, knocking them away. Even Tia was helping and using her kinetics, which she had inherited from her father, but there were so many of the convicts that Ash and Tia were barely holding them back. Kaiden was doing a great job of picking off the attackers with his pistol, but it seemed that every time he dropped one, two would take his place.

The other problem now was, Ash was using so much of her telepathy and kinetics that her headaches were starting to flare up fast, and she didn't have her suit to counter it, only a med kit, but she couldn't stop fighting or take Kaiden away either. Yet if she didn't take care of the headache now, she would become incapacitated by it, and it was already noticeable that her kinetics were starting to suffer from it as they weakened.

"Tia, I need your help. In the med kit, you will find a syringe and a small vial marked Asrinon. Fill the syringe with the fluid from the vial, and in the back of my neck is an injection port that I need you to inject the asrinon in," Ash told her telepathically as she continued to fire and use her kinetics. Tia looked scared to death now, but Ash told her that if she didn't do it, she would go down soon from pain. Tia crawled over, pulling out the med kit from Kaiden's pack, and did exactly what Ash had told her.

Then with Ash still shooting, Tia moved her hair away from her neck and saw the port. Ash held perfectly still as the young girl injected the medicine and then threw the syringe away as if it was something deadly and alive. Ash could feel the medicine burn, but it quickly went to work on the pain in her head, and now she was back to full power again.

"Thanks, Tia. You saved me," Ash said and could see the frightened girl smile. But by now, they were getting down to the last of their clips.

"Ash, I'm almost done with this clip and only have one more left after this," Kaiden told her.

"I know. That's all I have too," she replied and continued to fight with both her pistol and kinetics. Just then, behind them, a convict came at them with a knife from the dark of the abandoned building they were hunkered down in. Tia jumped up and met the large man head-on as Kaiden yelled at her. She moved like an expert and countered all his attacks with her own knife and then dealt him a few nasty slices. It was apparent she wasn't as strong or large as him, and he gave her a deep gash in her side, but she moved quickly and came around, stabbing him in the base of his skull. He toppled over with her still on his back. Tia headed back over to them with her hand on her side. Blood was now running out of the wound.

"Tia, no," Kaiden yelled, and Ash ordered him to see to Tia's wound. He didn't hesitate and rushed over to her, pulling back the slashed material. It would be a mortal wound if not treated soon, and he grabbed the med pack, pulling out a bottle of mediplast. He inserted the tip of the bottle directly into the wound, ignoring Tia's gasp of pain, and sprayed the gel into it. Soon, the wound was filled with green foam, and the bleeding stopped. Then he pulled out another syringe. Tia was trying to stop him so she could help fight some more, but he grabbed her arm and injected some painkillers and sedative into her.

"Why, Kaiden? I can still help," she said as she went out now.

He reached down and brushed her white hair from her face. "Because you have to live for me." He made sure she was protected, then ran back over to where he was before and once again started firing. He was now getting down to the last bit of his clip, and Ash had already run out and was just blasting with her kinetics as the convicts were advancing. One man ran toward them and was about ten feet when he suddenly dropped from a clean bullet hole in his forehead, and now the sound of a high-powered rifle reached them.

The convicts suddenly started dropping from behind as assault rifles were now going off. Ash suddenly heard an explosion and then a stinging sensation in her shoulder and saw she had been hit with something, but it was not serious. She immediately noticed that no one was using kinetics anymore, and when she tried, she couldn't as well. Kaiden fired the last of his clip and then came over by Ash. She knew that Fâd and her friends had reached them, so she moved back further into the abandoned building so they wouldn't get caught in the melee firing.

Ash had Kaiden protect Tia, which he was already doing, and she took a defensive position in front of him and handled any of the convicts who came over the concrete barrier that they were earlier hiding behind. She was now forced to fight using just her hands. She was doing fine, and convicts were dropping all around her, though a few times she took some hits.

Kaiden could see armored soldiers now moving easily through the crowd, and finally, the last of the convicts fell from a sniper strike. Ash was standing among a pile herself inside the abandoned building as the squadron moved around with their rifles poised to fire, making sure the area was secure. One of the large armored soldiers just stood there, looking toward the building they were in, and Ash ran out to him, leaping into his outstretched arms, crying.

Kaiden stood up now knowing that it was Fâd and them even with their helmets still on and walked out of the building with Tia cradled in his arms. He grabbed their packs and headed over to them. Two smaller soldiers saw him and quickly ran over to him. One of them lifted up Tia's shirt to see the wound and then ran a scan over her from their multitool. He pulled open a pack he was carrying and pulled out a syringe, filling it with some red liquid and injecting it right into the wound on Tia's side, and then looked up at Kaiden. "She's stable now, but we need to get her back. The wound punctured her kidney, and the injection I gave her will only protect the kidney for so long," he told Kaiden through his helmet.

"Captain, we need to go now. This young lady needs medical attention immediately," the other man in armor who came over to Kaiden told Fâd.

Fâd sat Ash down and signaled to move out as he handed Ash another assault rifle from his back, which he had brought for her. She noticed that it was hers and kissed, then stroked the side of it, telling her rifle how much she had missed it. Fâd couldn't help but start chuckling.

Fâd once again took point, which generally would have been Ash's position since she was the lieutenant commander for infantry, but since she wasn't in armor, she stayed behind Fâd for protection. Ash, though, instead of using hand signals, tapped into everyone telepathically and channeled Fâd's orders using herself to them in their heads, which was much more efficient than the comm links.

"I'm not sure I like this idea of you in my head," Nathan said jokingly.

"Now you know how I've felt for the last thirteen years," Fâd said to him, chuckling.

"Will you guys shut up? My gosh, we're trying to get out of here in one piece," Shin piped in.

"Hey, who are the other two guys?" Kaiden now asked.

"Forget that. Who's the girl? Looks like you scored, Kaiden," Nathan said.

"SHUT UP!" Ash said, and suddenly, everyone felt a sharp pain in their heads from it.

"What the hell was that?" Nathan asked, shaking his head in his helmet now.

"That was a warning. I can make it hurt worse if you don't shut up," Ash said, grinning, and glanced back at him. Fâd was also grinning in his helmet even though they couldn't see it.

Fâd coordinated their movements, and before long, they had covered almost all the distance back to where they had entered. But when they got to the large opening in the wall, there was a huge gathering of convicts around it, and more kept coming out from several directions.

"I don't have enough rounds left to handle all those kinetics," Dr. Shin told Ash and Fâd.

"That's not good. Fâd won't be able to block all of them, and mine aren't working now," Ash replied.

Just then, Artemis came down from the sky and unleashed a huge spray of armor-piercing rounds on the convicts, killing many and driving the rest away. Fâd took the opportunity and ordered to move. Everyone ran to the blown-out opening in the wall. Fâd, Ash, Nathan, and Cory set down another wave of gunfire at the convicts who had taken cover when Artemis fired on them. The ship then headed over to the other side of the wall and landed. Bridgett covered the doctors and Kaiden, who was carrying Tia, while Rachael picked off anyone from her secure perch on one of the rooftops that got on Bridgett's blind side.

They slowly started backing to the opening as Rachael rappeled down the side of a four-story building behind them and hit the release button on the climbing equipment that was built into her suit. The clamp released from up above, and the cable coiled back into her suit in a matter of seconds. She had already strapped her rifle to her back and was now firing with her pistol, heading for the opening, running through it. The rest, one by one, ran through with Ash and Fâd being the last ones. Fâd grabbed Ash around the waist, carrying her in his arm, as she continued to fire on the convicts, and he ran for the ship.

The ship was now hovering a few feet from the ground, and Fâd had to jump to reach it, still with Ash in his arms, and they both rolled into the bay as the door started closing. The ship rose from the ground, once again laying down fire from her forbs mech guns. The bay door sealed shut, and Fâd jumped up, removing his helmet, immediately throwing it aside, and raced over to where Ash was still lying on the floor, trying to catch her breath.

He fell down on his knees and pulled her into his arms as his lips came down on hers. She wrapped her arms around his neck and was kissing him back and crying at the same time. Finally, she stopped and looked at him, smiling with a tear-soaked face, and he hugged her tightly.

"That was fun, but I don't ever care to do that again," Ash said while Fâd was still holding her tightly. He looked down at her in his arms and started chuckling now.

"You have got to be another one of the craziest women I have ever known in my life," Fâd told her, still chuckling.

"Another one? Who's the other?" Ash asked.

"Rachael. You two are pretty equal on the nut scale," Fâd teased her and kissed her forehead as Ash started giggling. He stood up, helping her up, and could see how beat-up she looked. "Let's get you to the med bay, have Oscar and Lee look you over."

"How come they're here?" Ash asked as they headed over to the elevator.

"They got arrested with Rachael and Bridgett for fighting the operatives to help you three. It's amazing how many people get into trouble around you girls."

"Imagine that. How do we always seem to get caught, and you guys never do?"

"Because we're good," Fâd teased as the elevator took them to the second floor. They walked down the hall and into the medical bay, which looked very nice and well-prepared. Ash walked over to a large window that looked into another room, which was definitely a surgical one, where Oscar and Lee were in medical suits, operating on Tia. Kaiden was standing there, watching, when she and Fâd walked in; he didn't even look over at them but continued to stare into the room.

"How is she doing?" Fâd asked him.

"I don't know yet," Kaiden said, scared. Lee looked over at the window where everyone was watching from and gave them all a thumbs-up. Kaiden let out the breath he was holding and seemed to relax finally.

"Why don't you go get cleaned up and rest? Artemis will show you your assigned room, Lieutenant," Fâd said, smiling at him.

"Don't you mean Junior Lieutenant?"

"No," Fâd answered, and now Kaiden was grinning.

Artemis instantly appeared on a near portal pad and asked Kaiden to follow her. "This way, Lieutenant. You're really cute. Did you know that?" Kaiden blushed and looked back at Ash and Fâd, who were chuckling. Oscar came out of the operating room now and told Ash to come over and sit down on one of the examination tables. He made her remove her coat and shirt, which Fâd helped her with as well, and once she was down to her bra, they could see all the bruises on her.

Fâd grimaced when he saw them, especially around her ribs. Oscar ran a scan over her and then inspected the head wound that Kaiden had stitched up, which Fâd hadn't even noticed. "Well, there's nothing broken, just a lot of cuts and bruises. The gash on your head looks good. I was worried about that one. There was a lot of blood on the floor when they hit you," Oscar said and was now cleaning up the other cuts. Then he pulled out a syringe and filled it with some medicine.

"Another shot? I'm starting to feel like a damn pincushion. I have got needle marks all over me," Ash complained, but Oscar gave her a shot in the shoulder anyway, and she yelled at him because it hurt.

"Quit being a baby. That was nothing. You went through worse when you changed," Oscar told her.

"Why? What happened?" Fâd asked, now concerned, and Ash looked embarrassed.

"It was really quite interesting. We have the whole thing on vid. How do I explain this? Ash's change was worse than most due to her being a kinetic. Her powers actually sped up the process, but her human half had difficulty handling it at that rate of change. Her fever shot up to dangerous levels, and she nearly cooked herself from the inside.

"We couldn't take her to the hospital because of her kinetics and had to keep her nueralized because of it. But the good side of it all was, she only had to deal with it for less than twelve hours, and most of that time was spent unconscious, unlike most females, who have to endure the pain for over twenty-four and sometimes thirty-six hours," Oscar told them as if it was no big deal, but Fâd looked devastated.

"I am so sorry, Ash. I would have never if I had known that would happen to you," Fâd said, worried about her, but before Ash could reply, Oscar piped in again.

"Oh, everything's okay now, and you can reproduce like it was intended all along, which I noticed I do have the pills here for, so when you are ready, I can give them to you. I know that intercourse is a way that your two species oftentimes use to relieve stress, but you will not conceive until you take the pills. Of course, you are part vatoria, so who knows?"

Ash and Fâd both turned bright red from embarrassment and looked over at Oscar in disbelief. "Do you have no shame?" Ash said to him.

"What? I was just stating a fact," Oscar said, confused.

"That's a little personal, don't you think?" Fâd said but had a slight grin on his face.

"Yes, doctor-patient confidentiality. I would never discuss another's personal information with other crew members. I'm appalled you would think that," Oscar said and looked like someone had slapped him.

"That's not what we mean. Oh, never mind," Ash said, rolling her eyes, and stood up, feeling wobbly now. Fâd grabbed her to steady her.

"I want you to go and lie down and rest for a while. You'll find you will be getting sleepy anyway because I added a little incentive to the medicine to help with that," Oscar said. Ash could already feel the sedative.

"You ass! You gave me a sed…" She never got to finish that thought. Fâd caught her and lifted her into his arms easily, laying her head against his chest.

"Thanks. Otherwise, she would have never laid down," Fâd told Oscar.

"I know. She'll be okay, just really sore when she wakes up and mad. Give her these pills every four hours. They will help with some of the pain from the bruises and cuts," Oscar told him and gave Fâd a small bottle of pills.

"By the way, I never got to tell you, welcome aboard the *Artemis*. Is there someplace where we can drop you and your brother off?"

"In all honesty, Captain, if it's okay with you, we would like to remain on board. You need us," Oscar said, grinning up at the large watorian.

Fâd grinned down at him. "That we do, Doctor." Then he headed to the door, throwing a blanket over Ash, and walked through as it slid open. He headed up to his cabin and now noticed trunks in there that were Ash's. The crew must have brought them up from the cargo hold where they were loaded onto from the *Justification*. He walked over to the bedroom and carefully laid Ash down on the bed, then removed her boots and pants. She was just in her undergarments, and he pulled the blankets up on her. He sat there on the edge of the bed, still in his armor and with weapons strapped on, then leaned over, gently kissing her forehead.

Relief washed over him now, having her finally right here with him. He forgot to even mention her eyes. He had noticed them right away and couldn't believe how beautiful they looked. He was saddened that her gold ones were gone, because they were also beautiful, but now her eyes looked so exotic with the gold ring around the white and the gold flecks. He was just sitting there, watching her breathe and taking in her scent, which smelled like wild roses and fresh mountain breeze, his favorite, when he got a call on his comm.

"Captain, you need to get up here and see this," Cory said.

"I'll be right there," Fâd replied, heading out, and in no time was on the bridge. Everyone was now in uniforms but him, because he still hadn't gotten the time to change.

"What is it, Cory?"

"Take a look at this!" Nathan said and pulled up a screen over Sigma Six. Now over the planet were close to five battleships, three destroyers, and a large battlecruiser, all bearing the council insignia, depicting a white star with three oval multicolored rings encircling it, but nowhere was sentinel fleet.

Fâd opened a secure comm to sentinel fleet and waited for a response. Finally, after a few minutes had passed, he got one. "This is Rear Admiral Larson of the *Lithia*. Where are you guys?"

"We are just leaving Trinity space. What is happening over Sigma Six? Where is the fleet?" Fâd asked.

"Leaving. All pioneers are on board, and we are providing escort to passenger ships for new colony. What about you guys? Is everyone on board?" Larson asked anxiously, and Fâd could hear the concern in his voice.

"Yes, and then some. Everyone accounted for and well," Fâd replied with a grin.

"Wonderful. I will pass the information on to Vice Admiral Harper," Larson said, but Fâd could pick up something else in his tone.

"Father, what's going on? There's something you're not telling me."

"Have you heard from Sharni? Her destroyer and battleships are with us now, but no one has seen her for a couple days. I know she took a frigate to Alpha Prime five days ago to pick up some thermal couplings, but since then, I haven't heard from her, and she never said anything to me last I talked to her a few days ago about where she might be going from there," Larson said, and it was now very apparent that he was worried.

"No." Fâd looked over at Bridgett and Rachael, and they shook their heads as well. "The girls haven't heard from her either."

"All right. Well, she knows what she's doing. I'm sure she will contact us soon. It must be very important for her to remain silent like this. Council is back in control. There's nothing left here for us, so catch up. It's time to head to our new home," Larson told him.

"Affirmative, Admiral. We'll be there soon," Fâd said with a grin, and the comm went blank. He looked around, and all eyes were on him now. "You heard him. Let's go home." And everyone started grinning.

Back in the captain's cabin, Ash woke up feeling stiff and sore and stretched out gingerly, then moved over to the edge of the bed. She sniffed the air and now could smell Fâd everywhere. It was just like what Rachael and Bridgett had said, only Fâd smelled of fresh pine and chocolate, her favorite smells ever, and she was amazed at how that scent brought his image to her mind instantly.

She stood up and popped her back and neck, then went over and opened the closet. Some of her clothes were already in there, and she pulled out one of the infiltrator uniforms that the guys wore and realized it was in her size and quickly dressed. She figured Fâd must have gotten them for her at some time and put them in there. Once dressed, she walked over to the mirror on the dresser and pulled her hair back into a ponytail but noticed all the cuts and bruises on her face.

"Wow, don't I look great." She left the bedroom and walked out into the living quarters of the cabin, which had a bunch of her trunks in it. She felt a vibration on her multitool. She looked down and now saw a blinking small blue light. Shock flowed through her because it was not possible for this to be activated. A message coming over this link could only have come from her mother, because it was a direct link, totally untraceable and unhackable, but there it was, going off. She pressed the button, but the voice that came over it surprised her.

"Ash, are you alone?" Sharni said quietly.

"Yes. Sharni, is that you?" Ash asked, surprised.

"Yes. No time to chat. Listen carefully. I need your help. I have come upon some vital information that could mean the end of everyone in this galaxy if it is not stopped. I tracked where the source of it came from but need your assistance to extradite more information, not to mention a way back since my ship was shot down and I'm now in hiding," Sharni whispered into the comm.

"Yes, we will come and get you. Where are you?" Ash asked, worried about her.

"Earth!" Ash just stood there, not saying a word. This was the last place she would ever expect Sharni to go, not to mention that the end of all life was traced back to there. "Ash, are you still there?"

"Yes. We are on our way," Ash told her.

"I'm transmitting my coordinates to your secure comm link now. Be advised, Ash, the bodies that are behind this are very powerful and work in secret. They go by the name NOVA. Trust no one, and do not bring the fleet into this. They are being watched," Sharni said, and the link went silent.

Ash just stood there for a few minutes, then finally came out of her daze and raced out the door, barely giving it time to slide open, and onto the elevator. Once it slid open, she jumped out and ran over to Fâd, who was standing at his console, plotting a course and orders for each of the stations. He spun around when he heard the elevator open and now saw the look of dread on Ash's face.

"What is it, Ash?" he asked, worried.

"We need to head to Earth now. I'm sending you the coordinates," Ash told him and was punching up orders on her multitool as Fâd turned around and looked down at his console as they came across.

"What's on Earth that we need to get to right away?" he asked, putting in the coordinates to send to Nathan to plot for jump.

"Sharni!" Ash answered, and now Fâd was looking at her with narrowed eyes.

"Report," he asked, now all professional and the captain again.

"Sharni has uncovered some plot and traced the source to Earth but needs assistance from us to stop it. An organization called NOVA is somehow behind it."

"How do you know all this? When and how did you talk to her?"

"Just a few minutes ago, she contacted me on a comm link that was a direct, untraceable link to my mother's comm. She must somehow have known about it or also had the same linkup. She's in trouble. She got shot down and lost her ship," Ash told him with worry in her tone.

"I must tell the admirals," Fâd said and turned to his console to contact them.

"No. She said secrecy was the utmost importance and to trust no one. She told me not to tell the fleet because they are also being watched," Ash replied, and now her look changed from worry to fear.

Fâd looked down at her and then over at everyone else. They all nodded in agreement that this was a priority. He looked back at Ash. "Let's go get Sharni," he said, and Ash threw her arms around him, and he held her tightly.

"Plotting course for Earth!" Nathan said. Everyone took a deep breath as the *Artemis* jumped.

CODEX

BINDOS

THEY ARE OTHERWISE known as the galaxies' riffraffs. They are nothing but scavengers, and a lot of times, carians use them to move among council space to spy or acquire certain supplies and information for them since most races ignore bindos.

Not much is known about them but that they are small, not much taller than a ten-year-old human child, and all of them are rather cowardly and stinky. They are always in dirty biosuits, completely covered from head to toe since they only breathe helium-rich air, thus giving a high-pitched tone to their voice. They are also as round as they are tall, and nobody knows for sure what they look like under their suits. Only a pair of glowing red eyes are noticeable through the visor of their helmets. It is believed that they may resemble some type of bird, because oftentimes, when they speak, they let out a chirp between words.

Bindos have a waddling walk and move around in groups of three or four and oftentimes congregate around supply depots or seen asleep in back alleys at night. They do have a fondness for alcohol and frequent many nightclubs and bars, drinking through a tube in their suits until the club or bar's bouncers have to throw them out due to intoxication, at which time they actually get belligerent.

They contribute nothing to societies, and in their homeworld, Friel, they are oftentimes living in just small huts built out of whatever scraps of debris or even wreaked ships they can find. Carians mostly compensate them with these items as a means to get rid of them themselves, and the bindos use them. Bindos who do work for the carians fare much better in that they usually have a small ship that can get in and out quickly undetected and marks to be able to gain access to certain places throughout the different planets and colonies.

Not much is known about whether they are intelligent, but they do seem to be able to hide and blend in and gather valuable information and give it to the carians, so this at least shows some form of intelligence. Not much else is known about them, for no one has wanted to take the time to study them due to their offending aroma, which is believed to be a defense mechanism.

BIOSYMS

HALF-BIOLOGICAL, HALF-SYNTHETIC HUMANOIDS, biosyms are a product of a test tube created by the vatorias many, many years ago as medical assistants. Since then, they have evolved over time into a more complex, self-sufficient, sentient life-form, which through their appeal to council presidency gives them their own social standing, thus breaking away from vatoria control.

They were originally created using vatoria DNA, but when humans appeared, they were given access to an unlimited supply of human DNA through centuries of stockpiles of cryogenically frozen fertilized human eggs that were once used in in vitro reproduction but now has long since been abandoned due to medical breakthroughs in that area. Most cryogenic companies sell to the biosyms these stockpiles just to get rid of them and still be able to make a slight profit from it.

Biosyms, due to their advanced intelligence, have made genetic modifications and now create themselves also using synthetics and cybernetics as well. All their limbs are completely synthetic and cybernetic, including their eyes. Their skin is pale white, and in places, the synthetic tissues and muscles actually show through as a dark-gray coloration in the skin, giving them what look like stripes. Their cybernetic blue eyes are the only color in their appearance. Even their hair is gray and void of coloration. Biosyms are average in height, and due to their human DNA, they are not lacking in muscular makeup. In all honesty, they look just like humans, except void of color.

They are mostly known for their medical prowess due to their keen knowledge of gene therapy and modification. They are extremely intelligent, because their biological brains are actually hardwired to think at speeds that computers or some AIs (artificial intelligence) do. Because they are part biological, they do have emotions and can express feelings, such as anger, fear, desire, and in some cases, even love. Biosyms live mostly solitary lives due to their constant pursuit of knowledge, but there have been instances where some took up companionship with females of their kind. Of course, reproduction among themselves is impossible since they are all sterile, but they still can have intimate relations due to being anatomically the same as humans.

Unlike ferals and watorians, biosyms use technology to the max and are always striving to find ways to improve it, especially in the medical field, since aging is a major factor in biosyms' lives. They are awaken fully grown and age three years to every human's one, but they have since been able to change that to every two years to one and also increased their life expectancy to around seventy years instead of fifty, and one has to remember that humans live a lot longer now, as fifty has now become middle age for humans with all the new medical breakthroughs.

Biosyms have also been able to awaken at an earlier age and grow and mature along with other alien species, reaching maturity now around the age of eighteen and nineteen, which has aided in giving more time for advancement in knowledge and technology.

Biosyms are a lot of times counselors to the council presidency and even have a couple of members on the council. They call Alpha Prime their home planet, which is strictly council-run and protected. Most alien species have come to respect them for their keen knowledge and contributions of medical advancements, but noncouncil supporters don't trust them due to their strong ties with the council presidency.

BORVIANS

THIS ALIEN RACE makes up a majority of your merc groups and dislikes everyone; thus, they have no problem with taking what they want. Borvians are smaller than humans but stocky in build with coarse short black hair covering the majority of their bodies, except their face, palms, and feet. Their faces resemble a bat's with their bulbous large black eyes, razor-sharp teeth, and pointed small ears. They also have clawlike hands and feet and usually dress in leather armor and overcoats to hide the many weapons they carry. It is hard to distinguish between males and females unless a female is ready to mate, at which time she will display red streaks in her fur, becoming very pronounced on her head, and oftentimes causes hostilities among the males she is around for a short time.

Borvians do not set up domestic dwellings until they reach a more mature age, something comparable to old age in humans. This is when they seek out others of their age and set up colonies on some remote planet for raising their young. Younger borvians do not raise their own offspring. When a female conceives, she travels to a nursery, which is what these colonies are called, and gives birth, then leaves her young with them and continues with her mercenary lifestyle. Males never see or care to have anything to do with their young until they reach this older age. In fact, most young male borvians see the young as competition for future plunders and females and often-times will not think twice about killing them.

They are ruthless, and their merc groups have no problem attacking defenseless colonies, freighters, and even armed small frigates. Usually, when they raid, they leave very few survivors, but women hostages are always taken and sold on the black market and into slavery, because they fetch a high mark. They also are known to deal a lot with carians and do from time to time sell hostages to them or trade for technology. They generally shy away from anything associated with sentinel fleet due to the fleet having many ways of finding them and their bases of operation, thus wiping them out.

Borvians range all over the galaxy and don't call any one planet their homeworld. They have many highly organized merc groups that also incorporate many other life-forms into their organization and are a constant menace to the galaxy. It isn't until they reach their elder years that they actually become a contributing factor and actually perform legitimate work, but by this time, most are rather wealthy from their lives as thieves and murderers.

CARIANS

THIS IS THE galaxies' most vile and hated alien species around, a carnivorous reptilian race that has now extended their taste to humans. They are merciless warriors, who have no problem wiping out anyone or anything in their way, and over the years have amassed a large armada and fleet at their disposal with highly advanced technology through their many raids.

Carians feel that most life-forms are a waste of space and an abomination due to their religious beliefs teaching them that they are the true sentient life in the galaxy and that all others are nothing but disease and pestilence. Their goal is to wipe out most of the other alien species, especially humans, whom they see as nothing but a parasite bent on infecting the galaxy. They nearly accomplished their goal more than a century ago against council forces but were stopped by the rise of the separatist military faction sentinel fleet.

Carians walk upright on two legs and have clawed long fingers and hands. Their faces are flat, but they have elongated upper and lower jaws that are lined with rows of needlelike razor teeth on the inside that are used for tearing flesh since they are meat eaters and any living being is seen as a potential meal. Their noses are just slits in the center of their face, and they all have serpentlike red eyes. They have a row of small spikes running down from their neck to the middle of their back, and their builds look a lot like most lizards with the exception that they walk upright and are a little stooped over. Their one weakness is, they have retained the cold-blooded trait that most reptiles have.

The male and female of their kind are warriors and, like the watorians, excel in combat. Their leathery skin is tough and can handle much damage, and their redundant nervous system allows them to continue to fight void of pain, which is also aided by a regenerative, healing ability. Males are very tall, lean, and muscular and extremely strong, and depending on their maturity level, they range anywhere from bright red in color to greens and browns with red being the peak in a mature male, such as most elite males and clan leaders.

Females generally range in colors of yellows, blues, and greens and look just like the males, except not as tall or muscular. They, like the males, are excellent at hand-to-hand combat and are just as bloodthirsty. Carians wear heavy armor and carry an array of weapons with them at all times. Even the females wear like armament and also can handle many different types of weapons and hold command positions.

It is theorized that carians can reproduce quickly as they seem to have a never-ending supply of soldiers. It is also assumed that genetic inferiority is not tolerated, as there have been no carians ever seen who haven't been perfectly sound and strong. There has been talk lately, though, that carians are now capturing proturin scientists and biosym doctors, forcing them to experiment with gene modification and alteration to produce a more superior specimen among them.

In all, the carians are a severe threat with their stolen technology, constant supply of soldiers, and warped mentality, making trying to live a challenge for all life-forms.

COUNCIL

COUNCIL PRESIDENCY BEGAN as an alien-formed governing body, mostly made up of vatorians, feralosians, proturins, and even some borvians, overseeing many systems and planets under their control. Once humans came into the picture, they were readily accepted into the council and soon held high positions within the presidency. Before long, war broke out with the emergence of carians, and a large militia was built to help protect all life-forms against them. Council militia was mostly made up of humans since humans outnumbered the other alien life-forms six to one, but there were also watorians, vatorians, feralosians, and some proturins in the militia service.

The council forces held their own for many years, but then the council presidency feared the militia was getting too strong and started taking control of it. This caused the militia to weaken, and bad decisions were made that cost the military dearly. It got so bad that they started losing some of their key personnel as they completed their tours and left, starting up their own militia.

Council continued to fight, barely holding their own as the politics got worse and greed and power became the main focus. It took almost their defeat before they woke up and called for help, and sentinel fleet came to their aid, who was now the military might in the galaxy. Once they responded, they defeated and drove out the carians, but council was weakened, and their militia was almost nonexistent. So they had to contract the sentinel fleet for added protection for many of the outlying colonies.

Even the council presidency and quorum went through a house-cleaning during this time and started weeding out the corrupt councilmen, who almost brought about their destruction. In the meantime, the military took it upon themselves to build their might back up and soon had a fairly large armada and were now able to provide more protection to their other systems. This started causing a clash between them and sentinel fleet due to the fleet still having contracts with the council presidency, and open hostilities started happening.

Council presidency and quorum, upon hearing about this, realized they had ignored their own militia and that they were starting to get undermined as the military was starting to take full control. They knew they needed to act fast to avoid a confrontation with the powerful sentinel fleet, whom they still remained in contact with from time to time and on occasion worked with outside of the military's knowledge.

FERALOSIAN

CAT PEOPLE—OR FERALS, as humans call them—look like the large cats of Earth, except they are more humanoid than feline. Most males resemble lions, tigers, and leopards, whereas females take more after cheetahs, mountain lions, and jaguars. Both male and females have a flat face with catlike yellow eyes and the usual coloring of what feline they resemble. They walk upright on two legs and have paw-like hands but can use them like most other humanoids do with opposable thumbs.

Ferals are very large, even more so than watorians, and reach maturity around six or seven years of age, especially the male Leos. They are generally more your warlords and pride leaders. A male Leo resembles a lion in almost every way, except it has no tail and doesn't walk on all fours. They have long reddish manes that they generally tie into a ponytail at the back of their heads since it hangs down past their shoulders and also decorate it with many braids, beads, or colored feathers. The tiger and leopard males also are large but don't have the long manes, and they tend to remain more as your generals and soldiers than actual warlords, though some tigers have actually obtained that status.

Once a feral reaches maturity, they tend to leave their home-world, Titamos, and take up dangerous quests to build up a reputation and fortune so when they return home, they will have a better social standing among their clans and a better chance with females, since males outnumber them five to one. Oftentimes, due to this high ratio, males will fight among themselves over females; and usually, it is to the death, thus giving way to the image of their warrior-like attitude.

Ferals put a lot of effort into establishing their prides, and the more females in one's pride, the more the male's social standing and prowess increase. Of course, females ultimately choose if they want to join a specific pride and base their choice on the male's standing, fortune, and the young that he has already fathered.

Female feralosians are graceful and independent and take great strides to make sure of their choice in males. They are not as large as the males and are more docile and rely heavily on the pride male to take care of and protect them and their young. They produce live young that are reliant on them from the time they are born; thus, they produce milk for nursing like humans, but the young grow quickly due to the rich milk that their mothers produce. Within a pride, all females tend to all the young, whether it is their child or another's.

Females also take great pride in their appearance, for they want to be attractive to their mate as there is also a social standing among the pride's females even though the pride itself is a tight-knit family and every member plays a part in its well-being.

Males, on the other hand, generally tend to not show favorites so as to keep harmony among his pride. Males also generally tend to prefer to be around other pride males, usually sparring to keep their fighting skills sharp. They are always dressed in armor and armed with weapons, and it is only when they are home among their pride do they finally change into casual clothes but still remain armed with a pistol or a curved large knife.

Their clans are scattered all over the planet of Titamos, which has both open grasslands and forests. Some of the more prominent prides have established large cities and spaceports with their clans taking a more communal approach to society, thus also sharing in the benefits as well. Technology only plays a small part in their lives. They prefer to rely more on what natural resources their planet offers them. Of course, they still do use some technology, and feralosians are well-known for their armor and weapons design and manufacturing. They are not under sentinel or council control, preferring to remain neutral even though they oftentimes have a female on the council quorum. Truth be told, no one in their right mind would want to bother them anyway, unless they have a death wish.

PROTURINS

———◦⟨§⟩◦———

THESE ARE THIN aliens with average human height. They are easily recognized by their elongated heads with tentacle-like appendages hanging down at the back of their heads, giving the appearance of hair. Proturins have a flesh-colored leatherlike skin oftentimes accentuated with either red, yellow, or sometimes green patches or stripes on them. It is hard to tell males from females as they all look the same.

Their eyes are large and solid black rimmed with red, giving them the appearance that they have been crying. Their noses are nothing more than two slits opposite each other located in a central spot on the front of their face, and their mouths are the same, just a slit without lips. They have flat, blunt teeth used for grinding food and are mostly herbivores but, on occasion, will partake in the consumption of certain meats.

Proturins have three appendage-like fingers on each hand and opposable thumbs. They walk upright on two legs with their jointed knees located on the back side of their legs, making them look like they are always walking backward.

Physically, they are lacking and look frail, which isn't too far from the truth. Proturins are worthless in hand-to-hand combat, but give them a pistol or a small assault rifle and they can at least hold their own. Their big strengths are science and exploration due to their amazing and highly evolved intelligence. Being limited in the fighting end of the spectrum, they amazingly pose no fear and oftentimes find themselves in life-and-death situations, which is why they are associated with a short life span. But proturins actually have a life span of about sixty years or more, just like biosyms. They are generally social beings and love to meet and study new races and cultures and are not shy to ask all kinds of questions, usually ending up annoying the one they are talking to.

Back on their home planet, Rilos five, mature adults, male and female, are put together in groups of five or six and are sent out to explore, experiment, and make scientific discoveries to bring back to their homeworld, to then be reviewed, debated, and run through simulations and scenarios before releasing such knowledge to other cultures for sharing.

No one sees proturins as a threat; instead, just the opposite, as they have increased scientific breakthroughs for everyone. Especially, the carians see their great potential and on some occasions will capture some of the more well-known and influential scientists, forcing them to work for them to create diseases and viral weapons and to genetically experiment even on their own kind to improve and enhance the carian soldier. These poor doctors never live long, though, because carians are not patient, nor do they tolerate failure.

Another key point to proturins is, they never establish family units; instead, both male and females carry a scan card on themselves that has a genealogy chart that goes clear back for centuries. These are used in breeding requests. Back on the home planet, when a female is ready to procreate, she will go to the Hall of Records, which is a large library-type structure, and search through endless virtual records for the contributing male to help in the production of her offspring. Once she finds one she likes, she puts in a breeding request to their council, who then contacts the male.

The male has to accept, for it is considered a huge dishonor not to, and no matter where they are, they have to leave and return home to fulfill their obligation. Once mated with the female and it is confirmed she has conceived, he is allowed to leave and continue his studies. Gestation is about 180 days, and females give birth to live young that stay with the mother up to the age of thirteen and then go out on their own. The female does not mate again until their young leaves. Most of the time, the young proturin enters into an academy on their homeworld, depending on his or her level of intelligence.

The offspring at this age looks like a mature proturin but lack the coloring, which they don't get until around the age of seventeen or eighteen, which is when they are fully mature. Males do, though, keep in contact with their offspring from time to time and add their protégé's information and accomplishments to their genealogy records.

SENTINEL FLEET

DURING THE CARIAN and council war, a separatist militia rose up and became known as the sentinel fleet. Council militia was the only one during the war, and it was made up of many different alien races and humanoid life-forms, but the militia struggled in the war by allowing politics to make all the calls, which was not sound military advice. Eventually, over time, some humans, watorians, and vatorias had enough; and after putting in their required time of duty, they left the council military and started amassing their own fleet. Ships weren't hard to come by because council militia was also hurting for marks and started selling off some of their older and damaged battlecruisers, destroyers, and batteships to anyone with enough marks to afford them.

These ships were bought cheap, and with the aid of the watorian and even some proturin technology, they were rebuilt and refitted. Before long, they became powerful weapons of destruction. Three men in particular stood out among the newly formed fleet as one took up the role of fleet admiral and the other two as vice admiral and rear admiral, thus setting up the now sentinel command. These three men had fought together in the war against the carians under the council insignia for many years, and one was, in actuality, the other two's commander, and it was only fair to appoint him as fleet admiral. The other two were almost brothers, except one was human and

601

the other was a watorian. They both met in an orphanage, grew up together, enlisted together, and both fought in the infantry together. But their true love was space, and both wanted their own ships.

Yet all through the war, they remained an infantry, for they were unmatched in combat, and the one's strategic planning helped turn the tide against many carian ground assaults as the other one led those assaults and won. It was during this time that all three men managed to amass a huge amount of wealth and great fortune and used that along with some other contributors who also left with them help start up sentinel fleet.

In time, sentinel fleet got larger and had a huge armada at their command. Vice Admiral Thomas Harper, who was one of the founders, now commanded a massive battlecruiser called the Justification at the early age of thirty-three. Rear Admiral Gerrard Larson, another contributor, also had his own battlecruiser called the Lithia and at around the same age as his closest and best friend Harper. Now with massive weapons under their control, they in no time started changing the tide of the ongoing war. Council militia was losing and asked for help, and with the emergence of sentinel fleet, who came to their aid, they were finally able to defeat and drive off the carian invaders.

Over the next many years after the war, sentinel fleet only got larger; and eventually, the vatoria fleet joined with sentinel command. A decade later, they had amassed many more battleships and destoyers; and finally, a massive battle station was built, Valhalla, which was the size of a small planet and now housed sentinel command but minus Vice Admiral Harper and Rear Admiral Larson, who stayed aboard their battlecruisers but, on occasions, would attend command meetings when key issues would arise.

It was also during this time that since carian attacks had almost disappeared, human and other alien species spread out and recolonized other solar systems. Council militia was still too poorly equipped to protect all these new colonies located throughout the galaxy, so they contracted sentinel fleet to provide protection for these other colonized planets.

Eventually, council militia started trying to take control; but this time, it was aimed at sentinel fleet with council militia trying to dictate to them what they could and could not do. This inevitably caused hostilities between the two fleets, and it became very apparent to sentinel fleet that council presidency was losing power. It was also known that council militia was finally building back their armada, and sentinel fleet started pulling out the protection contract and allowing council to take back control to avoid a confrontation with them.

It was well-known among sentinel fleet that if things continued the way they were, a confrontation would eventually ensue. Sentinel fleet then decided in secret to search out a new solar system, thus leaving council space and starting over. The fleet knew that a confrontation would leave them weakened and council militia all but decimated; thus, they would be unable to defend themselves against raids from carians, who were now on the rise again, not to mention the now frequent attacks from merc groups.

The fleet sent out many scouting ships, and eventually, an uncharted system was found on the edge of the galaxy. In secret, they started building a whole new life for their people and followers. The fleet still remains today, providing protection to a few of the planets in council space until the time when the exodus call goes out to everyone who will join them and leave council-run space for good for this new world.

VATORIAS

———⁓———

THESE ARE AN elegant, aristocratic, and beautiful type of humanoids. They are average in height, comparable to humans, but they have certain attributes that distinguish them easily from other species. Vatorias are generally light-skinned with a slight tint of blue to it. They also have scroll-like gold markings that start around the corners of their eyes and travel down the side of their face, wrapping around their necks and fanning out over the rest of their bodies, ending on the tops of their hands and feet. They also have gold-colored eyes with brilliant, long white hair, giving them the appearance to most humans of what human fantasy calls elves, especially since all males and females are rather beautiful.

Vatorias are very intelligent and look almost fragile with their slender frames, but this is all a ruse as they are weapons experts and marksmen, and some even hold high military classifications in hand-to-hand combat. Vatorias also have their own military and ships but work jointly with sentinel fleet, which is where their true loyalties lie. They are prideful and try hard to keep their race pure without outside unions or adapting other cultures' customs.

They are capable of nonvatoria unions since their physical makeup is similar to humans, but this is highly frowned upon, and they go to great lengths to keep outside influences away through very elaborate betrothals while their children are young. Breaking such a betrothal is almost social suicide in their culture, and for a family that experiences this, it takes them many years to regain any social standing, thus causing most to not seek unions outside their own race because of it.

Once a true union among two vatorias is formed, it is celebrated for many days among the people. Producing young, though, is another matter entirely. Females do not conceive until they feel their mate can adequately protect and provide for them and their children. All males are somewhat sterile until the time the female is ready to reproduce. Then she puts off a scent that her partner can detect, thus causing him to become fertile for a short period of time. This condition has evolved over time and has been vatorias' way to keep their population in check.

Gestation among vatorias last eleven to sometimes twelve months, and the infant is born looking comparable to an eight-month-old human child. This is also due to female vatorias producing no milk for their young; thus, the child must be able to exist on the same food and substances that adults do.

One of vatorias' greatest qualities is, they're all telepaths; thus, their whole society communicates this way. Some are stronger than others and can communicate with more than one person at a time. Another more secret attribute is, some vatorias also exhibit natural-occurring kinetics, which they hide very well due to the fact that kinetics are an instant prison sentence among council-controlled space. Another key element in vatorias is, they openly embrace technology and use it everywhere they can; and through this, they have also increased their life expectancy. They don't live as long as watorians do but still live past two hundred years of age.

They are an old race and have always been around, which is why they pride themselves as being above all other life-forms. Their homeworld has always been the planet Krios in the Selen nebula. It is a beautiful planet lush with vegatation, spectacular waterfalls, and jungles, a tropical paradise where they have built elegant and exquisite huge cities plus many outlying villages with some of the more prominent lords and ladies residing over the centuries. Even though Krios is considered in council space, it is not controlled by council. Vatorias are their own governing body.

WATORIANS

This is a humanoid species closely related in every way to humans, except for having a few extra chromosomes in their DNA makeup, thus giving them acute senses, superior strength, and speed, making them the prefect warrior. Males look just like human males, except mature watorians are very large, and they also exhibit larger, pointed canines, thus giving them the nickname alien vampires. Yet their most distinguishing feature is, all males are extremely handsome, and no one knows the reasoning for this.

They are easily distinguished by their large muscle mass and height, white eyes, and shoulder-length hair, and some of the more accomplished warriors have fine braids hanging down in their hair with many different beads woven into the braids, signifying their many deeds. Older watorians who have achieved a certain status among their kind also start tribal markings around their right eye that go down the side of their face and end around their neck. They still retain some of their tribal customs, but since humans entered their space, they have since adopted a lot of the human-born customs and did away with a lot of their more primitive ways.

Male watorians start out just like male human children, but they are tall for their age and are always blue-eyed. It isn't until they reach the age of twenty-two or twenty-three that they go through a change. This is a time of maturity for all males and is a very painful time. Their senses become more acute as their bodies increase in height and muscle size as the muscle tissue hardens, making them able to withstand more damage in battle, thus increasing strength and speed without losing maneuverability.

They also increase their stamina, and the change is predominately signified by their eye color changing from the traditional blue to white, giving them the ability to see in the dark and increased distance. Their senses become even more acute, and they are able to pick up obscure scents that others cannot, making them great trackers.

It generally takes about a month for the change to fully complete its cycle, and most males become easily agitated, full of anger or combative during this time. The other known fact about watorians is, they live unusually long lives. It is well-documented that they can live past two hundred years of age.

Female watorians don't experience such changes unless through bonding. They generally mature around eighteen or nineteen years of age and are somewhat plain, blue-eyed, and large-boned and are close in height to the average female human. They also don't have the same characteristics as the males, such as the white eyes, pronounced canines, and great strength. But not all are plain. There are some who are very attractive, just like the males are handsome.

Females also excel in military training, but once they bond and start having offspring with their mate, they generally leave the service until their children get older. Another fact about watorians is, female watorians only choose male watorians as their life partners, whereas males oftentimes choose humans or vatorians, especially since males outnumber their females three to one.

Male watorians also experience imprinting their potential mate, which can occur as early as fifteen years of age, thus causing them to continuously be drawn to this person. The attraction increases as they age, and once they reach maturity, it becomes a driving force. If they do not pursue such bonding, they become agitated, aggressive, and at times, even hostile as the drive becomes more like a predator-prey type of feeling.

When males are ready for bonding, their teeth elongate twice as long temporarily, and they bite down into the soft area between the neck and shoulder, sinking their fangs into their mate, injecting a type of venom into them. This act has led to the common joke of being called the love bite, but its significance has more to do with reproduction than actual love and is an instinctive act for males as watorians bond for life and can only do this one time in their lives. Even if their partner dies, they will never be able to bond or want to again.

The venom that is injected is actually a DNA copy of the male but with an added bonus of genetic markers that travel through the female host, thus pulling any superior genes from the female and replacing the inferior ones in the male's DNA code that was injected. This new strand then attacks the host's reproductive organs and changes them to produce the new DNA. Thus, even if the female host is human, it will only produce a watorian child. In a way, it will be a cloned copy of the male but more perfected with some of the host's better genes, which it absorbed.

In female humans and vatorias, this change is very painful as their bodies literally combat the change and as their immune system fights the foreign bodies; but eventually, this is overcome, and even their uteri thicken to accommodate the larger and stronger infant. Nonwatorian female species generally suffer from anywhere to twenty-four or, in some cases, thirty-six hours as the changes occur, and most complain of severe abdominal cramping, slight fever, and headaches, but pain medications have been produced to aid with this.

Also, during this time, the change in nonwatorian females is marked by their eyes changing from their natural color to white, like the mature watorian males, and they gain increased stamina, heightened senses, and also the ability to see in the dark. Even female watorians also go through this change as well if bonded to a male watorian, but they don't experience anything near the pain nonwatorians do. It is believed this increase in the female's abilities goes back to the more primitive, animalistic nature of the watorians to aid in the protection of their offspring.

The other strange and contradictive attribute of watorians is, they are technical geniuses and rank first in technical breakthroughs, which is ironic due to watorians refraining from using technology in their day-to-day lives and relying more on good old-fashioned hard labor in their lives and living a simple tribal existence.

It is believed the reasoning for this is because watorians are legendary warriors and soldiers unrivaled in combat, and the quiet living is believed to help keep their natural hostile and aggressive behavior in check. They prefer to apply their technology toward spaceships, medical advancement, and agriculture. They are known for their skill at building and repairing spaceships, and many of sentinel fleet's ships that are out in space today are because of watorian technology. It is well-known that watorians are strictly in sentinel fleet as a lot of the fleet's higher-ranking officers are watorians.

It is not known where watorians originated from, but they have for years called Sigma Six their home planet, even before council took over. They live in tight-knit colonies, mostly sticking to forest or mountain regions and using only natural resources in their construction of their towns and dwellings. They grow their own food and raise their own livestock, and each colony is responsible for all their inhabitants' food supply. They do enjoy comfort and have a preference for the more rustic mountain resort kind of community that they have adapted from Earth's history.

ABOUT THE AUTHOR

———◆◇◆———

ROCHELLE L BLACK lives in Idaho where she met and married her high school sweetheart, and together, they raised three wonderful children and later on added grandchildren as their family grew in size. She loves camping, fishing, reading, and just spending time with her family and her two pugs.

Writing has always been her passion. Even as a young child, she wrote stories, and the school librarian would laminated them and turn them into stories for other children to read.

CPSIA information can be obtained
at www.ICGtesting.com
Printed in the USA
JSHW042318230621
16205JS00001B/1